D0442261

THE SATURDAY WIFE

Also by Naomi Ragen

The Covenant

Chains Around the Grass

The Ghost of Hannah Mendes

The Sacrifice of Tamar

Sotah

Jepthe's Daughter

Women's Minyan (a play)

The Saturday Wife

NAOMI RAGEN

ST. MARTIN'S PRESS
New York

This is a work of fiction. All characters and events portrayed in this book are fictional and any resemblance to real people or events is purely coincidental.

www.stmartins.com

Book design by Mary A. Wirth

LIBRARY OF CONGRESS CATALOGING-IN-PUBLICATION DATA

Ragen, Naomi.
The Saturday wife / Naomi Ragen.—1st ed.
p. cm
ISBN-13: 978-0-312-35238-7
ISBN-10: 0-312-35238-7
1. Jewish women—Fiction. 2. Rabbis' spouses—Fiction. 3. Marriage—Fiction. 4. Jewish fiction. I. Title.

PS3568.A4118S28 2007
813'.54—dc22

2007016179

First Edition: August 2007

10 9 8 7 6 5 4 3 2 1

Dedicated, with love, to

Hallel, Hillel, Ariella, Manny, Yotam, Elon, Aviyah, Matan, and Eliora

for bringing more joy and laughter into my life

than I ever imagined possible

ACKNOWLEDGMENTS

The genesis of any book is a strange and mysterious process. I would like to thank, equally and profoundly, the blonde in the miniskirt and tank top who got up onstage to dance with the toddlers during a Kosher Club week in the Dominican Republic, and Gustave Flaubert for writing *Madame Bovary,* which I took along with me on vacation. The confluence of these two is truly responsible for this book.

I would also like to thank the approximately ten thousand members of my e-mail list (www.naomiragen.com) for responding so generously to my request for help with my research. The hundreds of e-mails I received describing actual Bar and Bat Mitzvas and weddings, as well as shul wars and stories of rabbis, their wives, and their congregations, were wonderful, and I've used them all (well, almost). Without this input, the book you read wouldn't have been the same. I especially thank the wonderful rabbis and rabbis' wives who wrote me, as well as the intrepid and talented bloggers, the incomparable Renegade Rebbitzen and Ezer K'negdo, and others for information and inspiration.

As for those few on my e-mail list who wrote me nasty letters declining to participate until they knew more about how I was planning to use this material, I hope you are now feeling satisfied that you cannot be held responsible.

I thank my agent, Lisa Bankoff, for her unending support and encouragement through this and many other projects.

I thank my talented and very patient editor, Jennifer Weis of St. Martin's Press, for her enormous help and editorial guidance, as well as for suggesting in the back of a New York taxi that I make my main character a rabbi's wife. It has made all the difference.

I thank my son Asher for taking time off from finishing his doctorate at Harvard (I had to get that in) to read and comment on this book.

I thank my dear husband, Alex, for telling me jokes for the last thirty-six years. I finally got to use a few. If you don't think they're funny, his e-mail address is available.

Naomi Ragen

JERUSALEM, 2007

If we disregard due proportion by giving anything what is too much for it . . . the consequence is always shipwreck.

—PLATO

THE SATURDAY WIFE

PROLOGUE

It is not an easy thing for an Orthodox Jewish girl to be saddled with the name of a Gentile temptress responsible for destroying a famous Jewish hero. When Delilah's father filled in her name on the Hebrew Academy day school application form, the rabbi/administrator assumed it was a mistake, a feeble attempt on the part of some clueless, nonreligious Jew to find a Hebrew equivalent for Delia or Dorothy:

"You are aware, Mr. Goldgrab, that, in the Bible, Delilah seduced Samson and is considered a wicked whore by our sages?" he pointed out, as gently as he could.

"Well, now, you don't say?" Delilah's father drawled, his six-foot-two-inch frame towering over the little man, who nervously clutched his skullcap. "Just so happens it was my mother's name."

Our first meeting with Delilah was in second grade out on the punchball fields of the Hebrew Academy of Cedar Heights on Long Island. Punchball was a Jewish girl's baseball without the bat. You just made the hardest fist you could and *wham!*—started to run. When you hit that rubber ball, you took out all your anger, all your angst, all your frustration. You ran and ran and ran and ran, hoping you'd hit it hard enough so that no one could catch it or you and send you back to first base—or, worse, throw you out of the game altogether.

The privilege of hitting the punchball was not to be taken for granted. Each recess, teams were picked anew by captains, who were, by mutual agreement, the prettiest and richest girls in the class. Everyone who wanted to play lined up and just waited for the magic summons. And as in life, some girls—like rich, snobby Hadassah Mittelman—were always the captains, and some girls, like me, were never asked to play. Never.

We knew who we were and finally slipped away. But there were others—like Delilah—who sometimes made it in. Girls like her always had it the hardest. To *almost* make it was a far crueler fate that to be permanently relieved of hope.

The world was a simple place back then, neatly divided between those of us who got the little blue admission cards in the mail at the start of each new term because our parents had paid the full tuition and those who got them at the last minute, only after much parental groveling and pleading had pried them from the tightfisted grip of the merciless rabbi/administrator in charge. It was a world divided between those who had cashmere sweaters and indulgent fathers who dropped them off at school in their big cars because they lived in even more upscale neighborhoods farther out on the island and those who shivered in scratchy wool on public buses coming from the opposite direction.

Delilah took the bus, but she also had a cashmere sweater, the most glorious color pink, that seemed to float around her shoulders like angel hair. Rumor had it that her mother had actually knitted it for her from scratch, a rumor that cruelly denied her the status conferred by ownership.

This was no doubt true. Mrs. Goldgrab was a woman of scary heaviness, with bad skin and glasses with rhinestone frames that made her eyes contract into hard river stones. She worked a forty-hour week in some low-level office job that computers have permanently wiped off the employment map, and in her spare time, was a seething cauldron of unfulfilled social ambitions, thwarted at every turn by impassable roadblocks. One of the largest was her husband: a tall, lanky man with a shocking Texas accent who worked as a mechanic in a local car repair shop. If anyone ever ran into him in his uniform and mentioned it, Delilah was mortified. Over the years, she adopted the same attitude toward him as her mother: he was something she had to put up with, but he wasn't an asset.

From the beginning, Mrs. Goldgrab had plans for Delilah. Big plans. She wanted her to be popular with the right girls. To be invited to their birthday parties. She hoped to be able to drop her off at Tudor mansions in Woodmere and be casually invited in for coffee, where she would chitchat with the mothers who wore pearls and Ann Taylor suits even on weekends, women who existed—along with the longed-for invitations—only in her lower-middle-class imagination. Even Hadassah's mother wore jeans on weekends. And no one wanted to chitchat with Mrs. Goldgrab, not even her husband.

We always envied Delilah that sweater—to this day. Except that now we understand it had meant nothing to her. What she had wanted was a store-bought sweater, the kind Hadassah Mittelman wore. In fact, she wanted to *be* Hadassah Mittelman, the rabbi's beautiful daughter, who lived in a house with a full suit of armor standing in her hallway, guarding the grand staircase upstairs to her designer bedroom, with its ruffled canopy bed. Delilah didn't want to visit that house. She wanted to move in. Maybe we all did in those days. The difference was that Delilah never got over it.

So before you judge her for the horrible things she did, please try to remember this: All Delilah Goldgrab Levi ever really wanted was to be included when they called out the names of those who were allowed to play.

{ ONE }

The thing people never understood about Delilah was that she always considered herself the victim of a painfully disadvantaged childhood, something that mystified her hardworking, upwardly mobile parents. There were few who knew how deeply she mourned her endless humiliations: winter clothes chosen from picked-over reduced racks in January sales instead of shiny new in autumn; a sweet sixteen celebrated in a bowling alley instead of in a hotel with a live band; Passover seders at home prepared by her sweating mother instead of in the dining room of exclusive resorts; summers lying on the public beach instead of trips to Israel and Europe. A childhood of last year's Nikes, drugstore sunglasses, fifteen-dollar haircuts, and do-it-yourself French manicures whose white line was always crooked. . . .

On the rare occasions that she sat in self-judgment, such as before the Yom Kippur fast, she never felt these longings marked her as selfish, materialistic, or shallow. On the contrary, she considered herself an idealist, someone focused on the really important things in life: true happiness, true love. As she saw it, she was simply being honest with herself. And someone who "really loved her" would be the kind of person who would stop at nothing to help her overcome the trauma of her youth, her mother's cheap fashion accessories—those fake pearls, those nine-karat gold amethyst rings. Someone who "really loved her" would understand and appreciate how profoundly she needed a house, not an apartment, preferably with a swimming pool, in addition to business-class jaunts to five-star resorts in the Caribbean and Hawaii.

She felt this way despite all the best efforts of our synagogue and schooling to convince us of the fleeting worth of material things, as opposed to the eternal reward—in this life and the next—of spiritual attainments.

In general, Delilah's relationship to religion was somewhat complex. She wasn't a natural rebel. She actually loved the elaborate meals, the dressing up for the synagogue, the socializing afterward. On the other hand, she absolutely refused to accept the fact that bearded rabbis had the right to decide for her how long her skirts and sleeves would be, what she could and couldn't read, or watch on TV or in the movies, or what kind of dates she could have (i.e., serious ones, leading to early marriages, as opposed to frivolous recreational ones like riding roller coasters in Playland).

Like most people, she snipped and tugged and restitched her religion to make it a more comfortable fit. She didn't feel guilty about this. Why should she, she told herself, when the rabbis themselves had done a good deal of tailoring? Take the relationship between the sexes. On the one hand, the Bible taught that men and women were both created in God's image as equals, but on the other, Jewish law was male chauvinist in the extreme, notwithstanding millennia of rabbinical apologetics to disprove the obvious.

Men were the leaders, high priests, rabbis, judges. While rabbis claimed that they were simply expounding on eternal laws derived from God-given sacred texts, the laws always seemed to come out to the men's advantage. For example, sitting shiva. During the seven days of mourning for a parent, wife, or child, rabbinical law said a man wasn't permitted to do anything; he had to be served and taken care of. But if a woman was sitting shiva—surprise!—the same law said she was allowed to get up and wash the floor and cook dinner.

Despite these feelings, Delilah never considered herself a feminist, refusing to join those of us who railed against being banned from donning a prayer shawl and phylacteries or from learning Talmud. She'd just roll her eyes and yawn. "That's all I need. More religious obligations."

The biblical heroines she admired were not the tough, powerful matriarchs, but Esther, who'd soaked in precious bath oils for six months, mesmerizing the king and becoming queen of Persia; and Abigail, who sent war-weary King David camel-loads of food and drink, thereby giving her tightfisted husband, Nabal, a fatal heart attack, thus leaving herself rich and free to marry David, which she was only too happy to do. To Delilah's thinking, these were stories with a deeply spiritual message for women.

Betty Friedan and Simone de Beauvoir bored her. Equal wages were all right, but it was better if your husband earned enough so that you never, ever had to work if you didn't want to. Truth be told, her vision of the perfect world would have been a party in *Gone with the Wind* where women wore ball gowns to barbecues and men brought them plates of delicious food; a place where all women had to do was smile and be pretty and men fell all over themselves to please and amuse them.

All through high school, Delilah was in training for this role. If only you could have seen her then: those manicured toenails with the red polish so carefully applied, those tanned slim thighs, the blond hair braided in cornrows with turquoise beads, the tiny bathing suit like two slashes of color, the eyes that flashed at you like tanzanite, deep blue flecked with gold. She was so deliciously slim, so adorably sexy, it made you stop and stare, the way one stares at a flashy lightning storm or a gaudy tropical sunset. And she knew it.

How could she not? Men and boys flocked around her, and she giggled and flirted indiscriminately with all of them, even the young Puerto Rican janitors hired to clean the floors and bathrooms of the Hebrew Academy of Cedar Heights.

"Everyone does exactly as they please," she'd say cryptically, tossing her head. "Even the ones who parade around showing off their holiness with all those head coverings and fringed garments, yarmulkes and wigs. Secretly, they also do exactly what they want and find excuses afterward." When we protested mildly, she told us to grow up.

While we had all more or less decided by the end of high school what we wanted to be, Delilah remained vague. Her mother wanted her to take some education courses and become a teacher. But something as small and unimaginative as that wouldn't suit her at all, she said. Besides, she didn't like the outfits or the hair and makeup that went with it. You couldn't get away with much in front of a class full of yeshiva kids with a rabbi/principal peeking in on you every few hours. And what if the kids asked you questions, let's say, about the Resurrection of the Dead? Or if the Messiah was coming? She knew she was supposed to believe with perfect faith, but honestly, she had never been able to get her head around such ideas. What, would they come out of their graves, like in *The Night of the Living Dead*? Or like that mangled factory-worker who comes knocking on his parents' door in *The Monkey's Curse*?

And this Messiah. Did he know he was the Messiah? A person is born, gets toilet trained, eats hamburgers, and then—what, finds out he's going to bring peace to the world and change all human life as we know it? Would it be like Moses and the burning bush, where you are just minding your own business trying to keep the sheep from falling off a cliff when God suddenly calls your name and gives you your assignment? But then, how could you tell it was true and you weren't just another candidate for lithium?

She could always be a public school teacher, she supposed. But everyone knew the Teachers' Union stuck new teachers in hellholes in Brooklyn and the South Bronx, places where a white Jewish blonde getting into a new car was like waving a red flag in front of a bull. She tried to envision herself like Michelle Pfeiffer in that movie where she gets all the drug-addicted Puerto Ricans to become honor students because she's so tough, but kind and she really, really believes in them. But she couldn't imagine working in a public school and not wearing pants, which the rabbis absolutely forbade and which she still hadn't figured a way around. Michelle could never have worked those miracles in a skirt with all that sitting up on the desk with her legs crossed.

The decision to enroll at Bernstein Women's College, affiliated with the well-known Bernstein Rabbinical College, had been made after long discussions with friends and counselors. Although the tuition was thousands of dollars a year and she could have gone to any city college for free, she was advised by all that she wouldn't like city colleges. They were too big, too impersonal, full of public high school riffraff. There was no social life. The bottom line was she was afraid to venture out, despite her bravado, from the sheltered yeshiva day school environment she had known, to face the real world, where her new sophistication would be laughed at by hip young New Yorkers who slept together and indulged in drugs and all kinds of other perversions she could only just imagine with equal parts loathing and envy.

But there was one thing you had to give Bernstein, the one true incontrovertible fact which made all those student loans a worthwhile investment: it was turning out to be one, long *shidduch* date.

Everyone was a matchmaker: the girls, the teachers, the teacher's cousins, the girls' cousins. It was the official bride pool for Bernstein Rabbinical College as well as Yeshiva University, with its well-regarded medical and law school, a fact well-known to all the parents shouldering the burden of their daughters' unjustified and outlandish tuition.

Many of the girls were out-of-towners from tiny Jewish communities where available religious Jewish men were either under ten or over forty. Enrolling at Bernstein rescued them from horrible Young Israel weekends in Catskill hotels and being relentlessly pursued by the proverbial kosher butcher from Milwaukee: over thirty, overweight, and oversexed. Here, in a relaxed and respectable atmosphere, every Ruchie could find her Moishe. And vice versa.

The out-of-towners were usually the sheltered daughters of rabbis, pretty and sweet and innocent, with very little dating experience. Most of them had endured at least a year of long-distance courtships in which relatives and friends and professionals had found matches for them in places like Monsey, Brooklyn, or Baltimore. The dates arranged necessitated expensive cross-country plane trips, a situation that understandably left most of them languishing in solitary gloom on Saturday nights. When they moved into the dorms at Bernstein, they thought they'd died and gone to heaven.

In contrast, the native New Yorkers, used to a plethora of possibilities, found the fix-ups from Bernstein and Yeshiva University left much to be desired. Most of the guys were short and pale and wore glasses. They showed up dressed like they were on their way to a Rabbinical Council of America convention. Moreover, most were victims of severe rabbinical brainwashing on the subject of physical contact with the opposite sex outside of marriage. The *negiah*, or "touching" laws, were basically one loud NO! NOT ANYPLACE, ANY TIME, ANY BODY PART, UNDER ANY CIRCUMSTANCES! This left some of the young men severely challenged on this subject, making Delilah feel as if she had a rare communicable disease. Even the most adventurous managed little more than casually stretching an arm out onto the back of her subway seat.

Gee, that was a thrill.

Some, at least, had looked normal enough: a crocheted skullcap, a nice sweater over an open-collared shirt. There was one universal problem, though. Anyone willing to be fixed up was almost always someone who couldn't find a date on his own. And for good reason.

Delilah kept on going, though, always allowing herself to be persuaded by the hard or soft sell of the people who were setting her up, that this one "was different." And why shouldn't she trust them? After all, they had nothing to gain from making her miserable. In fact, most of them were involved in matchmaking because they considered it a good deed. Indeed, there is a widely held belief among religious Jews that achieving three successful matches earns one a free entry pass to the best neighborhoods in the World to Come.

The system in Bernstein worked this way: The guys would come into the dorm lobby and give their name and the name of the girl they were taking out to the housemother, who would then call up to the girl's room, announcing him. The girl would then come down to the lobby and tell the housemother the name of the boy. Sometimes, seeing the girl who spoke his name, the boy would sit perfectly still until he could quietly slip out the front door.

It was quite a show. When she had nothing better to do on a Saturday night, Delilah delighted in hanging around the lobby to watch. Which is how she got involved with Yitzie Polinsky.

The boy was striking: tall and very slim, with broad shoulders and thick rock-star hair that fell adorably over his eyes. He wore a dark skullcap that melted right in and was hardly noticeable at all. His jeans were faded in all the right places, and to top it off he had on a black turtleneck and a kind of bomber jacket of brown leather.

You could tell the housemother didn't approve at all. But when he gave her his name, her eyes lit up: the son of the very famous Rabbi Menachem Polinsky of Crown Heights. The housemother pushed her reading glasses to the top of her gray wig, looked him over again, lips pursed, and then shrugged. Allowances had to be made. She called up to the girl.

Delilah recognized her name: Penina Gwertzman, a cute little out-of-towner from Kansas or some other impossibly goyish place. Petite, with long dark hair and an ample figure, she was from a very religious family and had been carefully brought up. Yitzie wasn't her type at all. He was Delilah's type.

She watched as Yitzie's eyes took in Penina's body in long, slow strokes. Satisfied, he smiled and got up, sauntering over to her, his hands in his pockets. The nearer he got, the more Penina tugged nervously at her long pleated skirt, as if willing it to grow a few more inches.

What a waste, Delilah thought, watching them walk out together into the night, already making plans.

{ TWO }

In the morning, Delilah made inquiries. "I heard Penina went out last night with Yitzie Polinsky," she mentioned casually to her roommate, Rivkie. "How did it go?"

Rivkie, who had not a suspicious bone in her body and who considered any kind of gossip a mortal sin and so never listened to or repeated anything of value, said she thought she'd heard something not so good about it. Coming from such a source, Delilah knew it was going to be major, major breaking news.

She knocked on a few doors of reliable yentas and got the goods: a disastrous date that had ended scandalously, with tears and angry phone calls and possible repercussions for Yitzie, who was slated to follow in his father's footsteps, if only he could shed his yeshiva-bum reputation.

Yes! Delilah thought, thrilled.

She settled her face into the right lines of worry and concern and knocked on Penina's door. "I just heard. Are you all right?"

The girl's big, obviously cried-out eyes, welled. "Does everybody know?"

Delilah took a step back. "No! It's just that I happened to be waiting down in the lobby and saw him come in. I mean, that leather jacket. . . . He looked a little dangerous to me, so I asked to make sure you were OK."

Penina's face was stiff.

"It's just . . . I've had some bad experiences myself."

The girl suddenly melted into an angry puddle of damp emotions.

"It wasn't my fault!!" she cried passionately. "They told me he was a brilliant Torah scholar from a very important family, who was going to take over his father's congregation one day soon." She blinked and two large tears rolled down her fresh pink cheeks.

Delilah caught her breath in joy. "What . . . did something . . . happen?"

"He said he was taking me to the Village. I didn't know what village! I thought he meant Boro Park. But it wasn't. . . . I didn't see a single Jew. Then he took me inside some restaurant. But it wasn't a kosher deli or anything. It was really dark. And I didn't see anybody eating, or smell pickles—you know. It smelled like . . . liquor. There was a stage, and some girl with very uncombed frizzy hair was singing! Imagine, Yitzie Polinsky—the son of Rebbe Polinsky, who everyone calls a saint, who is known to be so stringently pious people are terrified of him and they worship him—imagine *his son listening to a woman's voice*, which everybody knows is forbidden! Anyway, we sat down at this little table. I couldn't see a thing. So"—she wiped her eyes, taking a deep breath—"at first I thought I was imagining it, but then I realized he had his hand on my knee. And then he put his other hand on my shoulder, and his fingers started playing with my hair and then moved underneath my collar. . . ."

Delilah bit the inside of her cheek, handing the girl a tissue. "Oh!" She shook her head in outraged sympathy. "The creep." She waited impatiently what she hoped was a suitable moment of commiseration. "And then what happened?" she asked eagerly.

Penina's eyes looked up over the tissue with sudden suspicion. "What do you mean? Of course I told him to take me back immediately!"

"Oh, yes. Of course, of course! That's exactly what I . . . thought. Meant. I mean, what else could you do? Did he?"

Penina stared down at the tissue, then blew her nose again miserably. "He said he had to make a phone call first. I waited and waited, but he never came back. I wound up paying the check, and I didn't even have enough money left to take a taxi! I had to use the subway. I was petrified!" She sobbed.

Delilah made an O with her lips and held it. "I have a good mind to call him up and tell him off. You wouldn't happen to have his phone number, would you?"

"You would do that? For me? But we hardly even know each other!"

"Doesn't our holy Torah tell us, 'Before a blind man put no obstacle'? It's my sacred religious duty. We wouldn't want another innocent young girl to go out and have such an experience, would we? I mean, he has to be stopped!"

Penina blinked. "Sharona Gottleib fixed me up. She said her grandmother was friends with his grandmother. . . . I'll never speak to her again!"

Delilah sighed heavily. "I understand." She patted the girl's soft white hand with its little fourteen-carat birthstone ring from Mommy and Daddy. "I will talk to Sharona. Trust me, I know exactly how to handle this."

Penina stared at her, her eyes welling once again. "You would do that? For me? Meet with him and tell him off?"

Delilah patted the little hand. "*Kol Yisrael aravim zeh le zeh.*" All Israel is responsible one for the other.

~ ~

She found out where his father's shul was and arranged to sleep over at a friend's house nearby. She wore a demure outfit that covered everything. Still, she sensed the cold eyes of matronly disapproval pointed like lasers at the top of her blond head to the bottom of her spiked heels as she walked down the narrow aisle of the women's section in Reb Menachem Polinsky's synagogue. She took a seat near the high *mechitzah*—the religiously mandated barrier piously separating the men from the women. It ran the entire length of the synagogue, giving the men almost the entire room, and confining the women to a small, cramped space. As usual, the more Orthodox the synagogue, the more demeaning and uncomfortable the women's section. Still, she was just grateful that at least she was in the same room with Yitzie, as some stringency kings had created synagogues where the women were shunted off to side rooms in completely different parts of the building, where only a handful could see or hear anything. Discreetly, she lifted the little curtain and peered inside at the men's section.

There he was, dressed in the traditional Hasidic Sabbath outfit: the satin waistcoat with its braided string belt that separated his holy upper body from his profane lower half, the dark, wide-brimmed hat. He wore a magnificent prayer shawl over his shoulders. His father, the old man with the white beard who stood at the center at the bimah, seemed to be running the place, the way everyone was falling all over themselves to be respectful to him.

Well, well, she thought. A real saint.

She waited for him in the room where they served the kiddush—the traditional after-prayer refreshments—but the synagogue was so over-the-top *frum,* it had separate rooms for men and women. So she waited outside. He came out, a few paces behind his father, surrounded by men. But when he saw her, he lifted his head and a secret look passed between them.

She called him that night. She was the blonde who had been standing outside his father's synagogue, she told him, and she had something she needed to talk to him about. They agreed to meet in the Village. When he showed up, he was again dressed in his leather jacket.

"I'm just here to tell you what a bum you are" was her opening line.

"You're fast. Usually, it takes women at least one date to find that out." He smiled.

"That girl you dumped last Saturday night? Well, she happens to be a friend of mine."

"She was pretty anxious to get rid of me. So I helped her out."

"You stuck her with the check and left her stranded."

"What happened to women's lib? Don't you girls carry cabfare?"

"She only had enough left for the subway, you creep." She laughed.

He took a step closer. "And you came here to tell me off, is that right?"

"Well, what other reason could I have?" she asked demurely, lowering her eyes.

He took her arm and tucked it between his bended elbow, patting her hand. The forbidden feel of his male skin against hers was exciting, as well as the fact that he'd done it on his own, without asking permission. Some of her other dates had actually asked straight out, "How religious are you?" Idiots. What did they expect a girl to do, give them a road map and a list of directions? To tell them, Not religious at all, just do anything you want? Her answer was always the same: "Very." The date ahead never failed to be a disaster.

Yitzie thrilled her. They met in places she had never been. Top of the Sixes, where she ordered her first daiquiri, which made her feel all warm and happy. Avant-garde movie theaters showing films by Godard that were so shocking and lewd she'd once actually run from the theater. To make it up to her, he'd bought her tickets to the opera at Lincoln Center. Orchestra seats. She'd worn a very form-fitting dress covered with silver glitter with a high collar of white silk and matching white cuffs, which she'd sneaked past the dorm mother under her prim black winter coat. She'd piled her hair on top of her head. Later, while she was in the lobby waiting for him to get her a Coke, two obviously tipsy middle-aged men had approached her with lewd smiles, about to say something when Yitzie showed up and they steered abruptly in the opposite direction. She looked at herself in the glass windows of the lobby. She looked ravishing and a bit slutty, she thought, wavering between embarrassment and delight.

She was in Yitzie's spell, or maybe he was in hers, she couldn't decide. He graduated slowly from slinging his hand across her shoulders in the secluded booths of dark little bars, to twining his fingers through her hair, to grasping her waist as they walked, slightly tipsy, down the streets of Manhattan. And then he began to pick her up in a car.

They drove out to the Rockaways and parked by the deserted summer bungalows. When he'd first suggested it, she'd told herself he was being romantic. She envisioned holding hands and watching the waves roll in while he whispered compliments into her pink little ears. The first time he kissed her, his tongue pressing between her teeth, she was so busy gagging she didn't feel his hand wander under her skirt. She was wearing a girdle and stockings, more solid than a chastity belt. But his hands moved so quickly. She couldn't believe someone could actually unhook a bra without having to put his hands under her blouse—which she would *never* have allowed, of course—but there she was, unhooked.

All the while, he kept telling her how beautiful she was—how irresistible, how much he loved her—in this slow, worshipful, sweet voice. She was deeply conflicted, part of her giving in immediately, the other part shocked and outraged and threatened.

Then something happened, physically, she hadn't expected. She felt all her juices begin to flow, inexorable and unstoppable. She felt light-headed and strange. Not herself. And the space they were in felt safe and private.

Who was to know? She let her arms fall to her sides, letting him use his hands on her as one lets a musician play an instrument: She watched, thrilling to the chords that resonated within her, absolutely new. She throbbed with a deep, resounding bass.

Her classes at Bernstein became a vague hum. She'd finally enrolled in the associate program to become a dental hygienist, enjoying the idea of leaning over strange men and telling them to open wide, but the classes were a bore. She could barely keep her eyes open through Dental Hygiene Theory I, Dental Materials, Infection and Immunity, Ezekiel and Gaonic Literature II. All she wanted to do was close them and dream of the night to come.

Things progressed rapidly. Yitzie was like a drug. He was everything she really wanted. Exciting and unconventional, but from a good family who had *yichus* and money. She daydreamed of how this was all going to end with a marriage proposal. They were, after all, so "good together." They had so much in common. She knew she could keep him happy.

But whenever he wanted to take it up the final notch, explore the last frontier, she kept pushing him away, adamantly refusing to go that extra step that would mark her forever as an uncapped bottle of Coke, as a rebbitzin once told them in high school. A girl who had lost all her fizz before her wedding night.

The laws of the Torah about maintaining virginity—as taught in yeshiva—were uncompromising. A girl who willingly bedded a man was a whore. And even if she was forced into it, she still had to marry the creep and he wasn't allowed to divorce her, ever. That was a punishment for the rapist, her rabbis had explained, never really getting into why a girl would want to be tied to such a man the rest of her life. If you pushed them on it, they'd get all excited, and finally shout at you that a woman's position during biblical times made it imperative for her to have a husband, and who would marry a deflowered, single girl?

Where it all got really sticky, as far as she could see, was when you decided to marry someone other than your lover. If the husband was clueless, expecting you to be a virgin and found out otherwise, he was within his legal right to throw you out without a dime. Which is why in biblical times the girl's parents saved the sheet from the marriage bed to display to town elders should just such a problem arise. Nowadays, though, DNA testing made presenting the bloody sheet as proof of virginity a bit more tricky. So Delilah knew she had to be cautious.

But she was in love with him. And he—he was . . . ? She couldn't make up her mind.

Sometimes he seemed totally enthusiastic, like a rabid sports fan fanatically immersed in witnessing the achievement of that last winning goal. And sometimes he seemed distracted, even bored. Sometimes he said hurtful things, like, "Another blintz, another inch," pinching her flesh in various places. His moodiness confused and depressed her. It took quite a bit of self-coaching for her to talk herself out of her bouts of pessimism and fright. She was, however, successful. She planned their future. He had no interest in taking over his father's congregation, which was fine with her, because she had no interest at all in being a rabbi's wife.

The mere sound of the Yiddish term *rebbitzin* filled her with distaste and dread, conjuring up images of overweight Jewesses in bad wigs wearing dowdy calf-length skirts and long-sleeved polyester blouses. She remembered the rabbis' wives who had been her teachers in yeshiva high school, those mirthless paragons of virtue dedicated to squeezing out and discarding the last ounce of joy from living, the way you squeezed a sweet orange, leaving behind only the empty bitter shell. God, God, God, and more God, combined with a life of doing *chesed*—good deeds—i.e., distasteful and inconvenient favors for ungrateful people you hardly knew and who would never reciprocate. That was the ideal of Jewish life according to her pious teachers, who, if they had had a magic wand, would have waved it over all twenty of them as they sat in class, turning their clothes navy blue, their hair into long braids, and their thoughts to bearded rabbinical students who would touch them only two weeks out of the month until they got pregnant, and then it was anybody's guess.

Only Rebbitzin Hamesh, her teacher for Jewish thought, filled her with admiration. While she viewed with pity her excess weight, her stiffly sprayed, formally coiffed wigs, and her matronly clothes and thick ankles, she nevertheless found her witty and charming in a pale-lipped pious way. Delilah was certain Rebbitzin Hamesh would wind up in heaven with a rich reward.

Once, Rebbitzin Hamesh invited the girls over on a Friday night. She'd worn a blue-velvet ankle-length housecoat and an elaborate head scarf. The house had been well swept with colorful touches, surprisingly beautiful rugs in bright greens and reds on the floors and walls. The house had smelled of roast chicken and warm sweet apple kugel. There had been a large lovely china closet filled with beautiful silver ritual objects. And

Rebbitzin Hamesh had not looked miserable or tasteless as she sat there with her ankles crossed, her clean cheeks shining like ripe apples as she read her prayer book and waited for her husband to return from synagogue with her well-scrubbed children.

But it had been so quiet, so very, very quiet. Like being in paradise already. Or like being dead. Rebbitzin Hamesh, Delilah thought, was too young for this kind of life. Anyone under eighty was too young. And that, Delilah decided, was the problem with worrying about earning your heavenly reward too early. It was then she made up her mind to live until she died. Rewards in the Afterlife, Heaven or Hell, were hard to imagine, let alone sacrifice the here and now for. It was like that television show, *Let's Make a Deal.* Do you trade the perfectly fine refrigerator you have in your hand for curtain number three, which might or might not have a new car, thereby risking getting stuck with a broken-down wagon filled with straw? Ah, the eternal question.

One night, Yitzie took her to a friend's apartment "for a Chanukah party." It was in an apartment house in Kew Gardens. No one answered the door when they knocked. Surprisingly, she saw he had a key. When he opened the door, there was no menorah. No latkes. No dreidels. No friends. They were alone together.

By the light of the menorah he dug up somewhere in a closet ("Otherwise, I'm leaving!") he sat down beside her on the very worn but comfortable old sofa, where he piously reminded her of the Jewish custom of relaxing while the candles still burned. He apologized for upsetting her. And then, almost more quickly than she could have imagined, things got completely out of hand. She didn't even recognize herself, the feelings streaming through her like a tsunami breaking through, washing out her brain like some flimsy beach structure that just floated out to sea, unpinned from its moorings. His clothes were everywhere. His hands were everywhere. And then, suddenly, her clothes were everywhere too. It was all happening so fast, she wasn't even sure she knew, exactly, what was going on. At least, that is what she told herself then, and later. She felt stunned, enthralled, humiliated, embarrassed, curious. When it was over, she stood up, looking down at the couch pillows. She touched them. Were they damp, dry? Were the stains old, new?

Frantically, she pulled on her clothes.

Afterward, Yitzie was very romantic, very concerned. On the way back to Bernstein, he stopped a block away. There, in the shadowed alleyway of an office tower, he held her close and kissed her just the way she'd always imagined in her fantasies. Yet, alone, sitting on her dorm-room bed, she felt a sense of deep shock and horror.

She undressed and took a shower, fingering her body tenderly, as if it belonged to someone else, someone childish and vulnerable. She examined herself, her clothing, the dark blue skirt, the white lamb's-wool sweater. She was not in any pain; still, the idea of what might have happened was profoundly terrifying to her.

Was it a sin? she wondered. And if so, which one?

She was free and single. And sex without marriage wasn't actually forbidden anywhere, as far as she could tell, whatever blather they'd thrown at her in high school. True, she hadn't gone to the ritual baths, but that was more Yitzie's problem than hers, sin-wise. She began to calm down, soaping herself and standing in the downpour of lovely hot water until all her bad thoughts just washed away. It was just nature taking its course. She shrugged, a secret little smile curling her lips as she allowed herself to think, How lovely! How lovely! And now that they had *done it* (she began to convince herself of that fact, although she was by no means sure; it had all happened so fast, and she was so totally inexperienced), she was now certain, beyond a doubt, that chuppah and *kedushin*—a marriage canopy and a sacred wedding ceremony—were on the horizon, the next step for the two of them.

She would be Mrs. Yitzie Polinsky, daughter-in-law of the renowned Torah sage Rebbe Menachem Polinsky of Crown Heights. And Yitzie? He would find his place in law or accounting or be taken in by one of his father's wealthy Hasidim as a trainee and later a partner in some lucrative import-export business. There would be a lovely home in Jamaica Estates, one of those mock Tudors that Donald Trump's father had put up and that were going for a million or more these days. They'd put in a swimming pool—she had to have a swimming pool—and beautiful Henredon French country-style furniture. She already had a scrapbook filled with ads for exactly the pieces she wanted. She'd have a large china closet filled with wonderful silver ritual objects, and all those creamy, gold-edged porcelain pieces made especially for Jews by Lenox: the seder plate, the kiddush cup, all of which would never be used and would pass untouched to her children, who would also never use them. She'd have a charge account in Lord & Taylor and Macy's. And they'd have great sex and a house filled with little yeshiva boys and pretty yeshiva girls. And everyone who'd been unkind to her in high school would eat their hearts out.

So she didn't object when Yitzie suggested another "party" at the same friend's house. But this time, when they got there, he took out a camera.

She stared at it. He kissed her and then started to unbutton her blouse. It was just that she was so beautiful, he explained rapidly. He wanted a picture of her like this, to always remember, for when they got old.

The idea that he was thinking so far ahead into the future thrilled her. "You know, Yitzie," she cooed, "we really should do something about this if we love each other so much. Why don't we just get married?"

She saw his eyes twitch as he continued to smile and fiddle with her buttons.

Had he not heard her? she wondered, as she suddenly leaned out of his reach.

He sat back. "What's wrong?"

"I asked you a question."

He made a sound like *mmmmhummyeehmm*.

"What does that mean?"

"It means you're interrupting me."

She snatched the camera and threw it against the wall.

"What the . . . ?" Yitzie jumped up. "That's a Canon!"

"I want an answer."

He was on his knees, gathering up the pieces, appalled. He looked at her, his eyes narrowing. "Are you sure?"

"Yes, I'm sure!" she told him hotly, as her heart sank.

He shrugged. "It's been fun, but you've gotten the wrong impression."

Her face paled. "What impression is that, Yitzie?"

"That we're a nice Orthodox Jewish couple from Brooklyn who's just blowing off a little steam until we fall back into the fold."

That's exactly what she'd thought, except for the Brooklyn part. She was, after all, from Queens, a major difference as far as she was concerned. "I know that! Who said I want that?"

He touched her face; his eyes held a sardonic gleam. "Don't you? Aren't you just dying to pick out your colors and move into my family's two-family in Crown Heights where we can live until we have the down payment for our own house in some swanky Jewish neighborhood, walking distance to the local shul?" He sneered.

She shrugged off his hand. "So what if I am? Who do you think you are, Mick Jagger? You're Rabbi Polinsky's son, the one who wears a *streimel* and *kapota* every Saturday, like some Polish nobleman from the Middle Ages. Sooner or later, if you wait around, they'll fix you up with some short rabbi's daughter with thick stockings from Beit Yaakov. She'll make you turn off the lights and put a hole in a sheet."

His hands fumbled around, looking for a cigarette. He lit it and lay down on the bed, exhaling large smoke rings that rose and broke against the dirty white ceiling. The smell of smoke was suffocating. "You know, Delilah, that hole-in-the-sheet thing? It's a myth."

She began to cough. He ran one finger up her arm from wrist to elbow. "I'm going to miss you," he said.

She thought perhaps she hadn't heard him right.

A few weeks later, she missed.

Well, that was putting it pessimistically, she told herself. After all, she didn't always get it on the day it was supposed to come. There were a million reasons. I mean, she wasn't a clock the way some girls were.

But then four more days passed. And a fifth.

She called Yitzie, but all she got was an answering machine. She left ten messages, one every half hour. Then she went knocking on Sharona Gottleib's door.

Sharona opened it. She looked annoyed. "Well, well."

What had she ever done to her? But there was no time for game playing.

"Listen, I've got to get in touch with Yitzie. He doesn't answer the phone—"

Sharona pulled her in and shut the door behind her, her fingers painfully tight around her wrist. "Not so loud, you idiot!"

"You don't understand."

She arched her brow. "No, huh? Late, are we?"

Delilah sank down on the bed. "Well, maybe. But I'm not even sure we had . . . that we did . . . What am I going to do, Sharona?"

"I tried to warn you. But you wouldn't listen."

Was that true? Delilah searched her memory and came up with a few snooty remarks thrown in her direction by Sharona when she'd asked for Yitzie's phone number. Something like, "You are making a huge mistake.

He's poison." She'd chalked it up to jealousy. Or to Sharona feeling she wasn't as good as Penina, not worthy of the great Yitzie Polinsky.

"But you were the one who fixed him up with Penina! If you felt that way, why did you do it?"

Sharona's face went rigid. "I had no choice. He's got some photos of me."

This information sank in with horror. "Oh, no! Sharona, what am I going to do?"

Sharona went to the door and opened it. "You'll figure it out."

Oh, God. Oh, God. Oh, God.

She lay back on her bed, the blinds drawn, the sounds of New York City street traffic rolling over her as if she were lying spread-eagled on 42nd Street and Sixth Avenue. Instinctively, she stretched her fingers over her stomach, as she tried to imagine the future. Was it her imagination, or was it already rounder, fuller?

She saw herself waddling through the halls, her sweaters stretched over a basketball-sized lump. She imagined the shocked and horrified stares of her classmates, the good yeshiva girls, the out-of-town rabbis' daughters, as they whispered just behind her. She saw herself summoned into Rebbitzin Craimer's office, the way she would ease her bulky pregnant body into the narrow chair as the old yenta lectured her about being a bad influence, a disgrace to the good name of the institution. What could she answer? She'd even have to agree!

And then they would throw her out of school with no degree, all that tuition and studying about plaque down the toilet, and all her student loans coming due with no way to pay them off! Her father (her mother, she was sure, would not be around, having died of a heart attack the moment she'd heard the news) would grudgingly take her in, and she'd have to listen to his snoring and watch him sit around in those sleeveless undershirts he liked, his skinny chest and hairy arms flailing as he tried to comfort her. She'd have to listen to his advice: Go back to Dallas or Houston. You'll be better off. Sorry I ever came to this city. They've got plenty of rabbis down in Texas. Don't worry. You'll find rabbis.

Or perhaps she'd throw herself on the mercies of the city's welfare system and rent a little apartment, a fourth-floor walk-up where she'd sit terrified behind thrice-bolted doors, hoping crackheads and dope fiends wouldn't break it down and kidnap her and her baby, selling them both into white slavery. A place where for recreation, she'd watch the roaches race each other across the kitchen counter. None of her friends would visit her. She'd be an outcast.

Hot tears dripped into her pillow as she rolled over onto her side.

There was another way. A trip to a clinic—they were clean and efficient, and it wouldn't be worse than going to a dentist—and before you could say Yitzie Polinsky, the little bugger would be an ingredient in some new antiaging cosmetic venture.

Her baby. They'd suck it out of her.

She'd seen that book with the pictures of fetuses inside the womb. Whatever those crazy women's groups told you about freedom over your body, it was a baby. It had a head, and a little tush, and tiny fingers and those tiny closed eyes. And they'd just Hoover it out of her, like some mess that needed cleaning up.

It was then she'd felt the entire true weight of sin crash down on her. Whatever she'd done in her life so far, she hadn't actually done anything hurtful to God. But killing a baby, even the froglike beginnings of a baby, because it was too inconvenient and embarrassing, would be a true sin. The God she seldom thought about, but always believed in, would not be able to forgive that. And for the rest of her life, she would have to live in a world in which she knew she had done this terrible thing, until the day she died, at which point her true punishment would only begin.

According to some woman who'd undergone a near-death experience—a bunch of bricks fell on her head while she was walking in the street—and had explained it all on *Oprah*, when you died you had this moment when you were forced to sit back and watch your life, like a movie. You couldn't close your eyes, because you had no eyelids. God would be watching her watch herself as the film showed her walking to the clinic, filling out the forms, lying down on the table. It would show her letting them, *telling them*, to rid her of this God-given life. A child, hers and Yitzie Polinsky's.

She was more frightened than she had ever been in her life.

"Can I put on the light?"

It was her roommate, Rivkie.

Rivkie Lifschitz was blessed with all things. She was from a respected well-to-do family and already engaged to an acknowledged Torah scholar. Perhaps because life had treated her so gently, she had also become a kind and generous human being. She was the kind of girl who learned the Torah portion of the week and managed to extract some beautiful moral lesson even from those difficult sections that dealt with body sores full of pus and the minutiae of the laws involved in animal sacrifices. "Blind or broken, or maimed, or having a wen or a dry or moist scab, ye shall not bring these near unto God and as an offering made by fire shall ye not bring aught of them unto the Altar." Even in this, Rivkie Lifschitz would manage to find some redeeming little detail, something about the priest's wife, and how the rabbis say that a man's house is his wife. How a woman completely bears the character of the home, and how holy that is. And a woman who is the wife of a temple priest—or his daughter—has a higher degree of holiness. . . . Only Rivkie could ferret out these details.

Once, she'd even had a discussion with Rivkie about *bedikot*, those mandatory self-examinations pious women performed for a week following their menstrual period to check if their vaginal discharges were completely free of blood before immersing in the ritual baths and resuming relations with their husbands. If the inserted cloth came out white, no prob. If it came out red, big prob. But if it came out yellow or brown, a woman had to ask a rabbi to examine it and decide whether she could count it as a clean day, and go on toward the finish line and her husband's arms, or if she had to return to Go, and start counting all over again.

"It really isn't as bad as you think. You can FedEx it to any rabbi in the country. He doesn't even have to know who you are. Or you can give it to the rebbitzin."

"You've got to be kidding!"

Rivkie had looked at her, surprised. "Look, we're all just trying to do God's will because we love Him so much. If He is asking us to separate until we can count seven clean days, we have to do it in the best way possible, because He is so good to us, and asks so little. . . . It would be terrible to separate a couple more than is necessary, and terrible to allow them to be intimate when it's against God's will. It's part of a rabbi's job description to help couples keep their marriage holy in God's eyes. And if I, as the rabbi's helpmate, can help him, or help the women in my congregation feel more comfortable about asking, then it would be a tremendous good deed, no?"

That was Rivkie. The perfect future rabbi's wife, whom no detail of ritual observance, no matter how gross, demeaning, or disgusting, could derail her from her earnest pursuit of true holiness.

No one could dislike Rivkie. It was impossible. She was so giving, so sincere. And even though you might smile behind your hand at her earnestness and the way she bounced around the world with love and enthusiasm, there would be no way you could fault her. There wasn't a mean or selfish bone in her body. Whatever she learned, she put into practice.

They'd been roommates for about six months. They hadn't spoken much. This, Rivkie chalked up to the fact that Delilah was a little older than she was and perhaps from a family of lesser means, which forced her to be extra busy earning money to finance her studies. The few times they had had a conversation, Delilah had wound up borrowing clothes, which Rivkie was only too happy to lend her—overjoyed, in fact.

She felt guilty sometimes for coming from such a wealthy family, being engaged to such a wonderful young man, having her health and her whole future ahead of her. She wanted to thank God every waking minute, and any good deed she managed to do she felt gave God back some pleasure. She felt this way even when her clothes came back to her wrinkled and stained—or failed to come back at all, which she viewed as an even bigger mitzva, because Delilah obviously needed new clothes badly, enough to take someone else's.

Rivkie sat down at her bedside, shocked. "Delilah, what's wrong?"

Her voice, so sweet and kind, filled with true concern, demolished the floodgates. Delilah sat up and sobbed—loud wet sobs full of the breathless sucking up of phlegm.

Rivkie, horrified, put her arms around her and patted her back. "Can't you tell me what's the matter? Maybe I could help you?"

At this, Delilah sobbed even louder.

Rivkie hugged her. "You don't have to tell me. But you should tell God. Talk to Him. Explain it to Him. Ask Him to help you."

Delilah looked up with surprise. Taking the tissue from Rivkie's hand, she considered it. Yes! Yes! This was the answer. Who was compassionate and kind and forgiving? Who, after all, caused new life to be created in the first place?

Most of all, who could perform miracles?

Yes, yes, yes!

She put her arms around Rivkie's slim shoulders, noting through her misty eyes that she was wearing a new blouse, one that had yet to be hung up in the closet, and that it was a very nice material. Silk? And that color, sort of a summer green. She wiped her eyes carefully, not wanting to get water spots on it that might ruin it, because she had a skirt that was the perfect match. . . . "Thank you, Rivkie. You've saved me. That's what I'll do. I'll pray." She saw her roommate's eyes shine through undropped heartfelt tears.

For a moment, Delilah felt her heart pierced by the knowledge that such innocence and sincerity existed in the world. She didn't doubt for a minute that if she poured her heart out and told Rivkie everything—which, of course, she had absolutely no intention of doing; she wasn't a complete idiot—the girl would not sit in judgment.

She suddenly remembered what her teachers had once told them about Judaism being a system in which human beings attempt to imitate God. Until this moment, she had never understood what such a thing could mean. Rivkie, like God Himself, would without question react with sympathy and compassion.

Delilah was suddenly flooded by an aching desire to be a person like that, someone who went through life cleanly, openly, helping others, at one with God and other human beings. Perhaps it was not too late? Jews believed in repentance and clean slates and having your sins wiped away.

She would pray to God. She would ask His forgiveness, ask Him to solve this problem to which she could find no solution that would not lead to even worse problems. She would hand the whole sordid mess over to Him. And if He answered her, she would finally and absolutely know there was a God, and He wasn't just a mythical being, like the tooth fairy or Santa Claus, a concept created by the popular imagination because human beings have to have explanations, and because they want to believe that their lives have some purpose, some meaning. She would bury all her skepticism, her doubts, and be reborn.

She got up.

"Do you want me to go with you?" Rivkie asked.

She shook her head. "No. I need to do this alone."

She took her purse and put on a pair of sunglasses to hide her eyes, since it didn't seem appropriate to begin repairing her makeup. Then she walked slowly around the corner to the synagogue.

Of course, it was locked. For a moment, all her good feelings evaporated. Why was it, she fumed, that churches were always open, always filled with quiet darkness, candles, etc. etc., and synagogues never were? And even if she waited around in the faint hope that some beadle might come by and unlock it for men wanting to say their afternoon prayers, still, she'd be the only woman there, and all of them would stare at her.

So where now? Where could she go that was dark and secret and spiritual? Where she would feel free to express her deepest soul and ponder the mysteries of the universe, God, and faith? She looked up and saw the movie house. They were playing *Star Wars*, which she had been planning on seeing again anyway.

The movie was just starting, but the theater was practically empty. She took a seat in an empty row at the far end of the aisle near the front, where anything she said aloud would be swallowed by the Dolby sound blasters. There was some kind of loud galactic fight going on.

"Please, God, I know I haven't been behaving myself the way You'd want," she whispered, then stopped. It sounded like she was talking to a school principal. She took a deep breath. "Dearest Father in Heaven," she began. But it sounded so phony, so Holy Scroll Press, that religious publishing house that translated Hebrew prayers into unbearable English and published books professing to be compilations of standard Jewish laws but were actually modern reinventions so stringent and reactionary they made Maimonides look like a flaming liberal. She sat back quietly, exhausted, and watched.

Obi-Wan Kenobi and Qui-Gon Jinn, who had only good intentions, who were actually sent to make peace and stop the trade blockade of a perfectly innocent little planet, were about to be killed for no good reason. She felt angry tears drop at the terrible injustice of the world, where innocent people with good intentions—*had she ever had any other kind? Had she not been, at the very moment disaster struck, planning to be a good Jewish wife and mother, taking care of a family in a large and comfortable house?*—were pursued mercilessly by evil.

She put her hand over her stomach. Well, a baby couldn't be called evil. It was a consequence but not an evil consequence. Just very inconvenient and embarrassing.

Her prayer was not going well at all, she realized, taking her eyes off the screen just as they landed on Tatooine and met Anakin Skywalker. . . .

She closed her eyes, gripping the seat in front of her with both hands.

"I'm not good at prayer," she whispered. "It's hard for me to concentrate; my mind is always wandering. But I'm scared, God. Really scared. I know I deserve to be punished for all the bad things I've done"—*clothes strewn over the floor, body parts touching intimately*—"but I really, really want children some day. But in the right way. With a visit to the ritual baths, and a marriage canopy, and a marriage contract handwritten by a scribe on vellum, signed by witnesses. Please forgive me for even considering aborting a child, if I am . . . if I am . . ." She hesitated, then stammered the word out loud. "Pregnant!" She looked around, frightened she'd been overheard. But people's eyes were on the screen. She sighed, her heart racing. She put her palm over it. "You are smarter than I am. Please find some way to help me out on this. I don't want to hurt an innocent child, or my future husband, or my parents." She took a deep breath. "But if I have a baby now, I will be thrown out of the Jewish community. I will never be able to marry a decent man, to be a good Jewish wife and mother. And I know that's what You want for me, isn't it?"

So far, she didn't see how God could be impressed, since she was even boring herself. And so God, who must hear this kind of stuff 24/7, must be snoring. She felt a sense of desperation, as if she were watching a delicate operation and the patient was flatlining and the doctors were using those electrodes, or whatever, to zap the heart one last time before calling it a day.

She leaned forward, a new sense of desperation making her body stiff and electric with passion. "Please, God, get me out of this! If You do, I swear on everything holy that I'll change!" She rapidly went down a checklist. "I'll pray every morning. I'll starve myself on all the minor fast days. I'll wear skirts that cover my knees and blouses that cover my"—briefly, she considered saying *wrists*, but there was no way—"that cover two fists above my elbow. I'll marry a good Jewish man and I'll be the best wife, the best religious Jewish wife and mother. You won't be sorry. Please help me!"

She felt a sudden warm flow between her legs. The skirt, she realized, was ruined. But her life was saved. It was a good trade, especially considering it was Rivkie's skirt.

Her life, she knew, was about to undergo a transformation.

~ ~

That morning, she carefully culled her closet of anything above the knee, anything red, anything too form-fitting. She culled and culled and culled. Finally, she put on the only white long-sleeved blouse she owned along with a skirt that reached mid-calf, which was possibly Rivkie's. It certainly could not be hers; she couldn't even remember ever trying on such a skirt, let alone actually buying it. Combing and twisting her long hair into a bun, she took out her prayer book and sat on the edge of her bed, praying. When she was done, she kissed the prayer book and put it down.

Rivkie looked her over approvingly. "So, you feel better?"

Delilah nodded. "God has answered my prayers. I don't know why. I didn't deserve any special favors."

"You know, when God tells us to imitate Him, that's what He means. He does favors for us not because we've earned or deserve them but out of infinite compassion and mercy. That's why *chesed* is such an important part of being a Jew. Do good deeds because it's the right thing to do and you have the opportunity to imitate God. That's the only way we can ever pay Him back for everything He does for us. He gives us the sun, and He only asks that we light a little candle."

Rivkie's words, although full of every cliché religious teachings had to offer, somehow touched Delilah's wounded soul.

"Rivkie, I have to change my life. I want to be just like you. I want to have your goodness. I want to go out with only good, religious boys. Men with good hearts. I want to reach out to people and help them. I want to get married. Can you help me, Rivkie? Can you?"

{ THREE }

When Chaim Levi was five years old, his grandfather, a Holocaust survivor and the venerated rebbe of a small *shteibel* in Ocean Parkway, enrolled him in a yeshiva in Williamsburg where the rabbis' beards were long and gray and they conversed as if the village in Poland they'd grown up in had been relocated, not wiped off the map.

Chaim's father, an electrical appliance salesman in Canarsie, beardless and dapper, was a man who respected tradition but knew which world he was living in. Still, out of respect and pity and guilt, he bent his will to his father's, hoping the old man might find in his grandson what had been lacking in his son.

Chaim was a handsome little boy, with big dark eyes and a shy, sweet smile. Not particularly bright, but good-natured and pleasant, as only the favored, longed-for man-child of a family starting from scratch could be (*kaddishel*, they called him, someone able to say the prayer for the dead for them), little Chaim went to yeshiva with an expectant smile, never doubting approval.

At first, he didn't really understand the meaning of the long, heavy ruler in the hands of the bearded little rebbe, who slapped it against his palm as he walked up and down between the rows of seated boys. But soon, Chaim caught on. *Smack!* For not getting your mouth around the Hebrew vowels of the biblical verse fast enough. *Smack!* For not reciting the daily prayers with enough devotion. *Slam! Smack! Crack!* For not paying attention, for fidgeting in your seat, for forgetting to kiss the prayer book. . . .

Around the room the little rebbe went, gesturing impatiently for each to give him their hand. Once in his possession, he would grip the small palm between his thumb and forefinger, slamming the ruler down on the nails as often as it took to bring a howl. That accomplished, the hand would be released. Then, astonishingly, the rebbe would jut his head forward and point to his cheek, indicating where the victim was expected to plant a grateful kiss to thank him for his instruction.

At recess, when the boys finally escaped into the yard to play baseball, calling the plays in Yiddish, there never failed to appear another little *rebbeleh*, a gnomelike figure in a tallis and tefillin, who would rush into the yard and insist on reciting his morning prayers at the top of his lungs, demanding that the boys stop playing and respond *Omeyn* in all the right places. By the time the praying was over, so was the recess.

Chaim complained to his parents, who secretly raised eyebrows and exchanged worried glances but nevertheless publicly backed the teachers. He began to wet the bed. He broke out in hives. He bit his nails to the quick, then let the ragged edges bleed.

He tried to learn, practicing the Hebrew words. He tried to sit still. To pay attention. But when the rebbe (*wham!*) wished—for Chaim's own good, of course—to (*WHAM!*) help free him of the unaesthetic and distasteful habit of nail-biting (*wham! Wham! WHAM!*), he felt a little volcano suddenly erupt in his brain. He ran to the window of the classroom and jumped down to the adjoining fire escape. Looking over his shoulder, he quickly ran down two flights to the street. Once there, he carefully spread-eagled himself on the pavement.

Carefully, he opened one eye, just in time to see the rebbe swoon, his ruler clattering to the ground. The boys, hanging out the window, cheered.

With his parents' and the yeshiva's full agreement, another school was found for Chaim, an Orthodox Hebrew day school, where smooth-cheeked American rabbis cracked jokes, and public school teachers in high heels and red lipstick came in the afternoons to teach them about the Statue of Liberty and the *Mayflower.* A place with a gym and a basketball court and vending machines.

His grandfather was heartbroken.

But when the boy was actually able to recite Talmudic passages in Aramaic and knew the difference between a Rashi and a *tosefot*, he relented. Little Chaim had taken a detour but was nevertheless on an upward path toward taking over his grandfather's congregation. An *illuy*, a Talmudic genius, he wasn't. But when he put his mind to it—or was coerced or bullied into putting his mind to it—he managed to keep up with the class, although he never rose to more than a middling student.

He had little imagination, but he was good at memorizing. He memorized whole passages from the Talmud, which sometimes convinced a certain kind of dreamy and unduly optimistic teacher that he had a special aptitude for it. Truthfully, most of the time, he had no idea what the passage was about that he rattled off with such ease. He couldn't decipher it and wasn't interested in it. The give and take of Talmudic discussions he viewed with trepidation, fearing they would reveal his intellectual deficiencies. Still, he always managed to get A's in Talmud, which thrilled his grandfather.

When Chaim entered high school, his grandfather offered to pay his entire college tuition if he would consider getting *smicha*, rabbinical ordination. It was the old man's fervent hope that, when his time came, his grandson would step into his shoes, shepherding and nurturing the beloved congregation he would leave behind.

It was a generous offer, but Chaim wasn't so sure. To put it mildly, his grandfather's modest synagogue did not reek of enticing possibilities. His mental image of the place conjured up dusty, mostly empty pews and creaky tables laden with anemic sponge cake and plastic cups of cloyingly sweet wine, all set out to fete a congregation transferring with alarming rapidity from rent-controlled Bronx apartments to paid-up plots in Forest Lawn. The demographics of the neighborhood had changed. The building had future Baptist Temple written all over it.

All his friends were interested in careers in computers or accounting, neither of which thrilled him either. Basically, all he wanted was something respectable, where he wouldn't have to work too hard and which would provide him with a reasonable and steady income, enough to afford a two-family house in a better section of New Jersey, a Chevy station wagon, a JC-Penney charge card, and tuition at Hebrew day schools for his children.

What else did he need, really?

When it came to religion, he was not a cynic, like so many of his classmates, who were only in the lifestyle until they could escape their parents' clutches. He was simple in his faith, a sincere, Torah-observant Jew, a person who prayed and practiced, studied and struggled. A person who sometimes succeeded, sometimes failed, repented and tried again. And all through his growing years he eventually developed a trust that his faith would see him through every joy and sorrow. It didn't always make sense to him, the myriad laws, the intricate web of custom and lore that ruled every minute of his life, but it felt comfortable, like an old house that has its creaks and leaks but nevertheless embraces one with its sheltering arms. As for God, He was a comfortable, familiar presence, someone who sat next to him on the couch when he watched television, and who jogged alongside him in the park.

He never understood Maimonides' God, that cold, far-off, unknowable Being, more an intellectual exercise than a Father, who had nothing to do with the heart. He believed in a God Who listened to phone calls, heard prayers and whispers, and was not above lending a helping hand when the occasion required it.

Chaim was comfortable in his own skin, happy with his place in the world, the little niche he'd been born into. A poor imagination is sometimes a blessing. In Chaim's case, it helped him to ward off frightening visions of a future full of fierce ambitions to accomplish outlandish scenarios in which he would be the main character.

The idea of taking over from his venerated grandfather, someone he truly loved and respected and in whom he felt great pride, seemed preposterous. A rabbi? Someone who stood at the front and had all eyes glued to him? Someone others looked to for guidance and wisdom? He didn't see himself as a do-gooder or a leader or even a politician, all of which he understood were invaluable qualities in a pulpit rabbi. He much preferred—and planned for—the simple life of the follower and had no doubt he would eventually discover a leader whose devoutness, charisma, and brilliance would shine out like a lighthouse, leading him in the right direction.

His parents were satisfied. The last thing they wanted was for him to take over his grandfather's annoying and penurious congregation of pensioners, who kept pennies in jars and cooked meals on one burner. His mother, who knew a thing or two, was especially appalled by the idea of such an un-American profession for her one and only son, a job that promised bad pay, no advancement, and plenty of aggravation. She wanted him to be a dentist, which in her mind lacked all such drawbacks. His father wanted him to be happy and, if possible, to sell stereo systems.

At some point during his sophomore year in high school, he realized that math—necessary for both computers and accounting—was not his best subject. As for dentistry, he learned from a distant cousin, who had recently set up an office in Queens, that tuition to dental school rivaled that of medical school—that is, if you could get in, not a small question considering his grades. And even if you passed all the hurdles, you were still left with buying all that expensive equipment, unless you wanted to hire yourself out to an established office and work for someone else "forever for nothing," as his cousin put it to him. The student loans and the bank loans for the machinery would take years to pay off. Besides, people's breath in your face . . . the sound of the drill . . . the smell of those metals and powders and gummy pastes . . . ?

The summer between his junior and senior year, another cousin found him a job up in the Catskills as a busboy at a strictly kosher hotel. He lied about being eighteen, so they hired him. It was a nice enough place for the guests, but the staff lived in ratty, mosquito-filled bungalows and were fed leftovers by hotel owners who took the epithet "cheap bastards" to a new level. The food first went to the adults. A day later, whatever the adults hadn't managed to eat was served up in the children's dining room. Whatever the kids were bright enough to bypass showed up on the staff's plates.

So of course the waiters and busboys never saved anything, effectively ending the leftover problem. In fact, they felt spilling out the day-old milk before it was foisted on the unsuspecting babies (not to mention themselves) was a mitzva. When the owners somehow got wind of the situation, they started going through the trash. They were experts at eagle-eyed discoveries of unsqueezed lemons, which they insisted be washed off and served again.

The guests, however, were decent people, and the tips made the summer stay worthwhile, providing most of them with a good chunk of their college tuition and living expenses. So, Chaim stayed on. It turned out to be a fateful decision, because that summer, he experienced a revelation that changed his life forever.

One weekend, the hotel hosted its annual convention of the Council of American Orthodox Rabbis. Hundreds of Orthodox rabbis and their wives descended upon the resort from all over the country. Chaim had expected dignified men in dark suits, black hats, big skullcaps, and dark beards, men who were shy and retiring, whose weighty conversations would revolve around serious moral issues.

Instead, they arrived in shorts and flowery, big-printed Hawaiian shirts. Rabbis on vacation, he realized, were more or less like everyone else on vacation, with wives in short summer dresses and bikinis by the pool. The hotel was filled with loud laughter and card-playing. He hardly saw one of them crack open a book, let alone a heavy Talmudic tome. And in between, they would saunter into the auditorium and discuss "The Future of American Judaism."

It was then Chaim had his revelation: Rabbis were ordinary human beings. Nothing special. I could do this, he thought. But why would I want to?

One of the old-timers, a professional waiter who'd been around, told him that they used to have the National Council of Synagogue Youth conventions the week before the rabbis' convention, and then treat the most sincere kids to stay over and be inspired. But soon they switched the order, so the rabbis and their bikini-clad wives were gone before the kids got there.

And indeed, a week later, the kids showed up. A few of the rabbis stayed behind to organize seminars on Jewish values and modesty and service to the community. They changed into dark pants and white open-collared shirts. The fresh-faced, wide-eyed kids in their mid-to-upper teens, who had come from all over the country, gathered in small seminars in banqueting halls and on the lawn. The waiters poked one another and made snide remarks about jailbait. But Chaim, who in general didn't have a sense of humor about such things, said nothing. And then one evening, when he had cleaned off his table and eaten his dinner, he wandered into one of the seminars and sat down quietly in the back.

The rabbi giving the lecture was short and youthful, with immense energy that seemed to lift him off the ground as he spoke. "The most important two things in life are renewal and courage. Turn the page and begin again, as if you are starting from scratch; as if the world had never been created, and you are at that moment creating it. I'm not saying this is easy. I'm not telling you that you won't fail sometimes, that you'll never get depressed. Never give in to depression, whatever the reasons! Even if you feel the years have flown by and all your mistakes have just piled up, never despair. This is the greatness of our Creator: His compassion has no end. He will never give up on you, so never give up on yourselves. He knows who we are—He made us, didn't He?—so even the worst person, the biggest crook, the most evil gossip, is God's child, and God looks at him and, like a father, always hopes he'll turn it around. It's never too late.

"To be a Jew is to remember that we are in charge of makeovers. Not the kind with the hair and the nails. Universe makeovers. We take terrible situations where there is only evil—people who are unkind to one another and full of hatred—and we transform lives. We change things. And we start by changing ourselves.

"You, the youth of tomorrow, the leaders and rabbis and doctors and artists, you are going to make over the world you were born into. You are going to give it new hope, new chances to be the beautiful moral place our Creator envisioned when He separated the water from the dry land, when He set down Adam and his wife Eve. In every generation, you are Adam and Eve in Eden, able to start again."

Chaim studied the enthralled, uplifted faces of the young people around him. He too felt uplifted. To be a rabbi like that! To stand in front of a group of people and fill their hearts with hope, their minds with good intentions and proper desires. To lead people forward to a new place where they would be happier, kinder, and more just, making the world that much happier, kinder, and more just. It was a noble thing, was it not?

Could I? he wondered. Was it at all possible? What did it take to become a real rabbi? And did he have it in him?

He didn't know.

But as he looked over college brochures and added up the numbers for tuition and board at places like NYU or Columbia, the realization struck him that Brooklyn or Queens College were in his future, along with some express ticket to nowhere called a BA in education or sociology. So when his grandfather repeated his long-standing offer to underwrite Chaim's tuition at Bernstein Rabbinical College if he was accepted to their Rabbinic Ordination program, it suddenly seemed like a reprieve.

Bernstein expected its rabbinical students to get a secular degree as well. And having *smicha* didn't force one to actually become a practicing rabbi. Many a lawyer, store owner, and insurance salesman on Ocean Parkway had *smicha*.

In addition, at Bernstein he'd be assured of a steady social life, a stream of willing Orthodox girls who attended Stern College or Bernstein Women's College, many of them from well-to-do newly religious families, girls who, unlike those in the fancy Hebrew day school he'd grown up with (who wanted handsome Orthodox future doctors), would be only too thrilled to meet a nice Jewish boy from Brooklyn who came from a rabbinical family. At Bernstein these girls would be thrown in his direction in droves. No senior—however bad his teeth, poor his personality, or ordinary his family—would be permitted to get his diploma without a wife, and preferably a small noisy child, sitting in the audience to applaud him.

And some of these girls, he'd heard, the ones from down South or the Midwest, were real lookers.

He began his studies with the serious, dogged determination that had seen him through high school. He took classes in Talmud, contemporary Jewish law (*halacha*), and Introductory Rabbinic Survey. In addition, the school required him to concomitantly earn a master's degree in either Jewish education and administration, social work, or psychology, which he could opt out of only if he was willing to take six intensive semesters of advanced Talmud study, which was for him not an option, thanks. He opted for social work, which is what he thought being a rabbi was all about anyway.

In his rabbinic studies, he worked diligently, memorizing what he could and avoiding class participation whenever possible. He could repeat what you told him, almost word for word, but when asked to elucidate the law, to leap ahead to original conclusions, he was lost.

His teachers, compassionate men who had seen their share of losers, knew with whom they dealt. Keeping in mind the joys and struggles of their own early scholarship, as well as the apocryphal story of Akiva, the ignorant shepherd who was over forty when by sheer diligence he began a study program that turned him into Rabbi Akiva, one of Judaism's greatest scholars and leaders, they were not without hope. Rabbi Akiva had said that the image that had inspired him to greatness was that of water dripping on a rock until it finally made a hole. When they looked at Chaim, they saw the rock, imagined their words as water, and hoped for the best.

They gave him passing, if not wonderful, grades that would permit him to continue, so that other rabbis would have to deal with the situation and have it on their conscience each Yom Kippur. In this way, he passed from class to class and rabbi to rabbi until his four years were almost over and, except for one semester on a particularly difficult segment of the Talmudical tractate *Yoreh Deah* with a young teacher who graded him objectively and without compassion, he managed, miraculously, not to flunk anything.

In his social work courses he did especially well, finding a real affinity for the course material, which had no apparent discipline, scientific basis, or true information that one couldn't figure out simply by using average common sense. He felt triumphant, and looked ahead to a promising future out in the world, where grades would cease to matter, and no one would be checking his scholarship with a magnifying glass. All they would see was the *klaf smicha*, the traditional ordination certificate handwritten by a scribe on parchment, with his name carefully spelled out in calligraphic letters to prove his worthiness and competency to head an Orthodox congregation.

As his course work wound down and he began to envision his future, his thoughts turned more and more to the subject of marriage. Few and far between (in fact, he had never in his life heard of such a thing) was the congregation whose rabbi had no rebbitzin. Indeed, the interviews took the wife into consideration with almost equal weight. After all, she would be an integral part of his work. She would create the proper atmosphere in the synagogue, a hominess, openness, and warmth. She'd be up there in the front pew, setting an example with her diligent prayers, her friendly smile, her many well-disciplined children, her compassion, her modest clothing, her great hat, wig, and so on. She would set the style for the women, showing the ideal of wife and mother that each needed to aspire to, just as the rabbi set a shining example to the men with his good nature, good deeds, and scholarship.

Yet he never thought about the woman he would marry in terms of a work partner. He wanted, first and foremost, someone he could love and who would love him. He wanted someone he felt attracted to sexually. There had to be some chemistry, hormonal flows, a little tickle in his stomach. He liked nice legs and a shapely body, the same as any other man. He had been going out nonstop for years, date after date. He'd dated the sisters of fellow rabbinical students, the out-of-town rabbis' daughters (he hadn't gotten the lookers), even, desperately, some granddaughters from his grandfather's congregation. But nothing ever came of it. At most, it fizzled after date three.

Almost always, it was he who put an end to it, with blessings and relief.

He tried to analyze why this was so and came to the following conclusion: It was like the plate of roast chicken and mashed potatoes they put in front of you at a decent restaurant—perfectly adequate, probably good for you, but completely disappointing.

Why was it, he bemoaned, that he saw hundreds of beautiful, exciting, luscious girls every, single day—on the subway, in department stores, and on the crowded streets of Manhattan, Brooklyn, and Queens—and one was never tossed his way? How could it be that the laws of chance should have been so slanted against him?

So when his roommate, Josh, told him about his fiancée's roommate, a girl sincerely interested in finding a marriage partner, he didn't exactly leap at the chance.

"I don't know, Josh. I'm so tired of blind dates."

All those days comfortably behind him, Josh laughed sympathetically. "Here," he said generously, whipping out a photograph of his darling Rivkie sitting on the bed of her dorm room with several girls. "It's one of those."

Chaim studied the photograph. He recognized the pale sweet face of Rivkie. His heart sank as his eyes ran over two similar girls—both dark-haired and excellent rebbitzin material, he had no doubt—but then he stopped, zeroing in on a blonde who looked into the camera with no smile at all. She seemed to be staring right at him. And there was no doubt about it: She was definitely a looker.

{ FOUR }

He went to Bernstein Women's College that Saturday night. He shaved closely and, on his roommate's advice, borrowed a nice blue sweater to wear over slacks, instead of his good Sabbath suit, which had a spill of schnaps on his lapel from that morning's kiddush. His hair was combed back and neat, but not greasy. His eyes were eager.

"Chaim Levi for Delilah Goldgrab," he told the housemother, who looked him over with a tentative smile of approval. Obviously, she had seen worse.

He sat on the sofa edge and fidgeted with the gray tweed upholstery beside other fidgeting young men, most of whom looked severe and distinguished in their black suits and homburg hats. Future sages of America, he thought miserably, cursing the little brat who had pushed passed him toward the pretzels and damaged his suit and probably his future.

Graduation and rabbinical ordination were just around the corner. He was eager to try out his skills with a congregation, feeling more and more certain that this was his calling in life. His job applications needed to be filled out; otherwise he'd have no choice but to work in the Bronx for his grandfather. This was not his first choice by any means, but it was something he could fall back on; he felt fortunate to have it. Among his classmates, he knew, there were many eager applicants for the few assistant rabbi and teaching positions available in normal geographical locations around the country, classmates who were smarter, better qualified, and more articulate than he. Leaving the space for Spousal Information blank was a sure way to ruin his chances. Nevertheless, job or no job, he told himself, there were limits to what a man could force himself to do, what he should be expected or required to sacrifice. This certainly included giving up any hope of happiness by marrying a woman for whom he had no passion.

He'd searched diligently through the sacred texts for backup and enlightenment on this score. What he'd come up with was advice that ranged from: *Rise up, my love, my fair one and come away. For, lo, the winter is past and the rain is over and gone. The flowers appear on the earth; and the time of singing is come . . . My beloved is mine and I am his.* To: *And I found more bitter than death the woman.*

It was confusing, Chaim thought, shaking his head, particularly since both sentiments were expressed by the same man, considered moreover to have been the wisest one of all, Solomon himself. Chaim's teachers had sometimes taken pains to explain away the discrepancies by pointing out that Solomon had written these things at different stages in his life. Still, Chaim wondered about taking marriage advice from a man who'd had a thousand wives and hadn't been happy with any of them.

He stared through the partition at the girls emerging from the elevator, all of them bright-eyed, attractive, and modestly dressed. Perky, he thought, depressed. He had been dating their clones for years. The sincere, "deep" conversations about the duties of Jewish parenthood and the sacredness of the home. And all the while, there was this subtle undercurrent of probing remarks designed to dig out how much money his parents had, where he expected to live, and if he would be learning full-time and expect her to be a Woman of Valor—breadwinner, bread baker, and babymaker rolled into one obviously saintly package—or if he would be bringing in some money too and, if so, how much and doing what?

Of course, none of these questions was asked openly and none of the answers was given frankly. All these conversations were always held on the highest moral ground, cloaked in the most impressive and saintly verbal packaging. Words like *tafkid be cha'im* (life's calling), *messirat nefesh* (dedication of one's soul), *gemilut chasadim* (charitable good works) were bandied about like the little hard candies thrown down at a Bar Mitzva boy to celebrate his successful reading of the Torah portion before the congregation, candies that often hit you in the head and accomplished minor concussions.

Then the elevator door opened and there she was. Or at least, he certainly hoped this one was his. He stood up. She was a vision in a slim skirt and green silk blouse, her blond shoulder-length hair tumbling to her shoulders in a mass of golden curls. He swallowed hard, mesmerized, thrilled, and incredulous at his good luck. He couldn't wait for her to give his name to the housemother. When she did, he took a step toward her. "Delilah?"

She looked up. He was taller than she, but only by a few inches, nothing like Yitzie. Nor did he have that sexy, rock-star slenderness around the hips or that certain way of moving—fluid and a bit dangerous—that never failed to give her those little pinpricks of electric shock. She took a deep breath, accepting that there would be no thumping heart, no flowing juices. Instead of that, there would be a perfectly respectable, good-looking young man, with a conventionally handsome face, fine dark eyes, and a square manly chin. Someone who would look good to her family and friends under the marriage canopy. A genuine Orthodox Jewish catch.

She began to imagine herself as a pious rabbi's wife. It's what she had been praying for, the opportunity to reform herself, to wash the slate clean. Besides, she was acutely aware that her shares on the *shidduch* market were in a highly volatile state right now. All that was needed was for some busybody to start a little rumor about her unhappy romance. It was like when people began to question whether butchers were really selling glatt kosher meat. Once there was doubt, prime ribs became chopped meat and it was all you could do to give them away.

She smiled at him. He smiled back, his kind open face guileless, his eyes almost childish in their innocent, unfeigned delight. He hid nothing, she thought, surprised and a bit contemptuous. He was hers. He would be easy to manage, not the touchy type who took offense or held a grudge or got angry—unless you banged him over the head with a hammer. And even then. The hair was too short, and that outfit . . . Still, she had seen much worse.

He watched as her sparkling blue eyes slowly took him in with approval. His sweater, he realized, had been the right choice. She wouldn't have liked a suit.

"Chaim?" she asked, and her white teeth, perfect and small and straight under cushiony lips, peeked out at him in a tiny secret smile. Oh, how he wished he could widen that smile, see those teeth in all their porcelain glory!

Is it necessary to expound upon the process of falling in love? The butterflies that wander through the digestive tract? The sweaty palms, the tickle below the belly button? The eyes that light up the object of desire like car headlights falling into a fog, all smoke and mirrors and nothing quite real? Let's just say it: From that moment on Chaim Levi was smitten. As such, he didn't understand anything that was happening.

They walked out into the New York night of twinkling lights and crowded streets, cars zooming, and couples walking arm in arm, their feet clicking against the pavement. He took her to a kosher delicatessen where religious couples on first dates often came. It was noisy and full of teenagers, and he regretted his choice immediately. He ordered pastrami on rye. She demurely ordered a salad, which she poked at tentatively, saying she had eaten so much all day, she wasn't really hungry. His sandwich smelled really good, she said appreciatively. With a great show of reluctance, she finally agreed to take half, feeding it to herself in greedy little bites. Pressed, she also agreed to order dessert, a gooey pecan pie that disappeared from her plate with surprising swiftness.

"I have a sweet tooth," she murmured, blushing a little with embarrassment.

She was so shy, he thought, entranced. So delicate, he thought in wonder, watching the color deepen on her pale golden skin as he spoke to her of his dreams and plans. She seemed immensely interested in everything he had to say, hanging on his every word as if it resonated with some hidden, kabbalistic meaning.

Basking later in the afterglow of the evening, he realized she hadn't spoken about herself at all. She remained as much a mystery to him as when he'd set out that evening to meet her.

"So, *nu*?" Josh asked. When Chaim smiled but didn't answer, Josh tilted his head and nodded. "Oh, I see. But I should warn you—"

Chaim's ears pricked up.

"She's got a bit of a reputation."

"Delilah?"

"Well, just a few things, nothing serious—" Josh squirmed, aware that he should have had this information long before proposing this match.

Chaim interrupted him rather sharply. "Doesn't this fall under the category of evil gossip? Isn't it sinful?"

"When it comes to information about a *shidduch,* we are allowed to tell all. It falls under the category of *Before a blind man, place no obstacle.*"

Chaim, who wished to remain a blind man where Delilah was concerned, tried another tack. "Not all information is reliable."

"Oh, this is. It's from Rivkie."

The paragon of virtue herself. Now his curiosity was piqued. This was no idle gossipmonger, no catty, loose-lipped female out to destroy for the sheer joy of feeling her own power. No. If it came from Rivkie, and if she thought it important enough to send on to Josh, who thought it important enough to share, it would be stupid of him not to listen. And yet . . . the girl's body, her face, her golden hair, her mesmerizing eyes. If the information was compelling enough, it could paralyze him, making it impossible for him to reach out and take her, like the brass ring. And he had been on so many merry-go-rounds, ridden so many painted horses with their short dark sensible hair, bright eyes, and housewifely bodies that would no doubt balloon into a perfectly round *balaboosta's* after the first child was born. He wanted her.

"What?" he asked impatiently, because he had to.

"Well, she has been around the block, if you know what I mean. She had a boyfriend, and I understand the breakup wasn't fun. She was pretty hysterical about it."

"A boyfriend?"

This was unusual. Religious girls didn't have boyfriends. They had dates with prospective marriage partners. After a certain number of such dates—two or three for the extremely pious, maybe a dozen or so for lesser souls—a decision had to be made, a proposal offered that needed either to be accepted or refused.

"Breakup? You mean, she refused his proposal?"

Josh winced. "Not exactly. He never asked her. And they went out for quite some time."

Chaim studied him. This was not good. Protocol demanded that a relationship between a man and a woman be based on investigating the possibility of marriage, getting engaged, arranging the wedding details, then getting married. Anything else was *pritzus*, in other words, screwing around. A girl involved in a longtime relationship that had not resulted in marriage was one of two things: an unfortunate victim of an unscrupulous and non-Godfearing boy who had led her on; or a willing participant in a very unsavory and unacceptable liaison that marked her as nonkosher marriage material.

Chaim nodded, disturbed but not defeated. As he saw it, he now had two choices. Like a rabbi asked to judge whether a chicken was kosher, he could probe and probe its insides, examine its viscera, turning it over and over until he found some reason to call it *treife*. Or he could look at the chicken's owner to see if he was a rich man or a poor man, deciding how much he needed the chicken. Thinking of her, Chaim decided on the latter tack. Under no circumstances was he willing to call this chicken *treife*. That being the case, he thanked Josh for his honesty and his help, broadly hinting that he needed no more information.

"I appreciate what you are trying to do, Josh, really. But I know you and Rivkie would never have arranged for me to meet Delilah in the first place if you'd thought there was something wrong with her behavior."

That, of course, put Josh into a serious bind. What could he say? That he had not been aware of any of this until his Talmud study partner, who knew Yitzie from the neighborhood, had mentioned it in passing? And that only then had he squeezed the information out of Rivkie, who was on close terms with both Penina Gwertzman and Sharona Gottleib and had reluctantly sought the source of her roommate's heartbreak—with the best of intentions, of course. Josh of course forgave her for not being worldly enough to understand the implications of such behavior. But to admit his error, he realized, would be to jeopardize his own infallible reputation, as well as that of his future wife, who had set this whole *tsimmes* boiling in the first place. Besides, all things considered, Chaim's other marriage prospects were not brilliant, and Delilah Levi seemed to be his heart's desire. Was it not written that *Forty days before conception a heavenly voice cries out, "This man for this woman?"* Who was Josh to argue?

He didn't, nodding in silent acquiescence and hoping for the best.

Two weeks before the wedding, Rivkie bumped into Delilah and Chaim on a street in Manhattan. Delilah, Rivkie thought, looked great. She was wearing a blue cashmere sweater and a slim skirt of supple black leather that ended just above her knees. She had on blue eyeshadow and liner, and fabulous red lipstick that Rivkie admired but would never, ever, have had the guts to wear. Rivkie noticed how Chaim looked at her. His yearning was almost palpable, like that invisible energy field around the body Chinese doctors are always fiddling with.

Delilah, who hardly ever went to class anymore and who hadn't been in the dorm room for weeks, was all smiles and hugs and kisses on the cheek.

"I'm having a beautiful dress made, in that building over there, on the sixth floor," Delilah said, looking up and pointing toward a factory loft on Seventh Avenue. "We got it wholesale. First I tried it on in Saks, and then my mother got our neighbor to get it from the factory. He's a button salesman, so he knows the wholesaler. And all I had to do was invite him to my wedding. It cost me a fraction!"

The skin of her throat was smooth and white as she arched her neck, pointing upward at the factory loft where, even as they spoke, her Queen for a Day dress was being hand-stitched by Guatemalan seamstresses in daily danger of INS raids. Rivkie watched Chaim watching her. And when Delilah turned around and spoke to him, she saw how he bent low and leaned in close with his ear toward her, looking into the distance and smiling vaguely, as if he were listening to music.

Delilah held out her engagement ring, a modest little thing but one that obviously thrilled her. "It's a marquise," she said, stroking it. "Isn't that a nice shape? I mean, for the price of a marquise you can get a round stone twice the size." She shook her head in delight. Only then did she remember Chaim. He didn't seem to mind.

"Rivkie, meet Chaim. He's going to be a rabbi," she said, and Rivkie could see that Delilah expected her to be astonished, and that she herself was astonished no less.

{ FIVE }

Ah, the wedding. Minor slights that had led to major family feuds and cutting decades-old silences had suddenly been forgiven. Animosities begun over Passover seder invitations and Rosh Hashanah cards and condolence calls withheld or insufficiently appreciated, were set aside. There was hope that all hard feelings would travel the labyrinthine road toward reconciliation, making their final exit via a white envelope containing a generous check. And so, forgotten relatives had been pursued in far away places like Hyattsville and Toronto. New cousins had been discovered. Old friends had been looked up. Addresses and phone numbers had been relentlessly tracked down with archival diligence through phone books and the Internet.

The guests came in alphabet subway trains from Brooklyn and Far Rockaway, in taxis from the Bronx, and in new Chevrolets from far-off Connecticut and Pennsylvania. They arrived early, or late, by Amtrak, Greyhound bus, and El Al flights from Tel Aviv. They poured into the hotel's genteel lobby, gaping at the ceilings, marble floors, and vases of flowers, before crowding the elevators down to the banquet hall. They flooded through the open doors like salmon swimming against the current in a desperate effort to reach the breeding grounds.

The glatt kosher caterer, who'd recently split with his brother-in-law in a backstabbing family coup, obviously had something to prove. The room reeked of gobsmacking culinary art: pirate ships with gangplanks and flags sticking out of the red flesh of carved-out watermelons; little marzipan Swiss villages nestled between chocolate mountains covered with whipped-cream snow that jiggled precariously as overcome children butted their heads against the table for a better look. And that was just the smorgasbord.

The older women wore long, pious polyester skirts and matching jackets from Boro Park. They wore elaborate gowns shaken out of mothballs from a child's Bar Mitzva or wedding or Loehmann's back-room bargains with slashed-off designer labels. They wore hats with feathers and satin bows. The most religious wore human hair wigs, newly washed and set in festive big-hair styles.

Some of the younger married women also wore wigs, but they were long and smooth and sexy, in daring shades of blond and red, bouncing around their shoulders as they walked or danced. But mostly, unlike their mothers, they wore fashionable head scarves tied with exotic panache the way girls out on the settlements do in Israel. They wore flashing engagement rings and matching diamond wedding bands, and intricate gold necklaces with matching bracelets from H. Stern or Fortunoff.

The singles in their late teens and early twenties, cousins and friends of the bride and groom, milled around, shooting each other shy, searching looks. The young men's hair had been cut, their beards trimmed or their cheeks newly shaved. They wore dark suits and ties like the groom—except for the Israelis, who came in inappropriate sweaters, or short-sleeved white shirts with no ties, and pants that didn't really fit. On their heads they sported dark wide-brimmed hats, or crocheted skullcaps with geometric designs, or the silly white yarmulkes left in a basket by the door for those who had come in with nothing at all.

The girls they eyed so optimistically had just been to the beauty salons or had blow-dried their hair themselves until their arms ached. They'd had their nails done and their eyebrows tweezed and wore makeup that ranged from an artistic touch here and there to heavy coats of every conceivable goo and paste.

They wore long dresses from the post-Christmas reduced racks at Lord & Taylor, Macy's, and Filene's. Or well-cut suits from Ann Taylor or Talbot's petite section, which are hardly ever on sale, and then only in size two or fourteen. They wore gold bangle bracelets and little shiny gold necklaces with five-cornered stars, or Chai or names like Sarah, Rivka, Chana, and Rachel spelled out in golden Hebrew letters made by Israeli jewelers.

And then there were the outcasts, the great unwashed, the children of cousins whom one simply cannot uninvite; who always show up at family celebrations in lesser or greater numbers, dressed in jeans and sneakers and uncombed hair or low-cut dresses with sequins missing; who look like they have just gotten up from the couch after watching a Sunday movie and who never seem to feel underdressed or out of place or even aware of the chagrin and pain their insulting carelessness is causing their hosts. They are the people everyone does their best to pretend aren't there at all, particularly those who invited them.

Toward the back, away from the band, in the best seating area, sat the small cluster of Gentiles: the black woman in a sleeveless Donna Karan dress, looking fabulous; the long-haired programmers; the short red-haired accountant. They smiled with discomfort at one another and the people around them, wide-eyed in the fashion of tourists to Indian reservations, who are anxious to observe the folkways of the natives with stalwart respect.

Teeming hordes of children, looking well-combed and uncomfortable in their shiny, stiff shoes and elaborate outfits, chased one another around the hall, stealing cakes and nuts off plates like locusts, tugging at their parents' legs. The little boys ran wild in white shirts and manly ties, while the little girls wore either miniature versions of whorish fad fashions or old-fashioned picture-book dresses that made them look like dolls.

Up and back they ran, holding sloshing glasses of Coca-Cola, which they refilled at an alarming rate, pushing aside the older men, who waited patiently and diffidently to ask for their glass of scotch and a glass of semi-dry white wine or rum Coke for their wives. The women would drink half a glass and put it down, already feeling themselves growing dizzy and drowsy from the unaccustomed experiment with alcohol that didn't consist of one sip from a communal wineglass Friday night.

There was mixed seating—that is, men and women, husbands and wives and children, all seated at the same tables. But there was also a small section in the rear with a *mechitzah*, so that the more distinguished rabbis wouldn't be forced to sit with their wives. The rebbitzins sat together with their marriageable daughters, all wishing to make a public display of adherence to the most pious stringencies in Jewish law, stringencies invented by the fortunate men who sat all day in study halls and thus had all the time in the world to rescue God from His horrible mistakes in neglecting to include such laws in His Torah and Talmud.

The men's tables included the elderly rabbis and their sons and grandsons, and even some of the more *farchnyokt* friends of the groom, who looked over the elderly scholars the way some men ogle single girls, savoring the possibilities. The thrill of talking to the great Rabbi So-and-so! How they would astonish their friends (and perhaps some unlucky prospective bride on some far-off *shidduch* date) with this tale. How they had brought up some intricate point of law and how the great Rabbi So-and-so had cocked his head and nodded approval as he listened, spellbound, to an explication. Imagine!

Religious men are the worst name-droppers. They will spend half a date regaling you with their exploits in cornering some octogenarian who is—or one day might be—a member of the Council of Sages, whose photos or garish oil portraits appear on posters in Crown Heights, Williamsburg, Geulah, and Bnei Brak like rock stars.

But if a man isn't interested in women before he has a wife, in all likelihood he is bound to be even less interested once he gets one. So any single guy at a wedding who prefers to sit next to bearded sages is not, generally speaking, a good marital prospect.

You see them sometimes, walking four paces in front of their wives and children in parks and zoos during the Intermediate Days of Festivals like Succoth and Passover, barely turning their heads to catch what their wives are saying. They are the ones who take the seat next to the cabdriver, leaving their wives to manage the task of stuffing themselves, a baby, a two-year-old, a carriage, and luggage into the back.

The single girls made their way around the hall, searching for someone who would give them a ride home. That is always the most urgent need when attending a Jewish wedding in Manhattan. You simply do not want to ride out to Brooklyn or Queens on the New York City subway system after 10 P.M. In fact, you do not want to ride anywhere on the New York City subway system at any time, period. The second reason, though, was always more important. You wanted to walk out with your pick from the most eligible single men, ensuring a good hour alone with him. It was considered a party favor, much more urgent and useful than catching the bride's bouquet.

Everyone agreed that the singles crowd at Delilah's wedding was promising, filled with Bernstein and Yeshiva University students, candidates for rabbinical ordination, and third-year dental, law, and medical school students, not to mention the few who already had their degrees in science, engineering, and accounting.

The music began, and Chaim, held at either elbow by his smiling father and chuckling father-in-law, was escorted toward his bride for the bedecking ceremony. He walked clumsily, his legs trembling, his face serious and intent, giving the appearance of one being dragged to his fate, as his friends clapped and sang all around him.

Delilah sat on a throne, flowers strewn around her, her face radiant with triumph. The blond down on her face caught the light, bathing her in a kind of golden shine like those photos of Marilyn Monroe, making her irresistibly beautiful and desirable. You could see the men in that room skip a step and miss a clap as they neared her, breathless.

Chaim too. He seemed mesmerized. The moment when the Jewish groom traditionally avoids Jacob's error by looking carefully into the bride's face to be sure it is really her and not her plain elder sister, before covering her face with the veil, went on almost embarrassingly long. Chaim just kept staring until finally, with an almost imperceptible look of exasperation, the bride finally reached up and pulled the veil down herself.

Delilah's wholesale gown was lovely, a luxurious silk satin, covered with beaded lace, with a long lace-edged train and little puffed lace sleeves tied at her upper arms with a bow. Many religious girls tend to line such sleeves. Obviously, Delilah had opted to skip it, and her flesh shone through the lace like honey. On her head she wore a little hat, like a medieval queen's headdress—very original—covered with the same lace and a double veil of stiff netting.

There were some frowns of disapproval among the older wig- and hat-wearers about the lacy sleeves, but if Delilah noticed she certainly didn't seem to care. She floated down the aisle with the joyous self-congratulation of a Camilla Parker-Bowles while on either side her mother and mother-in-law, carrying candles, made attempts to keep up with her.

Mrs. Goldgrab's face was like an enormous twinkling ornament atop a Christmas tree. Swathed in her sequined rose-colored gown, she threw smiles and waves in all directions. Chaim's mother, on the other hand, walked with her head down, staring at her shoes, an aggravated smile pasted on her lips.

Some of the guests stood or sat attentively through the long ceremony with its many blessings, while others retreated to their places at the tables to examine the first course—a cold dish left waiting on the table so as to hurry the festivities along, ensuring the surly waiters an early exit.

It was a nice ceremony, very traditional, conducted by the groom's venerable grandfather, whose hand shook as he handed the wine-filled silver goblet to the groom, who handed it to his father, who handed it to his mother, who finally lifted the bride's veil and helped her take a sip. Two drops fell slowly, barely noticeable except to the most discerning and those looking for bad omens, staining the white lace.

Escorted by musicians and the dancing, singing friends of the ecstatic bridegroom, the young couple were led off to a private *yichud* room, as was the custom, for their half hour of alone time before rejoining the festivities.

In the meantime, the first course, following the cold plate, was served, a choice of salmon filet or chicken livers in a phyllo dough. And although everyone was already stuffed from the buffet, they opened their mouths wide and devoured this too as everyone waited for the young couple to rejoin the festivities so the dancing could begin.

Rivkie, who had come with a much put-upon and reluctant Josh, was on her way to the bathroom when she noticed Delilah sitting alone on a couch in the lobby, just staring at the tiny wine stain on her dress, rubbing it with her finger. She seemed slightly pale. Chaim was nowhere to be seen.

"Beautiful wedding!" Rivkie called out to her tentatively.

Delilah smiled in vague acknowledgment.

"Where's your new husband?"

Delilah looked up. "Oh, Chaim? He went to talk to a rabbi, some urgent problem—God knows what now. You know, they delayed the ceremony half an hour because one of the letters in the marriage contract wasn't clear enough? Or maybe it was the date. Try to get a roomful of rabbis to agree on anything . . . and nothing moves until they make up their minds." She shrugged. She seemed listless. "Are you having a good time?"

"Wonderful. Everything is beautiful. The food is great. I love the band . . . and your dress is heavenly."

She brightened. "They stained it with the wine, but I'm sure dry cleaning can get it out. Not that I'll be needing it again anytime soon." She laughed, but you could tell she didn't think it was particularly funny.

And then Chaim showed up, a little sweaty and nervous, with a big smile. Behind him were photographers and friends and a man carrying a flute.

Seeing the crowd, a transformation came over Delilah. Like a toy with a new battery, she bounced up, daringly taking Chaim's hand—bride and groom traditionally avoiding physical contact in public—as the cameras clicked away. Color flooded her cheeks. She threw back her head and laughed as the music started up, dancing her way into the banquet hall. Then everyone got up to form circles, the women bearing away the bride, and the men the groom. As they parted Chaim turned, looking back longingly in her direction.

Delilah stared eagerly straight ahead, never looking back at all.

{ SIX }

As the last relatives finally left and the catering staff folded up the soiled linen, Chaim and Delilah made their way upstairs to their hotel room. It was not the bridal suite, but a room specially ordered to suit the needs of the religious bride and groom. So, unlike most wedding suites, it had twin beds, not a double.

They were both a bit awkward, a bit overwhelmed.

Delilah sat down in an armchair in her wedding dress, the bag with the cards and checks in her lap. It was a nice room, even if it was a little cramped, she thought, just a tad disappointed. She stared at the wedding gifts that lay piled up in a corner, all their festive wrappings and bows a bit frayed by being dragged around. Her head swam from glasses of champagne and rum Cokes and even a Bloody Mary, all of which she had managed to order and somehow actually consume.

Chaim approached her shyly, taking the bag from her hands and laying it on top of the table.

"Plenty of time for that in the morning," he said, deadly earnest, reaching out to squeeze her.

Well, she thought, looking up at him. Well, well.

Gently, she pushed his hands away. "I'll just be a minute, darling," she told him, getting up and escaping into the bathroom with her overnight bag. Inside the bag were two nightgowns. One was a filmy white see-though bridal number with an equally filmy white dressing gown. The other she had noticed when another girl shopping in Macy's had held it up to show her girlfriend, saying, "If I wore this, my boyfriend would kick me out of bed." When they'd both stopped laughing and put it back, Delilah had bought it. It was a long pink number, totally opaque, with a high neck and long sleeves.

Quickly, she stuffed the white gown back into the bag and hung the other up on the door hook. She stepped into the shower, shivering under the stream of hot water. Even as she dried her clean hot skin afterward, she still felt goose bumps as she slid the pink gown over her head. Carefully, she reached into the bag and took out something else she had specially prepared.

"Shut off the lights, Chaim, will you?" she called through the closed door.

"If you want," he answered, without enthusiasm.

She turned off the bathroom lights and then opened the door. The room seemed pitch dark. Chaim was already in bed. He moved over to the edge, reaching out for her.

"You are still dressed!" he said, disappointed, as his hands touched the material.

She reached back. He was totally nude.

"I . . . thought . . ." she stammered. "You're a rabbi!"

"Maimonides says clearly that whatever a man and wife do together in the sanctity of their marriage bed is perfectly fine."

"Whatever?" she said doubtfully.

"Whatever," he repeated decisively. "There is no shame, no boundaries. Everything is kosher. We are married. You went to the *mikva.* We can just enjoy ourselves. Now, why don't you take that silly thing off? Please, honey?" he wheedled.

"Well, if you're absolutely sure, just . . ."

"What?"

"I think we should put a towel down first. The hotel staff," she murmured.

"I'm sure they've seen everything." He laughed, touched by his bride's delicacy of feeling. He felt worldly and lusty next to her hesitation. It was just as it should be, he thought. He would be gentle with her, since she was obviously scared. And why not? A religious Jewish bride, so sheltered, so pure! Anything else would have been strange and suspect.

"I brought my own towel, from home," she said. "That way, I can just take it with us. I wouldn't want to steal a hotel towel. Please, just move over, will you?"

He rolled over, watching her outline as she bent over the bed, smoothing down the towel.

"Do you want me to put on a light?"

"No!" she shouted, and once again he felt moved and impressed by the touching urgency of her panic.

He chuckled. "It's okay. Shhhh. I'm sorry, forgive—"

She pulled the nightgown over her head, taking his breath away. By the faint light of the bedside radio and the streetlamps, he examined his bride, absolutely mesmerized, stunned by the outlines of her slim waist and thighs and generous breasts as she got into the bed and sidled up next to him. In a moment, he was lost in the silken feel of her skin, the scent of her warm body, like no other perfume, impossible to bottle. He felt himself transported to another place, a heavenly sphere he had never even dreamed of. Only a poet could have such dreams, he thought as he pulled her close to him, delighting in every new, thrilling adventure that beggared his poor imagination.

He wanted to immerse himself in every aspect of her otherness, to command it, to own it, to make himself part of it. He ran his hands over the taut youthful waist, tracing how it billowed out into her slim hips and softly rounded thighs. Those warm secret thighs!

He was owner and lover and, like a man who has purchased a priceless work of art, he felt both the pride of acquisition and the frustration of knowing this thing was outside him, unknowable. *Baal,* he thought, the ancient Hebrew term for husband which meant *owner*. It was also the name of an ancient Canaanite god. She was his, and she would worship him and adore him as all things male, her first and only man, he comforted himself, thrilled, relying on the sex advice sprinkled with delicacy throughout the ancient Jewish canon. The moment he took her virginity, he would be her *baal* in every sense.

He tried to pace himself. He wanted to be considerate, not to frighten her or—God forbid!—hurt her in any way. All this had been impressed upon him by mentors provided for him in the yeshiva, kindly rabbis and older married students who had volunteered for bridegroom consultations. He tried to control himself, but to his surprise he found himself clutched and held and pressed and fondled. He was thrilled, even as it dawned on him that slowly, but surely, he was no longer in control. He thrust against her, and to his surprise there didn't seem to be anything standing in the way. But before he could give that another thought, great paroxysms of uncontrolled feeling and sensation took hold of him, blotting out all rational thought. He felt himself pulled up and up and up and then suddenly released, allowed to free-fall down the precipice. He lay back, panting and almost unconscious.

He reached out to touch her, but she was already gone into the bathroom to wash herself off. The towel, too, was gone. Reluctantly, he moved over to the other bed, as is the custom, the bride and groom separating the moment that the "red rose" appeared. She would need to count seven clean days before they could meet again. It was maddening. It was Jewish law.

They had breakfast in bed, a sinful luxury, he thought, a bit embarrassed to let in room service, who rolled in a serving cart with juice, bread, jam, little boxes of cereals, silver carafes of milk and coffee, and a basket of fragrant warm muffins. She wore one of his undershirts, her blond hair tousled and adorable over her shoulders, her eyes heavy-lidded and satisfied.

"Are you all right, my love?" Chaim asked her, concerned.

"A little sore. There was a lot of blood. Good thing I remembered the towel," she murmured.

He felt guilty and proud and manly.

She pulled the tray toward her and began to eat.

"Whoa, aren't you forgetting something, my love?" he remonstrated gently, a bit surprised. She hadn't gone to the bathroom to ritually wash her hands, spilling water over each lightly held fist three times, to rid her body of the lingering impurity of nighttime spirits, a ritual followed by every Orthodox Jew, who believed touching anything with such hands would not only be sinful but unhealthy.

She hesitated. "Oh, I did that earlier, my love," she said breezily. "When you were still asleep." She kissed him, even though it was forbidden. He opened his mouth to protest, then shut it. Then she took a knife and spread some jam on a muffin.

"My darling, those muffins . . . they are from the hotel bakery; they don't have any rabbinical *hechsher*, so we can't know if they're kosher."

"But it's just flour, oil, water, and sugar. What could be wrong with it?" she asked him, already feeding herself tiny pieces as she pulled it apart.

"But, really, darling, you shouldn't."

She looked up at him, annoyed.

Should he press her, he wondered, his new bride? Was it worth having a fight over, the morning after their wedding, when no doubt her nerves were frayed? There was such a thing as a pious fool, he told himself, the man who won't rescue a drowning woman because he is too religious to touch a female that isn't his close relative. He wasn't a fool, he told himself. Besides, she was probably right; there wasn't anything forbidden in them. Really, who would make the effort to locate and bake with pig fat in New York City in these cholesterol-conscious days?

He let it go but made a point to wash and dress, feeling he had to set a good example. "I'm going out on the balcony to daven," he told her, taking his prayer book and tefillin with him. When he was finished with his morning prayers, he came back in.

He longed to take off his clothes and get back in with her under the covers. Instead, he sat in a chair across from her, silently eating his certified-kosher Kellogg's breakfast cereal with milk and drinking his coffee and freshly squeezed orange juice, thinking all the while how adorable she looked in his undershirt, her white thighs perfect, her ankles slim, her toenails sparkling with color. According to Jewish law, it would be almost a week before he'd be able to so much as touch her again.

It was maddening.

After breakfast, they ripped open the envelopes and added up their cash and checks, smiling, feeling overwhelmed with happiness and riches. They laughed at the wedding gifts, groaning over the third toaster and fourth blender, exclaiming over the intricately carved silver ritual objects.

With each tearing away of wrappings, Delilah felt the injustices of her deprived childhood recede farther back in memory, their sting softening. Images and memories of middle-income red-brick housing projects, bad haircuts, and dime store shopping trips were tossed onto a mental junk pile, to await the garbage trucks of forgetfulness that would hopefully clank along soon, dumping the lot into a landfill soon to be smoothed over and readied for the building of the lovely mansion that she would inhabit for the rest of her life. Soon, she hoped, the whole lot would be incinerated, so that it would all finally seem like a bad dream, as if it had never happened at all.

She had a sudden, wicked thought that her parents, most of all, were on top of that pile, never to hinder or badger or push her again. She'd invite them over a few times a year, she thought, until they were stuck in wheelchairs in old-age homes and she'd be forced to visit them. And she would, if she wasn't too busy.

They took a short trip to the bank to open an account and deposit the loot; then they checked out of the hotel, getting the bellboy to help them load their belongings into a taxi. They tipped him generously, using some of the bills that had been stuffed into the white envelopes, which they decided to stick in their wallets instead of sensibly storing in their new account.

Their first home was a small apartment in the Bronx near his grandfather's synagogue, where Chaim would be employed as assistant rabbi until the next listing of job openings for rabbis was sent to him from his alma mater, which ran an employment service for its graduates. The listings were sent out every six months. Although he had tried to find another position before the wedding, he had had no success. People like Josh, of course, had been snapped up by well-regarded congregations in the suburbs. But for lesser luminaries, the opportunities were less than abundant: an assistant rabbi in Nebraska, a youth leader in Terre Haute. He'd decided to do the sensible thing and wait.

He was a bit deflated when they walked into their first apartment, both of them carrying packages like an old married couple home from their weekly shopping trip. The moment should have been magic; he wanted to carry her over the threshold like something in an old *I Love Lucy* episode, playfully groaning under her delicious weight, her warm body next to his. He felt deprived and resentful, even as he faithfully did his best to adhere to the strictest letter of Jewish law, being careful not to touch her, not even to sit next to her on the couch or hand her a plate.

Unlike most of his coreligionists, who only knew what was allowed and what was forbidden, he possessed the knowledge to make fine distinctions between Divine and rabbinic law: what was really a sin, and what was a rabbinic attempt to prevent sin. Now, more than ever, he was painfully aware of the discrepancies. There was nothing wrong with touching her, according to Divine law. It was the rabbis who had come up with this particular prohibition, one of those they considered "building a fence around the law." These were laws meant to create a moat into which men might fall should they even move in the wrong direction. They were a barrier to help men from falling prey to urges that might push them to actually—God forbid!—transgress the Divine will as understood from the Five Books of Moses.

In the eyes of the rabbis who'd created this particular fence, the progression from handing a woman a dish to undressing her and taking her to bed was immediate, inevitable, and forgone. A done deed.

The stringency kings had, as usual, added their own outlandish roadblocks a few hundred miles forward of the rabbinic fence, even forbidding a father and daughter over the age of three from being alone in the house together. But instead of creating a society of saints, their overzealousness and suspicion of human nature was creating a society of perverts, Chaim thought, people who defended and praised such prohibitions, who claimed to understand and agree with such thinking. Ironically, it was these people who were constantly popping up in the headlines for being caught indulging in every perversion known to man. But that was true in all religions. Safe in the privacy of their own homes and secure in the knowledge that their victims will be gagged by the strongly enforced communal code of silence that holds the washing of dirty laundry in public to be a worse sin than actually soiling it in the first place, religious zealots of all stripes find the border between strict religious morality and absolute depravity unguarded and easily crossed.

Chaim was not a stringency king. He believed in moderation in all things, but he was also deeply committed to Jewish law. The avoidance of physical contact was nerve-racking for them both, Chaim assumed. Surely, she must hate it as much as he did. "I'm sorry, my love," he kept whispering to her. "I wish I could . . ." and there he interjected a long series of predicates over which even Delilah found herself blushing.

My, my, she thought. Who would have suspected? She looked at him with a growing fondness.

The successful hurdle of her bridal night complications left Delilah sweet-tempered and unusually congenial. While she was not particularly thrilled to be living in an apartment in the Bronx, she was grateful Chaim would have an immediate income until a suitable position with a lovely home in some leafy, pine-scented suburb came their way.

For the first week, she wandered around the rooms of her little home, touching all her new things. Everything thrilled her: the flatware with their colorful enamel handles, the dinnerware set for twelve with all the matching serving pieces, glasses of all sizes in sets of six, stain-resistant white tablecloths, brand-new no-iron polyester/cotton sheet sets, and dozens of towels. She looked proudly over her new china closet filled with wedding silver and lovely crystal bowls and porcelain. In fact, when they delivered her formal dining room set—something her mother had never been able to afford—she waited for the delivery men to leave and then sat down by the table, rubbing her hand across the sweet-smelling polished wood. She found tears of joy streaming down her cheeks as she contemplated her good fortune and the beautiful life that surely lay ahead of her.

Carefully, she dusted the shelves of their new wooden bookcases, filled with her husband's library: the tricycle-sized volumes of the Talmud and dozens and dozens of other Hebrew tomes: the Pentateuch, books on Jewish law, Jewish history, philosophy, and custom. There were also more popular works, the sound-bite Judaism books that gave you a mitzva a day to do, a Jewish ethic a day to explore, a Jewish value a day to review, and 1001 Jewish jokes for speechmakers. Joining them were Dale Carnegie's *How to Win Friends and Influence People*, Norman Vincent Peale's *The Power of Positive Thinking*, and even some novels left over from various periods in his youth and from various college courses: *Marjorie Morningstar*; *Inside, Outside*; *The Winds of War*; *The Chosen*; *Moby Dick*; *Bleak House*; *The Iliad*; *The Macmillan Handbook of English*; *Eichmann in Jerusalem*.

She brought few belongings of her own: clothes, music disks, her computer, photographs, her high school yearbook, which showed her in a short booster outfit (she never made cheerleader). There were also some of her own favorite books: *Valley of the Dolls*, *Gone with the Wind*, *Jepthe's Daughter*, *Little Women*, and *The Rainbow*—which, along with a few other books by D. H. Lawrence, actually belonged to the public library out in Rockaway.

She had another few months of school to go before she graduated and earned her dental hygienist's license. Her plan was to get a job in some very affluent dental practice and work there for clothes money until she got pregnant. She looked forward to working, trying out her skills, earning her own money. Being married didn't make her feel like an adult. The opposite. She felt as if she'd gone straight from her parents' home to her husband's home, despite the three years of dorming, which never really counted because she'd been obliged to go back home for weekends.

Each morning before leaving for school, she'd prepare Chaim's breakfast, which she'd leave on the table in a covered plate awaiting his return from morning prayers. Chaim would sit down by the table in the empty house, missing her, as he ate his lonely cornflakes and drank his black coffee, before settling himself into the work of assistant rabbi, which consisted of spending long hours in front of open volumes with tiny Hebrew lettering as he laboriously prepared his maiden speech before his grandfather's congregation.

He felt the sweat curl the tiny hairs on his forehead as he delved into the weekly Torah portion, searching for a sentence on which to build a twenty-five-minute talk that would display his erudition, wisdom, and wit. He wanted to enlighten, but also to entertain. When he finished, to his dismay, he found he had twenty minutes of erudition, five of wisdom, and none of entertainment. He closed the books, kissing them and putting them away.

Maybe it wouldn't matter, he told himself. After all, most of these people were used to his grandfather's rambling sermons on the finer points of Talmudic exegesis delivered in an accent that was hard to decipher if you weren't familiar with the speech patterns of American immigrants from that particular corner of the Sudetenland. Besides, most of them didn't hear very well and tended to use speech time to nap, girding themselves for the *mussaf* prayers that were to follow, most of which had to be done on their feet, exhausting for people of that age.

His plan was to win over the congregation not with speeches but with good deeds. By visiting the sick, bringing succor to the bereaved, being friendly and interested in the lives of his grandfather's flock, he knew he could bring them a caring energy that only youth could provide. His grandfather never got around much anymore, his weekly visit to a nearby chiropractor the only outing he continued to make on a regular basis.

Their first Sabbath, Delilah agonized over what to wear to the synagogue. Should she wear a wig, the only one she owned, a long, blond number purchased for exactly such an occasion, or a stylish hat in which most of her own hair would show? Or should she wear one of those horrid hair snoods so popular in Boro Park among the women who took the Woman of Valor song literally (*Charm is a lie, and beauty is worthless; a God-fearing woman brings praise upon herself*). She had one in her closet, purchased to wear to the ritual baths if she wanted to shampoo her hair before she got there, saving time. It was black with little silver sparkles, hugging her head like those towel turbans in the shampoo ads, making her look like an Italian film star in the forties. The wig, on the other hand, made her look like Farah Fawcett when she was plastered on the bedroom walls and lockers of every horny teenage boy in America. She finally chose the hat, which, though it showed most of her long hair, still looked the most respectable, with its cool white straw, band of apricot silk, and large apricot bow.

Choosing the clothes had been less problematic. She took out a lovely apricot silk suit, purchased as part of her trousseau, with a pretty scarf. It was an outfit that covered up everything without looking dowdy.

The women's section was one flight up, a few pews tucked into an alcove like an afterthought. Its front row—the only one from which a glimpse of the men's section and the actual service itself was visible—had a *mechitzah* of wooden shutters and lace curtains so thick it was almost impossible to see anything. Generations of frustrated women, however, had done their best to open it up. Many of the slats were broken, and numerous holes had been poked in the lace.

As she walked down the narrow aisle toward the front, Delilah saw the aged faces turn toward her and toward one another, nodding and smiling with pleasure. She was everybody's just-married granddaughter, she realized. She felt a wave of approval and happiness and love beamed at her from every corner as she heard the whispered word for bride, *kallah*, echo off the walls in all directions.

She smiled with real joy at the old faces shining with love, feeling like a princess graciously accepting the homage of her people. She wondered where to sit. Not wanting to hurt anyone's feelings by rejecting the places they patted hopefully beside them, she chose an empty pew in front. As she sat facing forward, she could feel the buzz moving all around the room, finally landing at a spot on the back of her neck, where dozens of old eyes rested with curiosity and unexpressed friendliness.

When she took out her prayer book, she felt the room shift as the women leaned forward in anticipation, waiting to see if she would turn to the right page. And when she rose to pray, taking the obligatory three steps backward and three steps forward that usher in the Eighteen Benediction prayer—steps that separate Orthodox Jews from their well-meaning, but ignorant, Jewish born-again cousins or from curious secular visitors or Gentiles—she could hear the small hiss of relief.

A *shaine maidel*. A beautiful girl.

A *frum* girl. A religious girl.

The rabbi's granddaughter-in-law!

A good match for his brilliant, pious grandson Chaim, their future leader. She could feel their happiness for the good fortune that had befallen their beloved rabbi and his family. It pricked the layers of her heart, making her feel that she didn't want to disappoint them, the way Princess Diana hadn't wanted to disappoint her cheering, devoted subjects, no matter how that Royal thing worked out.

When Chaim got up to speak, she felt herself grip her prayer book as she watched him walk down the aisle and climb up to the podium. He wore a black Sabbath suit and a wide-brimmed hat. He looked like a generic yeshiva boy, she thought, a bit dismayed. The yeshiva day schools disgorged them in colorful crocheted skullcaps, sweatpants, and basketball jackets, and Bernstein got hold of them and turned them into dour, serious, prematurely aged men in dark suits and glasses. There were legions of them, all interchangeable, like those stuffed or plastic effigies mass-produced in the wake of some hit movie. At least he was clean-shaven, she comforted herself. A beard would have been the last straw.

She was anxious for him to do well. She sat back, listening at first. It was about buttons, she realized. Should a button sewn onto a shirt as a spare—the extra button—be considered *muktzeh*, untouchable, on the Sabbath? She stuck with him for a while, listening as he detailed the problem. *Muktzeh* was a rabbinical category in which all things forbidden to use on the Sabbath by Divine decree also became forbidden to touch by rabbinic decree. And if one lived in an area in which one couldn't carry on the Sabbath, because there was no *eruv* (a fictitious boundary which encircled an area making it one and thus permitting one to carry from one place to the next), could one wear a shirt with such a button?

She looked around nervously, wondering if everyone was as excruciatingly bored as she. Discounting the nappers, she realized with relief that the men had their eyes fixed upon her husband with approval and pleasure. And while the women did shift nervously, their chatter rising above the volume and intensity generally to be expected in the women's section of Orthodox synagogues during the rabbi's speeches, it seemed all right.

And when Chaim finished, closing his book and kissing it, wishing everyone "Good Shabbes," and his grandfather got up to hug him, as if he were a Bar Mitzva boy, the synagogue erupted with interjections of goodwill and praise: *"Yasher koach."* "God bless you." "The apple doesn't fall far." The men's voices rang out, and the women stopped fidgeting. A few came over to Delilah to shake her hand, and their wrinkled arthritic fingers—like old white parchment—were cool against her young warm skin. "You must be so proud!" they told her. "A wonderful job!"

Delilah felt touched and filled with reciprocal warmth.

And then the service was over, and the people filed out as fast as their canes and walkers would allow them, navigating the staircase to the first floor social hall where gray-haired ladies in old-fashioned hats had laid out paper plates with various types of herring and gefilte fish stabbed with toothpicks, plates of dull sponge cake, and stale-looking Stella d'Oro cookies that smelled of anise. No one touched the food until the old rabbi arrived, pouring the red sweet Malaga wine—so thick you could cut it with a knife—into a silver cup, making the kiddush benedictions over it. That taken care of, the ladies brought out steaming platters of brown potato kugel and *cholent*—a dark meat-and-bean stew cooked overnight—which had enough fat in it to clog the last open space in any artery still actually allowing blood to pass through.

Delilah stood by Chaim's side as one by one the members of the congregation filed past, smiling at her and shaking Chaim's hand as the venerable rabbi they adored looked on benevolently. It was lovely, she thought, to be the center of so much positive attention.

She tried to tell herself she was lucky. That she had everything. That she'd been blessed. That it wasn't so bad she hadn't had a honeymoon, some tropical getaway where she could wear a bikini and lie near sparkling pools of turquoise water, lathered with suntan lotion, as sarong-clad men and women plied her with icy smoothies and fresh pineapple speared with festive paper umbrellas. That she could live with the two weeks of physical separation each month; that it would give her private time to read and watch TV in bed when he couldn't lay his hands on her. In fact, secretly, she thought it might be a relief.

In bed, she had noticed, his passion rose quickly and tanked accordingly. He had a self-congratulatory way of smiling afterward that she found irritating. He always rose fastidiously and returned to his own bed, leaving her behind to deal with sticky sheets and rumpled blankets. At first, she had been annoyed about the two-bed thing. "Why can't we just lie side by side on either side of a big bed when I'm a *niddah*?" she'd grumbled. But his response had mollified her. "If I could lie next to you and not sin, I wouldn't be a man."

But later, as time went by, with about half of each month with no physical contact at all between them, she began to feel peeved and insulted and abandoned. She would long for the ritual immersion that would have them resume their physical intimacy, no matter how flawed. In between, she saw him sneaking glances at her naked body like a guilty schoolboy. His yeshiva upbringing had created in him the perennial adolescent where anything concerning sex was involved, a permafrost that would last through all the stages of his life, never ripening into maturity.

She was compartmentalized in his life. Like most religious men, he managed to adore and ignore her simultaneously with breathtaking ease. He congratulated himself on marrying such a pretty, agreeable woman. But it was the idea of her he admired. She was decorative as well as practical, like a good appliance, able to perform many separate functions. He believed in separate "spheres." He believed it was noble and right for him to let her run hers and not to interfere. And vice versa.

He believed in all the old chichés—that women were superior beings, that they were more sensitive than men, on a higher level, blah, blah, blah. But of course, in their own "kingdom," he thought, adopting the language of patriarchal apologists who enthusiastically rationalized why women were entrusted with the tedium of housework and child care and men were fashioned for sitting on their backsides in study halls. Text after text, scholars never tired of trying to compensate for sentencing women to eternal drudgery, which they themselves abhorred, by dreaming up fancy ways of labeling it, easing their consciences and allowing them to view their self-serving little world of men-gods as a fair, nay noble, thing.

Countless rabbis, through hundreds of generations stretching back through time to the Temple itself, had been involved in the conspiracy. The separate-but-equal theory divided man and woman into the masters of their own universes, carefully delineating the realm of his kingdom to include anything but cooking, cleaning, and wiping up the various discharges and sticky liquids of children. As the wonderful German Rabbi Samson Raphael Hirsch put it, "A wife takes over obligations which comprise the great task of mankind, making it possible for her husband to accomplish more perfectly the part that is left to him. That's why it is written:

a helpmate, opposite him. If the helpmate were another man, that wouldn't help."

Delilah wasn't philosophical, but she was a realist. Jewish men—particularly Orthodox Jewish men—had fashioned the perfect little universe for themselves, and they were not about to give it up no matter how reactionary or unfair it was in this day and age.

To those who met her in the hallways at Bernstein about this time, she seemed reconciled to her new role. In fact, for the first time since they'd known her, she seemed really happy.

It's amazing how fast things change.

SEVEN

Delilah's mother, Marilyn Meyers Goldgrab, was the middle daughter of American Jews whose Russian grandparents had come over on big immigrant ships during the czars' pogroms. Despite the attempts of the German Jewish immigrants who preceded them to ship them off to Jewless hinterlands where their faithful adherence to the rituals of the Jewish religion would be less embarrassingly visible, and might, hopefully, soon shrivel and die without Jewish communal life, they had stubbornly stayed put in the great Jewish city of New York. They had also stayed strictly Orthodox in practice, raising their sons and daughters to value Jewish custom and Jewish scholarship.

Marilyn's parents—a housewife and an insurance agent—were limited in their means, but nevertheless had high aspirations for their children, for whom they wanted the best of everything. Her mother sewed her clothes and carefully braided her hair. Although they couldn't afford a private parochial school education, and Marilyn had been sent to public school, they made sure she faithfully attended Sunday and after-school Hebrew programs at her Brooklyn Orthodox synagogue.

This was fine with Marilyn. But as she started high school and began to attend Orthodox Jewish youth programs, she became acutely aware of the social disadvantages of her background. Those who had attended the expensive Hebrew day schools and summer camps tended to date each other and to look down on the public school kids, however observant.

For years she tried her best at the Thursday night midtown Manhattan indoor ice skating rink, where young Orthodox singles mingled. But she brought home only sore ankles and bruised pride—not to mention cold sores—for her trouble. Then, when high school had come and gone and she found herself dateless at Brooklyn College, one of her friends suggested investing in a weekend at Grossinger's up in the Catskills, the great, kosher watering hole of mateless Jewish singles on the cusp of morphing from youthful attractiveness into carefully made-up desperation. Marilyn's panic-stricken parents hurriedly laid out the money.

And it was there, on her first try, that she met Joe Goldgrab.

He was her waiter.

Joe had a past that Marilyn liked to call "colorful," at least in front of her family. The child of Jewish parents from Tyler, Texas, he had wanted to be a dress designer, then a sailor, and then a movie producer, and in the middle he had been drafted to Vietnam. After four horrendous years in the military, he had gone back home, only to find he was a piece of a jigsaw but the puzzle had changed. He wound up in New York, where he lived in dives and washed dishes until one of the more sympathetic waiters tipped him off about the big money and big knockers available to him in the Catskills during Jewish holidays.

He had been disappointed on the first count, but not the second.

He had smiled and brought her an extra dessert. She had smiled back. And later that weekend, when the men at her table were busy wooing the skinny straight-haired blondes, graduates of Ramaz and Flatbush Yeshiva, whose parents owned two-family homes and thriving businesses, Marilyn went walking on the grass with Joe. They sat by the pool in cold Adirondack chairs and looked up at the amazing stars. She found his Texas twang charming and his ambitions in fashion design and moviemaking thrilling. His military experience, which under normal circumstances would have anointed him with a huge black X as a marriage prospect, filled her with compassion. As he told it, he had been tricked into joining ROTC by slick on-campus recruiters dangling scholarships and National Guard duty, people who had disappeared along with signed promises not to draft him, replacing his college career with the jungles of Southeast Asia. Sure, he'd been bitter at first, he told her. But there were worse things than serving a country that had taken in his ancestors and protected them from the bullies of the world.

His words touched her.

Soon, he was taking her out weekends, to the theater and to bars, places Orthodox men seldom went. And although he was not what she, or her ambitious mother, had had in mind, both mother and daughter recognized the budding tire that would slowly envelop the youthful slim hips of the younger as it had the elder, realizing it was going to be Joe, or nobody. With her mother's encouragement, she told herself, "I can make him into whatever I want him to be."

Joe, far from home, liked Marilyn's parents, her warm house filled with the smells of chicken soup and *knaidlach*, and her warm, generous, yielding body, which gave a man something to hold on to instead of skin and bones. They got engaged. They got married. It was all a whirl of white—dresses, cake frosting, flowers. They rented a little apartment in Brooklyn near her parents. She dropped out of college, took a course in shorthand and typing, and got a job in an insurance office. He took a course in fashion design at FIT. The other students were a decade younger, savvy New Yorkers. Behind his back, they snickered at his hopelessly dowdy evening dresses, which could be envisioned only on aging, slightly overweight British royalty. He finished the course and got a job pushing around racks of dresses in Seventh Avenue knock-off shops, a job that had come with a nice title and many, many promises, none of which materialized.

She got pregnant. She gained and gained and gained. And with every pound, he lost more and more interest in their marriage and in their life. Big shouting matches ensued. Her parents got involved. The word *divorce* hung in the air like cold smoke from a recent cooking fire.

But when his first child was born, a boy, a new light came into his eyes. The baby was a little blond blue-eyed darling. Joe adored his son with an excess of love that spilled over onto the woman who had given birth to him. He had wanted to create something special in the world: a masterpiece of beauty and charm that was his own vision. With the child, his failures seemed to have been atoned for.

He reconciled with his wife, but insisted they move away from her parents. And so they found a place out in the Rockaways, near the ocean. He had always been clever with his hands. He got a full-time job in a car repair shop and took up part-time alcoholism. He tried to be a good father to make up for being a disinterested husband.

By the time Delilah was born, her parents had settled into their private Cold War, their dreams exploded into rubble. Like the inhabitants of Dresden, they built a new life on top of the debris. Using their dead hopes as fertilizer to help raise a new generation, they would never cease to burden their children with the task of fulfilling their own unfulfilled desires and expectations from life, all the while insisting "they only wanted the best" for them.

Delilah's brother, Arnie, was totally uncooperative, finding meaning in the dangerous, poverty-stricken idealism of kibbutz life. He left for Israel as soon as he was legally able, married a kibbutznik, and limited his connections to his parents to holiday phone calls and thank-you notes for care packages containing American coffee, tunafish, Entenmann's donuts, and children's clothes.

Delilah had been Marilyn's last hope.

The engagement of her daughter to Chaim Levi, future rabbi, and the grandson of a distinguished, if little-known, leader of a synagogue, initially filled Delilah's mother with a heady sense of victory. While she had never envisioned her future son-in-law as a religious leader, scion of a rabbinical family, she was nothing if not flexible, willing to unhitch her dreams from one wagon and hitch them to another, as long as there was a horse.

Marilyn's rosy vision of her daughter's future prospects were based on those rabbis she'd met who were the principals and administrators in her daughter's school—dapper little men who wore suits and smelled of aftershave, who knew how to squeeze the last dime of tuition out of pretension-filled parents—and the fathers of some of her daughter's classmates who lived in the Five Towns, one of the most affluent Orthodox areas in America.

In her mind, she conveniently edited out all the rabbis stuck teaching Bible and Prophets to fourth-graders—men struggling with mortgages on small frame houses in deteriorating neighborhoods—as well as her own rabbi, who worked in a tiny dwindling congregation in an expanding ghetto; a congregation that could barely afford to keep the synagogue in plastic cups, let alone pay their rabbi a decent wage. When these things intruded on her vision, like the pesky insects that ruin a lovely photograph by landing on your nose, she swatted them away with a determined murderous hand.

No, with Chaim, all their dreams would come true. A beautiful house connected to a magnificent synagogue, where her son-in-law would stand in front of the Ark of the Torah, distinguished and revered. Her daughter would sit in the front pew, endlessly admired, envied, and imitated. And she, the rabbi's mother-in-law, would sit next to her in a stunning hat. And when she got up, everyone would get up. And when she sat down, everyone would sit down. And the children—her grandchildren!—would be the sons and daughters of the rabbi and the rebbitzin. And her daughter, aside from giving a few parties at her lovely home, which would be catered by staff, would have the leisure to improve her mind and do countless good deeds, all the while shopping in Lord & Taylor for beautiful modest clothes, because, as the rabbi's wife, she'd need to set an example. And her son-in-law would have plenty of time to spend with his family, not like men who work nine to five. A few sermons, some back-patting, shmoozing, nice words at funerals that could be endlessly recycled, a few blessings under marriage canopies for which he would receive a generous check (and a full free catered dinner to follow, not to mention the smorgasbord that preceded). Actual working days would be limited to Friday night and Saturdays, with the rest of the week practically a paid vacation.

With this in mind, she slowly relinquished the cherished visions of the successful diamond importer, the high-paid lawyer, and the brain surgeon, destined to put her charming blond daughter into a mansion in Short Hills, New Jersey. She had made the engagement and wedding plans with joy, borrowing freely and expansively to usher her child into the long-awaited, triumphant future.

Her first visit to her daughter's first home, a few weeks after the wedding, sent her into a tailspin. Her vision of the Bronx had been upscale Riverdale with the million-dollar mansions. Her vision of her daughter's first home had been a three-bedroom condo. For several moments, she stood stock-still, staring at the recently whitewashed graffiti on the front of the building in the crumbling neighborhood. In shock, she labored up the dark stairwell to the second story, a slow fury building inside her as she entered and took in the tiny rooms, the small kitchen with its old appliances. She sat down on the couch and wondered how she could have been so misled.

"Isn't it nice?" Delilah said, smiling, waving her hand as if to introduce her mother to her new luxuries: the silver and porcelain, the Cuisinart, the Castro convertible with the new curtains to match.

"When," her mother said, taking huge gulps of air, "are you going to be able to move?"

And thus began the relentless campaign of Marilyn Goldgrab to see that her daughter got everything she deserved in life, the kind of things that her snooty classmates and their snooty parents took for granted. Her daughter was as good as any of them and twice as beautiful, she thought. She had had the same expensive education, the same clothes, albeit cleverly obtained at a fraction of the price, but whose business was that? And she therefore had every right to claim the same good life that was the deserved consequence of such faithful adherence to the rules. And Chaim, by hook or by crook, was going to give it to her.

Several times a week, her mother called Delilah, conversations that were full of unsolicited advice, hurtful and insulting admonitions, and dire prophecies. In short, Mrs. Goldgrab was driving her daughter crazy.

"Just don't talk to her," Chaim would say. "Keep it short. Tell her you're busy, that you'll call her back."

Delilah, who could really never stand her mother's pushy, demanding nature, wanted to do much more. And so, inevitably, there was a blowup. Hurtful, unforgivable truths were revealed in great, screaming arguments, and a soothing but troubled silence followed that lasted several weeks, until holidays and family celebrations intruded, necessitating a quick reconciliation. Marilyn called again, less frequently and more cautiously, nevertheless managing to preserve the needling subtext that was clear from everything she said.

"Your friend Adina is moving to Teaneck. I hear the houses are really beautiful there. I think her mother said it was a two-story colonial with a finished basement. . . . And your cousin Myra's husband—the one who went to work for your uncle Sam in his import business?—well, he just bought some license from Diesel to make watches, and now he's designing watches and selling them by the thousands, and soon they are moving to Great Neck . . . a house with a swimming pool!"

Like the centipede that enters the ears of people in horror movies, slowly taking over their brains and driving them insane, she felt her mother's words seep into her thoughts.

And then Chaim's mother began to visit her new daughter-in-law on a regular basis. She brought cookies and fattening but delicious kreplach and *knaidlach* and *rogelach* in large plastic containers meant for catering halls. And she never left before leaving behind a piece of her mind as well.

Like Emma Bovary, Delilah "accepted her wisdom; her mother-in-law was extravagant with it." They spoke to each other like people in a documentary about family life: with exaggerated consideration. But when Chaim's mother began a sentence with "I have to be honest with you," Delilah cringed, knowing that something disagreeable and insulting was on its way like a projectile, a Kassam rocket catapulted with reckless abandon into the soft flesh of populated areas.

The woman was relentless. Her criticism ranged from the kind of floor wax Delilah bought (too expensive) to the way she washed her dishes. "That set I bought you is porcelain, it should be hand-washed or the gold trim will turn dull."

Chaim, caught in the middle, tried to mediate and wound up getting himself exiled to his own bed even during the precious days when he could finally move into hers. Finally, there was the inevitable explosion, and his mother stopped bringing her plastic-covered caloric masterpieces. Instead, they went less frequently to her house to eat them.

Delilah, kept busy with classes and synagogue functions, didn't have too much time to brood. But eventually, she got bored. This was no fun, she thought. She tried doing more. She began preparing elaborate Friday night meals, inviting the synagogue president, the cantor, and his wife. But they were both in their seventies, on strict diets that precluded salt, sugar, fats, red meat, and just about anything else worth eating. Besides, she realized, what was the point of buttering them up? Her husband would be rabbi of this synagogue anyway; it was his by inheritance. And this life was going to be her life, until further notice.

She looked out her windows at the treeless streets and old brick buildings. She examined her apartment, whose novelty had already worn off and whose deficiencies showed through with devastating clarity.

She brooded, suddenly hearing her mother's voice without a phone.

And so the snake of discontent entered the garden of Delilah and Chaim's newlywed bliss through gates as wide as barnyard doors. In fact, it was inevitable, even without Marilyn.

The summer of Delilah's sophomore year in high school, the school's Hebrew department had arranged a class trip to Israel. It was very expensive. But even those parents who couldn't really afford it felt ashamed not to let their kids participate. So, along with many others, Delilah's parents took out loans, packed her suitcase, and sent her off.

Everyone had a great time wandering through the ancient ruins and the modern malls, riding up to Masada and standing teary-eyed by the Wailing Wall. On the flight back, sitting just two rows ahead of her, Delilah encountered her vision of the New York Orthodox Jewish couple who had it all.

She couldn't take her eyes off them.

She imagined they were coming back from a lovely vacation at five-star hotels, no doubt returning to Cedarhurst or Woodmere or another of those Long Island enclaves where mansions vie with each other on park-like lots nestled behind high stone fences, everything dappled by huge shady trees. New York's Orthodox Beverly Hills. They were both tall and slim and were traveling with two children, surprisingly advanced in age, considering the parents still looked like recent yeshiva high school graduates. The daughter was about fourteen, the son maybe nine.

The mother was a smoky blonde with long hair. Even after ten hours of being squashed on El Al, her hair still framed her face in perfect ellipses. You could still detect in her the yeshiva girl cheerleader that the disgruntled rabbis kept exhorting—to no avail—to lengthen her skirt. Now she wore a white cashmere sweatshirt with a hood and a pleated gray tweed skirt and black textured stockings that only legs like Angelina Jolie's could pull off. Her face was WASP princess: upturned nose, deep blue eyes. Delilah wondered if she'd had plastic surgery or if it was the same genetic magic that had Jews from Uzbekistan looking Mongolian and Jews from Great Britain like Margaret Thatcher.

Delilah drank her in like a free airline Diet Coke.

The husband, too, was gorgeous in his Banana Republic khakis and a blue striped shirt—Hugo Boss?—which had probably not been bought at discount at Century Twenty-One but at full price at Lord & Taylor's or Barney's during a busy lunch hour. He could no doubt well afford it. He was doing very well, thank you very much, Delilah thought, conjecturing if it was venture capital, heart surgery, or law, practiced from some office with ten-foot-high windows that looked over New York City like a personal backyard. He wore a discreet crocheted skullcap in no-nonsense black.

She imagined how they would gather their Louis Vuitton luggage and load it into their SUV. How they would drive and park in front of a wonderful old house, a place that had been meticulously redecorated and enlarged with enough basement and attic space to house several more families their size without the least discomfort. It would be a house they'd bought from anti-Semitic WASPs who'd simply died out or frittered away their money or retired to an adults-only golf community in Phoenix or Florida, a place where guards kept out the grasping poor and sticky-fingered, noisy grandchildren had strictly enforced visiting hours.

They were in love, she imagined, or, at least, content with each other and the life they'd built: walking-distance-to-synagogue communities, Ivy-prep yeshiva day schools, holiday trips to Israel on the New Year and Succoth, and Kosher Club jaunts to Acapulco or Grand Cayman on Passover.

And they deserved it all because they were good people, generous people.

Oh, my, yes.

They gave and gave and gave and gave. To Israel. To the handicapped. To political parties that supported Israel. To their synagogue. They were the most hounded and solicited beings in America and their checkbooks always stayed open. And in due time, they would grace fund-raising dinners for this or that as the honorees. She would look fabulous in a custom-made dress that was deceptively simple yet beautifully made and cost a fortune.

But they were not adventurers. They would not risk some idealistic move to the barren, fractious, terror-filled Middle East, no matter how their hearts swelled and tear ducts worked overtime each time they sang Israel's national anthem, "Hatikvah," meaning the hope:

Deep in my heart a Jewish soul yearns.
Our eyes to Zion look forward.

Right.

They were like their parents before them, like her parents—sensible. America was a gift one held on to for dear life.

It was everything she wanted in life, Delilah realized, her eyes shining.

On that same plane, just behind her, was yet another Orthodox family. They too had been on vacation and had also enjoyed their trip, except they had most probably not slept in hotels with stars of any kind but on mattresses on the floors of various Israeli relatives.

The woman was about the same age as the woman who sat in front, except that she looked it. She wore a pious hair covering of crocheted nylon that hung down her back, covering all her hair. Her husband wore a dark suit and a white open-collared shirt that seemed a bit yellowed from too many machine bleachings. He spent the flight pouring over religious texts with tiny Hebrew lettering. There were twice as many children, of all ages, who needed constant care. The husband helped, cheerfully and so ineffectually that the wife soon took over, sighing, freeing him to stroke his beard and read on.

Delilah imagined their many heavy, torn, unmatched suitcases, which relatives who came to take them home would manage to stuff into banged-up Fords. Some of the children would sit, unseat-belted, on top of them, until they drove to their cramped rented apartment in Kew Gardens or Boro Park, a place with many bookcases, bunk beds, a large dining room table, and convertible couches.

They would talk about this trip until their next one—perhaps a decade away. And their next vacation would be a ride to Hershey, Pennsylvania, and one night in a Comfort Inn.

Each time Delilah passed them in the aisle on the way to the lavatory, she cringed. Only if she were already dead and it was part of some afterlife punishment cooked up especially by God to make her pay for all her sins would she ever agree to be part of that scenario, she told herself.

She tried to anazlyze why. After all, they looked perfectly happy.

It was then she had her revelation: Heaven and Hell, she realized, were the same place. It was, for example, a room with a long table, and all people did all day was sit around and study. For the saints, it was Heaven. For the sinners, it was Hell.

She glanced over her shoulder as the poor woman in the polyester snood stood up, trying to rescue her baby from her two-year-old, who was poking the infant in the eye with his El Al–supplied crayons. This, she thought, was her vision of Hell.

And so, when Delilah woke up one morning, five months after her wedding, drenched in sweat from the realization that—without major intervention—this was exactly the life that loomed ahead of her, she must have been desperate. Which, of course, always explains many sins, but does not necessarily excuse them.

EIGHT

And so, a little over five months after Chaim's shirt-button sermon, as they were walking home after yet another shiva call (they'd been averaging one or two a month), Delilah turned to her new husband and said, "I can't stand this anymore."

Chaim looked at his new bride, astonished. "What's wrong?"

She turned her ring around her finger nervously. "What's *right*? This shul is falling apart, and the people are going with it. It's going to bury us alive. And this crumby apartment in this old building. The Bronx! And the polluted air. I want my own house. A backyard for the children. . . ."

He stopped dead in his tracks, focusing only on her last words. Was she trying to tell him some happy news? Oh, wouldn't that be wonderful! His face lit up.

"Uff, don't be an idiot! I'm not pregnant, and there is no way I'm getting pregnant in this neighborhood, in this apartment. A child in this shul would be like one of those wonders in Believe It or Not museums. I'm tired of going to funerals! I'm tired of being nice to talkative old biddies who have nothing to do all day but crochet you sweaters that don't fit and bake me cakes that would turn me into a fat old cow, just like them, if I ate a fraction of them!"

He looked crushed. Could this really be coming out of the mouth of his dear, delicate young wife? Such cruelty, such ungenerous words, about people who had done nothing but shower them with kindness? People who listened appreciatively to his sermons? Who treated Delilah like a favorite granddaughter? He stared down at the pavement, slowly putting one foot in front of the other.

Everything had been going so well, he'd thought. He'd been incredibly lucky to have a job so quickly. Most of his fellow classmates were still scrounging around for some teaching job in a yeshiva day school, which—if they were lucky—could be finessed into an assistant rabbi job five years down the line. He was already there, with a synagogue primed for him to take over.

And the apartment, what was wrong with the apartment? It was big enough for the two of them, after all. How much room did two people need? They even had an extra bedroom they were hardly using, a place for guests. . . . He glanced over at his wife, annoyed, then noticed two big tears snaking down her cheeks. He was alarmed, confused, his heart melting.

"Please, Delilah. Don't." He handed her a crumpled tissue. "What is it you want me to do?" he asked her helplessly.

"Find another job! Somewhere out of the city, in some nice little community with lots of pretty houses and trees."

Chaim, who only a few months before had wanted nothing more than to do just that, was suddenly loath to consider the idea. Despite his earlier fears, he now found himself almost addicted to the easy adoration of this congregation. Their warmth and praise were a balm for his jittery fears of inadequacy, fears that had plagued him all during his rabbinical studies. Like a child cuddled in the bosomy warmth of maternal approval, the longer he stayed, the more reluctant he became even to consider wrenching himself away by sending out his résumé.

He was succeeding. He had as much money as he thought he needed. Why take chances? Besides, it was by no means certain there really was any other place out there that would be eager to take him in.

"I can't believe you want me to give up my place in my grandfather's synagogue. Why, it would break his heart. Besides, when he retires, I'm in line to take over. I have no competition."

"If they keep losing members at the rate they're going, when *he* goes, there won't be a congregation!"

"But I could attract new people, young people! Don't you see? It's a wonderful opportunity, Delilah! Besides, I've heard stories about how the boards of some synagogues treat their rabbis. You are constantly under their thumbs or they'll cut off your head and cancel your contract. If you try to do your job, actually teach them something, deepen their observance, get them actively involved in supporting Israel, they get tired of you, and then they get annoyed, and then they get vengeful. And out you go, back on the unemployment line. At least here, we have Grandfather to stand buffer. They wouldn't dare fire Reb Abraham's grandson. We're safe here, darling."

"So, what are you telling me? That for the rest of my life all I have to look forward to is another roach-infested apartment in yet another Bronx walk-up? Is that it?"

What could he say to that? As long as he was connected to this synagogue, they would always have to live in a neighborhood within easy walking distance, because Orthodox Jews don't drive on the Sabbath. "I'm sure we could find something nicer. Maybe not Riverdale, but something—"

"Riverdale is the only place in the Bronx worth living, and this synagogue is nowhere near Riverdale and never will be, and you know it! It's in the Bronx. THE BRONX!" She raised her voice, causing passersby to pause a moment and look their way. They hurried forward in silence, waiting to continue in the privacy of their own home.

They drew the curtains and closed the windows.

"I didn't marry you to live in some dusty slum! I have my own plans, my own dreams, and if you really loved me, you'd want me to be happy!"

"Of course I want you to be happy. But what in all of this didn't you expect? I told you everything: about my grandfather and his synagogue and the offer he'd made me. We picked out this apartment together. I don't understand you, Delilah! None of this was forced on you; you agreed to everything!"

Delilah was quiet, trying to think of a reply that wouldn't make her the bad one, the selfish materialistic one. But she couldn't. Everything Chaim said was absolutely true. When faced with this reality, there was only one thing for her to do, one thing every wife can and must do when forced into such a corner: *change the subject.* The more irrelevant and unrelated the topic, the better, especially if it allows one to hurl hurtful truths that are sure to make one's husband blow his top, saying things he'd never believe himself capable of, things that will appall him when he calms down, making him forget what the argument was about in the first place, and forcing him to beg forgiveness, eat dust, and crawl for a very long time.

"If he wasn't your grandfather, they would have fired you already! Those sermons. . . . Buttons! Who wants to hear about buttons? The world is going up in smoke, terrorist attacks, natural disasters left and right, and you? You talk about buttons. Don't you see how you put them all to sleep, even the ones who try to stay awake? You get away with it because they don't dare fire you. You are just afraid to go to a place that will judge you like anybody else, a place where you'll have to stand on your own two feet!"

Chaim turned white and sat down. "Is that what you really think? Is that really true?"

She was braced for insults, not immediate surrender. It was their first fight and his quick capitulation filled her with equal parts of regret and contempt. She calmed down, afraid she'd overplayed her hand. After all, the last thing she wanted was to undermine his confidence. How would that help her get on the fast track? "Oh, it was just that one sermon. You've been getting better, really, like last week—when you talked about the ten tribes. . . ." She only vaguely remembered that, since she automatically tuned him out whenever he got up to speak now.

He looked devastated, but it couldn't be helped. She was entitled to the life she wanted. And it couldn't be lived in a Bronx apartment as the wife of a rabbi who spent his time at funerals. "You have so much to give. You could change lives. The people here . . . their lives are behind them. You need to be in a place with young people, young families. You could do so much good."

"They slept through it? Is that true?" he repeated, his eyes glassy, not hearing a word. Perhaps she was right. He *was* a dismal failure. He knew he wasn't all that bright, but he had worked so hard. This was his first congregation, and they were used to his brilliant, pious grandfather. Still, he had thought he was holding his own. At least he hadn't heard any complaints. But maybe they just didn't want to hurt his grandfather's feelings.

Perhaps all this time they too had been laughing at him behind his back, just like his wife.

Delilah and Chaim didn't speak for the next few days, except for business.

"Pick up the challahs."

"Don't forget the dry cleaning."

"Mrs. Farbish called and wants you to visit her husband in the hospital."

The pangs of regret began to hit Delilah about the third day. She wasn't sorry for what she'd done. She was sorry that this had been the result. Only one thing was worse than being stuck in this dump with Chaim; being stuck in it with a Chaim who wasn't speaking to her.

She wanted things to go back to normal. She wanted things to change completely. What she needed, she thought, was a plan.

Rivkie and Josh, she thought.

She'd last seen them three months before at their wedding, which was held at a posh country club in Westchester. Josh was now assistant rabbi in a beautiful synagogue there, a place with seven hundred young families, all of them professionals who lived within walking distance of the synagogue. She was dying to see Rivkie's house. And Josh had connections in the rabbinic and yeshiva world. He was from a rich prominent family. He might know which one of the jobs listed on Bernstein's Rabbinic Alumnus Employment Bulletin would be willing to take Chaim, with the proper references, which clearly, as a friend, he would be able to supply. It wouldn't be asking much. Just a little help. After all, Josh already had a job in some leafy suburb. Why would he begrudge the same to a dear, close friend like Chaim?

It wasn't being needy and pushy, she told herself as she dialed Rivkie's number. It was networking.

~

"I think we have no choice but to invite them," Rivkie told Josh.

He put down his pen and looked up from his book. "Rivkie, you are such a wonderful, kind person, but really, *is* this necessary?"

Rivkie nodded. "Yes, I think it is."

Delilah, who had made no effort to stay in touch since her wedding, had suddenly begun a relentless campaign to become her best friend. She called three times a week, long, rambling, intimate conversations about things Rivkie didn't want to know. If the information had been about others, Rivkie would have been able to beg off by truthfully claiming she didn't listen to gossip. But as it was, Delilah was talking about herself. Her latest purchases. Her sex life. Her brilliant innovations in the wonderful classic old synagogue where her husband, Chaim, would soon take over as rabbi. And always, she had ended the calls by saying how much she missed Rivkie. How she was dying to come out and spend some time with her. This had been going on for weeks. Until finally, her facade of giddy success and self-congratulatory pride gone, replaced by raw misery, Delilah had said point-blank, "Chaim has next Shabbes off; can we come to you? If I spend one more weekend with these old folks, I'm going to get bunions and grow a mustache."

"I can't just blow her off. After all, we were their matchmakers."

He shifted uncomfortably.

Chaim had never been a close friend, just an acquaintance for whom he—and most of his classmates—had felt a sort of undefined pity: he tried so hard, and achieved so little, always hanging on by his fingernails. Now he had married a girl with a checkered reputation, blond hair, and a pretty face, a girl whom no one—except Chaim—thought a suitable wife. It was like being forced to eat a dish full of bad ingredients prepared by a lousy chef simply because you'd lent someone a cookbook.

"Chaim is a fine person," Josh said carefully.

"Apparently, he's very unhappy with his job. It seems to be mostly with seniors."

"Seniors are wonderful. I'll take ten seniors for every teenager," he grumbled.

He was sitting at the dining room table perusing a lengthy Talmudic discussion from which he planned to prepare a program for his teenage Saturday afternoon discussion group. They were a difficult bunch, full of questions, doubts, and heresies, especially the girls, who were a hard sell on anything to do with the place of women in the traditional Orthodox synagogue service. You couldn't really blame them, since women had no place at all in the traditional Orthodox synagogue service, except as observers behind bars, lacy curtains, pretty wooden screens, or other inventive methods of keeping them at bay. Go explain that to intelligent teenage girls, many of whom were fluent in Hebrew from their expensive day school educations. Explain why they couldn't read the Torah, couldn't be called up for any of the shul honors, couldn't even kiss the cover of the

Torah as it was paraded around the men's section, barely visible to the women behind the partition.

The rabbi, who had tried a number of times to talk to this group, now refused to go back, as did the other two teachers hired for the Sunday school and Bar Mitzva program. As assistant rabbi and newcomer, the task had fallen to him. Just the thought of facing them filled him with aggravation. And now this.

"Why are they so desperate for our company all of a sudden? They haven't been in touch for months."

She shrugged. "I can't answer that. But Josh, my dear, I think we need to be generous. We are, after all, so blessed." He clasped his hands in front of him and looked at them. "And I think"—she paused delicately—"they might be going through a bit of a transition. You know, being married isn't so easy for everyone, like it is for us." She smiled at her husband, who took her hand and kissed it.

He had endless admiration for his wife's good heart and patience. He told himself that—like the patriarch Abraham—he should heed everything his wife tried to tell him. But this was too much. A whole weekend with those two!

"Can't we put it off?" he begged.

"It won't be so bad. You'll be in the synagogue most of the time anyway. It's just Friday night and Shabbes afternoon. I can invite some other guests. You won't even notice them," she promised, kissing him on the top of his head. "It's a real mitzva. And we can use all the blessings we can earn right now."

He put his hand on her growing stomach, and gave in.

~ ~

Delilah was thrilled. Here was a chance to socialize with another rabbi's wife. To check out what life was like out in the suburbs with a different kind of congregation, one where little kids ran around, babies cried, and pretty young mothers whispered secrets to one another, showing off their latest new hats and stylish suits. A chance to show off her own latest hat and stylish suit. And most of all, a chance to network.

Chaim, too, was pleased. He liked and admired Josh, despite the unfortunate little incident before his wedding. Josh was considered an *illuyi*, destined for greatness. He was also a good person, who kept to the strict letter of the law in anything having to do with his ethical and social behavior. He was from a wealthy family but never made a big deal about it, even though it was well known that he had turned his back on taking over his father's multimillion-dollar diet-drink company to become a struggling rabbi. Josh had never shown him anything but kindness. But the discrepancies in their prospects, backgrounds, and personalities were not conducive to friendship. Josh was royalty. Chaim was one of the peasants. Chaim had always acknowledged this fact without resentment or jealousy, as a given.

The invitation was unexpected.

"But why have they invited us? Why now?" he asked, puzzled.

"She's been after me for months. I guess she's lonely. You know she's always considered me her best friend. And I'm just so busy during the week, I don't even have time to pick up the phone and talk to her. We never get a chance to see each other. I invited them here, but you know, he can never get away. He's assistant rabbi, or something," Delilah said casually, deciding between two outfits. The skirt on one was longer but hugged her behind, as opposed to the one with a looser skirt that hit right above her knees.

"I'm also assistant rabbi. What makes you think *I* can get away?"

"But your grandfather . . . he wouldn't stop you. You've—we've—been here every Saturday for months." Her voice rose petulantly.

Seeing where this was going, and considering that it really wasn't too much to ask—he should be flattered and might even enjoy it—Chaim gave in.

They put their suitcases into their little Ford Escort, and drove off.

Delilah looked out the window at the ugly red bricks, the billboards, the housing projects, and the few bedraggled trees on the Drive. She took in the graffiti on the sides of the buildings, the rusting fire escapes, the self-storage units, the eyesore of old bricks painted an appalling red, white, and blue. They passed the White Castle on Bruckner Boulevard; the pawn, cash, and loan stores; the horrid rusting cars raised on pedestals in front of used car dealerships and muffler shops. They passed Co-op City, a housing project that rose like some set in a futuristic horror movie, where a hapless mankind is imprisoned and forced to live like ants in gargantuan prison complexes. And then, suddenly, it was all behind them.

Highway signs flashed by indicating Mount Vernon, one quarter mile; Scarsdale; Mamaroneck. Lakes of mirrorlike water held reflections of beautiful fall colors from overhanging trees. Bridges reached over the road like filigreed bowers. And all along there were glimpses of huge, wondrous homes, larger than any family could ever need, deserve, or use, nestled on huge private lots. Homes with pumpkins on front lawns, and yellow, red, and green forest trees in backyards. The cars that passed them on the highway were gleaming and rich, with suit jackets hung on backseat hooks, driven by men heading home from upscale Manhattan offices who would park in front of trendy updated farmhouses painted maroon, or renovated Colonials with white siding, trimmed in black shutters: places with manicured bushes and huge artistically placed poinsettia, their red leaves like torches leading up to the front gate.

It was all out there, Delilah thought. Prosperity and peace and success all tied up with a big red bow and a mortgage.

"Are you sure this is it?" Delilah asked Chaim, as they pulled into the driveway. She looked out, disappointed. She'd been hoping for more, while at the same time prepared to feel horribly jealous and put upon if it met her expectations. As it was, it turned out to be a relatively simple and modest brick house on a generous plot of tree-filled property on a quiet cul-de-sac.

It was much nicer inside, Delilah saw immediately. The living room had a fireplace surrounded by rough-hewn stones, with built-in holders for logs. There were oak bookcases, comfortable couches, and a whole separate room just for dining room furniture. "Wow," Delilah said, when she walked in.

"We didn't have much choice. We needed something within walking distance to the synagogue, and they didn't have much on the market. It's really more than we wanted to spend," Rivkie said in a rush, almost apologetically.

"You mean you bought it? I thought the synagogue—?"

"No, they only provide a house for the rabbi. Assistant rabbis are on their own. And mostly the bank owns it." She smiled uncomfortably, already feeling the weekend stretch out ahead of her in endless tedious blocks of time, through which she would have to be on constant guard. She didn't want Delilah's envy, or her friendship, or her confidences. She wanted to do the right thing, to offer loving kindness to another human being who seemed troubled and wanted (insisted?) on her intervention and help.

Delilah dressed carefully for dinner, deciding to wear a wig because Rivkie was wearing a wig. She put on her most pious suit, the one with the ankle-grazing skirt, then went downstairs to light Sabbath candles. Rivkie had already set up two candles for her on the tray next to her own elaborate silver candelabra, the traditional gift of a mother-in-law to her daughter-in-law before the wedding. It was gorgeous, and held at least eight candles. Rivkie only lit three. "I'll add another with each child," she explained, blushing.

Delilah dutifully lit her candles, waving her hands over the flames, covering her eyes as tradition required. When she finished, she saw that Rivkie was still deep in prayer, her eyes shut, as she silently mouthed heartfelt requests for good health, happiness, and good fortune for everyone she knew, an addendum to the candle-lighting blessing that pious women created for themselves over the centuries, convinced that the heavenly gates of mercy were open wide at that moment in time to the prayers of Jewish women.

Delilah studied her tranquillity, her sincerity, her really, really nice engagement ring, wondering why the words always felt like overchewed gum in her own mouth, a tasteless, meaningless exercise you were only too happy to spit out and be done with. She envied Rivkie her peace of mind, her convictions, the easy way in which things always seemed to work out for the Rivkies of the world. She felt bitter that her own life had been one panting uphill struggle.

It was so unfair. Which is why, she thought, the Rivkies and Joshes of the world were not being generous when they helped people like her, but simply being just. This was the very least they could do. And so when you asked a favor of them, you were simply giving them an opportunity to behave in a way that was required of them, after all. Excessive gratitude was not only unnecessary, it was counterproductive, the heavenly reward for good deeds being inversely proportional to how much praise and fawning gratitude they netted you from the recipients of your largesse. By not falling all over herself to thank them, she'd be doing them a favor, Delilah told herself, getting ready to pursue her latest goal.

But just when the coast seemed clear, someone knocked on the door. It turned out to be the wives of the Talmud Torah teacher and the beadle, both of whom had been invited to dinner, Delilah realized to her chagrin.

She smiled her way through helping to set the table, as the women chattered on about their most recent experiences in their charity work (visiting the sick, helping new mothers, collecting clothes for the poor). When they turned to her and asked in a friendly way what she was involved in, she said, with great conviction, "Old-age homes."

Dinner was lively, with lots of singing around the table and many learned discussions among the men, while the women automatically jumped up to clear and serve, without resentment. The women seemed to know each other well and were constantly referring to study groups, exercise classes, and book clubs they were part of. They all lived within a few blocks, no doubt in similar homes, she thought enviously, with big yards and leaves to rake and the smell of burning wood.

Saturday morning they rose early to the singing of birds. Josh and Chaim left for synagogue together, while Rivkie and Delilah had a leisurely breakfast. Delilah tried to be chummy and familiar. Rivkie did her best not to offend her but had no intention of paying for unwanted intimacies by supplying similar information of her own. This annoyed Delilah, but she chalked it up to Rivkie's boring piety.

The synagogue was packed with young families, baby carriages, toddlers. The other young women greeted Rivkie with warmth, hugging her. They were gracious to Delilah as Rivkie's guest. It was like being back in school again, Delilah thought, except, being the rabbi's wife, you would never get left behind on the punchball fields without being chosen. They'd have to pick you. In fact, you'd be the captain, and you'd pick them, your attention and affection a prize to bestow on the fortunate. You were important, because the rabbi was important. And holy. Don't forget holy. If he was holy, so was she, she thought, smoothing her hair beneath her hat and pulling down her skirt. Yes, this is what it would be like to be the rabbi's wife in a real congregation, one that was filled with potential celebrations instead of tragic losses.

Kiddush after the service was catered in a large and airy social hall. In honor of the day's Bar Mitzva boy, there were trays of piping hot potato, noodle, and spinach kugels; individual quiches; platters of vegetables with dips; and fresh salmon on beds of parsley. The dessert table held giant fruit displays, chocolate-dipped strawberries, and beautiful little petits fours.

They were so full by the time they reached home, they couldn't even imagine lunch. But there it was, a beautiful buffet laid out in all Rivkie's best Mikasa wedding china. Thankfully, there were no other guests. She felt happy and sleepy and content, unwilling to pressure her hosts or disrupt the pleasant atmosphere. There'd be time for that later, she told herself.

And as they lay down for the traditional Saturday-afternoon nap in the comfortable guest room, which smelled of lavender and newly ironed sheets, she realized just how lonely she'd been the last few months. And just how much she really hated the Bronx, her apartment, and the synagogue full of old people.

She reached across the bed, taking Chaim's hand. "Are you having a good time, Chaim?"

Half asleep, he murmured, "I suppose so. But I prefer the city."

She drew back, scowling. In the dappled shadows of the afternoon, his figure in the bed suddenly didn't seem human anymore. He seemed like a bottle wrapped in cloth. And his head was the bottleneck, she realized, something she would have to pull herself through, kicking and screaming, to get where she wanted to go.

Delilah chose the quiet private third meal of the day to make her move. Seated across from her hosts at a table filled with coffee and cake and various salads, Delilah said, "We had such a lovely time. This is such a great congregation. So many young people! Chaim is always saying if he had a young congregation, he could do so much. You know that image of writing on blank paper, rather than paper that's got writing all over it?"

Chaim, who had never expressed—or felt—any such thing, just stared at her.

"Really, Chaim? Would you prefer youth work?" Josh asked him.

"Well, I can't say I wouldn't like it. I just don't have much experi—"

Delilah laid her hand on his arm. "You know Chaim, he makes modesty into a fault. He has so much experience! The NCSY youth groups. Yavneh. Hillel House," she said, smiling, winking, and waving her arms in all directions.

Chaim, who had never worked with any of those groups, coughed until Rivkie brought him a glass of water.

"He is wonderful with the seniors. But he is wasted in the Bronx. Wasted. You wouldn't know of another congregation that has an opening, would you, Josh? In some small, pretty place like this? A young congregation?"

"Well, usually you need about four or five years as assistant rabbi before you can even apply for a position as rabbi," Josh explained.

"Usually, but not always," she said cryptically, with a secret smile.

"I suppose, theoretically, that's true." Josh nodded, wondering how long they would be held captive before the Sabbath was out and they smiled their goodbyes and the Ford disappeared down the road.

"I don't think an ad in the Rabbi's Forum of *Bernstein's Bulletin* is theoretical. It looked pretty practical to me," she said, pulling out the paper. "Especially if someone with your connections and reputation could pull a few strings—"

"Really, Delilah," Chaim murmured, mortified.

"Oh, I'm sorry." She looked around, innocent and bewildered. "Did I say something I shouldn't?"

"What congregation is it?" Josh asked, his curiosity getting the better of him.

She smoothed the *Bulletin* down and licked her finger, turning the pages. She jabbed at it, the way one would spear a particularly delicious hors d'oeuvre. "There!"

Josh took the paper and read. "You aren't talking about the ad for that synagogue by the lake, are you?" His look was incredulous.

"*Young, affluent community, interested in open-minded spiritual leader*," Delilah read. "How can you tell where it is?"

"They've been running that ad for months," Chaim informed her.

"Congregation Ohel Aaron. In Connecticut," Rivkie said quietly, raising her eyebrows at her husband and quietly taking Delilah's hand in solidarity. "She couldn't possibly have known that," she admonished him.

"Well, maybe not," Josh conceded. "But Chaim, surely, you've heard the story."

"What story?" Delilah demanded, turning to her husband.

"The story of why Congregation Ohel Aaron of Swallow Lake, Connecticut, will never get a rabbi," Chaim said quietly. "Isn't it time we got back to the synagogue for the evening prayers?" Josh nodded gratefully, and the men started the song that ushers in Grace After Meals, putting an abrupt end to the discussion.

Later that evening, when they finally stood at the door to say their goodbyes, Josh put his arm around Chaim's shoulder. "It's an honor for you to follow in your grandfather's footsteps. He has quite a reputation. I envy you."

"Thank you, Josh. They are enormous shoes to fill," Chaim said gratefully.

Delilah felt all her dreams slowly stop, the way the bubbles of Coke stop when the bottleneck slows them down and the cap puts an end to their escape.

She kissed Rivkie. "I'll call you," she murmured, clutching her a little more tightly than was appropriate.

Rivkie nodded uncomfortably. "I'm sure you will."

The moment they were in the car on the open road that led inexorably back to the Bronx, Delilah turned to her husband and said stiffly, "Tell me, Chaim. Why is it that Congregation Ohel Aaron in Swallow Lake, Connecticut, will never get a rabbi?"

NINE

In the 1950s, the Orthodox Jews of Connecticut joined the national movement out of the inner cities into the suburbs. Jews began showing up in places they were hardly ever seen or wanted. By then, the offspring of Eastern European Jews were already college educated, working in their families' businesses, or successfully developing their own. They sought an area outside of Hartford or New Haven, where they could build and enjoy their prosperity. And so they found their way to beautiful Swallow Lake. They built a large, imposing synagogue and called it Ohel Aaron, after a major donor. They built large, imposing homes with lake views and private boat docks.

Studies in the 1980s revealing that 52 percent of Jews in America were intermarrying sent shock waves through the American Jewish community. Jews began to rethink their values, the education they were giving their children, and the dilution of religious rituals in their synagogues and in their lives. Many decided to send their children to religious day schools.

When a decade later the dot-com bubble provided new wealth to many, yeshiva high school graduates bought into the Swallow Lake community at an unprecedented rate. One of them was a stock market trader who later wound up serving ten to fifteen in a federal penitentiary. To atone for his sins, he built an elaborate Orthodox Jewish day school on part of his Swallow Lake estate, naming it after his parents, who had both died of heart attacks.

The school was soon attracting the offspring of Orthodox Harvard Law and Business School alumni, Orthodox heart surgeons and cancer specialists, and Orthodox venture capitalists. Joining them were Jewish immigrants from South Africa, Iran, and the former Soviet Union, people who, while not Orthodox themselves, were not put off by the Orthodox way of life and were hopeful the day school would prove a bastion to keep their children from the drugs and sex that were rampant in other schools. They were also attracted to the school's reputation for getting kids into the Ivy Leagues. And most of all they wished to join other Jews who could afford homes in the high six- to seven-figure category.

When the aging rabbi of Ohel Aaron had a heart attack, they searched high and low for an Orthodox rabbi who would meet all of the community's needs. The problem, as usual, was that no one could agree on what, exactly, those needs were.

The day school graduates wanted the kind of rabbi they were familiar with from the synagogues of their youth, places with oversized barriers separating men and women; a rushed, rather melancholy, songless service; the words read in Hebrew so fast they sounded like watermelonwatermelonwatermelon. They wanted a rabbi they could look up to, an éminence grise with an iron will, who would be uncompromising and didactic in anything related to law or ritual. Someone who, when you pointed to a phrase in the Talmud, could complete it by heart and tell you the rest of the page for good measure. Preferably, they wanted the scion of a rabbinic family, or at least someone who had served a prestigious congregation and had earned a reputation for honesty, piety, warmth, and leadership.

The immigrants, however, had quite a different view of the situation. They saw Saturday as their day off. While they were willing to join the synagogue service in order to network, and didn't mind putting their wives where they could be neither seen nor heard for a few hours, what they absolutely didn't want—and would not tolerate—was being subjected to weekly exhortations about what they ate, how they lived, or anything else connected to the Ten Commandments, five of which couldn't possibly fit into their lifestyles. They wanted a rabbi who would look the part, but would be friendly and understanding. Someone who would kid around and take things easy. Someone who knew not only how to tell a good joke, but how to listen to one (even if it was just a little off-color). In exchange, they were prepared to let him pick their pockets for whatever cause he wanted.

Enter Rabbi Hershel Metzenbaum and his wife, Shira.

Rabbi Metzenbaum was in his mid-forties, a charismatic and distinguished scholar who had made a name for himself as a prominent member of the Council of American Orthodox Rabbis. He was also down-to-earth and friendly, a hands-on person who truly loved being a rabbi. Young people, particularly, were drawn to him, as he had an easy and respectful attitude toward them. He could play basketball and discuss the latest Star Wars movie. As a result, he headed numerous boards of numerous Orthodox Jewish youth groups.

As the rabbi of a small congregation in the Midwest for ten years, Metzenbaum had done wonders in gathering together unaffiliated Jews, reformed Reform Jews, and local Jewish college students from nonreligious backgrounds, not to mention the youth of his synagogue, helping to build a community dynamic that saw his synagogue grow and prosper, as new families bought houses in the vicinity simply to be able to be part of his congregation. He was adored.

The president of Ohel Aaron had heard about him from his brother, a prominent plastic surgeon in Ohio, who had attended one of Rabbi Metzenbaum's many weekly classes. The Synagogue Search Committee, impressed, put his name at the top of their list.

Rabbi Metzenbaum was used to receiving offers from search committees looking for rabbis. Until now, he had fended them off. But at this particular moment in time, many factors contributed to his reconsidering his commitment to stay put. The salary situation in the Midwest was going nowhere. His house was really too small for his growing family, but a larger mortgage was out of the question. And the kids—all five of them—were attending private Hebrew day schools. The two who were in high school had been forced to board in New Jersey, because there was no local Orthodox high school. Even with a rabbinic discount, the tuition for his five kids was sending him to the poorhouse.

Sensing his vulnerability, the board told him the job in Swallow Lake came not only with a large beautiful house which would be his—rent and mortgage free—for as long as he was rabbi, but also with free tuition for all his children in the elite local Orthodox day school, which included an excellent high school as well. But what tempted Rabbi Metzenbaum most of all was his perception that here was a rare opportunity, the kind most rabbis look for all their lives: a young, growing community, a place full of affluent, prominent people who would form an important stop on the fund-raising tours of every major Jewish organization. As rabbi, he could easily parlay his local popularity into national prominence, which would ensure him prestigious board memberships and thus an opportunity to influence the direction of Jewish education and community life all over the country. Moreover, it was a place where, when he chose to retire, he would be called Rabbi Emeritus and showered with compliments and a comfortable pension that would leave him the rest of his days to learn Talmud and write popular works of condensed Torah wisdom for busy Jews with short attention spans.

And thus, despite his long and revered position in the community, Rabbi Metzenbaum accepted the invitation of the Swallow Lake board to fly down with his family, all expenses paid, for a long weekend to explore the position. They put him and his wife and children up at the lovely home of the synagogue president, with its private swimming pool and tennis courts. They fed him lavish meals. They introduced the children to their peers and the rebbitzin to the sisterhood.

Sizing up his hosts, Rabbi Metzenbaum prepared his maiden sermon with meticulous care. He began with two good jokes, followed by an editorial from *The New York Times*, worked in a few minutes' worth of Talmud, and a few more minutes of light reminiscences of his childhood and memories of his grandparents, ending with a moral punch line, followed by another good joke. And he did it all in under twenty minutes. It was an enormous success.

He spent the Sabbath shaking hands and smiling at everyone, bending his head to listen intently to stories, compliments, jokes, and various normal and abnormal requests. He was friendly. He exuded modesty and compassion. Everybody loved him, except for those few misfits that exist in every congregation who never go along with the majority as a matter of principle; they warned that he was insincere, too religious, or not religious enough.

Shira Metzenbaum also made a favorable impression. She seemed attractive but in a dowdy religious way, which gave her a certain asexuality that relaxed the sisterhood. She smiled and was sincerely interested in the community, making an effort to learn everyone's names. She seemed willing—no, eager—to participate in the sisterhood activities. And the kids were bright and attractive, an asset to the community.

Both the Orthodox faction and the new immigrant faction were happy, and the Search Committee made Rabbi Metzenbaum an offer he couldn't refuse. Soon the Metzenbaums were making tearful announcements, being hugged and kissed and embraced at kiddush functions full of home-baked cakes and plastic cutlery. Far from being resentful or angry, his congregation sincerely wished their beloved rabbi and rebbitzin every happiness and success. Like proud parents seeing off a successful son, as much as they mourned for themselves, they rejoiced in his good fortune, accepting that it was the inevitable step he deserved to take to better his life.

The Metzenbaums attended a lavish going-away party, where there were many toasts, many tears, and many sincere testimonials. They sold their house, packed up their furniture and kids, and moved cross-country to begin their new life.

The rabbi poured himself into his work, getting to know all the movers and shakers, especially the members of the board: Solange and Arthur Malin, who owned a media empire; Amber and Stuart Grodin, who together had designed floppy novelty bears filled with a crunchy fragrant stuffing that became wildly collectible and dominated the aisles in every drugstore; Dr. Joseph Rolland, the world-famous heart surgeon, and his fashionable wife, Mariette; and the Borenbergs, Felice—a savvy businesswoman who had made a killing in her center aisle pushcarts at malls all over America, and Ari, her third husband and former employee.

The rabbi and his wife were a bit overwhelmed by the lavishness of the community, but the rabbi warned the rebbitzin she'd better stop sucking in her cheeks in contempt and disapproval when they showed her their game rooms, their home movie theaters, and their indoor pools with the retractable roofs. She had better remember not to remark with amazement on the self-cleaning wireless remote toilets, whose covers automatically lifted when you entered, and closed and flushed when you left. And she had better stop staring like a hick in Manhattan at the twenty-foot-high limestone fireplaces and the octagonal libraries made of Brazilian mahogany. He reminded her that they were there to focus on the community's spiritual requirements, and that even the most materially blessed could be very poor and needy when it came to their religious lives.

He told himself that this was an important group that could be led in a direction that would cause them to cherish their heritage, and to use their power, influence, and money to benefit the Jewish people. It was a group that was asking his help to go in a new direction.

He did what had worked so well in the Midwest: he began offering weekly classes for the men and boys. Attendance was poor, at first, but grew. Surprisingly, it grew most significantly among the high school boys, who found in the rabbi's sincere love for the Torah—particularly its ethics and morality—a spiritually viable alternative to rock music and Indian mysticism. Most of all, the rabbi was willing and able to give these youngsters what they needed most, something that their wealthy parents simply could not: time. He played basketball with them. He invited them over for little *melave malka* parties Saturday night. He knew what books they were reading. He was willing to counsel them on any subject and offer them help with any problem. He was willing to call their teachers and intervene on their behalf with their parents. He was tireless. And the kids loved him.

Shira Metzenbaum worked right alongside him. For if any woman since the beginning of time could be said to embody those true qualities needed to be a rabbi's wife, his partner in leading a congregation, it was Rebbitzin Shira Metzenbaum.

She not only cooked and baked and cleaned, she infused these tasks with holiness by constantly reminding herself that she was employing these womanly arts to bring misguided congregants closer to God. She was happy to have people join her on the Sabbath and on holidays; she loved a full house. There was never a Sabbath meal that did not include either board members she needed to impress, synagogue misfits she was attempting to remold, or complete strangers she was herding into her little flock. There was never a new mother to whom she did not take a casserole, investigating her mothering skills, or a sick person she failed to comfort by reading Psalms to counteract their obvious sins. There was no funeral or unveiling she didn't attend, no shiva call she failed to make, sitting silently in the house of mourning or offering tactful words of consolation: "It's a blessing you have other children."

As the rabbi tended to the young men, she drew around her the young girls, giving classes in modesty, chastity, Torah, and the Prophets. Soon, the girls were having long talks with their mothers. Gone were clothes that showed too much cleavage, too much knee. Soon, the rebbitzin and her followers began demanding a *mechitzah* that was taller, denser, and blocked the view completely. Certain women stopped using makeup on the Sabbath, surprising the men, who had never seen their wives look that bad. They insisted on trading in their king-sized beds for twin beds, slapping their husbands' hands away if they tried to so much as embrace them or kiss them during two weeks out of the month.

Words like *ruchnius* and *gashmiyus*, spirituality and materialism, began to pepper the speeches of teenagers, who looked around at their parents' lavish lifestyles with new eyes and new contempt. And then a few of the teenagers to whom the rabbi had been particularly close decided to attend yeshiva programs in Israel for the summer. When the summer ended, two of them called their parents to say they'd decided to stay there and join the Israeli army instead of making use of their early admission acceptances to Harvard and the University of Pennsylvania. Later that year, another one of the boys dropped out of Yale and went to live on the Lower East Side, enrolling in a yeshiva. He began wearing a black velvet skullcap, then a black hat and a long black coat. He grew long side locks and an unkempt beard. Soon, he refused to eat anything in his parents' home because he didn't think it was kosher enough. He adamantly refused to even consider returning to finish college, although he had only a year to go and the tuition had already been paid.

The final straw came when the daughter of Solange and Arthur Malin dropped out of Barnard and disappeared. She surfaced in Jerusalem at Michlalat Devorah, announcing she was engaged to a yeshiva student with whom she was planning to have ten kids and whom she would be working to support (presumably with her parents' generous help) for the rest of his life so he could sit and learn. The next day, the synagogue board of Ohel Aaron convened an emergency meeting.

Voices were raised. Hands slammed down on the table. A few punches were thrown. But in the end, when a vote was taken, it was overwhelmingly decided that the rabbi and his wife had to go. Given that the rabbi's contract had four more years to run, and the clause for early termination was going to cost the synagogue most of the funds they'd set aside to redo the catering hall so it could hold six hundred instead of only three hundred, the matter was turned over to Joshua Alterman, a Park Avenue lawyer known for defending white-collar criminals, some of whom were now his neighbors on Swallow Lake. It was Joshua who carefully reread the contract, finding the clause that hinted no penalty had to be paid if the rabbi—or his family—could be found liable for the termination. Brainwashing children into joining harmful cults, he suggested, would fit the bill nicely.

They gave Rabbi Metzenbaum two weeks' notice.

The rabbi and rebbitzin debated hiring a lawyer, but before they could do anything the synagogue sent a van to pack up their belongings and changed the locks on their house. The children were thrown out of the day school.

The scandalous treatment of the Metzenbaums in Swallow Lake soon became a cause célèbre, hotly debated among America's Orthodox Jewish communities and beyond. Soon, long articles appeared in *The Jewish Observer*, denouncing the Ohel Aaron congregation as a disgrace, and their treatment of Rabbi Metzenbaum and his lovely pious wife as tantamount to murder. As the very learned author and main stringency king of Boro Park explained—naming all the Ohel Aaron board members—embarrassing someone in public is considered akin to murdering them. *Midstream* hosted a written debate: "The Case of Swallow Lake: Has Orthodoxy Reached Its Nadir?" Even the religion editor of *The New York Times* decided to put in his oar, explaining to *Times* readers why an Orthodox congregation would fire a dynamic leader for encouraging young people to study in a yeshiva in Israel, or marry a yeshiva student, an article that made Orthodox rabbis and congregations everywhere cringe, made Conservative congregations giggle, and was pinned up on the bulletin boards of Reform synagogues throughout the country.

Soon JORA (Jewish Orthodox Rabbis Association) and RAOR (Rabbinical Association of Orthodox Rabbis) issued a call to boycott the congregation, telling their memberships that no rabbi should accept the now-vacant post of rabbi of Ohel Aaron until the poor Metzenbaums—jobless, living in the cramped basement of her parents' Canarsie home—received both an apology and monetary compensation. Rabbinic organizations refused to run the congregation's want ads for a new rabbi until informed by caustic letters from the Park Avenue law firm of Deal, Deal, Alterman and Goodstein that they were opening themselves up to lawsuits. While they immediately backed down and ran the ads, the word was out that Swallow Lake was a congregation to which no self-respecting rabbi should agree to go.

And that is why Congregation Ohel Aaron of Swallow Lake has been without a rabbi for two years, Chaim explained to Delilah, parking the car in front of their dusty apartment house late that Saturday night.

Delilah sat in the dark. Her eyes gleamed.

TEN

All that winter, she pleaded with him to answer the ad. “What can it hurt?”

He looked at her, amazed and appalled. “You can’t be serious. Don’t you understand? They are being blackballed! Anyone who took the job would be a pariah! It would ruin his reputation, maybe get him thrown out of the Council of Orthodox Rabbis of America altogether! I’ve already told you how it would hurt my grandfather. And just think how offended this congregation would be. Why, they’ve been so kind to us, Delilah! It would be like spitting in their faces!”

Delilah, who didn’t have much patience with other people’s emotions, being caught up so passionately most of the time with her own, looked at him coldly, her eyes narrowing. “Do you know what your problem is, Chaim? You have no ambition. You are willing to rot away here in this dive because you are afraid to spread your wings and fly.” She said this with a measure of accuracy that made her words doubly painful. “So, Ohel Aaron fired its rabbi. So what? Plenty of congregations fire rabbis! So it wasn't justified, at least according to all the busybodies out there writing articles. But think of this: Out of all those people who want to boycott Swallow Lake, is there even one who actually belonged to that congregation? Even one that had to sit through one of Metzenbaum's sermons or eat his wife's cooking on a Friday night? Josh is just so narrow-minded. There are two sides to every story. Isn't that what you always say? That we shouldn't judge someone until we are in their shoes? Huh?"

He saw she was furious and wished he could do something about it. But applying for the job in Swallow Lake was so beyond the pale, it never seriously entered his mind. His rabbinical life would be over; he'd be attacked by his fellow rabbis. People he respected and wanted to befriend, like Josh, would shrug their shoulders when his name was mentioned. No one would accept his rabbinical decisions. They wouldn't allow him to officiate at weddings. He would never be able to join a rabbinical court and arrange divorces. His career path would be blocked forever.

"Please, Delilah, be reasonable," he begged her helplessly. "Besides, even if I applied, there is no reason they should consider hiring me. Rabbi Metzenbaum was a respected rabbi for ten years. He's published books. He was elected president of all kinds of organizations. I haven't even been an assistant rabbi for one year! We would gain nothing and lose so much. Please, my love, try to understand."

She wanted to smash him over the head for his mild reasonableness, as the fury of thwarted hopes rose up from her bowels. In her mind, she saw the lovely house on the lake in Connecticut fade from view, replaced by used-car lots, smokestacks, and graffiti-smeared brick buildings. In the background, far off but clearly discernible, she heard the lilt of her mother's aggravated nagging, which would now follow her through eternity, reminding her how she could have done—oh, so much better.

Tears of misery tracked her face.

He stared at her, completely at a loss. When he tried to embrace her, she impatiently elbowed him out of her way.

Spring showed up. The bedraggled trees in the Bronx streets and alleyways sent forth a few anemic leaves. There was a drive-by shooting just down the block. And before they knew it, the season changed, transforming into the unbearably hot summer.

Delilah graduated in June with a license to practice dental hygiene. But instead of looking for a job, she did nothing. The idea of scrapping off bicuspids in the mouths of strangers suddenly nauseated her. She sat in her kitchen, swatting the flies, looking listlessly out the window into the street. She made no effort to get dressed, wearing her nightclothes into the late afternoon. Then she'd eat lunch and go back to sleep for the afternoon without washing the dishes from the morning or the previous evening.

One morning, her mother-in-law, who had the skill of a military cryptologist when it came to her son's laconic phone calls, turned up unannounced. She rang and rang the doorbell until Delilah finally heaved herself out of bed. Half asleep, she carelessly threw a short robe over her babydoll pajamas and opened the door.

Mrs. Levi took one look at her daughter-in-law, and one look at the house, before her face turned beet red. "What is the matter with you, Delilah? Look at yourself. Look at this place. You are a rabbi's wife! What if the president of the sisterhood should come to visit you?"

"She's ninety years old and would have congestive heart failure by the time she reached the second landing," Delilah murmured, groping for the coffeepot, which lay hidden under a mountain of unwashed dishes.

"Are you . . . you're not . . . pregnant? Is that it?" Chaim's mother offered hopefully, sending forth the only possible reason she could think of that might in any way excuse this behavior and allow her to feel charity or compassion for this girl, whom she had never liked and never wanted her son to marry.

"Absolutely not, thank God!"

Mrs. Levi turned purple, and began to choke. "Well, I never . . . had no idea . . . a religious woman, to feel that way . . . God just shouldn't punish you!"

"Don't worry. He already has. Look around you, Mama Levi." Delilah swept her arms expansively around the room. "This is what I've got to look forward to for the next fifty years, if Chaim and his grandfather have anything to say about it."

"You picked this apartment out! I distinctly remember the day you signed the lease! You said it had nice, big rooms." The older woman clutched the wall, feeling faint and alarmed. She could never have imagined her daughter-in-law behaving this way. While there had never been much love lost between them, Delilah had always made an effort to keep up appearances, to act the part of the good, religious daughter-in-law, not that she hadn't seen right through it. Still, on those too rare occasions she and her husband had been invited over, Delilah had always been well dressed and made up—even if it was with that horrid red "Hey, sailor" lipstick. The house had always been neat, if not exactly clean, with all the wedding gifts displayed, a few of them even shined and dusted.

"Yes," Delilah agreed. "I really know how to pick 'em, don't I?" she drawled, lighting up a cigarette and blowing smoke rings at the ceiling.

"When did you start smoking? It's a filthy habit." Mrs. Levi coughed, waving the smoke away frantically. She opened a window.

"That's right, Mama. The fresh air of the Bronx. So much better than Lucky Strikes," Delilah said, inhaling deeply as she sat down. The truth was, she'd bought her first pack just the day before. Although she thought the look was right for her present state of mind, she hated what smoking did to her well-cared-for teeth and pristine breath. But at the moment, the sacrifice was worth it. She crossed her legs and rested the side of her head on her hand, passively observing her mother-in-law's meltdown.

"So the real you has finally come out!" Mrs. Levi shouted. "I want you to know you never fooled me! I had your number from day one. I gave you a prince and you turned him into a *shmatte*!" she screamed.

"Excuse me, but that was the condition I got him in!" Delilah shouted back. "A *shmatte*. That's Chaim. A real, bona fide *shmatte*! Now get out of my house. I've had all I'm going to take from you and your precious son! Leave!"

Chaim's mother felt suddenly ill. She sat down heavily in the nearest chair.

Delilah got up. "Are you . . . all right, Mama?" she asked nervously, envisioning the call to 911, the paramedics, the flashing lights, the neighbors on the stoops, a frantic Chaim asking her all kinds of difficult questions, and—if they managed to revive the old crow—getting all kinds of contradictory answers. "Look. Don't get upset. I'm sorry. I'm just not myself."

The older woman stared at her coldly. "You've never, ever, been more yourself, Delilah. You are just like your mother. A pushy, materialistic, social climber. Except you have a better complexion, and haven't gained all that weight. Yet."

Delilah took two steps toward her, her fists clenched.

Mrs. Levi got up stiffly. She went over to the china closet and took out the lovely silver candlesticks that had been her wedding gift to her son's bride. She found a plastic bag on the floor—there were plenty to choose from—and put them inside. And then, wrapping her wounded dignity around her like a pashmina, she walked stiffly out the door, slamming it behind her.

Chaim, who had taken a teaching position in a local yeshiva to supplement their income, came home at five. He found his wife asleep. He also found they had new neighbors: a family of roaches had moved into one of the soup pots that had been lying around since the previous Sabbath. There was nothing to eat. No one had done the shopping. The refrigerator was empty.

He had gotten a frantic, completely incoherent phone call from his mother, calling him a *shmatte* and claiming his wife was a floozy. Even for his mother, it was a bit much. He had tried to calm her.

He loved his mother and respected her, as the Torah required. But from the beginning she had had a problem with his wife. She complained about her blond hair, calling her a "bottle blonde." But she had also told him, many times, that he didn't have what it took to be a rabbi. Now that he had incontrovertible proof that neither of these statements was true, he felt fully justified in ignoring her. Besides, an aging mother is never a match for a luscious new bride, a truth that mothers-in-law all over the world would do well to remember before they commence firing, even in self-defense.

He sat down in the living room and wondered, for the first time, if his marriage, upon which he had placed so many hopes, was falling apart. How had he failed this woman, whom he loved so much? he wondered. And what could he do to make her happy?

He cleaned up the kitchen, then went out and bought some take-out food and a bunch of yellow roses. He set the table, took the food out of the boxes, and warmed it up. Then he tiptoed into the bedroom and sat by her side at the edge of the bed, even though she was in the unclean part of the month. He felt reckless and a bit desperate. He smoothed back her lovely golden hair, breathing in the intoxicating scent of her warm, womanly body.

"Delilah," he whispered.

She opened her eyes, saw him sitting there, and felt a sense of alarm. "Get off, you know you're not allowed!"

He didn't budge. She stared at him.

"I love you," he whispered. "I'd do anything for you. I just want you to be happy."

"You don't care about me at all, Chaim." She shook her head, wondering what he could possibly be thinking if he was willing to sin. It was the first time she'd glimpsed an indication that he was capable of such a thing. The sight of it filled her with both a malicious satisfaction that she had gotten through to him, as well as a strange contempt. The lure of his religious piety during her short-lived repentance had been the bait that had hooked her, she realized. It was the one thing she'd really admired about him.

"Don't you see, I care more about you than I care about all the rabbinical prohibitions, all the fences around the Torah. I've broken them down, trampled on them, for you."

She failed to see what possible good this did her. "So your religion is a fake, the same way your love is?" she asked, annoyed, trying to move away from him.

He took a deep breath, keeping his temper in check. What good would it do to tell her off? She'd just be even angrier, if that was possible. "At least, come have something to eat. I've made dinner, cleaned up."

She sniffed the air. Chinese. All that grease, and you felt twice as hungry when you finished. But so what? She relented, feeling famished. If she got hungry, she'd eat again. What difference did it make if she got fat and ugly? Considering the eyesight of the people she was being forced to spend her time with, no one would notice anyway. She sat opposite him, eating silently and hungrily, filling her plate with noodles and rice and sweet-and-sour tofu made to look like pork. She ate and ate.

"Please, tell me how I can make things better."

She looked across at him. His face was the epitome of longing and misery and helpless yearning, the face of a dumb creature caught in a trap. She felt pity, but nothing else. He, after all, had willingly put his foot into the vice, while she had been lured there with decoys and false promises, she told herself.

The patent unfairness of this as a description of their courtship and marriage did not intrude upon her self-pity. Her equal responsibility for having chosen Chaim as a husband, and this apartment and neighborhood as a home, seemed to her less blameworthy than his having actually married her and dumped her in the Bronx with no hope in sight. Ever since the weekend at Josh and Rivkie's, she'd scanned the horizon like a shipwrecked sailor, hoping for some glimpse of a seaworthy vessel that might land in port and carry her off to the land of her dreams. But there was nothing, nothing. For this, too, she blamed him.

Life was not supposed to be like this. The man you married was supposed to make you happy. He was supposed to know your needs, without being told, and to do everything he could to fulfill them. Like Michael Douglas and Catherine Zeta-Jones. Like Tarzan and Jane. Like Superman and Lois Lane. Like Prince Charming and Cinderella. And it wasn't just a fairy tale. All you had to do was go to any synagogue in Scarsdale, and you'd see pews and pews full of Orthodox women who lived in mansions, wore designer clothes, and had vacations in Acapulco, live-in maids, and jewelry straight out of the ads in *Town and Country*. Why couldn't fate have arranged that for her? Found her a man who'd have whisked her off to Scarsdale, or Short Hills, or Beverly Hills? Why was she, who was so pretty, so blond, with such voluptuous curves, now stuck in three rooms, maidless, wearing rayon and polyester blends and tiny cubic-zirconium studs? All her treasures were wasted, thrown out, given away for pennies, to a man who took her to live in a Bronx apartment and fed her Chinese food out of boxes!

And then, she noticed the roses. A dozen of them. Such pretty flowers. Such a romantic gesture. She buried her nose in them, and the heavenly scent enveloped her like something out of a good dream. She looked at her husband, and then over his shoulder at the kitchen sink. All the dishes had been done, even the greasy pots with the burned-on fat that she had no intention of cleaning, ever. It was all sparkling. In a sudden impulse, she reached out to him. He clasped her hand to his heart, then brought it up to his lips, kissing her fingers one by one.

As their fingers intertwined, the wicked joy of transgressing a particularly annoying rabbinical precept made them feel young and bold and carefree and reckless. It wasn't such a terrible sin, to touch a woman when she was unclean, he told himself, looking at her sparkling eyes, trying to quiet his growing sense of unease. It wasn't like taking her to bed, God forbid! It was just a teeny, tiny step over the fence. He had absolutely no intention of wandering around in minefields.

"So, Chaim, does this mean . . . ?"

"What, my love?"

"That you'll look for another job?"

He looked into her eyes, losing himself in a calm blue sea of ravishing possibilities. What did she want to hear? What should he tell her? he thought, trying his best to navigate toward a safe shore. "If you are really so unhappy, I will, my love. But in order for me to find a job, I will have to keep this one a little while longer."

She took her hand back and placed it in her lap. "How long?" she demanded, her eyes narrowing.

He thought rapidly. "Another year?"

She got up and twirled around, heading for the bedroom.

He got up and went after her. "Well, nine months then. If I can write on my résumé that I've been assistant rabbi for over a year, we'll have a chance of actually getting some offers."

She stopped and turned around. "And then you'll write to Swallow Lake?" She smiled.

Such a beautiful smile, Chaim thought. Such lovely white teeth. Of course, she was a dental hygienist. She knew how to take care of them. Her mouth was a temple of order and cleanliness and plaqueless good smells. And her body. . . .

"Chaim?" she repeated impatiently, her lovely smile shutting down like an unplugged computer.

He thought about it. Nine months was a long time. Perhaps the boycott would be lifted by then. Or they'd become a Conservative or Reform synagogue, in which case they'd have plenty of candidates, no doubt better qualified, flooding them with résumés. Why fight about it now? "Well, if the job is still open, yes. I'll do that too."

"Do you promise?" That smile, that delicious smile, was back.

"I give you my word, *b'li neder*," he said, using the rabbinical formulation for swearing without actually promising anything that you couldn't take back.

Delilah, who understood the formula, also knew that there were many, many exquisite methods of torture that could be employed if he even thought about going back on his word. Moreover, since she could piously refuse to go to bed with him now, it wasn't as if this almost-promise was actually going to cost her anything. All around, it was a good deal. It was the tip of white sail in the distance she'd been looking for. It might take a while for the ship to arrive, but at least, she told herself, it was on its way.

ELEVEN

The very next day, she jumped out of bed, deciding that life was worth living after all. She cleaned up the house, using rubber gloves and putting on her Walkman. She played Donna Summers' "She Works Hard for the Money" (*Some people seem to have everything*!); the Weather Girls' version of "Big Girls Don't Cry"; and Sade's "Mr. Wrong." When she got to Bruce Springsteen's "Janey, Don't You Lose Heart" (*you say you don't have no new dreams to touch*), she sang along, feeling tears come to her eyes. That Bruce, he really, really understood her. More than her parents, this husband of hers, or any of her friends.

She was full of love, passion, hope, youth, longing. She loved life. She wanted to do right by God, her parents, her in-laws, even Chaim and his grandfather and this synagogue full of doddering old folks. But she also wanted to squeeze some fun out of the planet before she got old and fat, like her mother, who'd spent her life stuffing her dreams down her children's throats, making everyone around her miserable.

She thought of her mother coming to the door of those beautiful houses that belonged to her classmates, pathetic in her fake pearls and discount high heels, waiting patiently to be invited in and how she never was; her mother at the wedding in that custom-made dress with the sequins, her hair done just so, waiting for people to look at her and think. "Well, isn't she something? Aren't her children something?" And how all anyone had noticed was her bad complexion and her fat stomach. And now, her daughter, the rabbi's wife, was living in a roach-infested apartment building in the Bronx, from which she couldn't move, because according to the rules of God she had to be within walking distance from the synagogue, the only synagogue in the world where her husband was willing and able to get a job because he had family connections. A synagogue where there was not a single woman that couldn't be her grandmother.

She put the radio on with a pounding full bass and sang along with Britney Spears ("Oops, I Did It Again!"), deciding that she might as well get a job. At least it would get her out of the house for the next nine months, and she'd be able to earn some money toward the wardrobe she'd need when she moved to Swallow Lake.

Through Bernstein's placement service, she found a dentist in Riverdale in an absolutely beautiful home on Goodridge Avenue in Fieldston. You couldn't believe this was the Bronx. It was like using the word *woman* to describe both Uma Thurman and Marilyn Goldgrab. The clients were all professionals or academics associated with nearby Columbia or Barnard, or they were people who lived in Riverdale. She found herself happy to be getting dressed in the morning and going out. And very soon she had a regular clientele, mostly middle-aged men who came in monthly for a cleaning, even though it really wasn't necessary. They flirted with her and complimented her, but as soon as they found out she was a rabbi's wife, they disappeared.

But then, one Friday night, Chaim showed up with a young man. He was respectable, not one of those homeless people who sometimes wandered in off the street during the cold winter months, looking for shelter and a little Saturday-morning booze. He was Jewish, and not a Hare Krishna or a confused Methodist out-of-towner, which also sometimes happened. He had wandered into the old synagogue simply out of curiosity, the way people sometimes step into churches to view the stained glass. He was unfamiliar with the Orthodox service and uncomfortable among all the old men. He'd had your basic American Bar Mitzva education, which succeeds so beautifully in leaving the student with a lifelong ignorance and lack of curiosity about anything related to the Jewish religion. Ascertaining all this, Chaim, thrilled, invited him home on the spot for Friday-night dinner.

"This is Benjamin Eckstein," Chaim said nervously, recalling her reaction the last time he'd brought home an unexpected Sabbath guest. ("So what if Abraham sat outside his tent and dragged in every passing camel? Does that mean I'm running a soup kitchen?" she'd shouted at him. The guest, an elderly shut-in who'd twitched all evening, had luckily been hard of hearing.) "He's new in the neighborhood and is thinking of joining our synagogue," he added quickly.

But Delilah didn't need any convincing. She just smiled demurely and set another plate at the table.

All through dinner, she studied him.

He was about twenty-eight, twenty-nine, she guessed, taller than Chaim but not tall. He looked like a clean-cut rock star, his face covered with a fashionable dusting of light blond stubble. He had a strong jaw, a sensuous mouth. His blond hair had been cut short but combed straight up with gel by a very hip hairstylist. He wore a corduroy jacket with leather patches on the elbows and a long wool scarf that was very Parisian-Left-Bank-starving-student. He had pale furtive blue eyes and pale lashes.

He was recently divorced and his wife had gotten the Manhattan condo, he told them with a certain air of melancholy, implying an unfairness on which he was too decent to dwell, although the truth was it had been hers to begin with. He described a job at a small advertising agency in Manhattan that sounded like creative director, when he was actually a freelancer. There were no kids. He made it sound as if the choice of an apartment in the Bronx had been an existential, almost spiritual choice, rather than a financial necessity. "I think the area has something really interesting going on," he told them, pouring the last of the wine into his glass and finishing it. He told long rambling stories about advertising rates and the cola wars. Chaim listened appreciatively. He loved hearing people's stories, and he enjoyed not having to entertain anyone, since he was "on" all weekend.

Delilah found him intensely interesting, despite the fact that she couldn't have cared less about anything he had to say. She made a special effort to sparkle and twinkle in his direction, speaking at length about her favorite commercials and how an infomercial on the shopping channel had once convinced her to buy a brush that spun around automatically, but it had broken down after three months and they wouldn't give her the money back.

He, too, tuned her out.

Yet all the while, voices inside them kept up a continuous murmuring communication that had nothing at all to do with what inanities their lips were forming. Secret knowledge passed between them through furtive, hidden glances; through eyes that narrowed and flashed, and did everything but outright wink. Like a promo for a new movie, these voices hinted at all the highlights and delights that awaited them if only they bought tickets to the show.

He began showing up at the synagogue regularly, secretly searching the pews for Delilah. It took him awhile to realize that almost no women showed up for services Friday night. So he started attending Saturday-morning services as well.

He was lonely and bored. The only women he met were blowzy middle-aged secretaries and jailbait from some of the modeling agencies. He didn't like models, he decided, after numerous attempts, one of them serious enough to have landed him in divorce court. They were women who liked to talk but didn't know how to listen, and for whom you functioned mainly as a mirror. While it was thrilling to wear one as an accessory out in public, where people could envy you, they soon became more trouble than they were worth, like stunning new shoes that killed your feet.

Delilah, on the other hand, was real, he told himself. He caught tantalizing glimpses of her through the lace curtains that hung along the wooden latticework that separated the men from the women, her face suffused in radiant light. The old, blazing chandeliers, the silver chalice covering the sacred Torah scrolls, the elderly rabbi's long, white beard, the patina of heavy golden-hued wood—all of it together seemed to create an aura of saintliness that rubbed off on her the way a cat leaves its scent on its owners.

He focused on her prayer-murmuring, lipstick-less mouth, her charming retro hats, her modest but well-fitted suits. And that blond hair! And those big blue eyes! And the white skin! And the unbridgeable moat between them! It was deliciously tempting in all its contradictory allure. He felt elated by the possibilities and at the same time challenged, depressed, safe, and hopeless at the improbability of breaking down the walls that surrounded her.

Delilah, equally bored, was flattered and amused by him and eager to play the game. She made sure to pull back the little lace curtain, pretending to want a better view of her husband, or the elderly rabbi, all the while aware of Benjamin's head turning in her direction. At kiddush, she felt his shadow move across her plate as she filled it with kiddush junk food: cookies, various oversalted or oversweetened morsels from cellophane bags. She looked up and smiled into his eyes just a fraction of a second too long. It was he who lowered his gaze first, shuffling off to the other end of the room to speak to the rabbi.

"Why don't we invite Benjamin for lunch?" Chaim suggested.

"Who?" she answered innocently.

"Benjamin. You know. The art director. The divorced one. He's all alone."

"Oh, I don't know," she said reluctantly, a small thrill hiding at the pit of her stomach.

"Don't you like him?" Chaim asked her, surprised.

"It's not that, it's . . ." She shrugged, trying to look annoyed. "But if you want. If you think—"

"No, no, it's not important . . ."

"But if *you* want," she continued, with a new insistence in her voice that thoroughly confused him.

Chaim, by now, was used to being confused. In fact, he considered it whimsical and charming that he could never understand a single, solitary thing when it came to his wife's motives, moods, interests, or desires. "Are you sure you don't mind?"

"No. Why should I? If I've cooked already for four guests, what's one more?"

He opened his eyes wide, but didn't say anything.

Benjamin was delighted to accept the invitation. He wore a dark suit that fitted him well, she thought, and a blue striped shirt with a tie that was knotted a little too tightly. She saw the red streaks of a too-close shave on the delicate skin of his neck just above his collar and how his light skin reddened in the winter wind. It filled her with tenderness.

He brought them a bottle of rare kosher wine for which he'd traveled all the way to lower Manhattan in the hope of future invitations. He'd run home after services to fetch it, looking forward to the opportunity of handing it to her, acutely aware that it would be their first physical contact.

"Oh, look, Chaim, French kosher wine!" Delilah said, delighted, delaying the transfer of the bottle from Benjamin's hands to hers a little longer than absolutely necessary. Her touch went through him like an electric shock. He moved his hand so quickly that the bottle almost fell.

She pressed her lips together, hiding a smile as she dipped to rescue it.

"Ah, a true *Oneg Shabbat.*" Chaim nodded. "But it looks very expensive. You shouldn't have. I'll be afraid to invite you if it forces so much trouble on you!"

"No trouble at all," he lied.

Two of the shul's board members and their wives—kind, aristocractic, German Jews who spoke with a thick accent—had also been invited. Benjamin sat at the end of the table, casting sidelong glances at Delilah as she passed up and back, serving the food, conscious of how her shoulder arched beneath her dress as she brought in the trays and set them down. The first course was some kind of mushy-looking whitish thing covered with horseradish. "It's gefilte fish," she murmured, breathing softly in his ear as she put the plate in front of him. Her fingernails were well trimmed and painted a delicate shade of clear pink that made them look shiny and clean, like a newly washed child's, he thought. And her cheeks, pink and hot from the steaming kitchen, gave her a moist youthful glow. She smelled like vanilla.

There was a sudden knock at the door.

"Zaydie!"

Chaim's grandfather walked in with a gracious smile. He hardly ever visited and then only during weekday holidays, like Chanukah and the Intermediate Days of the Festivals, when taking a car was permissible and Chaim's parents could drive him over. That he had made the effort to walk several blocks and climb up two flights of stairs was remarkable and a bit disturbing. Chaim, touched and concerned, ushered him in with great reverence, giving up his own seat at the head of the table. "This is such a long walk for you. Why did you strain yourself, Zaydie?"

The old rabbi coughed and looked down at the table. "I spoke to your mother. She's . . . well . . . she thought it would be a good idea if I came to see you a little more often. I hope you don't mind. Please, go on with your meal."

"I was just about to serve the chulent, Zaydie," Delilah said, laying a plate for him, not looking into his eyes. She hurried into the kitchen, leaning heavily against the sink for a moment. What could Chaim's mother, that *klafta,* have told the old man? She could just imagine. She shrugged. Well, what of it? What could she do?

She served Chaim's grandfather first and then went over to Benjamin.

"Would you like meat or potatoes?" she asked him, and for some reason it sounded intimate, like a separate, secret conversation that involved only the two of them. Her eyes glanced at him sideways, a small smile on her pursed lips.

The old rabbi's eyes glanced up, studying them.

Benjamin caught the end of the heavy platters, helping her support them. They gave each other a quick but meaningful glance as their fingers touched. "Oh, whatever you give me will be fine," he said softly.

The old man suddenly pushed his chair back from the table. "I'll go now," he said, getting up abruptly.

"But why, Zaydie?" Chaim begged him, upset and confused. "You just got here! Please don't go!"

But the old man was already at the door.

People began to leave after that, a sense of impropriety and discomfort suddenly poisoning the atmosphere like someone rudely exhaling from a big cigar as all around people choked on the smoke. They quickly said the Grace After Meals, and were gone.

"Why don't I bring some tea and cake?" Delilah said brightly when only Benjamin was left. She, Benjamin, and Chaim sat together around the table, drinking tea, speaking casually, as Chaim, trying to be hospitable despite his sense of lingering discomfort, talked in a friendly way about his adventures with various shul committees about upcoming synagogue functions.

Always, the topic returned to the morning prayer service. They needed at least ten men—a minyan—to hold a prayer service. It was a disgrace, a disgrace!—that in a community of this size they had trouble finding ten men. Every morning! The absence of mourners required to say Kaddish for the departed souls of parents—the mainstay of Orthodox morning prayer services everywhere—left them at a distinct disadvantage, most of their congregants having lost their parents decades ago. Benjamin, who felt he should now offer to get up at five every morning to attend, shifted uncomfortably in his seat. There was no point in offering if he had absolutely no intention of keeping his word. And yet—

"I'd be happy to join," he found himself saying, aware of her eyes on him and the small nod and smile with which his words were acknowledged.

"That would be great!" Chaim rubbed his hands together appreciatively, already feeling better, fully rewarded for his efforts to integrate this stray. "Really wonderful."

"More tea? Or coffee?" Delilah murmured to Benjamin. Their eyes held.

Chaim, already busy pouring over the Torah reading of the week, smiled but didn't look up. "Thanks, my dear. Coffee."

As the liquid cooled in their cups, Delilah and Benjamin sat across from each other in the living room, she on the sofa, he in the armchair, reading magazines. "I think this is a beautiful ad," Delilah said as she thumbed through a women's magazine, trying to find in it something that would connect them. She wanted to sound sophisticated.

He took the magazine from her, pretending to study it. It was a silly ad, he thought, predictable and corny: a family in white shirts sitting on the grass. It could be selling anything from detergent to perfume to milk of magnesia. "I see what you mean." He nodded seriously. What lovely eyes she had! That color, like a jewel, with tiny gold flecks. "It takes special eyes to notice this kind of thing."

She found herself blushing.

"Well." Chaim yawned, oblivious, stretching.

Benjamin, who had only his lonely apartment with its unmade bed waiting for him, reluctantly began to realize that he too was expected to leave. At the door, she handed him a package.

"Here, another piece of cake. I know how single men are. They have empty refrigerators," she scolded him, her hands touching his. His fingers pulled back as if scorched. When he got home, he unwrapped the package, eating the cake greedily, crumb by delicious crumb.

He took to jogging past her house Sunday mornings.

Delilah, her hands encased in rubber gloves as she scrubbed the grime of the city from her neglected windows, felt herself start when she saw him run by. How slim he was, she thought. His shoulders and stomach were like a college student's in his running outfit, his hair still adolescent in its thick golden shine. She gazed at her reflection in the glass, studying her face: still young, still sexy. She pouted at herself until she heard Chaim open the door as he returned from the morning minyan.

"Could have sworn that was Benjamin . . . strange guy. He hopped over to the other side of the street when he saw me coming."

"Maybe he's embarrassed he didn't show up for minyan," she said, her eyes lowered.

"Yeah, that's probably it. But, then, what is he doing hanging around here?"

"He's jogging!"

"But he's got a park right across the street from his house."

She didn't answer him. Why should she? He didn't expect her to know anything. Besides, she wasn't sure she did. It could be a coincidence. He had plenty of women in that ad agency, all those *Sex and the City* wannabes breathing down his neck.

Be realistic, Delilah.

But it was so much fun to think about. Much more fun than thinking about her next scrape and polish. Or her next *chesed* project.

If you were the rabbi's wife, you always had to have a *chesed* project. Feed the hungry, visit the sick. The more time-consuming and distasteful, the more worthy the project. So far, she had resisted anything with hospitals. Chaim got stuck with all the sick calls; considering that the entire congregation practically took weekly vacations in Mount Sinai the way other people went to Florida, he spent endless time in sickrooms.

They had been after her to do the old-age homes, the openmouthed snorers sitting in their diapers in wheelchairs. The mumbling, insistent ones who grabbed you and made you their slaves. Get me this. Pick up that. Wheel me there.

She wasn't going back to the Moscowitz Hebrew Geriatric Center. Only one afternoon, and it had taken her three shampoos to get the smell out of her hair. She liked kids well enough. She offered to find some Jewish ones and do something with them.

"That doesn't actually sound like much of a plan," Chaim said mildly.

"So you think of a better one!"

"I don't know," he said, exasperated. "Maybe you could help some of the shul members with their shopping. Or take them to their medical appointments—so they won't wind up in the hospital."

"Old people," she griped.

"Well, it's their pensions that are putting food on our table and paying our credit card bills, my love. Show a little compassion. We'll be old one day too."

She looked up at him, suddenly stricken with conscience pangs. He really was a good person, she realized, ashamed of herself. He really did care about other human beings. And she, in taking on the job of being his partner, had to be a better person in spite of herself.

"All right. I'll take them shopping. I'll even do makeovers."

"Honey . . ." he cautioned.

"Just kidding."

She began by making a few phone calls, asking for advice from the president of the sisterhood, who liked her. She got a list of names and went about calling them, asking if they'd like her to join them the next time they went shopping. But that's not what they wanted. What they wanted was for her to pick up their shopping lists and do their shopping for them.

So, after work, she hurried to make dinner, then ran down to pick up their lists. Then she took the car and drove from store to store, buying farina and canned green beans and Metamucil, standing in lines and carrying heavy brown bags to the car. And, of course, she bought the *wrong green beans*, the ones with salt. They all had salt, except for one brand, sold in a little health food store where it was impossible to find parking. In the end, the old biddy even refused to pay for it. "I'll just have to throw it out. All that salt could increase my Lenny's blood pressure. Is that what you're trying to do, give him a heart attack?! What kind of help is this, anyway?"

Without telling anyone, she stopped picking up the shopping lists. Chaim was deluged with phone calls from outraged congregants who had immediately gotten used to the idea of having a personal shopper and were now furious at having their old lives back.

"You work for the shul, not me. I quit," she told him when he protested. "You go search all over town for low-sodium vegetables."

Being left with no choice, he came to a compromise, offering to drive them around to their stores. But this meant he needed the car and Delilah would have to take the subway to work. She was furious.

"Why is it I'm always the last person on the list, the last one you worry about being nice to?" she fumed. "Why does every stranger in this place, people who hardly say hello to you, who don't care about you at all, always have to come before me, your own wife?"

He shrugged helplessly. "I'll try to work something out. Please, Delilah, just be patient!"

But as she entered the subway station, there was Benjamin, waiting on the platform. They approached each other a little awkwardly at first. But then, meeting every morning, he got more talkative. He told her about his childhood, the inevitable grandmother who lit Sabbath candles, the grandfather who was "very religious," which Delilah knew could mean anything from eating chicken soup to wearing a *streimel and kapota*. You never knew what people meant by it. What Benjamin meant was that his grandfather wouldn't eat pork in the house, only in restaurants.

What had brought him to their synagogue? Delilah asked.

"I don't know. I was feeling kind of lonely, maybe. At loose ends, with the divorce and all. I was thinking about families and rituals, and I just happened to pass your synagogue. It was dark outside and the building was all lit up. I just walked in. Your husband was so friendly. He seemed really glad to see me."

"He is glad. The synagogue needs new blood."

"The old people seem to love him. To love both of you," he hurriedly corrected himself.

"Sure," she said wearily. "But let's not talk about the synagogue. Let's talk about you and your relationships. What kind of woman are you looking for?"

He swallowed hard.

"Don't be shy. This is what rabbis and their wives in Orthodox congregations often do for members of their congregations," she assured him. That was it! A *chesed* project! He was obviously unhappy. Perhaps she could help him? "Tell me about your ex-wife."

He spoke at length, in intimate whispers, making up things as he went along, editing out his penchant for short-lived affairs, creating a persona that was similar to his but deeper, more steadfast, more moral.

She listened with deep concentration, offering Dr. Phil–type clichés that made her feel both virtuous and wise and salved her conscience.

He looked at her, taking in the pious high collar, the demure covered knees, the silky blond hair beneath the charming beret. How does one seduce such a woman? He entertained the idea idly, not so much making plans as daydreaming. He pondered her, and his predicament. She was, after all, the rabbi's wife, like Caesar's, above reproach. But he could tell she was fed up with her husband and her life, even if she couldn't. A woman like that could be dangerous, he knew. And he certainly wasn't ready for anything sticky or complicated—not after having just extricated himself from a mess of lawyers and court appearances and fights over CDs and dishes.

But there is a certain unmatchable allure religious women have for a certain kind of secular man. In a world filled with licentiousness—women who wore practically nothing and wrapped their legs around the backs of chairs to sell everything from computer chips to chocolate chips in once-respectable magazines—a woman who covered her body had an infinite charm. Then, too, the constant threat of deadly sexually transmitted diseases made the virtues of sexual chastity as secretly appealing to the sex-glutted psyche of the modern man as short skirts and sexual availability were to his father and grandfather.

He knew that in her code of ethics adultery was as bad as murder, a commandment etched in Moses' tablets by God's own finger, brought down amid fire and brimstone. And yet, the thrill of trying! Imagine winning over such a woman! And truthfully, he admired her for all the qualities he imagined religious women have, bestowing them all upon her in his imagination, never once dealing with the fact that, if she yielded to him, she would no longer possess that which had attracted him to her in the first place.

But then, who among us can think clearly when our brains are awash in hormones?

After weeks of subway rides, the furtive stretching of hands along the back of her seat, the moving of thighs just an iota closer so that their coats touched, he decided he would declare himself. Then he decided not to. Then he gave himself ultimatums, deadlines, only to forget about them, or extend them or rethink them. He was terrified to move too quickly, afraid she would take flight.

Delilah began to dress more carefully for work, to try out different shades of lipstick, different hair clips. She'd adjust her hat at new angles, eyeing herself seriously in the mirror, turning her head first to the left and then to the right, smiling seductively at her image. Sometimes, as she lay in bed in the mornings before getting dressed, she thought of how she had asked him about his beard and how he had leaned toward her intimately and said, "I thought religious women liked men with beards."

"Maybe they do," she'd answered boldly, "but I don't."

The next day, he had shown up clean-shaven.

It had thrilled her. She began to daydream. What if Chaim should be rushing across the street, and a bus should come along! Oh, the horror of the ambulance, the blood, the hospital! But then it would eventually all be over. A coffin. A funeral. And she would mourn him. She could already see her eyes unattractively red, in great need of drops. But she'd also heard that widows lost weight because all they did was smoke and drink coffee. And then she would be allowed to stop mourning. And she would have a little condo in Manhattan, and a husband who wrote advertising copy for expensive magazines. A man who had weekends off, and had no congregants swarming around him that needed to be fed like pigeons in the park, who, the more you gave them, the more they left their droppings all over you . . .

And then, one morning, as she and Benjamin were sitting cozily on the subway, laughing, his arm draped across the back of her seat, she looked up and saw Mrs. Schreiberman, vice president of the sisterhood, who reached into her bag and took off her reading glasses, replacing them with her distance glasses. As Delilah saw it, she had two choices: one, to lean back on Benjamin's arm and ignore the woman completely; or, two, to wave casually, like this was normal. As forest rangers will tell those traipsing through national parks who might run into an eight-hundred-pound grizzly bear, the worst thing she could do was jump up and run.

She waved. But the little smile on her lips faded as she stared into Mrs. Schreiberman's shocked and outraged face. She had apparently decided not to play games. Delilah stiffened, giving Benjamin a quick nudge with her elbow. He looked up, realizing what was happening. If he had had the presence of mind to wave also, Delilah just might have pulled it off. But as it was, he looked as conscience-stricken as if he had been found in bed with the rabbi's wife, instead of just sitting next to her, fully clothed, in a public subway car.

Mrs. Schreiberman pressed her lips together and nodded to them both, a quick pained nod acknowledging that people like them existed in the world, and Delilah thought: uh-oh.

She considered going over to speak to her, but since she had no doubt been inundated with phone calls from disgruntled former *chesed* recipients who had gotten the wrong green beans and then been abandoned altogether, she thought better of it. What were the chances the woman would spill the beans and talk to Chaim? And even if she did, what could she possibly say? That his wife had taken the same train as a synagogue member? Sat next to him? Shared a laugh? Was it her fault the old bag got her jollies from imagining wicked scenarios?

When Chaim got home that night, the warm scent of baking and the wafting hot odor of soup greeted him at the door. To his shock, the house had been tidied, and the piles of women's magazines that usually covered the sofa and coffee table had disappeared into neat piles on well-dusted shelves. There was music coming from the stereo—some Hasidic boy's choir from one of the few CDs that actually came from his collection. Delilah, who was usually busy watching television when he got home, or soaking in the tub, was actually dressed. She looked very pretty, her smooth blond hair sliding over her shoulders like liquid honey, her lipstick freshly applied.

"Dinner will be ready in a minute, Chaim. Why don't you go wash? I have some rolls hot out of the oven."

"Everything is all right, isn't it? I mean, it's not a birthday or anniversary or celebration, is it?" he asked her anxiously.

She stood there, busy stirring something in a pot, not looking up at him. "No, nothing like that. Why would you even say something like that? What, I never make you dinner? I never clean up the house? It's got to be some special occasion?" Her voice trembled a little.

Now, he'd insulted her, he thought, slapping his palm against his forehead. She finally acts the way a wife is supposed to, and all he can do is be suspicious of her motives. Didn't Jewish ethics demand that one "weight the judgment of every man toward the good"? Was it not written, "Do not cause your wife to cry, as God counts each one of her tears"?

"A pleasant home, a pleasant wife, and pleasant furnishings enlarge a man's mind!" Chaim blurted out joyfully.

Delilah turned to look at him. She studied his rosy cheeks, like a schoolboy's, his wide, unfurrowed forehead, his innocent dark eyes, the sweetness of his untroubled smile of happiness. She smiled back. "Here, Chaim. Come sit down. You look hungry."

They sat across from each other at the table, in companionable silence.

"So, how did your day go?" he asked her, slurping the good vegetable soup with gusto. The sound of it sloshing around in his mouth made her a bit nauseous. She wrinkled her nose.

"Oh, nothing special. I met Benjamin on the train to work. He was telling me some funny stories about one of the models. . . . And right across the aisle, I saw Mrs. Schreiberman. So Benjamin and I wave to her, and she looks at us as if she's caught us making out. These old biddies live a rich fantasy life, let me tell you."

Chaim put his spoon down and wiped his mouth with his napkin, the implications of this conversation slowly breaking on him the way an egg oozes out of a broken shell, turning everything in its path into a sticky, gooey mess.

"Delilah, is there something you aren't telling me?"

She thought about that. What was she hiding? That she had been going to work with Benjamin every morning? That she had been leaning into his arm, which more and more found its way across the back of her seat? That she had been discussing with him the most personal aspects of his sex life? Does a woman have to share everything with her husband?

"Listen, Chaim, we go to work about the same time every morning. That's just the way it worked out since you started taking the car. And yes, we do talk about intimate topics because . . . because I'm trying to counsel him! He's lonely. He needs a *shidduch*. And so he speaks to me about his life. Isn't that what a rebbitzin is supposed to do? Listen and try to help?"

The picture clarified in his mind. His mouth formed an O. His mind formed an *Ah!* And his heart formed an *Oy*.

What now? If Mrs. Schreiberman spread this around the synagogue, and it got back to his grandfather . . . The congregants were very loyal to their old rabbi and very fond of his grandson. But Delilah had made it clear she found them boring, a burden, even a source of jokes. She flaunted her youth in their faces. And while they would have been willing to forgive her many lapses with the tolerance that comes with the wisdom of age, he wasn't sure she would ever be forgiven if the matter wound up public knowledge that would in any way taint or hurt his grandfather.

"Maybe I should speak to her," Chaim murmured, "before it gets out of hand. Explain to her about the—about your . . . counseling." He swallowed, and his voice dribbled off, melting into silence, taking with it his determination and conviction. What if he brought the subject up with her and she'd already forgotten all about it? He chewed his nails.

"Chaim, have your steak. It's fresh from the oven."

He looked up at Delilah, her pretty face, her eyes—blue as a mountain lake in summer—the tiny waist, and the voluptuous breasts. *A pretty woman means a happy husband. The count of his days is doubled*, the Talmud wrote. Then again, it also wrote, *A wicked wife is like leprosy to her husband.* The great rabbis in the Talmud were also clueless when it came to women, he thought. Why did he expect to be any smarter?

He picked up his knife and fork and cut into the tender juicy meat that melted like butter on his tongue. He took a large helping of creamy mashed potatoes and salad, dressed with a wonderful vinaigrette.

Whatever was going to happen tomorrow was going to happen. Tomorrow.

"Why don't we have a nice, relaxed evening, my love? I'll help you with the dishes, and then—" He glanced toward the bedroom. They were in their lucky two weeks out of the month. Like sailors who were gone from home six months out of the year, no matter what kind of a marriage they had, at least half the time they were happy.

TWELVE

When things that should bring one's walls tumbling down do not, the unexpected reprieve sometimes brings about the exact opposite one would anticipate: not relief and gratitude and rehab, but the idea that one can take even greater risks and get away with it.

Delilah, having weathered the discovery of her delicious little secret without suffering any of the dire consequences, instead of being penitent and taking her undeserved opportunity to redouble her caution, learned the opposite: having escaped she became more, not less, daring.

The morning train rides stopped, Chaim deciding to give her back the car and discontinue the shopping trips. The old people were remarkably understanding—or else they knew something. Or perhaps it was the common idea that while it was perfectly fine to burden the rabbi's wife with their errands, it was unseemly to bother the rabbi himself.

Delilah, far from viewing the car as the opportunity to safeguard her reputation, envisioned it opening the door to even more exciting possibilities. She decided to buy theater tickets. She would invite Benjamin to join her at a matinee on Broadway. It was a sudden impulse, one that came to her because she happened to hear "Cell Block Tango" from the musical *Chicago* playing on the radio at the dentist's office. Something in the wording ("He had it coming all along") struck a responsive chord. And suddenly she remembered a conversation she'd had with Chaim about the theater very soon after their wedding.

Modern Orthodox Jews, unlike their black-coated black-velvet-skullcap-and-oversized-fedora-wearing Ultra Orthodox brethren, do, for the most part, participate in the modern world. They have television sets, are sometimes *Seinfeld* and *Star Trek* fanatics, and will watch—if not admit to enjoying—*Sex and the City*. (Caveat: This is not to say that there are not many, many secret *Sex and the City* fans among Ultra Orthodox Jews, who simply hide their TVs in the closet.) However, the wearing of a religious symbol on one's head *does* build in a shame factor that makes the public viewing and enjoyment of barely dressed women and raucous scenes of a sexual nature difficult and embarrassing for modern Orthodox Jews, let alone rabbis. If you add to that the glorification of murder, adultery, and the liberal use of the kind of profanity that would have made pimps blush not long ago, most Hollywood movies and Broadway plays had become off limits to the skullcap-wearing community, velvet or crocheted.

"I just don't feel comfortable," Chaim explained. "You never know what you are going to see. Or hear! All those disgusting four-letter words. . . . Remember that movie *It's a Wonderful Life*? When beautiful little Bedford Falls turns into sleazy Pottersville? Well, the whole world has become Pottersville. The old black-and-white movies are all right. But movies and the theater these days? No rabbi can be seen in such places."

She understood him. But the idea that her entire life was now subject to a hidden committee who would be judging the appropriateness of all her actions, including anything she chose to see or hear on her own free time, was simply infuriating. And unlike her husband, she wasn't stuck with a big neon light on her head that flashed I'M A HOLY MORAL PERSON, AN ORTHODOX JEW. She viewed herself as free, even if Chaim wasn't. The fear of God, still firmly planted in some little corner of her heart, making her tremble during the closing prayers on Yom Kippur (*who will live, and who will die; who in his time and who before his time*) did not extend to weekday entertainment choices. The God she loved and believed in was a very busy, preoccupied, and long-suffering Deity, who couldn't possibly be checking the titles of the videos she borrowed. Her God was saving His time and energy to track all the really horrible acts being committed in the world: men who slept with their daughters; corporation heads who used up pension funds for million-dollar birthday parties; Muslims who slit the throats of their sisters; rabbis and priests who buggered small children. She figured, when He finished with all of them, He might have time to deal with her movie choices, which gave her plenty of time.

She took the train to Manhattan, took out money from the ATM, and bought orchestra seats to *Chicago* for a matinee the following Wednesday. Then she called up Benjamin and offered him a ticket. He said he had something at work that day, but he'd try to get out of it.

The truth was, he was confused. This was taking it a step further. Why he wasn't absolutely thrilled, he wasn't sure. Could it be because she had preempted him, thus wounding his male pride? Or had he started the process of rethinking the whole situation? He was feeling restless lately, with his go-nowhere job, his cramped Bronx walk-up, his sexless affair. The idea that he was now going to have to fit into her designs, fulfilling her impulses on demand, further eroded any sense of congratulation he might have felt in this proof of the progress he was making in pursuing the untouchable woman who was the rabbi's wife.

Nevertheless, he agreed. He wanted to see *Chicago*, and the tickets were very expensive.

Even though it was a matinee and she expected to be home in plenty of time, a sudden urge prompted her not only to hide her trip to the theater from Chaim but also to tell him her boss might ask her to work an extra shift at the clinic that day, so she might be home really late. She didn't explain this to herself, having found it was better not to tell herself everything.

Wednesday morning, she got up early and prepared Chaim a big breakfast: hot cereal with cinnamon and crushed walnuts, toasted whole wheat English muffins, a tomato-and-feta-cheese frittata. He sat there, pleased, slowly chewing, talking about some shul member who wanted to donate his house to the synagogue because he was a Holocaust survivor and had no one to leave it to. He had asked Chaim's advice.

"But I don't know. Maybe I should tell him to leave it to Israel or to shelters for abused women. I don't know what to tell him."

Something about his confusion, and the sincerity of his struggle with something that would have presented no moral dilemma for most people, touched her.

"Chaim, maybe you'd like to go to the theater with me today? A friend of mine has two tickets for a matinee—"

"But I thought you said you had to work late?"

"I could call in sick. We could go together. Come on, it'll be fun!"

He smiled and kissed her hand. "I don't go to the theater. You know that. What play is it, anyway?"

"*Chicago.*"

"Whew. That's definitely off limits. Those costumes. And murder and adultery. Religious Jews shouldn't be watching that," he said, shaking his head.

The primness of his dismissal made her jaw tighten.

"Maybe we could go to see *Golda's Balcony*. Or *Fiddler*."

She ignored that. "So, you don't want to?"

He stared at her, shaking his head. "Why would I?"

That was certainly true, she thought, relieved. So taking Benjamin wasn't actually taking anything away from Chaim.

She parked the car and met Benjamin in front of the theater. He wore a long camel-hair coat that looked handsome, if a bit worn. He had his fingers in the pockets and his thumbs beat a nervous tattoo against his thighs. She didn't approach him right away, standing on the side to watch him, wanting to examine him a little more closely, to decide what exactly it was that attracted her.

But the more she stared, the more confused she became. He was good-looking, true, in a very Gentile kind of way that had never before attracted her. But it wasn't his looks, not really. When they were together, a little voice inside always whispered with irritation, "So what?"

Truthfully, she liked him better when he wasn't around. She liked the idea of him, the daydreams she wove around him, with herself in the center and him fluttering like a moth, irresistibly drawn to her charms. His attraction to her was his strongest, sexiest quality.

He, on the other hand, felt the opposite. As much as he occupied her thoughts when they were apart, she disappeared from his. He actually managed to forget what she looked like from encounter to encounter. But when he saw her, he always felt a little thrill.

She looked so pretty, her complexion a lovely, rosy color from the cold and her body unfashionably shapely and soft, with real breasts and real hips. It was the way a women's body should be and had been, until designers and ad men decided to turn women into hipless, flat-chested, coltish adolescent boys, he thought.

For the first time, he offered her his arm. She decided not, hanging back. Then she decided—why not?—slipping her arm through his as they went off in search of their seats. What did it matter, after all, if their fully clothed bodies politely touched?

The show was wild. The costumes—if you could call those little bits of torn string a costume—draped provocatively over those perfect bodies; all that bumping and grinding. The music and dancing, the clever irony of plot, involving corrupt politicians, lawyers, and journalists, combined to make it a great show. Chaim might have enjoyed it too, whatever he said. But his public persona—the pious rabbi with the dignified public stature—would have insisted on coming along too, sitting between them, crushing both their joy with the weight of scandalized disapproval. If only her husband had been able to leave his public persona behind every now and then, she mused, inside the same Borsalino hat box that held his black Sabbath hat.

As an Orthodox woman, she understood the public need to defend modest dress and condemn loose women. She herself would not have wanted to actually wear any of those outfits she saw on stage. Still, she couldn't go along with Chaim's ban on Broadway, because that would be a slippery slope. First came Broadway shows, next was bathing beaches with bikini-clad women, then in-flight entertainment. And then where would she be? Stuck in a colorless Oz with no ruby slippers; inexorably hemmed in, trapped, by all those fences around the Torah that Chaim was always talking about.

Everyone had to decide on his own fence, Delilah thought. And some blessed creatures should always be allowed to roam the range with no barriers at all. Fences, after all, just gave certain people the urge to climb over or crawl under. In her personal experience, the only barriers that stopped someone from going where he shouldn't were the ones that did severe tire damage, putting you and your vehicle out of commission. FORBIDDEN. KEEP OUT! was like waving a red flag in front of a bull. If you thought you might get away with it, including tiptoeing successfully through a minefield, then fences simply became a welcome challenge, a way to show you knew better than the fence makers what was, and was not, good for you.

After the show, they exited into the snowy city streets, his blond head bare of any covering. It was the first time she'd ever gone somewhere accompanied by a bareheaded man. She found it strange yet liberating. When you walked in the city accompanied by a mate possessing unmistakable religious symbols on his person, people tended to draw in their chests tensely, as if your mere existence demanded that they make some kind of decision, choosing one thing over the other. Now, if people stared, it was simply because they were such a handsome couple, both young, both blond.

The out-of-towners especially, in their inappropriate-for-every-occasion clothing and obscure sports-team caps, looked at them with envy, she thought, instead of the veiled, vague hostility that came her way whenever she ventured out into Manhattan tourist spots with Chaim.

"Let me take you out for dinner," Benjamin offered. He liked her. She made him laugh, but she was never coarse. He like the innocent pleasures she fought with herself over enjoying, the way her clothes always left so much to the imagination. She thought she was daring and yet, she was at heart such an innocent. He began to remember why he had been drawn to her in the first place. There was something devastatingly attractive in a woman who struggles with her better instincts all the time and loses.

She turned to him, blushing. How much fun that would be! A proper dinner out. But it would have to be in a kosher restaurant, she realized. No matter in which fenceless fields she roamed, she was not about to trespass into anything clearly, black-and-white sinful, like eating unkosher food. But in a kosher restaurant, someone she knew was sure to spot them.

"Too public?" he surmised. She nodded. "So, why don't I go into Broadway Deli and buy lots of takeout, and we can put it in the car and take it to my place and eat in peace."

He wanted her to go up to his apartment. That was all she heard.

She hesitated.

"Listen, maybe I was out of line. But let me go in and buy you some food for dinner, just to thank you, and then you can just drop me off on your way home."

That seemed reasonable, she told herself, already disappointed, as if he'd rescinded the invitation.

They drove along the busy Manhattan intersections, not saying much, because they both knew they were entering a no-turning-back zone. When they got to the Bronx and neared his building, he turned to her, putting his hand on her arm.

"Please, Delilah. Come up with me."

Her thoughts jumped around in her head, doing back flips and somersaults, running forward, banging into brick walls, then going around and around until finally stopping with exhaustion. The idea of returning early to her staid married life in the drab apartment she hated, to the placid husband who bored her with his goodness, made her feel like an insect caught in amber. She felt sleepy and unwilling to resist any temptation that came her way.

"Just for a minute," she told him, parking the car a block away, in a neighborhood she was sure was out of the radius of walking distance to their synagogue. She looked around her furtively as she walked with him toward his apartment. Only when they got inside did she concentrate on what she was seeing. His building was even worse than hers, with graffiti all over the walls and run-down hallways perfumed by cheap cooking oil. Only a brass door plate announcing DR. AVRAM MENDES, SECOND FLOOR gave the building its solitary touch of respectability.

"You have a doctor in this building?"

"A chiropractor who is at least one hundred and fifty years old, they say. I've never actually seen him come out of his apartment. He might have died ten years ago, for all anyone knows, and be lying there, rotting."

She looked up at him, surprised. What did she know about him, really? He could be one of those serial ax murderers, the ones that have a signature. Maybe he was the kind that wandered into synagogues and wound up strangling rabbis' wives. Maybe there was a whole file on him that would become another episode on *Law and Order.*

"Delilah?"

He was smiling at her, his feet on the stairs. She smelled the pastrami and sour pickles in the brown bags from the deli. She loved pastrami. She followed him up. His apartment was larger than hers—or maybe it just looked that way because it was so sparsely furnished. There was an old white couch with some colorful Indian pillows. An exotic animal-print throw rug on the floor. Framed prints of what looked like advertising posters on the wall. "Are those your ads?" she asked, hoping to be impressed.

"Some of them," he said, waving vaguely in their general direction.

"Wow, they're beautiful!" She was overwhelmed by talent of any sort, people who actually created something from nothing. She wandered into the kitchen. He was already taking the food out of the containers, putting them into plates and bowls.

"Um, is this your meat set or your milk set of dishes?"

"Huh?"

"You have two sets of dishes, don't you? Meat and milk?"

He shrugged. "Sorry. Just the one."

She stared at the food. If it was cold, she'd be able to eat it. But not if it was hot and had been put into a dish that had once held ice cream. The biblical prohibition of not cooking a calf in its mother's milk had, through the centuries, turned into one of the most exacting and wide-ranging set of laws separating meat from milk, to the extent that religious Jews waited up to six hours to allow milk to enter their mouths again after they'd eaten the flesh of cows, chickens, turkeys, ducks, bison, and any other living creature except fish, just in case some meat might still be caught between their teeth.

"Listen, why don't you let me do that?"

She searched through his barely filled cupboards for paper or plastic plates, or maybe just some glass bowls, which the rabbis had decided were nonporous and thus could be used for both meat and milk dishes, if thoroughly washed in between. Luckily, the deli had packed plastic flatware. She carefully transferred the cole slaw and potato salad.

He sat down, watching her, amused. Here she was, back in rabbi's-wife mode, making sure she had a perfectly kosher meal in the most unkosher of settings.

"Finding everything you need, dear?"

She looked up at him. *Dear?* Such a husbandly term, she thought. It made her feel strange. She unwrapped the sandwiches and placed them on paper plates. He sat down across from her at the all-purpose table he used for dining in his living room, reaching out for some food. A sudden, heavy silence fell on them both. Delilah looked around her. She was alone with another man, a man who adored her. A man who was probably expecting something more than a sour pickle.

And would she give it to him? Would she pole-vault over the fence and land straight into the quagmire of unforgivable commandment breaking, where she would be transformed for all time from a creature that tiptoed close to the edge of volcanoes to one who had actually fallen right inside, all her convictions, what she told herself about herself, going up in smoke, singed and blackened and unrecognizable?

And would it be worth it?

She thought back to the dates she had had with Yitzie Polinsky, the thrill that had filled her body at his touch, the sense of release and satisfaction she had felt in his arms. How he had made her laugh. . . .

Yitzie.

The bum.

Was Benjamin another Yitzie? Would she again be reduced to begging God for a miracle to save her from ruin? And, more importantly, was the risk worth taking? Were the rewards worth desiring? She looked at him: his fair skin, his long fingers. Then she looked around the house. He lived like a tramp, she realized. And the posters that he had hung on the walls were, she realized, famous ads for vodka or cosmetics she had seen hundreds of times in many magazines, absolutely nothing original.

"Let me get you something to drink, Delilah. Rum Coke? Bloody Mary?"

"Sure," she said, suddenly needing less clarity.

All she wanted was a little excitement in life. Something to break the routine. To take her out of herself and give her a glimpse of the possible, a future where the sun rose and set by a new horizon. But the more she looked around—the broken floorboards, the scratches on the Plexiglas coffee table, the missing knob on the kitchen cabinet door—the more she felt she had taken a step backward, not forward.

She drained the glass he put in front of her and felt the soothing flow of alcohol loosen the tight knot of dismay pulling ever tighter in her chest. Her body felt warmer, calmer. Her mind was less judgmental, more open to suggestion.

"Why don't I put on some music?" Benjamin suggested.

He was now on familiar turf, his role in this scenario a comfortable fit for his talents. He wrote advertising copy, created ad campaigns to convince people to do and think all kinds of things for all the wrong reasons. He seduced them to smoke by convincing them it would make them appear smart and muscularly independent and daring to the opposite sex; to eat high-cholesterol sweets because it would make them part of a crowd of youthful, healthy, beautiful people; to purchase cars that would put them in endless debt because it would show how successful and rich they were. And now he was busy creating an ad campaign that would convince the rabbi's pretty wife that sleeping with him would make her life easier and more enjoyable.

He shut off the overhead lighting and lit a few lamps, an amazingly simple gesture that instantly created an atmosphere of intimacy and romance. He put a music disk into the stereo.

"Frank Sinatra!" Delilah exclaimed, finishing her second drink and reaching for a pickle. She started to hum along, then sing outright, finally getting up. "I did it my waaaaaaay!" she sang, sudden tears filling her eyes.

Uh-oh, Benjamin thought.

She put her arms around him and sobbed. "I'm such a bad person. Such a bad, bad, awful person!" He felt the shoulder of his new Ralph Lauren shirt dampen and wondered if she was wearing waterproof mascara. He put his arms around her and kissed her on the temple, smoothing back her soft shiny hair. It smelled like almonds and honey, he thought, wondering what kind of shampoo she used and who wrote the ads. They stood in the middle of the living room, clinging to each other as the music played. He patted her softly, then let his hands run smoothly up and down her back. She arched toward him like a cat.

She was tired, tired of everything, of the hypocrisy of it all, of straining toward a happiness that never seemed to get any closer, of craving money and a nice house and a passionate love life. She was tired of playing the dutiful little rabbi's wife in her modest hats and wigs and long-sleeved over-the-knee clothing; tired of cleaning out people's neglected, debris-filled mouths, flirting with elderly men, and kowtowing to their judgmental wives.

She wanted to smash something. To hit Chaim over the head for his consistency, his placid acceptance, his calm ability to wake up every morning and get through the day. Why not, then, just smash her life?

She felt the arms of the man around her. He was a cipher. Not important at all. She didn't care about him, not really. She didn't even know who he was, with his *treife* kitchen and no mezuzah on the door. He might as well be a goy, a Gentile prince. He didn't even have money. And, she finally realized, he probably didn't have a very good job either, if he was living in some run-down Bronx walk-up decorated with cliché posters produced by other, really successful ad men.

But what did any of this matter? She needed someone to fall in love with, someone who would destroy the channels through which her life flowed, allowing her to irrevocably change direction. He was at the moment the only one available. It would be good, she thought, her hands reaching up to caress the back of his head.

It would be good enough.

She felt his hands harden their grip around her, leading her into the bedroom.

She followed, almost in a daze, allowing herself to be led. He bent over her, kissing her full on the lips. She tasted the pastrami. She pushed him back.

"What?"

"I—I've got to *bentsch*," she told him.

"You've got to . . . *what*?"

"*Bentsch*. To say Grace After Meals."

He sat down on the bed, flabbergasted. "By all means." He waved her off.

She sat down by the table, trembling, wiping his kiss off her mouth. She took a little Grace After Meals book out of her purse, the souvenir of some cousin's wedding.

"Blessed art thou, O God, King of the Universe, who feeds and sustains the whole world with grace, compassion, and pity."

She felt the flush of shame crawl up her throat, turning her face hot.

"Fear God, you who are sanctified to Him, for there is no want for them that fear Him. Young lions have always become poor and suffered hunger, but they who seek God shall never want for any good thing. Avow it to God that He is good, and His love endures forever. You open Your hand and satisfy the desire of every living thing. . . ."

She finished, wiping her full eyes. And there was Benjamin, leaning on the doorpost to the bedroom, completely naked. She stood up, grabbed her purse, and ran out the front door and down the staircase.

Just as she neared the last landing, the door to the doctor's office opened and someone stepped out into the dark hallway. She veered to the side, nearly knocking him over.

"Delilah?"

She stopped and turned around. Horror washed over her. *Oh, no!* she thought. *No, no, no!*

There stood Chaim's grandfather, coming out of his weekly visit to the chiropractor. She stared at the old rabbi, her cheeks burning. Then she looked over the old man's shoulder. There, just above, running down the steps after her, was Benjamin, wearing a half-opened bathrobe. She motioned to him in hysteria.

"Delilah! Wait, don't go! I'll put my clothes back on!"

She watched helplessly as the old rabbi slowly pivoted, looking up the stairs behind him.

She turned and ran, down the steps and out into the street, not looking back. She sprinted to her car, her heart pounding as she rummaged frantically through her purse, searching for the car keys. Her hands trembled. She felt faint and breathless as a slow panic rose in her chest. In what seemed like an hour, she finally managed to open the car door, start the engine, and drive off.

When she got home, Chaim was already there.

"So, quite a day, no? You must be exhausted."

She stared at him.

"Your double shift at the clinic? All those patients?" he repeated, puzzled.

She didn't hear him. It was as if he were one of her patients, his mouth stuffed with dental cotton and instruments, trying to make himself understood.

He came to the bedroom. His forehead was wrinkled. He was moving his lips.

"I'm not feeling very well, Chaim. I think I'm—" She barely made it to the bathroom before throwing up her entire dinner.

He was immediately concerned. "Do you want me to call a doctor? Do you have fever?"

She wished he would just shut up; his solicitations and good-natured concern were making her feel even sicker. She put on the shower, blocking him out, waiting for the inevitable and terrible ringing of the phone, which would usher in the apocalypse.

I have to think, think, she told herself. It's not so bad. What does he know, the old man? Then she remembered that look he had given her and Benjamin at lunch and his abrupt leave-taking. In slow motion, her brain did a retake of the slow turn of his head toward the stairs.

She was lost. This was the end. He was old but nobody's fool. And if he had heard the rumors from Mrs. Schreiberman, he would feel it his religious obligation to tell his grandson of his suspicions, because a man was not allowed to live with a woman suspected of committing adultery. The fact that nothing had happened wouldn't matter.

Once Chaim threw her out, who would take her? Damaged goods. A divorced woman. A rabbi's wife thrown out of the community. They wouldn't even allow her to pray in an Orthodox synagogue. They'd whisper behind her back for the rest of her life. And all those girls from high school who had considered her a bleached blonde from a poor family, a girl who would never be their social equal, would gleefully tell one another, 'Did you hear what happened to Delilah? Didn't we all know it?"

She heard the phone ring. She heard Chaim gasp. And then she heard him pound on the bathroom door.

"Delilah!"

She took a deep breath and wrapped herself in a towel as attractively as possible, giving herself a quick once-over in the mirror before opening the door.

His eyes were wild. Her heart sank.

"It's my grandfather. They've taken him to the hospital! He's had a stroke!"

Delilah stood absolutely still, her brain computing all the possibilities. Finally, she moved toward her heartbroken husband, laying a hand on his shoulder and looking deeply into his anguished eyes.

"Major or minor?" she asked him.

THIRTEEN

Reb Abraham hung on for several days. The family held vigil next to his bedside. Attached to an intubation tube that went down his throat, he looked at them silently with open eyes that seemed to yearn for a method of communication. Everyone tried to talk to him, but he gave no response until Delilah, very reluctantly, entered the room. The transformation was remarkable. Color rushed into his white cheeks.

"Look, he's so happy to see you!" Chaim exulted. "He looks better already!"

Mrs. Levi pursed her lips sourly, amazed and chagrined.

Then the old man tried to sit up, his hand shaking uncontrollably. He snatched at the intubation tube, trying to pull it out of his mouth. Delilah froze. The family, alarmed, rang for the nurse, who injected some kind of sedative into his intravenous tube, and he sank back into oblivion. And then, on the morning of the fourth day, Chaim's phone rang. It was his father, telling him it was all over.

Chaim was distraught. He blamed himself. If only he had taken the time to accompany the old man on his weekly appointments, to help him climb the stairs. If only he had checked more thoroughly the treatments the old chiropractor was foisting off on him as therapy. Obviously, that quack had to be responsible; after all, his grandfather had collapsed right outside his door.

His grandfather's sudden, precipitous demise was horrifying. Despite his extensive grief-counseling experiences, there was a fundamental and inescapable horror tinged with guilt in seeing someone he loved lose his grip on life. Age didn't matter. Seeing the upright body—always so dignified and tall—suddenly reduced to pale flabby flesh, bloated from excess fluids, expanding and contracting with the mechanical whir and sob of the intubation machine, was traumatic. The hospital visits, in which the doctors assured the family that all manner of medical tortures were absolutely necessary and unavoidable and might possibly result in a cure, were brutal. He felt intuitively that his grandfather was in pain and that all the medical establishment was really doing was making it impossible for him to leave this world with some peace and dignity. So that when, finally, the struggle ended, it came almost as a blessing.

But loss is loss, a tearing apart that is wretchedly wounding. Chaim mourned the loss of the old rabbi with all his heart. He leaned on Delilah, who behaved with such exemplary consideration that even her mother-in-law, who had spent the entire week sending guilt-inducing waves of hostility in her direction, finally relented. And when, soon after, Delilah made the announcement that she was expecting, even Chaim's mother smiled and hugged her, putting aside her suspicions and holding her tongue, realizing she had been upstaged. Besides, there had been enough grief in the family. A baby was exactly what everybody needed.

Chaim behaved as if his wife had been touched by a miracle. New life, just when he was in the depths of despair over death. Delilah's pregnancy blessed him, filling his mind and soul with new hope. He prayed it would be a boy, someone who could be named after his grandfather, a man he had loved and admired his entire life, as it was considered a special merit to the deceased if he had a namesake within the first anniversary of his death.

And then, before he had caught his breath, the congregation began to fall apart. In rapid succession, the membership began to scatter, moving to nursing homes and retirement communities. He just couldn't understand how it had all happened so quickly.

The first inkling that something was amiss had come during shiva. He had tried to talk to the congregants who came to pay their respects, but they were silent, stiff and uncomfortable, anxious to leave. All except for Mrs. Schreiberman. She showed up every day, full of venom, spouting incoherently cryptic sentences like "You can fool an earthly judge but not the heavenly court!" and "Poor man! Poor man! He died of a broken heart!"—looking straight at Delilah. And then one day she tried to attack the rabbi's young wife, charging at her with a rolled-up newspaper. "You little bitch. You know what you did. You killed him, you floozy!"

Delilah had had to run to her bedroom, barricading herself inside, while Chaim called the medics. The old woman had been ushered out, taken home, and heavily sedated until her daughter showed up, and, not knowing what else to do, placed her in the mentally challenged wing of an excellent nursing home. Chaim had chalked it up to grief, but rumors and interpretations of the incident ran through the congregation like wildfire. Within six months, the congregation was down to thirteen members, and the board voted to sell the synagogue building, the proceeds of which were donated to Israeli terror victims.

Chaim was shell-shocked. Confused, bereft, and financially vulnerable, just at a time when a baby was on the way, he clung to Delilah. Finally succumbing to her tearful entreaties to apply for the job in Swallow Lake, he very reluctantly, and despite his better judgment, decided to try his luck.

To his surprise, they put him on a waiting list. Despite the ban, the search committee had, apparently, still found plenty of candidates. But when they finally invited him and Delilah down for the weekend, things went amazingly fast.

{ FOURTEEN }

Swallow Lake in May: the mirrored, calm surface. The large oaks leafing out. The dogwoods and crab apples in full bloom. The yellow flowering buttercups. The forests of oak and hickory. The smell of lilacs so thick and heady every breath makes you feel as if you are swallowing large glasses of perfumed alcohol. Intoxicating.

"Delilah, isn't this unbelievably beautiful?" Chaim gasped, thinking that, whatever happened, it was a joy simply to visit such a place.

It was like a picture postcard from the most WASP-y dream imaginable, Delilah thought. In fact, it made Woodmere and Cedarhurst look like middle-class Jewish suburbs.

The scenery was great, she agreed. But it was the houses that really interested her. Those homes, those fabulous homes, Delilah thought in wonder. The Colonials, the farmhouses, the Arts and Crafts cottages, the Tudors, the brick Georgians. They were straight out of some E Hollywood *Houses of the Stars* program. Houses so large, on plots of land so enormous, it didn't seem quite possible for anything smaller than a municipality to actually own and inhabit them. And the maintenance. Talk about attention to detail: the perfectly painted shutters, the newly painted clapboard siding. The bluestone walkways, the gleaming monolithic glass windows overlooking infinity pools, lakes, sunsets. And the landscaping: shrubbery, flowers, and trees in perfect harmony and design.

"Wow, wow, wow!" Delilah repeated, overcome. This, she thought, is heaven.

She felt a tinge of sudden irrational anger. Why, she asked herself, couldn't she have been born into one of these houses? Better yet, why couldn't she have married a man who inherited one, or had a sibling who was a dot-com genius who'd bought one for her, or won the lottery herself and built one? Why had she been condemned to live out her days in little 600-square-foot boxes? But then the anger passed and she was filled with joy.

"I can't wait to see the inside of one of them." She squeezed Chaim's hand. He looked at her. Her face was shining like a child's presented with a large gift-wrapped box. He tried to remember the last time he'd seen her looking like that. It was that moment, just before they'd walked down the aisle, when he couldn't bear to pull the veil over her face. And now she was carrying his child, he thought. This woman he loved so much and had been trying, with no success, to make happy.

Until this moment, he hadn't been nervous about this job interview, because he really didn't want this job, so fraught with complications and controversy. But now, looking at Delilah's happy face, he exhaled, returning her squeeze, touched by a new determination to do everything in his power to get her what she wanted.

"We're here."

They pulled up to the entrance of a lakefront estate. The gates were ornate grillwork edged in gold leaf. And they were firmly shut. Not a living soul was visible anywhere.

"Now what?" Delilah asked Chaim, who shrugged, as mystified as she at the ways of the extremely rich. "Maybe there is a button to push somewhere? Go out and look, Chaim."

There was, indeed. Chaim found it and pushed. A disembodied and suspicious voice asked them who they were and what they wanted. Soon the gates magically slid to one side, allowing them to drive through.

The house was fronted by a circular driveway, at whose center was an island of exotic plants.

"Please don't say *wow* every five minutes," Chaim begged her.

Delilah, who was about to say *wow*, closed her mouth.

The front door was answered by the lady of the house, a tall, blond-haired stick of a woman who could not possibly have been any thinner without an IV attached to her arm and round-the-clock medical supervision. Her face was a battleground in which formal hospitality, suspicion, and sincere dismay struggled for prominence.

"I'm Solange Malin," she said, with faint traces of a British accent, a mask of politeness finally winning out, which was fine with Deliliah, who preferred phony good cheer over frank nastiness any day. Their hostess extended her hand in welcome. Chaim stared at it uncomfortably, wondering if he should overcome his pious scruples about touching a woman or risk offending the wife of the president of the synagogue's board from the word *go*. Delilah saw him hesitate. She hurriedly reached over him, pumping the bony fingers while secretly kicking him in the ankle. He shook the woman's hand.

"An honor to meet you, Mrs. Malin. I've heard so much about you and your husband. Your charitableness and good deeds are well known to everyone in the Jewish world."

Delilah's heart swelled like a mother watching her child get the lines right in a school play.

Solange's eyes crinkled in pleasure at the compliment. She smiled. "Not at all! Everyone on the board is dying to meet you. And please accept our condolences on the loss of your grandfather. I understand he was a very important rabbi, leader of a well-known New York synagogue? We read all about him in the *New York Times* obituary. They called him 'One of the last great European scholars,' and they called the synagogue a landmark. And you, I understand, are his successor?"

Chaim, to whom this was news, nodded, surprised. "He was a wonderful man. And yes, I'm his only grandson."

"Such a privilege! Please, let me get someone to help you with your luggage. Anna-Maria?" she called over her shoulder.

"No, please. It's not necessary. All we have are these overnight bags," Chaim protested.

"Oh, well. That's fine then. Please, let me show you to your room."

The entrance hall was truly breathtaking, with a winding staircase leading to a square upstairs gallery on which large, magnificent canvases of bold modern art caught your eye from every corner. Off the entrance hall was a huge dining room, which seemed to be undergoing a massive upheaval.

"Excuse the mess. I'm redecorating. Please—" she gestured up the stairs, as if anxious to have them settled and out of the way.

When she showed them to their room, Delilah tried very, very hard, not to say *wow*! It was twice the size of their Bronx apartment, with a huge double bed, French doors leading to an open balcony, a huge dressing room, and an enormous private bathroom with a Jacuzzi, sauna, and heaven knows what else. Only one thing seemed odd: There were about ten heavy dining-room chairs scattered around the place. But the room was so large, Delilah hardly noticed them.

"Oh, my!" Solange Malin gasped. "No, this is not right! I'm so dreadfully sorry!" She pressed an intercom and said, very firmly, "Anna-Maria, would you come up here, please?" They all stood around uncomfortably, shifting from leg to leg, waiting to see the reason for this sudden fall in the friendliness barometer.

"What, in heaven's name, are the chairs doing here?" she asked the squat, brown woman who walked in, her brows already lowered in bull-like defiance.

"You tol' me, get dining room ready. I take out chairs," the maid said sullenly.

"But I didn't tell you to put them in here!"

"We put in here, always," she said stubbornly.

"Well, take them out immediately. Don't you see we have guests?"

The maid didn't budge.

"Anna-Maria?" Solange Malin demanded, an octave higher.

"They heavy."

It was a standoff. After a moment of silence, the mistress of the house got on the intercom again. "José, can you come up here, please, and help Anna-Maria."

Soon the chairs were marching out of the room under the straining torsos of two huffing servants, who were exchanging choice phrases in Spanish under their breath, glancing at Chaim and Delilah and their employer with barely contained malevolence.

"Well, I hope you'll both be comfortable here now." She smiled.

"Oh, this is more than comfortable. We can't thank you enough,"

Chaim said sincerely, feeling a sense of vague discomfort as he looked at the straining backs of the two employees.

"I don't know about you, but I'm ready to dive into that Jacuzzi. Wheee!" Delilah said with glee as soon as Solange Malin took her leave. She began unbuttoning her blouse.

"Delilah!"

"What? We've got plenty of time. Why don't you take off your clothes and join me. It looked awfully roomy." She giggled, only to turn around and find the two servants gaping at her.

"Mis. Us. Shee. U. kam. U. moo," Anna-Maria said urgently.

She clutched her blouse together, raising her eyebrows at Chaim, who stared back helplessly. They went through this about four times until Delilah finally realized the woman was here to usher them out of paradise into yet another bedroom. Delilah could see the hatred just behind the woman's eyes as she helped them gather their things together. She wondered why Solange Malin put up with this kind of live-in enmity. If she ever got enough money to hire servants, she thought, she'd fire them faster than they could say *Adios!*

The new bedroom was more magnificent still. And it had twin beds.

"I thought you'd be more comfortable in here," Solange said, suddenly reappearing. The two Mexicans stared impassively at the floor, no doubt wondering—as were Chaim and Delilah—why she hadn't just moved them here in the first place, since they were mobile and the chairs were not.

The new room was black and white and red. On the walls were framed photographs, everything rather blurry in shades of red.

"Chaim used to take pictures like that until he went digital. They come out perfect now," Delilah said.

"They're Desmond McClintocks," Solange said stiffly.

Delilah looked at her blankly.

"The abstract photographer? The one who just had a retrospective at MoMA? Do you like them, Rabbi?" she said, pointedly ignoring Delilah.

"Oh, they're wonderful," Chaim said hesitantly. "So . . . so . . ."

Red, Delilah thought, her face burning with embarrassment.

". . . evocative," he finally said.

"Oh, what a charming photo," Delilah said, trying to recoup, suddenly picking up a small framed photograph on the nightstand. It was of two little girls in plain dresses that seemed way too big for them, covering them up from neck to ankle. Their hair fell over their shoulders in long tight braids. "They look just like those little Hasidic girls in Jerusalem! Don't they, Chaim? Is this also by the same famous photographer?"

Solange grabbed it out of her hands in a tight-lipped silence that left Delilah breathless, wondering what rule of the very rich she'd broken now.

"I didn't remember I'd put it in here," Solange murmured. "As a matter of fact, my son-in-law took it. They're my granddaughters. And they live in Jerusalem."

There was a big period at the end of that sentence. Chaim and Delilah heard it clearly and asked no more.

"This is our best guest bedroom." Solange nodded, making them wonder what had transpired to get them an upgrade so soon. "I thought twin beds would be more comfortable," she added, as if reading their thoughts.

"It's very kind of you to take so much trouble," Chaim said.

"Not at all! We are very excited about having you both here. Our community has suffered a great deal with this whole, scandalous Metzenbaum business. We are hoping for some new leadership. Not fanatics out to brainwash people and alienate them from their children"—she picked up the photograph and stared at it in silence—"or busybodies out to condemn our customs and practices. We need team players who are warm and responsive, who will join actively in our community and our way of life." She turned her head, looking at Delilah carefully. "Some rabbi's wives these days refuse even to join the sisterhood. They think it's beneath them because they have high-powered jobs, law or medical practices, or they're VPs of some computer company. Career women," she said with a sniff, as if the air had suddenly been fouled. "That's not who we're looking for here."

Chaim shifted uncomfortably.

"Oh, I know what you mean. It's terrible." Delilah jumped in eagerly. "I know quite a few rabbi's wives who are always thinking about themselves. But I have always believed that being the wife of a rabbi is the highest calling any Jewish woman could possibly have. It's an opportunity and a privilege to serve a community."

"Well." Solange's nose unwrinkled, the air suddenly fragrant again. "I'm so glad you think so. Perhaps if you have some time before dinner, you'll allow me to show you around?"

"That would be wonderful," Delilah assured her, thrilled. She couldn't wait.

"I'd better go now. If you need anything, I'll just be downstairs. Otherwise, I'll see you in time for candlelighting." She nodded, forcing a smile on her lips and taking the photo with her.

Two wonderful Tibetan wooden lion carvings stood on either side of a low carved ebony wood table. Chaim tried hard to tiptoe around them, terrified he might bump into one and knock it over. It was like being given a bed in the Metropolitan Museum, he thought uncomfortably.

The furniture was beautiful, even if the decorations were a bit weird. But this bedroom had no Jacuzzi, Delilah noted with disappointment. What it did have, she discovered to her joy, was a magnificent porch with two rocking chairs overlooking the lake and a bookcase full of magazines. Big, fluffy robes were hanging in the bathroom, along with the softest, thickest towels she'd ever seen. Delilah took a long soak, using the French bubble bath and the Italian shampoo, then curled up in a white wicker rocker. She could see the turquoise blue of the swimming pool sparkling down below and hear the gentle whack of tennis balls bouncing off the red clay courts visible over the hill.

She was supremely happy, all her angst suddenly melting, all her worries, anxieties, bravado, defenses, and heartbreak over things she'd never be able to solve magically evaporating.

She couldn't understand Solange Malin, who was obviously nursing some heartbreak, despite her palace. All the conventional wisdom about how money isn't everything, how a house is just a shell was just baloney, Delilah thought. There was no human need that owning this house and land couldn't fill, as far as she was concerned. Anyone who couldn't be deliriously happy here might as well join Osama bin Laden's merry men in their caves.

"Chaim"—she caressed his face, looking deeply into his eyes—"I've finally found all the answers."

"What were the questions?" He laughed, caressing her back.

They sat next to each other quietly, each thinking their own thoughts. This was the way their relationship should be, Delilah thought, like two potted plants, next to each other but not in each other's space, each of them growing and blooming at their own pace, enjoying each other's foliage without insisting on sending out spores that would colonize and take over. They were both so different, but in a good way, she told herself.

Both of them had been taught that a person's goal in life should be to serve God. But the older she got, the more complicated that became. It seemed that at every given moment, there was some other extremely complicated and usually inconvenient and difficult thing that needed to be performed *in exactly the precise right way* or it—and you—were worthless.

For example, Grace After Meals. There was an entire little book of things you had to say to thank God for your food after every meal. But on holidays, you had to add a special paragraph. On Chanukah and Purim, another one. And on the new moon, still another. And even if you said the whole book, if you forgot to add precisely the appropriate paragraph, then your prayer was worthless and you needed to say the *entire thing all over again.*

She sighed.

Someone once said that if the Jews celebrated Christmas, there would have been at least three, four-hundred-page volumes of Jewish law—with commentaries—describing exactly how tall the tree had to be, what color, how long it needed to be in the house, and when and how you were allowed to throw it out. There would be a long list of commandments and prohibitions concerning the decorations and the exact angle that they had to be hung, with commentaries on the different rabbinical schools of thought—both stringent and lenient—concerning candy canes.

She glanced at her husband. Chaim never seemed to have any doubts or hang-ups. Often, Delilah admitted to herself, she envied him this. She took his hand and kissed it. "Chaim, please get this job. It would be so good for both of us. And I promise you, this time I'll do better. I'll make you proud of me."

Chaim put his arm around her, squeezing her shoulders. "I'll do my best, my love."

~ ~

That evening, just after lighting the Sabbath candles, Chaim and Delilah were given the grand tour of the house and grounds. There were many impressive works of art and many beautiful pieces of furniture. Solange, acting as docent, pointed out the big expressionist canvases by Gregory Armenoff, a Roger Shinomura woodblock, a fantastic Romare Bearden collage, as well as wonderful Israeli works by Lea Nikel, Dorit Feldman, and Menashe Kadishman. One entire room had been given over to dreamlike glass masterpieces by Dale Chihuly.

But when the tour was over, Chaim admitted to himself that the thing he envied most were the views from the back porch over Swallow Lake just as the sun was setting. Good thing the Tenth Commandment talked about coveting one's neighbor's house, not his scenery, he thought with a smile. As far as he knew, that wasn't a sin. As for Delilah, she felt her entire being awash in an almost hypnotic sense of longing. Oh, to acquire and own and use and take for granted such riches! Even to live nearby. It would be everything she ever dreamed of.

They waited in the entrance hall for Arthur Malin, who was chairman of the synagogue board, who was going to walk with them to the synagogue. Chaim realized his hands were sweating. He felt as if he were about to meet Donald Trump, not sure he wouldn't point a finger and yell, *You're fired!*

What kind of man owned this palace, he wondered? A person who was not only rich, but cultured and intelligent, with amazing good taste. And what kind of rabbi was he looking for?

They waited and waited, until, suddenly, a voice called out, "Shaindel, where's the apple cider?"

Solange blanched. "He likes to call me that. It's my Hebrew name. He's the only one," she explained, flustered. Chaim and Delilah kept their faces passive, but reached out to pinch each other when she wasn't looking.

Arthur Malin walked into the hallway, glass in hand. "A refrigerator the size of Milwaukee and no juice." He shrugged. He seemed amused. When he saw them he stopped, his face lighting up with a kind smile.

"Hello, hello. Welcome. Good Shabbes." He greeted them warmly, in a heavy Brooklyn accent.

Delilah gulped. He looked like one of her favorite high school *chumash* teachers. "We were just admiring your collections, Mr. Malin."

A maid they hadn't seen before came over hurriedly, pouring him some apple juice. He took it from her gratefully, his eyes lighting up. "*Gracias,* kid," he said, gulping it down and giving her the glass since she seemed to be waiting for it. Then he turned to Delilah. "You like? Good. I don't know much about it. We have a guy that helps us pick things out. He goes for the bright colors, and all the little pieces of material and wood glued on with the *shvartzas*—by what's-his-face—Reardumb?"

"Avrom!" Solange said sharply, her British accent suddenly gone with the wind. Then she seemed to remember herself, glancing at them nervously. "I mean, Arthur," she corrected herself, the Queen's English suddenly making a reappearance. "Please! You know that you and I are the ones who make the final decisions." She turned, smiling. "We just love Bearden."

"Yeah, we decide everything, especially what color ink to use on the checks!" He laughed uproariously, slapping his knee. "Oy, that was good. What do you want, Shaindel? They should think we're big art mavens? I embarrassed her, right? I always embarrass her, my darling wife. He put his arm around Chaim's shoulder. "So, Rabbi, *vus macht du*?"

"We are both doing great. Such a beautiful place. I'm ready to pitch a tent and squat," Chaim said jovially, liking Arthur more with every word he said.

"Rabbi, you don't have to pitch a tent. We already have one, a big one."

"Arthur . . ." Solange raised her brows in warning.

"It's our synagogue!" He roared.

Delilah blanched. "You don't mean the rabbi and his family live in the synagogue?"

"Well, what do the two of you live in now?"

"We have a very nice apartment," Delilah began, wondering if they were already in negotiations.

"All six hundred square feet of it." Chaim laughed.

"Do they come that small? I'd forgotten." He smiled, shaking his head. "I grew up in Bensonhurst, Brooklyn. My parents' apartment was bigger than that, but not much. Here, even the cars get more room to themselves."

"My husband has a very special sense of humor," Solange broke in. "Of course, the rabbi's house is very nice. A two-story Colonial, about two thousand square feet, with a full finished basement. It's very comfortable."

"They'll see it, Shaindel. I promise."

Delilah exhaled. Two thousand fricking feet, she thought, exulting. And a finished basement!

The plan was to walk to the synagogue, where Chaim would give his first speech, and afterward join the board members at the home of the Rollands for Friday-night dinner, where they could all get to know one another.

The walk took them past the Swallow Lake Country Club. It had a 13,000-square-foot fitness center, sandy beaches, eight tennis courts, and an Olympic-sized pool and marina, Arthur Malin informed them. He was a founding member, he said. He believed in physical fitness. All those days sitting in yeshiva on his *tuchas* had convinced him that body and soul needed to be nurtured simultaneously. He seemed in excellent shape, despite creeping baldness and a challah-eating paunch.

All the way there, he regaled them with stories about his yeshiva days in Brooklyn and how the rabbis told his parents he'd wind up in jail. "The rabbis were always trying to convince us not to go to college but instead to sit and learn Talmud the rest of our lives and have the community and our rich fathers-in-law support us. Once, Rabbi Pupik gets up and says, 'You know what happens to boys who go to college? They wind up becoming organic chemists. And do you know what organic chemists do? All day they spend with their hands in what comes out of behinds. People behinds, animal behinds.' Then he'd roll up his sleeves and pantomime it, holding it up to his nose, licking it with his tongue. We were all adolescents, we were rolling around on the floor going, *Uch, uch, uch!*" He laughed. "I'll tell you what. Maybe we didn't become Talmud scholars, but not one of us became an organic chemist!"

Instead, he'd gotten into real estate, learning the business from his mother's uncle. And then, just on a fluke, he'd started purchasing radio stations one at a time when nobody wanted them. Delilah found the whole story a little hard to follow but understood he now headed a media conglomerate that supplied news and entertainment to a vast number of people in the United States and elsewhere.

And while he didn't say so, Chaim already knew that he was also one of the most giving and generous men in the world, involved with a vast number of charities, both Jewish and non-Jewish, with a particular interest in the handicapped. He was one of those people who earn your respect and overcome your prejudices, Chaim thought. As much as those with no money would hope to at least be able to boast of a superior moral edge over their very wealthy counterparts, the truth was that it is equally possible, and far more likely, he believed, for a rich man to be a good person than a poor one—tightfisted grasping hands, let's face it, being more of a problem among those who have grabbed little than those who have grabbed much.

"Oh, my goodness!" Delilah gasped, when she saw Ohel Aaron.

Huge vertical columns of concrete, interspersed with thin ribbons of stained glass, rose into the air, meeting at a point in the center that looked as if it had been tied with some kind of gigantic leather belt.

Arthur Malin shrugged. "I know, I know. It's supposed to be an Indian tepee. The first Jews in Swallow Lake wanted to do something that fit into the environment and would be respectful of local traditions. *Ich vast?*"

It looked, Chaim thought, like a huge ice-cream cone that had been turned upside down and smashed into the pavement by a vengeful three-year-old. "Well, it's the inside that's important," Chaim said.

"That's even worse," Arthur Malin admitted, opening the doors.

He was right. It was vast and rather gloomy, lit by massive wooden chandeliers straight out of the Ahawaneechee Lodge. All that was missing were the antlers and other dead hunting trophies. The bimah, which stood at the center, seemed to be made out of bark-covered log cabin blocks. The Ark of the Torah, hewn out of a massive redwood trunk, seemed to be covered—could that actually be?—in leather. On either side, huge electrical fixtures in the shape of flickering torches finished the effect of a Comanche tribunal gathered to do a war dance.

It took every ounce of self-discipline Chaim could muster not to ask, Are you sure this is Tent of Aaron, and not Pocahontas?

"Let me guess. The *mechitzah* is made of feathers?" Chaim whispered to Delilah.

"He'll hear you!" she hissed.

As it turned out, feathers would have been more traditionally acceptable according to Jewish law than what he found: solid panels of beaten bronze, each one in the shape of a different wild bird, placed at widely spaced intervals that allowed men and women to see each other clearly. He gulped in panic. According to Jewish tradition, the birds were for the birds. There was no question in his mind that any Orthodox rabbi worth his salt must absolutely refuse to officiate over a synagogue service in such a place. He glanced at Delilah, who sat in the front row looking at him hopefully, her face beaming in excitement and expectation. He walked in heavily. This wasn't his pulpit—yet. There would be time to make changes, if and when he got the job, he told himself.

Delilah looked around her, delighted. There were many women of all ages, and at a Friday-night service, which was traditionally almost entirely male. Usually, this meant either that the congregation was young and sassy and used the synagogue as a social watering hole or that the women were in love with their rabbi. In this case, she had no doubt they'd come to gather early impressions by inspecting them both. She smiled until her mouth ached, her entire body tensed and ready.

There is always a little break in the Friday-evening service, when afternoon prayers are over and evening prayers cannot yet begin. In most synagogues, this time slot is filled by the rabbi giving a short learned discussion on some obscure point in Jewish law, saving, as rabbis do, the major heart banger for the larger gathering on Saturday morning.

Chaim stood up and walked to the podium. The place was packed, he realized with pleasure. Quite an achievement in a relatively small place like Swallow Lake, when, all over the country, synagogues—and churches—were empty 363 days a year; and Bar and Bat Mitzva kids disappeared faster than free champagne the minute they'd unwrapped their presents and recovered from their hangovers.

Delilah sat tensely at the edge of her seat. Chaim hadn't discussed his sermon with her. *Please, please,* she thought, her heart clenching, *don't blow this! Just get this job and I'll be the best wife, the best rebbitizin, I promise.*

"The rabbi and his wife were cleaning house," Chaim began, with no introduction, "when the rabbi came across a box. 'What's in it?' he asked the rebbitzin. She said, 'Leave it alone. It's private.' Well, what can you do? A rabbi is also a person; he was curious. So one day, when she was out shopping, he ran to find it and opened it.

"Inside were three eggs and two thousand dollars. He waited patiently for her to come home, and then he demanded to know what it meant. 'Every time you give a bad sermon, I put an egg in the box.' "

" 'Twenty years, and only three eggs! Not bad! But what about the money?'

" 'Every time I get a dozen eggs, I sell them to the poor for a dollar.' "

He waited for the laughter to die down before raising his hand. "I hope I don't get an egg for this one. But before I start, I'd like to tell you another story.

"A young Talmud scholar was invited to become rabbi in a small old community in Chicago. On his very first Sabbath, a violent debate erupted as to whether one should or should not stand during the reading of the Ten Commandments. They asked the new rabbi to decide. 'What's your custom here?' he asked them. But no one could tell him. So the next day, the rabbi visited the synagogue's oldest member in the nursing home. 'Mr. Fine, I'm asking you, as one of the oldest members of the community, what is our synagogue's custom during the reading of the Ten Commandments?'

" 'Why do you ask?' asked Mr. Fine.

" 'Yesterday, we read the Ten Commandments. Some people stood, some people sat. The ones standing started screaming at the ones sitting, telling them to stand up. The ones sitting started screaming at the ones standing, telling them to sit down. They insulted each other, threw chairs, slammed doors, threatened to leave the synagogue, and called me an idiot—'

" 'That,' said the old man, 'is our custom.' "

Chaim followed his jokes with a short speech that discussed the Torah portion of the week, combining it with a good-natured attempt to inspire more ethical behavior among neighbors when it came to borrowing and returning things, which everyone found equally amusing and useful and not overly flat-handed or judgmental.

Not everyone was happy. Some thought the speech was too lightweight, while others thought it was too preachy. But that is normal in all congregations.

Watching a new rabbi approach a congregation is like watching an acrobat on the high wire. Not content to just watch him rush across the abyss to safety, we demand that he stop in the middle, open an umbrella, and sit down on a chair that totters this way and that, while down below we judge his skill and daring and entertainment value. Most of us hold our breath wishing for the rabbi's success, although—admit it—disaster is much more fun to watch, and there is always another rabbi waiting in the wings just in case, ready to take over as soon as the body of the old one is removed.

But there was something so sincere and naive—and pathetic?—about Chaim Levi that even those with the most cynical hearts rooted for him to succeed.

The women were very nice to Delilah. They were gratified and flattered at her absolute unfeigned enthusiasm and delight with everything she had seen in the community. She was a yeshiva graduate. And although she was blond and young and pretty she was also obviously pregnant, wearing one of those "good girl" pregnancy dresses with the high collars and little bows. And a wig. The more they probed, the more they realized she was nothing like their last rebbitzin, and they—and their husbands—need not fear aggressive classes in family purity or campaigns to import the ethos of the stringency kings and their revisionary attitudes toward keeping women in their place. She seemed like a friendly open girl who liked a good manicure and colorist and yet would be willing to play the role of community organizer when asked. She seemed, in short, like a good team player.

The men who interviewed Chaim were satisfied that he knew how to learn Talmud and had a fundamental grasp of religious law. He smiled a lot. But when they asked him about his vision for the congregation, his mind went completely blank. After a long awkward silence, he answered, rather sheepishly, "I think a rabbi should try to serve the congregation's needs. I think he should listen more than he talks."

To his surprise, they hired him on the spot.

FIFTEEN

Delirious with joy, Delilah moved into her new home, leaving urban decay, suspicious glances, and a checkered past behind her. The home she moved into had a lovely living room with a bay window, a formal dining room, and an imposing wood-paneled study for Chaim. It had a huge master bedroom with a working fireplace and three smaller bedrooms. In the backyard, there was a well-kept lawn with some nice shrubs and a picnic table. For days, she wandered around, feeling as if she was an intruder who would soon be caught and evicted. She touched the walls, wiggled her toes in the carpets, drank lemonade in the garden. She was sweet and good-natured to Chaim, preparing good dinners and giving him little hugs and kisses as she rapturously unpacked her belongings and set them up around the house. There was so much room! She slid across the parquet in stocking feet like a ten-year-old blissfully home alone.

She was so happy, she felt grateful to God, her stars, and every other power over the universe and her personal destiny. This was a new beginning, she told herself, assuaging the waves of regret that sometimes enveloped her. For the first time in her life she began to appreciate her religious instruction. For if there was one thing you learned in yeshiva, it was how to deal with sin and guilt. No matter how awful you were, there was no thread so scarlet that it could not be bleached as white as snow.

Unlike Catholics—who made a group project out of it—Judaism was strictly do-it-yourself in the repentance department. You started by admitting your terrible deeds, regretting them, and making yourself a promise never to do them again. Only when that was done could you hope to approach God and ask Him to wipe the slate clean. Unlike Catholics, however, Jews never got that comforting *Say ten Hail Marys* that ended the matter. Barring a burning bush, you were more or less in a state of perpetual doubt as to whether you'd been forgiven. Which is why the words *Jewish* and *guilt* are so often found in close proximity.

Delilah had been shocked and horrified at the turn of events in the Bronx, particularly her part in what had befallen Reb Abraham. But working on herself, she had learned to live with it. After all, he had had to go sometime. No one lasted forever. And she hadn't really done anything wrong, it was simply appearances that had been incriminating. Furthermore, if the old man had been as sincere in practicing moral restraint as he had been in preaching it, he would have given her and Benjamin the benefit of the doubt, despite the admittedly unfortunate and weighty circumstantial evidence. And while she certainly wasn't happy he had taken it all so hard and had wound up giving himself a stroke, she had to admit the timing, in any event, had been perfect. It had proved the magic bullet needed to make the Bronx congregation disappear, and her husband soften up.

Chaim, it was true, had suffered. But look where he was today! The rabbi of a rich and important and thriving congregation in such a beautiful spot, a place that loved him and treated him so well. Why, just the other day Mariette Rolland had told her that her husband was a "blessing" to Swallow Lake! And Felice Borenberg had mentioned how much she loved to listen to him speak.

One day, she knew, he would thank her.

Full of gratitude, having put the past behind her, she was determined not only to become a good rabbi's wife but the *best* rabbi's wife. Chaim, having landed this position, was suddenly the focal point of her admiration. She wanted to help him, to become queen to his king over the moral lives of the people around them.

She smiled and said hello to everyone, even those who treated her coolly. She made weekly sit-down dinners for twelve. She agreed to open her house to monthly sisterhood meetings. She stayed on the phone for hours listening to problems and offering solutions. She even prepared and gave a *shiur* for women on the Torah portion of the week.

And then, one morning, she found she simply couldn't get out of bed. Her limbs felt like lead and her head swam. She felt hot, thirsty, depressed, confused.

"You are doing too much! I tried to tell you to slow down. Darling, don't forget you're pregnant."

"I'm fine. Pregnancy isn't a disease," she told him curtly, quoting Mariette Rolland, who'd recently told her all about how she'd canceled only one day of work appointments to give birth to her last daughter.

She suffered strange cravings, waking Chaim at 2 A.M. to search for passionfruit sorbet and peanut-butter brownies. She fell prey to bouts of depression: "I look like a cow! My mother has nicer ankles! And just look at my stomach, my boobs. . . ."

Chaim stared at her, shocked and dumbfounded. The truth was that pregnancy had brought a blush of radiant health to Delilah that made her body softer and rounder, her skin gleam with a luscious dewy softness. She looked sexier than ever. And if everyone was looking at her, he had no doubt as to why.

"Delilah, darling, you're more beautiful than ever, really" he did his best to assure her.

"Don't lie to me, Chaim! I know everyone's staring at me, thinking how ugly I look! And I'm sick of these goody-goody dresses with the Peter Pan collars and bows! I'm sick of these sensible low-heeled old-lady shoes. I want my body back! I want this *thing* out of me!"

He couldn't reason with her. And then, one morning, he overslept, missing the morning minyan. That same week, he found his eyes closing and his head nodding when he tried to prepare his sermon. He awoke with a start several hours later with nothing accomplished.

He didn't know what to do. He had zero experience with pregnant women, viewing Delilah as a delicate piece of china carrying a soft-boiled egg, imagining that the slightest jarring motion would do irreparable damage to both. With a touch of desperation, he sought out someone who could advise him. The only person who came to mind was Josh, who had been through this only recently himself.

Josh was surprised to hear from him. Once Chaim had gone against the ban and accepted the job at Swallow Lake, they'd lost contact completely, much to Josh's delight. "Well, this is really not such a good time for me."

"Please, Josh, I'm in trouble," Chaim confessed.

"What's wrong?"

"My wife—that is, I—*we* are expecting our first child. Delilah is very worried—depressed—and frankly I'm not getting any sleep. This is a new job. I'm afraid the congregation will begin to grumble."

Josh put his hand over the phone and hissed to his wife, "It's Chaim Levi. Delilah's pregnant and driving him crazy." She shook her head, backing away. "Please . . ." He made a begging face.

Rivkie took the phone. "Hi, mazal tov, Chaim! How wonderful. . . . Hmm, hmmm. . . . Yes, some women have harder times than others. Why don't I call her? . . . No, no bother at all, I'm happy to help. I apologize we haven't been in touch. You know what it's like, or you will, a new baby—"

Delilah was not particularly happy to hear Rivkie's voice, the voice of judgment. She hadn't forgiven their silence when Chaim got the job at Swallow Lake. But Rivkie was very sympathetic and supportive, and Delilah found herself actually enjoying discussing her feelings with someone who wasn't a member of the congregation with an ax to grind, someone with whom she could be completely honest.

"I'm frightened, Rivkie, and I feel like hell. I'm throwing up. Even the smell of Sabbath food makes me want to puke my guts out, let alone preparing these meals for guests. And I can't stand all these needy phone calls, all this meaningless shul chitchat, when all I want to do is just go to sleep! If I only had the weekends off, but that's when we're most *on*."

"I know. It's hard. But people will understand if you're honest and give them a chance. Tell them how you feel. Drop out for a while. It's OK. You are in for such an exciting, wonderful experience! Start focusing on the fun aspects of having a baby. Have you planned your nursery and layette yet? Why don't you go shopping? And most of all, you've got to get yourself a doula."

"A what?"

"It's a Greek word that means—well, helper, servant—slave, anyhow, not really sure. They are women who help you through the birth. I had one. She was wonderful, *baruch Hashem.*

"You mean, a midwife? I already have a doctor."

"No, no. She doesn't have any actual medical training at all. She doesn't deliver the baby."

"Then what *does* she do?"

"Well, before the birth she gives lessons to the couple so the husband can share and participate in the birthing experience. She gives massages with aromatic oils. She sings and dances and says special prayers to ease your spirit and comfort you. And once you're in the delivery room, she—"

"She comes to the delivery room? What does she do there? I mean, if she has no medical training. All you need is an epidural, right?"

There was silence on the other end of the line. "We don't believe in epidurals. Giving birth is a sacred experience, a gift from God. When you get all drugged up, you cut yourself off from the connection to God, and your body—"

Delilah's heart missed a beat. "You mean to tell me you went through labor and delivery cold turkey?"

"It was a fabulous experience, believe me! Extremely spiritual. Never have I felt closer to God, more like His holy vessel. I'm not saying it wasn't hard. I mean, they call it labor, right?" She chuckled. "And of course there was some pain," she admitted dismissively, "but that just made it more real. Believe me, I wouldn't have missed it. And my doula was wonderful."

Where did she get this stuff? Delilah thought enviously. She could just see herself repeating those words in a lofty and pious tone when the young women of Ohel Aaron came to her for advice. In general, anything she could lift from Rivkie would be wise, she told herself. She didn't actually want the doula—it sounded pretty grim—but what she did want was to impress people on how she had breezed through her pregnancy and childbirth on spirituality alone. Besides, you could always get rid of the woman and have an epidural if things didn't work out.

She took down the woman's name and phone number and then refocused the discussion in a more useful direction. "Where did you go to shop?" she asked.

Rivkie was full of useful information. "But you know, Deliliah, the Jewish custom is not to make any preparations at all and only buy baby things once the baby is born."

"Not even diapers?"

"Nothing. But you can take down ordering information."

So, one afternoon, she got Chaim to drop her off at a mall with a Pottery Barn for Kids. There, Delilah made a remarkable discovery: A baby was made to be accessorized! She imagined herself standing over a white French-provincial baby crib, smiling with maternal joy at her designer-dressed infant angelically asleep in its color-coordinated sheets, bumper, and blanket, a matching rug at her feet and matching wallpaper all around. She took a catalog and furiously wrote down numbers.

She looked around at the other pregnant women who wandered with shining eyes among the treasures. They too were lumpy and thickened. But among the women carrying small babies or wheeling toddlers in carriages, a fair number were already back to being thin and young, she noticed, cheering up, imaging herself back to normal too, the only remnant of her pregnancy a double-D bra cup and glowing hormone-enriched skin.

She went on a cancellation spree, telling everyone she needed her rest so the dinners and sisterhood meetings and long phone calls and the *shiur* were all off until further notice. When a panicked Chaim mildly suggested she might try to stay a little more involved, she said, "Rivkie did the same thing when she was pregnant. She says it's perfectly all right. People will understand."

To Chaim's surprise, everyone did. They were extremely understanding, even sympathetic. Besides, no one had the stomach to start interviewing new candidates all over again, and word had gotten around that the new rebbitzin wasn't the world's best cook and her attempt at a *shiur* had been basically to steal a whole chapter straight out of one of those books by Nechama Leibowitz, the Bible scholar, which most people had read already long ago. So they were only too happy to forgo her dinners and lectures.

Remarkably, the less Chaim and Delilah did, the more their popularity rose. The women loved how the rabbi was taking care of his pregnant wife, and the men deeply sympathized with his plight. The fact that his sermons seemed to go from lightweight to featherweight was not only accepted but appreciated. Who wanted moral discomfort and inspiration disrupting their otherwise relaxed and pleasant weekend anyhow?

Within a few weeks, Delilah underwent a remarkable transition: She seemed to blossom. Her nausea lifted, and she began eating like someone just coming off a five-month stint on Weight Watchers, wolfing down food in alarming amounts. She sank back into her new role as baby maker like a pasha into his pillows

Chaim, stretched to the limit from doing laundry, shopping, cooking, and cleaning, in addition to his work as rabbi, often wondered what she did all day. Every time he saw her, she was sitting around with her hand on her stomach, rifling though yet another baby catalog, adding more numbers to her list. She insisted on hiring a local doula, recommended by Rivkie's doula.

"I don't know. She's very expensive. Do you really need her?"

"Don't you want this to be a spiritual experience for me, Chaim? After all, it's God that is forming this child in my womb. I want to feel God during my labor. And if I'm all doped up, how can I do that? Besides, Rivkie said it was fabulous."

He dragged along with her to private coaching lessons, where the doula—a petite dreamy yoga instructor with prematurely gray hair covered by a pious snood—lectured him on understanding his wife's emotional needs and helping to ease her physical pains. He learned to coach her through contractions, to remind her of breathing techniques. He was taught to dab her lips with ice, to support her back, to adjust her pillows. Chaim, surrounded by demanding women, did everything that was asked of him, reluctant to say a word. He was simply grateful that now both he and Delilah were sleeping through the night.

They had begun to think their lives would go on this way forever, when one night, while they were in a movie theater and she was halfway through a box of popcorn, Delilah leaned over and gave the box to Chaim, complaining, "My stomach is killing me."

He was immediately alarmed "Maybe we should go home."

"No, I want to see how this movie ends."

By the time the closing credits were flashing on the screen and they got into the car, she had the worst stomachache she had ever had in her life.

"I'm swearing off popcorn forever," she said.

By the time they got home, she was in agony, barely making it to the bathroom. It was there she saw the tiny blood-tinged mucus and understood that her labor had begun.

"Call the doula! Get my bag!"

In the midst of a maelstrom of horrible physical pain that filled her with panic, she heard Chaim's calm voice. "Relax, darling. Everything is under control. Just take a shower if you feel up to it. Do you need help getting dressed? Remember to breathe. Do you want me to massage your back?"

She grabbed his cheeks like pincers, squeezing and shaking him back and forth.

"*Get me to the hospital, you idiot!*" she screamed.

The ride took forty minutes. Her contractions were coming sixty seconds apart, with peaks that lasted close to two minutes. The pain was intense, disabling, paralyzing. Chaim, his cheeks still stinging, was afraid to open his mouth. He was actually happy to see the doula, who arrived with a small bag and a large Zen smile.

"I know you are in pain, Delilah. But try to remember, your pain has a wonderful purpose. It's actually a gift. It's a blessing, this pain. It's preparing your body. Just think, if your body wouldn't be prepared, how would your baby be released into the world? Thank God for the pain, Delilah. Say a prayer, thanking God for it, for His kindness. Appreciate and give thanks for every contraction—"

"Get that woman out of here before I kill her!"

The doula's smile faded. "Perhaps you'd like a Shiatzu massage?"

"If she lays a hand on me, she's a dead woman!"

"Oh, dear." The doula sighed. "This is a difficult situation. Let's try some visualization techniques . . . or maybe you'd like me to sing? I've got a tambourine with me. Here, let's try. Think of your womb opening, allowing the sacred passage of this blessed new soul into the world: *Pisku li, shaare tzedek, avoh bam, Odey yah.* Open for me the gates of mercy, I will enter and bless You," the doula sang, shaking her tambourine.

"I want my doctor! I want an epidural!"

"Now, now, you know how we feel about epidurals. . . . Here, let me try some aromatherapy. Let me see." She rummaged through her bag. "I've got some lovely lavender, some sage. . . ." She opened some bottles, spilling the liquid into her palms, rubbing her hands together to warm them. "Now, just a touch of this on your forehead and behind your ears—"

Delilah grabbed her hand and bit down on her fingers.

The doula screamed. "Oh, my God, oh, my God, there's blood!"

"Say a prayer for *that* pain, you incompetent piece of garbage!! I should have known. I'm going to kill Rivkie!"

"Nurse!" The doula wept.

"Oooh, that looks nasty," the nurse agreed. "You'd better get yourself down to emergency." Weeping in pain, the woman fled.

"Please, Chaim, get me a doctor, get me an epidural. Please, I'm begging you!"

"Delilah, the doctor's on his way. He'll be here any minute," he explained helplessly. "Maybe she wants me to adjust her pillows?" he asked the nurse, frightened.

"I'll adjust your head, you imbecile!"

Finally the doctor arrived.

"Thank God! Please, doctor, give me an epidural, Demerol, anything!"

"Well, let's just take a look, shall we?" the doctor said calmly, poking around familiarly in her private parts. "Oh, my."

"What? Is something wrong, doctor?" Chaim asked, terrified.

"No, not at all. But she's too far along for an epidural, I'm afraid."

"*What do you mean!*" Delilah screamed.

"Well, you said on your form you were planning on bringing a doula, so we assumed you wanted a natural childbirth, which is why we didn't offer you an epidural when you first came in. Also, either you waited too long to come in or the birth is going very fast. In either case, it's impossible to give you one now. It's much too close to the birth. It might injure the baby."

"*No. Please!*"

"Delilah, be brave! Remember, God is with you! It can be a true spiritual exper—" Chaim tried.

"I'M GOING TO REDO YOUR CIRCUMCISION WHEN I GET OUT OF HERE, YOU MORON!"

Delilah closed her eyes. The pain was worse than anything she had ever in her life imagined possible, except when she fantasized about what they did to you in Auschwitz. *This was Auschwitz!* Why hadn't anyone told her it was going to be this bad? That Rivkie, that doula—they had all had children, they knew! *Liars.* And God? Where was God? And then it dawned on her: The curse of Eve! "In horrible pain will you deliver children" or something like that. This *was* God's will. His plan. But what about the curse of Adam? "In the sweat of your brow you'll bring forth bread." When was the last time she saw her husband—any man—sweat? Men had gotten a reprieve. But the curse against women went on and on and on and on. . . .

From the corner of her eye she saw Chaim sitting, small and exhausted, in the corner of the room with his face in his hands. A rabbi. God's little helper, she thought malevolently. They were all in it together. A conspiracy. God and her husband and that doctor and brainwashed religious women! And she had fallen for it like a dope. As she figured it, in the sin department, whatever she had done was nowhere near what had been done to her. If anyone had to repent for doing horrible things, she wasn't at the top of the list. From now on, all bets were off.

As she looked at her husband, he seemed to grow smaller and smaller, until finally she had the sensation that he wasn't a man at all, not even a person, just an insect, a fly on the wall, whom she hoped someone would swat away.

She started to scream and wouldn't stop until they finally wheeled her into the delivery room. Her son was delivered, with shocking speed, after only three pushes, the strength of which made her experienced obstetrician open his eyes in wonder. Never had a child been expelled faster or with more determination from a mother's womb.

"It's a boy!"

"Figures," she muttered.

"Do you want to hold him?" the nurse asked her.

"I'll catch him later." Delilah grunted, turning over and falling into a dead sleep.

SIXTEEN

"Deli, where should I put the flowers?" Mrs. Goldgrab asked her daughter.

"Don't touch them, and don't call me Deli. I'm not a pastrami sandwich," Delilah growled.

It was bad enough she had roped herself into this sit-down dinner a week after giving birth, but to have her mother not only in the house but trying to rearrange things according to her taste was quickly sending Delilah over the edge. Now, awaiting her guests, the baby all washed and dressed in a lovely baby sailor suit, blessedly asleep in his beautiful new carriage, she tried to take a deep breath and remember why, over Chaim's objections, she was overtaxing herself, insisting on doing it this way.

"Look, Chaim, I've never had the whole board over. Now I've got household help, which I won't have in a few weeks. And everyone will ooh and aah over the baby, and even if I screw up they'll say, 'Oh, she just gave birth.' So, let me do it now."

She'd also decided to invite some friends, feeling she not only needed some allies but some messengers who would spread the news of her triumph to all her old schoolmates. Who knew that the only person who would accept would be Tzippy, a school friend she was never overly fond of, whose greatest asset was that she always seemed to accept Delilah's invitations and actually show up? She was not only coming but bringing a friend, someone Delilah had never met. The Malins had agreed to host the two for the weekend after Delilah explained that Tzippy was her "best and closest friend." That way, they could attend the Saturday-morning circumcision ceremony in the synagogue,

"So, how can I help you, darling?" Mrs. Goldgrab said, peeved.

"Just stay out of my way! Don't rearrange anything, and don't talk to anyone!"

The older woman, insulted but not surprised, took a large brownie off a plate and went out to sit on the back porch to feed herself chocolate comfort and nurse her grievances.

Having her mother and father in the house was just about the last straw. She had readily come up with a number of imaginative and convincing reasons to explain their absence, but Chaim had been scandalized. "We can't very well hold a bris without inviting our parents. It's wrong to deny that respect to them. Besides, what will people think, that we're orphans? Or black sheep?"

The thought of her mother sitting down next to Solange Malin and striking up a conversation about any subject of interest to her mother was breathtaking in its possibilities for disaster. Oddly, while she disliked her mother-in-law intensely, she was less concerned about Mrs. Levi proving an embarrassment. Like it or not, she had grudging respect for Chaim's mother, who could certainly hold her own in any company.

In fact, Chaim's mother had so far proved extremely helpful. After dressing the baby, she had skillfully set the table and helped arrange the catered food on the platters. Since Delilah's pregnancy, there had been an undeclared truce between them. As in so many cases of this kind, once a daughter-in-law becomes a grandchild factory, all bets are off and grandmothers eat crow, a fact it would do well for mothers of the groom to bear in mind before beginning any sentence to the bride with "I'll tell you very frankly."

You might be able to live without your daughter-in-law. You might even be able to manage without your precious son. But no one in her right mind is going to forgo a relationship with that soft little last-chance package of big eyes and baby fat you've waited so long to cuddle to your milkless breasts.

All this, Delilah knew well. But being shrewd if not wise, she discerned that good behavior on her part at this moment in time would yield rewards far richer than simply seeing Chaim's mother grovel. And as she looked at her little boy, so beautifully groomed and ready for inspection, she saw that she'd been right.

Delilah wandered around her home, inspecting.

During the months that had gone by, she'd developed a different set of eyes. After her first visit to the Malins, she had thrown out her globe lamp and the collection of ceramic cats with pink fur. After the Grodins, the little glass vases filled with plastic flowers and the plastic refrigerator magnets had gone. And after the Rollands and Borenbergs, Chaim had had to argue with the truck driver from Goodwill, who had knocked on the door ready to move out their entire bedroom set, his parents' wedding gift. The problem with it, she tried to explain to him, and with their Mikasa china pattern (which she was secretly and deliberately breaking piece by piece), was that everything matched. Matched sets—furniture, china, silverware—were embarrassingly middle class, she had learned from her visits to Felice Borenberg and Mariette Rolland. She wanted to start over, mixing patterns, filling her bedroom and living room with antiques, no two pieces the same, but all polished to a high shine.

Her taste was changing. Unfortunately, her finances were not keeping up.

Now—as Delilah was well aware—no one wants a rabbi or his wife to live better than the average congregant. A rabbi is supposed to represent contempt for material things. He is supposed, by his very being, to point the way toward a happiness that is not measured by what you have, but who you are. On the other hand, a congregant does not want to feel like Scrooge visiting Bob Cratchit.

What Delilah was planning to do—and really it was the right and commendable thing for her to do—was to convince the board that the rabbi's wife was hardworking and had excellent taste, and that the only thing standing between her and the exploitation of her potential as premiere hostess to the Swallow Lake community was cold, hard cash.

She looked forward to plunging back into the role suspended by her pregnancy of wonderful rabbi's wife. It would be nothing like it was in the

Bronx, she convinced herself, because the needs of the rich were altogether different.

First of all, they didn't treat you like slaves, because they actually had slaves, people they paid to insult and order about; people who had to pick up their groceries and tend to them when they broke an ankle or simply felt bored. And you weren't constantly in hospitals, because if there was one thing rich people knew how to do, it was take care of themselves.

They exercised and ate blueberries and strawberries and oatmeal and brown rice and fresh salmon and green tea. They went to spas, slathered themselves with expensive mud from the Dead Sea, had Norwegian gods who massaged away their tensions and cellulite, and yoga teachers who kept them supple. They avoided pneumonia by wintering in Hawaii and avoided assorted melanomas by applying extremely expensive sunblocks that left them looking like pale toast rather than pumpernickel. They used hypnotists to convince their subconscious they didn't like smoking, so lung cancer was out. They remembered flu shots and vitamin supplements and practiced meditation. And most of all, they didn't have infusions of industrial sewage to pollute their water or belching factories to destroy their air quality.

It was easy to stay out of hospitals if you were rich and cautious.

Since they had their physical well-being pretty much under control, Delilah imagined she'd try to win her place in the community by showing them how to develop their spiritual side. She asked Chaim for his advice. As usual, he had been no help at all.

"Just be yourself. You're fine. You do plenty." He tried to comfort her. "You don't have to please anyone but yourself."

Right.

What she needed was a *chesed* project, she decided. Some series of good deeds that would occupy her time and prove to the community that she deserved their respect for being their proxy in all kinds of worthwhile and unpleasant tasks that needed doing. Soup kitchens would have been perfect, if only there was anyone in Connecticut who was hungry.

She remembered the famous story of the rabbi of the Reform temple in the next town, who decided that on Thanksgiving the community should prepare turkeys and pies and all the trimmings "for less fortunate members of the community." He and his wife and several members of the congregation loaded the food into a van and started looking for the poor. Problem was, they turned the car in the wrong direction. The houses just kept getting more and more palatial, with not a poor person—Jewish or otherwise—anywhere in sight. So, finally, they made some phone calls, turned the car around and drove three hours until they finally, wearily, unloaded the feast on a bunch of startled Baptists, who were pretty much full from their own meal.

Then she thought: fund-raising.

That had all kinds of fun possibilities. Dressing up in fabulous new clothes and having your hair professionally colored and styled in order to hit the malls for free "favors," getting jewelry and nice clothes and vacations donated for raffle tickets. There was only one main problem. You had to have something to raise money for.

Well, Israel, of course. There was always someone over there who was recovering from some horrible outrage, physical or emotional. Poor kids. Better: poor Black Jewish kids. Hospitals. Terror victims. Better: poor terror victims just out of hospitals who were unemployed, divorced, or widowed with children (two terror victims!) with empty refrigerators. Victims of left-wing government atrocities who'd had their homes bulldozed, the same homes that previous left-wing governments had built with other charity money.

Whatever. Israel was a gold mine.

But then, like any gold mine, you had many miners: The six-figure salaried professionals in expensive suits from United Jewish Communities and Israel Bonds, people whose expense accounts and cushy business-class trips and overnight stays at fancy hotels were on the line. People with motivation. Or the powerhouse women volunteers from Hadassah. People who knew what they were doing, who had experience and connections.

A rank amateur couldn't very well compete with them and win. Besides, when she dropped the idea casually on Solange Malin, her reaction had been pointed and hostile: Perhaps if the rebbitzin had time on her hands, she might consider fund-raising for the shul. Yeah, to raise the rabbi's salary. Talk about worthy causes! But you couldn't very well consider that a *chesed* project, now could you?

"Too tacky, even for us." Chaim shook his head.

So, there she was, with no acceptable *chesed* project. And she the rabbi's wife, the community role model for sainthood.

It bore down on her, the weight of unmet expectations, of disappointed desires, of unearned admiration. She wanted desperately to make a good impression.

She knew that Chaim had not been their first choice. That they'd wanted the grandson of the legendary European rabbi who had founded the famous Yeshiva. As it turned out, the community who'd won him, had gotten much more—or much less—than they'd bargained for. He'd wound up embroiling them in a major scandal involving after-hours rabbinical "counseling" to widows, divorcees, and, yes, married women in good standing. He would have gone on his merry way if one hadn't become obsessed, stalking him wherever he went, so that even his wife, Rebbitzin Clueless, finally had to wake up and say, Whoa. Now lawyers and lawsuits were pelting them like hail.

So, as she saw it, Chaim had been quite a bargain. For aside from not being particularly bright, and not really having all that much to contribute to his congregation's spiritual life, he was basically harmless. He told some good jokes and didn't make enemies by pushing unpleasant agendas, like forcefully denouncing intermarriages or scolding people for not sending their kids to Israeli summer programs. He was happy to give eulogies and make short speeches at Bar and Bat Mitzvas—in which he invented Nobel Prize–winning accomplishments and character traits for twelve- and thirteen-year-olds. As far as she could tell, he was well liked by most everyone except the chronic complainers, who exist in every shul filled with unreasonable expectations, who wanted a rabbi who is a mentor, a leader, blah, blah.

As if. Congregations didn't want leaders; they wanted shleppers, rabbis who were always scurrying to catch up with their fickle needs. Today, they wanted the women called up to the Torah. Tomorrow, they'd want sushi at shul events. The next day they'd want armed guards with Uzis to roam the shul complex . . . and the rabbi was expected to fall in and support the powers that be. Except that those powers were always shifting.

Their lives, she realized, were built on beach sand. And she, no less than he, was responsible for keeping the powers that be from washing them out to sea.

The unexpected situation she had fallen into by becoming the wife of a rabbi had dawned on Delilah in stages. Stage one, she had been filled with the romantic illusions carefully nurtured in the classrooms of her youth, places where rabbis and rabbis' wives held sway. Life, they'd explained, was to be lived in order to earn great rewards that could only be cashed in after you died, in the "next life." A woman, unable to earn much spiritual change on her own with the measly religious duties that fell her way—drops from the great ocean that washed over the men—could nevertheless increase her bottom line by supporting her husband's myriad religious duties. And the greater the husband, the more credit the wife earned. The wife of a rabbi who was a scholar, head of a great congregation, a leader of men, never had to worry about her spot in the World to Come. It would be an orchestra seat, center stage.

For this, sacrifices had to be made. Like not being able to express yourself freely, having to dress and behave like a dowdy pious matron. Most of all, you had to defer to your husband, helping to feed the myth that every word that fell from his mouth was a pearl of wisdom.

And then came stage two, the realization that a rabbi was just a man, a husband, who had his moments, good and bad, all that Talmud study notwithstanding. That when he pronounced "too much salt in the kugel" or "that dress seems a little too tight around the hips," it was not the word of God. That he was capable of locking himself in his study for hours to compose a sermon about the virtues of compassion, kindness, and peacemaking, only to emerge and threaten the rowdy kids next door with bodily harm if they didn't shut up.

But, then, there were also the times when she saw him secretly donate money from his own pocket to help out divorced moms, or send kids to summer camp, or pull strings to get teens into rehab centers. Times when she felt she might actually be earning World-to-Come credits by supporting him and being part of his work.

And then came the last stage in which the shocking realization dawned that, like it or not, she had no choice: being married to the rabbi, she, too, was an employee of the shul. It was two for the price of one. A package deal. The salary he was paid, and the good life they enjoyed, devolved on her shoulders as well.

She looked out to the back porch where her mother was sitting, with its view of the forests and backyard swings. At first, just the idea of a backyard and front yard, of your own trees and plants, had made her so happy, she'd find herself just sitting outside, tearing up over her good fortune. But now, she was already beginning to feel the small ping of discontent. The beautiful lake view was blocked. The backyard was adequate but small. There was no swimming pool. No Jacuzzi. No sauna.

And while the bedroom was three times the size of the one they'd had in the city, their bathroom had one sink, not two, and it was tiled with plain-colored tiles, nothing imported from Spain or Mexico or Portugal. The refrigerator was a Westinghouse, not a Sub-Zero.

Despite the twinges of discontent, Delilah was still telling herself that she was happy. And in many ways, she was.

Why, just that morning she had lain in bed examining the cards and gifts that had not stopped pouring in. There was a gorgeous sequined diaper bag by Isabella Fiore from Mariette Rolland, who had exquisite taste in everything. The Malins had sent over a classic pram, navy and white patent leather with an adjustable backrest, an air flow adjustment device, and a genuine porcelain medallion, a gift of the congregation. The Grodins had sent over their novelty bears, about ninety-five different models, while the Borenbergs had sent clothing by Minimun, which, someone had explained to Delilah, looked ordinary but cost a fortune.

Despite her sore body, she'd leaned back, sighing with satisfaction and happiness. Even though she was married to a man who catered to the needs of endless strangers, people who claimed and received his time, energy, worry, and interest twenty-four hours a day, seven days a week, she felt she could make her marriage, and her life, work in a place like Swallow Lake.

"Why don't you ask some of the women tonight about a suitable *chesed* project? Maybe they'll have an idea," Chaim had suggested that morning. She'd stared at him, stunned. Finally, her husband had a good idea. This alone, she thought, was worth a celebratory dinner.

SEVENTEEN

The Grodins arrived first, bearing a bottle of expensive wine. Amber was a large woman who wore custom-made clothes that seemed to float over her body benignly, giving away no secrets. Like many heavy women, she had a strikingly lovely face that people bemoaned, as if it were a tragedy. "Such a shame!" they'd say. "Such a beautiful face! If only she could lose a little weight, she'd be such a knockout." Since Amber had been overweight from the age of thirteen months, she had been waiting her entire life for someone to call her beautiful without an addendum.

Her husband, Stuart, was equally heavy and gave the impression of being a laid-back guy with a killer sense of humor. Nothing could have been further from the truth. Far from being easygoing and self-satisfied, he was the opposite: a kind of fat Richard Dreyfuss in *The Apprenticeship of Duddy Kravitz*, constantly looking for a new angle to exploit, seeing in every social relationship the hidden opportunity for scoring.

Whenever he was together with the rich birds in his neighborhood, he never ceased hoping they'd molt when he was around, leaving behind some golden feather he could scavenge and cash in. Sometimes it was a stock tip, but often it was just the small talk that went on between very wealthy men, about investment advisers and commodities and real estate opportunities. He lunged for the information like a Venus flytrap, before anyone could catch on.

He was always a little nervous around people like the Malins, feeling that he was a fake, a one-trick pony, who had had some luck that could always peter out. He and Amber had been in the novelty business for years—producing instantly breakable and forgettable objects—until they hit the jackpot with the bears.

"Delilah, sweetheart, mazel tov! Let me see the baby. . . . Oh, Stuart, look at this baby!" Amber cooed, looking him over. They had one grown son who lived in Miami whom no one had ever seen. There didn't seem to be a daughter-in-law in the offing or a grandchild on the horizon.

"Cute," Stuart agreed, giving the baby a quick little look over, then nervously canvassing the room. "Are we the first?"

Delilah nodded. "But they'll be home from shul soon. Please, sit down."

She didn't offer them anything, because traditionally one didn't eat or drink Friday nights before hearing kiddush over the wine, which would only take place when the rabbi walked in and the meal began.

The Borenbergs came next. Felice was in her late forties, but you would never have guessed it. She was tiny and wore her hair down her back almost to her waist, like a fairy princess. The cost of dye necessary to keep it that shade of platinum could have put a deserving student through medical school, Amber once snickered to Solange, who was only too happy to join in, resenting the woman's overt sexiness along with everything else about Felice.

Women of a certain age, Amber and Solange were in whispered agreement, should cut their hair to a sensible length instead of running around like Venus on the half shell. Whenever Felice walked into the women's section, the two of them—and many many others—seethed at the way the head of every man in the synagogue turned to look at her. Men never realized how tacky that kind of behavior was, Solange and Amber agreed. But they never said any of these things to her face because Felice was constantly throwing the most wonderful parties in her exquisite home. She always had the best cook, the most wonderful gardener and florist, the most efficient and pleasant household help that stayed with her for years. Amber and Solange would have been devastated to be cut from her guest list.

Felice was also a terror on the StairMaster and never skipped her private pilates and yoga sessions, giving her the figure of a junior high school cheerleader. That was bad enough. But what was truly unforgivable was that she had actually founded the multimillion-dollar company that allowed her to maintain her lifestyle at Swallow Lake, rather than having married the man who did.

A rabbi's daughter who had wound up at Harvard Business School, she had come up with the brilliant idea of putting pushcarts along the center aisles of malls, in which she sold everything from back massagers to pearl jewelry, amassing countless millions. She had actually been written up in *Fortune* as one of America's foremost entrepreneurs. There had been three husbands, the first two long gone and forgotten. She had a number of children away at college, leaving behind only her baby, now a pimply sixteen-year-old sophomore in the local yeshiva high school. She had sold half her shares in her thirties and had been pursuing a life of leisure ever since. Her current spouse, Ari, was the son of Israelis who had left the country when Ari was ten in search of the American dream. And although Ari had been back only twice in the last twenty years to visit his grandmother and relatives, he considered himself the resident expert on anything to do with Israeli politics, culture, or economics, insisting on having the last word on Middle East history and politics. He was at least fifteen years younger than Felice, the only man on the board who still had all his hair in its original color.

"I hope I'm not too late to help," Mariette Rolland said briskly, as she walked in alone. Her husband, Joseph, the heart specialist, was a man whom no one ever actually saw, although his existence was a well-established rumor. Mariette was cover-girl beautiful, with strawberry-blond hair cut into a shoulder-length bob.

A clinical psychologist with a thriving practice, she was also the mother of four children—a fifteen-year-old son and three very beautiful daughters aged sixteen through twenty-three, the oldest of whom was already married and the mother of two babies.

She was also very kind. She never gossiped. She contributed generously to every imaginable charity, as well as baking cakes for them, and opening her home for countless fund-raisers. She gave dinner parties for her husband's medical colleagues. She ran support groups for women with osteoporosis. She volunteered at battered women's shelters, taught quilting, and took gourmet cooking classes. All this, she managed singlehandedly as her husband jet-setted all over the globe, attending medical conferences and tending to an international roster of patients, including a member of the Saudi royal family, making him one of the few Jews to have gone in and out of that country alive.

Mariette did it all with aplomb, patience, good nature, and good cheer. She was also one of the few women who insisted on a token head covering for her hair, out of respect for the rabbinical injunction. She always found the perfect hat to match every single one of her perfect outfits, which was in itself enough to make you want her dead.

"Delilah, how are you? Tell me how I can help. Oh, look at the baby! Such a little darling. How was the birth?"

"Oh, it was an amazing spiritual experience. You know, I didn't have any drugs. I had this doula. And I never felt closer to God, believe me. I felt He was directly responsible for everything that was happening to me."

"How inspiring! Usually a first birth is pretty difficult," Mariette said, impressed.

"It all depends on your spiritual strength." Delilah nodded. "*Baruch Hashem.* It's an experience I'll never forget. In fact, I'm thinking about giving a *shiur* about it."

"Mariette, that's such a lovely suit! Wherever did you find it?" Amber asked enviously.

"I got it in this little shop in passy the last time I was in Paris." She sighed mournfully.

Mariette's married daughter lived in Paris, so she had a perfect, morally iron-clad reason to travel there often. In between her shopping trips to the Galeries Lafayette, there were often side jaunts to Provence and the French Riviera. But she made it a point to disavow any enjoyment from her travels. "I am counting the days until my family finds their way back to America, or even to Israel, believe me!" she'd say fervently, shaking her head as she fingered the exquisite rose-shaped sequined buttons on her suit jacket—such as can only be found in Paris. "Such anti-Semites," she'd murmur, shrugging helplessly, steadying her upper lip. "But what can I do? She's my daughter." In answer to any question that broached the subject of when her daughter was actually planning on leaving France, she'd exhale slowly, explaining for the umpteenth time that there was a business that needed to be sold, some big factory her son-in-law had inherited, was now in charge of, and was unfortunately unable to sell. "Everyone has their burdens." She'd smile bravely, planning her next trip.

There was the obligatory oohing and aahing over the sleeping infant, who slept under the watchful eye of the au pair, who stood by ready to whisk him out of sight and hearing range the moment he showed any actual signs of life.

EIGHTEEN

"Delilah, look who I've brought," Chaim said cheerfully as he walked in from shul, accompanied by the Malins and two women. Delilah walked over to him, a big smile on her face. She gave the strangers—whom she assumed were shul strays—the barest of smiles and an offhand nod, before turning her attention fully to the Malins.

"Solange, Arthur, thanks so much for the beautiful carriage! And for hosting my dearest friend! I can't wait to see her!"

A strange look came over Solange. "You're very welcome, Delilah. Your *friends* also couldn't wait to see you!" she said, gesturing pointedly toward the strangers.

"Don't you recognize me, Delilah? It's me, Tzippy."

Delilah took in the woman's gelled black hair that stood up in spikes, the ends tinted blond, the low-cut vintage dress, the chains with numerous symbols. For a split second, the rather overweight, studious girl with glasses she remembered from high school peeked out at her.

"Tzippy? Is that really you?" she said in a tiny, hoarse voice. She felt breathless, as if she'd swallowed a fish bone and was afraid of inhaling it into her lungs.

"Yes, it's really me. And this is Fréderique." She reached out, threading her fingers lovingly through the hand of a petite blonde in a red pantsuit and bringing it to her lips.

Delilah froze in horror.

A gay person in the Orthodox community is like a beer-guzzling Muslim in a mosque: totally impossible for the faithful to publicly embrace. While the rest of the world might have moved on, and even certain Reform and Conservative Jewish congregations in New York, Los Angeles, San Francisco, and Boston might have graciously finessed their way around it, most people in the religious Jewish world continued to view homosexuality in biblical terms, i.e., as an abomination worthy of, if not currently punishable by, stoning. The more widespread its acceptance, the more Orthodox religious leaders pointed to it as proof of the current decadence of modern life, and to themselves as guardians of the last bastion left standing against it. The depth of one's horrified rejection was often the yardstick to one's piety.

"It's so good to see you! Mazel tov on the baby!" Tzippy went on cheerfully, oblivious, hugging her. "I don't know if this is the right time to announce it—I know you're not supposed to mix one *simcha* with another—but I just can't resist: I also have a mazel tov coming to me!" she looked lovingly at Fréderique. "We're engaged!" she announced. "We hope to have a commitment ceremony as soon as our rabbi gives birth. We'd be honored if you'd be one of our chuppah holders."

People standing within hearing range turned astonished faces in their direction. Delilah shrank.

"I was really surprised you called. Frankly, I'm not in touch with most of the girls we grew up with anymore. Nothing personal, just, you know, nothing in common. And even my family—well, you can imagine. Intermarriage is bad enough. But intermarriage with a same-sex partner who's Catholic and French—which is almost as bad as being German these days—was too much for them. So we thought it was a pretty important statement, didn't we, Fréderique? I mean, you being the rabbi's wife and all of an Orthodox congregation and still being willing to invite us and introduce us to your community as your friends."

"*Best* friends," Solange said slowly. "Isn't that what you said, Delilah?"

"She told you that?" Tzippy beamed at Fréderique, who beamed back. "I had a pretty big crush on her too."

Delilah stepped back, dizzy, rapidly reevaluating all those times she'd worn her bikini and shared a beach blanket with Tzippy during the summer of her sophomore year.

"*Bon soir*, I've heard a lot about you," Fréderique said, looking her up and down. "And it was all true."

Delilah touched her sweating forehead.

"Is that French I'm hearing?" Mariette called from the other side of the room. "*Ça va?*" she ventured, moving toward them, smiling. Having used up her entire French vocabulary except for *How much*? *My size is the American size eight*, and *Give me a low-calorie soft drink*, Mariette returned to English. "I'm afraid my French is pretty bad," she said. It was not. It was nonexistent. "So, are you two roommates? I remember how much fun it was when I was in college to bunk with a roommate—"

"Yes, we live together, but not as roommates," Tzippy began instructively, as if she were about to deliver the main address at the Gay Pride parade.

Delilah suddenly plucked her peacefully sleeping infant unceremoniously out of his carriage. He howled.

"Oh, what do you know? He's hungry again. And I just fed him! What an appetite!" Delilah said in a booming voice over the baby's screams, putting an end to all conversation. "Chaim, why don't you seat everyone? I'll just feed him and be back in a jiffy." She ran up the stairs to the bedroom.

Felice arched a brow, while Solange and Amber went silent, staring at their feet. The lesbians and the disappearing act were bad enough, but nothing compared to not having provided place cards and having left the responsibility for seating in the hands of a husband at the last minute. That could only be characterized by one hyphenated word: low-class.

Chaim looked anxiously around at the knots of people, wondering how to untie them and where they were supposed to go.

"What a wonderful idea!" Mariette declared brightly. "So much better than boring place cards. This way, we can all decide. You don't mind, Rabbi Chaim, if we take it out of your hands? Now, let's see, I am dying to sit right next to Arthur—you don't mind, Solange, do you? And why don't you and Stuart sit over here. And Felice, you and Amber can be here, next to Chaim's mother and father. And Mrs. Goldgrab, what about here?" Mariette kindly and charmingly filled in for her AWOL hostess, making it all seem like great fun, instead of a major screw-up. "Tzippy, Frêderique, why don't you sit together over *here*," she said, placing them firmly in one corner with smiling efficiency so no one would be forced to speak to them.

Delilah leaned up against the bedroom door. The baby flailed, moist and angry, getting justifiably redder and more furious by the minute. She undid her bra and compressed her generous nipple into its tiny mouth, effectively shutting him up.

A dyke, she thought with horror. Tzippy Rosenfeld, who'd sat next to her in *chumash* class learning all about the Temple offerings! Quiet, unattractive, frizzy-haired Tzippy, full of sardonic humor no one got! And she'd been introduced to the Swallow Lake board *as the rebbitzin's dearest friend!*

Delilah sat down, her nipple aching from all the unaccustomed tugging. Perhaps it wasn't as bad as she thought. Perhaps not everyone had overheard them. As for the hand-holding, after all, good women friends often held hands as a sign of innocent affection, didn't they? And lots of people dressed strangely these days. It was Britney Spears pollution. Chaim certainly didn't seem as if he'd noticed anything strange. But she got scant comfort from that. First, because he never noticed anything, and second, because even if he had he'd still be incapable of snubbing someone, anyone, even if his life—or, more importantly, his job—depended on it.

And then, finally, another realization dawned on her: They'd be staying overnight at the Malins! Although she was fuzzy on the details—what, in heaven's name, was there for two women to do with each other, after all?—a cold shudder of terror crawled up her spine. What if they woke Solange or Arthur's mother, who would discover them in flagrante delicto?

She sat on her bed filling with despair, imagining how the information would spread like wildfire all over the community Delilah so wanted to impress with her goodness and piety. She could see with clarity how all the eyes in the women's section would turn to stare at her, people whispering in shocked low tones behind her back how the rebbetzin's friend, *her very, very best friend in all the world, the only one she'd invited to her son's bris out of all her many, many friends*, had performed acts of lesbian lewdness under the roof the president of Ohel Aaron.

Delilah shook her head. "A tragedy. Such a solid, religious girl. She won second prize in the Bible quiz! She was engaged to an accountant from Boro Park and studying to be a—a librarian. At Brooklyn College." Delilah stared at her hands. "She's been my *chesed* project now for years."

"Head trauma?" Mariette asked sympathetically. "You get all kinds of personality changes," she told the others.

Delilah nodded sadly. "She was praying so hard one Yom Kippur she actually tipped right over from the women's balcony into the men's section. Head first into the bimah. It was terrifying."

"Well, I'll be damned!" Delilah's father boomed

Solange's mouth dropped open. Mariette and Felice exchanged wondering stares.

"Most unfortunate." Arthur shrugged. "How kind of you, Rebbitzin, to be so loyal. Poor thing."

"Yes." Mariette nodded. "Emotional support is so important to trauma victims. It's a really worthy *chesed* project."

"That's the way I brought her up, to do good. It's our way of life," Mrs. Goldgrab piped up, poised to elaborate until she caught a glimpse of Delilah's half-lidded, sidelong glance, which reminded her of a crocodile just about to have lunch.

Chaim, who had been listening to all this in dumbfounded wonder, suddenly cleared his throat. "Speaking of *chesed* projects," he interjected quickly. "Delilah has been searching for a new one for our community. I told her she should ask all of you."

"A *chesed* project! Why, you are going to have your hands full with your new baby, my dear. That is the biggest *chesed* project any woman can take on," Solange said loftily.

"Be real, Solange!" Felice waved her hand dismissively. "You can go crazy in the house all day with a screaming kid. First of all, get a babysitter, so you'll have a few hours a day for yourself. And whatever you do, don't get involved in hospitals. All those germs!"

"And you don't want to get involved in fund-raising either, believe me. It's too time-consuming," Mariette pointed out. "And the competition is cutthroat."

"I've got an idea! What about collecting clothes for Israeli terror victims?" Amber said.

"Oh, clothing drives are so passé. Besides, why would old clothes do anything for terror victims?" Solange asked.

People were shifting nervously, beginning to wonder if she was eve
ing back, when all of a sudden, Delilah suddenly reappeared. He
looked slightly red, and she had a sweet, sad smile on her wan fac
someone who has witnessed the last act of a Shakespearean traged
emerged purified and uplifted by the cathartic horror of it all.

She sat down at the other end of the table, facing her husban
managed to avoid looking at or speaking to either Tzippy or Fréde
the entire evening. Even though Chaim tried to be hospitable, incl
them in the conversation whenever he could, they began to shift u
fortably, exchanging meaningful glances. Finally, just before de
Tzippy suddenly answered her cell phone, even though no one had
it ring. It was urgent family business, she apologized, rising fro
table together with Fréderique, which necessitated their immediat
parture.

They said their goodbyes. Delilah walked them to the door.

"So sorry you've got to go!" Delilah said brightly. "But thank
coming!"

"You mean thanks for leaving, don't you?" Tzippy said, looking a
for what she knew would probably be the last time.

"You always did have a strange sense of humor."

"Relax, Delilah. There's no need to pretend. We get the picture."

Delilah's smile faded. "And don't you pretend you don't know w
going on here. You went to yeshiva. Our jobs are on the line here."
sighed. "Look, I'm really sorry. I just never imagined. . . . It's nothing
sonal. Goodbye. I wish you both luck."

"So long to you too, Delilah," Tzippy answered, looking at
steadily. "I wish you luck too. Take it from me you'll need it. A person
only pretend to be something they're not for just so long."

"What is that supposed to mean?" She bristled.

"Oh, I think you know, *Rebbitzin*," Tzippy murmured meaningf
"But hey, to each his own closet." They closed the door behind them.

She came back to the table and sat down, smoothing her skirt
neath her.

"Lovely girls," Solange murmured.

Delilah nodded. "I know what you are all thinking. But if it had
been for the accident—"

"What happened?" Amber asked.

"But what about handbags!" Delilah burst in suddenly. "Designer handbags!"

"Designer Handbags for Terror Victims," Felice mused, rolling the phrase over on her tongue.

Delilah leaned back, pleased. "Well, I was looking at some of those horrible pictures of bus explosions, you know? And on the sidewalk was this handbag, just lying there. And I began to think of all those Israeli women who had lost their handbags . . . and you know, if you give victims money, they'll just spend it on the house or on food. They would never go out and buy themselves a really, really beautiful handbag. They wouldn't allow themselves that pleasure, and as we all know, a special handbag can do so much for a woman's feeling about herself."

"That," Ari said slowly, shoving yet another slice of kugel onto his already overcrowded plate, "has got to be the dumbest idea I ever heard."

"What do you mean!"

"How can you say that?"

"Spoken like a man!"

Each of the women jumped on him, causing his fork to pause in midair before it could deposit its next unnecessary load. He looked at them, astonished. "You can't be serious. Come on! I'm Israeli, I know what I'm saying. Israelis have stubborn pride. They hate charity."

"Has anyone ever mentioned this to the UJC?" Stuart murmured

"All right, all right. Explain the logic of it to me," Arthur said calmly, raising his palms upward, ever reasonable and wanting to spare his hostess further humiliation.

"Well," Delilah began eagerly, "let's say you were depressed over your appearance, as I imagine some terror victims are—all that stress, not to mention physical injuries." She shuddered.

"And maybe no matter what clothes you wear, you still feel fat or you can't find your size," Amber joined in.

"But a beautiful handbag never has to fit, and it makes every woman feel special," Felice concluded.

"Exactly," Delilah agreed triumphantly.

"What do *you* think, Rabbi Chaim?" Ari said, suddenly turning to him.

Chaim looked from the disbelieving eyes of the men to the agitated and defensive eyes of the women, finally staring straight into those of his wife, who looked back at him, expressionless, waiting.

"Well." He gulped. "Let me tell you a story. Ninety-year-old Moishe is dying. There he is, in his bed, getting ready for his last hour on earth, when suddenly the smell of newly baked fudge brownies comes wafting up the stairs from the kitchen. This was his favorite. There was nothing he loved to eat more than fudge brownies. So, with his last ounce of strength, he lifts himself up off the bed, clutches the wall, and slowly makes his way out of his bedroom and down the steps, gripping the railings with both hands. Finally, his strength almost gone, his heart beating with his last breaths, he leans against the kitchen door frame and stares in.

"There, in front of him, is a wondrous sight: hundreds and hundreds of fudge brownies. 'Oh, my God, maybe I'm already in heaven!' he thinks. 'But if I'm still alive, then this is the greatest act of *chesed* from my wonderful wife, who knows me so well and has been at my side for over sixty-five years. My darling wife who wants to make sure I leave this world a happy man. I cannot disappoint her.' With one final superhuman effort, Moishe lunges toward the brownies but ends up on his knees near the table. His old hand trembling, he reaches up to take one, his mind already beginning to imagine the explosion of chocolate in his mouth, the thick fudgy taste that will soon fill him with final joy, when all of a sudden—*wham*—his wife whacks his hand away with her mixing spoon.

" 'What are you doing!' he cries out to her.

" 'They're for the shiva.' "

No one said a word, the women looking aghast while the men tried out tentative little smiles.

"With all due respect, Rabbi," Ari finally broke the silence. "What's that supposed to teach us?"

Chaim looked up, surprised, his forehead suddenly glistening with moisture.

"Isn't it obvious, Ari?" Arthur Malin broke in, raising his eyebrows. "No matter what state a person is in, there is always something that can bring him joy. Is that what you meant, Rabbi?"

Chaim nodded his head gratefully.

"Amber is right. Clothes have to fit. Different people like different syles. And I'll tell you something else, trying on clothes is depressing. It's not fun. But a beautiful handbag. It's a wonderful, original idea. Like brownies for the dying," Arthur concluded, smiling encouragingly at Chaim.

So he wasn't the brightest star in the sky, and his wife was even dimmer, Arthur Malin thought to himself. But he would rather have the community collecting pocketbooks than brainwashing their young people to join the black hats. He thought of his grandchildren in their broken-down apartment on a poor Jerusalem side street, their father jobless and probably going to stay that way, living on handouts from America. At least Rabbi Chaim would do no harm.

"I can give you a few handbags, and I know some other women who will be happy to contribute, Delilah." Felice offered.

After services the next day, they held the bris. They named their son after his great-grandfather, Abraham. It was a very moving ceremony in which the entire community participated. Afterward, there was a sit-down luncheon in the catering hall served on china plates that were a far cry from the plastic forks and paper shnaps cups of the Bronx.

NINETEEN

Delilah's dreams of spending her time searching for designer handbags to cheer Israeli sufferers of posttraumatic shock were not exactly working out as she had planned. In fact, being a rabbi's wife in Swallow Lake wasn't turning out as she had planned.

She realized this the morning of the sisterhood meeting. She was in the kitchen, preparing the evening's food, which Solange had suggested be a dessert buffet in a baby shower theme, because one of the sisterhood members had just found out she was pregnant. So there were going to be baby bottles holding little tulips, and diaper-pin napkin holders, a large stuffed animal in a diaper holding the silverware. There would be parchment paper cones of peanut brittle held in ice-cream-cone holders and tall martini glasses with little silver scoopers holding jellybeans. There would be a blueberry-lemon crème brûlé tart, chocolate peanut-butter diamonds, fudge-covered brownie cheesecake, chocolate-dipped almond horns, cupcakes, plum crumble cake, fresh fruit cut up to look like lollipops, and a peach and berry crisp.

The baby was screaming, so she picked him up and balanced him on her hip, as she creamed the confectioner's sugar into the butter. The phone was ringing.

"Chaim, can you get that? *Chaim?*"

It kept ringing.

"Hello?"

"Rebbitzin Levi?"

"Yes, who is this? Shhhh. . . . No I'm not shushing you, it's my baby. How can I . . . ? Oh, Mrs. Stein. You really should discuss that with my husband. . . . I'm sorry he's so hard to catch, but he's. . . . Yes, I realize that it's important. . . . Of course, I'll remind the cleaning staff to wash off the plants in the synagogue lobby before your son's Bar Mitzva. . . . No, I don't think it's petty, not at all. You have out-of-town guests; of course you should feel comfortable. *Ssssssssshhhhhh!* No, no, really, it's the baby—"

Was that the damn doorbell ringing?

"CHAIM!" Where was he?

"Sorry, I've got to go. 'Bye."

She hung up the phone and ran to the door.

"Oh, Mrs. Cooperman. How are you?" She smiled as best she could at the young woman on her doorstep, who wordlessly handed her a white envelope, turned her back, and fled. Delilah held it in her fingertips gingerly, imagining the piece of cloth tinged with vaginal secretion inside, releasing it over the pile of mail on the dining room table meant for Chaim.

The baby was not going back to sleep, she realized, sitting down and pulling out her breast. She sat down on the couch and closed her eyes as the infant nursed, pulling on her nipple, which was sore and cracked. She put him over her shoulder to burp. He let loose a large wad of goo, which, as usual, managed to miss the diaper and run down her shoulder, thus destroying yet another blouse.

No, things were not going as she'd imagined. For starters, there she was sitting in the front pew in the synagogue, a sitting duck, listening to all the whispers as Chaim was speaking, wondering if they were laughing at him or angry at him or just ignoring him and discussing where to buy shoes, as he gave his weekly sermon. At first, she had concentrated on his every word, tense and defensive, cringing when she heard him say anything the least bit controversial that might wind up with some incensed synagogue member accosting them at kiddush to bawl him out. But as hard as she listened, it was impossible to predict. Once, he told a touching story about the daughter of a friend who had celebrated her twenty-first birthday in Jerusalem by preparing a Sabbath dinner for friends. He compared that to the twenty-one-year-olds who celebrate by getting drunk in bars with friends. Who could have predicted that this would lead to a half-crazed congregant cornering him over the potato kugel, shouting, "Not every American kid gets plastered on his birthday! What are you trying to do, talk all of us into sending our kids to Israel where they'll be blown up by suicide bombers?"

After that, she'd tune out his speeches completely. It was bad enough she had to show up at the synagogue every Saturday morning, baby or no baby, rain or shine. And it wasn't enough just to come, she had to show up in the best possible outfit, with a matching hat or wig that covered all or most of her hair.

Never in her wildest dreams had Delilah ever imagined she'd wind up covering her hair. The custom, as far as she knew, had started with the biblical phrase in Leviticus that described the *sotah* ordeal that a woman had to undergo if her husband suspected her of committing adultery but didn't have any actual proof. The poor floozy was taken to the temple where, the Bible says, "The priest shall present the woman . . . before God and uncover the head of the woman." How that had morphed into every married woman being obliged to shave her head—or wear a wig, or tuck every last strand of her hair inside some dorky-looking snood—was beyond her. But there it was. Her own theory, adopted from a talkative and rebellious classmate who had wound up marrying a Gentile, was historical: Given the fact that only prostitutes had not worn a hat in the Middle Ages, medieval rabbis had found some way to update biblical Judaism to be in tune with the times. Unfortunately, Orthodoxy's innovations sort of froze in the fourteen hundreds. So when women all over the world stopped covering their hair, Orthodox rabbis forgot to update. Now, women were stuck with two impossible-to-explain ideas: that a wig was more modest than your own hair and that being the only woman in the entire city to wear a hat—thus calling undue attention to yourself wherever you went—was a source of modesty.

As a girl, she'd only seen the most pious rabbis' wives and her Torah teachers wear wigs. Other religious women teachers had worn hats, although with visible reluctance, and the hats kept getting smaller and smaller as time went by.

Strangely, although her mother's generation and even her grandmother's had neatly done away with the hair-covering custom altogether, it was her generation that had set themselves the reactionary goal of bringing it back, something like Iranian girls making a revolution to put themselves into veils and under the thumb of the mullahs and imams.

How many discussions had she had with her Bernstein Seminary classmates on whether or not they would cover their hair when they got married? How many hours had been wasted describing the merits, exploring the major moral significance, and plumbing the religious joy of buying either a hat to match every outfit or a fantastically expensive custom-made wig usually reserved for chemo patients who had lost all their hair? Whatever the conclusion they came to, most agreed that—outdated custom or no—it was a religious obligation you simply couldn't wiggle out of. Some girls even claimed it had nothing to do with modesty; that it was one of those unfathomable Divine decrees, like the red heifer, whose sprinkled ashes somehow had the mystical power to cleanse the nation of sins and impurities.

But as far as Delilah could see, forcing women to cover their hair was no red heifer; it was simply a gimmick—one of many—that rabbis had dreamed up just to make married women uglier than unmarried women, so that men could easily tell them apart, ostensibly for the purpose of encouraging them to keep their hands off the married ones.

Wig wearing wasn't helpful in the least to this endeavor, which is why the stringency kings wanted to outlaw wigs. For many years they had waged a guerrilla war against the wig stores and *shaitel* makers, coming up with ever more imaginative ways of doing battle. Their ultimate coup was achieved by spreading the rumor that wigs contained hair donated by women as part of the idolatrous worship of Hindu deities. The resulting wig burnings that took place all over the religious world—reducing many a panicked matron to ugly head scarves and wig store owners to bankruptcy—filled them with rapturous satisfaction. But the rumor was eventually quashed, and the sale of wigs shot back up to normal. This time, though, wigs had to carry a rabbinical stamp of approval ascertaining no Hindu deities had been deprived of their due.

Many of Delilah's friends viewed the prewedding wig-and-hat-buying spree as just one more lovely, religiously sanctioned prenuptial extravagance. They would no more have dreamed of forgoing it than they would have given up the sterling silver candelabra they had coming to them from their mothers-in-law.

But as married life rolled on and all that wig wearing gave them headaches, ruining their natural hair; and the effort to find a hat that would match every single outfit began to drain their ingenuity—not to mention their cash—they began to realize what a fine mess they'd gotten themselves into. By then, of course, it was much too late. If a bride never covered her hair, that was one thing. But if she covered it and then decided as a married woman to uncover it, that was a major religious statement that needed to be accounted for among friends, family, and community, a monumental showdown that most religious women didn't have the stomach for, even when their husbands backed them up.

Not that many husbands did. Given that their own religious status would be vulnerable to a staggering blow should their wives suddenly feel the joy of having the wind blow through their hair, such a man was rare. Except for the singular man of moral courage who sympathized with his wife's frustration or had the intellectual honesty to admit the silliness of the prohibition, most men were perfectly thrilled to maintain religiously sanctioned control over their wives' femininity.

Delilah had also bought into the hats and the wigs but had become disillusioned rather sooner than most. She immediately discarded her head covering while in the privacy of her home, ignoring the example quoted in the Talmud of the sanctimonious and insufferable matron who declared the secret to her success in mothering some outrageous number of priests in the Holy Temple had been entirely due to the fact that "the walls of her house had never seen a strand of her hair." But that was just an opinion, not Jewish law. All rabbis agreed that you only had to cover your hair outside the house. If any man came over, she threw on a scarf, of course.

However much she longed to go back to wearing her hair the way she had as a single girl, she was painfully reconciled to the fact that it would be tricky if not impossible now that she was the wife of a congregational rabbi and all eyes were upon her, grading her saintliness. How could people rely on a rabbi who couldn't maintain strict adherence to Jewish law even in his own home?

While she chafed under the prohibition, she made do by constantly wearing an exquisite blond wig, custom-made at enormous expense to fit her perfectly. She looked so stunning in it, she left Chaim alone. Unfortunately, constant wear and many washings and blow dryings had taken their toll; the wig, alas, had lost its appeal. In fact, it was actually beginning to look like a wig, which is the last thing any religious woman wants. Equally unfortunately, the thousands of dollars necessary to replace it were simply not available. What she was left with was buying the kind of out-of-the-box human hair/polyester weave worn by Hasidic women, Halloween revelers, and call girls, styling and length being the key differences.

She tried turbans. She tried snoods. She tried berets. She tried baseball caps worn frontward and backward. While all these things were workable, if not beautiful, adequate to run errands and wash the floors, they simply would not do when she made her slow triumphant walk down the center aisle to the front of the women's section to the seat marked with a brass plaque: RESERVED FOR THE RABBI'S WIFE.

Hats, at least the kind worn by the women in her congregation, cost a fortune. And clothes like theirs an even bigger fortune. But what could she do? Living among the very wealthy, being invited to another Bar and Bat Mitzva or wedding almost every month, she needed something respectable and festive to wear. And since everyone she knew in the community came to these affairs, she couldn't very well wear the same outfit each time, now, could she? Besides, it would wear out eventually, unless it was made of iron. Couple that with the constant gifts that she and Chaim had to come up with, the extra quantity and quality of food she had to buy for the unending stream of guests, the high heat and electric bills for the large house, not to mention the babysitters needed when she had to accompany her husband to unveilings, evening events, shiva calls, and many other duties that necessitated leaving little Abraham behind, and they were effectively broke most of the time.

She considered going back to work, but when you took child care into account it wouldn't have left her that much. And somehow the business of being the rabbi's wife, while unpaid, was slowly encroaching on more and more of her time.

She once sat down and calculated where her week went. The weekends of course were shot. Not just Saturday, but all day Friday and much of Wednesday and Thursday had to be spent shopping for food and cleaning up the house and cooking for a steady stream of weekend guests who came expecting to be served three opulent sit-down dinners, beginning Friday night and ending late Saturday night when they all cleared out.

And even shopping for food was not a simple thing if you were a rabbi's wife. There was that time, after a sleepless night with a colicky baby, she'd rolled out of bed and shlepped to the supermarket, only to be hailed from across the aisles by a "Yoo-hoo! Hello, Rebbitzin! My goodness, you look awful! Have you been showering?" Or the time she was accosted in the frozen food section by a woman who stared into her shopping cart, examining each item's *hechsher* to see if it was kosher enough. "I'm surprised you are buying things marked with a star-K instead of an OU, not to mention the half circle-K." She sniffed, scandalized. "My husband says the rabbis supervising aren't reliable. He won't touch a crumb, not a crumb, if it's not stamped with an OU. Do your guests know what they're eating?" Or the time she was a second away from her turn on the checkout line when a shul member grabbed her by the shoulders and insisted on regaling her with an half-hour's worth of disgustingly graphic medical details, hinting broadly that she needed someone to drive her to her appointments and hold her hand during treatments. Or the stranger in a polyester jogging suit wearing a large cross, who—seeing her head covering—barred her from picking up nail polish remover, insisting on knowing if she was Jewish and, if so, why she didn't believe in Jesus.

Sundays were spent going to unveilings or funerals or condolence calls. Mondays were when the week began again with obligations and other synagogue-related work that she had never had to worry about in the Bronx among the aged.

For example, women started showing up at her doorstep, demanding her attention and wordlessly handing her white unmarked envelopes. The first time it happened, Delilah opened the envelope, thinking it might be a donation to the synagogue, but all she found was a bit of stained white cloth. Slowly, it dawned on her where this material had been and where the stain had come from.

She confronted Chaim, fuming. "Read my lips. No-way-José am I going to examine some woman's vaginal fluids and tell her if she can or can't have sex with her husband. I am not touching these disgusting things. Tell them to leave me alone!"

"Listen, Delilah," Chaim had answerered reasonably, "most rabbis' wives are happy to do it. It's a woman's thing. And women feel more comfortable talking to another woman. But if you can't, you can't. Just give them to me."

She was only too happy to do so. But she was still stuck with being the go-between, giving them back to the women, telling them the results, and explaining the consequences. In the worst case, it could mean another two weeks of sexual abstinence and dealing with a frustrated husband—girl, you don't want to know . . . While Delilah sympathized, no way was she interested in becoming privy to whether or not each one of them would or would not be having sex with their husbands, thus becoming a living repository of the entire community's sex life. Nor did she particularly want the entire community to keep tabs on hers.

This was not as easy as it sounds in a community with only one *mikva*. Although efforts were made to hide the entrance to the ritual bath from the street, still, once inside, everyone she met there knew exactly when she'd be having sex with her husband, the rabbi. In addition to that, they had the opportunity to inspect how short her nails were (the very pious cut them to the quick on *mikva* night, making long nails and manicures impossible) and how she looked without her hair and absolutely no makeup of any kind.

Moreover, the "*mikva* lady," that stalwart institution of religious life, chosen from the ranks of the needy and overly pious but not overly bright, made privy to information of the most personal nature, could not always be relied upon to be discreet. "Hello, Mrs. Goldberg, I haven't seen you in months," said at full volume in the supermarket, for example, announced a pregnancy to the community like an engraved invitation to participate in the most intimate details of someone's private life.

Then, of course, there was the monthly sisterhood meeting. During the intensive Metzenbaum era, it had been moved from the synagogue to the rabbi's house, because Shira Metzenbaum didn't have enough to do, and now no one saw fit to move it back. And it was not just a meeting, she was led to understand; it was an event.

The food that she had to prepare had to be as imaginative as the way she served it. Each meeting had to have a "theme," to help keep the women interested in coming back, she was advised. Last month it had been a Ladies Who Lunch theme, with flower-filled shopping bags from Nordstrom's and Lord & Taylor, and wigs and hats on Styrofoam heads, elaborately decorated to look like some of the synagogue members. She'd prepared white carrot and sweet potato soup, persimmon tuna salad, and little chocolates she had to make in special plastic molds that turned out dreidels and menorahs and other symbols of the season. Often, Delilah cursed her hyper Martha-Stewart-in-a-wig-on-uppers predecessor, feeling *schadenfreude* for the woman's present life in Canarsie.

It wasn't just the preparations that were driving her crazy. During one sisterhood meeting, she'd found two women in her bathroom discussing the hair dye and prescription medication they'd found in her medicine cabinet. At another, a woman she hardly knew told her that her baby was looking "much better" than when he was born, when he'd been "like the puppy in the litter you throw away." After another, she'd found a silver cake server missing, and then a whole Wedgwood plate. And then there was the woman who had asked all kinds of personal questions about Chaim, finally admitting that her first rabbi had been touchy-feely Moishe from New Jersey, who had had his wife killed by a hit man, and her second, a rabbi in Florida, who had been arrested as a pedophile, so she was just trying to make sure it wasn't her fault the third time around.

And in between, day and night, there were the phone calls—*brring, brrring, brrrring!*—day in and day out. The woman who called them at 1 A.M. to complain that her little Lenny had been traumatized by getting a doughnut with pink icing at the *Oneg Shabbat* party. The man who was incensed that the Lion of Judah giving category in the latest United Jewish fund-raising campaign was between twenty and forty thousand dollars, leaving "those who are just as pious but not as rich" out in the embarrassing cold. Could the rabbi deal with that? Can you give the rabbi a message? Can you remind him? Can you talk to him about it? Could you possibly mention that in his last sermon he spoke too long, too short, about a topic we don't care about, do care about, but not to that extent, in that way? Can he talk about twelve-year-old girls getting nose jobs in time for their Bat Mitzvas? Can he talk less about Israel; more about Israel? Can he stop supporting the right-wing fanatics, who won't compromise, and who will get the Jewish people wiped off the planet? Can he stop supporting left-wing fanatics, Israeli peace nuts, who are giving in to our enemies and are going to get us wiped off the planet? Can he stop putting so much pressure on our young people, who are going to wind up with black hats and beards, unemployed and with ten kids? Can he put more pressure on our young people, who are going to be drug addicts and get lost in rave parties in India?

Blah, blah, blah, like she actually had nothing better to do than to consult with Chaim on his boring sermons.

And then there were the phone calls that were actually for her. A cousin of a synagogue member, a very nice thirty-two-year-old girl with a good job as an editor at a big New York publishing firm, was looking for a very attractive lawyer or doctor who was also Orthodox but open-minded. Would she know of somebody suitable? Could she set it up?

Gee, honey, if I knew anybody suitable who matched that description, why would I give him to you? I'd take him myself, she thought. "Not right now, but let me write down the information," she'd answer sweetly, making no effort to get a pencil. Why bother? Go find a modern Orthodox man in his thirties who wasn't holding out for a girl who would think as highly of him as his mother, looked like Kate Winslet, was as saintly as the matriarch Sarah, and had the domestic skills of Martha Stewart. Listen, she wanted to shout at these men, the girls are all five-foot-two dark-haired teachers or social workers who will never cook you a kreplach or kiss your feet the way your mother did. Get over it!

And then there were the men who couldn't wait to get married, who would marry anyone: the divorced men. The stingy, over- or undersexed grouches with bad tempers, body odors, and hanging bellies full of brisket and donuts who had already made one woman miserable but were anxious to make it two. They too were on the phone, seeking her help.

Even the mothers and fathers of college students, who should, for Pete's sake, have been able to fend for themselves, were calling her, demanding she find suitable matches for their offspring so they wouldn't bring home a *sheygets* or a shiksa from their ivy-covered campuses, along with their 3.9 grade-point averages and wildly expensive degrees. Some of these callers were super-religious, people who insisted on knowing the color of the girl's mother's Sabbath tablecloth. Was it white—acceptable, conservative—or any other color? And did the family have two or three sit-down meals on the Sabbath? (The third meal—which no one could possibly fit into an average stomach—being considered a sign of extra piety.) And was the boy actually going to use his law, accounting, or computer degree or put it aside and let his wife support him forever while he twiddled his thumbs and spoke on his cell phone from Talmudic study halls?

And then there were those people who saw her as the representative of the entire Jewish religion, people who would read the newspaper and then call her up to ask indignantly how a rabbi could run off with a former Russian Orthodox nun who had once been a flamenco dancer, shack up with her in a Miami condo, and leave his wife and congregation behind? "He said it was because his wife sometimes ate shrimp, but I'm not buying it!" they'd shout.

And all this, mind you, she was supposed to deal with on top of her newborn.

The baby. Little Abe.

That was a whole other story in itself. She looked down at the infant in her arms, sucking away like a leech. It had taken Delilah only several weeks to realize that, among her many interests and talents, mothering was not among them. She was as surprised to learn this as the next one.

Like most of us, she had always assumed that the ability to mother was a raw, animal instinct, hormonally supplied by the same chemicals and brain synapses that came along with the birth of a child. The truth was that the insistent, desperate cry of a newborn, added to the insistent, desperate cries of members of her congregation, was just about driving her over the edge.

"He hates me!" she yelled at Chaim, bursting into his study when he was putting the final touches on his weekly sermon on how husbands should be compassionate and unselfishness and helpful. "Just look at his eyes. Look!"

"Delilah, I can't concentrate with all that crying. Could you possibly take him outside for a while?" he'd say, not looking up until she shoved the baby into his arms and disappeared.

After these outbursts, she'd be overcome with guilt. She'd sit in her bedroom, listening to her albums and weeping until she had no more tears left. Then she'd go into the bathroom, wipe her eyes, and examine the sad state of her skin and the tire around her middle that simply refused to vanish. She'd return to Chaim, retrieve her son, and cuddle him tenderly in her arms, crooning lullabies and whispering to him.

She would never, ever, she told herself, do anything that would remotely harm the baby. Why, just the idea that a single hair on his little head might be pulled filled her with horror and pity. In fact, every time the child went to sleep, she remembered that she was deeply in love with him. She'd sit for hours, examining him, every minute detail. But she had to admit, he disappointed her. He had his grandfather's little eyes, which seemed to stare at her accusingly, her mother's big nose, her mother-in-law's thin dissatisfied lips, and her husband's dark hair. She would have preferred a girl with a beautiful little face, big blue eyes, and darling blond curls. A little doll she could buy adorable baby J-Lo dresses for with matching hair bows.

But she took some pride in having created a son. Little Abraham was a credit to her. She had produced him, after all, when she could just as easily have produced a girl as first-born. Orthodox Jews, no matter their well-concealed disappointment and shocked denials, were no different than the members of most other religions and cultures on this point. Let's face it, girls are not considered much to celebrate. There's no ceremony. No gathering of rabbis and friends to welcome her into the tribe. And even though politically correct modern Orthodoxy has been embarrassed into sanctioning the *mesibat bat*, or girl party, and the Bat Mitzva, everyone is in on the fact that it is just a pale-flaccid little consolation prize.

He was her pride and joy, she reminded herself. If only he wasn't so much work. If only she had more time. . . .

"Normal people look forward to weekends! What do I get on weekends? I get to be inspected, to serve armies of house guests, to visit cemeteries. I'm a prisoner here. Getting away for the weekend, or for holidays, is always impossible!"

Chaim, used to Delilah's tantrums, had learned to tune them out.

However, later that evening, after she'd said goodbye to the last of the sisterhood members and loaded the dishwasher and vacuumed the carpet, she leaned against the doorpost of his office and said, very calmly, "Did you know that Andrea Yates was class valedictorian? Captain of the swim team? In the National Honor Society? A nurse in the cancer ward?"

He'd stared at her in horror. Then he picked up the phone and made immediate arrangements for a private meeting with Arthur Malin.

Soon after, the synagogue board voted to provide the rabbi and his wife with some weekly hours of child care and housekeeping and to give Delilah a free yearly membership in the Swallow Lake Country Club.

As with many kind gestures, this move also proved the wisdom of the saying that no good deed ever goes unpunished.

{ TWENTY }

Delilah Levi walked through the doors of the Swallow Lake Country Club with the exact opposite feeling with which she walked through the doors of Ohel Aaron: the delicious sensation of being invisible, instead of a walking poster for Virtue of the Week. With her brand-new skin-hugging Lycra shorts and tank top, her brand-new New Balance cross trainers, and a headband that made her look like a Jane Fonda video backup girl, she joined the aerobics classes, letting herself go, shimmying and grapevining across the floor as she admired herself in the mirror-lined room. She loved the way she looked, her blond hair loose or up in a ponytail, her figure rapidly going back to its prepregnancy youthfulness, the stomach and waist melting away. There, among other women her age who didn't know who she was, she felt released from the burdens of her fishbowl existence.

It was a great revelation to learn that she was as lonely in the Swallow Lake congregation as she had been in the Bronx. Here too, the movers and shakers on the board were grandmothers. As for befriending the younger women, it was complicated. She wasn't their equal. She was supposed to be their superior, or at least to maintain that myth. A synagogue hired a rabbinical family to put on a pedestal, to be looked up to and imitated. To breach the distance, to become chummy, exposing the reality behind the perfect picture, could jeopardize that illusion and, she worried, her family's position in the community.

While she couldn't avoid every single woman in her congregation, she quickly learned to steer clear of the country club in the very early hours when Mariette came in; and the one afternoon a week Solange used it. Felice, who had a private trainer and a home gym, never showed up, nor did Amber, who wasn't into exercise.

Relaxed and temporarily unburdened of the plethora of rabbinical prohibitions concerning her body, dress, voice, and flesh, which only had force when men were around to stare and listen, she left her anxieties behind in the bubbles of the Jacuzzi and the pool of sweat in the sauna. Soon she was striking up conversations with strangers her age, gossiping about clothes and movie stars and men, sending caution to the wind in her hunger for companionship, telling herself it was good enough if they didn't look too familiar.

One woman in particular caught her attention. She was about the same height and body build as herself, a sexy blonde she had never seen before. Her hair had been colored by a genius; it was the most delicate shade of ash blond with marvelous natural highlights. Her body was tight, like a dancer's, and as voluptuous as Pamela Anderson's. There had no doubt been a boob job. Nobody with the possible exception of Barbie had boobs that big and hips that slim. And the nose? That too had been surgically snipped to shiksa perfection. And boy, was this woman in shape! When the rest of the class was groaning from the stomach crunches, she was still crunching away even more effortlessly than the instructor. Delilah often followed her around the gym like a groupie. One day, she managed to meet her at the lockers.

"You are in such wonderful condition. What's your secret?"

The woman threw her exercise bag over her shoulder, turned, and looked at Delilah curiously, her eyes flicking up and down, leaving no part unregistered. "You are?"

Delilah wiped her sweaty hand on her tank top and held it out. "Delilah. Delilah Levi."

The woman smiled and shrugged, declining to take it. "I've got a thing about germs. Nothing personal. Joie Shammanov."

A bell, low and resonant, clanged in Delilah's head.

Shammanov.

For months she had been hearing about the fabulously wealthy Russian businessman who had bought the biggest estate in Swallow Lake and had been building on it ever since. Shammanov, it was said, would be in court for a hundred years battling the county's municipal authorities for having broken every single zoning law to build what was rumored to be Xanadu on uppers. But no one knew for sure because, to the chagrin of Swallow Lake's leading citizens, who were dying of curiosity, no one had been invited to the house, despite numerous overtures. The Shammanovs were Jewish but had no intention of becoming part of the community, spokespeople who answered the phone said firmly.

Like his estate, Shammanov himself was also shrouded in mystery. Although he had been featured on the cover of *Fortune* magazine, the article had revealed very little, calling him secretive, a shunner of limelight. According to *Fortune*, his wealth had come from his near monopoly on shares of the privatized oil fields in his native Turdistan, following the fall of the Soviet Union. He was said to own banks, real estate, airlines, hotel chains, and innumerable corporations. His wealth, Amber had whispered, was equal to the gross national product of certain small countries.

Delilah whistled in nervousness. "Wow, interesting name!"

"So is yours."

"Please, let's not get into it. It's been a pain my whole life. It was my grandmother's name and my father insisted—"

"Parents." Joie pursed her lips in disgust. "I really sympathize. I've got the same kind. Never happy unless they are making you miserable."

Delilah, who wasn't prepared to go that far, decided nevertheless not to blow this bonding opportunity. "I guess we just have to live our lives and put up with them," she agreed. "Love what you've done with your abs. You've got such . . . definition."

"Really?" Joie looked at her arms, pleased. "You think? You also look great. I envy those stomach muscles."

Coming from the crunch queen, that was high praise indeed. "Oh, thanks!" Delilah gushed, thrilled. "I just had a baby, and I'm dying to get rid of these extra pounds. They are so stuck on."

Joie stared at her. "Oh, I also just had a baby! I thought I'd never lose them."

"You look fantastic!"

"Thanks. I have to get ready for my son's Bar Mitzvah."

"You have a son who's thirteen years old? You look like twenty yourself." Delilah said, truly amazed and not a little envious.

The woman turned to her, put down her bag, and smiled. "Oh, he's not mine. He's my husband's, from his first marriage. You are so nice! Not like most of the snobs I've met here. They are so full of themselves. And most of them go to that synagogue with the men on one side and the women on the other. I never saw such a thing."

Delilah shifted uncomfortably. "Actually, it's not so bad."

The woman's face dropped. "Oh. Do you go there too?"

Delilah nodded. "I'm the rabbi's wife."

Joie slapped her forehead. "Oh, so sorry! I'm just such a blabbermouth. My husband always tells me. He's Russian and very outgoing, and I'm always saying the wrong thing, screwing up his multibillion-dollar deals left and right." She held out her hand. "Please, forgive me?"

Delilah took it gratefully. "There's nothing to forgive. Believe me, I know it seems weird to outsiders: the separate seating, the hair covering, the no phones, no cars, no cooking on the Sabbath."

"It's not weird, it's just that I'm so ignorant and prejudiced. I think you have to grow up in a family that has respect for religion, for traditions. And I didn't. My parents weren't at all respectful. And I think I lost out a lot because of it."

"Well, it's never too late to learn." Delilah couldn't believe she heard herself say this, in perfect imitation of a rebbitzin on the make for lost souls. "Oh, no, forget I said that!"

"Why?"

"Because this is the one place on the planet where I don't have to do this."

"Do what?"

"Convert people to the true faith. I can just forget I'm hemmed in by all these weirdo rules, by all these rabbis, and just wiggle and crunch and grapevine and boogie. I know I could put on a tape and do it in my bedroom, but I find if I have people to compete with, it keeps me going. It gets so lonely, you know, with a new baby, and my husband is never around."

The woman's face softened. "I know exactly what you mean." She hesitated. "Look, I was just heading home. If you've got a few minutes, why don't you come over to the house for a cup of coffee? I've also got this home movie theater, and we just got a preview copy of this year's Oscar nominees. . . ."

The idea of making a friend of the elusive Joie Shammanov, who incidentally had a home movie theater and movies not yet available even in DVD and whose husband was making multibillion-dollar deals, intrigued Delilah. Besides, she was always happy to inspect and then eat her heart out over the glories of yet one more Swallow Lake estate.

A blue Bentley was waiting at the entrance for Joie Shammanov. A chauffeur got out and opened the door for her. Delilah followed behind in her beat-up Ford.

When Delilah Levi drove past the polished bronze gates, under beautiful scrollwork that spelled out USPEKHOV, she began to feel a little like Dorothy at the end of the yellow brick road. Rising to her right on a low hill stood a breathtaking Romanesque-style castle straight out of Fantasyland in Orlando, Florida. To her surprise, the Bentley drove right past it, turning off and continuing down the road toward the lake.

She couldn't believe her eyes when the car pulled up to a huge lakefront mansion.

"Joie, what does *Uspekhov* mean?"

"It means success." She smiled.

They'd built a brand-new second house on the property. Talk about excess. It was mind-boggling. But she reminded herself not to go around saying *omigod* and to make believe she saw this kind of thing all the time, so as not to put off her new friend with any hick behavior.

She needn't have worried. As it turned out, Joie was only too happy to discuss her wealth. Over lattes served on a deck overlooking the lake and an infinity pool, Delilah learned that the Shammanovs' purchase of forty acres of lakefront property had included a 7,500-square-foot French château that neither of them really liked. But instead of tearing it down and rebuilding, they'd decided to simply put up a second house, nearer the lake. They had been building for over a year, but the place still wasn't quite finished, although Joie was happy to report that the 45,000-square-foot home was already estimated to be worth well over $90 million. They had a screening room, a Japanese garden with 500 rare species of trees flown in from Japan, office facilities, a gym, and a library. The living room alone was over 3,000 square feet, with an adjoining reception hall large enough to seat 150 people for dinner or hold 200 people for a cocktail party. There was a 70-foot pool with an underwater sound system, as well as a trampoline room, an Art Deco theater, and goodness knows what else. Joie said even she didn't really know.

"This is my husband's thing. He loves to build. He's never going to finish this house. Every time I think we're almost done, he finds something he doesn't like, or he gets a better idea and tears everything out and starts over. We ordered Brazilian rosewood for the library? After it was all built, he decides it's too dark, so he throws the whole thing out and orders a different wood. And the tiles in the kitchen, handmade in Mexico? He saw something similar somewhere, which made him mad, so he had them all taken out and ordered tiles from this tiny factory in Portugal." She laughed, her eyes grim. "So many of them broke on the way over, he had to order them fifteen times before he had enough."

After coffee and a few delectable scones, Delilah said delicately, "Love to see this place sometime."

"Would you? Oh, sure. If you've got time, come now."

Oh, the marble floors! she thought in rapture. What had they done to get rid of those pesky grouted lines? How did they get it to shine seamlessly, like glass? And how did they get those designs, the red and cream and white marble laid out in an intricate pattern like some handwoven rug? And how did they get the walls to look like some Chinese lacquer box? And where did they find those chandeliers, and that furniture, all oversized like a scene out of some forties Hollywood movie? It was extremely costly and yet, overwhelmed as she was, even Delilah recognized everything was a just a tiny bit off. A little too much, a little bit old-fashioned. A little bit Arab or Eastern European in its decadence, where huge sums had been poured into projects that, instead of showing off the owners' impeccable good taste, did quite the opposite. It was like those sultans known as boobs of the rain forest, who give solid gold watches custom-made to hold tacky nude photos and then throw in CDs, some cheesecake, shortbread cookies, and a candle. The Queer Eyed folk would have wrung their hands.

Nevertheless, the sheer enormity of the place, and its mind-boggling expense, rolled over Delilah like a large vehicle going full speed. It was simply on a scale too grand to envy, the way no one actually envies Queen Elizabeth her Buckingham Palace. It wasn't a place anyone could actually aspire to own or even if they did, would really want to live in, the way no one would actually want to live in Grand Central Station, even if it could be remodeled as a private residence. Unlike the homes of the Malins, the Grodins, the Rollands, and the Borenbergs, fabulous estates that one nevertheless felt were possible to get your greedy little hands around—given the right luck—this house was quite a different story. It was a place only a person with unheard-of appetites and a truly fabulous imagination, matched by an equally bottomless pot of money, could have envisioned, let alone build.

"It's like the castle in that old black-and-white movie," Joie said.

Delilah looked at her blankly.

"*Citizen Kane.*"

"Oh, of course." She smiled. Who in heaven's name watched black-and-white movies? She resolved to take it out of the video library next chance she got. Hopefully, Ted Turner had gotten around to colorizing it.

"Want to see the baby?" her hostess said suddenly, apparently bored with the tour.

Delilah, who would have much preferred to continue opening doors and prowling hallways, nodded. They took an elevator lined in mirrors and marble up a few flights.

The nursery was done up exquisitely in pastel nursery-rhyme themes. An enormous pink dollhouse you could actually walk into was filled with stuffed animals and lovely dolls. There were rocking chairs and window seats and soft carpeting that matched the walls and curtains. In the center of this fairyland sat an old woman with enormous breasts holding an infant swathed in clothing more suitable for a little Eskimo in an igloo than for a child in a heated nursery. The baby was cute: blond, with large blue eyes. She was about six months old. She looked up at her mother in wonder.

"Here she is, my little Natasha," Joie said, smiling at the baby, her arms outstretched. The woman, unsmiling, grasped the child closer.

"Let me have her, Yelena," Joie demanded.

There was a volcanic storm of Russian, whirling up a notch in belligerence with each passing moment. The old woman shook her head and then her fist, shooing them both away.

Joie turned on her heel and walked out, slamming the door behind her.

"Gee, you're a saint! If *my* babysitter pulled that, I'd fire her on the spot."

Joie looked up. "That," she said slowly, "is my mother-in-law."

"Oops. Sorry."

"Don't be. I wish I could fire her. She makes my life a living hell."

"You know, Joie," Delilah said thoughtfully, "the Jewish religion is very clear about a man leaving his father and mother and clinging to his wife. There is actually a phrase in the Bible that says exactly that. And our rabbis teach us that a man mustn't let his mother get between him and his wife. His wife comes first."

Joie looked at her, transfixed. "A verse? In the Bible? Really?"

Delilah nodded. "I could show it to you."

"That would be fantastic. Viktor had a very religious Jewish grandfather. He was a rabbi, Viktor says. Viktor has a lot of respect for religion—but you know, brought up in the Soviet Union, he had no one to teach him. His father was an atheist. But Viktor loved the old man, who died when he was just a little kid. He talks about him all the time."

"You know, my husband would be really happy to learn with your husband."

"Learn?"

"Oh, that's just the way we Orthodox Jews put it, when we talk about religious instruction. It's considered a joint effort. Teacher and student learn together."

"Really? You think your husband would be willing to teach Viktor that verse in the Bible, about the clinging and about the mothers-in-law?"

"Joie, I don't think it, I know it. My husband has a heart of gold. He's always telling me we should be encouraging more people to join our synagogue."

"Well, if your husband can get my husband to part with his mother, I would be grateful to you for the rest of my life."

That was the moment when Delilah Levi and Joie Shammanov became instant best friends.

A week later, Chaim began learning with Viktor Shammanov. And two weeks after that, the elderly Mrs. Shammanov found herself with a one-way ticket on a plane to Miami.

{ TWENTY-ONE }

Great unhappiness can only come about when one has known great happiness. This is the irony that people refuse to understand when the wheel of Fate turns and gives them their heart's desire. The cocktail waitress who bets a few dollars in Vegas and winds up with the jackpot. The nebbish who asks the girl of his dreams to marry him and gets a yes. The plain girl with the glasses who lands the captain of the basketball team (a common occurence, by the way; just look around you). All these people, God bless them, are primed for the worst of disasters, while the rest of us—who shlep along with average luck and average successes and failures—are immune.

That is not to say one should not rejoice in one's good fortune. As Henry James taught us in the most frightening of horror stories ever written, "The Beast in the Jungle," the anticipation of disaster can, in itself, become the disaster. To paraphrase King Solomon in Ecclesiastes, rejoice in your good times, because time and chance happen to all.

This was Delilah's good time, the best time in her life. There were picnics and pool parties at the Shammanovs. There were shopping trips to New York and stays in private hotel suites. There were manicures and pedicures and private masseuses who came to the Swallow Lake mansion and were just as happy to do two women as one. There were daily outings and private confessions. The good times were limited only by Delilah's child-care arrangements; Joie had no such restrictions. Once she packed her mother-in-law off to Florida, she hired a daytime au pair and a nighttime au pair and even an au pair for her dog. "He is very jealous of the baby as it is. We don't want to make it worse."

Far from judging her friend or even envying her, Delilah rejoiced in her good fortune. While she knew that the average person would have been appalled at the meager amount of time Joie spent with her daughter, Delilah tended to agree with Joie that the time she did spend with Natasha—usually when the child was fresh from being bathed and diapered and fed—was "quality" time.

Delilah wondered what it would be like to foist her son off on somebody else whenever he was dirty and hungry and cranky, and to get him back clean, fed, and smiling. Why, they would only see each other at their best! And while she knew there were those who would condemn her for being a bad mother, she wondered if in the best of all possible worlds all children wouldn't be better off bonding with their parents under such ideal circumstances. Imagine a world full of adults who had only known smiling, relaxed mothers! Why, they could close down the UN—that humongous waste of time and money whose only useful function, as far as she could tell, was to provide freedom from parking tickets and assorted felonies to Third World bureaucrats. And they could forget about nuclear nonproliferation treaties, because why would calm, smiling, satisfied adults want to build bombs to murder other calm, smiling, satisfied adults and their perfect offspring?

Every woman, Delilah, thought, should have a Joie Shammanov. She never ceased to rejoice over this unexpected relationship. She had a best friend. A shopping partner. Someone who made her feel smart and good and didn't judge her.

Joie, for her part, seemed very happy to have Delilah's constant companionship. Her marriage to a Russian Jew and her relocation to the very Jewish Swallow Lake had left her like a fish out of water.

Because the fact was that Joie Shammanov, until very very recently, wasn't Jewish.

Born Jill O'Donnell in Lodi, New Jersey, to a housewife and a construction worker with a bit of a drinking problem, she ran away from home when she reached sixteen. It wasn't a horror story. She wasn't abused; she didn't have a drug problem or an unwanted pregnancy; she was simply bored. The life of a New Jersey teenager—stupid parties, backseat romantics, cramming for exams, worry about SAT scores—just weren't enough for her.

She wound up working in a clothing store in Manhattan, living with the owner and two other girls whom he put up in his Manhattan apartment. He took turns with each of them, which was fine with Jill, because it was better than putting up with the owner all by herself and it was a very nice apartment after all.

When she was eighteen, she moved out and decided to try her hand at modeling. But she wasn't tall enough and, truth be told, wasn't pretty enough, given the raving beauties from all over the world who were her competition in New York City. Her nose was a bit thick and her eyes rather narrow. But she had a beautiful figure and stunning hair, so every once in a while the agency found her work as a hair or figure model, where they needed just parts of her instead of the whole thing.

It wasn't enough to live on, so she moonlighted in a bar in one of the downtown hotels. And it was there, one night, that she happened to serve a bunch of Russians. They were all overweight and absolutely interchangeable. But when the evening was over, one of them handed her a $500 tip and his card.

"Call me," he said.

She didn't, having no interest in expanding her already sizable knowledge of heavy drinkers. The next night, he showed up again, this time alone. He sat in a corner, nursing one drink until closing time. He then gave her a $1,000 tip and another card.

Still, she didn't do anything. He was too muscular, she thought. Too foreign. Too old. He came in every single night, and each night he upped his tip. After a week, when she still hadn't called, he disappeared.

She took the money and went on the mother of all spending sprees. She paid off her credit card debts. Then she bought a coat at Bendel's for $2,000. A pair of boots for $1,500. She had her hair and nails done and used some to have her teeth whitened.

By the end of the second week, she was broke again.

The following month, a car pulled up to the bar and a chauffeur came in with a box with her name on it. He left it with her boss, who called her into the back. It was Russian sable. Stunned, she slipped it on, sliding her hand down the heavenly softness, into the silk-lined pockets. Inside was a velvet box holding a diamond and emerald bracelet. There was also a note that said he would pick her up after work.

She didn't wait until after work. She grabbed her purse and walked out of the bar and never looked back. She went straight to her apartment and packed a suitcase with all her new things, then went straight to the Greyhound station, and bought a ticket on a bus to San Diego that was leaving in three hours.

After the first hour, she got hungry, so she bought herself a hamburger. As a blonde in a sable eating a hamburger at a Greyhound bus station, she attracted quite a bit of attention, which she rather enjoyed. She finished the food. She found a comfortable seat away from any weirdos and thought about San Diego: the beaches, Marine World, the year-round sunshine. And then she thought, I probably won't need a fur coat in San Diego. Which was just as well, because she'd probably need to sell it so she'd have money to rent an apartment. She didn't really have enough for more than a few days in a good hotel. And the more Jill O'Donnell thought about life on her own in San Diego, the more she thought about the man who had given her the coat and the bracelet and who seemed to have money coming out of his pores. She compared him in her imagination to other men, the kind she'd meet in San Diego; young, blond, and flat-stomached who spoke nonaccented English. They would all basically want the same thing from her, which she would or wouldn't want to give them to a lesser or greater degree. And none would be as generous.

She sat there, trying to remember what he looked like, trying to imagine what would happen when he came to pick her up and she wasn't there. First, she felt sad for him, imagining his disappointment. And then, suddenly, she felt frightened. She had, after all, walked off with tens of thousands of his dollars and had given him nothing in return. Then, suddenly, she looked up and saw them. The terminal was suddenly packed with them, like some scene from *Angels in America*, except instead of angels it was full of fat Russians who seemed to have appeared out of nowhere. Or maybe it was just her imagination. She began to sweat. She took off her coat and tucked her bracelet inside her sleeve. Then she picked up her suitcase and hailed a taxi back to the bar.

She stood outside, waiting for the car to show up. When it did, she got in.

TWENTY-TWO

"Delilah, the phone has been ringing off the hook. I have had at least twelve different people in the synagogue call me up, furious. You aren't returning phone calls! You aren't giving me their messages! You aren't taking their envelopes, or answering their questions, or discussing their matchmaking needs! They say you are rude. That you've stopped inviting people over, that you aren't going out into the community enough, making enough of an effort to attract new members to join the synagogue."

Delilah listened, her face impassive. When he was finished, she looked up calmly. "I'm really, really sorry to hear that, Chaim. I have some suggestions for them. Why don't you tell them all that they can just kiss my mezuzah!"

"Delilah!"

She leaned back indifferently, taking out a pack of cigarettes, lighting one up, and blowing large smoke rings toward the ceiling. She'd taken up smoking again. She was trying to imitate Joie, how she held a cigarette, the way she tilted her head back *just so,* exhaling with world-weary ennui.

Chaim's arms waved frantically, dispersing the smoke in all directions. "And what is this with the smoking already? If you don't care about yourself, think about me, about the baby, for goodness' sake. You're filling *our* lungs with tar and nicotine deposits too."

"So, I'll smoke outside."

"Please, Delilah. What's gotten into you? The shul has been so generous. They've paid for household help, a babysitter, and time off. Is this how you show your appreciation? Be fair!"

"Fair? You want *me* to be fair? Tell me this, Chaim, while we're talking about being fair. How fair is it that some women get husbands who buy them Harry Winston diamond bracelets and some get men who grit their teeth when they shell out fifty-nine ninety-nine for gold earrings at Macy's during the Presidents' Day sales? How fair is it that some wives have cooks and chauffeurs, and—oh, four or five maids, and some have to beg and be grateful for four hours of housecleaning a week, if that much? That some women get their hair colored in Frederic Fekkai, and some do it themselves over the bathroom sink?"

She threw back her head, took another deep puff, and exhaled, studying Chaim through the haze of smoke, watching as his body and face faded, becoming blurry and indistinct, like some screen saver disappearing from a computer screen. Who was this guy, she thought, surprised, this person she was tied to for the rest of her life, who didn't provide her with a single thing she really wanted?

"Delilah, what's gotten into you?" Chaim shouted, astonished.

She didn't want to be a rabbi's wife, she suddenly realized. She wanted to be the wife of a rich man who would spoil her, the way all the women in her congregation were spoiled. The way Joie Shammanov was spoiled. Why did she have to be the good one, the moral one, the kind one, the generous one, the hard worker, the woman of virtue? Had she ever pretended to have *any* of these qualities, ever valued them, or aspired toward them, like the goody-goodies in Cedar Heights, the ones with the calf-length skirts who stayed after school for extra brainwashing in *mussar* and how to improve your judgmental skills and guilt quotient? No, it was all just a big accident, a big celestial joke—and it was on her, she realized.

"They are complaining that you are spending all your time with Mrs. Shammanov—who isn't even a member of our congregation—doing who knows what: neglecting the congregation, not to mention your family. That you are acting like some airhead high school girl. It's got to stop!"

Finally, miraculously, she was having a little fun, enjoying the pleasures she would only get to have in this life vicariously if at all, and there was a conspiracy afoot to deprive her even of that! She stubbed out the cigarette viciously into the carpet. "Look, get this through your skullcap. Joie Shammanov is the best thing that has ever happened to me. Why should I give her up—give any of it up? So that you can keep on playing social worker, psychiatrist, and Catskills entertainer to a bunch of self-indulgent whining *machers* and their wives who treat us both like low-level employees? They may own you, but they don't own me."

Just then, the phone rang. Chaim picked it up.

"Hello, Solange, how are you? . . . Good, good. Yes, well *now* is really *not* a good . . . Of course, of course. I understand. She's right here. I'll put her on." Apprehensively, he handed Delilah the phone. *Please,* his eyes implored.

"Solange, Delilah here. . . . Well, let me just interrupt you, Solange, to tell you what *I* was thinking. I was thinking that the sisterhood meeting should really go back to being at the synagogue where it belongs. . . . Oh, you like it better in someone's house? Well, then, Solange, maybe you can have it at yours. And while you're at it, you can get your chef and five slaves to decide the menu and the theme, and cook it and serve it and clean up afterward. And then the sisterhood can check out *your* hair dye and steal *your* plates!" She slammed down the phone.

Chaim went white.

They didn't speak for three days. And then Chaim came home early. He brought a bottle of wine, some flowers, lit some candles, brought in take-out someone had picked up for him especially from the Broadway Deli in Manhattan: Delilah's favorite restaurant, he remembered. He arranged for a babysitter. "Come, let's have a quiet dinner and talk, Delilah," he coaxed her.

He sat down across from her. They ate in silence. "Delilah, I've straightened it out. I called Arthur Malin. He is such a mensch. And he knows Solange can be a bit of a character—"

"She's a *klafta.*"

He took a deep breath. "Now, now, don't be unkind, dear."

Chaim groveled. He apologized. He explained. He was as nice and understanding as he could possibly be. He even apologized for not having thought himself of moving the sisterhood meetings back to the shul or somewhere else. He even, in the end, agreed, that Solange Malin was, and had always been, a *klafta*.

Delilah listened wordlessly, amazed. "Well, I have to say this for you: you're trying."

He certainly was. After an emergency call from Arthur, the two men had sat together and decided the best course to take. He was now taking it.

"I have an idea, my dear."

OK, she thought, putting down her pastrami on rye, which brought back some mixed memories. She swallowed and tapped her mouth with a napkin, all the better to open it good and wide if circumstances should so require.

"Maybe you could influence the Shammanovs to join our synagogue. The board would be thrilled. Everyone has been dying to meet them. And then, perhaps, if the Shammanovs became more active, in a little while I could ask for a raise, and all the other things. . . . We would be able to afford more household help, child care—"

"You want me to talk them into coming to our synagogue?!"

"Yes, why not? Didn't you tell me there is a boy who is almost Bar Mitzva age?"

"But they're not religious at all! She's a convert!"

"Think about it, Delilah. I know you've become her friend. Now, as her friend, wouldn't you be helping her by bringing her and her family closer to their roots, their heritage? The Jewish people are strengthened every time another family joins a synagogue and becomes part of the community. And of course, I admit it, this would be such a good thing for us—for the synagogue, of course—but not just that. Even rich people can be lonely. Why don't you invite them over for Friday-night dinner? We'll invite the board. You can even have it catered if it's too much for you to manage."

Somewhere inside she understood that all this was perfectly reasonable. But the truth was, she felt stingy about sharing her friend, about destroying the special relationship they shared. Most of all, she didn't want to introduce Joie Shammanov to Rebbitzin Levi; she wanted to keep the two worlds separate.

"Please, Delilah?"

She narrowed her eyes and looked at him squarely. "Chaim, I also have an idea. How would you feel about not being a rabbi?"

He looked at her blankly. "Not be a rabbi? What would I be then?"

"Well, you could be many things. A businessman, for example."

"I don't know anything about business."

"What's there to know? Do these people look like such geniuses to you? Listen to this business: You go to some clothing line, you know, some jeans manufacturer, Diesel."

"Diesel?"

"Or another one, whatever," she said irritably. Was it Joie or her mother who had told her all about this? Never mind, she told herself. Even Marilyn knew something some of the time. "It doesn't matter. And you buy the rights to the name. And then you get some cheap belts or watches from some factory in China, and get them to put Diesel on it, or any other name, and you sell it in all the big department stores. You just have to tell them how to make the watch or the belt look. And that's easy. I could do that myself."

"You want me to be a watchmaker?" He shrugged helplessly.

"You are totally missing the point! What I'm saying is that these business ideas are a dime a dozen. They are easy. You just have to understand how to do it. You need a friend in the business world to help you get started. I'm sure Mr. Shammanov—" She had never actually met the elusive husband of her friend, but Chaim didn't have to know that.

"But I don't want to be a businessman, Delilah, I want to be a rabbi. It's all I've ever wanted to be. I wouldn't be good at anything else." He cradled his head in his hands, his shoulders round with defeat. "Delilah, what do you want me to do?"

This simple question, asked in all innocence, which should have touched her heart and filled her with remorse and pity, alas, did just the opposite.

"*To do*? What do I want you *to do*? Well, I'll tell you. For starters, I want you to put up office hours and unlist our home phone. I want you to get a day off every two weeks so we can go somewhere together. I want you to arrange for more than a measly one-week vacation during the summer. I want you to demand they get a junior rabbi to take over the youth minyan and the Bar Mitzva program!"

He lifted his head and stared at her. "Are you deliberately trying to get me fired? Is that it? Because if you are, you'd better think about it. I took this job because you wanted me to. And when I did, I became a pariah. If I need another job, I've got the mark of Cain on my forehead. We'll wind up in some tiny community with no Jewish school and a twenty-member congregation that meets in our basement. You'll be baking all the cakes and making *cholent* for the entire congregation every Saturday. And everyone will have to stay with us until the Sabbath is over because it will be too cold and too far for them to walk home. Heck, they might sleep over Friday nights too, with their entire families."

She listened to him in horror, her heart skipping a beat. "No one is going to fire you. I mean"—she hesitated—"what makes you think that? You are doing well, aren't you? I mean, I haven't heard anything—"

"Delilah, you aren't listening. There is a whole group that wants to get rid of me. They never wanted me in the first place. Some say I'm not serious enough. Not enough of a scholar. Not bright enough. And the others are complaining I'm too serious. They are furious I closed down the kiddush Club, that custom they had of going out before the Torah reading and finishing off a few bottles of Scotch and then staggering back in."

"Why did you close it down?"

"Well, remember that Shabbes when I said 'How are you?' to Selwyn Goldbart and he said, 'F— you?' Whereupon I reminded him that the traditional greeting was Good Shabbes?"

She nodded.

"That's when I decided the drinking had to stop."

"I don't see why that means *I* have to do things differently."

"Because"—he paused ominously—"I'm not the only one they're complaining about."

There was silence, the information sinking in with a large thud.

"You mean to say—after all I've been doing—that they've still been . . . someone has been complaining . . . about me?"

"I kept defending you, but I can't anymore. You haven't offered to teach any classes for the women, your dresses are too short, and your wigs are too long. And you aren't setting a good example to the other wives and mothers because of all the time you are spending having fun. Be realistic. All they need is a good excuse, and you are giving it to them."

"So, after all I've put up with! And this is what they say about me?" A little plume of red smoke wafted in front of her eyes that wasn't coming from her cigarette. "Who, exactly, did you hear this from?"

He shook his head and shrugged.

She grabbed him by the shirtfront. "Tell me!"

"Well, the Grodins."

"Amber and Stuart? What's their problem?"

"You aren't taking an active enough role socially, to bring people together."

"So he can pick their brains and empty their pockets. Who else?"

"Mariette."

She was wounded. "Mariette?"

"Well, you never did follow through with the designer handbag thing—"

"I've been busy!"

"And Felice Borenberg mentioned something to her husband about your wardrobe being inappropriate for the rabbi's wife. And Solange said the same thing to Arthur."

"They're just jealous because I look so good," she said, with no small measure of truth. Nevertheless, she felt a stab of panic. The entire board was complaining about her! What would she do if they fired Chaim? If she had to leave Swallow Lake, just now, when everything was going so well? Where would they go?

She studied her perfect manicure.

Why, those little shits, she thought. Who did they think they were dealing with, *mikva*-pure Shira Metzenbaum? Maybe one day she and Chaim would walk off into the sunset into something far more lucrative and less intrusive. But no one was going to send them packing, not if she could help it.

She thought of the dinner party she would arrange and the phone call to Solange Malin she would have to make. She considered how she would introduce the board to Viktor and Joie, and how on a visit to their home she would give the women of Swallow Lake something to drool over that would fill their hearts with discontent and their minds with greedy visions of what was possible, if only their husbands could approach the wealth of the Shammanovs. They would never again be happy with their 3,000 square feet once they saw the Shammanov's 45,000 square feet, their acres of lakefront property, their Japanese gardens. If she never accomplished another thing, that was an experience she felt sure would do their souls good (she knew it would do *her* soul good). And if Joie and Viktor really did become active members of the synagogue, they would no doubt be invited to join the board, replacing some of the others. And then no one would dare to criticize her or even suggest firing Chaim.

And in the end, they would all agree that she, Delilah, was a wonderful rabbi's wife and that the congregation was lucky to have her and her special skills.

TWENTY-THREE

Solange was chilly but correct. And Joie Shammanov was unaccountably delighted and grateful to get the invitation. In fact, she seemed thrilled.

"Viktor has been after me to make some friends, to get us more involved socially. Who will be coming?"

Delilah described the board members, and Joie seemed extremely interested. "But I have to warn you, Joie, they are all twice our age."

"I don't think that matters, do you? Have you seen their homes? How do they dress? What cars do they drive?"

Delilah was only too happy to tell her everything she wanted to know. And in the end, Joie even offered to send over her own chef to help Delilah plan the menu and do the cooking.

"That would be fantastic!"

The chef was a fairly new French import. He had fabulous ideas. "What about ze Peking duck and ze green papaya salad in a rich ginger and cardamom sauce, and zen ze pan-roasted squab stuffed wiz truffle and soft polenta, wiz per'aps an Armagnac-scented *jus*. Charlotte *aux fruits de saison* profiteroles *au chocolat*?"

She discussed it with Chaim.

"I don't know, Delilah. Is this guy Jewish? Does he know anything about preparing a kosher dinner?"

"What difference does that make? We'll buy all the ingredients. He'll use our utensils. I'll be in the kitchen to supervise him. What in this menu sounds problematic?"

"No, nothing—well, truffles."

"I thought they were like mushrooms?"

"They are not *like* mushrooms. They *are* mushrooms. But it's an interesting halachic problem. What blessing do you say over them? The Talmud in Berachos 40b states that even though mushrooms grow on the ground, they don't get their nourishment from the soil. But the *Aruch Hashulchan*, among others, hold that if one made a mistake and recited the blessing over vegetables on mushrooms, it's nevertheless acceptable—"

She rolled her eyes. "Chaim?"

"Oh, yes, what were we talking about?"

"So they are kosher, right? You can eat them?"

"Yes, of course."

"And Joie's chef can do the cooking?"

"Delilah, I'm really *not* comfortable about a non-Jew doing the cooking. I'm sure he wouldn't do anything deliberately, but there is always something he might not understand."

She stood still and lowered her head. "Well, if you really think so."

Chaim, who had expected a huge argument, was taken aback. She was, after all, doing this for him, and it was going to be an enormous amount of work. Why shouldn't he try to make things easier for her? "Look, I don't want to take a stringent view for no reason. As the great Reb Yechiel Halevi Epstein used to say, 'To say *forbidden, forbidden, forbidden* doesn't take a great scholar. But it takes talent, wisdom, and understanding to take a lenient view and say *permitted.*' I suppose it would be all right. Do you promise to supervise him carefully and not let him bring in any food or utensils?"

"I promise! Thanks so much!" She hugged him.

"And please, Delilah. Don't make yourself crazy. The people who don't like us now, won't like us even after they've eaten a wonderful dinner," he said with a shrug.

She bought all the ingredients, which cost a fortune. She hired a serving girl to help her for the evening, and even rented a uniform for her. She bought a lovely toile tablecloth and matching napkins and had a professional service draw up place cards using hand calligraphy. Joie's florist sent over the flower arrangements, and the whole house smelled of lavender and roses and lilacs and peonies. Joie's dressmaker made Delilah a fantastic wraparound dress the color of her eyes, copied from the latest styles seen on the runways in Milan and Paris, from which Joie had recently returned with the real thing.

"Are they here already?" Stuart Grodin asked, his eyes staking out the territory, while Delilah and Amber kissed the air outside each other's ears.

"Who?" Delilah asked innocently.

"Why, the Shammanovs," Stuart said, rubbing his hands together, like a baseball player getting ready to hold the bat and hit the ball out of the park. "I understand you know them well, Delilah?"

She smiled mysteriously. "Yes, we've become dear friends."

"What are they like? What's the house like?" Amber pressed her.

Delilah smiled, ignoring the question. "Would you excuse me, Amber? I need to be in the kitchen."

The chef was working his magic. Everything smelled wonderful, and he seemed to be managing just fine. "Go, go." He shooed her out the door.

She heard the door opening and closing, Chaim greeting more guests.

It was the Malins, the Rollands, and the Borenbergs. Mariette came around and kissed her. She had a tall handsome stranger with her, who turned out to be the elusive Dr. Rolland.

He had thick, salt-and-pepper hair, perfectly and recently cut, an aquiline nose, a strong jaw, and firm, young skin, except for a few distinguished creases on his forehead. He was really tall and broad-shouldered and athletic, Delilah thought, as his heavy-lidded blue eyes peered at her beneath thick, dark lashes. In short, a ladies' man with all the qualities needed to fulfill his potential. He gave Delilah a hug, his hand dipping just a bit too low.

"Good to finally meet you." He smiled.

"Yes, finally. You certainly do wander," she said, firmly moving his hand off its target.

Mariette's eyes were suddenly cool.

"Wherever did you find that dress, Delilah?" Felice Borenberg demanded.

"Why, yes, dear. It looks as if it were made for you!" Solange said enviously, as Amber looked on, her lips pursed in disapproval.

"It was. Made for me," she said nonchalantly.

"Well, I had no idea you were getting your clothes custom-made these days. It must cost a fortune," Felice said, raising her eyebrows at Solange.

"Joie Shammanov has the best little dressmaker. She did it for me practically as a favor. Please, come in. Let me take your coats."

"Everything all right in the kitchen, Delilah?" Chaim whispered.

"Everything is fine. I was just in there a minute ago!"

"Please, you promised!"

"I can't be everywhere, Chaim!"

She rushed back into the kitchen. The first course was already being plated: a fantastic mixture of duck and papaya salad. The chef stood at the stove stirring the ginger sauce. The scent alone made Delilah's mouth water. They smiled at each other.

"*Fantastique, non*?"

She nodded, smiling. "Fantastic." The bell rang again. She heard Joie's high-pitched laughter, and then a deep, unfamiliar bass. She rushed into the hall.

"Joie! So good to see you!" Delilah hugged her. "They are all dying to meet you! So, how does it look so far?" she whispered.

"Everything looks fab," Joie whispered back. "Delilah, my husband, Viktor."

Viktor Shammanov was a bear of a man, with the back and shoulders of a body builder, the kind that are so pumped up they seemed to be constantly leaning forward in a Mr. Universe see-my-muscles pose. He had to be at least six foot three. His hair—spread over the top and back of his head in thinning, unnaturally black waves—swept over his forehead from a strange side part. His face was part pit bull, part Khrushchev. And although he wore a suit of impeccable cut, a silk tie, and shiny black shoes, still he resembled one of those guys on *The Sopranos.* He took Chaim into his arms and hugged him, kissing him vigorously on both cheeks. "Viktor Shammanov. Good to meet you, Rabbi! My vife, she spends the day now with your vife. Is good!"

"Yes, it's great. They've become great friends. Mr. Shammanov, let me introduce my wife, Delilah."

Delilah waited in apprehension for the grizzly to pounce. He didn't. He didn't even hold out his hand to her.

"Am grandson of big rabbi, Ukrainian rabbi. I know not to touch rabbi's vife." He bellowed with laughter, his voice bouncing off the walls like a sonic boom.

"Very good, very good!" Chaim rubbed his hands together nervously. He suddenly noticed another couple standing by the door. He'd never seen them before.

"Please, come in, won't you? I'm sorry. You are?"

"Khe doesn't speak English." Viktor unleashed a flood of Russian. "Khe is cousin, bodyguard. And khis vife. Also cousin."

The man took off, prowling around the house, looking for assassins. Delilah quickly added two more settings to the table.

"Let me introduce you to our synagogue board, Viktor," Chaim said, making the introductions. He went through the names, and each person then stepped up like a petitioner at the court of some Oriental potentate, almost curtsying as they shook his hand and nodded to his wife. Only Joseph Rolland took Joie's hand and kissed it, causing Viktor Shammanov to stop what he was saying and stare. Dr. Rolland soon stepped back.

"In Russia, you take khand of another's man's vife to your lips, and you die," he said casually. There was a sudden silence. Then he bellowed with laughter. "Kidding, just kidding," he boomed.

Everyone exhaled.

"Please, everyone, why don't we just wash and then sit down to dinner?" Delilah said, with perfect poise.

"Vash? Am I dirty I need to vash?" Viktor asked, looking around him with mock shock like a Catskills comedian.

"I know it sounds strange, but it's a religious custom. We wash before saying grace over the bread, the way the priests in the Holy Temple washed before preparing sacrifices on the altar," Chaim explained companionably, taking Viktor's arm and leading him off to the special basin built into an alcove of the dining room for exactly this purpose. Everyone followed. Delilah then helped them find their place cards and be seated. Chaim said blessings over the bread, then tore off some pieces and dipped them in salt, handing a piece to each guest, as was the custom.

Delilah rushed back into the kitchen. "Is everything all right?"

"Of course, madame," the chef said, taking a large swig from a very expensive bottle of wine bought especially for the evening. It was, she noted, already half gone.

"We've got two extra guests. Maria, you can start serving now," she told the help.

The girl lifted the plates up to the chef, who ladled generous amounts of sauce on top of each. She carried them to the table and began to serve.

Viktor handed his plate to his bodyguard, who tasted it. Everyone stared, wondering how long Viktor would watch him not dying before agreeing to eat. He didn't wait very long. "Food vonderful!" Viktor announced. "I loff good food."

"Yes, I have quite a few business contacts in Russia, and they all know how to eat," Stuart Grodin said obsequiously.

"You khav bizness, in Russia? What kind bizness?" Viktor asked.

Stuart was thrilled. He started discussing the subcontractors for his bears, who were going to manufacture them under license and distribute them all over Eastern Europe.

"Bears? You sell bears to Russians? Like snow to Eskimos!" Viktor roared. "You vant bizness in Russia, is only vun bizness. Only vun bizness in vorld."

Everyone leaned forward a little in their seats, placing their utensils down so as not to make a single sound that might obscure the answer.

"Oil! Oil bizness. You heard of Turdistan? You khear what happen to oil after communists? All people get certificates, oil certificates in Turdistan. Every family have certificate. But don't need certificate. Need—" He rubbed his thumb and forefinger together. "So me and brother, ve buy certificates. Ve get friends to buy certificates. Now ve own oil company. Now ve drill, make oil company bigger. Ve sell certificates. Our friends, all very rich. Like Sultan of Brunei!"

"Can others buy these oil certificates? Is it like stocks and bonds?" Stuart asked eagerly.

He tilted his head, then shook it. "Is very difficult. Need to organize. Only Russian peoples who lives in Turdistan can buy. Is almost impossible for people like you to buy. You buy bears!" He looked around the table, smiling. No one smiled back. "Vhy so serious, you Americans? Ah, yes, I know vhy." He looked around the table expectantly.

"Viktor, are you looking for something?" Chaim asked.

"Vodka! Ve make toast!"

Delilah ran to get the bottle out of the liquor cabinet, together with the shot glasses.

"Varm vodka?" Viktor bellowed. "In Russia, vodka cold, like Kremlin in vinter!" He filled his shot glass and raised it aloft. "Ten years ago I go to Moscow on buziness. Vladimir vent, also Yuri." He turned to his wife. "You remember Yuri? The vun vit daughter Galina, who haff trouble vit kidneys from eating bad pork, vun vit small face, vun who married police captain? . . . In Russia, very important to have relative police captain, very khelpful to many buzinesses; also bear buziness, also oil buziness. Ve did vell, so ve vent into restaurant to celebrate. They don't know how to fix kebab, but bread and soup and pirochki vas excellent. Ve make big buziness. Ve sign big contract. Ve become very, very rich. And ve move here, to America. I find vife in America. I have my beautiful daughter Natasha in America. Ve build house in America. In America, you can be Jew. I bring my son to live in America. I vant Bar Mitzva. I don't know khow to make Bar Mitzva. And now I meet Rabbi Chaim, and khe vill khelp me make Bar Mitzva for my son. And all you my friends, my American friends, you vill come to my son's Bar Mitzva. I velcome you to my khome, as you velcome me to your khome in America. I raise glass to Rabbi Chaim." He poured everyone a drink. Then he threw back his head and downed it, wiping his lips across his sleeves. "And now, raise glasses, drink to Svallo Lake, to friendship!" He poured another round.

Delilah signaled to the serving girl to start clearing off the table and to bring the next course. Her head was already swimming from the pure alcohol now coursing through her veins. She walked into the kitchen to supervise.

And then she spied something. It was a little container. She lifted it. CRÈME FRAÎCHE, it said. "Hello? Where did this come from?" she asked the chef.

"I bring it *avec moi* from Paris, Madame." He gave her a superior and knowing smile. "*C'est impossible* to find decent crème fraîche in America."

"You were told specifically not to bring in any food!" Her head swam. "What's in it?"

His lips thinned with insult. He looked down his nose. "Just ze cultured cream. It make ze sauces very smooth, very *riche*."

"Cream? Cream! In all the sauces? Don't tell me you put this in the duck salad sauce, and the sauce that went over the squab, and into the profiteroles!"

He drained his glass of wine and poured himself another, finishing off the bottle. "But of course!" His brow wrinkled in displeasure. "In France, zis is well known." He shrugged, that go-to-hell French shrug of nasty waiters and impatient shopowners.

She clenched her fists. "But none of the recipes you showed me even called for cream!"

"Recipes!" he mocked. "Who writes zis? Ze little cook, ze *New York Times*. Ze great chef? We do not read zeez silly instructions."

"You nincompoop! I told you, I'm a rabbi's wife! We are Orthodox Jews! All our guests are Orthodox Jews, you French nitwit. We don't mix meat and milk. I told you that!"

His whole body stiffened with offense. He bowed. His hand waved over the kitchen dramatically. "Pardon, madame, but I do not see ze meat here. Only ze duck and ze chicken!"

"I'm going to kill you!" She lunged at him. He picked up the carving knife and moved back, waving it at her. Delilah grabbed the hired girl and hid behind her. He started swearing very rapidly under his breath in French, the word *Juifs* appearing again and again, in what was apparently not a paen of praise to David Ben-Gurion or Moses. Then he threw down his apron and walked out the kitchen door, slamming it behind him.

She leaned against the wall, trembling.

She thought of the religious men and women sitting around her table, the synagogue-owned table in the house of the community's spiritual leader, its rabbi. And she was his helpmate, the person who sat by his side, who was supposed to help the congregants keep God's commandments.

She had, it seemed to her, a clear choice. She could go in and tell them what had happened, insulting Joie and Viktor, whose chef, after all, had managed to screw up, sending everyone home early with nothing to eat. Chaim would make her throw out all her dishes, after he berated her with a million *I told you so*s. Solange and Mariette would arch their brows and nod at each other at the debacle. And who knew what the decision would be, the next time the board took a vote?

Or, she could . . .

She looked at the delectable squab already arranged on the plates, covered in sauce. She searched the pans to find a piece that had not yet been plated and doused. There was only one left. She took out a clean plate and placed the squab on it, adding the vegetables. "I'll take in this one. You take in the rest," she told the girl.

Then she reached for the almost empty container of crème fraîche, opened the garbage can, and buried it deep inside, covering it with debris. She picked up the plate and carried it into the dining room, placing it in front of her husband.

"Ah, I get special service. A true woman of valor!" Chaim said, kissing her hand.

"You see, little voman, this is vay vife treat husband," Viktor boomed, squeezing Joie's knee.

Delilah smiled at him and sat down, looking down into her own plate. Slowly, she scraped the sauce off the squab with her knife, eating tiny, relatively sauceless pieces as best she could.

"Umm, this is just scrumptious!" Solange exclaimed, putting a sauce-drenched morsel on her tongue.

"Yes, divine. The sauce is so creamy and rich. I've never tasted anything like it," Mariette said, savoring each piece. "You must get us the recipe, Delilah."

Delilah nodded silently, not looking up.

"Come. Ve toast some more!" Viktor called out.

Chaim downed his fourth glass. He staggered to his feet, shakily holding up his shot glass. "Now—now it's my turn. Shhhh, shaa." He waved at everyone. "Sit down! To all my wonderful friends in Swallow Lake, who have entrusted me with their spiritual growth and who have allowed me to become a part of their lives and the lives of their families, so that we might be true to our heritage and our holy Torah, fulfilling all the commandments of our God."

My God, were those tears in his eyes? Delilah thought, horrified.

"And to my wonderful wife who has made this fabulous evening possible, bringing together old friends and new, nourishing us with a gourmet kosher"—Delilah started to cough—"meal." She coughed louder and louder.

"She's choking!"

"Somebody do a Heimlich maneuver!"

"I vill do it!" Viktor sprang up.

"No, I'm fine—don't," Delilah protested, terrified as she watched Viktor Shammanov lumbering drunkenly toward her, getting ready to squeeze her in half. "I'm fine. Something must have just gone down the wrong pipe, that's all." She smiled, wiping her eyes. "See?"

Viktor smiled and sat down. "Finish toast!"

"Ah, yes." Chaim nodded. "To my wonderful wife, who has been a true helpmate, like Sarah to Abraham, like Rivkah to Isaac, like Rachel to Jacob. . . ."

Like Eve to Adam, Delilah thought.

"May God bless her! It's not easy to be a rabbi . . . so many things I'd like to do, and it's impossible . . . to please everyone . . . and some people are jerks, you can never please them, and some are just drunks, like the kiddush Club members, and the ones who tell me they go for lap dances because it helps them fulfill their God-given duty to pleasure their wives . . ."

Felice turned sharply to her husband, Ari, who stared down at a fork he was digging into the tablecloth. Joseph Rolland cleared his throat.

"Chaim!" Delilah said sharply, pulling him back down into his seat.

"Er . . . I think maybe it's time for dessert?" Arthur pointed out.

"What did you say, time to desert?" Stuart Grodin laughed.

"Is that a true story?" Mariette turned to Delilah. "About the lap—"

"Wait, wait, I'm not finished," Chaim muttered, struggling back up to his feet. "And to the women who want to know if they should tell their husbands one of the kids isn't theirs or if it would be a mitzva to keep the information to themselves . . ."

"Oh, ho!" Viktor roared.

"And of course, to my beautiful, difficult wife . . ."

She elbowed him. "You already did me!" she hissed. "Sit down!"

He ignored her. ". . . whom I love, and who makes my life miser—"

"Chaim!"

"To Delilah. I raise my glass to her and to all of you!"

"To Delilah!" The men roared, while the women studiously avoided looking at each other.

Delilah drank another shot of vodka. The room was swimming in front of her. Solange looked suddenly fat. And Mariette looked like she was wearing devil's horns. Or maybe that wasn't Mariette; maybe it was just her own reflection in the glass of the china closet.

{ TWENTY-FOUR }

People remember what they want to remember. And while everyone had had a great time at the rabbi's house meeting Viktor and Joie Shammanov, they soon forgot the circumstances of their initial meeting, remembering only that they were now dear friends of the fabulous Shammanovs. In fact, soon it felt as if they had known them forever.

Joie made an effort to invite the women over to her home at least once a week, preparing fabulous meals. After some coaching from Delilah, she got rid of her French chef and hired one who had once worked in the Catskills at a kosher hotel. She had Chaim over to supervise making her kitchen kosher. And even when he went a bit mad with a blowtorch, effectively ruining the inside of their $6,000 Gaggenau oven, she told him not to worry about it, and just replaced it. The silverware and glasses could all be made kosher by plunging one into boiling water and by just soaking the other. The dishes, of course, were a bit of a problem; there is no way to make porcelain dishes kosher if they have held milk and meat or pork or shellfish. But even Joie, caught up as she was in fitting into her new community, balked at throwing out an entire set of $200-a-plate Hermes Toucans dinnerware, with its $1,500 soup tureen. What they did was order additional plates to use when the synagogue came over.

Sightings of Viktor Shammanov in earnest conference with the board members and others from among the most prominent citizens of Swallow Lake became more and more frequent. Meanwhile, the women of the synagogue board had taken it upon themselves to advise Joie Shammanov on how to make a Bar Mitzva.

"I once went to a Bar Mitzva where they turned the entire synagogue into a circus tent, and the Bar Mitzva boy greeted the guests on an elephant. . . . They had flame eaters, clowns, and jugglers," Amber told her excitedly.

"And I was at one where they turned the place into an African jungle, with grass floors and tribal dancers flown in from South Africa. All the food was African too. It was something to remember," Solange remarked.

"That's nothing. I was at one where they flew everyone to a safari game park in Kenya. But we wound up waiting on line for hours to get in. It turned out there were two other Bar Mitzvas in front of us," said Felice.

"You don't want to go to Africa," Mariette counseled authoritatively. "Joseph and I were there once, for some conference. The minute we finished breakfast, the monkeys descended on the tables and ate all the packets of sugar! They were all over the place! It was disgusting. And that's not the worst of it." She lowered her voice conspiratorially. "I was reading their local fashion magazine, and they had a full-page advertisement for *rape insurance*! They promised to bring you AIDS medication first thing the next morning," she whispered, shuddering.

Joie's eyes widened.

"Then again," Solange said brightly, breaking the stunned silence, "you could always rent a fabulous place right here. Like Radio City Music Hall. Or Madison Square Garden. Then you could put the name of the family up on the marquee. It's great fun!"

"Been done." Felice shook her head. "They even hired the Rockettes to dance with the Bar Mitzva boy. The police had to rope off half of Manhattan."

"That's peanuts! Did you read about that music producer who built an entire synagogue in the south of France just for his son's Bar Mitzva and afterward just took it apart? He flew in Beyoncé Knowles and Justin Timberlake!" Delilah said delightedly. "I read all about it in *People* magazine at my last gynecologist's appointment."

Joie lifted her head. "Oh," she said, "that does sound like fun!"

"But does it sound to you like a *religious* occasion?" Solange tilted her head.

"Doesn't it?" Joie looked at Delilah, who was already deep in daydreams, envisioning herself in a pink bikini lolling about on the beaches of Cannes. She looked up, suddenly realizing that everyone was staring at her, waiting for an answer.

"I can't see anything wrong with it," Delilah said.

Solange looked puzzled. "But didn't Rabbi Chaim say he was against this kind of thing?"

"Why do you say that?" Delilah felt her underarms break out in sweat.

"Well, he gave a whole sermon about it about a month ago. Were you there, Amber?"

"Oh, yes, *that* sermon." She arched her brow.

"Oh, sure!" Delilah nodded. "I know what you are talking about now," she said, her mind a complete blank. "But I don't think he was talking about the same thing."

"No? Then what did he mean when he said that these kids end up spending two years going to multiple parties every weekend, that they get used to drinking and eating too much and getting all these party favors, so that afterward when the parties stop, they are just so blasé about everything they wind up taking drugs and getting into all kinds of trouble just to keep themselves amused?"

"Yes, that's exactly what he said," Mariette agreed. "I remember, because a lot of people were complaining about it afterward. People who'd had Bar and Bat Mitzvas. They were very hurt!"

"Well, you see, I'm sure you misunderstood, because there is *no way* Rabbi Chaim would *ever* say anything controversial that would hurt people's feelings," Delilah pointed out, relieved. "He probably meant they shouldn't attend too many every weekend. But one would be all right."

"So you are saying that your husband is in favor of a Bar Mitzva party like the one in France, the one that cost millions?"

"I think I can safely say that my husband would never condemn anyone because of how much money they have, or if they wanted to spend it on fulfilling one of God's commandments. You know, there is this concept of . . . of"—she thought back to her yeshiva days, desperately searching for solid ground—"of *hedoor mitzva*."

The women tilted their heads quizzically.

"It's the idea that you should go a little overboard when you're doing God's commandments. Like . . . let me see—you know, like choosing an *etrog* for Succoth."

Joie looked at her blankly. "Succoth? *Etrog*?"

"Oh, it's the Feast of Tabernacles, a seven-day holiday in which we are supposed to 'dwell in booths.' So we make this little hut, a sukkah, outside our homes, and we let the sun bake our heads, the rain and snow fall in our soup," Delilah went on.

"Whatever for?" Joie shook her head.

"Oh, uhm. Well," Delilah racked her brain. "It's . . . it's supposed to teach us to have faith in God. And that a home, no matter how solid and expensive, can't really save you from the rain or the sun. . . ."

Joie blinked, looking back at her house. "That's exactly what a home *can* do."

"Yes, I know. But—"

"What she means, my dear, is that living in a flimsy hut for a week is supposed to make us understand that we need His help and protection, because, you know, a house can be gone in an instant. Hurricanes, floods, tornadoes," Mariette told her, nodding sagely. "Isn't that what you were going to say, Delilah?"

"For sure. Now, where was I? Oh, the *etrog*—that's a citron. It looks just like a lemon, except it doesn't have any juice, and not much taste, but it smells heavenly. For some reason, the Bible chooses the citron, and a few other things, to symbolize the holiday. You are supposed to hold them in your hands and shake them in all directions."

Joie blinked.

"Well, anyhow, God says to take a citron, any old citron. But people decided it would honor God more if we made an effort to find the *perfect* citron, the one with no spots or blemishes. One perfectly shaped, not too big or too small. And sometimes, people go around with magnifying glasses when they shop for their citron. They can spend thousands of dollars on one. They think it's a way of honoring God. You could say the same thing about going over the top in a Bar Mitzva."

Solange and Felice looked at each other, their mouths falling open.

Mariette shook her head. "You can't be serious! I was once at this Bat Mitzva in the Plaza Hotel. To enter the reception, you had to pass through a corridor lined with eight-by-ten-foot photos of this twelve-year-old girl doing various dance and acrobatic moves. I mean, I applaud the concept in theory. But a twelve-year-old girl really shouldn't be blown up to eight by ten feet. She had braces and acne. And when we got into the reception, there were all these well-known chefs standing at different serving stations, preparing food. There were fountains of champagne. And when we were finally stuffed to the gills and sat down, the lights were lowered. And there comes this litter, supported by six-foot "slaves" in loincloths, and on top is the Bat Mitzva girl dressed like Cleopatra. And then it *really* got ostentatious," Mariette said. "That can't possibly be a good thing spiritually. You didn't mean that seriously, did you, Delilah dear?"

"Well," Delilah swallowed, feeling herself challenged, "at least it's something that little girl will remember, isn't it? Maybe she'll remember what fun she had and want her own daughter to have a Bat Mitzva!"

"That's good enough for me!" Joie nodded. "You know, I have to be honest with you all, this wasn't something I was looking forward to, but now I can truthfully say it's going to be great fun! The only question is where to do it." She chewed softly on the nail of her forefinger, deep in thought.

"What about Israel?" Solange suggested.

"Oh, I . . . don't. . . ." Joie shook her head.

"Why not?"

"Well, for one thing, you can't get prime ribs in Israel," Felice pointed out. "Ask my husband. He goes on and on about how skinny the cows are there."

"And if you forget something, there's no Lord and Taylor or Nordstrom's," Amber said. "You're stuck."

"I had a different kind of place in mind. Something spiritual, with lots of sea and sand and sky," Joie explained.

Solange cleared her throat. "You know, Joie, Israel is on the Mediterranean coast. There are miles and miles of beaches there."

"Is that true? I had no idea!"

"It's also a very spiritual place. It's a holy place to three major world religions," Solange went on, heating up.

"But Joie doesn't mean *that* kind of spiritual!" Delilah stood up.

Solange looked at her, shocked. "Don't you think Israel is the most appropriate place for a Bar Mitzva, Delilah?"

"Well, sure, if you want to go that way."

"What other 'way' is there?"

"I just mean, that different people get spiritually worked up about different things. Now, you might feel spiritual about Jerusalem. But Joie might feel spiritual about a beach in Barbados, or the Dominican Republic, or the Cayman Islands."

"Ooh, that's a great idea, Delilah! We could fly everyone down and rent a whole wing at a resort. Put up a tent on the beach!"

"That does sound nice," Amber agreed.

"It sounds fabulous, Joie. Just fabulous." Felice nodded.

In the end, everyone agreed, even Solange, who was as sick as everyone else of the icy Connecticut winter and needed a tan. You couldn't, after all, wear a bathing suit at the Wailing Wall.

"Oh, this is going to be so much fun! Thanks everybody so much for your help!" Joie kissed them on both cheeks and gave Delilah's hand a special secret squeeze.

Delilah gratefully squeezed her back.

TWENTY-FIVE

In the beginning, Delilah had been panic-stricken that Joie's newfound acceptance into the community would water down, or destroy, their own special relationship. But that hadn't happened. In fact, Joie seemed to want to be even closer to Delilah, taking her shopping and buying her extravagant gifts—like a Louis Vuitton handbag, the famous monogram in striking colors on a white background, with tan leather handles and little gold zippers and locks that didn't actually lock anything. It was fabulous.

"Chaim, look at this!" she said, overcome with joy, caressing it.

He took his head out of his book. "A handbag."

She rolled her eyes. "Not just any handbag. It's a Louis Vuitton Damier Speedy Alma from the canvas multicolor collection. It costs a fortune."

He put down his book. "It's very nice. So I guess your *chesed* project is going well then?"

"*Chesed* project?" she looked at him blankly.

"Designer Handbags for Terror Victims. That's what it's for, right?"

As if. She clutched it to her breast. "No, it's a gift. To me. From Joie."

"A gift? And it costs a fortune, you say? Exactly how much of a fortune are we talking about?" he asked, looking at her steadily.

"I don't know," she lied. She knew exactly how much, since she had looked it up in the on-line catalog.

"Well, if it's over a hundred dollars, you really shouldn't accept it."

"Over a hundred dollars?" she looked at him contemptuously. "You can't get a Louis Vuitton key ring for a hundred dollars."

"How much, Delilah?"

"One thousand five hundred thirty-nine dollars and fifty-three cents."

"What?" he exploded. "You can't accept a gift like that! It's going back."

"She'd be deeply hurt and offended. And embarrassed. Don't our sages tell us that embarrassing someone is almost as bad as killing them?" She tucked the handbag protectively under her arm.

"Then you'll have to add it to your *chesed* project. How many bags do you have already?"

She had a cheapo Prada pink begonia pouchette that Solange had unloaded, a *very* old classic quilted Chanel in a horrible dark blue from Mariette, and a beat-up Fendi from Amber in some weird lilac shade. Felice had been the only one who'd come across with something she'd coveted: a silver snakeskin and leather Argent bag, which was actually cute, if you liked silver snakeskin. "I've got a few," she answered defensively.

"How many, Delilah?"

"Four. So far."

"That's it?" Chaim said. "After all these months? Only four? Think about it, Delilah! How is it going to look if you suddenly show up with an expensive designer handbag in front of all these people you've been asking to donate? You are going to make us a laughingstock, or worse."

She fingered the handbag thoughtfully. She hadn't thought of that. He was right, she realized. She didn't answer him. But the next day, she told the babysitter to stay a few extra hours. She rode Amtrak to Penn Station and then took the subway to Canal Street on Manhattan's Lower East Side. She walked down the street, humming, looking into the crowded shops filled with Oriental merchandise.

It didn't take long.

"Psst. Youbyvuton?" Little Chinese women clutching cell phones accosted her on every street corner, looking like extras in one of those Japanese kung fu mafia flicks. "I ge goo pri!" they insisted, in reassuring tones. She nodded, allowing herself to be whisked off to a side street. The woman whipped out a laminated page with every Louis Vuitton handbag imaginable. She spotted the Alma.

"How much?" she said, pointing.

"Forty dolla!"

"That's high!"

"OK. Thirty dolla. Goo pri for you?"

She nodded. "I'll take one of those and one of these," she said, pointing to another model, in black with colored letters.

The woman returned with a plain plastic bag. Inside were the two handbags.

"Sixty bucks?"

The woman nodded. Money changed hands.

She knew better than to take them out and examine them on the street, in case an undercover cop was around. On the way back to the subway, she went into a store on a side street and bought three Louis Vuitton lookalike wallets. Each one cost her ten dollars. The real ones cost four hundred. Each.

When she got home, she took out her booty and examined it. Her purchases even came with their own monogrammed felt holder, just like the real ones. And inside the bags and the wallets there was a label that said LOUIS VUITTON, PARIS. She looked at the fake, and then she looked at her original. It was almost impossible to tell them apart. OK, it was *totally* impossible to tell them apart. What people never realized about Louis Vuittons until they shelled out thousands of dollars and brought them home was that most of the real models weren't even leather, just laminated cloth.

"Delilah?" Chaim said, when he saw her wearing her new purse.

"Relax. I picked up a fake on Canal Street. Pretty realistic, no?"

He looked it over. It looked exactly like the one Delilah had shown him the day before. "Are you sure this is fake?" he asked suspiciously.

"My goodness! Only a man would ask that. Of course it's a fake! It's obvious. Just look at the stitching; it's got two extra stitches. And the zipper? I mean, come on!"

He shrugged, lost. "Well, you know it's against the law to buy these. You could get arrested, Delilah. Not to mention the fact that it is totally unethical."

"The only police that would arrest me over this are the fashion police. Relax, Chaim. This is America."

"It's stealing. It's wrong. You've got to take it back."

"To whom, the Chinese Mafia?"

"Promise me you'll never do it again?"

"I promise." She meant it too. Who wanted a fake, even a very good one? It was like cubic zirconium, or a really well-dressed whore. The fact that nobody could tell the difference didn't change what they were.

The sisterhood looked over the rebbitzin's new handbag with envy. But anyone who asked was told it was a fake. From Canal Street. To salve her conscience, she added the two fakes to her collection. She couldn't see what difference it would make to victims of terror, who, she was sure, would be equally delighted with these bags, since Israelis, being over there in the Middle East, wouldn't know the difference anyway. Besides, Palestinian terrorists, those beasts, had absolutely no respect for either human life or really, really important designer handbags. It would be such a shame if a real, brand-new Damier Speedy got caught up in a terror attack.

To help speed donations to her project, Joie agreed to give a luncheon buffet at Uspekhov. Delilah was thrilled. To please Joie, she went down the synagogue list, paying personal visits to almost everyone and duly noting the size of their lots, the upkeep of their homes, the quality of their furnishings, and the cars in their garage. From these women, she received further lists of names of non–synagogue members, whom she approached and visited, until she was able to compile a true A-list of the most well-to-do people in the community and its surroundings. She went over the information with Joie, and together they prepared the guest list. The invitations were eagerly accepted, and the best-dressed, best-jeweled, richest women of Swallow Lake soon flowed through the iron gates of Uspekhov, touring the estate.

It was a huge success, Delilah's designer and almost-designer handbag collection swelling to hundreds of bags. She was thrilled. And so was Joie.

Soon after, the Shammanovs were suddenly everywhere. They were the honorees at the annual Hebrew Day School fund-raising dinner, pushing aside Arthur and Solange, who had spent years toiling to help balance the budget of that money-eater. They were announced in the highest category of the Lions of Judah circle for the UJC fund-raising campaign. They were seated to the right of the Israeli ambassador at the five-star Israel Bonds Dinner in Hartford. They were on the cover of *Lifestyles* magazine.

They were photographed with Steven Spielberg and Demi Moore and her very young husband at a benefit for the Shoah Foundation. And there was a smiling photo of them accepting a medal of honor from former President Clinton and a smiling Hillary at a B'nai Brith dinner.

Discussions were held and it was decided, although not unanimously, that Viktor and Joie Shammanov be invited to join the synagogue board.

All the while, the members of Ohel Aaron felt their hearts rise and fall, buffeted equally by waves of envy and admiration. Suddenly, their homes began to feel cramped, and they started to find contractors to add porches and finish basements. They hired landscape designers and began importing dwarf trees from Japan. They watched the fashion channel for the latest designer shows in Milan and Paris and then rushed to get their dresses made by Joie's dressmaker.

And then the community held its breath in hushed anticipation as they waited to see who among them would get an invitation to the Bar Mitzva of the Shammanovs' son, Anatoly. All over the community, wild rumors abounded. A synagogue was already under construction in Macchu Pichu, fortress city of the ancient Incas, in a high saddle between two peaks in northwest Cuzco, Peru, they whispered to each other in wonder. Llamas would bring up the kosher foie gras. Or Viktor was building his own island, like Sealand, in the middle of the ocean with the help of his oil rigs, a place where he would declare himself king and give out passports to all the guests, giving them tax-free status for the rest of their lives. The Bar Mitzva boy would be brought in by aircraft carrier, or strapped to the back of a great whale. Destiny's Child would be there, and/or Shania Twain, Michael and Janet Jackson, Celine Dion, the entire cast of the Cirque du Soleil from Las Vegas, Britney Spears, Nicole Kidman, and Natalie Portman and her Israeli boyfriend. They would argue, debate, and discuss, rumors flying, becoming more and more fantastical with every day that passed.

The hunger to be on the guest list soon became ravenous.

Delilah and Chaim were spared the suspense. Their invitation had been personal. Delilah had already begun shopping for cruise wear.

"Shorts? You're buying shorts? I'm not so sure we should even go," Chaim told her, scandalized and depressed over the whole thing.

She was stunned. "Not go? Are you insane? Why not?"

"Because I'm the rabbi, and there will be some members of the congregation who won't be invited, and they deserve services on the Sabbath. Who will provide them if I leave?"

"So for one Sabbath there will be no speech! Believe me, they'll survive."

"It's not just that. They'll probably invite all the people who run the service. The cantor and the Torah reader and the *gabbai*—"

"So what? All the synagogue needs is ten people to hold a service! Believe me, there will be more than ten who aren't getting invitations. They'll manage. For Pete's sake, you aren't going to make me miss this, are you? Because that would be cruel, Chaim, really cruel. Besides, the Bar Mitzva boy is going to need your support. You need to stand next to him as he's reading, in case he forgets."

That was certainly true, he thought morosely. Little Anatoly, with his thick Russian accent and even thicker brain, would need all the help he could get. "There is only one way that kid is going to get through this without humiliating himself and his parents: if he doesn't open his mouth."

"You're his teacher! How can you say that? He's got to read something. You just have to try harder. After all, you've got another two months, no?"

"If I had another two years I still wouldn't manage. The kid's got a wooden ear. And he doesn't remember anything."

"But he'll have it written in front of him, no? He doesn't have to memorize, does he?"

"No, thank God for that. But he does have to remember in which direction to turn the page. He can't even remember that!"

"So that's not a reason to be upset with him. He's just a kid, after all."

"I'm not upset with him. I'm upset with how this whole extravaganza is affecting the community. I know what will happen: All the women in shul will be running around in bathing suits on Shabbes, and the men will sit around the pool playing cards! I just don't understand it." He shook his head. "When I first spoke to Viktor, he seemed perfectly willing to have something modest, here in the synagogue. I don't understand where they got the idea for this circus."

Delilah cleared her throat. "Actually, it was Amber who had the idea about the circus," she murmured, examining her manicure. "Look, Chaim, isn't it better that they spend money on a religious ceremony than spending it on something else that would be more frivolous, like . . . like . . ." But she couldn't think of a single thing that would be more frivolous.

"Religious ceremony? You mean the half hour in the synagogue? The rest is just one big, ostentatious, overblown, see-how-much-money-I've-got festival! You know what? It would be better to tell everyone in the world not to have a Bar or Bat Mitzva at all. To skip it. Believe me, most of these boys and girls would have a much better chance at actually becoming thoughtful, spiritual adults without one!"

She gasped. "How can you say that? What about *hedoor mitzva*?"

"That doesn't mean spending the most money on something! You know, rabbis in certain Hasidic sects have put a ceiling on how much people can spend on weddings. They say, if the wedding has more than one hundred and fifty people and is held in too expensive a place, they won't attend or officiate. They did it because they didn't want people to go into debt or be ashamed, and because it was becoming impossible for parents to marry off their children. That's *hedoor mitzva*."

"Well, that's all very nice, but it's too late now. You can't embarrass the Shammanovs by staying away and by saying these things out loud."

"I've already said all these things out loud," he sighed, "but, obviously, no one was listening."

~ ~

The feeling was dawning on Rabbi Chaim Levi that not only was he not doing any good, he had actually become just one more facilitator for all that was going wrong in the Jewish world. The Shammanovs' Bar Mitzva was just the tip of the iceberg.

He remembered the Bat Mitzva invitation he had gotten the month before, directing him to a Web site. He had dutifully logged on and looked it up. There he was confronted by a photo of Selma and Max Gutfreund's chubby twelve-year-old daughter Leah in a sleeveless white top, bra strap showing, who managed to give him a braces-filled come-hither look over her bare tattooed shoulder. When he clicked on her picture as instructed, she breathily announced that he was invited to her "golden girl rock concert" and invited him to click onto her video.

Mesmerized with horror and fascination, he clicked.

There he found the child wandering through a mall with a group of her prepubescent friends holding shopping bags as she wiggled her hips and threw back her hair, singing. The lyrics, which he tried hard to decipher, went something like:

If I was rich, I could be a bitch,
I'd never go slow, yo, because of my cash flow, wo!
So don't be a smarty, come to my party.

There was a picture of Leah sitting with provocatively crossed legs on a motorcycle as she sang an off-key rendition of a song that went: *Give me a chance to make you happy, your lovin' me is the key.*

And then he saw something else. There was a link entitled MY RABBI. His heart beating, he clicked on it. There he was confronted by a picture of himself and of the synagogue. *I want to thank Rabbi Levi. He's a super cool dude! Like, he's taught me everything I know.*

He felt like laughing. He felt like weeping. He was furious, mortified, and overwhelmed. He felt like retraining, becoming an electrician or a plumber or any other profession in which you can enter a situation with a competent tool box and fix the bloody problem; a profession where the people who hired you actually respected your expertise.

Instead, he allowed people to enter his synagogue week after week and to leave feeling good about themselves, whether or not they deserved to. He was unable to provide them with true values, true direction. Not that he hadn't tried.

There was that time he had talked to the congregation about the importance of shiva calls to the bereaved. A young widow had complained to him that few people had made condolence calls, and one who did had cornered her young son and told him, "Your father was so good that God needed him more," bringing the child to hysterics, lest he too behave himself into an early grave. Another shul member, who hadn't bothered to show up at all, had come over to her in the supermarket and said, "You were just so together that we didn't think you needed a shiva visit."

He had exhorted his congregation, chastised them, explained to them, entreated them to please *please* visit the bereaved during their week of mourning, not to speak unless spoken to, and to be respectful.

And what had been the result of this heartfelt sermon? A group of synagogue members, together with a sprinkling from the board, had accosted him during afternoon prayers, demanding that he apologize because certain people were now embarrassed and were thinking about leaving the synagogue altogether! And a synagogue, they explained to him ominously, can't afford to lose dues-paying members.

The days when a rabbi got a post for life, and when a congregation would not have dared to oppose him, were over, he thought. Most rabbis felt the yapping at their heels every minute of every day. They felt constantly under review, their every speech fodder for both their enemies and their friends, and that they need only say the wrong thing one too many times to turn friends into enemies and themselves out onto the unemployment lines.

But it wasn't just the fear of losing their jobs. They didn't want to leave because they were invested in the community, caring deeply about the lives of its individuals and families. They wanted to make a difference, and they felt that if only they could hang on just a little while longer, they and their congregation would turn the corner and a great expanse would open before them, a safe harbor in which to dock the ship that swayed and trembled, buffeted by heavy winds and changing tides. If they could only be good captains and navigate correctly, there was no telling what good could be accomplished, how many could be rescued from drowning in heartache or getting eaten by the reconnoitering sharks of modern vices.

He knew he was never going to be an intellectual giant, author of memorably profound works of scholarship. He was fine with that. He had a very simple plan, a very modest life's goal: to do some good. To bring to the people around him some of the largesse of their heritage, to sustain them with the fruits of goodness that came to people who knew who they were, and how they were connected to their history and culture and God. So many ills of the modern world—destroyed families, miserable single men and women looking for connection, angry directionless teenagers seeking solace and meaning in mind-altering drugs—could be healed by spirituality. The Torah had answers. He wanted so much to give them, but no one would let him.

Places of worship and communities had turned into hotbeds of strife and competition and a way to show off material wealth. And many times congregants, who were unable to keep up with the Schwartzes or the Malins or the Rollands, were pushed beyond their means into bankruptcy or worse—economic activities that bordered on the unethical or downright criminal. Perhaps it was inevitable, given the cost of day school tuition, monster mortgages, and unrelenting excesses in lifestyle adopted by many communities as the norm and relentlessly foisted upon all those wishing to remain members in good standing. The striving for excess had created a culture that dripped with excess, a culture that was the opposite of everything Judaism valued and cherished and taught.

Despite his better judgment, he had let circumstances and his wife bully him into taking on a congregation that had been blackballed by everyone he respected. Since taking the job at Swallow Lake, he'd been frozen out of alumni events at Bernstein, which had taken him off their mailing list. The heartfelt letters he had received from his grandfather's friends and colleagues, urging him to reconsider, had gone unanswered. He had placed all his eggs in the nest of Swallow Lake. If this didn't work out, he didn't know what he would do.

He wondered, for the first time, if perhaps Delilah was right. Maybe he should try his hand at something else, some little business he could work hard at and build up, a job that would supply him with what he needed to keep his wife happy in nice clothes and jewelry and household help. A job that would let him buy a roof that couldn't be whisked away the moment he failed to supply the flattery necessary to keep afloat the overblown ego of some self-important *macher*. A home he could call his own, in a neighborhood full of normal people who didn't need three thousand square feet of living space filled with in-your-face excess. A place where people took care of their own children, made their own gefilte fish for Passover, and served it by themselves to beloved family members around their own dining room tables. A place where people didn't think it was what they owned that was important, but what they gave.

Maybe, he thought, I can't create such a place in Swallow Lake. But maybe, just maybe, it already existed somewhere else in America—or in Israel—untouched, forgotten by time, and hidden off somewhere, like Brigadoon. If he could find it, perhaps there still was a chance he could manage to do some good and be happy.

But for now—he sighed—he had to get Viktor Shammanov's son ready for a Bar Mitzva that would no doubt have much bar and very little mitzva.

TWENTY-SIX

Like Jews on the night of the final plague, ready to pack up and leave for the Promised Land, the members of Ohel Aaron tensed, waiting for the arrival of the coveted invitation to the Shammanovs' Bar Mitzva. Soon, there arose from each household a whoop of joy, or a bitter sigh of regret, as it became clear who had gotten the golden tickets and whose home the angel had passed over.

As those fortunate enough to have experienced it related, a limousine pulled up to the house and a tuxedoed servant holding a silver tray got out and rang the bell. On the tray was a single white orchid and a handmade music box. When you opened it, it played the "Cell Block Tango" from *Chicago*. There inside was a ten-page invitation, each page describing yet another event as well as the dress code they expected (sport casual, black tie for dinner, golf and tennis wear, swimwear). The idea of swimwear in the doldrums of a freezing East Coast winter was enough to warm the hearts of every lucky invitation holder. Invitees were given the date and time they needed to arrive at the airport, but no other information. The mystery of it all thrilled them.

There began, then, a certain shift in the communal dynamics. Those preparing for the trip began to meet in groups to discuss their wardrobes and their household arrangements. They chattered over the phone and in coffee shops and over their shopping carts in supermarket aisles. How many dresses? How many shoes? What kind of hats?

Gradually, those who had not received invitations felt themselves weeded out socially. And even though it was clear that the Shammanovs could not have invited everyone nor, in the very short time that they had become active in the synagogue, could they possibly have formed a reasonable or accurate opinion of anyone, the uninvited began to think people were looking at them differently, wondering: Why not them? What had the Shammanovs perceived about them that others had not yet been alert enough to discover?

Alas, there was more than a shred of truth to these perceptions. Despite the fact that it was unclear on what basis invitations had or had not been sent out, it was nevertheless assumed by those invited that those left out were in some way to be held responsible for their fate.

The uninvited heard the communal buzz, like a chain saw, cutting down their reputations along with the community's cohesiveness. Among themselves, they began to search out answers. It was a fact that certain synagogue members had been invited to meet the Shammanovs at the rabbi's home and at the Shammanovs' home. And who had been the driving force behind both events? They all came to the same conclusion: Rebbitzin Delilah Levi, dearest friend of Joie Shammanov.

Thus there began the communal wooing of Delilah Levi. Those who hadn't thought much about her until this time suddenly remembered to invite her over for tea parties and book clubs and trips to the city. Those who had actively disliked her now donated heavily to her *chesed* project, parting with fairly new and expensive bags with a groan. They offered her their au pairs to help babysit her little boy, lent her their maids, sent flowers on her birthday, and cakes for the Sabbath. They stopped calling her at all hours of the day and night and made sure to come up to her in the synagogue and compliment her on her outfit, her hat, her husband's "brilliant" sermon, her little boy's amazing cuteness. They helped her get appointments with the best hairdressers and manicurists and cosmeticians. They showed up at sisterhood meetings. In short, they groveled.

But as time grew closer and invitations still failed to arrive, it became clear that mere hints were not enough. Like Hasidim who go to their rebbe, asking him to intercede with God on their behalf, those of a gentler nature humbly approached the rabbi's wife, pleading with her to find it in her heart to get them an invitation. This, of course, she could not do. After all, who was she to make up the Shammanovs' guest list? Besides, most of the people who were calling her had never even said two words to her before, so why should she put herself out now when they were falling all over themselves to be nice?

The others, mostly low self-esteem types, were unbearably hurt, depressed, angry, and consumed with a desire for revenge. As they could not see their way clear to being able to avenge themselves on the Shammanovs, they looked for the next best thing: either invitation holders or Rabbi Chaim and his wife, who had introduced the Shammanovs to the community in the first place. They suddenly began to find all kinds of faults with Rabbi Chaim's speeches, which in the past they had either ignored or enjoyed. They began to talk about the way the rebbitizin's hair stuck out of her hats, and the expensive new clothes she had suddenly started wearing, no doubt at the expense of dues-paying synagogue members. Rumors began to circulate about how the Levis had been run out of town in their last congregation. And someone who had known a roommate of Delilah's at Bernstein Women's College even whispered a thing or two that put all listeners into a state of delicious, openmouthed shock.

Busy choosing head coverings to match her synagogue dresses, her evening wear, her beach cover-ups, and her Sabbath afternoon clothes, Delilah was oblivious to the boiling cauldron of communal strife. But when someone left an anonymous note in the rabbi's mailbox, describing with malicious joy how they felt a religious obligation to inform him of all the things that were being said about him and his wife, Chaim finally had no choice but to interrupt her dreamy happiness.

"Who," he said, dangling a white slip of paper between his thumb and forefinger, "is Yitzie Polinsky?"

Her face lost color. "Oh, isn't that the baby crying?" She hurried up the stairs.

Slowly and deliberately, he climbed up after her. "Delilah?"

"Who's been buzzing in your ear, Chaim?"

"Would you like to see this anonymous letter someone slipped into my mail?"

She shook her head vociferously. "I went out with him once or twice in college. Rivkie fixed me up with him. But he turned out to be a yeshiva bum."

Chaim looked down at the letter in his hand, undecided. Finally, he shrugged and left the room. He didn't say another word to her until dinner, at which time he finished his veal cutlet, wiped his lips, and placed his knife and fork on his plate with careful precision. "This," he told Delilah, "has got to stop. Delilah, you've got to talk to the Shammanovs!"

"What, exactly, do you want me to say to them? That they have to invite the entire shul? What, are we in fourth grade? They'd have to charter three more planes and pay for three times the food!"

"This Bar Mitzva is destroying the community. People are bitter and jealous, and they hold us responsible!"

"Us? What do mean?"

"Well, after all, it was you who brought the Shammanovs into the community in the first place. You are the one who decided which of our neighbors would be invited to their home and to ours."

"I invited the people who have been nice to us. And the board."

"Exactly! You invited all the big shots and left out the ones who are just ordinary, good-hearted, hardworking members of my congregation!"

This, of course, was absolutely true. She'd left out the wig-wearers, the day-school PTA moms, the makeup-free mikva stalwarts, and the yentas with complaints. Delilah wasn't interested in the boring accountants and lawyers and Hebrew teachers. But then, neither were the Shammanovs.

When Joie had asked for her help in deciding the guest list, she'd seen it as a perfect opportunity to weed out the shleppers and put together a wonderful weekend with fun people who would know how to enjoy themselves without putting everyone (read: the rabbi's wife) on a big guilt trip for wearing a bikini or dancing or taking a swim. She'd suggested inviting women whom she thought would be amusing for Joie and, yes, for herself, young women who were rich and thin and sexy and who wore their designer clothes well and would know what to do at a concert by the legendary rock stars who would no doubt be entertaining them, no expense spared. Imagine: Mick Jagger, with his sneer and swagger! Or Ricky Martin with those hips, just inches away from her! She just couldn't wait.

"Chaim, what is it you want from me? You were the one who told me to go out into the community. To be friendly. To help you get new members, didn't you? So I did! *Now* what is it you want?"

He stared at her blankly. It was like shouting over the Berlin Wall. He shook his head and left, spending as much time as possible hibernating in his study until the wretched event would finally be over and peace and sanity would, hopefully, be restored to his congregation.

The day finally arrived. A limousine picked Delilah and Chaim up and drove them to the airport, where a huge refrigerated truck was loading into a cargo plane enough food to feed the U.S. Army in Iraq. A rabbi in a white coat and long beard was supervising.

"They are using Golden Caterers," Solange whispered.

"The ones that cater at the Waldorf and the Plaza?" Felice asked, surprised. "They absolutely never cater outside!"

"I've been watching the plane loading. Whole cows, dozens of them, glatt kosher; a farmload of chickens and turkeys! Pounds of caviar and kosher French foie gras—which is only produced once a year, so you have to get it just in time," Amber whispered back in awe. "And truffles, Swiss chocolate, raspberries, baking supplies. The chefs are flying out with all their pans and pots and utensils, and whole sets of dishes. They even brought along their own stoves and dishwashers, because they don't want to have to kosher the hotel's."

"Wow, what a production," Mariette marveled.

"Wait. I'm sure this is nothing compared to what they have planned," Felice predicted, something to which they all silently agreed. "Look, there's Delilah. My, doesn't she look fetching." Felice arched her brow. "If that skirt was any tighter—"

"Or shorter. Really, ever since she and Joie became such dear friends, the woman has—"

"Careful," Amber whispered.

Solange stopped abruptly, looking around her edgily.

It was like being in the Gulag. You didn't want anyone to overhear you saying anything that could even vaguely be interpreted as negative about either the rabbi or his wife. The rumor was going around that Lorraine Harris had said something in the gym to a friend on the treadmill about an outfit Delilah had dressed her baby in and almost immediately had gotten a call that the invitation had been rescinded. "The messenger actually came to Lorraine's house and asked for it back! They wouldn't even let her keep the music box!" Felice shuddered.

"All I was going to say was isn't it a wonderful thing that Delilah has become so close to the Shammanovs? For the synagogue, I mean..." Solange's voice trailed off.

They waited in smiling silence as Delilah strode up, air-kissing each of them. "Well, here we all are! What fun this is going to be!" Delilah whooped.

The women glanced at each other with strained smiles, being careful to stay politely behind Delilah and Rabbi Chaim as they joined the line of the privileged few invited to board the Shammanovs' own private jet. The rest of the guests had to content themselves with a normal charter flight.

The Shammanovs' private jet was like something out of the Victoria and Albert Museum, done up in red with lots of gold braid and oil paintings of faded pastoral scenes and nudes. There were only 50 seats on the plane, instead of the usual 120. There were private servants who prepared the meals and served them, and first-run movies.

Delilah looked around her. The entire board was there. The men were already huddled with Viktor. She noticed that each one of them made an effort to get him alone whenever they could, and that Viktor was constantly in clandestine whispered conferences with the richest people in Swallow Lake and the environs. She wondered what they were talking about, but didn't trouble her head too much about it. After all, the really important thing was that everyone was being incredibly nice to her.

She was almost ready to make her shipment of designer handbags to Israel's terror victims, and donations continued to pour in. Friends of Solange, Felice, and Amber kept asking her what she and Chaim were doing for their summer vacation; if they'd consider joining them at their private beach houses, country estates, or ranches in South America. She said she'd let them know.

She and Joie sat next to each other on the plane, talking about the latest movie-star-couple breakup, while their babies were cared for by Joie's daytime and nighttime au pairs.

"I've hired another au pair, who is waiting for us at the hotel. The concierge arranged it. She's going to be my water au pair, because you need someone to be especially careful with a baby near the water, and I get so sleepy in the sun. Also, if—God forbid!—one of the other au pairs gets sick, she can take over, because goodness knows I've got my hands full with supervising this whole shindig."

And then, before they knew it, the plane had landed, refueled, and taken off again. After hours over the open sea, it suddenly hovered above a series of incredibly green and magnificent islands. "Ooooh!" everyone gasped, third-graders on their first trip to Disneyland, as the plane came in for a landing amid palms and mountains and beaches. Dark-skinned girls in hula outfits waited on the tarmac. Hips swaying, they placed thick purple, white, and pink leis around the guests as they descended. "Don't worry about the luggage. It'll be brought to you," someone said, directing them to waiting limousines.

Delilah leaned back, sighing with contentment, as the car drove off. How far she had come from middle-income housing projects near the bay, she thought, holding her baby in her lap and threading her arm through her husband's. She rested her head against Chaim's shoulder. She felt a surge of gratitude toward him for being her partner and making all this possible.

He looked at her, surprised and touched, and patted her hand. "Happy, my love?"

She nodded. For the first time she felt it was really true. She *was* happy. She had everything she'd always dreamed about.

And it was just the beginning.

TWENTY-SEVEN

Hotel employees welcomed them tenderly, as if they were delightful friends who had been away too long. An unseen hand gently placed a tall glass filled with untold amounts of gaily colored alcohol and a little umbrella into her hand. She followed a bellboy through a spectacular outdoor lobby facing the sea until she reached her suite.

Oh! Delilah thought, looking around the suite. It was like an Entertainment Channel special featuring "celeb perks." She sank into the pillows of the couch, fingering the bows of a huge gift basket.

"Delilah!"

"Huh?"

"The baby, remember?" Chaim held out the sweating, unhappy infant to her.

She looked at him, annoyed. Little Abraham with his endless secretions and appetites. She took him reluctantly, shaking her head. "Look,

Chaim, if this weekend is going to work, I have to have someone to help me. Otherwise, I won't be able to do anything."

"What, exactly, are you planning to do?"

She thought fast. "Well, help Joie through it. Sit next to her in the synagogue during the ceremony, explaining things. You know she expects me to. And I can't do it with a crying baby."

He shrugged. "Well, I can't take care of him. I've got to be up there with the Bar Mitzva boy. He's going to need all the help he can get."

"Not you! I need an au pair."

"Can't the Shammanovs' three au pairs watch him?"

She shook her head. "Viktor wants them to concentrate on Natasha."

"Don't you have to bring one of those with you?"

"No, actually the concierge can arrange it. Joie told me all about it." She handed the baby back to him and picked up the phone.

The baby, hungry and hot, with aching ears, began to whimper.

"They say it's absolutely no problem," she said, hanging up the phone triumphantly. "They'll send us one. We can have her for the whole weekend."

"And the cost?"

She looked at him steadily. "Look, we are getting this entire vacation for free, so we can afford to splurge on this one little thing." She walked over, patting down his tie. "Come on, honey, otherwise I'll never get to go swimming or anything."

"Oh, so that's what this is really about! Delilah, it's just not appropriate for the rabbi's wife to be walking around in a bikini."

The baby was now screaming so loud he'd completely lost his breath, his face going frighteningly red. Reluctantly, she took the infant back, unbottoning her blouse and whipping out a breast. Little Abe, already familiar with the lay of the land, wasn't taking any chances; he latched on to the nipple quickly, hanging on with desperate determination.

"Ouch, that hurts! You little leech! Look, Chaim, don't be a fuddy-duddy. These are all fun people who won't mind a bit. I made sure of that."

"What?"

"I mean, Joie made sure of that."

"So it's true, then! You *did* pick the guest list."

"Don't be silly. Joie made the final decision."

"But you were the one who told her who'd be fun and who wouldn't?"

Delilah, who was holding the baby in one arm and rummaging through her luggage with the other as she looked for her bathing suit, cover-up, trendy baseball cap, flip-flops, and eyewear, looked up for a moment. "You say that as if it's a bad thing."

"Don't you understand?" he exploded. "You—no, *we*—are guilty of everything people have been accusing us of! And they are absolutely right to be furious."

"They're just jealous. You know what? Maybe they'll learn a lesson from all this. Isn't that what you always say, that God gives us troubles to open our hearts and make us repent and become better people?"

He stared. "And what, exactly, are the people back home trudging through the icy sludge supposed to learn from this, Delilah?"

She thought about it for a moment. "That they should be nicer to their rabbi's wife," she said, shrugging. "But when I get back, I promise you I'll give them every opportunity. After all, doesn't the Torah tell us not to hold a grudge?"

He shook his head, giving up.

The pool was surrounded by little three-sided tents, inside of which there were two chaise lounges. In one tent she spotted Viktor, deep in discussion with Stuart Grodin. She thought about waving to them, but they only had eyes for each other. The pool boy led her to an empty tent, handing her thick white towels and arranging her lounge covers. Delilah left the baby in his carriage and stretched out. Soon a dark-haired Hawaiian beauty came by.

"Mrs. Levi? I'm Lana, your au pair for the weekend. Aloha. Happy to meet you."

Delilah swung her legs over the side of the chaise. "And I'm *delighted* to meet you." She grinned, stretching out her hand. "Well, here he is, the baby. Abraham. Little Abe." She made appropriately maternal faces at the exhausted baby, who looked back at her, bleary-eyed. "He's a little knocked out from the flight. But here is some formula, and his bottles and pacifier, and his favorite giraffe."

And just like that, little Abe disappeared.

She leaned back, stretching out, allowing her robe to open, and cautiously peeked around to see if anyone had reacted. Seeing nothing, she took it off altogether.

It was a white suit, covered with tiny gold cross-stitch embroidery. She looked, she realized, absolutely luscious in it. Plates of pineapple were brought to her, and a bar menu. She chose a Heavenly Hawaiian Smoothee, made with frozen yogurt, fresh tropical fruits, and some kind of liquor. She wasn't an expert, but, boy, what a wallop! Considering that she was still experiencing the effects of the welcome drink, whatever inhibitions still lingered were soon sent on their way.

She leaned back, boldly lifting off the baseball cap. Covering her hair suddenly seemed ludicrous, considering the vast expanses of forbidden flesh now open for public viewing. She pushed back her sunglasses, surveying the new world. She had no idea that at the same time, the world was surveying her.

Just across the pool lay Dr. Joseph Rolland. From behind his sunglasses, he examined the rabbi's wife.

She was like a big, soft, sexy doll, he thought. Blond hair (this was definitely not a wig, he realized, delighted) lightened from darkish honey to fourteen-karat gold, the shadings competently but not expertly done. It was the kind of color a man with meticulous and expensive tastes might secretly sneer at after he'd had his good time. Her lips were full yet delicate, when not cheapened by a slash of some too-bright trendy shade as they were now. The eyes were a glorious blue but a little narrow at the corners, the only part of her face that really looked better with her obvious and carefully applied makeup. Without it, he considered, her face would look more deliberate and calculating, like an animal scurrying for escape or chasing its next meal.

The bathing suit was nice but, given his experience with keeping high-maintenance girlfriends happy, he knew it had been found on a bargain rack in an expensive department store because of some fluke of size or color or style that didn't mesh with popular taste. Yet it looked wonderful on her. She had the knack, which very few women have, of making clothes her own so that you couldn't imagine them on anyone else. No one would look at her and say, What a beautiful bathing suit! They'd say, What a beautiful woman!

He was quite surprised to see her at the pool in this state of undress. He knew she was careful never to put herself outside the religious pale. Nothing too low-cut or sleeveless or far above the knees. And her hair was always covered. He blessed his good luck as he studied her slim ankles and shapely calves, her curvy wide hips and slim waist, with just the right absence of any excess fat to make her truly delicious. She was turning to talk to the women on all sides who had gathered around her, her head high, her smile and laugh animated, her expression alternately amazed or scandalized, while all the while her eyes cast furtive, searching glances around her that acknowledged and ignored the male appreciation being beamed at her from all directions.

"Like some more sunscreen, honey?" Mariette offered her husband, as she covered her nose with white goo.

He jerked back to reality. "Huh! Oh, ah. Well. Sure. Thanks, Mariette," he murmured, allowing her to massage it into his chest. He saw Delilah glance up and stare in his direction. He nodded and waved. Mariette turned around to see who it was he was greeting. She saw Delilah lying there in her bathing suit, and her eyes narrowed.

Delilah lowered her head. Mariette had her hands full, she thought, flattered and scandalized. He was sort of cute though, she thought, in a very subdued and older-man kind of way. He looked as if he had had lots and lots of experience. But even those men eventually find their perfect match and settle down. Look at Warren Beatty. Look at Michael Douglas. Of course, they were usually close to sixty and being blown off by chorus girls when it finally happened, but *c'est la vie*. He was old enough to be her . . . *sugar daddy*, a small voice inside piped up. She gave the idea a slap to see if it would howl and go away, but it didn't. It just gave a squeak, to prove that it was real and flexible.

But even Delilah Levi had her limits, she told herself. Besides, if it was just money she was after, there were plenty of ways to get it. And plenty of younger men who had it.

She put on her robe, turning her attention to the small group that had gathered around her as the women of Ohel Aaron zeroed in on their favorite rebbitzin, the one who had made it possible for them to leave behind the freezing cold Connecticut winter for a few days on this ultimate, all-expenses-paid dream vacation in Hawaii.

Those lucky enough to find empty chairs near her sat down as if they were at the Western Wall and had finally maneuvered their way into touching distance of the holy stones. The others crowded in nearby, having no choice but to content themselves with turning their bodies in her direction so they could catch her every word and perhaps seize an opportunity to participate in the conversation. And when they looked at Delilah, they couldn't believe they'd never noticed how beautiful she was: a golden girl, her skin turning a little bronze as it tanned under expensive sun cream, supplied in the gift basket each guest had found in their room. Beautiful and young and wise. And smart! And funny! Why, they found themselves laughing and laughing at the least little roll of her eye or slightly raised inflection of her voice. They adored Delilah Levi, so kind and friendly and down-to-earth! Not one of those hypocritical fanatics whom everyone had to tiptoe around in case they bumped into her halo.

And Delilah liked them, for the most part. But not enough to put herself out. She was content to smile with noblesse oblige as she accepted offers of chocolate-covered macadamia nuts and *Cosmopolitan* magazines. She closed her eyes, letting the sunlight dance on her lids, listening to the sound of the waves crashing soothingly on the white beach sand below the pool.

As all religious people know, there are two ways to take any fortunate event that occurs in your life. The first is to accept it as a pure blessing from God, a reward for numerous good deeds. The second is to view it as God's way of emptying your mitzva-reward bank account, as He readies the roof to fall in upon your head for your sins.

But Delilah wasn't thinking about either possibility. She was simply living in the present, imagining it would go on this way forever.

{ TWENTY-EIGHT }

The next morning they gathered on the beach as instructed, waiting to be borne off to the mysterious venue of the Bar Mitzva to end all Bar Mitzvas. At that point, everyone was so psyched up, only a few would have been surprised if the ground had opened up and a rocket had emerged from an underground silo ready to launch them to the moon.

"Have you figured out the theme?" Amber asked Mariette, who shook her head.

Every Bar and Bat Mitzva has to have a theme. Becoming responsible for your deeds is such a downer. So people have a gangster theme, with each table commemorating another Jewish crook or murderer. Or a shopping theme, with each table representing a different store: Bergdorf's, Nordstrom's, Lord & Taylor. Or a Greek theme—which is a bit problematic, considering that Jews annually celebrate the victory of the Maccabees over the vicious Hellenization program that almost destroyed Judaism—but, hey, togas are so cute.

People were still not sure what the Shammanovs' theme was.

"First, I thought it would be maybe *Eighty Days Around the World.* But then you'd need a hot-air balloon, and I don't see any," Mariette said, scanning the area.

"It could be *Swiss Family Robinson,*" Felice murmured.

Just then they spied the sails in the distance, as a flotilla of boats headed toward shore and landed, one by one. Burly, handsome sailors, their tanned and muscled thighs set off perfectly by white shorts, jumped out to haul the boats in. One by one, the sailors approached the women, their smiles dazzling in their sun-kissed faces, as they picked up the valises and led the wives on board, their husbands following as an afterthought. Soon the entire Bar Mitzva party had pushed off from shore into the wide ocean.

"Oh, look at the whales!" Delilah shouted, squeezing Chaim's hand.

"Where?" Mariette demanded.

"Right there! See that spray of water?" Dr. Rolland exclaimed, pointing to the horizon as he moved toward the boat railing next to Delilah. She felt his shoulder brush against hers, his hip connect for a moment, but when she turned to him with a raised eyebrow, he seemed completely oblivious, looking out to sea, his hand clasped around his wife's waist. Delilah shrugged, moving away.

Soon the sea was full of whales, dashing around the boats, thrilling them.

"I don't know, they're awfully big. Isn't this a little dangerous?" Amber pointed out. "I mean, couldn't they turn our boat over?"

Just as she said it, a huge one brushed past the boat ahead of them, dousing the passengers with water.

"Oh, my clothes are soaked!" one woman wept, very not in the spirit of the party. But Joie wasn't having any of that. Soon the woman found herself in a lifeboat, speeding back to shore. Her husband waved to her. Joie took a megaphone: "And if anyone else gets wet, don't worry. We've got plenty of clothes on board! Relax!"

"Maybe the theme is *Jaws*?" Felice said, shuddering as the poor woman faded in the distance.

"Or *Mutiny on the Bounty,*" Chaim whispered.

Just then it came into view: a fabulous cruise ship flying Russian flags and flags with . . . with—no, it couldn't be—flags with the face of Anatoly Shammanov, the Bar Mitzva boy! Soon the guests were being helped from the sailboats up to the ship.

They were greeted by a group of Hawaiian musicians who began to beat their drums and play their slack-key guitars. Lovely girls in grass skirts and leis undulated all over the deck, giving out grass skirts to all the women.

"Everybody hula!" a deejay commanded them.

"Isn't this fun?" Joie shouted over to Delilah, who was busy fastening the grass skirt around her hips.

"The best!" Delilah shouted back, outswiveling the dancers as best she could.

Then the girls were replaced by men naked to the waist, juggling burning torches as hypnotic drums began to play. And then, suddenly, a loudspeaker invited them all to the right side of the boat.

They peered at the empty sea, where a tiny speck appeared in the distance. It got larger and larger.

"Look!" someone finally screamed, pointing into the sea. "Dolphins!"

There were dozens of them.

"Dolphins? Who cares about bloody fish? It's my Anatoly!" Viktor Shammanov boomed. And sure enough, seated on a little rubber throne, holding reins around the heads of the mammals and flanked by waterskiers who looked like former KGB agents, was the Bar Mitzva boy.

"Ve try to train vhale." Viktor shrugged. "But vhales not interested!"

The child looked terrified.

"Khere khe comes. King Neptune!" Victor roared, as the child shakily climbed up to the deck. He lifted the boy onto his shoulders and began to hula.

So, was that the theme? Pagan gods? Or was that just a little side remark, a joke, Rabbi Chaim wondered, looking at Viktor dancing wildly and Delilah undulating in her grass skirt. His eyes widened in alarm.

He was trapped, he thought. There wasn't a single thing he could do, cornered as he was with the entire synagogue board on a boat in shark-infested waters and a current that ended in Japan. He couldn't exactly walk out in protest, now could he? Whatever was going to be, was going to be. He looked longingly at the sailboats now casting off back to shore as the band struck up again and the hula lesson continued.

Finally, they were all given keys to their staterooms to prepare for the evening ahead. He took two aspirin and lay down, trying to compose himself for the Friday-night services still to come. His head felt like a drum on which a healthy native was pounding out an emphatic tribal message.

Services were held in the main ballroom, which had been transformed into a synagogue. It seated a thousand comfortably. Delilah looked around, realizing that they had been joined by numerous Russian-speaking families who were certainly not from Swallow Lake.

"It's all Viktor's friends and relatives." Joie rolled her eyes. "Russian families are very close."

The service went along well enough, Chaim thought. And afterward, they went to the second ballroom for dinner. Food and booze flowed incessantly like the sea down the gullets of the celebrants. And just when they were about ready to doze off, the cheerleaders came out. There were about twenty of them, healthy, voluptuous, young, in tiny skirts and sleeveless tops. They bounded onto the dance floor with their pom-poms, singing a cheer that incorporated the name Anatoly.

"Isn't great?" Viktor laughed. "Lakers' Girls."

"As in Los Angeles Lakers cheerleaders?" Arthur choked, stunned.

"Ve vant only best." Viktor smiled. "For Anatoly. Go, Anatoly, go! Girls teach you cheer."

The chubby teenager ran out into the center of the floor.

All the men got up and jockeyed for the best eyeful. Joseph, Arthur, Ari, and Stuart nudged one another. Delilah was there too, right in front, not wanting to miss anything, her arm around Joie's waist.

And then the girls disappeared and a live band began to play balalaikas and other traditional Russian instruments.

"But Viktor, I told you, Jews don't play music on the Sabbath. It's not allowed!" Chaim pleaded.

"Rabbi don't vorry! Musicians are not Jews—don't even like Jews! Are Russians. For Russians, it's not Sabbath!" Viktor laughed, linking arms with the dancers as they stamped out "Kalinka-Malinka," carrying him off.

Chaim looked over at this scene. Friday night, the beginning of the Sabbath, the holy day of rest.

"Rabbi! This is a desecration of Shabbes! You have to get that band to stop playing!" Arthur Malin demanded. "This is a disgrace! You have to talk to the Shammanovs!"

"Arthur, I tried—"

"Try again!" Arthur shouted, scandalized. "Get Delilah to talk to them!"

Chaim looked around for her. She was in the center of the dance floor, clapping. "Delilah," he hissed, taking her arm.

She turned around and looked at him. "Isn't this great?"

"What's the matter with you? It's a desecration of the Sabbath!"

"Why?"

"Because they are playing music!"

"But they're not Jewish! They can play!"

"No, they can't! Jews aren't allowed to pay people to work for them on the Sabbath. Everyone has to have a day of rest. Arthur Malin is furious."

"Arthur Malin has five maids who work for him on the Sabbath on a regular basis! All of these people have maids who work for them on the Sabbath. And besides, aren't the waiters working? Aren't the sailors who are running the boat working?"

"That's different!"

"Why?"

"It's—" He suddenly felt his head swim. He had to talk to Viktor again. To explain. He looked around for him, but his host was now in the center of an impenetrable knot of dancers, sitting on his haunches and kicking out his feet as he balanced bottles of beer on his head. Right next to him was Delilah.

He turned around, dizzy, groping his way toward the bar. "Double scotch," he said. He held the glass in his unsteady hand as he weaved his way through the long halls back to his cabin. He unlocked the door and looked in on his sleeping son.

"You can go now, thanks," he told the au pair. "I'll watch him." Then he stumbled to the veranda. The night air was mild and cool. He sat down in a deck chair, gulping down the liquor, watching the dark waves as they carried him farther into the night.

⁓ ⁓

The next day, the guests, hung over and exhausted, dressed in their good suits, their pastel hats, their custom wigs, their spike-heeled Jimmy Choos, their diamond earrings and brooches, made their way to the ballroom-turned-synagogue to witness the Bar Mitzva of Anatoly Shammanov.

All eyes were on Delilah, who was dressed in a pink brocade suit. She sat next to Joie, who wore a little black dress and a diamond-and-onyx necklace that looked like the Crown Jewels and cascaded down her generous cleavage like a waterfall inside a cave. A pashmina, brought along because Delilah had advised her friend that cleavage in the synagogue freaked out the rabbi, lay forgotten in her lap. Delilah didn't notice. She was totally preoccupied with examining the truly amazing creation on Joie's head: a hat with a large stylized horsehair flower and striped coque feathers.

"Love the hat!" Delilah whispered.

"Thanks! Love yours," Joie giggled.

Anatoly mounted the steps that led to the bimah, stepping up to the plate, as it were, to read the scripture of the week from the Haftarah. Unlike the whiz kids who read the entire Torah portion from the unvoweled and unpunctuated scrolls of the Torah, all he had to do was remember to read the transliterated Hebrew words of a short selection from the Prophets to the tune he'd been taught.

Chaim stood next to the child, wondering which of them was more nervous.

Anatoly cleared his throat. Then he began:

> "La ...... LA...... la.... la..... LA la la............ LA..... la............. la LA la...
> la LA...
> .... LA LA.."

Omigod. She saw Chaim wipe beads of sweat off his brow as he whispered to the boy, probably feeding him every incoherent word. At this rate, it was going to take hours. She slid down in her seat, casting nervous glances at Joie. But Joie was just looking at the boy with a fixed smile on her face, and was that—could it be—a yawn? Delilah exhaled. As long as no one broke down in tears, or ran away, or admitted defeat, it would be fine.

Joie leaned in and whispered. "It's a shame his mother didn't come."

Delilah looked around the packed room, surprised there could be anybody left behind in the Ukraine. "Why isn't she here?"

"Because she's a bitch. Besides, she's not Jewish, so all this upsets her. I mean, she had him baptized in the Greek Orthodox Church when Viktor wasn't looking." Joie grimaced. "Can you imagine? Viktor hit the ceiling, of course. He put the kid's head under a faucet and washed it off. 'He's my son, and he's a Jew, like me!' he told her."

Delilah swallowed hard, looking up at her husband, who stood sweating next to the boy at the bimah. According to Jewish law, a person was the same religion as his mother, not his father. "So he was converted, right? Anatoly, I mean?"

"Converted? Why? His father is a Jew. Anyhow, the rabbi who converted me said it wasn't necessary."

Delilah stared at her husband, standing with his arm around the Bar Mitzva boy, a Greek Orthodox Christian.

Forty-five excruciatingly long minutes later, the torture finally ground to a halt. The child was pelted by candies, and finally, finally, the fun could begin in earnest, as soon as the pesky restrictions of the Sabbath day were over. But first, they had to sit through Chaim's sermon. Delilah leaned back, sighing.

Chaim walked up to the podium. He coughed, then wiped his glistening forehead with a tissue. "When the Jews were in the desert, God asked them to build a tabernacle. Not because God needed a sanctuary. After all, God is everywhere. No, He asked it of us, because He knows the limitations of human beings. He gives us the sun, and what does He ask of us? To light a candle. A measly little candle. That's all."

Delilah looked up, suddenly guilt-stricken, the words playing in her head like a familiar tune. She had heard this before.

"But for many, even that is too much. Remember that when you feel the sun on your face every morning, when a healthy, beautiful new child or grandchild is placed in your arms. Remember all God does for you and the little He asks.

"Place yourself at His service, Anatoly, on this your Bar Mitzva day, the day a Jew becomes responsible for his own sins before God. Your parents are absolved. They are not responsible for your sins, and you aren't responsible for theirs. Now you control your life and your relationship to God. Give Him your devotion. Accept His demands on you." He hugged the child and motioned for him to sit down. Then he turned to the congregation. "Under His guidance, let us eliminate from our public and private lives every aspect that is not worthy of our relationship with Him. Those who resist God will be shattered."

Delilah looked around at the startled faces of the audience, who shifted uncomfortably in their seats. What was Chaim doing? she thought, alarmed.

"In the words of the great Samson Raphael Hirsch, joy is only to be found in the advancement of good and right. May your sons step into your place and may *you*, the parents, be *worthy* of emulation," he said pointedly.

"Don't depend on material prosperity to save you, or the approval of other people. The future depends on ethical and dutiful conduct."

Delilah darted nervous glances at Joie, who stared straight ahead, attempting to suppress yet another yawn. Delilah tried to motion to Chaim to speed it up, but he never even glanced in her direction.

Chaim closed his book and kissed it with reverence. "Anatoly, I congratulate you. May your parents be blessed through you and may you be blessed through them."

Delilah let herself exhale in relief.

While the prayer service continued, most of the women filed out. They strolled slowly around the deck, waiting for the men to finish so they could go into the dining room and partake of a magnificent kiddush, to be followed by a still more elaborate lunch, whose combined caloric intake would be enough to wipe out famine in a small African village. In the afternoon, they would groaningly fall into bed, sleeping through the numerous, annoying constraints of the Sabbath day until the sun sank into the sea, and the party they had flown halfway around the world to attend could begin.

Delilah found she was too excited to nap.

"Where are you going?" Chaim called after her sleepily.

"I'll be back soon. I just need to walk some of this food off."

She closed the door behind her.

"Well, hello," she heard over her shoulder. She turned. It was Joseph Rolland.

"Oh, Shabbat Shalom," she said primly. "Where's Mariette?"

"Now, now, we don't want to talk about Mariette, do we, Delilah?" He smiled at her, a smile he used confidently, whipping it out and dusting it off like a faithful surgical tool that had performed miracles numerous times, even on the comatose and half dead. Delilah, who had been hoping to run into Mick Jagger or Keith Richards, gave him a respectful nod-to-older-man, which—had it been taped and shown to the morality police—would have proclaimed her innocence.

This surprised and wounded Dr. Rolland, who was used to the magic of his white coat immediately transforming women into eager contestants on the win-a-night-with-Joseph-Rolland game show. It made him feel that he was losing it, that he was getting . . . old. He looked her over, her image suddenly transformed from an amusing dalliance into a seriously important project upon which much depended.

"Mind if I walk with you?"

She hesitated, then shrugged. What could she say?

"You know, I've been wanting a few moments alone with you for some time."

She looked down at her shoes. "Really? Why?"

"Well." He thought fast. "I don't think enough people really appreciate how difficult your job is."

"Oh, that's certainly true. It's really nice of you to say so."

Encouraged, he kept going. "I mean, the constant visitors, the politics, the catering to everyone's needs. And you are so young! It doesn't seem fair that those soft fine shoulders should have to bear so much."

Delilah straightened her back, feeling almost as if he'd caressed her. Where was this leading? she wondered. "No one forced me into it."

He inhaled, surprised by her resistance. He wasn't used to working very hard where women were concerned. But he liked a challenge, and his ego was involved, so he was willing to put up with it. "No, no, that's true. But sometimes our lives take turns that we don't expect. We drift along until one day, we wake up and find ourselves so far from where we thought we'd be, with so many needs that have gone unmet for so long. . . ." He stopped, his hands gripping the guardrails, as his eyes looked with what he hoped was mysterious longing off into the sea.

Delilah stood still. Was he for real? Rich, attractive Dr. Joseph Rolland, with the international jet-setting career and the wondrous mansion with its own gazebo, outdoor pool, and tennis courts overlooking the lake, had "unmet needs" that Mrs. Perfect didn't have a clue about? And he was standing here, opening his heart to . . . her?

She was, above all, flattered. "I know what it's like not to be understood."

He turned his full attention to her. "I sensed that in you from the moment I met you. That . . . yearning. That desire for something . . . better, deeper."

She began to protest mildly. He raised both hands, finding hers. "Sssh. Don't say anything, Delilah. I'm not asking anything of you. Just to be near you, when I can. To speak to you, when you'll let me. I've never met anyone like you. Don't try to talk me out of it. We're like two rivers, you and I, flowing along, and some force of nature has brought us together. There's something in our souls that are propelling us, making it happen."

She bit her lip, trying to hide a smile, considering the idea. It was all very well and good and might even be fun, she thought, like some afternoon soap. But quite aside from the whole morality of the thing, the Ten Commandments "adulteresses shall be stoned" issue, she did not want Mariette Rolland as an enemy.

"I am Mariette's friend," she murmured.

"And I am her husband and lover and the father of her children. This is much more difficult for me than it is for you."

Couldn't argue with that, although something was askew with the reasoning, she understood. "It's immoral."

"Morality! God tells the Jews to murder every last person in Amalek, men, women, children, even the cows and sheep. What's moral about that? A person has to listen to his God-given brains, his heart, not follow rules blindly! I mean, Abraham was willing to slit the throat of his only son. That's where blind faith leads you. . . . Some things are above morality."

Now she was thoroughly confused. The willingness of Abraham to sacrifice his only, beloved son when God asked it of him was considered the ultimate test, and Abraham had passed it with flying colors. His willingness was the foundation stone of the Jewish faith. "Above morality? Like what, for instance?"

"Like love, Delilah. Like once-in-a-lifetime, true, take-it-or-leave-it-because-it-won't-return-again love." This was his big finale. The title of his hit song. After discreetly surveying the area, he reached out and took her hand in his in wild abandon, pressing it to his heart.

She grabbed it back, massaging it as if it had been injured. "Are you crazy?" she whispered, giggling.

He smiled at her. "I haven't offended you, Rebbitzin Levi, have I?" He arched his brow.

She glanced at him sideways, in silence.

Going for broke, he reached out and put his hands around her waist. "Please, Delilah. Have mercy!"

Just then, a couple from the shul came jogging around the corner. Delilah turned her back on Joseph Rolland, whose hands fell limply to his sides. "Good Shabbes!" She smiled at them.

"Good Shabbes, Rebbitzin, Dr. Rolland." They smiled back, not slowing their pace but looking curiously over their shoulders.

Delilah and Joseph stood still, waiting for them to disappear.

"Come with me for a minute!" Joseph whispered to her urgently, taking her by the hand.

"You are insane! What if Mariette sees us?"

"She's snoring for the next two hours at least. Believe me, I know Mariette."

She followed him down the stairs into a small private alcove hidden behind a giant potted palm. He sat down, his hands on his knees, then leaned forward, pulling her onto his lap. She smelled his good cologne—she was a sucker for musk—and the dab of something lemony in his hair. A small feeling began in the pit of her stomach, as she remembered her days with Yitzi Polinsky and Benjamin, those sweet, powerful feelings that kept her in a state of drama and excitement, making her feel young, beautiful, and endlessly desirable.

She thought of her husband, also snoring away in bed, and the little boy who was all needs and wants who didn't see her at all. She thought of Mariette, always so superior, so perfect, and so full of advice, who'd stabbed her in the back with her criticism. She heaved herself up and walked away, back out to the deck, her nostrils flaring as she took deep, heady breaths of the sea air. She felt dizzy, grabbing onto the railing to steady herself. She looked out at the endless sea to where it met the endless sky. She was a tiny mote in the fleeting turnover of creation, insignificant and worthless as dust. Life was so incredibly short, and death so incredibly long. It was startling to her that only a little while ago, she thought Joseph Rolland a lecherous old jerk. And now? She looked up at his face that was close beside her. Here was a man who saved lives. A man who could hold a living human heart in his hands, putting it inside a heartless human being and allowing him to live.

Those hands, those wondrous hands, had touched her own. He wanted her. Loved her. He saw something in her that was worthwhile, a prize to be attained. She felt desired in a way that she had not felt for a very long time.

Inside, the raw unruly pull of passion slugged it out with reason, while all the while in the corner of her mind she was aware of Joseph's puzzled face close beside her, waiting.

She didn't want this to be like the others. She wanted something real out of this. Something serious and life-changing. She had to be sure that's what he wanted too.

"Can I ask you something?"

"Anything, my sweet."

"If I say no, will you just go on to your next conquest?"

He was startled. He hadn't given it any thought, although that was a pretty fair and accurate description. Still, if it was really fun, he might delay the inevitable.

"Is that what you think of me?" His eyes were tender, full of hurt.

"I'm sorry, Joseph." She reached up and touched his face. He took her hand, kissing the palm. Instinctively, she curled it into a fist.

She looked over his shoulder into a mirrored column, studying her face. Never had her eyes seemed more lovely and tender. Never had her lips seemed more tempting and desirable. This, this, was what life was all about. The excitement of the new conquest. The ability to test one's charms. The gift of mesmerizing and alluring.

Chaim treated her like he did one of his congregants: He paid attention to her in the hope that he could solve the problem and send her on her way. Most of the time, all he really wanted was to be left alone in his study to read. Of course, when he got the itch, she was suddenly remembered, or if she'd just come back from the *mikva* and it was his religious obligation. She didn't want to be some man's religious obligation. Not with those eyes. Not with those lips. She wanted someone who would fling the world over the abyss for her. All the novels she had read—*Anna Karenina*, *The Thorn Birds*—all the movies she had seen, were swirling through her head. They all made adultery seem funny and charming, exciting and interesting. And the husbands in these books and films were always so dull, so painfully clueless that one couldn't help feeling sympathy for the free spirit that wandered.

A person can only pretend to be something they're not for just so long.

Who had said that? Tzippy, she remembered, shuddering a little. Maybe she'd been right. Why should she not be the heroine of her own production? Why should she be stuck in the drab existence that had been forced upon her through no fault of her own when she had the ability, the talent, the looks, the daring, to hand herself another chance, another life?

He moved back. "Can you sneak away tonight? During the party? I know a place—"

"It's much too dangerous!"

"Life is full of worthwhile dangers, Delilah," he whispered, prying open her fingers one by one until her palm was once more naked and exposed. He pressed his lips full inside it.

"Not on the boat," she whispered.

TWENTY-NINE

Saturday night on the calmest ocean in the world, Rabbi Chaim stood outside the magnificent ballroom of a cruise ship, holding a cup of wine in his shaking hands, while two men beside him held a burning candle of twisted wicks and a bag of fragrant spices. As hundreds watched, Chaim closed his eyes and concluded the recitation of Havdalah, the traditional prayer that denotes the end of the Sabbath day and the beginning of a new week: "Blessed be You, God our God, King of the Universe, Who has made a distinction between holy and profane." He had a feeling the profane would be taking over in record time.

The ballroom doors flung open. Silver lanterns wreathed in white roses hung from birch branches. Trapeze artists flew through the air, turning somersaults and catching each other by the wrists. And who was that on stage? Three voluptuous Black girls wearing . . . well, one couldn't be quite sure, but something with strands of material and feathers and Lord knows what else, that covered roughly eighteen percent or less of what needed to be covered. They began to sing a song specially written for the Bar Mitzva boy, who was invited onstage. And then, as the child looked on, they began to bump and grind and wiggle their behinds in their signature way, moves that had earned them millions, international fame, and even music awards.

"No, no, no!" Chaim moaned, closing his eyes.

He felt someone hug him. "What's wrong, Rabbi? You don't like girls?" Viktor Shammanov grinned cynically, putting his arm around him. His eyes were bugging out of his head, drinking in the girls' bodies as if they were water and he was dying of thirst. It was then he realized Victor Shammanov was not the man he was pretending to be.

Chaim got up abruptly. "Excuse me." He weaved his way unsteadily through the crowd, drunk with shame and disappointment and helplessness. The party swirled around him, the serving stations, the huge video screens, the thousands of flowers, the noise from the stage, as one famous act followed another. Was that a white horse? Was that a small elephant? Was that David Copperfield, the magician?

Maybe, just maybe, he could get him to make the whole shebang disappear.

A very skinny, extremely long-haired, vastly tattooed guitarist was jumping up and down in black leather pants. The drums were something out of deepest Africa. And the guests, his congregants? They were all out on the dance floor, gyrating and bumping and grinding. There was one in particular, some blond bimbo in a really tight gown, her hair whipping from side to side as she shook, and wriggled, and boogied, practically lap-dancing her partner right on the dance floor. Who was she with? Could it be Dr. Rolland? He was also going wild . . . and the woman was definitely not Mariette. Chaim moved closer, angling for a better view.

No. It just couldn't be! He found a chair and collapsed into it, putting his hands over his face and feeling the blood rush into his head in shame and humiliation. Without another look, he got up and walked quietly back to his cabin.

"I can go now?" the babysitter asked, before he opened his mouth. He nodded, and she took off like a homing pigeon, thrilled, to find the source of the vibrating booms that filled the ship. Maybe she'd enjoy it, he thought, and he could claim *that* as a good deed when he stood before God and was grilled on how he could have let all this happen.

Like Aaron facing Moses just after the Golden Calf debacle, he thought desperately of some way to exculpate himself and transfer the blame, something along the lines of "What could I do, Moses? You know what these people are like. All I did was throw the gold into the fire, and oops, out came a calf!"

Not particularly convincing, was it? he thought, ashamed to face God.

And as Chaim Levi sat there in the dark, rocking his baby son in his arms, looking out at the dark sea for answers, many thoughts went through his head, many questions. Like chemical elements poured into a beaker, disparate ideas began to churn and fizzle and send up strange odors.

He thought about Benjamin. How strange a coincidence it had been that he lived in the same building with his grandfather's chiropractor. And how, after his grandfather's stroke, he never once telephoned or even paid a shiva call, simply vanishing. How Delilah had wanted him to go to the theater with her that night, and how she had come home so late and acted so strangely. He thought about the color in his grandfather's cheeks when Delilah walked into his hospital room, and how he had tried to sit up and pull out his tubes. How old Mrs. Schreiberman had physically attacked his wife and had to be hospitalized. And how Delilah had met the woman on the subway while she was sitting next to Benjamin, and how nervous she had been about it.

The ideas sloshed around in his head, bubbling, congealing, and changing colors as they began to react.

"Delilah, have you seen the rabbi?" Joie asked.

For the first time that evening, Delilah looked around for her husband.

"I don't see him."

"Can you find him, please? Viktor has a spectacular surprise for everyone, but he wants the rabbi to be there! Hurry."

Delilah didn't ask any questions. She wandered through the ballroom, then finally went back to their cabin.

As she opened the door, she saw the back of his head.

"Chaim?" She walked around. He had the baby in his arms. His eyes fluttered open. "Joie sent me to get you. Viktor has some important announcement to make and he wants to be sure you're there. Put the baby down and come. Where's the au pair?"

He didn't move.

"What's the matter with you?"

"Do you love me, Delilah?"

She stared at him. "How much have you been drinking?"

"Just answer me. For once in your life, tell me the truth."

She studied her nails. "I had your son, didn't I? I became a rebbitzin, didn't I?"

"Answer me!"

Oh, gee whiz, what now? "Chaim, I love you. Now, can we *please* just go back to the party? The entire ship is waiting for us."

"You don't, do you? I think I always really knew that, deep down. You think I'm ridiculous. I bore you."

Her mouth dropped open. "What's gotten into you?"

"I saw you out there on the dance floor, with Dr. Rolland."

Uh-oh. She tossed her head. "Dr. Rolland? So?"

"So? So a woman who loves her husband wouldn't dance with another man that way."

"Oh, grow up! I was just having a little fun!"

"I know all about it, Delilah."

"It?" For some reason, she started to get nervous.

"Yitzie Polinsky."

Her jaw dropped. Oh, boy. "There's nothing to know."

"Josh told me all about it before we were married."

"What? That sanctimonious piece of—!"

Chaim smiled sadly. "I was also angry at him. I didn't want to know." He looked into her eyes. His face was somber. "I don't care about that, Delilah. You didn't know me then. You were single. I want to know about Benjamin."

Her face went white. "Benjamin?"

"Why didn't he come to pay a shiva call? You knew him so well. He took the train with you every morning—"

"Oh, I get it. It's the old Schreiberman subway business! You're mad so you are bringing up ancient history. Is that it?"

"I went to see her, Delilah."

"Schreiberman? In the mentally challenged ward?"

"She told me some things that don't sound so crazy. That make everything fit together."

She inhaled, wondering what part to play. Outraged and Insulted? Hurt? Amused? (Harder to pull off but infinitely more fun as a part, she thought.) She decided on Innocent-Until-Proven-Guilty.

"You know, the Torah says if a person makes accusations, they have to back them up with facts."

"Oh, it would be easy to back up. All I have to do is find out if you really worked late that night. All I have to do is call your boss when we get back."

There went Innocent-Until-Proven-Guilty. "You wouldn't embarrass me by doing that!"

He looked at her shocked face. "Are you sure?"

She took a deep breath. "Look, Chaim, I can see you're upset. And you probably have every right to be. I agree with you that we need to have a long talk. But please, the Shammanovs are waiting. It's going to be humiliating for them if we don't show up soon. Please, please, can we just talk about all this later? After all, *they* haven't done anything to deserve being embarrassed in public."

"They've embarrassed themselves with this ridiculous, tasteless display of excess."

"Chaim, promise me you won't hurt their feelings? They're my friends!"

He thought about it. He got up and handed her the baby. He straightened his tie and tapped the top of his head with his cupped palm, checking that his skullcap hadn't slid off. He tucked in his shirt and buttoned his jacket and then, without turning around to look at her, walked out of the cabin.

Realizing the au pair had probably been let go for the night, Delilah groaningly put the baby down in his carriage, praying he wouldn't wake up and ruin her evening. Then she wheeled him into the banquet hall.

"There khe is!" Viktor boomed when Chaim walked in. "Rabbi, please, please, come up khere!" Viktor waved enthusiastically. "I vant to tell you, every one of you, I luff this man. Khe is a true friend. Khe take my son, my Anatoly, teaches him. Khe brings me khonor, pride, brings me back my grandfather's kheritage." He pounded his chest. "I am Jew. I am proud! Thank you, Rabbi!" He gave Chaim a bear hug.

"You're welcome," Chaim gasped.

"And my Joie, where is my Joie? And Delilah? Where is Delilah?" He motioned urgently for them to join him onstage. "I have announcement. In honor of son's Bar Mitzva, I build for Svallo Lake new synagogue. Not like tepee, like palace! I build new house for rabbi—beautiful house, with swimming pool. Until is ready, I give you extra house on Uspekhov for synagogue! Khere, I khave surprise."

The lights dimmed, and a huge screen was lowered. "*Khere it is!*"

The crowd gasped as the screen projected the image of a magnificent synagogue about three times the size of their present one. There were landscaped grounds and a sculpture garden. The screen flashed pictures of the new social hall, which looked like the lobby of the Bellagio Hotel in Las Vegas. He pounded his chest. "No donations! No fund-raising. I do this myself, for Grandfather!" Wild applause rang out. Confetti fell from the ceiling and the boom of a fireworks display lit up the windows with magenta and orange.

Delilah looked at the plans for her new house as they flashed on the huge screen, thrilled. Again and again, the drawings of the new synagogue, the banquet hall, the landscaped grounds flashed on, almost hypnotically. There was a moment of mass hysteria, as the drunk, exhausted crowd applauded and applauded and applauded until their fingers felt numb. Chaim looked around. Arthur Malin, his rage at Sabbath desecration forgotten, clapped along with the rest. Then Viktor took the microphone in hand once more.

"And vun more thing: I khave Superbowl tickets for all men. You come as guest of Viktor Shammanov. New England Patriots vill vin!"

A shout arose from the luxurious deck as it plowed into the calm waters of the night, a cry of surprise and awe the likes of which had not been heard on a cruise ship since the *Titanic.*

THIRTY

Back home in Swallow Lake, Chaim and Delilah settled the baby and unpacked their suitcases. They felt hung over, exhausted, and emotionally drained. Both were eager to avoid conflict. Ever since the Bar Mitzva banquet, they had been polite and distant, like bus passengers thrown together on a crowded Greyhound going from New York to California, wishing only to travel along pleasantly without additional stress.

Chaim had no time to deal with his personal life, because members of the synagogue had been calling him nonstop ever since Viktor's dramatic announcement, wanting to hear him gush about what a saint Viktor Shammanov was.

"I mean, it's just wonderful, don't you think?" rich accountants and lawyers and businessmen would blather through the phone lines, the same way those who had been to the Bar Mitzva had done in person on the plane all the way home from Hawaii.

"Well, it certainly is a generous offer that we should consider" had been his usual cautious answer.

This infuriated his listeners.

"Consider? What's to consider? A billionaire falls into our laps and wants to redo our shul, saving us millions; what's there to think about?"

"Well, first of all, do we really need a new synagogue?"

This incensed them even more. "We've been saying for years that the social hall is tiny. And the kitchen—no decent caterer would set foot inside it! Why should we look a gift horse in the mouth?"

Ask the Trojans, Chaim thought. But all he said was, "Well, I'm sure that the board will make the right decision. It's not up to me. I'm only the rabbi, after all."

"But Rabbi, with all due respect, I just don't understand! You and the rebbitzin should be thrilled! After all, you are the ones who brought the Shammanovs into the community! You introduced them and made them feel at home! None of this would have happened if not for you! Besides, hasn't he also promised to build you a new house?"

Something in those words, meant as praise, struck Chaim like a blow. He took a deep breath. "Perhaps we shouldn't accept such a generous gift. There are so many worthy causes that need support: terror victims in Israel, handicapped children, the poor, the aged. Just because there are resources to buy something doesn't mean one should buy it. Perhaps we should redirect Mr. Shammanov's generosity elsewhere."

At this point, the questioner usually gave up, exasperated, casting baleful and uncomprehending looks at the telephone or the rabbi, as the case might be, followed by an explanation of some unexpected and urgent reason to end the conversation.

Chaim locked himself in his study, writing furiously. He must write the sermon of his life, he exhorted himself. He must bring some sanity back to this community, before it drowned in its own Olympic-sized ego. Patiently, he sieved through the sources.

Was a man permitted to live excessively if he could afford it? Judaism, he found, was not in favor of asceticism. The Rambam had said, "No one should, by vows and oaths, forbid to himself the use of things otherwise permitted." In the Talmud it was written, "In the future world, a man will have to give an accounting for every good thing his eyes saw, but of which he did not eat."

There would always be poverty in the world. There would always be the suffering caused by disease and the malice of humans toward one another. The Torah commanded people to set aside ten percent of their wealth for charity, but the other ninety percent, a person was free to enjoy in any permissible way he saw fit.

Yes, all this was true. But who decided what was a fit way to enjoy God's blessings? Was it not the society in which one lived? One's neighbors? Should not the synagogue set the standard for moderation and being happy with what one has? For as it is written in Ethics of the Fathers: "Who is wealthy? He who rejoices in his lot in life."

Why shouldn't this community which had everything, including a perfectly adequate synagogue, simply rejoice in what it already had? Would Viktor Shammanov's gift really make anyone happier? Or would it feed into the community's ever-burgeoning demands upon itself, making each congregant mourn all those things they imagined they lacked, instead of praising God for the abundance that was already theirs?

The first rule of fund-raising is to know how to say no to a donor who wishes to donate something you don't want: the million-dollar statue of the late Herbert Cohen, to be placed at the entrance to the town's meeting hall; the Hospital for Stray Raccoons; the soccer stadium for ultra-Orthodox Jerusalem.

This is very difficult, because for the fund-raiser it means deliberately reducing your bottom line. But sometimes less really is more. This too, he thought, was a time to say: No, thank you very much. We have what we need. We should not be concentrating on walls and floors. We should be concentrating on how to fill the shells that are our homes and places of worship with the richness of meaning, values, and generosity toward our wives and children and neighbors and friends and employees that is expressed in the expenditure of time, and words, and caring personal acts, not the purchase of more things. Enough with the remote-controlled toilets, the three-hundred-dollar rubber beach sandals for three-year-olds, the infinity pools, the midget trees, the au pairs day and night, the ten-thousand-dollar koi fish, the army of servants you treat like slaves. Enough! Learn to find pleasure in your relationships with your family and your God. Learn to cherish what you have, not to pile on more junk you'll need to unload: things that will clog your basements and attics and brains and arteries, like plaque choking off the flow of lifeblood to the heart; things that will block and obscure what really matters in life!

He wrote furiously, nonstop, his armpits wet, his forehead glistening, his hands shaking.

Yes, Chaim thought, his chronic stomach pains leaving him for the first time since he got the invitation to the Shammanovs' Bar Mitzva. This is the speech he would make. Let them fire him! Let Delilah leave him! As he had once read on the door of a toilet stall in a vegetarian restaurant: *It is never too late to be what you might have been.* This is what he would say to them all. For once in his life, he would be a real rabbi, a mentor.

A week after the Bar Mitzva, Viktor Shammanov gathered up the men of Swallow Lake and took them on his private jet to witness the triumph of the New England Patriots in the Superbowl. While Chaim too was invited, he gently declined, claiming an inability to take off more time from his congregational work. Surprisingly, he got no special phone call from Viktor—or any of the other invitees—urging him to reconsider, a circumstance Chaim viewed with a mixture of relief and foreboding.

Delilah had come home with leis around her neck and a feeling of heaviness in her heart. The words that had passed between herself and her husband revealed to her how flimsy a structure her marriage really was. More a sukkah than a brick house set on concrete. She had never given her marriage—as a marriage—the least thought, viewing Chaim as she viewed the anchor person for the evening news: Whatever happened in the world, he would be there with his well-pressed suit and toothpaste commercial smile. The idea that her bond with Chaim could ever dissolve or disappear had not occurred to her.

Until now.

She pondered the unthinkable. What would it be like, she wondered, to dump Rabbi Chaim and run off with some rich, sexy, irreverent playboy, who knew how to dance and drink and do more than a quick close-your-eyes-and-wait-twenty-seconds-it-will-all-soon-be-over in bed? She thought about life with Joseph Rolland or even Viktor Shammanov. Joie didn't really appreciate her luck. A man that extravagant and adventurous. A man looking for meaning in his life. She finally had to admit to herself that was what she wanted, what she had always wanted: a Yitzie Polinsky, someone dark and dangerous who lived on the edge and took the world on his own terms. Not some scared rabbit hiding in some sunless warren, always a terrified hop, skip, and jump in front of some plodding hunter. This was all frighteningly new, thrilling information for Delilah as it bubbled up from her subconscious into her daydreams.

Yet despite the newfound clarity that her husband held few attractions for her, that he—in fact—bored her silly, she, like many women, was terrified of the idea of losing the roof over her head and the social acceptance and respectability that was the ground beneath her feet. Did she really want to go from "rebbitzin" to "divorcee" and "single mom" with a weekly Parents without Partners meeting in downtown Hartford after a day of scraping goo off the teeth of strangers?

To leap from Chaim into the sheltering arms of another man was one thing, to take a flying leap into the unknown, quite something else again. Chaim, as a rabbi, had adequate reason to send her on her way. No rabbinical court in the world would back her up once he revealed what he knew about Yitzie Polinsky, his suspicions about her relationship with Benjamin, and what he had witnessed between herself and Joseph Rolland. It wouldn't even matter if in the end he had not a single shred of evidence to back him up. Rabbinical court judges were notorious for their one-sided rulings in favor of husbands; they were all hanging judges when it came to even the merest appearance of impropriety on the part of the wife. This was based firmly on Torah law, which even had a special-Divine category called "the jealous husband." A man didn't need proof. All he needed were his suspicions in order to put a wife through humiliating and life-threatening trials. If she was innocent, of course, the bitter waters she was forced to drink made her fertile. But if she was guilty, they caused her "belly to swell and her thighs to waste away."

There was nothing remotely similar for the philandering husband unless he was involved with another man's wife, in which case both he and his paramour earned themselves a mandatory death by stoning. These days, of course, such a verdict was unenforceable. The result was that the man went scot free while the woman got divorced and ostracized.

If, one day, time and chance provided her with an opportunity she just couldn't turn down, in the form of a desirable suitor willing to provide for her the kind of life she had seen all around her since coming to Swallow Lake, she might willingly open the door and walk out. Until then, she had no intention of letting Chaim open it for her, kicking her out into a world of uncertainty, homelessness, poverty, and calumny. She wanted the decision—and the timing—to be hers. That being so, she felt she had no choice but to mend her ways and earn her way back into her husband's good graces.

The first thing she did was to talk to her former boss at the Riverdale dental clinic. He had been most understanding. That taken care of, she decided to start dealing seriously with her *chesed* project. She began to go through her handbags and pack them up for shipping. She contacted a number of well-known charitable agencies dealing with terror victims. But, for some reason that she couldn't figure out, none of them had any interest in becoming involved. In fact, unless she was imagining it, she heard muffled laughter in the background during her phone conversations with them, which she found shocking, considering that the subject was no laughing matter. She chalked it up to pressure. Anyone involved with such tragedies had to crack sometime.

She now possessed two hundred and seventy-four used—but more or less still very nice—designer handbags and nothing to do with them. She put in a call to the Israeli embassy. A very nice girl, whose English left much to be desired, explained that if she shipped them to Israel she'd have to pay tax on them, even if they were a charitable donation. Something about putting the local used handbag stores out of business.

"But Israel doesn't have any used handbag stores!"

"That's not entirely true," the girl said, getting a bit snooty. "Anyway, we don't think a designer handbag is the most important thing a terror victim lacks. Especially the ones that are still in the hospital, or orphaned, or widowed."

Well, she couldn't solve *all* their problems.

A bit desperate, she decided, very reluctantly, to call Rivkie, with whom she had had no contact at all since the doula businesss. But times were desperate; besides, Delilah wasn't the type to hold a grudge, especially if the person involved could still be useful.

"Hi, Rivkie, you'll never guess!"

She could tell Rivkie wasn't exactly thrilled to hear from her, but being Rivkie she was polite and kind. She had relatives in Israel who could give them out, she agreed, but Delilah would have to raise the money for taxes and shipping.

"How much do you think that will be?" she asked.

"Well, it depends on how much they estimate the bags are worth."

"Look, between you and me, some of them are fakes that are worth thirty bucks, and some are worth two thousand."

"Well, the tax on a two-thousand-dollar bag is going to be a lot of money, believe me. But if you get it together, let me know."

"Thanks, Rivkie." She hesitated. "Sorry I haven't been in touch. It was just so awkward and all. I mean, after the doula business. How is she?"

There was silence. "Her hand has healed."

"Oh. I'm glad to hear it. And how are things going with the two of you?"

"Fine, fine. Josh has just accepted a position as rabbi of the Lincoln Center Synagogue on the Upper West Side."

"Wow, Manhattan!"

"It's a nice congregation. Look, Delilah, I've got to run. Take care of yourself, and let me know if I can help you. 'Bye."

" 'Bye, Rivkie. And thanks. For everything. Oh, by the way, you don't happen to have any friends or relatives that live in Swallow Lake, do you? Someone you might have spoken to about me?"

There was dead silence on the other end. Then a tiny voice. "Why do you ask?"

"Because someone wrote Chaim an anonymous letter about Yitzie Polinsky."

"Delilah, I—I'm . . . well, I have to ask *mechilah*."

The traditional request for forgiveness that went around before the high holidays and Yom Kippur was rarely used at other times of the year, unless the penitent truly feared for their eternal soul.

"*Mechilah*?" Delilah asked suspiciously. "For what?"

"Delilah, I swear I didn't know it would get back to Chaim. Mariette Rolland is friends with my mother. And I might have mentioned it to my mother years ago."

"Rivkie, I have something to tell you."

"Yes?"

"Your clothes? They never actually fit me. They were too big, especially around the butt! And you can forget about *mechilah*. You can kiss my little ass, and that goes for your husband too!" She slammed down the phone.

Mariette Rolland. How appropriate, Delilah thought. She looked at the boxes and boxes of handbags. What to do with them? She picked up a Chanel and turned it over. Not bad. Someone would pay good money for it on eBay. A little light clicked on in her head. She piled them into cartons and put them down in the basement. Every day, she'd auction off one of them, until she had enough money to pay the taxes and shipping costs for the rest.

She got busy. She started cleaning the house, taking the baby out for walks. She skipped her aerobics classes and, instead, baked fattening cakes for myriad Sabbath guests.

"Chaim?" She poked her head into his study.

He looked up from his open books, eyeing her silently.

"I thought you might be hungry. I made a little snack." She placed a mug of hot freshly brewed coffee on his desk with a blueberry muffin, warm from the oven. "And Chaim?"

His eyes shifted from the food to her face, which was settled in pleasant docile lines. "I have made up lists of people we should invite over soon. Can you check them over and see if I've left anyone out?"

He looked down at the neatly typed pages, holding dozens and dozens of names.

"This looks fine, Delilah." He nodded correctly. "Now, if you'll just excuse me, I have some work. . . ."

"Oh, sure, of course. Sorry." She smiled, looking chastened and pathetic, he thought, as she closed the door behind her.

He looked down at the food. He couldn't bring himself to touch it.

{ THIRTY-ONE }

The Sabbath following the Superbowl, Chaim sat nervously in his chair, waiting impatiently for the moment he could rise and approach the podium. All the while, he anxiously patted his jacket pocket, like a best man fingering the rings, to make sure the pages of his speech hadn't somehow disappeared. Finally, the Torah reading was completed, along with all the post-reading blessings. This was his cue. He rose, taking the papers out of his pocket, and strode purposefully down the aisle and up toward the podium.

Just as he was about to mount the first step, Arthur Malin reached out and touched his arm. "Rabbi? I want to ask your kind permission to address the congregation this Shabbes. The board has something very special to tell them. Would you mind?"

Chaim looked down at the speech clutched in his hand. He had opened his mouth to object when he realized all the members of the board had now risen and were standing in front of him like an opposing football team, ready to tackle him to the ground.

"You don't mind, Rabbi, just this once?" Stuart smiled affably.

"Really, Rabbi, do us this favor?" Joseph nodded.

"You'll understand why in a minute." Ari rubbed his hands together.

Chaim looked at them and at the congregation. It was, after all, their synagogue. He was just the hired help. He bowed, turning around and walking back to his seat. He sat down heavily, crumpling the pages in his fist as he rammed them back inside his pocket.

"I thank the rabbi for giving up his pulpit for me. Thank you, Rabbi Chaim! I have wonderful news!" Standing in the front of the synagogue surrounded by the other male members of the board, a huge smile on his face, Arthur Malin announced: "The board held an extraordinary meeting after the Superbowl and agreed to accept the fantastically generous gift of the Shammanovs to build us a new synagogue and a new rabbi's house. We signed the papers yesterday. The new synagogue will have sixty-five-thousand square feet! A catering hall that is fifteen thousand square feet! It will have twenty-eight classrooms, a two-thousand-square-foot library, recreation rooms, screening rooms, a swimming pool, and a cafeteria—so you can eat after every minyan! In addition, there will be a fifty-six-foot-high waterfall in the lobby with a reflection pool that will symbolize our new theme: Mayim Chayim, living waters—and I must say, since this whole thing started off the coast of Maui, it's particularly apt." He chuckled.

The privileged ones who had been to Maui chuckled with him, while the others stared in shocked, morose silence.

"Construction begins next week and we should be enjoying—well, I don't know if that's the right word exactly, heh-heh—our Rosh Hashanah and Yom Kippur prayers in our new space. For his unbelievable gift, we would like to present Viktor Shammanov with a token of our community's thanks. Viktor, would you come up here, please?"

Viktor, seated in the front pew, bounded up to the podium, a huge smile on his face. "I luff this man! You are so kind to me and my family! Who vould have thought little Viktor from Turdistan would be in America, an American, in a synagogue? That khe would build synagogue in khonor of khis grandfather, such a kholy man!"

Arthur wiped his eyes, reaching out to hug the man. Viktor hugged him back. When Arthur was able to breathe again, he said, "On behalf of

Ohel Aaron, we wish to present you with this silver pointer that is used by the Torah reader. We think it is appropriate, Viktor, because in all you do you help point the way for our congregation, showing us what we all want to be."

Shouts of "Mazel tov!" "Bless you!" "*Yashar koach*!" "Wonderful!" rang out from every corner, or so it seemed to Chaim, who turned around, staring at the congregation. The truth was, he realized, that the well-wishers were strategically seated all over the synagogue to give the appearance of overwhelming adulation. In fact, the synagogue was deeply divided, an equal number of congregants sitting stone-faced, their hands clenched in their laps. For a moment, a swell of hope rose in his chest. Just then, he heard his name called: "Vere is khe? My rabbi?" Viktor shouted. "Khere khe is! Come khere, come khere." He waved. Reluctantly, Chaim got up and walked toward him. "This is reason I came to your synagogue. This man. Khe is responsible for everything!"

Select members of the synagogue broke out into a fury of foot stamping and applause. And even those unwilling to applaud the new synagogue, found it in themselves to unclench their fists and slap their palms together, joining in the adulation for their rabbi, with whom they felt they enjoyed a special bond, especially since he had been willing to forgo his Superbowl ticket to be with them. Still others sat facing forward without moving a muscle or changing their expression as they lifted their eyes to Chaim Levi, the man who had brought Viktor Shammanov to Ohel Aaron.

Chaim stood firmly sandwiched between Arthur and Viktor, facing the congregation, his physical presence blessing the enterprise, the speech in his pocket crumpling and growing moist from the sweat that now drained from every one of his pores.

In the women's section, Delilah sat shaking hands and air-kissing furiously, like a queen. She had done it. Pulled it off! Her husband was safe in his job. She was safe in hers. There would be no wandering now, no fear of unemployment. There would be a brand-new, huge, custom-designed house with every luxury, to rival those of even the richest members of the congregation. Chaim would forgive and forget. Their lives would be blessed, floating on calm waters forevermore. She glanced up eagerly at her husband.

He looked back at her, expressionless, then turned away. This small gesture landed in her stomach like a rock.

She looked at the fawning smiles of the women who surrounded her, women wearing clacking, pointed designer shoes, wildly expensive hats, and custom-made suits, suddenly remembering the bored eyes of the captains of the punchball teams when they finally turned in her direction, having no one left to choose. Finally on the team, she had fumbled the ball, let it drop, lost the point, and they had all turned their backs on her, pretending not to know her. Her heart froze. What did it matter how these women looked at her now, when her own husband looked away?

Why did everything she dream of, lean on, depend on, turn to straw the instant it came to fruition, collapsing beneath the weight of reality? she wondered. Was there truly no happiness in the world? Was everything, then, a lie? Love, faith, joy, constancy, sincerity? All those kissing her now, would they still love her tomorrow? Would they love her husband? Or was it a merry-go-round that constantly stopped and made you get off, forcing you to pay for new tickets if you wanted another little ride, another little taste of success?

She wanted someone to take her off the carousel, someone with strong firm arms who would lift her up and let her rest her weary head against his shoulder, whispering compliments and extravagant promises in her ear with unconditional love. She wanted to exhale and be safe and secure at last, she told herself, without conviction.

No, she realized, that wasn't it at all. That would be supremely boring.

And then the truth finally hit her. As Emma Bovary had finally figured out in the end, there was nothing worth having, nothing that lasted: "Every smile hid a yawn, every happiness, a misery. Every pleasure began to curdle, and every embrace left behind a baffled longing for a more intense delight."

An image arose in her mind: the neat little figure, the dark passionate eyes, a woman who had driven herself to madness and suicide, who had betrayed and been betrayed. An unfaithful wife, a bad mother, a silly self-destructive fool. And yet, a dreamer who was not afraid to envision a different life, no matter how others condemned her for it.

She took a deep breath and straightened her back. There would be a huge house. Her husband would be head of one of the largest synagogues in the area. People would point to her and say, "Rebbitzin Levi!" And all the punch ball captains and rabbi's daughters who had lived in Tudor mansions in the Five Towns would think of her when they sat alone, divorced or on their way to teach special ed in hellholes in Brooklyn. And when her name and her husband's popped up in the social columns with flattering pictures of her in dazzling dresses at charity events, they would envy her and be sorry they hadn't been nicer to her. They would understand that all along she had been playing the game alongside them, that she had been a good player, a worthy teammate, and that she too had won. Even if she didn't feel that way now, she told herself, she was sure she would feel that way tomorrow. After all, as someone much smarter and more successful than Emma Bovary had pointed out: "Tomorrow is another day."

The bulldozers came the following week. All the furniture, the sacred Torah scrolls and the prayer books had been moved temporarily into the spare house on the Shammanovs' property, where the synagogue would continue meeting until the construction ended.

People stood around in awe, a bit horrified, as the metal teeth bit into the side of the building, bringing down the concrete tepee with its ribbons of stained glass. With amazing ease, where the synagogue once stood, there was only a pile of chalky rubble, twisted metal, shards of brightly colored glass, and splintered wood. Billowing clouds of choking dust filled the air, fogging the windows and whitening the plants of the expensive homes in Swallow Lake. Maids and cleaning services would spend weeks of backbreaking labor erasing the evidence of the collapse.

Chaim stood outside, mesmerized, watching it fall, his heart filled with mixed emotions: horror, regret, and a tiny twinge of strange joy.

Delilah spent the morning at the country club, anxious to talk to Joie about the plans for the new rabbi's residence. To her surprise, Joie wasn't there. And when the congregation showed up at the Shammanov estate that Friday night to attend services, they found the gates locked and nobody home.

EPILOGUE

The collapse of the Ohel Aaron Congregation on Swallow Lake created a mushroom cloud reminiscent of those hovering over unlucky cities at the close of World War II, filled with controversy, heartbreak, and conjecture. The story, featured in every major newspaper and magazine in America, included photos of the bulldozed synagogue with a furious Solange Malin shaking her fist. Both *Newsweek* and *Time*, on the other hand, chose to use photos of Viktor Shammanov at the airport, ushering his blond wife and baby into a private jet just before they flew off to God knows where.

The whole convoluted tale of Viktor's business dealings—which turned out to be one huge international con job—was fodder for exposés in both *Fortune* and *Business Week*, which debunked all the facts, the same facts they had written about him earlier—which had convinced people to trust him in the first place. As it turned out, Viktor was selling shares in an oil company that the government of Turdistan declared belonged to them, denouncing Viktor and his company as worthless. But then, the entire government of Turdistan had also been declared a scam, the elections having been rigged and the opposition candidates fed disfiguring poison.

Viktor, of course, had done it all through a tangled web of companies incorporated in places like the Cayman Islands, the Seychelles, and other accommodating sun-kissed shelters. The Four Seasons Hotel in Maui was suing him, as were the cruise line, the catering services, the Lakers cheerleaders, Mick, Christina, Michael, and hundreds more, many of whom were forced into declaring bankruptcy.

And then, just as the dust was about to settle, the true, horrifying dimensions of the scam came to light. It was not just the synagogue that Victor Shammanov had bulldozed in Swallow Lake, but the lives of its most prominent inhabitants as well. From quiet conversations between accountants, lawyers, and financial planners, who shared the painful truth back and forth on cell phones and over alcohol-soaked dinners, the story came out. Unbeknownst to one another, the wealthiest residents, those who had been courted by Victor and his wife, invited to their home and their Bar Mitzva, had one by one persuaded Viktor Shammanov to overlook the rules and allow them to purchase shares in his company. Swearing each to secrecy, and with a great show of reluctance, Viktor had done them the great favor of accepting the substantial investments they pressed upon him.

Many of those defrauded were too embarrassed to admit it. And those who tried to claim a tax deduction on their losses aroused the interest of the Internal Revenue Service, who wondered where all that money had come from, prompting them to do a thorough audit going back many years, resulting in huge reassessments, fines, and even criminal charges.

Soon after, many FOR SALE signs began to appear on Swallow Lake's largest estates. Many were quietly repossessed by the banks or sold at auction. The kind of people who bought the homes were quite different from the original residents—local small businessmen and white-collar workers who smelled a fire sale and lined up for bargains.

The land where the synagogue had once stood became embroiled in lawsuits and countersuits because Viktor had managed to sell it several times over. The legal wrangling kept it a pile of weeds and rubble, an eyesore, for years to come. Eventually it was rezoned, and some builder put up condos and then a Baptist church.

In the beginning, Ohel Aaron members used the auditorium in the day school for services, until the dwindling student body forced the school to close its doors. Without a synagogue or a day school, the remaining Jewish families trickled out of the community to places like New York, Boston, and Hartford. Solange and Arthur wound up in San Diego, where they started a new day school. Ari and Felice quietly divorced. Ari is now working in a high-tech company in Ramat Aviv and was recently drafted into the Israeli army.

Amber and Stuart, who were hit worst of all, having invested every penny they owned with Viktor, declared bankruptcy, losing control of their teddy bear empire. But they managed to bounce back, designing a new doll that shakes its behind when you press a button, and reportedly have made countless millions with it.

Only Joseph and Mariette stayed behind in Swallow Lake. She stopped wearing her hats, and they no longer call themselves Orthodox. Her house, they say, is as beautiful as ever, and so is she. Still, she is alone much of the time.

As for Chaim and Delilah, they've become somewhat of a legend, the subject of rabbinical sermons from Johannesburg to Jerusalem and all points in between. Someone even made a movie about a hapless rabbi and his scheming wife, which everyone knew was based on all the newspaper articles about them. It poked a lot of fun at Orthodox Jews and was roundly condemned by embarrassed congregations everywhere, who accused the screenwriter and the producers of being "Jewish anti-Semites." It got Reese Witherspoon another Oscar nomination.

As for what really happened to Chaim and Delilah, stories—like Elvis sightings—continue to surface every few years, claiming to be the true, the only, authoritative version. What everyone agrees on is this: Immediately after the Sabbath when they were turned away from the ornate gates of Uspekhov, a furious crowd of shul members showed up at the home of their rabbi and rebbitzin, who, fairly or unfairly, were held entirely responsible for the disaster. Holding buckets of concrete, glass, and wooden rubble, they poured the contents on Rabbi Chaim's front lawn, all the while waving flashlights and screaming insults. Someone marked their front door with an X, and others ran after their speeding car with a bucket of tar and feathers.

After that, it all depends on whom you want to rely. One widely circulated report, published in the *Jewish Daily Press* (known by all as the *Jewish Mess*) had them driving directly to Tijuana, where they got a quickie civil divorce and an even quicker religious divorce, or *get*. Never did anyone get a *get* as fast as Delilah Levi, the story claimed. And Chaim, instead of gently tossing the scroll into her hands, as is the custom, pitched it so hard she wound up having to duck. Subsequent reports in that same paper had Chaim remarried a year later to a short, dark-haired Torah teacher with whom he went on to have other children in addition to little Abraham, over whom Delilah was only too happy to relinquish custody. Years later, another story about a Rabbi Chaim Levi appeared, describing the life of the Orthodox rabbi of a large, prosperous synagogue in Bogotá, Colombia. It described how he had learned Spanish and how he and his wife—a second marriage for both—lived in luxury with their eight children, surrounded by an adoring, respectful congregation and full-time personal bodyguards, who protected them from drug-crazed kidnappers.

Soon after that, someone who looked exactly like Delilah surfaced on the cover of a California business journal. She wore a very chic and modest black suit as she smilingly accepted an award for running the most successful new eBay venture, a Web site selling "gently pre-owned designer handbags." In the article, the woman accepting the award—who called herself Marlene Gold—talked about how she had begun her business after surviving a devastating divorce and losing custody of her only child to her vindictive ex.

She described how she'd started at the bottom and worked her way up. She talked about her mansion in Beverly Hills with its pool, her shopping trips to Paris and Milan for the shows, her fabulous vacations in sunny spots all over the globe. Despite the fact that she wore a magnificent wedding ring, she refused to give any details about her personal life, saying only that "she had a very handsome young husband, and two beautiful blond daughters." She had everything she wanted in life, she said, and moreover, she had earned it herself. Someone scanned the magazine cover and article, and for a while it circulated through the Internet to millions. Everyone who saw it and who had known Delilah agreed that, if it really was her, she looked fabulous and thin, and sexier than ever.

But the most recent article, which you must have read—everybody did—was the one in *New York* magazine. The reporter, a crack investigative journalist and a Gentile, tracked down a former classmate of Chaim's who had sent out the following shocking revelation to everyone on the Bernstein alumni e-mail list.

> Dear Friends:
> In light of the terrible sin of gossip and scandalmongering of which we have all been guilty over the years concerning our friend and colleague Rabbi Chaim Levi, who defied the ban on the Swallow Lake congregation, I would like to set the record straight once and for all. Chaim and Delilah Levi are still married, baruch Hashem, and the parents of five children. They are the rabbi and rebbitzin of a tiny shteibel somewhere in North Dakota, consisting of thirteen families, who all meet in the rabbi's basement for Sabbath and holiday prayers. Because the town is snowed in most of the year, the entire congregation regularly has not only kiddush but lunch and holiday meals at the rabbi's house, which the rebbitzin prepares, although congregants often bring homemade contributions. I know because I spent the Sabbath with them.

In the magazine interview, the classmate tried hard to convey the great joy and serenity the Levis had found in living in such a tiny Jewish community, as well as the great love of the congregation for their rabbi and rebbitzin. He described Rebbitzin Levi as

> the picture of the matriarch of an older generation, dressed in the modest clothing one would expect of a pious wife and mother, her dress loose and midcalf, her hair completely covered by a snood where only her blond bangs were visible, like those pious women of Boro Park and Meah Shearim. Numerous small children tugged at her dress as she ate with a healthy appetite from the heaps of cholent, kugel, and potato salad arrayed in plastic serving plates on a plastic tablecloth. There was much sincere laughter and the singing of many Sabbath hymns, as the children played board games and the adults conversed.

She looked, the classmate claimed, *perfectly content*.

The reporter, however, was not convinced. He wrote:

> The classmate, a very pious Jew who lowers his eyes when he meets other men's wives, is a man who seems to be defending the Orthodox world. It is not impossible that he views the creation and publication of this fairy-

> tale ending to a scandalous tale that has rocked the religious world for years as a good deed, a mitzva.

Furthermore, the classmate could not, or would not, provide an address and phone number for them, claiming he wished to protect their privacy, as they had "suffered so much from public scrutiny."

The reporter's cynicism produced a furor. Hundreds of letters to the editor arrived at the magazine. Those who defended the classmate's tale said they found it perfectly feasible that the Levis, having undergone such terrible trials, had stayed together and learned to love each other. Delilah's repentance and reformation further confirmed to them the beauty of the Jewish religion, which allows people to change and grow and learn from their mistakes.

But most people, including a good number who had actually known the Levis, were inclined to share the reporter's skepticism. They said they found the classmate's story *hard to believe*, either because they couldn't bear to think of Chaim still saddled with Delilah or vice versa. They also took issue with the idea that anyone, particularly a weekend house guest, could possibly know if someone was *perfectly content*.

But the best letter of all, people agreed, was from a woman claiming to be Delilah's former roommate and the rebbitzin of a large congregation. Her sentiments spoke to many when she wrote:

> It is not easy to be a rebbitzin. There are so many demands on your time, such a constant intrusion into your private life, and sometimes not much appreciation. Some people are just not suited to it. Wherever she is, we hope that Delilah has come to terms with the limitations of our lives and the impossibility of having all our dreams come true. If she has been forced, or has chosen, to live a simple pious life, we hope that the serenity to be happy with such a choice has come her way as well. And if she really has found the overabundance she craved, we hope that it doesn't give her high cholesterol or make her mean-spirited and that she is nice to her household help and takes care of her own children, at least some of the time. And that she remembers to say her prayers as sincerely and as often as she can.

"Once again, Jacques masterfully makes his familiar plot fresh, leavening it with both humor and poignancy. A welcome episode for the series's legion of fans."
—Booklist

The murderous Rapscallion army is on the move. Pursued by Lady Cregga Rose Eyes, the Badger Lady of Salamandastron, they are heading inland to take a great prize: the peaceful Abbey of Redwall.

But the Long Patrol—that fighting unit of perilous hares—is called out to draw them off . . . and fight them to the death if need be. And the lead sword of the Long Patrol will be taken up by the young, inexperienced hare Tammo—in one of the most ferocious battles Redwall has ever faced . . .

DON'T MISS THESE OTHER NOVELS OF "REDWALL"

Mossflower

Brave mouse Martin and quick-talking mousethief Gonff unite to end the tyrannical reign of Tsarmina—who has set out to rule all of Mossflower Wood with an iron paw . . .

"Packed with action and imbued with warmth . . . richly inventive."

—Kirkus Reviews

"Children are privileged to enter the rich world of Redwall and Mossflower. So are the parents who get to come along."

—The Boston Phoenix

continued . . .

The Pearls of Lutra

A young hedgehog maid sets out to solve the riddle of the missing pearls of legend—and faces an evil emperor and his reptilian warriors . . .

"Plenty of adventure."

—*Publishers Weekly*

"The Redwall Books . . . add a touch of chivalry and adventure reminiscent of the King Arthur stories."

—*The Arkansas Democrat Gazette*

The Outcast of Redwall

The abandoned son of a ferret warlord must choose his destiny beyond the walls of Redwall Abbey . . .

"Grand exploits . . . another rousing saga."

—*Booklist*

"Strongly plotted and spiced with a variety of secondary characters."

—*Publishers Weekly*

The Bellmaker

The epic quest of Joseph the Bellmaker to join his daughter, Mariel the Warriormouse, in a heroic battle against a vicious Foxwolf . . .

"Filled with rousing adventure, strong characters, and vibrant settings."

—*Boston Sunday Globe*

"Jacques spins another irresistible tale."

—*Booklist*

continued . . .

Martin the Warrior

The triumphant saga of a young mouse destined to become Redwall's most glorious hero . . .

"Wonderfully imaginative."

—*New York Times Book Review*

"Readers will rejoice."

—*Los Angeles Times*

Salamandastron

When the mountain stronghold of Salamandastron comes under attack, only the bold badger Lord Urthstripe stands able to protect the creatures of Redwall . . .

"A good yarn . . . grand climax . . . Jacques charms readers . . . another winner."

—*Booklist*

"Swashbuckling adventures told with great gusto in rousing words."

—*Chicago Tribune*

Redwall

The book that inspired a legend—the first novel in the bestselling saga of Redwall! The epic story of a bumbling young mouse who rises up, fights back . . . and becomes a legend himself . . .

"Charming . . . rollicking good adventure."

—*Fantasy Review*

"Reminiscent of *Watership Down* . . . *Redwall* is a thrilling tale of danger and adventure . . . an edge-of-the-seat, can't-put-it-down book with potential for classic status."

—*Parent's Choice*

Also by Brian Jacques

REDWALL
MOSSFLOWER
MATTIMEO
MARIEL OF REDWALL
SALAMANDASTRON
MARTIN THE WARRIOR
THE BELLMAKER
SEVEN STRANGE AND DEADLY TALES
THE OUTCAST OF REDWALL
PEARLS OF LUTRA
THE LONG PATROL

THE LONG PATROL

Brian Jacques

ACE BOOKS, NEW YORK

THE LONG PATROL

An Ace Book / published by arrangement with
Hutchinson Children's Books

PRINTING HISTORY
Published in Great Britain in 1997 by
Hutchinson Children's Books, London.
Philomel Books, Reg. U.S. Pat. & Tm. Off.
Philomel hardcover edition / 1998
Ace mass market edition / February 1999

Cover art by Troy Howell.

For information address:
Philomel Books,
a division of Penguin Putnam, Inc.
375 Hudson Street, New York, New York 10014.

The Penguin Putnam Inc. World Wide Web site address is
http://www.penguinputnam.com

ISBN: 0-441-00599-3

ACE®
Ace Books are published
by The Berkley Publishing Group,
a division of Penguin Putnam Inc.,
375 Hudson Street, New York, New York 10014.
ACE and the "A" design are trademarks
belonging to Penguin Putnam, Inc.

PRINTED IN THE UNITED STATES OF AMERICA

10 9 8 7 6

This book is dedicated to the memory of a nine-year-old boy, Jimmy Casey—the bravest warrior of all who never gave up, and who will live on in the hearts of all who knew him.

Brian Jacques

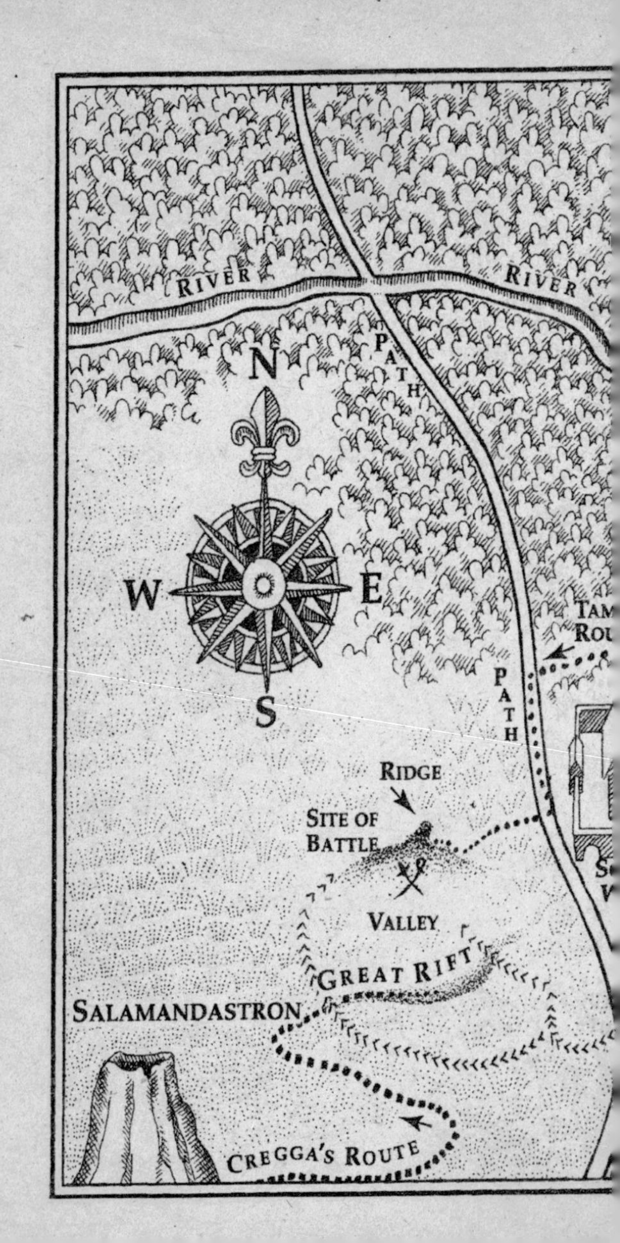
RIVER
RIVER
N
PATH
W
E
S
PATH
RIDGE
SITE OF
BATTLE
VALLEY
GREAT RIFT
SALAMANDASTRON
CREGGA'S ROUTE

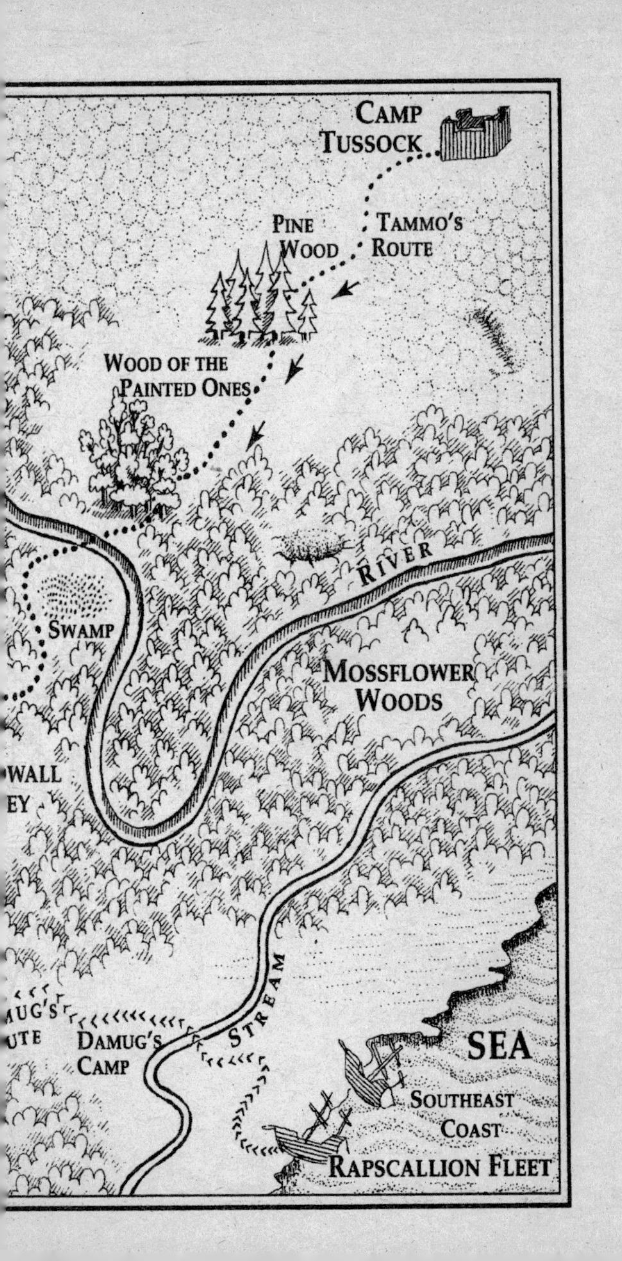

CAMP TUSSOCK
PINE WOOD
TAMMO'S ROUTE
WOOD OF THE PAINTED ONES
RIVER
SWAMP
MOSSFLOWER WOODS
WALL
EY
STREAM
UG'S
UTE
DAMUG'S CAMP
SEA
SOUTHEAST COAST
RAPSCALLION FLEET

Sometimes I sit here through the night,
Dreaming of those far-flung days.
I'll gaze into the fire's warm light,
As if into some sunlit haze.
And here they come, those comrades mine,
Laughing, happy, brave to see,
Untarnished by the dust of time,
Forever fresh in memory.
The way we marched, the feasts so grand,
I'll tell you of them all,
From Salamandastron's west strand,
And north up to Redwall.
Of high adventures each new dawn,
As side by side we stood in war,
This tale is told that you may learn,
Just what true friends are for.

The Ballad of Tammo

BOOK ONE

The Runaway Recruit

1

Melting snowdrifts with grassy knolls poking through made a patchwork of the far east lands as winter surrendered its icy grip of the earth to oncoming spring. Snowdrop, chickweed, and shepherd's purse nodded gratefully beneath a bright midmorning sun, which beamed through small islands of breeze-chased clouds. Carrying half-melted icicles along, a tinkling, chuckling stream bounded from rocky cliff ledges, meandering around fir and pine groves toward broad open plains. Already a few hardy wood ants and honeybees were abroad in the copse fringes. Clamoring and gaggling, a skein of barnacle geese in wavering formation winged their way overhead toward the coastline. All around, the land was wakening to springtime, and it promised to be a fair season.

It is often said that a madness takes possession of certain hares in spring, and anybeast watching the performance of one such creature would have had his worst fears confirmed. Tamello De Fformelo Tussock, to give this young hare his full title, was doing battle with imaginary enemies. Armed with stick and slingshot, he flung himself recklessly from a rock ledge, whirling the stone-loaded sling and thwacking left and right with his stick, yelling, "Eulaliaaaa! Have at you, villainous vermin, 'tis m'self, Captain Tammo of the Long Patrol! Take that, y'wicked weasel! Hah! Thought you'd sneak up behind a chap, eh? Well, have some o' this, you ratten rot, beg pardon, rotten rat!"

Hurling himself down in the snow, he lashed out powerfully with his long back legs. "What ho! That'll give you a bellyache to last out the season, m'laddo. Want some more? Hahah! Thought y'didn't, go on, run f'your lives, you cowardly crew! It'd take more'n five hundred of you t'bring down Cap'n Tammo, by the left it would!"

Satisfied that he had given a justly deserved thrashing to half a thousand fictitious foebeasts, Tammo sat up in the snow, eating a few pawfuls to cool himself down.

"Just let 'em come back, I'll show the blighters, wot! There ain't a foebeast in the blinkin' land can defeat me . . . Yaaagh, gerroff!" He felt himself hauled roughly upright by both ears. Lynum and Saithe, Tammo's elder brother and sister, had sneaked up and grabbed him.

"Playing soldiers again?" Lynum's firm grip indicated that there would be no chance of escape.

Tammo's embarrassment at being caught at his game made him even more indignant. "Unhand me at once, m'laddo, if you know what's good for you," he said, struggling. "I can walk by myself."

Saithe gave Tammo's ear an extra tweak as she admonished him: "Colonel wants a word with you, wretch, about his battle-ax!"

Tammo finally struggled free and reluctantly marched off between the two hulking hares, muttering rebelliously to himself, "Huh! I can tell you what he's goin' t'say, same thing as usual."

The young hare imitated his father perfectly, bowing his legs, sticking out his stomach, puffing both cheeks up, and pulling his lips down at the corners as he spoke: "Wot wot, stap me whiskers, if it ain't the bold Tammo. Now then, laddie buck, what've y'got to say for y'self, eh? Speak up, sah!"

Lynum cuffed Tammo lightly to silence him. "Enough of that. Colonel'd have your tail if he saw you makin' mock of him. Step lively now!"

Entering the largest of the conifer groves, they headed for telltale spiral of smoke that denoted Camp Tussock. It was rambling stockade, the outer walls fashioned from tree trunks ith a big dwelling house built of rock, timber, moss, and ud chinking. This was known as the Barracks. Moles, squir-ls, hedgehogs, and a few wood mice wandered in and out f the homely place, living there by kind permission of the olonel and his wife, Mem Divinia. Some of them shook their eads and tuttutted at the sight of Tammo being led in to iswer for his latest escapade.

Seated close to the fire in his armchair, Colonel Cornspurrey e Fformelo Tussock was a formidable sight. He was immac-lately attired in a buff-colored campaign jacket covered with ows of jangling medals, his heavy-jowled face shadowed by ie peak of a brown-bark forage helmet. The Colonel had one ye permanently closed, while the other glared through a mon-cle of polished crystal with a silken cord dangling from it. is wattled throat wobbled pendulously as he jabbed his pace ick pointedly at the miscreant standing before him.

"Wot wot, stap me whiskers, if it ain't the bold Tammo. ow then, laddie buck, what've y'got to say for y'self, eh? peak up, sah!"

Tammo remained silent, staring at the floor as if to find ispiration there. Grunting laboriously, the Colonel leaned for-ard, lifting Tammo's chin with the pace stick until they were ye to eye.

"'S matter, sah, frogs got y'tongue? C'mon now, speak 'piece, somethin' about me battle-ax, wot wot?"

Tammo did what was expected of him and came smartly to ttention. Chin up, chest out, he gazed fixedly at a point above is father's head and barked out in true military fashion: "Col-nel, sah! 'Pologies about y'battle-ax, only used it to play ith. Promise upon me honor, won't do it again. Sah!"

The old hare's great head quivered with furious disbelief, nd the monocle fell from his eye to dangle upon its string. Ie lifted the pace stick, and for a moment it looked as though e were about to strike his son. When the colonel could find , his voice rose several octaves to shrill indignation.

"*Playin'?* You've got the brass nerve t'stand there an' tell ie you've been usin' my battle-ax as a *toy*! Outrage, sir, outrage! Y're a pollywoggle and a ripscutt! Hah, that' it, a scruff-furred, lollop-eared, blather-pawed, doodle-tailec jumped-up-never-t'come-down bogwhumper! What are yeh?'

Tammo's mother, Mem Divinia, had been hovering in th background, tending a batch of barleyscones on the griddl Wiping floury paws upon an apron corner, she bustled for ward, placing herself firmly between husband and son.

"That's quite enough o' that, Corney Fformelo, I'll nc have language like that under my roof. Where d'you thin y'are, in the middle of a battlefield? I won't have you roarin at my Tammo in such a manner."

Instead of calming the Colonel's wrath, his wife's remark had the opposite effect. Suffused with blood, his ears wen bright pink and stood up like spearpoints. He flung down th pace stick and stamped so hard upon it that he hurt his foot paw.

"Eulalia'n'blood'n'fur'n'vinegar, marm!"

Mem countered by drawing herself up regally as sh grabbed Tammo's head and buried it in the floury folds of he apron. "Keep y'voice down, sir, no sense in settin' a ba example to your son an' makin' yourself ill over some battle ax!"

The Colonel knew better than to ignore his wife. Rubbin ruefully at his footpaw, he retrieved the pace stick. Then, fix ing his monocle straight, he sat upright, struggling to moderat his tone.

"*Some* battle-ax indeed, m'dear! I'm discussin' one *partic ular* weapon. *My* battle-ax! *This* battle-ax! D'y'know, tha young rip took a chip out o' the blade, prob'ly hackin' awa at some boulder. A chip off my blade, marm! The same battle ax that was the pride of the old Fifty-first Paw'n'fur Platoon of the Long Patrol. 'Twas a blade that separated Searats from their gizzards'n' garters, flayed ferrets out o' their fur whacked weasels, an' shortened stoats into stumps! An' who was it chipped the blade? That layabout of a leveret, that's who. Hmph!"

Tammo struggled free of Mem's apron, his face thickened with white flour dust. He sneezed twice before speaking. "I ain't a leveret any longer, sir. If y'let me join the jolly ol'

Long Patrol, then I wouldn't have t'get up to all sorts o' mischief, 'specially with your ax, sah.''

The Colonel sighed and shook his head, the monocle falling to one side as he settled back wearily into his armchair. ''I've told you a hundred times, m'laddo, you're far too young, too wild'n'wayward, not got the seasons under y'belt yet. You speak to him, Mem, m'dear, the rogue's got me worn out. Join the Long Patrol indeed. Hmph! No self-respectin' Badger Lord would tolerate a green b'hind the ears little pestilence like you, laddie buck. Run along an' play now, you've given me enough gray fur, go an' bother some otherbeast. Be off, you're dismissed, sah. Matter closed!''

Tammo saluted smartly and hurried off, blinking back unshed tears at his father's brusque command. Mem took the pace stick from her husband's lap and slapped it down hard into his paw.

''Shame on you, Cornspurrey,'' she cried, ''you're nought but a heartless old bodger. How could y'talk to your own son like that?''

The Colonel replaced his monocle and squinted challengingly. ''Bodger y'self, marm! I'd give me permission for Lynum or Saithe t'join up with the Long Patrol, they're both of a right age. Stap me, though, neither of 'em's interested, both want t'be bally soil-pawed farmbeasts, I think.'' He smiled slightly and stroked his curled mustache. ''Young Tammo, now, there's a wild 'un, full of fire'n'vinegar like I was in me green seasons. Hah! He'll grow t'be a dangerous an' perilous beast one day, mark m'words, Mem!''

Mem Divinia spoke up on Tammo's behalf: ''Then why not let him join up? You know 'tis all he's wanted since he was a babe listenin' to your tales around the fire. Poor Tammo, he lives, eats, an' breathes Long Patrol. Let him go, Corney, give him his chance.''

But the Colonel was resolute; he never went back on a decision. ''Tammo's far too young by half. Said all I'm goin' t'say, m'dear. Matter closed!''

Popping out his monocle with a wink, Cornspurrey De Fformelo Tussock settled back into the armchair and closed his good eye, indicating that this was his prelunch naptime. Mem Divinia knew further talk was pointless. She sighed wearily and went back to her friend Osmunda the molewife, who was assisting with the cooking.

Osmunda shook her head knowingly, muttering away in the curious molespeech, "Burr aye, you'm roight, Mem, ee be nought but an ole bodger. Oi wuddent be surproised if'n maister Tamm up'n runned aways one morn. Hurr hurr, ee faither can't stop Tamm furrever."

Mem added sprigs of young mint to the golden crust of a carrot, mushroom, and onion hotpot she had taken from the oven. "That's true, Osmunda, Tammo *will* run away, same as his father did at his age. He was a wayward one too, y'know. His father never forgave him for running away, called him a deserter and never spoke his name again—but I think he was secretly very proud of Cornspurrey and the reputation he gained as a fighting hare with the Long Patrol. He died long before his son retired from service and brought me back here to Camp Tussock. I was always very sorry that they were never reconciled. I hope the Colonel isn't as stubborn as his father, for Tammo's sake."

Osmunda was spooning honey into the scooped-out tops of the hot barley scones. She blinked curiously at Mem. "Whoi do ee say that?"

Mem Divinia began mixing a batter of greensap milk, hazelnut, and almond flour to make pancakes. She kept her eyes on the mix as she explained: "Because I'm going to help Tammo to run away and join the Long Patrol. If I don't he'll only hang around here gettin' into trouble an' arguin' with his father until they become enemies. Now don't mention what I've just said to anybeast, Osmunda."

The faithful molewife's friendly face crinkled into a deep grin. "Moi snout be sealed, Mem! Ee be a doin' the roight thing, oi knows et, even tho' ee Colonel won't 'ave 'is temper improved boi et an' you'll miss maister Tamm gurtly."

A tear fell into the pancake mix. Tammo's mother wiped her eyes hastily on her apron hem. "Oh, I'll miss the rascal, all right, never you fear, Osmunda. But Tammo will do well away from here. He's got a good heart, he's not short of courage, and, like the Colonel said, he'll grow to be a wild an' perilous beast. What more could any creature say of a hare? One day my son will make us proud of him!"

everal leagues away from Camp Tussock, down the far outheast coast, Damug Warfang turned his face to the wind. efore him on the tide line of a shingled beach lay the wave-vashed and tattered remnants of a battered ship fleet. Behind im sprawled myriad crazy hovels, built from dunnage and lotsam. Black and gray smoke wisped off the cooking fires mong them.

The drums began to beat. Gormad Tunn, Firstblade of all apscallions, was dying.

The drums beat louder, making the very air thrum to their leep insistent throbbing. Damug Warfang watched the sea, ounding, hissing among the pebbles as it clawed its way up he shore. Soon Gormad Tunn's spirit would be at the gates of Dark Forest.

Only a Greatrat could become Firstblade of all Rapscallions. Damug cast a sideways glance at Byral standing farther along he beach, and smiled thinly. Gormad would have company at Dark Forest gates before the sun set.

Gormad Tunn, Firstblade of all Rapscallions, was close to leath.

• • •

Greatrats were a strange breed, twice the size of any norma rat. Gormad had been the greatest. Now his sun was setting and one of his two sons would rule as Firstblade when he wa gone. The two sons, Damug Warfang and Byral Fleetclaw stood with their backs to the death tent where their father lay in accordance with the Law of the Rapscallion vermin. Neithe would rest, eat, or drink until the great Firstblade breathed hi last. Then would come the combat between them. Only on would remain alive as Firstblade of the mighty army.

The day wore on; Gormad Tunn's flame burned lower.

A small pebble struck Damug lightly on his back. "Lug worm, is everything ready?" he whispered, lips scarcely mov ing.

The stoat murmured low from his hiding place behind rock, "Never readier . . . O Firstblade."

Damug kept his eyes riveted on the sea as he replied "Don't call me Firstblade yet, 'tis bad luck!"

A confident chuckle came from the stoat. "Luck has nothin' to do with it. Everythin' has been taken care of."

The drums began to pound louder, booming and banging small drums competing with larger ones until the entire shoreline reverberated to their beat.

Gormad Tunn's eyelids flickered once, and a harsh rattle of breath escaped from his dry lips. The Firstblade was dead!

An old ferret who had been attending Gormad left the death tent. He threw up his paws and howled in a high keening tone:

"Gormad has left us for Dark Forest's shade,
And the wind cannot lead Rapscallions.
Let the beast stand forth who would be Firstblade,
To rule all these wild battalions!"

The drums stopped. Silence flooded the coast like a sudden tide. Both brothers turned to face the speaker, answering the challenge.

"I, Byral Fleetclaw, claim the right. The blood of Greatrats runs in my veins, and I would fight to the death him who opposes me!"

"I, Damug Warfang, challenge that right. My blood is pure Greatrat, and I will prove it over your dead carcass!"

A mighty roar arose from the Rapscallion army, then the hordes rushed forward like autumn leaves upon the gale, surrounding the two brothers as they strode to the place of combat.

A ring had been marked out higher up on the shore. There the contestants stood, facing each other. Damug smiled wolfishly at his brother, Byral, who smirked and spat upon the ground between them. Wagers of food and weapons, plunder and strong drink were being yelled out between supporters of one or the other.

Two seconds entered the circle and prepared both brothers for the strange combat that would settle the leadership of the Rapscallion hordes. A short length of tough vinerope was tied around both rats' left footpaws, attaching them one to the other, so they could not run away. They were issued their weapons: a short, stout hardwood club and a cord apiece. The cords were about two swordblades' length, each with a boulder twice the size of a good apple attached to its end.

Damug and Byral drew back from each other, stretching the footpaw rope tight. Gripping their clubs firmly, they glared fiercely at each other, winding the cords around their paws a few turns so they would not lose them.

Now all eyes were on the old ferret who had announced Gormad Tunn's death, as he drew forth a scrap of red silk and threw it upward. Caught on the breeze for a moment, it seemed to float in midair, then it dropped to the floor of the ring. A wild cheer arose from a thousand throats as the fight started. Brandishing their clubs and whirling the boulder-laden cords, the two Greatrats circled, each seeking an opening, while the bloodthirsty onlookers roared encouragement.

"Crack 'is skull, Byral—go on, you kin do it!"

"Go fer 'is ribs wid yer club, Damug! Belt 'im a good 'un!"

"Swing up wid yer stone, smash 'is jaw!"

"Fling the club straight betwixt 'is eyes!"

Being fairly equally matched, each gave as good as he got. Soon Byral and Damug were both aching from hefty blows dealt by their clubs, but as yet neither had room to bring cord and boulder into play. Circling, tugging, tripping, and stumbling, they scattered sand and pebbles widespread, biting and kicking when they got the opportunity, each knowing that only one would walk away alive from the encounter. Then Byral saw his chance. Hopping nimbly back, he stretched the footpaw rope to its limits and swung at Damug's head with the boulder-loaded cord. It was just what Damug was waiting for. Grabbing his club in both paws, he ducked, allowing the cord to twirl itself around his club until the rock clacked against it. Then Damug gave a sharp tug and the cord snapped off short close to Byral's paw.

A gasp went up from the spectators. Nobeast had expected the cord to snap—except Lugworm. Byral hesitated a fatal second, gaping at the broken cord—and that was all Damug needed. He let go of his club, tossed a swift pawful of sand into his opponent's face, and swung hard with his cord and boulder. The noise was like a bar of iron smacking into a wet side of meat. Byral looked surprised before his eyes rolled backward and he sank slowly onto all fours. Damug swung twice more, though there was little need to; he had slain his brother with the first blow.

A silence descended on the watchers. Damug held out his paw, and Lugworm passed him a knife. With one quick slash he severed the rope holding his footpaw to Byral's. Without a word he strode through the crowd, and the massed ranks fell apart before him. Straight into his father's death tent he went, emerging a moment later holding aloft a sword. It had a curious blade: one edge was wavy, the other straight, representing land and sea.

The drums beat out loud and frenzied as the vast Rapscallion army roared their tribute to a new Leader: "Damug Warfang! Firstblade! Firstblade! Firstblade!"

3

Some creatures said that Russa came from the deep south, others thought she was from the west coast, but even Russa could not say with any degree of certainty where she had come from. The red female squirrel had neither family nor tribe, nor any place to call home: she was a wanderer who just loved to travel. Russa Nodrey, she was often called, owing to the fact that squirrels' homes were called dreys and she did not have one, hence, no drey.

Nobeast knew more about country ways than Russa. She could live where others would starve, she knew the way in woods and field when many would be hopelessly lost. Neither old- nor young-looking, quite small and lean, Russa carried no great traveler's haversack or intricate equipment. A small pouch at the back of the rough green tunic she always wore was sufficient for her needs. The only other thing she possessed was a stick, which she had picked up from the flotsam of a tide line. It was about walking-stick size and must have come from far away, because it was hard and dark and had a luster of its own—even seawater could not rot or warp it.

Russa liked her stick. There was no piece of wood like it

in all the land, nor any tree that produced such wood. It was also a good weapon, because besides being a lone wanderer, Russa Nodrey was also an expert fighter and a very dangerous warrior, in her own quiet way.

Off again on her latest odyssey, Russa stopped to rest among the cliff ledges not far from Camp Tussock. Happy with her own company, she sat by the stream's edge, drank her fill of the sweet cold water, and settled down to enjoy the late-afternoon sun in a nook protected from the wind. The sound of another creature nearby did not bother Russa unduly; she knew it was a mole and therefore friendly. With both eyes closed, as if napping, Russa waited until the creature was right up close, then she spoke in perfect molespeech to it.

"Hurr, gudd day to ee, zurr, wot you'm be a doin' yurrabouts?"

Roolee, the husband of Osmunda, was taken aback, though he did not show it. He sat down next to Russa and raised a hefty digging claw in greeting. "Gudd day to ee, marm, noice weather us'n's be 'avin', burr aye!"

Russa answered in normal speech, "Aye, a pity that somebeasts blunder along to disturb a body's rest when all she craves is peace an' quiet."

"Yurr, so 'tis, marm, so 'tis." Roolee nodded agreement. "Tho' if ee be who oi think ee be, marm Mem at Camp Tussock will be pleased to see ee. May'ap you'm koindly drop boi furr vittles?"

Russa was up on her paws immediately. "Why didn't you just say that instead of yappin' about the weather? I'd travel three rough leagues 'fore breakfast if I knew me old friend Mem Divinia was still cookin' those pancakes an' hotpots of hers!"

Roolee led the way, his velvety head nodding. "Burr aye, marm, ee Mem still be ee gurtest cook yurrabouts, she'm doin' pannycakes, ottenpots, an' all manner o' gudd vittles!"

Russa ran several steps ahead of Roolee coming into Camp Tussock. Lynum was doing sentry duty at the stockade entrance. In the fading twilight he saw the strange squirrel approaching and decided to exercise his authority.

Barring the way with a long oak quarterstaff, he called officiously, "Halt an' be recognized, who goes there, stranger at the gate!"

Russa was hungry, and she had little time for such foolishness. She gave the husky hare a smart rap across his footpaw with her stick. "Hmm, you've grown since I last saw ye," she commented as she stepped over him. "Y'were only a fuzzy babe then—fine big hare now though, eh? Pity your wits never grew up like your limbs, y'were far nicer as a little 'un."

Mem Divinia wiped floury paws on her apron hem and rushed to meet the visitor, her face alight with joy. "Well, fortunes smile on us! Russa Nodrey, you roamin' rascal, how *are* you?"

Russa avoided Mem's flour-dusted hug and made for the corner seat at the table, as she remembered it was the most comfortable and best for access to the food. She winked at Mem.

"Oh, I'm same as I always was, Mem. When I'm not travelin' up an' down the country, I'm roamin' sideways across the land."

Mem winked back at Russa and whispered, "Your visit is very timely, friend. I have something to ask of you." Then, on seeing the Colonel approaching the table, she quickly mouthed the word "later." Russa understood.

Colonel Cornspurrey De Fformelo Tussock viewed the guest with a jaundiced eye and a snort. "Hmph! Respects to ye, marm, I see you've installed y'self in my flippin' seat! Comfortable are ye, wot?"

Russa managed a rare smile. "Aye, one seat's as good as another. How are ye, y'old fogey, still grouchin' an' throwin' orders around like they're goin' out of style? I've seen boulders that've changed faster than you!"

The conversation was cut short by Osmunda thwacking a hollow gourd with a ladle, summoning the inhabitants of Camp Tussock to their evening meal.

Mem Divinia and her helpers always provided the best of victuals. There was steaming hot, early-spring vegetable soup with flat, crisp oatmeal bannocks, followed by the famous Tussock hotpot. In a huge earthenware basin coated with a golden piecrust was a delicious medley of corn, carrots, mushrooms, turnips, winter cabbage, and onions, in a thick, rich gravy full of Mem's secret herbs. This was followed by a hefty apple, blackberry, and plum crumble topped with Osmunda's greensap and maple sauce. Hot mint and comfrey tea was served, along with horse-chestnut beer and red-currant cordial. Afterward there were honeyed barleyscones, white hazelnut cheese, and elderflower bread, for those still wanting to nibble.

Tammo sat quietly, still out of favor with his father, the Colonel, since the battle-ax incident. He listened as Russa related the latest news she had gathered in her wandering.

"Last autumn a great storm in the west country sent the waves tearing up the cliffs, and a good part of 'em collapsed into the sea."

The Colonel reached for cheese and bread with a grunt. "Hmph! Used to patrol down that way, y'know, lots of toads, nasty slimy types, murderous blighters, hope the cliffs fell on them, wot! Anythin' happenin' at Salamandastron of late?"

Tammo leaned forward eagerly at the name: Salamandastron, mountain of the Badger Lords, the mysterious place that was the headquarters of the Long Patrol.

Unfortunately Russa dismissed the subject. "Hah, the badger mountain, haven't been there in many a long season. Place is still standin', I suppose . . ."

The Colonel's monocle dropped from his eye in righteous indignation. "You *suppose*, marm? Tchah! I should jolly well hope so! Why, if Salamandastron weren't there, the entire land would be overrun with Searats, Corsairs, vermin, Rapscallions, an' . . . an' . . . whatever!"

Russa leaned forward as if remembering something. "Spoke to an owl last winter. He said a whole fleet of Rapscallions had taken a right good thrashin' on the shores near Salamandastron. Wotsisname, the old Warlord or Firstblade or whatever they call him? Tunn! Gormad Tunn! He was wounded near to death. Anyhow, seems they've vanished into thin air to lick their wounds since then. I've seen no signs of Rapscallions, but if I were you I'd sleep with one eye open, y'can never tell where they'll turn up next. Cruelest pack o' slayers ever to draw breath, that lot!"

"I don't think we need worry too much about Rapscallions," Mem interrupted her friend. "They only plunder the coasts in their ships. Strange how they never sail the open seas like Searats an' Corsairs. Who's the Badger Lord at Salamandastron now, have y'heard?"

Russa poured herself a beaker of tea. "Big female, they say, madder than midwinter, stronger than a four-topped oak, temper like lightnin', full o' the Bloodwrath. She's called Cregga Rose Eyes, wields a pike that four otters couldn't lift!"

Osmunda nodded in admiration. "Hurr, she'm got'n a purty name, awright."

Russa laughed mirthlessly. "There's nought pretty about it! That one's called Rose Eyes because her eyes are blood red with battle light. I'd hate to be the vermin that tried standin' in her path."

All eyes turned on Tammo as the question slipped from his mouth: "What's a Rapscallion?"

The Colonel glared at his son. "Barbarian-type vermin, too idle t'work, too stupid t'build a decent home. Like y'mother says, they only raid the coastlines, nothin' for you t'worry your head over. Mind y'manners at table, young 'un, speak when y'spoken to an' not before, sah!"

Russa shook her head at the Colonel's statement. "You an' Mem are both wrong. Rapscallions are unpredictable, they can raid inland as easily as on the coast. I saw their Chief's sword once when I was young. It's got two edges, one all wavy for the sea, an' the other straight for the land. There's an old Rapscallion sayin': 'Travel whither blade goes, anyside the sword shows.' "

The Colonel cut himself a wedge of cheese. "Huh! What's all that fol-de-rol s'posed t'mean, wot?"

"Have we not had enough of this kind of talk, swords'n'vermin an' war?" cried Mem Divinia, banging her beaker down on the table. "Change the subject, please. Roolee, what d'you make of this weather?"

The mole changed the conversation to suit Mem, who could see by the light in her husband's eye that he was spoiling for an argument with Russa.

"Ho urr, ee weather, marm . . . Hurr . . . umm . . . Well, ee burds be a tellin' us'n's 'twill be a foine springtoid, aye. May'ap missie Whinn'll sing ee song abowt et."

Mem coaxed a young hedgehog called Whinn to get on her

paws and sing. Whinn had a good voice, clear and pretty; she liked to sing and did not need much urging.

"Blow cobwebs out of corners, the corners, the corners,
Throw open all your windows
To welcome in the spring.
Now icicles are shorter,
And turning fast to water,
Out yonder o'er the meadow,
I hear a skylark sing.

All through the earth a showing, a showing, a showing,
The green grass is a growing,
So fresh is everything.
Around the flow'rs and heather,
The bees do hum together,
Their honey will be sweeter
When 'tis made in spring."

Tammo and the other creatures at the table joined in as Whinn sang the song once more, and there was much tapping and clapping of paws. The evening wore on, with everybeast getting up to do his bit, singing, dancing, reciting, or playing simple instruments, mainly small drums or reed flutes.

Owing to the amount of food he had eaten and the warmth of the oven fire, Colonel Cornspurrey had great difficulty keeping awake. With a deep sigh he heaved himself up and took a final draught of chestnut beer, then, swaying a little he peered sleepily at Russa Nodrey, and said, "Hmph, I take it you'll be off travelin' again in the mornin', marm?"

Russa looked as fresh as a daisy as she nodded to him. "Crack o' dawn'll be early enough for me. Thank ye for your hospitality—Camp Tussock vittles were as good as ever."

Shuffling off to the dormitory, Cornspurrey called back, "Indeed 'twill, keep the noise down when y'go, I'll bid ye g'night now. An' you others, don't sit up too bally late, work t'be done on the morrow."

4

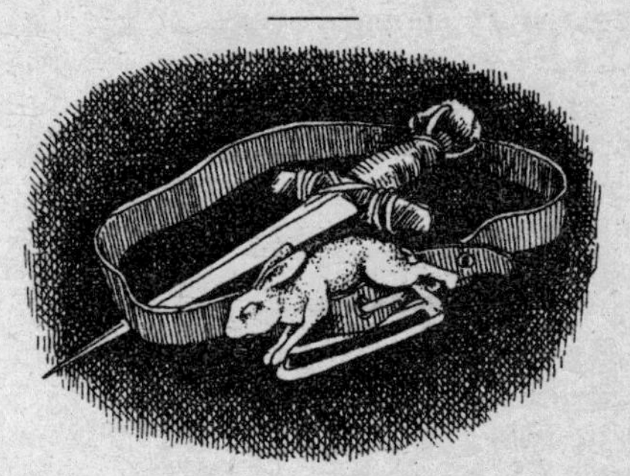

When his father had gone to bed, Tammo watched his mother and Russa conversing earnestly in low voices. He knew they were discussing something important, but could catch only snatches of their conversation.

"Nay, 'tis impossible, Mem. I travel alone, y'know that!"

"Well, there's a round score o' pancakes to take along if you'll help me, Russa."

"But I might not be goin' anywhere near Salamandastron!"

"Well then, take him as far as Redwall Abbey. He'll meet other warriors there, and the Long Patrol visits regularly. He won't be any trouble, I promise you. The Colonel's forbidden him t'go, but there'll only be trouble 'twixt the two of 'em if he has to stay."

"A score o' pancakes you say, Mem?"

"Make it thirty if y'like! He'll keep up with you an' obey every word you say, I know he will. Do it as a favor to me an' you'll always be welcome to a meal at Camp Tussock!"

"Hmm, thirty pancakes, eh, hah! And it'd be one in the monocle for that old waffler, somebeast disobeyin' his orders. Right then, I'll do it, but we'd best leave tonight an' be well away from here by the morn. I'll wait outside in the copse. Send him out when he's ready."

Russa departed, muttering something about preferring to sleep out under the stars. Mem Divinia started clearing the table.

"Come on now, all of you, off t'bed, mind what the Colonel said, work t'be done tomorrow. Tammo, you stay here an' help me to clear away. Good night all, peaceful dreams!"

One by one they drifted off to the big dormitory cellar, which had been built beneath the stockade.

Osmunda nodded to Mem. "They'm all gone abed now, marm."

Mem took a haversack from her wall cupboard and began adding pancakes to its contents. "Tammo, put those dishes down and come here. Hurry, son, there's not much time."

Mystified, Tammo came to sit on the table edge near his mother. "What'n the name o' seasons is goin' on, marm?"

Osmunda smacked his paw lightly with a ladle. "Do ee be 'ushed now, maister, an' lissen to ee muther."

Mem kept her eyes averted, fussing over the haversack. "Lackaday, I'm not sure whether I'm doin' the right or the wrong thing now, Tammo, but I'm givin' you a chance to see a bit o' life out in the world. I think 'tis time you grew up an' joined the Long Patrol."

Tammo slid off the table edge, disbelief shrill in his voice. "Me, join the jolly ol' Long Patrol? Oh, marm!"

Mem pulled the haversack drawstrings tight. "Keep y'voice down or you'll waken the entire camp. Our friend Russa has agreed to take you in tow. She'll keep you safe. Now don't be a nuisance to that old squirrel, keep up, and don't dare cheek her. Russa ain't as lenient as me an' she's a lot quicker on her paws than your father, so mind your manners. There's enough food in the haversack to keep you going for a good while, also thirty of my pancakes for Russa. Come over here, Tamm, stand still while I put this on you."

Mem Divinia took from the cupboard a twine and linen belt, strong and very skillfully woven. It had a silver buckle fashioned in the image of a running hare. Attached to the belt was a weapon that was neither sword nor dagger, being about half the length of the former and twice the size of the latter.

Tammo cast admiring glances at the beautiful thing as his mother set the belt sash fashion, running over his shoulder and across his chest, so that the buckle hung at his side.

The long knife had no sheath, but fitted neatly through a slot in the belt buckle. Carefully, the young hare drew the weapon from its holder. Double edged and keenly pointed, its blue steel blade was chased with curious designs. The cross hilt was of silver, set with green gems. Bound tightly with tough, red, braided twine, the handle seemed made for his paw. A highly polished piece of rock crystal formed the pommel stone.

Mem tapped it lovingly, saying, "This was made by a Badger Lord in the forge at Salamandastron; 'tis called a dirk. No weapon ever served me better in the days when I ran with the Long Patrol. Your father always preferred the battle-ax, but the dirk was the weapon that I loved specially. It is the best gift I can give you, my son. Take it and use it to defend yourself and those weaker than you. Never surrender it to a foebeast or let any creature take it from you. Time is running short, and you must leave now. Don't look back. Go, make Camp Tussock proud of you. Promise me you'll return here someday, your father loves you as much as I do. Fate and fortune go with you, Tamello De Fformelo Tussock—do honor to our name!"

Osmunda patted his ears fondly. "Furr ee well, maister Tamm, oi'll miss ee!"

Seconds later Tammo was rushing out into the night, his face streaked with tears and covered in white flour dust from his mother's good-bye embrace. Russa Nodrey materialized out of the pine shadows like a wraith.

"I hope my pancakes aren't gettin' squashed in that there bag. Looks like you've brought enough vittles with ye to feed a regiment for seven seasons. Right, come on, young 'un, let's see if those paws o' yours are any good after all the soft livin' you've been brought up with. Shift y'self now. Move!"

The young hare shot forward like an arrow from a bow, dashing away from his birthplace to face the unknown.

The new Firstblade of all Rapscallions sat alone on the creaking, weather-beaten stern of his late father's vessel, which lay heeled half over on the southeast shore. Damug Warfang had watched dawn break over the horizon, a red glow at first, changing rapidly as the sun rose in a bloom of scarlet and gold. A few seabirds wheeled and called to one another, dipping toward the gentle swell of the placid sea. Hardly a wave showed on the face of the deep, pale-green waters inshore, ranging out to mid-blue and aquamarine. A bank of fine cloud shone with pearl-like opalescence as the sunrays reflected off it. Now the wide vault of sky became blue, as only a fresh spring morn can make it; scarlet tinges of sun wisped away to become a faint rose thread where sea met sky as the great orb ascended, golden as a buttercup.

All this beauty was lost on Damug as the ebb tide hissed and whispered its secrets to the shingled beach. Probing with his swordpoint, he dug moodily at the vessel's timbers. They were rotten, waterlogged, barnacle-crusted, and coated with a sheen of green slime. Damug's pale eyes registered anger and disgust. A bristletail crawled slowly out of the damp woodwork. With its antennae waving and gray, armor-plated back ndulating, the insect lumbered close to Damug's footclaw. Vith a swift, light thrust he impaled it on his swordpoint and at watching it wriggle its life away.

Behind him breakfast fires were being lit and drums were be-inning their remorseless throb again as the Rapscallion armies vakened to face the day. Damug sensed the presence of Lug-orm at his back, and did not bother turning as the stoat spoke.

"Empty cookin' pots cause rebellion, O Firstblade. You nust throw the sword quickly, today!"

Damug flicked the swordblade sideways, sending the dying nsect into the ebbing sea. Then he stood and turned to face ugworm. The Greatrat's jaw was so tight with anger that it nade his voice a harsh grate.

"I know what I've got to do, slopbrain, but supposing the word falls wave side up? How could I take all of those back nere out to sea in a fleet of rotten, waterlogged ships? We'd o straight to the bottom. There's not a seaworthy vessel on nis shore. So unless you've got a foolproof solution, don't ome around here with that idiotic grin on your stupid face, elling me what I already know!"

Before Lugworm could answer, Damug whipped the sword-oint up under his chin. He jabbed a little, causing the blade o nick skin. Lugworm was forced to stand tip-pawed as Da-nug snarled, "Enjoying yourself now, cleversnout? I'll teach ou to come grinning at my predicament. Come on, let's see ou smile that silly smile you had plastered on your useless ace a moment ago."

The stoat's throat bobbed as he gulped visibly, and his words ame out in a rush as the blade of the unpredictably tempered Varlord dug a bit deeper. "Damug, Firstblade, I've got the an-wer, I know what t'do, that's why I came to see you!"

The swordpoint flicked downward, biting into the deck be-ween Lugworm's footpaws. Damug was smiling sweetly, his wift mood swing and calm tone indicating that his servant vas out of danger, for the moment.

"Lugworm, my trusty friend, I knew you'd come up with solution to my problem. Pray tell me what I must do."

Rubbing beneath his chin, where a thin trickle of blood howed, Lugworm sat upon the deck. From his belt pouch he lug out a small, heavy brass clip. "Your father used this because he favored sailin', always said it was better'n paw slog gin' a horde over 'ill'n'dale. If y'll allow me, Chief, I'll show ye 'ow it works.''

Damug gave his sword to the stoat, who stood up to demonstrate.

''Y'see, the Rapscallions foller this sword. The Firstblade tosses it in the air, an' they go whichever way it falls, but it's gotta fall wid one o' these crosspieces stickin' in the ground Wave side of the blade up means we sail, smooth side o' the blade showing upward means we go by land.''

''I know that, you fool, get on with it!''

Lugworm heeded the danger in Damug's terse voice. He attached the brass clip to the wave-side crosspiece and tossed the sword up. It was not a hard throw; the flick of Lugworm's paw caused the weapon to turn once, almost lazily, as morning sunlight glimmered across the blade. With a soft thud it fell to the deck, the straight, sharp blade edge upward.

''Y'see, Chief, it works every time 'cos the added weigh on the wavy side hits the ground first. But don't fling it 'igh in the air, toss it up jus' like I did, slow like, wid a twist o' yer paw. 'Tis easy, try it.''

Damug Warfang was not one to leave anything to luck. He tried the trick several times, each time with the same result The sword always landed smooth edge upward. Damug removed the brass clip and attached it to a bracelet he wore.

''Good! You're not as thick as you look, friend Lugworm.''

The stoat bowed his head respectfully to the new Firstblade saying, ''I served your father, Gormad Tunn, but he became old and strange in the brain and would not listen to my advice Heed my counsel, Chief, and I will make the name Damug Warfang feared by all on land and sea. You will become the greatest Firstblade that Rapscallions have ever known.''

Damug nodded. ''So be it. You are my adviser and as such will be at my side to reap the benefit of all my triumphs.''

Before Lugworm could voice his thanks, the blade was in his face, its point almost tickling his right eyeball. The smile on Damug's lips was cold enough to freeze water.

''Sly little Lugworm, eh? Counselor to mighty ones! Listen, stoat, if you even think about crossing me I'll make you scream half a season before you die!''

6

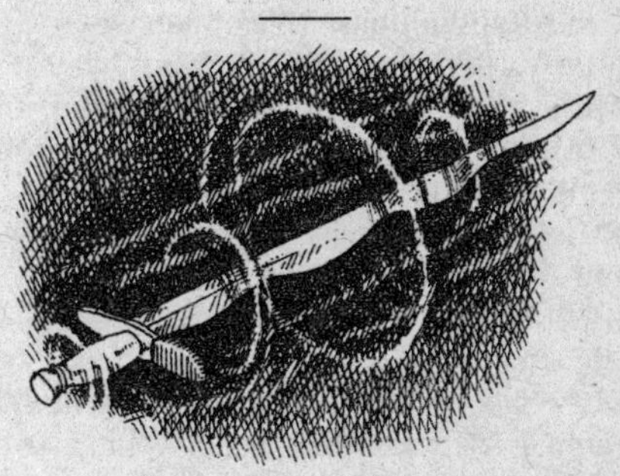

The rats Sneezewort and Lousewort were merely two common, low-ranked Rapscallions in the Firstblade's great army. The pair scrabbled for position on a clump of boulders at the rear of massed hordes of vermin warriors, who had all gathered to witness the Throwing of the Sword ceremony. They jostled and pushed, trying to catch a glimpse of what was going on in the stone circle where the duel had taken place. High-ranking officers called Rapmarks occupied the immediate edge of the ring, as was their right. The ordinary rank and file struggled, standing tip-pawed to get a view of the proceedings.

Sneezewort hauled himself up on Lousewort's back, and the dull, stolid Lousewort staggered forward under the added weight, muttering, "Er, er, wot's goin' on down there, mate?"

Sneezewort flicked his companion's ear with a grimy claw. "Straighten up, jellyback, I can't see much from 'ere. 'Ang on, I think ole Firstblade's gonna say sumpin'."

Lousewort flinched as his ear was flicked harder. "Ouch-ouch! Stoppit, that's me wounded ear!"

Staggering farther forward he bumped into a big, fat, nasty-looking weasel, who turned on them with a snarl. "Hoi! If you two boggletops don't stop bangin' inter me an' shoutin' like that y'll 'ave more'n wounded ears ter worry about. I'll stuff yore tails up yore snotty noses an' rip 'em off, so back off an' shut yer gobs!"

Damug's voice rang harsh and clear across the savage crowd of vermin gathered on the shore.

"The spirit of my father, the great Gormad Tunn, appeared to me in my dreams. He said that the sword will fall land side up and seasons of glory will reward all who follow Damug Warfang. Plunder, slaves, land, and wealth for even the lowest paw soldier of the mighty army of Rapscallions. I, your Firstblade, pass the words of my beloved father on to you, my loyal comrades!"

Sneezewort could not resist a snigger as a thought occurred to him. "Yeeheehee! 'Beloved father'? They couldn't stan' the sight o' each other. Huh, Damug'll be in trouble if'n the sword lands wavy side up after shootin' 'is mouth off like that, I tell yer, mate!"

The big weasel turned 'round, testing the tip of a rusty iron hook. "Damug won't be in 'arf the trouble you'll be in if'n yer don't put a stopper on that blatherin' jaw o' yourn, snipenose!" He turned back in time to see the sword rise above the crowd. There was a vast silence, followed by a rousing cheer.

"Land up! Land up!"

Lousewort thrust a stained claw into his wounded ear and wiggled it. "Stand up? Wot's that supposed ter mean?"

The big nasty weasel whirled around and dealt two swift punches, one to Lousewort's stomach, the other to Sneezewort's nose. They both collapsed to the ground in a jumbled heap, and the weasel stood, paws akimbo, sneering at them. "It means you need yer ears washin' out an' yer mate needs his lip buttoned! Any more questions, dimwits?"

Clutching his injured nose, Sneezewort managed to gasp out, "No thir, it'th all quite clear, thank yew, thir!"

Damug gave his orders to the ten Rapmarks, each the commander of a hundred beasts.

"Our seasons of petty coast raids are over. We march straight up the center of the land, taking all before us. Scouts must be continuously sent out on both sides to report any area that is ripe for plundering. Leave the ships to rot where they lie, burn your dwellings, let the army eat the last of our old supplies here today. We march at first light tomorrow. Now bring me the armor of the Firstblade!"

That night Damug stood garbed in his barbaric regalia, the swirling orange cloak of his father blowing open to reveal a highly polished breastplate of silver, a short kilt of snake-skin, and a belt fashioned from many small links of beaten gold, set with twinkling gemstones. On his head he wore a burnished brass helmet surmounted by a spike, with iron mesh hanging from it to protect his neck. The front dipped almost to his muzzle tip; it had two narrow eye slits.

Oily smoke swirled to the moonless skies as the lights of myriad dwellings going up in flames glimmered off the armor of Damug Warfang, Firstblade. Roaring, drinking, singing, and eating their last supplies, the Rapscallion regiments celebrated their final night on the southeast shores. They gambled and stole from one another, fought, argued, and tore the water-logged fleet apart in their search for any last bits of booty to be had.

Damug leaned on his sword, watching them. Beside him, Lugworm cooked a fish over glowing charcoal for his Chief's supper. He looked up at the Firstblade's question.

"Are they all ready to follow and obey me, Lugworm?"

"Aye sirrah, they are."

"All?"

"Save two, Chief. Borumm the weasel and Vendace the fox. Those two were allies of your brother, Byral, so watch your back whilst they're about."

Smiling humorlessly, Damug patted his adviser's head.

"Well answered, Lugworm. I already knew of Borumm and Vendace. Also I knew that you were aware of them, so you have just saved your own life by not staying silent."

Lugworm swallowed hard as he turned the fish over on the embers.

Lousewort staggered up over the tide line under the weight of a large circular ship's steering wheel. It was a great heavy piece of work, solid oak, decorated with copper studding, now moldy and green.

Sneezewort stood tending their fire, over which he was roasting some old roots and the dried frame of a long-dead seabird. He shook his head in despair. "Ahoy, puddenbum, where d'yer think yore goin' wid that thing?"

Smiling happily, Lousewort stood the wheel on its edge. "Er, er, looka this, it's a beauty, izzenit, mate? I'll wager 'tis worth a lot, thing like this. . . ."

Sneezewort snorted at his slow-witted companion. "Oh, it's a beauty, all right, and it will be worth somethin'. After you've carried it back an' forth across the country fer seven seasons an' found a new ship to match up wirrit. Great ole useless chunk o' rubbish, wot do we need wid that thing? Get rid of it afore ye cripple yerself carryin' it!"

He gave the wheel a hearty push, sending it rolling crazily off into the darkness. There was a crash, followed by the outraged roar of the big nasty weasel.

"Belay, who threw that? Ooh, me footpaw! I'll carve the blackguard up inter fishbait an' 'ang 'im from me 'ook!"

In their panic the two dithering rats ran slap into each other twice before tearing off to hide in the darkness.

Damug tossed the remnants of the fish to Lugworm and wiped his lips upon the orange cloak.

"Keep an eye open whilst I sleep. Oh, and pass the word around: I want every Rapscallion painted red for war when we march tomorrow, fully armed and ready for slaughter!"

7

ammo had never been so tired in all his young life. It was ree hours after dawn and they were still running. His foot-aws felt heavy as two millstones, and the weight of the hav-sack on his back, which had been fairly light at first, was ow like carrying another beast.

Those open plains that had always looked smooth and ightly undulating from a distance, what had happened to em? Suddenly they had become a series of steep hills and eep valleys, with small sharp rocks hidden by the grass, areas f thorny thistle and slopes of treacherous gravelly scree. The elcome sunlight of dawn was now a burning eye that blinded im and added to the discomfort of his already overheated ody.

Staggering and gasping for breath, Tammo slumped down n the summit of a hill, unable to go another pace forward. ussa Nodrey was already there, still upright, breathing calmly she viewed the prospect to the south. From the corner of r eye she watched the young hare with a tinge of admiration, hich she kept well hidden from him.

"Nothin' like a brisk trot, eh, Tamm? How d'you feel?"

Tammo was on all fours, head bent as he tried to regulat
his breath. He spoke still facing the ground, unable to loo
up. “Not too blinkin' chipper, marm. Need water, somethin
to eat, and sleep. Give anythin' for a jolly good snooz
marm!”

Russa crouched down beside him. “Lissen, young 'un, ca
me Russa, pal, matey, anythin' you like. But stop callin' m
marm. It makes me feel like some fat ole mother duck!”

Tammo glanced sideways at her, mischief dancing in hi
eyes. “I'll do that, matey, but you stop callin' me young 'u
or I'll *start* callin' you mother duck!”

Standing behind him, Russa smiled as she pulled the hav
ersack from his back. Despite her initial reluctance, she wa
beginning, if a little grudgingly, to enjoy Tammo's company

“Let's have this thing off ye, Tamm. We can't stop here
got to press on a bit afore we make camp.”

Tammo flexed his shoulders and moved to a sitting positio
“Why's that? This looks like a jolly good spot, wot?”

The squirrel pointed south, indicating another two hilly tor
“We've got to land up across there by midday. Right, here'
where yore eddication starts, young 'un . . . er, pal. Tell me
why should we make camp there instead o' here?”

Tammo pondered the question a moment. “Haven't a ball
clue, old pal. Tell me.”

Russa began shouldering the haversack. “Well, for a star
'tis too open up here, we c'n be seen for miles. A good cam
should be sheltered for two reasons: one, in case o' th
weather; two, t'stay hidden. Doesn't do t'let everybeast know
where ye are in open country.”

The young hare stood up slowly. “Hmm, makes sense
suppose.”

“You can bet yore life it does.” The squirrel winked a
him. “But afore y'go harin' off, let me tell you the rest. A
midday it'll be hottest, that's when we should sleep a few
hours an' save energy. We can eat'n'drink too afore we nap
sleep's good fer the digestion. If we ate an' drank now, we'
be travelin' on full bellies. It'd take us twice as long to ge
there in that state. All right, matey, let's be on our way. I'l
carry this 'avvysack fer a while—'tis only fair.”

Tammo started down into the valley, digging his paws i

against a shale drift. He felt much lighter and better for the brief rest. "Indeed 'tis only fair, considerin' the weight of your pancakes, old pal!" he called back.

Russa caught up and quickly took the lead. "Less of the old, young scallywag, or I'll put on a turn of speed that'll have ye eatin' me dust fer a full day!"

Tammo pulled a wry face at the squirrel's back. "What ho, young Russa, point taken. Lead on, but not too fast."

Russa shook her head as she skirted a patch of mossy grass, still wet and slippery with morning dew. "Rest yore jaws an' let the paws do the work, Tamm, seasons o' gabble! I never did so much talkin' in all me life. Save yore breath fer travelin', that's another lesson y've got to learn."

"Right you are, O wise one, the jolly old lips are sealed!"

"Good! Then shut up an' keep up!"

"To hear is to obey, O sagacious squirrel!"

"You've gotta have the last word, haven't yer?"

"Only because you're the strong silent type, great leader."

"I'll great leader you, y'cheeky-faced rogue!"

"Bad form f'r a Commander to insult the other ranks, y'know. Whoops! Yowch!"

Not looking where he was going, Tammo trotted into the area of mossy grass and slipped, landing flat on his back. Because of the steep incline, he rolled a good way downhill, until he was halted by a boulder.

Russa went by him, looking straight ahead, a smile playing 'round her lips. "Tut tut, I've already told ye, matey, y'can't lie down fer a nap until we make camp!"

Tammo learned a lot that first morning. By midday they were standing on top of the hill overlooking the spot Russa had chosen for a campsite. Down in the valley a little stream tumbled over a rock ledge, forming a tiny waterfall. There were wild privets and dogwood to one side, making a shady bower.

Hot and dusty, Tammo wiped a paw across his mouth at the sight of fresh water. He saluted smartly at Russa and said, "Permission t'go down an' chuck m'self in yonder cool water!"

The canny squirrel shrugged. "Suit y'self, matey, if'n that's what y'feel like doin'."

The young hare let out a joyful whoop and sped off downhill.

Russa backed off and, dropping out of sight, cut off at a tangent, approaching the glade from a different angle.

Ducking out of his shoulder belt and dirk, Tammo cast both aside and leapt into the water. It was ice cold and crystal clear. The sudden shock robbed him of his breath for a moment; then he gave vent to a yell of sheer delight. It was good to be alive on such a day. Gulping down the sweet fresh water, Tammo stood beneath the cascade with his mouth wide open, falling backward and splashing playfully with all four paws.

"Yerrah! Now dat's wot I likes ter see, Skulka, a young critter fulla the joys o' spring!"

Rubbing both eyes and snorting water from his nostrils, Tammo floundered upright to see who had spoken.

Two ferrets, big and lean and clad in tattered rags, stood on the bank, one with an arrow half drawn on her bowstring, the other with a spear stuck in the ground as he tried on Tammo's belt and dirk for size.

The young hare knew he was in deep trouble. Glancing around to see if he could spot Russa, Tammo pointed at his property. "Good day, friends! I say, that's my belt an' dirk you're jolly well tryin' on, y'know!"

The female kept her arrow centered on Tammo. Turning to her partner, she revealed a row of snaggled, discolored teeth in a grin. "Lah de dah, Gromal, ain't 'e got nice manners? Didyer know that's 'is jolly ole dirk'n' belt yore tryin' on?"

Gromal had fastened the belt around his waist, and now he was stroking the dirk handle and admiring the fine blade. "Ho, is it now? Well 'ere's the way I sees it, Skulka. That beast flung 'isself in our water widout so much as a by yer leave. Lookat 'im there, drinkin' away an' sportin' about as if it belonged to 'im!"

Tammo stood quite still in the stream and managed to force a friendly smile at the evil pair. "Accept my apologies, you chaps. Sorry, I didn't know the stream belonged to you. I'll just hop right out."

Gromal pulled his spear from the ground. "Aye, that's the ticket, me young bucko. You jus' 'op right up 'ere on the bank so's we kin search yer. Yore gonna pay fer the use of ur water. Keep that shaft aimed at 'im, Skulka. If'n 'e makes ne false move, shoot 'im atween the eyes an' slay 'im!''

Skulka drew her bowstring tight, sniggering. ''If 'e don't ve no more val'ables, then mebbe we c'n use 'im as a slave r a few seasons.''

A hardwood stick came whirling in a blur from the tree over and struck the arrow, snapping it clean in two pieces. ussa hurtled out like a lightning bolt, shoving Skulka into e water and launching herself at Gromal. She caught him a rrific headbutt to the stomach, and he crumpled to the round, mouth open as he fought for air. Tammo waded wiftly to the shallows, and as Skulka staggered upright, he ealt her a powerful kick with both footpaws. She fell back the water, and he sat upon her, applying all his weight.

Russa had relieved Gromal of the dirk; now she grabbed er hardwood stick and stood waiting for him to rise. He came p fast, seizing his spear and charging her. Almost casually he stepped to one side, dealing him three quick hard blows the back of his head as he rushed by her. The ferret dropped ke a log.

Ignoring him, she turned to Tammo and said, ''Best let at'n up afore ye drown her, mate.''

Tammo hauled Skulka dripping and spluttering from the tream. He shook water from his eyes, peering indignantly at ussa. ''I say, y'might've told me about these two before you t me flippin' well dash down here an' dive in the water, ot?''

The squirrel kicked Skulka flat, trapping her across the roat with the hardwood stick. Then she shrugged indiffer-ntly. ''I didn't know they were down there. Besides, you ouldn't wait to dash into the water. I never approach a camp-ite without checkin' it out first, mate, and so should you.''

Tammo heaved a sigh as he took his belt from the fallen erret. ''Another jolly old lesson learned, I suppose?''

Russa patted his back heartily. ''You jolly well suppose ight, me ol' pal!''

While the two ferrets sat on the bank recovering from their rubbing, Russa paced around them. She glanced across at ammo, who was carrying the haversack out of the shrubbery here she had left it. ''What d'you think we should do with these vermin, Tamm, kill 'em, or let 'em go?"

The young hare was shocked at the suggestion of cold-blooded slaying. "Russa Nodrey!" he cried, his voice almost shrill with outrage. "You can't just kill them! You wouldn't!"

The squirrel's face was impassive. "D'you know why I'm alive today? 'Cos my enemies are all dead. Make no mistake about it, Tamm, these two scum would've slain you just fer fun if I hadn't been here."

The ferrets began to wail imploringly.

"No no, we was just sportin' wid yer, young sir!"

"We ain't killers, we're pore beasts fallen on 'ard times!"

Russa curled her lip scornfully. "Aye, an' I'm a bluebird wid a frog for an uncle!"

Tammo placed himself between Russa and the ferrets. "You're not goin' to slay them. I'll stop you, Russa!"

The squirrel sat down and, unfastening the haversack, began selecting a few of Mem Divinia's pancakes. "Huh! No need t'fall out over a pair of nogoods like them. Please yoreself, mate, do what y'like with 'em."

Tammo flung Skulka and Gromal's weapons into the water, then he drew his dirk and pointed it at the cringing duo. "Get up an' get goin', you chaps. I never want to see your ugly faces again. Quick now, or I'll let Russa loose on you!"

Without a backward glance, the pair sped off as if pursued by a flight of eagles. Tammo put up his dirk. "There, that's settled!"

Russa filled a beaker with water from the stream. "So you say, me ole mate."

"What d'you mean, so I say?"

"Ah, you'll learn one day. I thought you were starvin'. Come an' get some o' these vittles down yer face."

They dined on pancakes spread with honey, beakers of stream water, and a wedge of cold turnip and carrot pie apiece. The sun was unusually hot for early spring, and Tammo felt rather giddy after their adventure. Finding a soft shady spot beneath the hedgerow, he was asleep in a trice. Russa sat with her back against a dogwood trunk and napped with one eye open.

8

When the sun was past its zenith, Russa woke Tammo. He felt marvelously refreshed and immediately shouldered the haversack, saying, "My turn to carry this awhile. Come on, pal, where to now?"

Still traveling south, the squirrel took him to the top of the next rise and pointed with her stick. "Little patch of woodland yonder, we should make it at twilight."

The going was much easier for Tammo. He enjoyed the sight of new places and fresh scenery, learning from his experienced traveling companion all the time. Russa seemed to come out of her normally taciturn self and was much more verbose than usual.

"Skirt 'round this patch, Tamm, don't want to disturb that curlew sittin' on 'er nest, do we?"

"Of course not, jolly thoughtful of you. Leave the poor bird in peace to sit on her eggs, wot?"

"Nothin' of the sort. If'n we crossed there that'd upset 'er, and she'd fly up kickin' a racket to warn us off. That'd give our position away to anybeast who was trackin' us."

"Oh, right. I say, d'you suppose there is somebeast after us?"

Russa's reply was cryptic. "I dunno, what d'you think?"

The squirrel was as good as her word. Long shadows were gone and twilight was shading the skies as they arrived at the woodland patch, which was considerably bigger than it had seemed from afar. Russa allowed Tammo to pick their campsite, and he chose an ancient fallen beech with part of its vast root system poking into the air.

Russa nodded approval. "Hmm, this looks all right. Want a fire?"

Tammo shrugged off his belt and weapon. "If you say so. Spring nights can be jolly cold, and besides, I'd like to have a hot supper, if y'have no objections."

Russa shook her head vigorously. "None at all, matey. There's plenty o' deadwood an' dry bark about. I'll see t'the fire, you unpack the vittles."

Flint and steel from Russa's pouch soon had dry tinder alight. Clearing a firespace around it, she added fragrant dead pine twigs, old brown ferns, and some stout billets of beech. Tammo found a flagon of elderberry wine in the pack. He warmed pancakes before spreading them with honey, and set two moist-looking chunks of plum cake near the flames to heat through. They sat with their backs against the beech, pleasantly tired, eating, drinking, and chatting.

Russa picked up Tammo's dirk and inspected it closely. "This is a rare weapon, mate. Is it your father's?"

"No, it was my mother's. She was a Long Patrol fighter, y'know. She said a Badger Lord made it for her in the forge at Salamandastron, the great mountain fortress. Can you tell me anythin' of the mountain, Russa? I've never seen it."

Reflectively the squirrel balanced the blade in her paw, then she threw it skillfully. It whizzed across the clearing and thudded point first into a sycamore trunk.

"Sometimes a thrown blade can save your life," she said. "I'll teach you how to sling it properly before long."

Tammo had to tug hard to pull the dirk from the tree trunk. "I'd be rather obliged if y'did. Now what about Salamandastron?"

Russa took a sip of wine and settled back comfortably. "Oh, that place, hmm, let me see. Well, a mountain's a mountain, much like any other, but I can give you the chant I heard the Long Patrol hares sayin' last time I was over that way."

Tammo piled a bit more wood on the fire. "You know the Long Patrol hares? Tell me, what do they chant?"

The squirrel closed her eyes. "Far as I can recall it went somethin' like this:

"O vermin if you dare, come and visit us someday,
Bring all your friends and weapons with you too.
You'll find a good warm welcome, let nobeast living say
That cold steel was never good enough for you.

You won't find poor helpless beasts all undefended,
Like the old ones, babes, and mothers that you've slain,
And you'll find that when your pleasant visit's ended,
You'll never ever leave our shores again.

All you cowards of the land and you flotsam of the sea,
Who murder, pillage, loot whene'er you please,
There's a Long Patrol a waitin', we'll greet you
cheerfully,
You'll hear us cry 'Eulalia' on the breeze.

''Tis a welcome to the bullies who slay without a care,
All those good and peaceful creatures who can't fight,
But perilous and dangerous the beast they call the hare,
Who stands for nought but honor and the right.

Eulalia! Eulalia! Come bring your vermin horde,
The Long Patrol awaits you, led by a Badger Lord!"

Tammo shook his head in admiration. "By golly, that's some chant! Are they really that brave and fearless, these Long Patrol hares?"

Russa threw a burning log end back into the fire. "Ruthless, they can be, but they keep the shores defended and the land safe fer peaceful creatures t'live in. C'mon now, mate, y'need yore sleep for tomorrow's trekkin'. Stow y'self over there in the dark, away from the flames."

Tammo pulled a wry face at this suggestion. "But I'm nice'n'warm here, why've I got to move?"

The squirrel's face grew stern. "Because I says so, now stop askin' silly questions an' shift!"

Tammo retreated into the surrounding bushes, muttering, "Nice warm fire an' I've got t'sleep back here, a chap could catch his death o' cold on a night like this, 'taint fair!"

Sometime during the night, Tammo was awakened by a bloodcurdling scream. He leapt up, grabbing for his dirk, which he had left within paw's reach. It was not there.

He stood in the firelight and looked around. His friend was missing too. Cupping paws around his mouth, the young hare yelled into the night-darkened woodlands, "Russa, where are you?"

With a bound the squirrel cleared the fallen beech trunk and was at his side, wiping the dirk blade on the grass. "I'm here. Keep y'voice down an' get back under cover!"

Together they crouched in the bushes. Tammo was bursting to question Russa, but he held his silence, watching the squirrel's eyes flick back and forth as she craned her head forward, listening.

From somewhere in the midst of the trees there came a shriek of rage. Russa stood erect and shouted in the direction whence it had come, "Yore mate's dead, ferret! Take warnin' an' clear off, 'cos I'm comin' after you next an' I don't take prisoners!"

Skulka's answering call came back, thick with rage: "It ain't over, old one, we'll get you an' yer liddle pal! Jus' wait'n'see!"

This was followed by the sound of Skulka crashing off through the ferns. Then there was silence. Russa gave Tammo back his dirk, saying, "It was those two ferrets we tangled with earlier today, mate. I knew they'd be back, 'specially after they saw you take our 'avvysack o' vittles out o' the bushes back there."

Tammo felt weak with shock. "Russa, I'm sorry. If I hadn't

let them see the haversack they would've gone off none the wiser."

The wily squirrel shook her head. "Wrong, matey, they would've tried to get us whether or not. I knew they was followin' us all day. 'Twas logical they'd make their move tonight when they thought we'd be asleep. So I took off into the trees wid yore blade an' bumped straight into the one called Gromal, armed wid a long sharpened stake, if y'please. So I had to finish it then an' there, 'twas him or me. But I'm a bit worried, Tamm."

Tammo was puzzled by this statement. "What's worryin' you, Russa?"

"Well, did y'hear the other ferret shoutin', she said *we'll* get you. We. It's like I thought, there must be a band of 'em somewheres about. I had a feeling I knowed them two from long ago, they always run with a robber band."

Tammo gripped his blade resolutely. "Right, mate, what's t'be done?"

Russa ruffled Tammo's ears rather fondly. "Sleep's to be done. Shouldn't think they'll be back tonight, but we'll take turns standin' guard. More likely they'll try an' ambush us out in the open tomorrow, so get y'sleep—you'll need it."

Night closed in on the little camp. The fire dimmed from burning flame to glowing embers, trees murmured and rustled, their foliage stirred by a westering wind. Tammo dreamed of his home, Camp Tussock. He saw the faces of his family, and Osmunda and Roolee, together with the young creatures with whom he had played. Elusive aromas of Mem Divinia's cooking, mingled with songs and music around the fire of a winter's night, assailed his senses. A great sadness weighed upon him, as though he might never see or feel it all again.

Russa climbed into a tree and slept the way she had for many seasons, with one eye open.

9

Extract from the writings of Craklyn squirrel, Recorder of Redwall Abbey in Mossflower Country.

Great Seasons! Now I know I am old. A beautiful spring afternoon, the sun smiling warmly over Mossflower Wood and our Abbey, and almost everybeast, from the smallest Dibbun baby to the Mother Abbess herself, is out in the grounds at play. While here am I, sitting by the kitchen ovens, a cloak about me, scratching away with this confounded quill pen. Ah well, somebeast has to do it, I suppose. Though I never thought that one day I would be old, but that is the way of the world, the young never do.

Let me see now, out of the Redwallers of my early seasons there are only a few left: Abbess Tansy, my dear friend, the first hedgehog ever to be Mother of Redwall; Viola Bankvole, our fussy Infirmary Sister; and who else? Oh, yes, Foremole Diggum and Gurrbowl the Cellar Keeper, two of the most loyal moles ever to inhabit Redwall Abbey. Counting the squirrel Arven and myself, that is everybeast accounted for. Arven is our Abbey Warrior.

Who would have thought that such a mischievous little rip would grow up to be so big and reliable, respected throughout Mossflower?

Alas, the seasons caught up with all the old crew who were our elders, and they have gone happily to the sunny meadows. Though they are always alive in our memories, those good creatures and the knowledge and joy they imparted to all. Sad, is it not, though, that our Abbey has lacked a badger and a hare for many a long season now? But I beg your indulgence, I am getting old and maudlin, I've become the same ancient fogey my friends and I would laugh at in our youth. Enough of all this! If I sit here much longer I'll be baked to a turn like the oatfarls in the oven. If my creaking joints will allow me, I'm going out to play with the others. After all, it is springtime, isn't it?

Abbess Tansy ducked as a ball made from soft moss and twine flew over her head. She wrinkled her nose at the tiny mouse who had thrown it. "Yah, missed me, Sloey bunglepaws!"

The mousebabe stamped her footpaw and grimaced fiercely. "A not 'uppose t'duck you 'ead, Muvver Tansy, you stannup straight!"

Behind Tansy a Dibbun mole picked up the ball and was about to throw it clumsily when Craklyn sneaked up. She took the ball from him and threw it hard, hitting Tansy on the back of her head.

With the soft ball sticking to her headspikes, the Abbess whirled around, a look of comic fury upon her face. "Who threw that ball? Come on, own up!"

Craklyn's expression was one of simple innocence. "It wasn't me, Mother Abbess!"

Tansy glared at the little ones playing the game. "Well, who was it, one of you rascals?"

The Dibbuns fell about laughing as a small mole named Gubbio pointed to Craklyn. "Yurr, et wurr ee flung yon ball, marm!"

Craklyn looked horrified. She pointed to Gubbio, saying, "No, it wasn't! You were the one who threw the ball! We saw him, didn't we?"

This caused more hilarity among the babes. The sight of the

Recorder fibbing like a naughty Dibbun was too much for them. They skipped about giggling, pointing to Craklyn.

"'Twas marm Craklyn, 'twas 'er!"

Abbess Tansy pulled the ball from her headspikes and pretended to lecture the Recorder severely: "You naughty creature, fancy throwing things at your Abbess! Right, no supper for you tonight. Straight up to bed, m'lady!"

It all proved too much for the Dibbuns, who threw themselves down on the grass, chuckling fit to burst.

Foremole Diggum in company with Arven the squirrel Warrior and several other moles passed by, headed for the south wall. They had been talking earnestly together as they went, but on seeing Abbess Tansy they stopped conversing and nodded to her as they hurried on their way.

"Afternoon, marm, an' you too, marm!"

Craklyn exchanged glances with Tansy. "They're up to something. Hi, Arven! What's the rush, where are you all off to?"

"Nothin' for you t'be concerned with, marm," Arven called back to her. "Just out for a stroll."

Immediately, Tansy took Craklyn's paw and began to follow them. "You're right, they are up to something. Out for a stroll, eh? Well, come on, friend, let's join 'em! Carry on with the game, you little 'uns, and no cheating!"

Behind the shrubbery that bordered the outer wall of the ramparts on their south side, Diggum Foremole and the rest were questioning a mole called Drubb.

"Whurr do ee say 'twas, Drubb?"

He pointed with a heavy digging claw in several places as he brushed hazel and rhododendron shrubs aside. "Yurr see, an' yurr, yonder too, roight along ee wall if'n you'm look close. Hurr, see!"

Craklyn and Tansy arrived on the scene. Straight away the Abbess started to interrogate Arven: "What's going on? There's something you aren't telling me about. What is it, Arven—I demand to know!"

The squirrel had crouched low at the wallbase, probing the joints of massive red sandstone blocks with a small quill knife. He looked up at Tansy, keeping his voice deceptively calm. "Oh, it's something and nothing, really. Drubb here says he ɩinks the wall is sinking, but he may not be right. We didn't ay anything to you, Tansy, because you've enough to do as ɩbbess . . ."

He was cut short by Tansy's indignant outburst. "The south uter wall of my Abbey is sinking and you didn't consider it erious enough to let your Abbess know? Who in the name of tricken oaks do you think I am, sir—Mother Abbess of Red-vall, or a little fuzzbrained Dibbun playing ball?"

Diggum Foremole touched his brow respectfully. "You'm orgive oi fer sayin', marm, but ee lukked just loik a fuzzy-rain Dibbun a playin' ball when us'n's passed ee but a mo-nent back, hurr aye."

Tansy drew herself up grandly, spikes abristle and eyes light. "Nonsense! Show me the wall this instant!"

The group wandered up and down the length of the high attlemented south wall for the remainder of the afternoon, alking and debating and pointing earnestly. The final conclu-ion was inescapable. The wall was sinking, bellying inward oo. They probed the mortar between the stone joints, stood n top of the wall, and swung a weighted plumb line from top o bottom. Then, placing their faces flat to the wall surface nd each one squinting with one eye, they gauged the extent f the stone warp. Whichever way they looked at it there was nly one thing all were agreed upon. The south wall was crum-bling!

10

Darkness was stealing over Redwall Abbey, and the lights of Great Hall shone through long, stained-glass windows, laying columns of rainbow colors across the lawn. Buttressed and arched, the ancient building towered against a backdrop of Mossflower woodlands. From bell tower to high roof ridge, it was the symbol of safety, comfort, and achievement to all the Redwallers who called it home.

Sister Viola Bankvole had never adopted the simple habit worn by most Abbey creatures. She favored flounces and ruffles, supported by more petticoats than enough. She made her way out of the Abbey's main door, holding up a lantern and tutting fussily as playful night breezes tugged at her cloak and bonnet. Brazen and slow, Redwall's twin bells boomed out sonorously, calling everybeast to table for the evening meal.

Abbess Tansy and her party were at the north wall gable, completing an exhaustive inspection of the entire outer walls.

Foremole Diggum patted the stones fondly. ''Burr! Thank ee, season'n'fates, thurr b'aint nuthen wrong with ee rest of'n our walls, marm, boi 'okey thurr b'aint!''

Arven held up his lantern, watching Abbess Tansy's face

xiously. "He's right, Tansy. The east, north, and west walls, cluding the gatehouse, stairs, ramparts, and main gates, are sound as the day they were built!"

The Abbess rubbed a paw across her tired eyes. "So they e, but that's little comfort when the whole south wall could pple at a moment's notice."

Viola came bustling up, bonnet ribbons streaming out bend her. "Mother Abbess! There's a full evening meal waitg inside that cannot start without your presence! My word, st look at yourselves, dusty paws, thorns and teazels sticking your clothing, what a sight! Craklyn, I thought you were pposed to be helping with the Dibbuns' bedtime. Goodness iows what time those babes will get up to the dormitory night when they haven't even been fed yet! Oh, and another ing . . ."

Arven's voice cut strongly across the bankvole's tirade: Enough! That will do, Sister Viola!"

Tansy took advantage of Viola's huffy silence to say, Thank you, Sister, we will be in to dine shortly. Meanwhile, ould you be good enough to take my chair and order the eal to start in my absence? But do not send the Dibbuns to ed. I have something to say for all Redwallers to hear."

Viola seemed to swell up with the importance of her mison. Nothing she could think of pleased her more than taking e Abbess's place, albeit only for a short time. The bankvole vept off back to the Abbey, cloak aswirl with the wind.

Craklyn watched her go as they made their way toward the bbey pond to wash. "Hmph! That bankvole, sometimes I ink a swift kick in the bustle would do her the world of ood."

Tansy stifled a smile as she reproved her friend. "Sister 'iola is a good and dutiful creature, and she can't help being bit overzealous at times. Mayhap we could all take a little sson from her devotion to detail."

The bustle and chatter of good company was always a keyote to Redwall dining. Great Hall was packed with Redwallrs, eating and conversing across well-laden tables. Golden nd brown crusts of batch loaves, nut-bread, and oatfarl shone the candlelight; tureens of steaming barley and beet soup, lled with corn dumplings, were placed at intervals, between hot cheese and mushroom flans and fresh spring salads. Flagons of spiced fruit cordial and dandelion tea vied for place with pear and chestnut turnovers, apple and cream puddings, and two huge wild cherry and almond cakes. Many of the elders sat Dibbuns on their laps, sharing their plates with the Abbeybabes. The young ones were jubilant at the chance to stay up late.

Arven and the moles came to the table in Tansy's wake. The good Abbess signaled Viola to stay where she was, in the big chair at the head of the table. Shoving Sloey the mousebabe and Gubbio the Dibbun mole playfully apart, Tansy placed herself between them on the low bench, saying, "Move aside there, you two great fatties, let a poorbeast in!"

Sloey looked up from her soup as she moved to make room. "Big fatty y'self, marm. Wot you be late for?"

Gubbio spoke for his Abbess as he munched a large slice of cake. "Apportant bizness, oi surpose."

Tansy ladled soup for herself, winking at the molebabe. "Aye, mate, apportant bizness it was!"

The meal continued in no great hurry, a low buzz of conversation accompanying it. Time was never a factor when victuals were being taken at Redwall. When Tansy judged the moment was right, she stood up and nodded to Viola. The bankvole rang a small pawbell which was on the table near where she sat. Talk died away and Dibbuns were shushed as Tansy addressed her creatures.

"My friends, listen carefully. As your Mother Abbess I have something to tell you. Now there is no cause for alarm, but Foremole Diggum, Arven, Craklyn, some other good moles, and myself have inspected the structure of our Abbey's outer wall is today. For some reason as yet unknown to us, the south wall is in a dangerous state."

Shad, a big otter who occupied the gatehouse as Keeper, was immediately up on his paws. "What's t'be done, marm?"

Tansy gestured to Diggum, and the Foremole answered for her: "Hurr, furstly us'n's needs to foind out whoi ee be unsafe, on'y then'll us be able to fixen ee wall."

With Tansy's permission, Arven was next to speak. "There's no need for anybeast to worry, but we must set a few sensible rules for the safety of all. From tomorrow we will fence off an area isolatin' the entire south wall. Please do not hang about near it. Carry on with your chores and pleasures as normal, and see that none of our little 'uns try to play in the area, because it will be dangerous for a while. Lots of stone and rubble are bound to be lying about when the wall is demolished."

An incredulous murmur arose 'round Great Hall.

"They're going to knock down the south wall, demolish it!"

Shad the Gatekeeper thwacked the table with his thick tail, silencing the talkers. "Hearken t'me! Wot's all the bother about? Stands t'sense that a wobbly wall 'as t'be knocked down afore y'can build it back right. You 'eard Abbess Tansy, there ain't no cause to worry!"

Pellit, a fat dormouse kitchen helper, shook his head knowingly. "Huh, just wait until the first vermin comin' up the path spots the wall knocked down. That'll be the time to start worryin'!"

A loud hubbub broke out as a result of the dormouse's observation, and argument and dispute took over until Great Hall was in uproar. Many of the Abbeybabes, upset by the noise, began wailing with fright.

Without warning, Viola Bankvole leapt up onto the table. Seizing a big empty earthenware basin, she raised it high and sent it crashing to the floorstones. The noise of it smashing to fragments caused a momentary silence. That was enough for Viola; she was in, her voice ringing out sternly: "Silence! Be quiet, I say! Have you no manners at all? You there, Brother Sedum, and you, Pellit, take these babes off to bed right now! The rest of you, stop behaving like a pack of wild vermin. Shame on you! Arven, you are Abbey Warrior, tell these silly creatures of your plans!"

Arven had made no plans at all, but he took the center floor and made them up boldly as he went along, his voice ringing with confidence to reassure the listeners.

"My plans, yes—I was just coming to that before all the shouting started. Foremole Diggum and his moles will take care of the demolition and rebuilding, together with any of you he chooses to assist him. The work will be carried out in shifts, so that the job will be completed as soon as possible.

Meanwhile I'm sure our friend Shad will contact the Skipper of Otters and his crew, and together with our own stout creatures they will form a force to guard and patrol the immediate area. Really, friends, there is no cause to worry at all. Many seasons have passed since any vermin bands were seen in this part of Mossflower Country."

Tansy clapped her paws in appreciation of Arven's fine speech, and soon the other Redwallers joined in, heartened by his words.

Late that night when most other creatures were abed, Tansy presided over a meeting of the Abbey elders in Cavern Hole, a smaller, more comfortable venue. While they were gathering she took the opportunity to murmur to Craklyn, "What price a swift kick in the bustle now, marm? I think Viola behaved magnificently tonight in Great Hall. There's a lot more to our Infirmary Sister than mostbeasts would think, d'you agree?"

The squirrel Recorder nodded vigorously. "Indeed there is, she can be a proper little firebrand when she wants. All right, Mother Abbess, I'll eat my words. I'd sooner shake her by the paw than kick her in the bustle!"

Deep into the small hours they sat debating the issue of the south wall, its possibilities and its perils. The meeting ended with Diggum's irrefutable mole logic.

"Hurr well, so be't. Us'n's caint do ennythin' 'til we foinds out wot maked ee wall go all of awobble. Oi'm thinkin' us'n's won't be able t'do that proper lest us gets a gudd noight's sleep."

Arven tossed and turned in his bed, the question of the wall troubling him greatly, until finally sleep took over and he settled down. In his dreams he was visited by Martin the Warrior, the guiding spirit of Redwall Abbey. Martin was the Warrior who had been instrumental in founding Redwall long ages before. The dust of countless seasons had blown over his grave, though his image was still fresh on the wall tapestry of Great Hall. It was often in times of trouble and crisis that he would appear in dreams to one or another Redwaller of his choosing, comforting and counseling them.

On this night, however, his words carried a warning to Arven. Looming through the mists of slumber the warriormouse strode, armored and carrying his legendary sword. Arven instinctively knew there would be a message for both him and the Abbey, and as he watched Martin draw near, a great sense of peace and well-being swept over him. He felt like some small creature folded within the security of a figure that was old, wise, compassionate, and above all, safe.

The Warrior spoke:

"Watch you ever the southlands,
And beware when summertide falls,
A price will be paid for these stones we hold dear,
Though war must not touch our walls."

Arven had no recollection of his dream the next day.

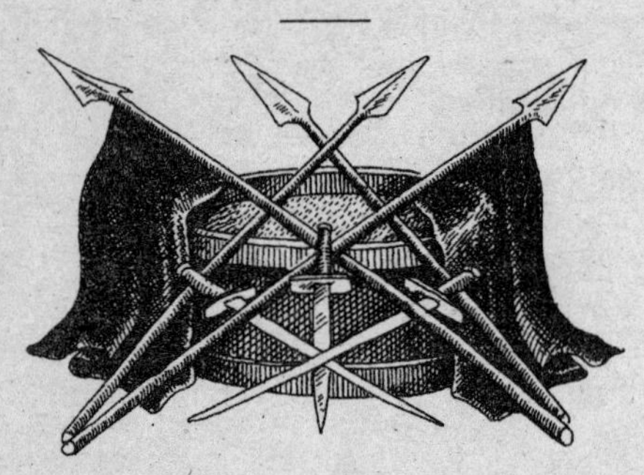

On the southeast coastline the mighty Rapscallion army crouched, saturated, cold, and hungry, amid the wreckage of their ships. Gray-black and bruised though it was, dawn proved a welcome sight for the dispirited vermin masses. Nobeast could have known that after they had burned their dwellings a storm would arrive in the night.

It came from the southeast, tearing across the seas with a vengeance, without warning. Battering torrents of rain sheeted down to drown the campfires 'round which the vermin were sleeping. Hailstones big as pigeon eggs were mixed with the deluge, while a gale-force wind drove the downpour sideways over the beach.

Shrieking and roaring, rats, ferrets, stoats, weasels, and foxes dashed about on the shingle, seeking shelter as the storm's intensity grew. Ships beached on the immediate tide line were seized upon by the mountainous seas and heaved out upon the waves, where they were smashed like eggshells as they crashed into one another. Rigging and timbers, ratlines and gallery rails flew through the air, slaying several unfortunates who were running panicked on the shore.

Only four vessels, beached high above the tide line, their ulls half buried by sand and shingle, were safe. Around the e sides of these ships the Rapscallions fought their comrades avagely, endeavoring to find shelter. Damug Warfang and his apmark officers, together with a chosen few, occupied the abin spaces, while the remainder fended for themselves out 1 the open.

By daylight the rain and hailstones had passed, sweeping pward into the land, though the wind was still strong and vild. Damug crouched over a guttering fire in the cabin of his ather's former ship, teeth chattering. Drawing his cloak ghter, he watched Lugworm heating a pannikin of grog over he meager flames.

"That looks ready as it'll ever be. Give it here!"

With his teeth rattling like castanets against the container, he Greatrat sipped gingerly at the scalding concoction. When e had drunk enough the Firstblade gave the remainder to ugworm, who choked it down before Damug could change is mind. Peering through the broken timbers, Damug cast his ye over the low-spirited Rapscallions roaming the shore.

"We'll move right away, get inland where the weather's a ouch milder. First grove o' woodland we find will do for a amp; fire, water, whatever food we can forage, then they'll e ready to gear up and march."

Lugworm fussed around his Chief, brushing dirt and splinters from Damug's cloak. "Aye, sir, they'll be fine then, ightin' fit fer a journey o'er to the west, ter pay that badger ack for yore father."

Whack!

The Greatrat's mailed paw caught Lugworm alongside his aw, sending him crashing into a shattered bunk. Damug was ike a madbeast: flinging himself upon the hapless stoat he eat him unmercifully, punctuating each word with a blow or ick.

"Don't you ever mention that beast within my hearing gain! We stay away from that cursed mountain! Aye, and hat rose-eyed destroyer, that blood-crazed badger! That . . . That . . ." He grabbed Lugworm by the throat and shook him ike a rag. "That . . . *badger*! You even *think* about her again nd I'll kill you stone dead!"

Damug Warfang hurled the half-conscious Lugworm from himself, slammed the door clean off its hinges, and strode quivering with rage out of the cabin. Grabbing a ferret called Skaup, he bellowed right into his face, "Get the drums rolling, and tell my Rapmarks to line up their companies. We march north. Now!"

Within a very short time the Rapscallion soldiers were formed up into columns five wide and marching away from the hostile coast.

Damug strode at the head of his army; on either side of him, six rats pounded their big drums. Ragged banners flapped wildly in the wind, their poles ornamented with the tails of dead foebeasts. The poles' tops were crowned with the skulls of enemies, and their long pennants bore the sign of Rapscallion, the two-edged sword.

Borumm the weasel and Vendace the fox were scouts, known by the title Rapscour. They marched to the left flank of the main body with twoscore trained trackers each. Borumm glanced back at the receding shoreline and the sea, saying, "Take yer last peep o' the briny, mate, this lot won't be goin' nowheres by water anymore. 'Is Lordship Damug don't like sailin'."

Vendace narrowed his eyes against the driving wind. "That's a fact, cully, an' I'll wager an acorn to an oak that 'e won't be 'eadin' over Salamandastron way neither. Taint only ships Damug's afeared of."

Borumm let his paw stray to the cutlass at his side. "A proper Firstblade shouldn't be afeared o' nought. But we'll frighten 'im one dark night, eh, mate?"

Vendace grinned wolfishly at his companion. "Aye, when 'e's least expectin' it, we'll find space atwixt 'is ribs fer a couple o' sharp blades. Then we'll be the Firstblades."

Borumm closed his eyes longingly for a moment. "Harr, we'll turn this lot right 'round an' make fer the soft sunny south coast an' rule it like a pair o' kings."

Lugworm stumbled along behind the last column, clasping a damp strip of blanket to his bruised throat. Being a Firstblade's counselor had its drawbacks. It would take him a day or two to get back into his Chief's favor, and meanwhile he ecided to stay as far away from Damug as possible.

Lousewort and Sneezewort marched just ahead of him, being in the back five of the last contingent. Lousewort caught ght of Lugworm and called back to him, "G'mornin', uggy, wot sorta mood's the boss in t'day?"

Lugworm tried to speak, but could manage only a painful urgle.

Sneezewort looked quizzically at Lousewort. "Wot did 'e ay, mate?"

The stolid Lousewort shook his head. "Er, er, 'e jus' said Gloggle oggle ogg,' or sumthin', I dunno."

Sneezewort prodded his mate. " 'Gloggle oggle ogg,' eh? hat's wot you'd a bin sayin' right now if'n you was totin' at stoopid big wheel along wid yer."

The big nasty-looking weasel's voice reached them from the ank marching in front. "Wot stoopid big wheel's that yer lkin' about?"

"Oh, the one I chucked awa—Wot wheel are ye talkin' bout, comrade? I don't know nothin' about any wheel, d'you, natey?"

Lousewort nodded obliviously. "Oh yep, you remember, neezy, my nice big wheel wot you throwed away. Owow! Vot are ye kickin' me for, mate?"

All morning the wind continued to blow, right until midnoon, when a drizzle started. Damug Warfang rapped out commands o the drummers.

"Speed up that beat to double march, there's a woodland p ahead."

The two Rapscours and their scouts dashed ahead of the Rapscallions to reconnoiter the spot. It was a prime campsite, vith a small pond containing fish, and lots of fat woodpigeons oosting in the trees. By late noon the army was completely heltered from the weather: rocky ledges, heavy tree trunks, nd overhead foliage sealed them off from cold, wind-driven ain. A feeling of well-being pervaded the camp, now they vere in a fresh location. This was luxury, after an entire winter pent on the hostile and hungry southeast shore.

Borumm and Vendace were snugly settled in, having spread n old sail canvas over the low curving limb of a buckthorn, with a rocky outcrop at their back. They sat cooking a quail over their campfire. Lugworm was with them, hiding behind a flap of the overhanging canvas, glancing nervously around at the passing Rapscallions.

Borumm chuckled at the stoat's apprehensive manner. Shoving him playfully, he said, "Wot's the matter, matey? You ain't doin' no 'arm jus' sittin' 'ere sharin' a bird with two ole pals."

Lugworm averted his face as a Rapmark walked by. "What'd Damug say if'n somebeast told 'im I was sittin' 'ere talkin' wid you two?"

Vendace shrugged as he tended the roasting quail. "We won't tell 'im if you don't. Stop frettin' an' 'ave some o' this bird. All you gotta do is tell us where ole Firstblade'll be sleepin' tonight an' how many guards'll be around, an' anythin' else y'think we should know. Leave the rest to us, matey."

Borumm whetted a curved dagger against the rock. "Aye, by tomorrer it shouldn't make any difference who saw yer talkin' to us. Damug won't be around to throttle yer again, 'e'll be searchin' for 'is daddy in Dark Forest!"

Sneezewort had a good fire going. He stirred the half-burned wood hopefully, watching Lousewort returning from the pond. He noticed that his companion looked very damp.

"Yore lookin' a bit soggy, mate. Didyer catch anythin'?" he called.

Lousewort slumped by the fire, waving away the cloud of steam rising from his ragged garments. "Er, er, I nearly did, but I got pushed inter the water."

Sneezewort picked up a small log and brandished it angrily. "Pushed in? Huh, show me the slab-sided blackguard wot pushed yer!"

"Er, er, it was that big nasty-lookin' weasel."

Sneezewort threw the log on the fire, sighing resignedly. "Ah well, that one's got 'is lumps comin' someday. So, you didn't bring any vittles back at all?"

Lousewort produced a pile of dripping pondweed. "Er, er, only this. May'aps we can make soup out of it."

His companion turned up a lip in disgust. "Yurgh, dirty smelly stuff, chuck it away!"

Lousewort was about to carry out his friend's order when his paw was stayed. Sneezewort stared unhappily at the mess of dripping vegetation, shaking his head, and said, "Take my ole helmet an' fill it wid water. Pondweed soup's better'n nothin' when yer belly thinks yore throat's cut!"

Damug belched loudly and settled back to suck upon the bones of the tench he had just devoured. From the shelter of an ash nearby he heard his title whispered.

"Firstblade!"

The Greatrat lay still, lips hardly moving as he answered, "Gribble, is that you?"

From his hiding place, the rat Gribble called in a low voice, "Aye, 'tis me. Lugworm's gone over to Borumm an' Vendace. From wot I 'eard they'll make their move tonight, Chief."

Damug Warfang smiled and closed his eyes. "Good work, Gribble. It always pays to have watchers watching watchers. I'll be ready. Go now, keep your eyes and ears open."

12

Russa Nodrey added twigs to the fire embers, peering upward at slatey skies that showed between treetops that morning. ''Hmm, doesn't look too good out there t'day. No point in leavin' camp awhile, those vermin'd probably ambush us afore we got out o' these trees.''

Tammo looked up from the beaker of hot mint tea he was sipping. ''Y'mean the rotten ol' vermin are hiding in these woodlands? I thought you said they'd ambush us out on the flatland.''

The wily squirrel pointed a paw at the sky. ''So they would if it were fine weather, but put y'self in their place, mate. You wouldn't stand out in the open soakin' an' freezin', waitin' fer us to come out of a nice dry camp like this. No, if'n you'd any sense at all you'd get under cover, out of the weather. They're probably creepin' through the trees toward us right now.''

The young hare dropped low, drawing his dirk. ''Are you sure that's what the rascals are up to?''

Russa added more wood to the fire. ''Sure as liddle apples, if I know anythin' about vermin!''

Tammo was amazed at his companion's calm manner. Then what're you standin' there loadin' more bally wood on e fire for? Shouldn't we be doin' somethin' about the situ- ion?''

Russa hid the haversack away beneath some bushes, then mmaged about in her back pouch. She tossed Tammo a sling d a bag of flat pebbles. ''Here, I take it y'can use that.''

Tammo loaded a pebble into the tough sinewy weapon, and vung it. ''Rather! I was the best slingshot chucker at Camp ıssock!''

Russa twirled her hardwood stick expertly. ''Right, here's hat we'll do. I'll take to the trees an' pick 'em off as you aw 'em out. Use the sling, leave yore blade where 'tis unless ey get too close, then don't fool about, use it fer keeps. Move ow, I c'n hear 'em comin'—sounds like there's enough o' e scum. We'll have our work well cut out, mate.''

Tammo heard a twig snap some distance away and heard a ırsh cry.

''There's one of 'em, come on!''

He turned to answer Russa, but she was not there.

Suddenly a rat came leaping over the fallen beech at him. ammo reacted swiftly. Swinging the loaded sling, he brought cracking down between his assailant's eyes. The rat fell bleaxed by the force of the blow. For a second Tammo froze, most paralyzed at the sight of the rat's broken body, half ıocked, half exhilarated at this victory and escape. But there 'as no time to think. Instinctively he began whirling his sling. eaping backward a few paces, he centered on a shadowy ɔrm in the shrubbery and let fly. He was rewarded by a sharp gonized cry as the slingstone smashed home. The young hare ırned and ran a short distance. He was stopping to load up is sling when a sharp-clawed paw gripped the back of his eck.

''Haharr, gotcha!''

There was a heavy clunking noise, and the vermin collapsed mply. Russa leaned out of the foliage of an oak, directly over /here Tammo stood. She waved the piece of hardwood at him.

''Best weapon a beast ever had, this 'un! Get goin', Tamm, ıere's more of 'em than I reckoned!''

The woodlands became alive with vermin war cries. An

arrow zipped past Tammo, grazing his ear before it quivere
in the oakwood. Then they came pounding through the wood
lands toward him, a score or more of snarling savages, bran
dishing an ugly and lethal array of weapons. Whipping
slingstone at them, Tammo took off at a run, only to find h
was headed straight in the direction of another group.

Whichever way he wheeled there were vermin coming a
him. Foliage rustled overhead, and Russa came sailing out o
a tree to land beside him, her jaw set grimly.

"I never figgered on this many, mate. The villains've go
us surrounded. Pity it had to happen yore first time out, Tamm
Still, there's one consolation—if'n we go together, I won't b
left t'carry the news back to yore mum."

Tammo felt no fear, only rage. Drawing his blade, he gritte
his teeth and swung the loaded sling like a flexible club
"Stand back t'back with me, pal. If we've got to go, then let's
give 'em somethin' to jolly well remember us by. Eulaliaaaaaaa!"

The vermin rushed them but were swiftly repulsed, such
was the ferocity with which the two friends fought. Four rats
went down from blade thrust, sling, and stick. Whirling to
meet a second onslaught, following hard on the heels of the
first, Russa stunned a weasel with the butt of her stick, grabbing him close to her so that he took the spear thrust of a
ferret behind him. Tammo whipped the loaded sling into the
face of another and slashed out to the side with his dirk, catching a rat who was sneaking in on him.

A big, wicked-looking fox swung out with an immense
pike. The heavy iron blade thudded flat down on Russa's head,
stunning the squirrel and knocking her flat. Tammo tripped
over a wounded rat and stumbled awkwardly. The vermin pack
flung themselves on the pair. Tammo managed to slay one and
wound another, then he went under, completely engulfed by
weight of numbers. Stars and comets rattled about in his head
as the butt end of the fox's pike flattened him.

Waves of throbbing pain crashed through the young hare's
skull. He struggled to lift his paws to his head but found he
was unable to. Noise followed, lots of noise, then an agonizing
pain across his shoulders. Opening his eyes slowly, Tammo

found himself facing Skulka. She was swinging the thorn-covered wild rose branch that she had just struck him with.

"Hah! I thought that'd waken 'im! Would yer like another taste o' this, me bold young warrior?"

Tammo's paws were tightly bound, but that did not stop him bulling forward and up, catching the ferret hard beneath her chin with a resounding headbutt. Her jaws cracked together like a window slamming as she fell backward.

A rat ran forward swinging a sword, shouting, "I'll finish 'im!"

Russa had recovered sufficiently to kick out at the rat with her tightly lashed footpaws, and he was knocked sideways, striking his back sharply against a tree trunk.

Rubbing furiously at his spine, the rat came at Russa, sword held straight for her throat. "I'll show ye the color o' yer insides fer that, bushtail!"

He was stopped in his tracks by the big fox's pike handle. "No, y'won't, cully. I want some sport wid these two afore we put paid to 'em. Now then, young 'un, where'd yer 'ide that bagful o' vittles you two've bin totin' around?"

Tammo glanced down at the pikepoint pricking his chest. He smiled contemptuously at his tormentor, and said, "Actually I stuffed 'em down your ears while you were asleep last night, figurin' that owing to the lack of brains there'd be plenty o' room inside your thick head, old chap."

The fox quivered with anger but held his temper. "You've just cost yer comrade 'er tail, and when I've chopped it off I'm gonna ask yer again. We'll see 'ow smart yer mouth is then, bucko. Skulka, Gaduss, grab 'old o' that squirrel . . ."

Suddenly the fox stopped talking and stared dumbly at the javelin that appeared to be growing out of his middle. A blood-curdling cry rang through the trees.

"Eulaliaaaaaa! Give 'em blood'n'vinegar!"

This was followed by a veritable rain of arrows, javelins, and slingstones. Taken by surprise, the vermin scattered. One or two who were a bit slow were cut down where they stood. From somewhere a drum began beating and the wild war cry resounded louder: " 'S death on the wind! Eulaliaaaa! Eulaliaaaaaa!"

The vermin had obviously heard the call before. Whimpering with terror they fled, many of them falling to the rain of missiles pursuing the retreat.

Tammo was busily trying to sever his bonds on the fallen fox's pikeblade, when the drums sounded close. He looked up to see a very fat hare striding toward him. Amazingly, the creature was making the drum sounds with his mouth.

"Babumm babumm barabumpitybumpitybumm! Drrrrrr-ubbity dubbity rump ta tump! Barraboomboomboom!"

A tall elegant hare with drooping mustachios, carrying a long saber over one shoulder of his bemedaled green velvet jacket, stepped languidly out of the tree cover.

"Good show, Corporal Rubbadub, compliments to y'sah. Now d'you mind awfully if one asks y'to give those infernal drums a rest?"

With a smile that was like the sun coming out, the fat hare threw up a smart salute and brought both footpaws down hard as he gave two final drum noises.

"Boom boom!"

The tall hare's saber whistled through the air as he spoke to Tammo and Russa. "Stay quite still, chaps, that's the ticket!"

The two friends winced and closed their eyes tightly as the saber whipped around them like an angry wasp. In a trice the cords that had bound them were lying slashed on the ground.

Russa smiled one of her rare smiles. "Captain Perigord Habile Sinistra to the rescue, eh!"

The hare made an elegant leg and bowed. "At y'service, marm, though I'm known as Major Perigord nowadays, promotion y'know. Hmm, Russa Nodrey, thought you'd have perished from vermin attack or old age seasons ago. Who's this chap, if I may make so bold as t'ask?"

Standing upright, Tammo returned the Major's bow courteously. "Tamello De Fformelo Tussock, sah."

"Indeed! Any relation to Colonel Cornspurrey De Fformelo Tussock?"

"I should say so, sah, he's my pater!"

"You don't say! Well, there's a thing. I served under your old pa when I was about your seasons. By m'life! Then you'll be Mem Divinia's young 'un!"

"I have that honor, sah."

Major Perigord walked in a circle around Tammo, shaking is head and smiling. "Mem Divinia, eh, great seasons o' salt, e prettiest hare ever t'slay vermin. I worshiped her, y'know, rom afar of course, she was ever the Colonel's, and me? Pish ish! I was nought but a young Galloper. Ah for the golden ays o' youth, wot!"

He broke off to listen to the screams of the fleeing vermin rowing fainter, then turned to Corporal Rubbadub and said, 'Be s'good as to call the chaps'n'chappesses back, will you, ere's a good creature."

Still smiling from ear to ear, Rubbadub marched off in the irection of the retreat, his drum noises echoing and rolling roughout the small woodland.

"Barraboom! Barraboom! Barraboomdiddyboomdiddy oomboom!"

The Major perched gracefully on the fallen beech trunk. 'Complete March Hare, ol' Rubbadub, took too many head vounds in battle, doncha know. Never speak, but the chap nakes better drum noises than a real drum, or four real drums 'that matter. Brave as a badger and fearless as a fried frog, hough, a perilous creature t'have on your side in a pinch."

Tammo remembered the term "perilous hare," so he gave he polite rejoinder, "As you say, sah, a perilous creature, an' vhat more could one ask of a hare?"

Perigord nodded his head and winked broadly at the ounger beast. "Rather! 'Tis easy t'see you're the Colonel's ffspring, though I think that fortunately you favor your nother more."

Tammo touched his aching head and leaned back against he beech.

Major Perigord was immediately apologetic. "Oh, my dear ellow, what a beauty of a lump they gave you on the old eezer—you too, Russa. Forgive me, chattin' away here like sea gull at suppertime. We must get y'some medical atten-ion. At ease in the ranks there, sit down an' rest until Pasque gets back. She's our healer—have y'right as rain in two ticks, vot! You're with the Long Patrol now, y'know, no expense pared!"

Despite his headache, Tammo managed a bright smile. 'Did you hear that, Russa? We're with the Long Patrol!"

To Tammo's utter amazement, when all the hares returned to camp, he counted only eleven, including Perigord and Rubbadub. The Major was amused by the look on his new friend's face.

"I can see what you're thinkin', laddie buck. Well, let me tell you, the Long Patrol counts quality high above quantity, wot! Here, let me introduce y'to our happy band. This is our Galloper, Riffle, fleet of paw and faster'n the wind. Sergeant Torgoch, a walkin' armory, collects weapons, 'specially blades. These two're Tare'n'Turry the terrible twins, can't tell 'em apart, eh, never mind, neither c'n I. Lieutenant Morio, our Quartermaster, can steal a nut from a squirrel's mouth an' make him think he's jolly well eaten it. My sister, Captain Twayblade, charming singer but rather perilous with that long rapier she carries. The delightful Pasque Valerian, best young medico t'come off the mountain, I've seen her fix a butterfly's wing. That chap there's Midge Manycoats. He's our spy, master o' disguise an' deadly with a noose. Then there's Rockjaw Grang, Giant o' the North, bet y've never seen a hare that size a season's march. That leaves m'self, whom y've met, an' orporal Rubbadub, the droll drummer.''

Rubbadub smiled widely, clapping his ears together twice ıd issuing a drum sound so that it looked as if the ears, and ɔt his mouth, had made the noise.

''Boomboom!''

Russa nudged Tammo and, nodding toward Torgoch, murured, ''That 'un's carryin' yore blade, mate!''

Amid the array of daggers, swords, and knives bristling om Torgoch's belt, the young hare identified his own eapon, its shoulder belt wound 'round the blade.

Tammo braced himself and faced the hare. ''Beg pardon, d lad, but I rather think that's my dirk you've got.''

The Sergeant took Tammo's weapon from his belt. Balancg it deftly on his paw, he smiled ruefully. ''I 'oped it ouldn't be, young sir, 'tis a luvverly blade. I took it orf a ermin oo didn't look as if 'e'd be usin' it agin. You'd best ve it back, y'don't see knives like this'n a lyin' about every ay. A proper officer's weapon 'tis, I'd say a Badger Lord ould've made it.''

Tammo was about to put on the belt when he suddenly sat own hard on the ground and began shivering. The ache in s head had become overwhelming. The tall saturnine Lieunant Morio nodded gloomily at Pasque Valerian and said, I'll light a fire an' heat some water. You'd best see to that oung 'un, he's got a touch o' battle shock. I recall m'self ein' like that first time I saw serious action.''

Pasque sat alongside Tammo, rummaging in her herbalist's ouch. ''Lie back now, easy does it. Here, chew on this— on't swallow it, though. Spit it out when you've had nough.''

It was a sort of sticky moss, bound together by some type f vegetable gum, with a taste reminiscent of mint and roses. 'ammo chewed slowly, and through half-closed lids he atched Pasque mixing herbs by the fire. She was the prettiest, ıost gentle creature he had ever encountered. Tammo reolved that he would get to know her better, then his thoughts ecame muddled as he drifted away into warm dark seas of lumber.

Night had fallen when he awakened, and a delicious aroma of cooking reminded him he was very hungry.

Perigord's sister, Twayblade, patted the log beside her. "Feelin' better now, young 'un? Come an' perch here. Rubbadub, bring this beast somethin' to eat, wot."

Instinctively, Tammo reached to touch his injured head. A massive paw engulfed his, and he found himself staring upward into the fearsome face of the giant hare, Rockjaw Grang.

"Nay, lad, th'art not to touch thy 'ead yet awhile. Best leave alone what our little lass 'as patched up. Sithee, coom an' set by t'fire."

Rockjaw picked Tammo up as if he were a babe and sat him down between Twayblade and Pasque, who smiled quietly at him and said, "I hope you're feeling better this evening."

Tammo flushed to his eartips and muttered incoherently, feeling completely awkward and embarrassed for the first time in his life. He wanted so much to talk with Pasque, yet his tongue would not obey his brain. Rubbadub saved the situation by marching up with a bowl of hot pea and celery soup with fresh-baked bread to dip in it.

He winked and grinned broadly. "Drrrrrrr tish boom!"

Russa raised her eyebrows. "Oh, he does cymbals too?"

The young Galloper Riffle refilled the squirrel's beaker. "Aye, marm, bugles also, an' flutes when he's a mind to. Ol' Rubbadub's a full band when the mood takes him."

Major Perigord turned to his troop good-humoredly. "Stripe me, but you're a dull bunch o' ditchwallopers! We ain't welcomed our guests with the anthem yet."

Tammo looked up from his soup. "The anthem?"

Midge Manycoats took out a tiny flute and got the right key. "Humm, humm, fa, sol la te, fa, fa, fa, that's it. Right, troop, the 'Song of the Long Patrol.' Like to hear it, Tammo?"

The young hare nodded eagerly. "Rather, I'd love to!"

With Midge acting as conductor and choirmaster, the little woodland camp with its flickering fire shadows, echoed to the famous marching air of the Salamandastron fighters.

"O it's hard and dry when the sun is high
And dust is in your throat,
When the rain pours down, near fit to drown,

It soaks right through your coat.
But the hares of the Long Patrol, my lads,
Stout hearts they walk with me
Over hill and plain and back again
To the shores of the wide blue sea.

Through mud and mire to a warm campfire,
I'll trek with you, old friend,
O'er lea and dale in a roaring gale,
Right to our journey's end.
Aye, the hares of the Long Patrol, my lads,
Love friendship more than gold.
We'll share long days and tread hard ways,
Good comrades, brave and bold!"

Rubbadub completed the anthem with a long drumroll and a double boom as Tammo and Russa thumped out their applause on the tree trunk.

The terrible twins, Tare and Turry, called out to Tammo, "Come on, come on, you've got to jolly well sing us one back!"

"Aye, so y'have, sing up, Tamm, you look as if y'could belt out a good ditty!"

Russa Nodrey noted the horrified look on Tammo's face, and smiled wryly at Perigord. "Hah! Look at 'im, that'n would sooner be boiled in the soup than sing wid yore pretty Pasque sittin' next to 'im!"

She spared Tammo further embarrassment by volunteering herself. "Ye can't expect that hare t'sing whilst 'e's recoverin' from an injury. I'll do my anthem for you, 'tis called 'The Song of the Stick.' Though I usually sings it when I'm alone."

Leaping up, Russa began twirling her small hardwood staff, tossing it in the air, catching it on her tail, flicking it back overhead into her paws, and spinning it until it became a blur as she sang:

"This ain't a sword, it ain't a spear,
An arrow, nor a bow,
'Tis just a thing I carries 'round
With me where e'er I go.

It cannot talk or grumble,
And never answers back,
But it can sniff out vermin
An' land 'em such a crack!

O my liddle stick o' wood, my liddle stick o' wood,
Whacks here'n'there an' everywhere,
No weapon's half so good,
An' I am tellin' you,
My friend so stout'n'true,
This liddle piece o' timber
Has always seen me through.

It'll wallop a weasel, sock a stoat,
Or fling a ferret from 'is coat,
'Twould knock a fox clean out his socks,
My liddle stick o' wood!"

The hares gathered 'round, applauding Russa, who was still performing tricks with the hardwood, which seemed as though it had a life of its own.

Tammo waved at her. "Thanks, matey, that was great!"

Russa came over to whisper in his ear. "I wouldn't do it fer any otherbeast, Tamm, performin' in public ain't my thing. So remember, you owe me one, pal."

When the meal and the entertainment were over, Major Perigord gave out his orders.

"Heads down now, chaps, we move out at dawn. Rockjaw, take first watch. Riffle, Midge, recky 'round a bit, see if y'can pick up the vermin trail for the mornin'. Compliments an' g'night, troop."

Russa and Perigord sat by the fire, long after the rest were asleep, conversing in low tones.

"What brings you an' the Patrol over thisways, friend?"

"Rapscallions an' Lady Cregga Rose Eyes's commands. We travel on her orders, Russa. Last winter we did battle with old Gormad Tunn an' his army, never seen so many vermin in me life, wot! Well, we gave 'em the drubbin' they richly deserved an' sent the scum packin'. Great loss o' life on both sides, but Rapscallions got the worst of it, by m'left paw they id! Our Badger Lady was like a pack o' wolves rolled into nebeast when the Bloodwrath came upon her. They took off ke scalded crabs an' we pursued 'em almost into deep water, ackin' an' smashin' at their fleet, did a fair part of damage) it. Hah, off they sailed, screamin' an' cursin' something readful!''

Russa stared into the fire. ''Evil murderin' beasts, 'twas all ley deserved!''

The elegant Major stroked his mustachios reflectively. 'Trouble is, nobeast seems t'know where the blighters went. Ve know Rapscallions don't sail out on the open seas, they ug the coasts an' make raids from their ships. So we're cer- ain they can't have had their fleet sunk out at sea an' got lemselves drowned, worst luck. Lady Rose Eyes is extremely vorried, y'see they've dropped completely out of sight, over thousand Rapscallions, with Gormad Tunn and those two vil sons of his, Damug an' Byral. Our Badger Lady figures lat the cads are layin' up someplace, plannin' a major come- ack. Huh, they won't come near Salamandastron again, but he's of the opinion, an' rightly so, that the great Rapscallion rmy'll find a target easier than our mountain. Russa, I tell ou, with a mob o' that magnitude they could create a veri- able bloodbath anyplace!''

Russa nodded her agreement. ''So she sent you an' yore roop out to track 'em down?''

Perigord stirred the embers with his sabertip. ''That she did, ld friend, and we searched most o' the winter until we located oday's gang. But they're only a blinkin' fraction of the main and, must've had their ship blown off course an' wrecked. I hink they're travelin' overland to join up with the others, hat's why we're trailin' 'em. Pity we had to show our paws y attackin' them today, but I couldn't let you an' young 'ammo be slain by those foul blackguards.''

Russa patted the Major's left paw gratefully. ''Thanks, Per- gord. I wasn't greatly bothered, but it'd be a shame t'see a ine young hare like Tammo butchered by vermin. I brought im along with me because 'tis his life's ambition to join the ong Patrol. 'E idolizes you lot.''

The hare squinted along the length of his saberblade. ''I ould see that. Bear in mind, both Tammo's mater'n'pater ran with the Patrol once. He comes of good fightin' stock, that young 'un. Officer material, I shouldn't wonder, wot?"

Both beasts sat silently, watching the flames die to embers. Russa finally stretched out in the shelter of the beech log and said, "If you take him with yer I'll come along for the trip. Promised his ma I'd look out fer 'im. Wot's yore next move?"

The Major unbuttoned his tunic and lay down. "Sleep what's left o' the night, I s'pose, then carry on trailin' the vermin an' see where they go. Though if they persist in travelin' south I'll have to stop 'em permanent—can't have those killers wanderin' up the path to Redwall Abbey. Lady Cregga'd have an absolute fit if she knew we'd let a gang o' bloodthirsty thieves anywhere near the Abbey."

Russa rolled over so that her back was warmed by the embers. "Fits right in with my plans. I was plannin' on visitin' ole Abbess Tansy, an' of course there's always the famous Redwall kitchens, no grub better in the land!"

Major Perigord Habile Sinistra licked his lips dreamily. "I'm right with you there, old sport!"

14

Arven was jerked into wakefulness by Shad the otter Gatekeeper. The burly creature was cloaked and carrying a lantern. "All paws on deck, mate, yore needed at the wall!"

Wordlessly, the squirrel donned his tunic and grabbed a cloak, then the pair stole out of the dormitory silently, loath to waken young Redwallers still sleeping.

Descending the spiral stairs to the ground floor, Shad explained what had taken place. "I was asleep in the gatehouse not an hour back when Skipper an' his otter crew arrived. Funny, I sez, I was comin' over t'see you today, messmate. Was you now, sez 'e t'me, well that *is* funny, Shad, 'cos I couldn't sleep fer dreamin' that summat was amiss at the Abbey, so I roused the crew an' set course for 'ere right away! Well, there's a stroke o' luck, sez I to 'im, you saved me a journey, matey, y'better come an' look at our south wall."

By then Shad and Arven were at the main door of the Abbey building. Pale stormlit dawn was breaking. A gale-force wind tore the breath from their mouths, buffeting both creatures sideways, and hissing rain glistened off the grass in the cold half-light.

Sheltering the lantern beneath his flapping cloak, Shad shouted at Arven, "Come an' see for yoreself!"

Leaning into the tempest, heads down and cloaks drawn tight, both beasts made their way to the south wall.

Skipper of Otters stood at the southeast end of the wall, he and his crew sheltering beneath a monstrous jumble of branches, limbs, twigs, leaves, and stone blocks. Arven nodded briefly to the otters, then, launching himself into the mass of foliage, he shed his cloak and climbed nimbly upward into the tangle. No squirrel could climb like the Champion of Redwall; in a short time Arven was vaulting out of the foliage onto the battlemented walkway that formed the walltop. Bracing himself against the stormy onslaught, he surveyed the damage and its cause.

Mossflower woodlands grew practically right up to the east wall, curving slightly at the south corner and petering out to give way to gently sloping grassland. Directly at the curve a great beech tree had fallen upon the end of the south wall. The ancient forest giant had stood there for untold seasons in high and wide-girthed splendor, only to be felled during the night by the irresistible force sent by weather's wildness.

Near the beech base, Arven could see where the top-heavy tree had broken. Long, thick wood splinters shone white in the rain like the bone fragments and shards of some dreadful wound. In its crashing fall the trunk had hit the wall, scattering battlements, walkway, and sandstone blocks, the tremendous weight hewing a large V shape into Redwall's outer defenses.

As Arven came springing back down to ground, Skipper draped the squirrel's cloak about his shoulders.

"Much damage, mate?" he asked.

Arven nodded. "Much!"

Skipper indicated his sturdy crew with a wave. "Well, much or little, it don't bother us, matey, we're 'ere to lend a paw in any way y'need otters. Where d'you want us t' start?"

Arven patted the faithful creature's back. "You're a good 'un, Skip, you and your crew. This Abbey only stands by the goodness and loyalty of its friends. But there's nothin' we can do whilst the weather keeps up like this. Come on, let's get you lot inside and find you some breakfast by the fire."

Skipper's craggy face broke into a smile. "Lead us to it, me ole mate!"

Mother Buscol was official Redwall Friar, and the small fat squirrel liked nothing better in life than to cook. She watched the hungry otter crew poking their heads around her kitchen doorway and hid her pleasure by scowling at them.

"Indeed to goodness, an' what do all you great rough beasts want, hangin' around my kitchens like a flock of gannets?"

Skipper winked roguishly at her. "Feedin', marm!"

Narrowing her eyes, she shook a ladle at him. "Hot oatmeal an' mint tea's all you're gettin' out o' me this morn."

Skipper came bounding in and swept Mother Buscol off her paws, planting several hearty kisses on her chubby cheeks. "Oatmeal an' mint tea is fer Dibbuns, me beauty. Where's the good October Ale an' a pan of shrimp'n'hotroot soup, aye, an' some o' those shorty-cakes fer afters? Cummon, tell me afore I kisses you 'til sundown. Haharr!"

Her slippered paws kicked the air as she beat the otter playfully with her ladle. "Lackaday, put me down, you great wiry whiskered oaf, or I'll clap you in a boiler an' make riverdog pudden of you!"

Behind her back, Shad had purloined a batch of hot scones, and now he slid past Mother Buscol, chuckling. "Where's yore manners, mate? Put the pore creature down an' we'll wait in Cavern 'Ole 'til brekkfist's ready."

Laughing, Mother Buscol went about her business. "Indeed to goodness look you, shrimp'n'hotroot soup with the best October Ale an' my good shortybreads. Whatever next?"

Dibbuns hastily finished their meal and trundled into Cavern Hole to sport with the playful otters.

"Skipper, Skipper, it me, Sloey, I jump offa table an' you catch me!"

"Burr, 'old ee still, zurr h'otter, oi wants to ride on ee back!"

"Teehee! We tella Muvver Buscol you steal 'er scones!"

Otters rolled and wrestled happily about the floor with the babes, tickling, swinging, and playfighting. Abbess Tansy and Craklyn came to see what all the noise was about, and Tansy shook her head at Skipper and his crew, sprawled on the floor.

"Really, sir, I don't know who's the worse, you or these babes. Come on, Dibbuns, be off with you. The elders need to talk with Skipper while he has his breakfast."

Foremole Diggum scratched his head as he inspected the plans Craklyn had drawn up on a parchment. "Umm, can ee go through et all agin, marm, then may'ap oi'll unnerstan' wot ee wants a doin'!"

The Redwall Recorder outlined her scheme for the second time. "As I said, the tree falling has started demolition on the wall, so it's not all bad. But how to move the tree so we can continue with the job? Here's my idea. First we need axes and saws to lop off all the top foliage of the beech, then, if it is not already broken clean of its stump, we must sever it. Once that job is done the tree must be supported by struts, to make sure it doesn't fall any further. Then the remaining wall can be removed, the tree trunk dropped and rolled out of the way. Clear?"

Diggum continued scratching his head. "Hurr, 'tis a pity oi be such a simplebeast, oi'm still all aswoggled with ee plan, marm."

Arven stood up decisively. "Oh, you'll get the hang of it as we go along, Diggum. What's the state of the weather outdoors now?"

Gurrbowl the Cellar Keeper and Viola Bankvole went outside. They were back shortly to report. "The rain has stopped, though it's still quite windy; sky over to the south is clearing. If the wind dies down 'twill be a fine afternoon."

Skipper quaffed his beaker of October Ale. "Right y'are, marm, then let's get those axes an' saws out o' the toolstore an' sharpen 'em up. We'll start work after lunch!"

Still mystified by the plan, Foremole Diggum decided to inspect the job from a different angle. He gathered together a few of his trusty moles for the task. "Yurr, Drubb, Bunto, Wuller, an' ee Truggle, oi figger et's toime us'n's taked a lukk at ee wall proper loik!"

Skipper was greasing a double-pawed saw when he noticed the moles leaving, carrying nothing but a few coiled ropes. "Ahoy, where d'you suppose they're bound?"

Arven glanced up from the axblade he was whetting. "Leave them be, Skip. I could see Diggum wasn't too happy with Craklyn's plan, so I suppose he's going to take a look for himself. You know moles, they always look at things in a different way from otherbeasts, and quite often theirs is the most sensible way. Maybe they'll find out something we don't know."

Foremole Diggum moved slowly along the wallbase on all fours, sniffing the ground, scratching the stone, and probing the soil with his strong digging claws. About midway along the south wall he stopped and, pointing to a spot on the sandstone blocks three courses up, addressed Truggle: "Roight thurr, marm!"

The other moles nodded wisely; their Foremole had made a good choice. Truggle produced a small wooden mallet and began striking the place Diggum had indicated. Diggum placed an ear against the ground, directly below where she was hitting, and listened carefully, ignoring the wind and the wet grass. When he had heard enough, the Foremole signaled Truggle to stop and straightened up.

Drubb blinked earnestly at Diggum. "Boi 'okey, gaffer, oi can tell by ee face you'm founded summat."

Foremole Diggum took a twig and stuck it into the ground on the place where his ear had been.

"Ho oi found summat sure enuff, doant know 'ow oi missed et afore. Wot caused ee wall to sink'n'wobble? Ee answer's daown thurr, 'tis a cave or may'ap summ sort o' chamber!"

Bunto shook his Foremole by the paw. "Hurr! Oi knowed ee'd foind ee answer. Wot now, Diggum, zurr?"

Foremole Diggum's homely face wrinkled into a cheery smile. "Us'n's got some diggin' t'do!"

Five sets of digging claws met over the twig.

"Who'm dig deep'n'make best 'oles?
Only us'n's, we be moles!"

15

Lugworm had done his work well. The two rat sentries guarding Damug Warfang's shelter of brush and canvas sat upright with four empty grog flasks between them. The crafty stoat had known that the strong drink would be irresistible to beasts standing guard through the cold lonely night hours. Lugworm watched them from his hiding place until he was sure the pair were sleeping soundly. Slipping away he found Borumm and Vendace waiting at the place he had arranged to meet them.

Borumm drew his curved dagger, impatient to go about his business. ''Everythin' ready, mate, coast clear?''

Lugworm nodded fearfully, wishing he had never been drawn into the conspiracy to slay the Firstblade. ''Aye, 'tis ready, but go carefully, Damug's a light sleeper.''

Vendace drew his blade, suppressing a snigger. ''Light sleeper, eh? Well 'e won't be after tonight!''

Lugworm edged away from the would-be assassins nervously. ''There, I've done me bit, the rest's up to youse two. But remember, if yer fail an' get caught, then not a word about me!''

Borumm the weasel kicked out, sending Lugworm sprawling.

Vendace stood over him, snarling scornfully. "Garn, git outta my sight, stoat, yore in this up to yer slimy neck. The only consolation you've got is that we don't intend ter fail, or git caught. Now beat it an' keep yer gob shut!"

As Lugworm scrambled away whimpering, the fox winked at his cohort. "We'll deal wid him tomorrer, no use leavin' loose ends lyin' about. If Lugworm can betray Damug 'e'd do the same fer us someday. Come on, let's pay the Firstblade a liddle visit."

Damug perched in the branches of the ash tree near his shelter, the rat Gribble crouching by his side. Together they watched the weasel and the fox as, daggers drawn, the pair slid by the two sleeping sentries, silent as night shadows. The Greatrat waited a moment, until he heard blades grating against the sack of stones he'd wrapped in his cloak and laid by the fire. Then he nodded to Gribble.

The rat blew two sharp blasts upon a bone whistle.

Pheep! Pheep!

Ten heavily armed Rapmark officers broke cover, rushed in, and surrounded Borumm and Vendace.

It was fine and sunny next morning, a perfect spring day. Damug allowed Gribble to dress him in his splendid armor; choosing a cloak that did not have dagger slits in it, draped it loosely across one shoulder, and strolled out to the woodland's edge. The entire Rapscallion army was marshaled there, awaiting him, each beast fully armed and ready to march, their faces painted bright red. The face paint served a double purpose: it instilled fear into those they chose to attack, and marked them so they would not strike one another down in the heat of battle.

Damug took up position on a knoll where he could be seen and heard. Whipping out the sword that was his symbol of office, he shouted, "Rapscallions! Are you well rested and well fed?"

A roar of assent greeted him. "Aye, Lord, aye!"

He smiled approvingly. Now his horde looked like true Rapscallions. They bore little resemblance to the cringing vermin who had wintered on the cold shores after their defeat at Salamandastron.

Damug yelled another question at them. "And are you ready to conquer and slay with me as your Firstblade?"

Again the wild roars of agreement echoed in his ears. He waited until they died down before saying, "Bring out the prisoners!"

Over a single drumbeat the rattle of chains could be heard. Covered in wounds from the beatings they had received, three pitiful figures, chained together at neck and paw, were led forward. It was Borumm, Vendace, and Lugworm, stumbling painfully against one another as they staggered to stay upright. Spearbutts knocked them down on all fours in front of Damug, and the vast crowd of Rapscallions pressed forward to hear Damug's pronouncement.

"Let these three wretches serve as a lesson to anybeast who thinks Damug Warfang is a fool. They are cowards and traitors, but I am not going to order them slain. No! I will give them a chance to show us all that they are warriors. At the first opportunity of battle, these three will lead the charge, their only weapons being the chains they wear. Those chains will stay on them, binding them together until death releases them. They will march, eat, and sleep all their lives in chains. Let nobeast feed them or comfort them in any way. I am Firstblade of all Rapscallions. I have spoken!"

The three prisoners were made to kneel facing Damug and thank him for sparing their lives. When they had finished he swept contemptuously by them. Waving his sword at two random vermin, he rapped out, "You there, and you, come here!"

Sneezewort nudged his companion Lousewort. "Git up there, thick'ead, Lord Damug pointed at you, not me!"

Lousewort approached the knoll where Damug stood. Sneezewort breathed a sigh of relief: whatever it was, Lousewort would be on the receiving end. The other beast Damug had indicated strode up before him. It was the big nasty weasel.

The unpredictable Warlord circled them both. "Give me your names!"

"Hogspit, they calls me Hogspit, Sire."

"Er, er, I'm Lousewort, yore Lordness!"

Damug leaned on his sword and stared at them closely. 'Lousewort and Hogspit, eh! And are you both Rapscallions, ue and loyal to your Firstblade?”

Both heads bobbed dutifully. “Aye, Sire!”

Damug laughed aloud and clapped their shoulders with his ailed paw. “Good! Then I promote you both to the rank of :apscour. You two will take the places of Borumm and Ven-ace, with twoscore each to command. Take your scouts and o now, travel due north, and report back to me every two ays on what lies ahead.”

Sneezewort was livid. He followed his companion, arguing nd shouting at him, “Lord Damug never pointed at you, ’e ointed at me, I’d swear ’e did. Wot would the Firstblade want /id a fleabrain like you as a Rapscour officer?”

Lousewort drew himself up importantly. “Er, er, less o’ 1at, mate, I ain’t no fleabrain, I’m a Rapscour now. So don’t o tellin’ me no more of yer fibs. Lord Damug pointed t’me, ou said so yerself, huh, you even shoved me forward!”

Sneezewort was hopping with rage. He ran at Lousewort, hrieking, “I’ll shove yer forward an’ sideways an’ back’ards s well, y’great lump o’ lard-bottomed crabmeat!”

But Lousewort was a bit too large and solid to shove. He tood firm, shaking a cautionary paw at his friend. “Er, er, top that, you, y’can’t shove me, I’m an officer now!”

Sneezewort advanced on him, sneering ominously. “So I an’t shove yer, eh? Who’s gonna stop me, Scrawfonk?”

Lousewort grabbed hold of Sneezewort and held him firmly. ‘Ooh, you shouldn’t a called me that, that’s a bad name to all anybeast! Er, er, I know who’ll stop yer, my brother of-icer. Hoi, Hogspit, there’s a low common pawrat ’ere, callin’ n officer naughty names an’ shovin’ ’im too.”

The big nasty weasel strode aggressively up and punched ;neezewort hard in the stomach. “Lissen, popguts, don’t let ne ever catch you givin’ cheek to a Rapscour. An’ you, blath-rbonce, don’t let ’im shove yer, see!”

Grabbing them both by the ears, Hogspit banged their heads ogether resoundingly. He strode off, leaving them both rue-ully rubbing their skulls.

Lousewort looked at Sneezewort dazedly. “Er, er, let that e a lesson to yer, matey!” he muttered.

A short while after the Rapscours had left with their scouts, the great army got under way. Drums beating to the pace of their march battered out at a ground-eating rate as the day advanced into warm sunny afternoon. Northward the Rapscallion host tramped, dust rising in a cloud behind their banners and drums—only three days away from the southernmost borders of Mossflower Country.

16

A young female hare named Deodar stood on a hilltop close to the west shore. She nibbled at a fresh-plucked dandelion flower, watching a Runner approaching from the northeast. Deodar knew it was Algador Swiftback, even though he was still a mere dot in the distance. His peculiar long leaping stride marked him out from all the others at Salamandastron.

Now he would appear on a hilltop, then be lost to sight as he descended into the valley, but pop up shortly atop another dune, traveling well, with his graceful extended lope serving to eat up the miles easily. The sun was behind Deodar now, hovering over the immeasurable expanses of sea that lapped the coast right up to the shore in front of the mountain. She waved and was rewarded by the sight of Algador waving back. Deodar sat on the sandy tor, enjoying the heat of the sun on her back.

Algador took the last lap at the same pace he had been running all day. He could run almost as fast as his brother, Riffle, the Galloper of Major Perigord's patrol. Breathing lightly, he sat down next to Deodar.

"Hah! So you're my relief. What'll this be now, miss, your third run o' the season?"

Deodar stood, flexing her limbs. "Fifth, actually. Where did you cover, Algy?"

Algador made a sweep with his paw. "Northeast from there to there. No sign of Perigord returning yet, and no signs of Rapscallions or other vermin."

Deodar closed one eye, squinting along the pawtracks her friend had just made. "Righto, Algy, I'll follow you out along your trail then cut west and come back, coverin' the jolly old shoreline."

Algador rose and turned to face Salamandastron farther down the coastline. Between patches of green vegetation growing on its rocky slopes, the mountain took on a light buff tinge. An extinct volcano crater jutted in a flat-topped pinnacle over the landscape. He nodded in its direction. "How's Rose Eyes, showed herself lately?"

His companion shook her head. " 'Fraid not, you'll have to shout your report through the forge door. Lady Cregga sees nobeast while she's forgin' her new weapon. D'you recall the day she broke her old spear, wot!"

Algador could not resist a chuckle. "Hahaha! Will I ever forget it, missie! Standin' neck high in the sea an' sinkin' two Rapscallion ships, was that ever a flippin' sight. I thought she'd have burst with rage when the spearhaft snapped an' she lost her blade in the water!"

Deodar took off into a loping run, calling back, "Can't stop jawin' with the likes o' you all day, must get goin'!"

Algador waved to her. "Run easy, gel, watch out for those shore toads on the way back, don't take any nonsense off the blighters. Take care!"

The sun's last rays were turning the sea into a sheet of fiery copper as Algador entered the mountain. Without breaking stride he took hallway, stairs, and corridors as though they were hill and flatland, traveling upward from one level to another. Sometimes he swerved around other hares and called out a greeting, other times he caught a glimpse of the setting sun through narrow slitted-rock windows. Arriving at a great oak double door, he halted, waiting until his breathing was ormal and mentally going over his report speech. Standing tiffly to attention, he reached out a paw and rapped smartly pon the door. There was no answer, though he could hear oises from inside the forge room. Algador waited a moment, nocked once more, and gave a loud cough to emphasize his resence.

A massively gruff voice boomed out, echoing 'round the orge room and the antechamber outside where the hare stood, 'I'm not to be disturbed. What d'you want?"

Algador swallowed nervously before shouting back, "Ninth pring Runner reportin', marm, relieved nor'west o' here this fternoon!"

There was silence followed by a grunt. "Come in!"

Algador entered the forge room and shut the door carefully ehind him. It was only the second time he had been in there. long unshuttered window, with its sill made into a seat, ltered the last rosy shafts of daylight onto the floor. Massive, ough-hewn rock walls were arrayed with weapons hung verywhere: great bows, quivers of arrows, lances, spears, avelins, daggers, cutlasses, and swords. A blackened stone orge stood in the room's center, its bellows lying idle, the hite and yellowy red charcoal fire embers smoking up rough a wide copper flue.

The hare's eyes were riveted on a heroic figure standing ammer in paw over a chunk of metal glowing on the anvil. ady Cregga Rose Eyes, legendary Badger Ruler of Salamanastron.

Her size was impressive: even the big forge hammer in her aw seemed tiny, like a toy. Over a rough homespun tunic she ore a heavy, scarred, metal-studded apron. The glow from e red-hot metal caught her rose-colored eyes, tingeing them carlet as she glared down at Algador. His long back legs uivered visibly, and he felt like an acorn at the foot of a giant ak tree.

The Badger Lady nodded wordlessly, and Algador found imself babbling out his report in a rush.

"Patrolled north by east beyond the dunes for two days, arm, spent one night by the river, saw no signs of anybeast. o track or word of Major Perigord so far, no sign of Rapscallions or vermin. Sighted a few traces of shrews yesterday morn, marm.''

Lady Cregga rested the hammerhead on the anvil horn. ''You didn't contact the Guosim shrews or speak to them?''

''No, marm, 'fraid I didn't. Traces were at least three days old, campfire ashes an' vegetable peelin's, that was all, marm.''

Cregga took tongs and replaced the lump of metal she was working back in the forge. Then she gave the bellows a gentle push, flaring the charcoal and seacoal into flame.

''Hmm, pity you missed the shrews. Their leader, the Log-a-Log, might have had some information for us. Never mind, well done. Ask Colonel Eyebright to come up here, will you?''

''Yes, marm!'' The young hare stood motionless to attention.

Lady Cregga watched him for a moment, then unusually she gave a fleeting smile. ''If you stand there any longer you'll take root. Go now—you're dismissed.''

Algador saluted and wheeled off so quickly he almost tripped over his own footpaws. Lady Cregga heard the door shut as she turned back to her work at the forge.

Cutting straight through the main dining hall, Algador made for the Officers' Mess. He accosted another young hare coming out, carrying tray and beakers. ''Evenin', Furgale! I say, is Colonel Eyebright in there? Got a rather important message for him.''

Furgale was a jolly type, obliging too. Placing the tray on a window ledge, he waggled an ear at the Runner. ''Say no more, old pip, I'll let him know you're here.''

Flinging the door open wide, Furgale danced comically to attention. Closing both eyes tightly, he bellowed into the small room, ''Ninth Spring Runnah t'see you, Colonel Eyebright. Sah!''

Eyebright was every inch the military hare, of average size, silver gray with long seasons, a smart, spare figure in plain regulation green tunic. Looking up from the scrolls he was studying, Eyebright twitched his bristling mustache at the messenger. ''I'm not deaf y'know, young feller. Send the chap in!''

Algador marched smartly into the Officers' Mess. ''Lady

Cregga sends her compliments an' wishes you to attend her in the forge room, Colonel, sah!''

The Colonel's eyebrows rose momentarily, then, fastening his top tunic button, he rose and put aside the scrolls. ''Very good, I'm on m'way!''

He eyed the Runner up and down, a kindly smile creasing his weathered features. ''Ninth Spring Runner, eh? Obviously enjoyin' the job, young Algy!''

Algador stood at ease, returning his Commanding Officer's smile. ''Very much, thank ye, sah.''

Eyebright's silver-tipped pace stick tapped Algador's shoulder approvingly. ''Good show, keep it up, won't be long before we have y'out gallopin' for a Long Patrol like that brother o' yours.''

Algador swelled with pride as the dapper Colonel marched spryly off.

Cregga nodded her huge striped muzzle to the window seat as she poured pennycloud and dandelion cordial for herself and the Colonel. They sat together, he sipping his drink as he watched the parched badger take a long draught of hers. ''Thirsty work at the ol' forge, eh, marm?'' he said.

The rose-hued eyes flickered in the forge light. ''That's not what I called you up here to talk about, Colonel. I had the Ninth Runner report to me this evening, and the news is still the same—all bad. No sign of Perigord's patrol, no word of Rapscallions, everything's too quiet. My voices tell me that big trouble is brewing somewhere.''

Eyebright chose his words carefully. ''But we've no proof, marm, mayhap things being quiet is all for the best. No news bein' good news, if y'know what I mean.''

The Colonel tried not to jump with fright as Lady Cregga suddenly roared and flung her beaker out of the window. ''Gormad Tunn and those two spawn of his are out there getting ready to plunge the land into war. I'm certain of it!''

The old hare kept his voice calm. ''Tunn and his army could be anywhere, far north, south coast, wherever. We can only do our best by protecting the west land and the seas in front of us. We can't just go marchin' out an' fightin' all over the place.''

Lady Cregga strode to the forge and, seizing a pair of tongs, she rummaged in the fire, pulling out the lump of metal she was working on. Laying it on the anvil she took up her hammer. "Colonel, how many hares would it take to guard Salamandastron and the shores roundabout?"

The Colonel's eyebrows shot up quizzically. "Marm?"

Clang!

Sparks flew as Cregga's hammer smashed down on the glowing metal. "Don't 'marm' me! Answer the question, sir—how many fighting hares could do the job, and are you able to command them?"

Eyebright stood up abruptly. "Half the force would be sufficient to protect this area. As to your second question, marm, of course I am able to command. Are you questioning my ability or merely insulting my competence?"

The Badger Lady let the hammer drop. Leaving the anvil, she came to stand in front of the old hare, towering above him. "My friend, forgive me, you are my strong right paw on this mountain. I did not mean to question your skills as a Commander. I spoke in haste, please accept my sincere apology."

The pace stick rose, pointing directly at Cregga. Eyebright's tone was that of a reproving father to an errant daughter. "I have served you well, Cregga Rose Eyes. Anybeast, no matter what their reputation or size, would be down on the shore now to give satisfaction, had they called my honor into question as you did. I forgive you those words, though I will not forget them. Marm, your trouble is that you are eaten up with hatred of Gormad Tunn, his brood, and their followers. You feel bound to destroy them. Am I not right, wot?"

Cregga hooded her eyes, gazing out of the window at the night seas. "You speak the truth. When I think of the gallant hares we lost on the beach and in the shallows of the tide on those three days and nights—and what for? Because Gormad thought his Rapscallion forces great enough to conquer Salamandastron. Aye, he tried to make cruel sport of us, the same way he has done to other more helpless creatures all his miserable life. It will not go on! Soon I will have made myself a new battlepike. If there is no news by then I intend to take half our warriors and go forth to seek out and destroy the evil that goes by the name Rapscallion. One day they will be nought but a bad memory in the minds of good and honest creatures. You have my oath on it!''

Colonel Eyebright left the forge room in resigned silence. Nobeast could swerve the Lady Rose Eyes from her purpose once her mind was made up.

Down in the dining hall, Algador was taking supper with his friends, all young hares the same age as himself. Furgale tore into a large salad, speaking with his mouth full, as there were no officers present.

''I say, chaps, when d'you suppose the lists'll be posted for new recruits to the jolly ol' Long Patrol?''

Cheeva, a young female, flicked an oatcake crumb at him. ''First mornin' o' summer, my pater says. Hope my name's on it. I'll bet Algy's top o' the bloomin' list, wot?''

Algador sliced into a hefty carrot and celery flan. ''Do you? I'll pester the life out of Major Perigord until he takes me as Galloper with Riffle. I think I'm old enough to beat the ears off him in a flat run now!''

Suddenly the room echoed with banging clanging noises, the din reverberating off the walls. Cheeva clapped paws to her ears, crying, ''Great seasons o' salad, who's makin' all the clatter?''

Algador had to shout to make himself heard. He called to Colonel Eyebright, who was passing through on his way to the mess, ''I say, sah, who's creatin' that infernal racket?''

The Colonel stopped by their table, gesturing to them to stay seated. ''Some badger or other at her forge, why don't y'go up there an' tell her to stop?'' He nodded at the smiling young faces turned toward him. ''I've a feelin' that you lot are goin' to find yourselves Long Patrollin' sooner than you think!''

At this announcement the young hares cheered wildly, eyes aglow, fired with hope and desire. Heedless of what lay ahead.

17

"Barradum! Barradum! Barrabubbitybubbityboom!"

Russa peered bad-temperedly from under the edge of a cloak that served her as a blanket. "Hoi, drumface, pack it in, willyer!"

Rubbadub marched over, his fat face wreathed in morning smiles. Placing a plate of hot food in front of the half-awake squirrel, he brought his cheerful features right up to her nose. "Boom! Boom!"

Tammo and the rest of the column laughed, spooning down an early breakfast of barley meal mixed with honey and hazelnuts.

Sergeant Torgoch did a very good imitation of a motherly female. "Come on, sleepyhead, rise an' shine, the mornin's fine, the lark's in the air an' all is fair, the day's begun, look there's the sun!"

Midge Manycoats skipped about like a Dibbun. "Oh, mummy, may I go out an' play? I'll pick some daisies for you!"

Torgoch's voice dropped back to that of a gruff Patrol Sergeant. "Siddown an' finish yer brekkfist, you useless liddle omadorm, or I'll 'ave yore paws pickled for a season's 'ard marchin'!"

Wiping his lips on a spotless white kerchief, Perigord buckled on his saber, and flexed his footpaws. "Listen up, troop, we're marchin' due south. Exercise extreme caution out on the flatlands, an' keep y'r eyes peeled for vermin. When the blighters have recovered their nerve I wouldn't be surprised if they chance another crack at us, wot!"

Equipment was packed away into haversacks, and weapons brought to the ready as the Sergeant harangued them. "Right, you 'eard the h'officer, form up an' stir yer stumps now!"

Grasshoppers rustled and bees hummed about early flowering saxifrage and heathers, and the sun shone boldly from a sky of cloudless blue. It was a glorious spring morning on the open moorland. Tammo strode along between Russa and Pasque; the squirrel had her stick, and both hares carried loaded slings. Up in front, Perigord conversed easily with Rifle, though his eyes roved restlessly over the landscape. "Pretty clear tracks, eh, wot? Seems they ain't bothered about coverin' their trail, I'd say."

"Aye, sir, mebbe they'll try somethin' when we reach that rocky-lookin' hill up ahead."

The Major kept his eyes front as he answered, "Hmm, or that little outcrop to the left—*Down troop!*"

An arrow zipped by them like an angry hornet as they threw themselves to the ground. Lieutenant Morio bounced up immediately. "Just one of 'em, sah. There he goes!"

The sniper, a rat with bow and quiver, had broken cover and was racing toward the rock-rifted hill. Perigord sat up, his jaw tight with anger as he saw a rip the shaft had torn on the shoulder of his stylish green velvet tunic.

"Just look at that, the blinkin' cad! Drop the blighter, Rock."

Rockjaw Grang set shaft to a longbow that resembled a young tree. He squinted along the arrow, stretching the flexible yew bow into a wide arc, tracking his quarry.

The rat halted, relieved he was not being chased. He unslung his bow and began coolly choosing an arrow. Rockjaw's shaft took him out like a thunderbolt.

The giant hare shook his head at the fallen rat's foolishness.

"Yon vermin should've kept a runnin'. 'Ey up, there's more!"

Four more broke cover to the right from behind a low rise; shooting off a few slingstones at the hares, they began dashing for the hilltop. Regardless of what orders they had been given, the vermin did not want to be caught out alone by the hares.

Perigord turned to Twayblade and Riffle. "Cut 'em off, try an' take one alive! Rockjaw, you an' Midge cover the hill. The rest of you—about face!"

Tammo shot Russa a puzzled glance. "About face?"

Sergeant Torgoch grabbed Tammo and spun him around roughly. "Don't question orders, young 'un, do like the h'officer sez!"

A band of vermin poured out of the woodland toward them. Tammo and Pasque whirled their slings as Perigord called out, "On my command, two slings, arrows, or one javelin, then go at 'em with a will. Steady now, let the blighters get closer . . ."

Tammo felt his teeth begin to chatter. He ground them together tightly and caused his head to start shaking. The vermin faces were plainly visible now, painted red with some kind of mineral dye. Yelling, roaring, and brandishing fearsome weapons, they rushed forward, paws pounding the earth. Perigord leveled his saber at them, remarking almost casually, "Let 'em have it, chaps!"

Tammo's first slingshot missed altogether; in his excitement he whipped the sling too high. His second shot took a weasel slap on the paw, causing him to drop his spear with a yelp. Then Tammo found himself charging with the Long Patrol, the war cry of the perilous hares ripping from his throat along with his comrades. Even Russa was shouting.

"Eulaliaaaaa! 'S death on the wind! Eulaliaaaaaa!"

They met with a clash, Perigord slaying the leading pair before they could blink an eye. Tammo thrust out at a stoat and missed; the stoat feinted with his cutlass, and as Tammo backed off his foe skipped forward and tripped him. The young hare fell. He saw the stoat launch himself in a flying leap, cutlass first. Levering himself swiftly aside, Tammo kept his paw outstretched with the dirk pointed upward. The stoat landed heavily on the blade.

Pulling his blade free, Tammo scrambled up, only to find

e vermin fleeing with Long Patrol hares hard on their heels.
Major Perigord and Rubbadub came marching up, the forer cleaning his saber on a pawful of dried grass. "Well done, oung 'un, got y'self one, I see!"
Tammo could not look at the vermin he had slain, and his ead began shaking again as he tried to face the Major.
Shrugging off his tunic, Perigord inspected the torn shouler. "I know how y'feel, Tamm, but he'd have got you if you dn't got him. Here, see."
He retrieved the stoat's cutlass and pointed to the notches rved into the wooden handle. "Count 'em, tell me how any you make it."
Tammo took the weapon and counted the notches. "Eighen, sir!"
Perigord took the blade and flung it away with a grimace f distaste. "Aye, eighteen, though they weren't all fightin' easts like you an' me, laddie buck. Those smaller notches ou saw were for the very old or the very young, creatures o weak to defend themselves. Don't waste your sympathy n scum like that one. Come on now, stop shakin' like tadpole lly an' give us a good ol' De Fformelo Tussock smile. Rubadub, beat 'em over to that hill yonder, we'll form up there."
Rubbadub's pearly teeth flashed in a huge grin as he arched off drumming the Long Patrol to him.
"Drrrubadubdub drrrubadubdub dubbity dubbity dub. Baoom!"
Perigord and Tammo stared at each other for a moment, en burst into laughter.
The patrol squatted on the hilltop, Pasque Valerian tending one or two minor injuries that had been received. Twayade swished the air regretfully with her long rapier. "Sorry e didn't take any prisoners, Major, but those vermin weren't kin' any prisoners either, the way they were fightin', so e'n'Riffle had to give as good as we jolly well got."
Perigord watched from the hilltop as the remaining vermin rew small in the afternoon distance. "No matter, old gel, we an still track 'em. As long as we cut 'em off before they each Redwall Abbey. What d'you make o' those villains, ussa, pretty sharp thinkers, wot?"
The squirrel munched on an apple, nodding. "Aye, 'twas a

clever move they made. Clear tracks to this hill, then the must've split up a couple of hours afore dawn an' circled bac Leavin' a few to the left'n'right to distract us, the rest of th crafty scum went back to the woodland so they could ambus us from be'ind. Knowin' we'd be expectin' them to be waiti for us, hidin' about here on this hilltop."

Rockjaw Grang was watching the retreating vermin an counting their numbers. "Sithee, there's still enough o' yo beasts to make a scrap. They must've numbered fifty or mo when we first met 'em, sir. By my count they still got'n thirt two."

"Hardly enough for eleven bold chaps'n'chappesses lik us," Riffle snorted scornfully. "Thirteen if y'count Tamm ar Russa. I say, thirteen, is that unlucky?"

Lieutenant Morio stood up, dusting off his paws. "Ay unlucky for them when we catch up with 'em. Everybeast f now, Pasque?"

The beautiful young hare was closing up her medicin pouch. "Yes, Midge took a slight cheek wound and Tur nearly lost the tip of an ear. I've seen to them both. No there's only the Major's jacket, but I can do that this evening."

The twins, Tare and Turry, ragged Tammo unmercifully.

"Heehee! Lookit the long face on ole Tamm!"

"Bet he wishes he'd been wounded, just so's Pasque coul bandage him up an' bathe his brow a bit!"

"If I were him I'd chop me nose off, that'd get her atten tion!"

"Aye, she'd say, 'Goodness nose, what've they done t your handsome hooter?' Hahahaha!"

Pasque joined in the fun. Grabbing Turry she began rebar daging his ear fiercely. "Hello, what's this ear? Goodnes knows, your bandage has come loose. Here, let me tie it a b more snugly!"

Turry squeaked as he tried to get away. "Ow ow! You'v cut off all the blood to me ear! Stoppit!"

Sergeant Torgoch loomed over the playful young one "Now then, young sirs an' miss, I'll cut off all yore ears an cook 'em for me supper if yore not all formed up an' read t'march two ticks from now. Up on yore paws, you idle lo

Where d'you think y'are—on an 'oliday for 'ares? Move y'selves!''

Pasque marched at the rear with Tammo. She smiled and waved to the Sergeant. To Tammo's surprise, he smiled and winked at her.

Tammo scratched his ear, completely puzzled. ''Is he always like that, shoutin' one moment an' smiling the next?''

''Sergeants are all the same,'' the young hare chuckled. ''Bark's worse than their bite. Torgoch is my favorite Sergeant, he's always there to look out for you if you get in any trouble.''

18

The remainder of the day went smoothly enough, with the patrol following the vermin track steadily. Late afternoon brought them to the banks of quite a sizeable river. Major Perigord halted them within sight of it.

They crouched in a patch of fern, viewing the scene ahead. Through a screen of weeping willow, elder, sycamore, and holm oak, the river made a welcoming sight, with patches of sun-burnished water showing amid cool islands of tree shade. Tammo was wondering why they had halted and concealed themselves, when he heard Perigord and Twayblade discussing their next move.

"Looks very temptin' indeed, eh, gel?"

"Exactly, good spot for an ambush, I'd say."

Tammo remembered the last time he had rushed forward to water. The hares were right, this time he would be on his guard.

The Major issued orders in a whisper. "Sergeant Torgoch, take young Pasque an' scout the terrain downstream. Cap'n Twayblade, do likewise upstream, take one with you."

"Permission t'go with you, Cap'n. *Please*, marm, I'd like a chance t'be a real part of the patrol!"

Twayblade could not help smiling at the eager Tammo. "Stripe me, but you're a bright'n'brisk 'un. Still, one volunteer's worth ten pressed creatures. C'mon then, young Tamm."

Leaving the edge of the fern cover, Twayblade drew her deadly long rapier and stooped low. "Follow me, Tamm, duck an' weave, take advantage of any cover, keep your eyes open an' do as I do. That is until I give you an order, then it's do as I say!"

Tammo enjoyed learning from an expert. He kept low, rolling behind mounds, bellying out to crawl over open spaces swiftly, then stopping dead and remaining motionless, disguised among bushes. Never traversing in a straight line, they headed east, keeping with the outer edge of the tree fringe until Twayblade decided they had gone far enough. She flattened herself against a gnarled dwarf apple tree, and for a moment Tammo lost sight of the Captain. She blended in with the tree bark until she was almost invisible to the casual observer, and only by staring hard could the young hare make her out.

"Great seasons, Cap'n," he chuckled admiringly, "you nearly vanished altogether then! Mayhaps you'll teach me that trick, marm?"

Twayblade shook her head vigorously. "Not me. Little Midge Manycoats is the chap, he'll teach you all about disguise an' concealment, he's the best there is. Righto, let's make our way to the riverbank an' follow it back down t'where we left the patrol. Everythin' seems to be safe enough hereabouts, but let's not get careless, Tamm. Keep that splendid blade o' yours at the ready, wot!"

They took a drink at the river's edge; the water was cold and sweet. Splashing through the shallows, they cooled their footpaws as they went. Tammo noticed a good patch of watercress, fronds streaming out around a limestone rock beneath the water. He did not stop to gather it, but noted the spot and carried on in Twayblade's wake. The rest of the journey back was pleasant and uneventful, and they arrived at the ferns as noontide shadows lengthened.

The Captain made her report: "Well, well, I see you lot've had a nice little nap whilst we were gone, wot! Nothin' to report, the coast's clear up that way."

Torgoch and Pasque returned; the Sergeant threw a brisk salute. "River narrows downstream, sah, lots o' rocks stickin' up. That's where the vermin made their crossin', still wet pawprints on the stones. We'd catch 'em up by midnight if the patrol got under way smartlike, sah."

Perigord judged the sun's angle. "I think we'll make camp here, Sergeant. No sense in chasin' our tails off, wot. Early start tomorrow, good fast march, an' I've little doubt we'll encounter 'em about high noon. Camp down, troop."

Insects skimmed and flitted on the river surface in quiet twilight, and the campfire flickered warmly. Tammo and Russa opened their haversack. The squirrel dug out the last of her pancakes and distributed them, saying, "Warm these over by the fire, toast 'em up a mite, they're good!"

Rockjaw spitted his on a willow twig and held it over the flames. "How's the soup a comin' along, Rubbadub?"

Corporal Rubbadub pulled a wry face as he took a sip from his ladle. "Brrrrumbum dubadub!"

Lieutenant Morio raised an eyebrow. "As bad as that, eh? Nothin' hereabouts we can add to it?"

Tammo rose and winked at them. "Wait there. I spotted some fresh watercress earlier on. Won't be a tick!"

It was slightly eerie being alone in the gathering gloom as Tammo made his way back upriver. Once or twice he thought he heard noises, and each time he drew his blade and halted, listening, but the only sounds he could make out were those of the flowing water. The young hare gripped his weapon tightly, chiding himself aloud, "Not very good form, sah, behavin' like a ditherin' duckwife!"

Squaring his shoulders, he loped onward until the limestone rock showed pale and ghostly through the gloom. Wading out to it he gathered pawfuls of the fresh watercress, lopping it off below the waterline with his dirk. Carrying the delicious treat back to the bank, Tammo stuck his blade in a sycamore trunk and began tying the cress in a bundle, using his shoulder strap to secure it.

Four dark shapes dropped out of the branches overhead, making Tammo their target. Footpaws whamming onto his back, shoulders, and head drove Tammo flat, stunning him. Before he had a chance to recover and fight back, a cruel noose slid over his head, pulling tight about his neck. Cords were whipped skillfully around his paws. Tammo was unable to cry out; groggily he tried to head-butt one of the wraithlike figures, but a heavy stick struck him in the midriff. Doubled up and fighting to suck air through his wide-open mouth, Tammo was shoved roughly into a cradle made from woven vines. In a trice he was hoisted up into the tree foliage, high among the leafy branches. A dirty gag was bound around his mouth, and the noose loosened.

Savage green-black faces came close to his, lots of them—they seemed to be everywhere.

"Mayka move! Goo on, beast, mayka move! Choohakk! Cutcha t'roat an' eatcha iffya mayka move!"

A paw stroked Tammo's long ears, and a deep grating voice chuckled, "Choohoohoo! Dis a nicey wan, dis wan ours!"

19

On the afternoon that the weather cleared and brightened up there was great activity in Redwall Abbey. Armed with axes, saws, and pruning knives, the creatures set about the task of dismantling the beech tree that had collapsed upon the already unstable south wall. Arven and Shad the Gatekeeper took a long, double-pawed saw, and between them they tackled the heaviest limb they could reach.

Viola Bankvole stood by as Infirmary Sister, with an array of unguents, salves, bandages, and medicines, in case of injuries. Mother Abbess Tansy had given her permission for any willing Redwallers, young or old, to join in. She remarked to her friend Craklyn as they watched the beech being decimated. "Far better to let everybeast take part, don't you think? It makes a heavy chore into more of a social activity."

The squirrel Recorder had her doubts. "We need more organization, Tansy. Look at Sloey and Gubbio—they're sitting perched up on that branch with hammers, knocking away at twigs, the little turnipheads!"

Tansy smiled fondly up at the two Dibbuns. "Oh, leave them, they can't get into much mischief doing that."

Craklyn pointed lower down the same branch. "But see, Brother Sedum and Sister Egram are trying to saw through the bottom of the same branch. Look out—there it goes!"

The branch snapped with a sharp crack, Sedum and Egram fell backward with a joint yell, and the two Dibbuns squeaked in dismay as they plummeted earthward.

"Haharr gotcha!"

Lithe and brawny, Skipper of Otters dropped his ax and leapt beneath the branch to catch Sloey and Gubbio in his strong paws. Giggling helplessly, the three of them fell into the mass of leafy foliage, the Dibbuns crowing aloud with excitement, "Again! Do it again! More, more!"

Skipper sat up rubbing his head. "Ouch! You liddle coves—watch where yore a wavin' those 'ammers!"

Viola was over like a shot. "I knew it, some creature was bound to get hurt! Come away from there, you naughty babes! And you, call yourself a Skipper of Otters, have you no sense at all? Stop scrabbling about in those leaves with the Dibbuns this instant!"

She swept Sloey up in her paws, and the mousebabe, who was still waving her hammer, which was no more than a small nut mallet, bopped the good Sister an unlucky one between the ears. Viola turned her eyes upward, gave a faint whoop, and sat down hard.

Skipper shook with laughter as he gave orders to some other Dibbuns who had just arrived on the scene. "Ahoy, mates, git bandages an' ointment, fix pore Sister Viola up, she's sore wounded!"

Full of mischief, the Abbeybabes needed no second bidding.

Viola floundered about helplessly on the grass as they poured ointment on her head and dashed 'round and 'round her until she was swathed in bandages. Tansy and Craklyn had to turn away, they were chuckling so hard. Then Tansy caught sight of the cook.

"Mother Buscol, perhaps you and Gurrbowl would like to set up the evening meal out here? There's lots of deadwood from the tree for a fire. Couldn't we have a chestnut roast and baked parsnips? Craklyn and I will help—I know, we'll make honey and maple apples. Is there any strawberry fizz in the cellars? That would be lovely for our workers!"

Grumbling aloud, the fat old squirrel trundled off to the kitchens for her ingredients. "Lackaday, an' what's wrong with a kitchen oven, may I arsk? Indeed to goodness, look you, a full picnic meal for who knows 'ow many creatures an' everywhere 'tis nought but bushes an' bangin'. Come on Gurrbowl, we'll 'ave to see what can be done!"

Goodwife Gurrbowl the Cellar Keeper shook her head severely at Sister Viola as she passed. "Moi dearie me, b'ain't you'm gotten no sense, Viola, a playin' wi' ee Dibbuns an' gittin' eeself all messed oop loik that!"

Skipper and his crew, with Arven and the more able-bodied Redwallers, set to with a will, chopping, sawing, and hauling heavy branches. The work went well. They struck up a song as they toiled:

"Oh, seed is in the ground an' up comes a shoot,
Seed is in the soil an' down goes a root,
Here comes a leaf an' there goes a twig,
Seasons turn as the tree grows big!

Saplin' bends with the breeze at dawn,
Wearin' a coat of bark t'keep warm,
Growin' lots o' green leaves 'stead o' fur,
Birds go a nestin' in its hair.

Some gets flow'rs as they spread root,
Some gets berries, some gets fruit,
Trees grow t'gether in a glade,
All through summer that's nice shade.

Lots o' trees do make a wood,
Just the way that good trees should,
Ole dead trees when they expire
Keep my paws warm by the fire!"

They had scarcely finished the song when a voice rapped sternly from the deepest section of the foliage, "That's still no reason to cut down a tree, is it?"

Skipper looked at Arven strangely. "Did you say somethin', mate?"

"No, I thought it was you for a moment, Skip."

The voice sounded out again, quite irritable this time. "Honestly, where there's no feeling there's no sense. I'm trapped in here, you great pair of buffoons. In here!"

Skipper thrust himself into the foliage. "Sounds like an owlbird t'me!"

A deep sigh escaped from the leafy depths. " 'Owlbird?' Did I call you an otterdog? No! Then pray have the goodness to at least get the name of my species right. Owl, say it!"

Skipper shrugged his brawny shoulders. "Owl!"

"Thank you!" the voice continued. "Now are you going to stand about jawing all day or do you think you and your friends can muster up the decency to get me out of here?"

Right at the heart of the foliage was a thick dead limb with a deep weather-spread crack in it, and wedged there was a female of the type known as Little Owls. She had wide gray eyebrows and huge yellow eyes, which were fixed in a permanent frown.

Arven climbed over a limb and nodded amiably at her. "Good day to ye, marm. You'll excuse my sayin', but we never cut down your tree, the storm knocked it down."

The owl moved her head from side to side huffily. "So you say. All I know is that I'm not three days in this nest, hardly settled down, Taunoc gone hunting for beetles, when the whole world collapses in on me. Knocked unconscious, completely out! I've only just regained my senses, due to your infernal banging and knocking, of course!"

Skipper put down his ax guiltily. "An' are ye all right, marm?"

The owl was a very small one, but she puffed herself up until she filled the entire crack, glaring at the otter. "All right? Do I look all right? Clutching on here, half upside down, doing my level best to stop three eggs spilling out and breaking all over the ground. Oh, yes, apart from that and being knocked out, I suppose I'm all right!"

Tansy and Craklyn pushed into the foliage, all concern for the owl's predicament.

"Oh, you poor bird! Three eggs and your home's destroyed!"

"Viola, come quick! Arven, Skipper, hold this branch

steady. Stay still, my dear, we'll have you and your eggs out of there safely in no time at all!''

The Redwallers flocked in to help; carefully they extricated the Little Owl from the crack. The nest, with its three eggs intact, was lifted out as gently as possible. Then, chopping away twigs and foliage, they led the bird out into the open.

Tansy found out that the owl's name was Orocca. They brought her to the fire, placing the nest on a pile of blankets. Orocca was small but looked formidably strong and fierce. She ruffled her feathers and sat on her nest, staring aggressively at everybeast, the pupils of her immense golden eyes dilating and contracting in the firelight.

Mother Buscol gave her warm candied chestnuts, hazelnuts crystallized in honey, and some strawberry fizz. ''Indeed to goodness, bird, you need sweet food to get over your shock. Eat up now, look you, there's plenty more.''

As Orocca ate voraciously, Viola approached her with herbs and medicines. The owl shot her a glare that sent her scuttling. Timidly she stood behind Skipper and called to Orocca, ''When will your egg babies be born?''

The answer was terse and irate. ''When they're ready, and not a moment before, silly!''

Foremole Diggum and his team arrived at the fire. Diggum clacked his digging claws together in delight. ''Hoo arr, lookee, Drubb, 'unny apples an' chesknutters by ee foire! Gurr, us'n's be fair famishered. 'Scuse oi, marm, 'opes you'm doant objeck to molers settin' 'longside ee?''

To everybeast's surprise, Orocca actually smiled at Diggum. ''Please be seated, sir, I enjoy the company of moles immensely. I find them wise and sensible creatures, not given to ceaseless chatter and inane questions.''

Foremole and his crew sat, heaping their platters with food.

Arven scratched his head in bewilderment. ''Orocca doesn't seem too fond of us, yet she took to you straight away. What's your secret, Diggum?''

Foremole's homely face crinkled into a knowing grin. ''Hurr, oi 'spect 'tis our 'andsome lukks, zurr!''

Striving to keep a straight face, Arven sat next to Diggum. ''Oh, I see. But pray tell me, sir, apart from admiring yourself in a mirror, what else have you been up to this afternoon?''

The mole poured himself a beaker of strawberry fizz. "Us'n's been a diggen, oi'll tell ee wot oi found, zurr!"

Later on Arven sought out Tansy, who was in the dormitory with Mother Buscol, bedding down Dibbuns for the night. Peeping 'round the door, Arven watched in silence, recalling fondly his own Dibbun times. The Abbeybabes lay in their small beds, repeating after Abbess Tansy an ancient poem. Arven had learned it from Auma, an old badgermother, long ago.

He listened, mentally saying the lines along with the little ones.

"Night comes soft, 'tis daylight's end,
Sleep creeping gently o'er all,
Bees go to hive, birds fly to nest,
Whilst pale moon shadows fall.

Silent earth lies cloaked in slumber,
Stars standing guard in the skies,
'Til dawn steals up to banish darkness,
I must close my weary eyes.

Safe dreams, peace unto you, my friend,
Night comes soft, 'tis daylight's end."

Mother Buscol stayed with the yawning Dibbuns while Tansy drifted quietly outside to see what her friend wanted. Together they descended the stairs and strolled out into the beautiful spring night, and Arven related what Diggum Foremole had told him.

"Diggum and his team located the exact spot where the trouble with the south wall began. Today while we were dealing with the tree, he and his moles began excavating. I've arranged with him to show us what he found."

Holding lighted lanterns, Diggum and his stout crew awaited them at the edge of a sloping shaft they had dug into the ground near the wallbase.

Tugging his snout courteously to Tansy, the mole Chieftain greeted her. "Gudd eventoid to ee, marm, thurr be summat yurr oi wanten ee t'cast thy eye ower. Oi'll go afront of ee an' moi moles'll foller, keepen furm 'old o' yon rope.''

Sensibly the moles had pegged ropes either side of the shaf walls, forming a strong banister. Gingerly, everyone followed Diggum into the shaft. The earth was moist and slippery underpaw.

Following Diggum's advice, Tansy held tightly to the ropes By lantern light she saw that the shaft leveled out into a smal tunnel, where she was forced to crouch, her gown sweeping its sides.

''Burr, oi'm sorry you'm 'abit be gettin' amuckied oop,' Foremole murmured apologetically. '' 'Tis only a place fit fur molefolk, marm.''

The Abbess patted the broad back in front of her. ''Oh, 'tis nothing a washday won't solve, friend. Lead on, I'm dying o curiosity to see what you've discovered.''

When she did see it, Tansy was almost lost for words. She stood awestruck at what the flickering lantern light revealed.

''Great seasons o' sun an' showers, *what is it?*''

BOOK TWO

A Gathering of Warriors

20

Between them both, Hogspit and Lousewort knew virtually nothing about scouting ahead for the Rapscallion army. Their promotion to the rank of Rapscour was greeted with scorn by the twoscore vermin trackers each had under his command. All day they had trudged steadily north, with the eighty vermin ignoring their commands pointedly. They went their own way, foraging and fooling about, pleasing themselves entirely.

Lousewort was completely bullied and cowed by Hogspit; the big nasty weasel took every available chance to beat or belittle his fellow officer. Lousewort bumbled along in Hogspit's wake like some type of menial lackey.

It was about early noon when they breasted a long rolling hill with a broad stream flowing through the fields below it. Hogspit immediately gave his verdict on the area.

"It'll do fer a camp tonight, I s'pose, good runnin' water an' plenty o' space. Wot more could Damug ask fer 'is army?"

Lousewort gave his opinion, for what it was worth. "Er, er, not much shelter, though. Wot iffen it rains?"

Hogspit fetched him a clip 'round the ear. "Iffen it rains

then they'll just 'ave ter get wet, blobberbrain. That's unless you've got ideas of buildin' lots o' nice liddle wooden 'uts t'keep 'em dry."

Lousewort thought about this for a moment. "Er, er, but there ain't no wood around, mate, an' even if there was it'd take too lon—Yowch!" He jumped as the weasel booted him hard on the behind.

"If brains wuz bread you'd a starved to death afore you was born!"

The conversation was ended when a weasel came panting up the hillside and pointed down to where the stream curved 'round the far side of the tor. Throwing a smart salute, he rattled out breathlessly to the two officers, "Boatloads o' scruffy-lookin' mice down that way, sirs!"

Hogspit swelled his chest officiously, sneering at the messenger. "Ho, 'tis 'sirs' now, is it? A lick o' trouble, a coupla foebeasts, an' all of a sudden we're officers agin, eh! Right then, 'ow many o' these scruffy-lookin' mouses is there?"

Lousewort tried hard to look like a commander of twoscore as he parroted Hogspit's last words. "Er, er, aye, 'ow many is there?"

The big weasel silenced him with an ill-tempered stare before turning back to the tracker. "Never mind goin' back t'count 'em. Get the others t'gether quick an' meet us down there. Cummon, dunderpaws, let's take a look!"

Lying in a hollow not far from the stream bank, both Rapscours saw the vessels come 'round the bend. There were six long logboats, each carved from the trunk of a large tree, and seated two abreast at the oars were small creatures, their fur wiry and sticking out at odd angles. Each of them wore a brightly colored cloth headband and a kilt, held up by a broad belt, through which was thrust a little rapier. Others of them sat at prow and stern atop supply sacks, and all of them seemed extremely short-tempered, for they argued and jabbered ceaselessly with one another. Only an older creature, slightly bigger than the rest, remained aloof, standing on the prow of the lead boat surveying the river ahead. In all, there were about seventy of them crewing the long logboats.

Hogspit rubbed his paws together. Grinning wickedly, he glanced back to see the tracker leading thirty vermin into the efile. The weasel sniggered with delight. Thirty Rapscallions vould be more than enough to take care of a gang of scruffy-ooking mice. He stuck a grimy claw under Lousewort's nose, ssuing orders to him.

"Huh, this'll be simple as shellin' peas. You stay 'ere with his lot, I'll go out there an' scare the livin' daylights out of hose mouses. Be ready t'come runnin' when I shouts yer!"

Swaggering out onto the stream bank, Hogspit called out to he oldish creature in the prow of the first craft as it drew evel, "Hoi, graybeard! Git them boats pulled in 'ere. I wants er see wot you've got aboard—an' move lively if y'know vot's good for yer!"

For a small beast, the leader had extremely dangerous eyes. He held up a paw and the crews ceased rowing. Steering the row 'round with a long pole, he waited until his craft was lose enough, then vaulted to dry land on the pole.

One paw on his rapier, the other tucked into his belt, he ooked the weasel up and down. His voice, when he spoke, vas deep and gruff.

"Lissen, swampguts, I know wot's good fer me, an' what's board these boats is none o' yore business—so back off!"

Hogspit was amazed at the small beast's insolence. Swelling ut his chest, he laid paw to his cutlass handle. "Do you know vho yer talkin' to? I'm Rapscour Hogspit of Damug War-ang's mighty Rapscallion army!"

The creature drew his small rapier coolly, quite unim-ressed. "Then clean the mud out yore ears an' lissen t'me, Spit'og, or whatever name y'call yoreself. I wouldn't know Damug wotsisname or his army if they fell on me out of a ree! I'm Log-a-Log, Chieftain o' the Guosim shrews. So pull teel if y'fancy dyin'!"

Hogspit whipped out his cutlass and charged with a roar.

In the hollow, Lousewort felt his belt tugged urgently by a at, who squealed, "Is that it, do we charge too?"

Lousewort pulled free of the rat's tugging paw. "Er, er, no, want t'see wot 'appens."

Log-a-Log faced the oncoming Rapscour until he was al-most on top of him, then, stepping neatly aside, he tripped Hogspit, lashing his back smartly with the rapier blade as the ig weasel went down.

The shrew circled him teasingly. "Up on yore paws, y'grea pudden, or I'll finish ye where you lie!"

His face ugly with rage, Hogspit scrambled up and bega taking huge swings at the shrew with his cutlass. Each tim the blade came down it was either on the ground or thin air The shrews in the boats sat impassively watching their leade making a fool of the bigger creature.

Turning aside the bludgeoning cutlass with a flick of hi rapier, Log-a-Log mocked his opponent. "It must be a poo outlook fer this Damug cove if'n this is the way he teache his officers t'handle a blade. Can't yer do any better, bucket bum?"

Slavering at the mouth and panting, Hogspit cleaved down holding the cutlass with both paws. The blade tanged off rock, sending a shock through him. He spat at his enemy snarling, "I'll carve yer guts inter frogmeat an' dance on em!'

Log-a-Log wiped the weasel's spit from his headband, eye flat with menace. "Nobeast ever spat on me an' lived. could've slain ye a dozen times. Here! There! Left! Right Up'n'down!" Whirling about he pricked Hogspit each tim he spoke, showing him the truth of the statement. Halting, th shrew curled his lip scornfully at the Rapscour and turned hi back on him, saying, "Gerrout o' my sight, vermin, you'v done yoreself no honor here today!"

Swinging the cutlass high, Hogspit charged at the shrew' unprotected back. At the last possible second Log-a-Lo turned and ran him through, gritting up into the coward' shocked face, "No skill, no sense, and no honor, now y'v got no life!"

21

When the drumbeats ceased that evening, Damug Warfang was standing on the stream bank with the entire Rapscallion horde spread wide around the valley behind him. He sat down on the head of a drum the rat Gribble had provided. Facing him in three ranks stood the remains of the trackers, with Lousewort at the front.

The Firstblade shook his head in disbelief at the tale he had heard. "Three hundred shrews in twenty big boats, are you sure?"

Lousewort nodded vigorously—his life depended on it. The others nodded too, backing him up.

"Let me get this clear," Damug continued, "they ambushed you, slew thirty of my trackers and a Rapscour, then got clean away?"

The nodding continued dumbly.

"And not one, not a single one, was slain or taken prisoner?"

More nods. The Greatrat closed his eyes and massaged their corners slowly. He was tired. Four times he had been over the same ground with them, and still they stuck firmly to their story. He glanced at the carcasses of the thirty-one vermin lying half in, half out of the stream shallows, creatures he could ill afford to lose, slow and stupid as they had been.

Turning his gaze back to Lousewort and the living, he sighed wearily. "Three hundred shrews, twenty big boats, eh? Well take my word, I'll find the truth of all this sooner or later, and when I do, if the answer is what I think, there'll be some here begging me for a swift death before I'm finished with them. Understood?"

The nodders' necks were sore, but still they bobbed up and down wordlessly.

Damug indicated the slain. "You will dig a pit twelve times as deep as the length of my sword, and when you have buried these bodies you will stand in the water all night up to your necks. Nor will you eat or drink again until I give the order. Gribble, detail two officers to stand watch on them."

Dying campfires burned small red blossoms into the night all around the valley, throwing slivers of scarlet across the swift-flowing stream. Stars pierced moonless skies, and a wispy breeze played about the sleeping Rapscallion camp.

Vendace gritted his teeth as the file scraped his neck. "Keep yer 'ead still," Borumm hissed at him impatiently as he worked on the fetters binding them together. "It won't take long now!"

Lugworm was already free—it was he who had managed to steal the file. Fearfully, the stoat whispered to the fox and the weasel, "You'll 'ave ter work faster, we ain't got all night!"

Borumm stifled the rattle of the neckband with both paws. The chains chinked softly as they fell from Vendace's body. The fox massaged his neck, eyes glittering furtively in the darkness. "Shut yer snivelin' face, stoat. C'mon, let's get movin'. We need t'be across that stream an' long gone by dawn."

Clinging to the rocks in midstream, Lousewort and forty-odd trackers struggled to keep their chins up above water, sobbing and cursing as the cold numbed their limbs and the icy flow threatened to sweep them away. Already some of their number, the weaker ones, had been drowned by others trampling them under in their efforts to stay alive.

Two Rapmark Captains sat hunched in sleep over a small fire on the bank. A ferret ground his chattering teeth as he glared in their direction. "Look at 'em, snoozin' all nice'n'warm there, while we're freezin' an' drownin' out 'ere. It ain't right, I tell yer!"

Lousewort hugged a weed-covered nub of rock, coughing water from both nostrils miserably. "Er, er, mebbe they'll let us come ashore when it's light."

Snorting mirthlessly, a sodden rat pulled himself higher to speak. "Who are you tryna fool, mate? 'Ow many of us d'yer think'll be *left* by tomorrer? Whether 'e knew it or not, Damug sentenced us to die by pullin' this liddle trick!"

The two sleeping Rapmark Captains were fated never to see dawn. They kicked briefly when the chains of Borumm and Vendace tightened about their necks. As the officers slumped lifeless, the escapers relieved them of their cloaks and weapons. Then, grabbing a coil of rope, Borumm plunged into the stream and waded out to where the wretched vermin clutched feebly at the rocks.

Securing the rope to a jagged rut, Borumm held it tight, and hissed, "You know me'n' Vendace—we're your ole Rapscours. We're gettin' out of 'ere, and anybeast feels like quittin' Damug an' his army can come along. That one ain't the Firstblade his father was!"

A ferret took hold of the rope as Vendace and Lugworm waded up. "I'm wid yer, mate! An' so would you lot be if y've got any sense. Warfang treats 'is own army worse'n 'is enemies. Lead on, Borumm!"

Vendace silenced the general murmur of approval. "Keep the noise down there. I'll make it to the other bank wid this rope an' lash it tight 'round a rock. Y'can grab on to it an' make yore way over, but be quick, there's no time ter lose!"

Pulling themselves paw over paw along the taut line, the escapers made their way to the opposite side of the stream. Borumm perched on a rock with the last few, but when it was Lugworm's turn to take the rope, Borumm pushed him aside.

"Where d'yer think yore off to, slimeface?" he snarled.

The stoat's voice was shrill with surprise. "It was all part o' the plan, we escape together, mate!"

There was nowhere to run. Borumm grinned wolfishly at him. "I ain't yore mate, an' I just changed the plan. We don't take no backstabbers an' traitors wid us. You stay 'ere!"

Borumm swung the bunched chains savagely, and Lugworm fell lifeless into the stream before he even had a chance to protest about the new arrangements. Lousewort was shocked by the weasel's action. "Ooh! Wot didyer do that for? The pore beast wasn't doin' you no 'arm, mate!"

Borumm was not prepared to argue. There was only himself and Lousewort left on the rock. He swung the chains once more, laying Lousewort senseless on the damp stones. Swinging off on to the rope, the weasel hauled himself along, muttering, "Sorry about that, mate, but if'n you ain't for us yore agin us!"

22

›ubbling and hissing furiously, the tank in Salamandastron's ›rge room received a red-hot chunk of metal. Lady Cregga :ose Eyes held the piece there until she was sure it was suf- ciently cooled. Then, slowly, she withdrew the wet gray steel. : was an axpike head, the top a straight-tipped, double-bladed pearpoint. Below that was a single battle-ax blade, thick at ıe stub, sweeping out smoothly to a broad flat edge, the other ide of which was balanced by a down-curving pike hook.

The Badger Warrior turned it this way and that, letting it ise and fall as she tested the heft of her new weapon. Satisfied ıat everything about the lethal object suited her, Cregga be- an reheating it in the fires of her forge. The next job was to ut edges to the spear, ax, and hook blades—not sharpened dges, but beaten ones that would never need to be honed on ny stone.

She straightened up as the long-awaited knock sounded pon the door, followed by Deodar's voice.

"Tenth Spring Runner reportin', marm, relieved on the ʼestern tide line this afternoon!"

The rose-eyed badger had waited two days to hear a Runner's voice. She recognized it as female and roared out a gruf reply, "Well, don't hang about out there, missie. Come ir come in!"

The young haremaid entered boldly, slamming the door be hind her and throwing a very elegant salute. "Patrolled nort by west, marm, returnin' along the coast. No signs of vermi or foebeast activity; still no sign or news of Major Perigord' patrol whatsoever. Spotted a few shore toads but they kep their distance. Nothin' else to report, marm!"

Cregga put aside her work, great striped head nodding res olutely. "Well done, Runner, that's all I needed to know Stand easy."

Deodar took up the at-ease position and waited. The Badge Lady picked up her red-hot axpike head with a pair of tongs "What d'you think, missie? 'Tis to be my new weapon."

The hare gazed round-eyed at the fearsome object. "Peril ous, marm, a real destroyer!"

Setting it to rest on the anvil, Cregga squinted at the Runne "Answer me truly, young 'un, d'you think you're about read to join the Long Patrol?"

Deodar sprang quivering to attention. "Oh, I say! Rather! mean, yes, marm!"

A formidable paw patted Deodar's shoulder lightly. "Hmm I think you are too. Do you own a weapon?"

"A weapon, 'fraid not, marm, outside o' sling or short dag ger. Colonel Eyebright ain't fussy on Runners goin' heavy armed."

Cregga's big paw waved at the weapons ranged in rows o the walls. "Right, then let's see you choose yourself some thing."

She checked Deodar's instinctive rush to the weaponry "No hurry, miss, take care, what you decide upon may hav to last you a lifetime. Go ahead now, but choose wisely."

The young hare wandered 'round the array, letting her pav run over hilts and handles as she spoke her mind aloud. "Le me see now, marm, nothin' too heavy for me, I'll never be a big as Rockjaw Grang or some others. Somethin' simple t carry, quick to reach, and light to the paw. Aha! I think this' jolly well fit the bill, a fencing saber!"

Cregga smiled approvingly. "I'd have picked that for yo myself. Go on, take it down and try it, see how it feels!"

Reverently, Deodar took the saber from its peg and held it, feeling the fine balance of the long, slightly curving single-edged blade. It had a cord-whipped handle, with a basket hilt to protect the paw. So keen was its edge that it whistled menacingly when she swung it sideways.

Suddenly Lady Cregga was in front of her, brandishing a poker as if it were a sword. "On guard, miss, have at ye!"

Steel changed upon steel as they fenced around the glowing forge, Cregga calling out encouragement to her pupil as she parried blows and thrusts with the poker.

"That's the way, miss! Step step, swing counter! Now step step step, thrust! Backstep sideswing! Keep that paw up! Remember, the blade is an extension of the paw, keep it flexible! And one and two and thrust and parry! Counter, step step, figure of eight at shoulder level! Footpaws never flat, up up!"

With a quick skirmishing movement the badger disarmed her pupil, sending the saber quivering point first into the door. "Enough! Enough! Where did you learn saber fighting, young 'un?"

Deodar looked disappointed that she had been disarmed. "From my uncle, Lieutenant Morio, but evidently I didn't learn too well, marm."

Cregga pulled the saber from the door, presenting it back to Deodar hilt first. "Nonsense! If you'd learned any better I'd have been slain. What d'you want to do, beat the Ruler of Salamandastron on your first practice?"

The young Runner took the saber back, smiling gratefully. "No, marm! Thank you for this saber—and the lesson too."

That same night the list of new recruits was posted at the entrance to the Dining Hall, and everyone clamored around it to see who had been promoted to the Long Patrol. Drill Sergeant Clubrush, who was responsible for day-to-day discipline among the younger set, sat near the doorway of the Officers' Mess with Colonel Eyebright. The hares were old friends, being of the same age and having served together many long seasons.

Eyebright tapped his pace stick gently against the table edge. "Stap me, but I wish Lady Cregga hadn't ordered me t'post that confounded list. Just look at 'em, burstin' their britches to be Patrollers, all afire with the stories they've heard, an' not a mother's babe o' them knows what they're really in for, wot?''

The Sergeant sipped his small beaker of mountain beer. ''Aye, sir, 'taint the same as when we was young. You didn't get t'be a Patroller then 'til you 'ad t'duck yore 'ead to get through the doorway. I recall my ole pa sayin' you had t'be long enough t'be picked for Long Patrol. I'd 'ave gived those young 'uns another season yet, two mebbe, 'tis a shame really, sir.''

The Colonel turned his eyes upward to the direction of the forge. ''Mark m'words, Sarge, 'tis all Rose Eyes's doin'. I've never known or heard of a badger sufferin' from the Bloodwrath so badly. I've had it from her own blinkin' mouth that she's bound to march off from here with half the garrison strength to destroy Tunn an' his Rapscallions. Have y'ever heard the like? A Ruler of Salamandastron leavin' our mountain t'do battle goodness knows how far off. She'd have had us *all* go if I hadn't dug me paws in!''

Clubrush finished his drink and rose stiffly. ''Beggin' y'pardon, sir, I'd best get 'em organized afore supper. Oh buttons'n'brass, willyer lookit, there's young Cheeva sobbin' 'er 'eart out 'cos she wasn't posted on the list.''

Eyebright nodded sadly. ''She was far too young, her pa an' I decided we'd leave her a while yet. Better Cheeva cryin' now than me an' her father weepin' when Cregga's bloodlust brings back sad results. You go about y'business now, Sarge, I'll see to her.''

Drill Sergeant Clubrush marched smartly into the midst of the successful candidates, bellowing out orders.

''Keep y'fur on now, young sirs an' missies! Silence in the ranks there an' lissen up please! Right, anybeast whose name's bin posted up 'ere—in double file an' foller me. We're goin' up to Lady Cregga's forge room where I'll h'issue you wid weapons I thinks best suited to gentlebeasts. No foolin' about while yore up there . . . Are you lissenin', Trowbaggs, I'll 'ave my beady eye on you, laddie buck! Keep silence in the ranks, show proper respect to the Badger marm, an' mind yore manners. Tenshun! By the right . . . Wait for it, Trowbaggs . . . By the right quick march!''

As they marched eagerly off, Colonel Eyebright went to sit next to the young hare Cheeva, who was sobbing uncontrollably in a corner. The kindly old officer passed her his own red-spotted kerchief.

"Now, now, missie, this won't do, you'll flood the place out. Come on now, tell me all about it, wot?"

Cheeva rocked back and forth, her face buried in the kerchief. "Waahahhh! M . . . m . . . my n . . . n . . . name wasn't p . . . p . . . posted on th' r . . . r . . . rotten ole li . . . li . . . list! Boohoohoo!"

Eyebright straightened his shoulders, adopting a stern tone. "Well I should hope not! It was the unanimous verdict of the officers who made out that list that you be kept back. D'you know why?"

" 'Co . . . co . . . cos I'm t . . . too yu . . . yu . . . young! Waaahahaaarr!"

The Colonel's trim mustache bristled. "Balderdash, m'gel, who told y'that? The reason is that we decided you were real officer material, needed sorely on this mountain, doncha know! Suppose Searats or Corsairs launched an attack on us whilst that lot were off gallivantin'. Who d'you suppose we'd be lookin' for to take up a trainee commandin' position, eh, tell me that? Long Patrol isn't the be all an' end all of young hares like y'self who want t'make somethin' of themselves. Ain't that right, young Deodar?"

Without Cheeva seeing him, the Colonel winked broadly at Deodar, seated nearby. She had had no need to go to the forge room for a weapon; she was polishing her saber blade with a rag. Deodar caught on to the officer's little ruse right away.

"Oh, right you are, sah, I'd have been rather chuffed if I was picked t'be a trainee officer at the garrison here."

Cheeva looked up, red-eyed and tear-stained. "Would you really?"

Deodar snorted as if the question was totally ridiculous. "Hah! Would I ever? How's about swappin' places—I'll stay here for officer trainin' an' you go bally well harin' off with that other cracked bunch?"

Colonel Eyebright shook his head sternly. "Sorry, miss, orders've been posted, you've got to go. Soon as I've got you lot out o' my whiskers I'm goin' to start Cheeva's officer trainin'. First task, nip off an' wash that face in cold water, miss. Can't have the troops seein' anybeast of officer material boohooin' all over the place, can we, wot?''

Cheeva gave back the kerchief and ran off half laughing and half weeping. " 'Course not, Colonel, sah, thank you very much!''

Eyebright wrung out the spotted kerchief, smiling at Deodar. ''Good form, gel, thanks for your help. And don't polish that saber away now, will ye!''

After supper the new recruits laid their paws upon the table and began drumming loudly until the dining hall reverberated to the noise. This was the prelude to a bit of fun traditional to Long Patrol.

Colonel Eyebright played his part well. Striding from the Officers' Mess, he held up his pace stick for silence.

When it was quiet he began the ritual with a short rhyme.

''Who are these strange creatures, pray,
Say who are you all,
Stirring up a din an' clatter
In our dining hall?''

Young Furgale rose in answer in time-honored manner.

''We are no strange creatures, sah,
But perilous one an' all,
Tell Sergeant we're the Long Patrol,
We've come to pay a call!''

The Colonel bowed stiffly and marched back to the Mess, where he could be heard announcing to the waiting Clubrush:

''Wake up from your slumbers, Sergeant, dear,
I think your new recruits are here.''

Wild cheering and unbridled laughter greeted the appearance of Clubrush. He dashed out of the Officers' Mess, roaring and glaring fiercely like the Drill Sergeant of every recruit's nightmares. On these occasions a Sergeant always wore certain things, and Clubrush had dressed accordingly. 'Round his waist he wore a belt with dried and faded dock leaves hanging from it—these were supposed to be the ears of recruits that he had collected. 'Round his footpaws he trailed soft white roots—recruits' guts. Over one shoulder was a banderole of cotton thistles representing tails. All over the Sergeant's uniform were pinned bits and pieces of herb and fauna, supposedly the gruesome bits he had collected from sloppy recruits.

Scowling savagely, he paced the tables, singing in a terrifyingly gruff voice as he went:

"You 'orrible lollopy sloppy lot,
You idle scruffy bunch!
I'll 'ave yore tails off like a shot
An' boil 'em for me lunch!

You lazy loafin' layabouts,
'Ere's wot I'll do fer starters
If you don't lissen when I shouts,
I'll 'ave yore guts fer garters!

O mamma's darlin's, don't you cry,
Yore dear ole Sergeant's 'ere,
Those foebeasts, why, they're just small fry,
'Tis *me* you'll learn to fear!

I'll 'ave yore ears'n'elbows,
You sweepin's o' the floors,
An' long before the dawn shows,
You'll 'ave marched ten leagues outdoors.

O dreadful 'alf-baked dozy crowd,
I'll stake me oath 'tis true,
Long Patrol Warriors, tall'n'proud,
Is wot I'll make of you!"

Sergeant Clubrush's fierce demeanor changed instantly as he patted backs and shook paws of the young hares crowding round him.

"Welcome to the Patrol, buckoes, you'll do us proud!"

• • •

Cregga Rose Eyes had a handle for her axpike—a thick pole, taller than herself. The wood was dark, hard, and sea-washed, like that of Russa's stick. Long summers gone, somebeast had found it among the flotsam of the tide line. Now the Badger Lady rediscovered it, lying with a pile of other timber at the back of her forge. She worked furiously, far into the night, shaping, binding, fixing the awesome steel headpiece to its haft, speaking aloud her thoughts as she bored holes through wood and metal for three heavy copper rivets.

"Sleep well, Gormad Tunn, sleep on, Damug, Byral, and all your Rapscallion scum! I am coming, death is on the wind! On the day when you see my face, you and all of your evil followers will sleep the sleep from which there is no awakening!"

23

Tammo had been gone too long for Russa Nodrey's liking. She caught Perigord's glance as she took up her stick. "No-beast takes this long t'gather a few pawfuls of 'cress, Major. Somethin's wrong—I'm goin' to take a look!"

Perigord buckled on his saber. "Tare, Turry, Rubbadub, guard the camp an' supplies, the rest o' you chaps, off y'hunkers an' come with us!"

Traveling swiftly and silently they spread out, covering trees, riverbank, and shallows carefully. It was not long before they picked up Tammo's trail. Captain Twayblade found the rock where she too had noted watercress growing underwater.

Pasque waved wordlessly from a short distance up the bank. Keeping voices to a barely audible murmur, they gathered 'round her. "A bundle o' watercress. He was here—see, 'tis tied up with his shoulder belt."

Midge Manycoats inspected the trunk of a nearby sycamore. "There's a knifepoint mark here. Looks like Tammo stuck his blade in this tree!"

A pebble struck Rockjaw Grang on the side of his neck. "Owch! 'Ey up, somebeast's chuckin' stones!"

Out of the darkness above, a volley of small stones peppered Perigord's troop, followed by rustling in the high foliage, sniggering laughs, and reedy voices calling, "Tammo! Tammo! Choohakka choohak! Where poor Tammo?"

Russa shouted aloud at Perigord, "Let's get out o' here!"

The Major shot her a puzzled look. "Wot, you mean retreat, run away?"

Shielding herself from the stones with an upraised paw, the squirrel winked several times at him. "Aye, let's run fer it afore we're battered t'death!"

Perigord suddenly caught on; he cut and ran into the shallows. "Retreat, troop, everybeast out o' here, quick as y'like. Retreat!"

The Long Patrol were not used to running from anything, but they obeyed the command. Pounding upstream through the shallows, they halted out of range of the rain of pebbles.

Then Twayblade turned on Perigord, her long rapier flicking angrily at the air. "Retreat from a few stones'n'pebbles, what are we, pray—a flight of startled swallows?"

Perigord laid the blame firmly at Russa's paws. "Ask her!"

The squirrel looked from one to the other. "Well, if y'stop lookin' all noble an' outraged for a tick I'll tell ye. Really 'twas my fault. I've traveled this riverbank afore, an' if'n I'd been thinkin' clear I'd have stopped you pitchin' camp where the Painted Ones roam."

Twayblade ceased twitching her rapier. "Painted Ones?"

Russa's bushy tail stood up angrily. "Aye, Painted Ones. Tribes o' little tree rats is all they are, though they paints their fur black'n'green an' lives in the boughs an' leaves 'igh up. Huh! Some o' the villains even attaches bushtails to themselves an' masquerades as squirrels, the liddle blackguards, not fit t'lick a decent squirrel's paws! But they're savage an' dangerous, almost invisible when they're among the treetops. Young Tammo's in a bad fix if y'ask me!"

The saturnine Lieutenant Morio nodded his agreement. "But no doubt you've got a plan, marm?"

Russa had. She explained her strategy then slid off among the trees, leaving the hares to carry out their part of the scheme.

Sheathing his blade, Perigord began gathering flat heavy

pebbles. "Slings out, chaps, load up an' give 'em stones for supper!"

Meanwhile, Tammo lay bound and gagged. The leader of the Painted Ones was digging teasingly at him with the point of his captured dirk, giggling wickedly each time his prisoner flinched.

"Ch'hakka hak! 'Ear you friends, alla gone now, soon dissa one cutcha up wirra you own knife. Den we eatcha! Hakka-chook!"

Tammo had heard Russa and the hares and felt a mixture of anger and sadness when Perigord shouted retreat and they ran off. Now he felt alone and deserted, certain too that something horrible was about to be inflicted upon him by the sadistic little tree creatures, who seemed very confident and contemptuous of landbeasts.

Then Tammo's heart leapt as he heard the night air ring with a familiar war cry:

"Eulalia! 'Tis death on the wind! Eulalia! *Charge!*"

Whacking, cracking, whizzing all around him, a veritable load of slingstones tore upward into the foliage. One rock big as a miniature boulder whipped by him, snapping off branches in its path. Good old Rockjaw Grang!

Turning his head to one side, Tammo peered into the gloom and saw small black and green figures retaliating, loosing pebbles from their own slings at the bold enemy below.

Russa had reached the far side of the trees. She skipped nimbly up into a stately elm and turned toward the distant din of battle. Thrusting the hardwood stick into her mouth she bit down on it and took off like a fish skimming through water, building up her speed as she raced through the treetops. Bright eyes cut through the darkness as she traveled even faster, the limbs and leaves passing in a blur, knowing that swiftness was the key to her mission. Sighting the back of the first Painted One, Russa grabbed her stick in one paw, still hurtling through the top terraces of foliage at a breakneck pace. She cracked the hardwood stick down between the rat's ears, then, changing her angle at the same time and shooting in a downward curve, she battered mercilessly at anybeast in her path.

The hardwood stick was like a living thing in her paws,

whacking heads and paws and cracking limbs. Overhead Russa spotted a glint of steel as a stream of orders was shouted down through the treetops. "Chakkachook! Killa! Killa!" Swooping upward, she disposed of two more rats with a quick side-to-side jab to their faces. Bulling into the leader of the Painted Ones, she laid him senseless with a single rap to his skull.

Russa grabbed the dirk and slashed through Tammo's bonds. "Quick, get behind me an' lock y'paws 'round my waist!"

With a swift kick she sent the Painted Ones' leader from the bough they were standing on. As soon as he started to fall, Russa leapt after him, with Tammo holding grimly on to her and shouting, "We're comin' doooooooown!"

Leaves, twigs, branches, limbs tore madly by in a rushing kaleidoscope of brown, black, and green. Tammo's heart seemed to fly up into his mouth as all three plummeted earthward, Russa's footpaws practically resting on the back of the rat as his body smashed a path down to the ground for them. They landed with a thrashing crashing sound, flattening an osier bush as the three bodies hit it.

Major Perigord whirled a slingstone upward, remarking as he let the pebble fly, "Just dropped in to join the jolly old scrap, wot? Bravo!"

Letting go of Russa, Tammo flopped awkwardly onto the ground. Apart from various scratches he was surprised to find himself unharmed. Russa yanked the battered and unconscious tree rat leader upright and pushed him into Rockjaw's open paws.

"Make light, get me a lantern, somebeast, 'urry!" she cried.

Tinder and flint hastily fired a lantern Riffle had brought. Bidding Riffle hold the light close to their captive, Russa grabbed the leader by one ear, hauling his head upright. Then she pressed the dirkpoint under his chin and called upward, imitating the tree rats' speech, "Chakkachook! Dis beast a dead'n, we cuttim 'ead off, you chukka more rocks. Dissa beast tellya true, chahakachah!"

The slingstones stopped and a mass wail went up from the foliage.

"Yaaahaaaagg! Norra kill Shavvakamalla! Yaaahaaaagg!"

Rockjaw Grang slung the senseless leader over his shoulder.

'Shavvakawot? Sithee, 'tis a big name for a lickle rat!''

Sergeant Torgoch smiled at his friend's broad accent. ''Take im back t'camp. We'll get a good night's sleep with their hief as 'ostage, wot d'ye say, sah?''

Drawing his saber, Perigord began backing his troop out of ie area. ''Capital idea! But we'd best keep up the threats, just make sure they know we mean business. I say, are you hurt, ld lad?''

Tammo was limping on his right footpaw. ''Little sprain, ah, I'll be right as rain in a bit.''

The hares backed off, shouting horrible threats into the ees. ''I say, you rips up there, leave us alone or we'll scoff our jolly old leader. I'm quite serious, y'know. Chop chop, um yum, eatim alla up, as you blighters say, savvy?''

''Yaaaaahaaaag! No eata Shavvakamalla! Yaaahaaa-aaagghh!''

''Hah! Y'don't like that, do you? Well keep your bally dis-ance or it's fricassee of tree rat for brekkers!''

''Aye, an' we'll use the leftovers t'make tree rat turnover er lunch, it'll go nice with a bit o' salad!''

''Actually I'd rather fancy a slice of tree rat tart. D'you hink there'd be enough of him left t'make one, eh, Rock-aw?''

''By 'eck, goo an' get thy own tree rat, Cap'n. I'm doin' ll the carryin', so this 'un's mine. Bah goom, 'e'll make a rand tree rat 'otpot with a crust o'er 'is 'ead!''

''Yaaaahaggaaaah! Nono tree rats 'otpot, yerra no eatim!''

Major Perigord called a halt to the teasing. ''Quite enough ow, pack it in, chaps—those rotters've got the message, I hink. I say, Rockjaw, I hope you were jokin' about tree rat otpot. We're not really goin' to eat the blighter, y'know.''

Rockjaw Grang plodded along with his burden, muttering a ingle word:

''Spoilsport!''

24

The remainder of the night passed uneventfully, though Peri-gord's troop knew they were being watched from the treetop by the Painted Ones. Pairing off, the hares took turns to guar the camp and keep an eye on the still-unconscious prisoner.

Tammo and Pasque were on second watch. They sat to gether, keeping the fire fed with twigs and dried moss.

Tammo eyed the captive's slumped figure uneasily. "I say d'you think the rascal will come 'round before mornin'? H looks pretty much of a heap, maybe the fall finished him off?"

Pasque felt the pulse on the rat's neck and checked hi breathing by holding a thin blade of grass close to his mout and nostrils. "Not t'worry, he'll live, though whether or nc he'll ever be the same after you an' Russa landin' atop of hir remains t'be seen. Now—I'd best take a look at that footpav you've been hobblin' about on."

Tammo dismissed the idea airily. "Oh, that? Hah! 'Twa nothin' really, I'm fine, thanks!"

Pasque Valerian began pulling herbs and dressing from he bag. "Sorry, but I've got to fix it up, Major's orders. If yo have to travel on that paw all day tomorrow it'd become worse an' you'd slow us all up. So hold still.''

Pasque damped warm water on dock leaves and crushed gentian stems, binding the poultice to Tammo's right footpaw with a thin brown cloth strip. When she was done, Tammo was pleased with the result. The bandage was firm but not tight, and he could use the footpaw quite freely without twingeing pains.

''Golly, that feels like a new paw now. My thanks to you, marm!''

Pasque fluttered her long lashes comically. ''Why, thank ye, young sir, though if you had any of your mother's pancakes left I'd charge you two of 'em for my services!''

The leader of the Painted Ones stirred. ''Whuuchakka huunhh! Whuuurrg! Shavvakamalla hurtened much lotsa!''

Pasque reopened her medicine bag, showing open disdain for the creature as she treated him. ''Hmph! Hurtened much lotsa, is it? Y'wicked little runt, I'd have hurted you much lotsa more if I could've got a clear shot at you. Here, sit up'n'drink this!''

Averting his head, the rat tried to push away Pasque's medicine. Tammo came to her aid. Grabbing the protesting vermin's jaws he forced them open, pushing the rat's head back.

''Carry on, chum, pour it down the filthy ol' throat, an' I hope it tastes jolly awful. Give the bounder a bigger dose if he tries spittin' it out!''

Between them they fixed up the rat's injuries. Tammo, working under Pasque's directions, proved capable with bandage and splint, though whenever his friend was not watching, he would give the bindings an extra sharp tug, causing the rat to groan. Pasque took the groans as a sign that more medicine was needed, and she dosed him well.

''Oh, do stop moanin' an' whinin', you cowardly little bully. Thank the fates you're still alive an' bein' treated by civilized hares!''

Morning dawned warm, with the promise of a hot sunny day. Steam rose in drifting tendrils from the mossy riverbank as Corporal Rubbadub marched about, sounding reveille.

"Rubbadubdub, dubbadubbity dub, baboom baboom baboom!"

The Painted Ones' leader clapped both bandaged paws to his aching head and glared pleadingly at Rubbadub, who merely smiled and leaned close to the rat's ear, to give him the full benefit of his skills.

"Boompity boompity boom!"

Major Perigord stretched languidly, issuing morning orders as he did. "Rise'n'shine, troop. 'Fraid we can't take the chance of breakin' our fast hereabouts, what with the flippin' forces o' darkness up there in the arboreal verdance, waitin' to take a crack at us an' rescue ol' Shavvaka wotsisface. We'll cross the river lower down an' don the nosebag when we're well away from here. Those painted chaps can have their boss wallah back once we've crossed the river. Break camp, Sergeant."

Torgoch, looking fresh as a daisy, saluted stiffly. "Right y'are, sah! Midge, Riffle, move y'selves. Tare'n'Turry, make sure that fire's well doused before y'leave. Rockjaw, sling that h'injured vermin over y'shoulder. Officers lead off, other ranks bringin' up the rear!"

Rockjaw threw the rat over one shoulder, chatting to Lieutenant Morio as he did.

"Wot does the Major mean by 'arboreal verdance,' sah?"

"Hmm, arboreal verdance, lemme see, I rather think it means treetops, leafy green ones."

"Oh! Then why didn't 'e say treetops?"

"Why should he when he knows how t'say words like arboreal verdance?"

Rockjaw cuffed the moaning rat lightly. "Hush thy noise, or I'll give thee summat to moan about an y'won't see your arboreal verdance again!"

They crossed the river at the ford, which was littered with huge rocks, providing good stepping-stones. Behind them the foliage rustled and trembled as the Painted Ones followed, anxious as to the fate of their Chieftain. Perigord soon dispelled their fears by frog-hopping the hobbled rat back to the last stepping-stone, where he left him to be rescued by his own kind. But not without a severe warning.

Fearlessly the Major drew his saber and pointed it at the

swaying tree cover. "Listen up now, every slackjawed one o' ye! My name is Major Perigord Habile Sinistra, but don't for a moment think that 'cos I'm left-pawed I can't use this blade! If y'don't improve your ways I'll return here, me an' my warriors, an' we'll chop y'all up an' eatcha, got that! We didn't eat your leader simply because he's a coward an' a bully an' that'd make him taste bad. If I were you chaps I'd set about findin' a new commander today! Now if you've understood all that, an' you probably haven't if you're as dense as ol' Shavvachops here, then take heed because I'm perilous an' don't make idle threats. I bid ye good morn!"

Throwing up an elegant front salute with his saber, Perigord wheeled on one paw and marched back to his patrol.

Torgoch nodded admiringly. "Does yore 'eart good t'see a h'officer with steel in 'is backbone layin' down the law to vermin, don't it, Rock!"

The giant hare dusted off his shoulder as if he had been carrying some unspeakable bundle of garbage there. "Aye, by 'ecky thump! But if'n I'd a been him I'd 'ave told 'em I'd chop off their arboreal verdancy. Sithee, that'd make yon vermin sit up straight!"

Breakfast time slipped by unnoticed. Having picked up the vermin trail, the patrol marched swiftly onward over the grasslands in the fine spring morning. Between them, the twins Tare and Turry struck up a lively marching chant.

"As I marched out one sunny day,
O lairo lairo lay!
I met a hare upon the way,
O lairo lairo laydee!
With ears like silk, and eyes so brown,
And fur as soft as thistledown,
She smiled at me an' that was that,
My poor young heart went pitter pat!

O pitter pat an' eyes of brown,
She looked me up an' looked me down,
I ask you now, what could I do,
I said, 'Please, may I walk with you?'
We walked together all that day,

O lairo lairo lay!
As laughingly I heard her say,
O lairo lairo laydee!

'Pray tell to me, O brave young sir,
Are you a wild an' perilous hare
Who thinks of nought from morn 'til night
But march an' sing an' charge an' fight?'
O march an' sing, O perilous hare,
So I said to this creature fair,
'To march an' fight is my intent,
The Long Patrol's my regiment!'

And then upon that sunny day,
O lairo lairo lay!
She turned from me an' skipped away,
O lairo lairo laydee!
She said, 'I fear that we must part,
Sir, I would not give you my heart,
That Long Patrol, alas alack,
Those hares march off an' ne'er come back!'

O ne'er come back an' Long Patrol,
While rivers flow an' hills do roll,
I'll march along my merry way,
An' look for pretty hares each day!"

Two hours into noon, woodlands were sighted. However, this was no copse but vast expanses of mighty trees.

Russa picked up the pace, smiling fondly. "Yonder lies Mossflower, an' the Abbey of Redwall within a few days. What d'yer think o' that, young Tamm?"

Before Tammo could answer, Perigord interrupted sharply: "Only a few days to the Abbey, you say? By the left! We'd best put on a stride an' catch up with those vermin!"

Doubling the pace to a swift lope, they headed toward the shady green vastness of the sprawling woodlands. The first thing Tammo noticed on entering Mossflower was the silence. It was complete and absolute. The sudden call of a cuckoo nearby made him start momentarily. Overawed by the ancient wide-girthed splendor of oak, beech, elm, sycamore, and other towering giants, the young hare found himself whispering to Russa, "Why is it so bally quiet in here?"

The squirrel shrugged. "Dunno, I've never given it a thought. May'aps because out in the open y'can hear the wind, an' distant sounds travel on the breeze, but in 'ere, well, 'tis sort o' closed in like."

Stirring the moist carpet of dead vegetation with his saber-tip, the Major commented, "Cap'n Twayblade, let 'em rest their paws awhile here and scrape up a quick snack—no cookin' fire. Russa, you come with me and we'll track ahead. They've left plenty o' trail in this loam."

When the pair had left, Tammo sat with his friends in dappled sunlit shadows. They munched dried apples, nuts, and oatcake, washed down with beakers of water.

"I've never been to Redwall Abbey, what's it like?" he whispered to Pasque.

"Can't help you there, chum. I haven't either. Neither has Riffle, Tare'n'Turry, or any of us younger ones. Cap'n Twayblade has."

The Captain put aside her beaker. "Well, I'll tell you, chaps, I don't wish to appear disloyal to Salamandastron, but Redwall Abbey, by m'life, there's a place an' a half! I was only there once, with Torgoch an' Rockjaw, we were carryin' dispatches from Lady Cregga to the ol' Mother Abbess, congratulatin' her on a onescore season Jubilee, as I recall. Anyhow, we arrived at Redwall in time for the feast. Remember that, eh, Rock?"

The burly Rockjaw Grang grinned and nodded, speaking in his odd way. "Bah gum, that were a do I'll not forget! Sithee, I've ne'er clapped eyes on so much luvly grub in one place: puddens'n'pies, cakes, turnovers, pasties, tarts, you name it an' it were there. Trifles, cream, cheeses, soups, an' more kinds o' fresh-baked breads than y'could twitch an ear at! But by 'ecky thump, I've tasted nought like that October Ale they brew at yon Abbey. . . ."

He sat with a dreamy look on his craggy face as the Sergeant contributed his reminiscences. "Ho yerss, they 'ad all manner o' fizzy cordials an' berry wines too. We sang an' danced an' feasted for more'n three days. I declare, you ain't never met such obligin' creatures as those Redwallers, 'omely an' friendly as the season's long, they was. If'n I'm still around when I gets too old to patrol, I'd like nothin' better than to retire meself to Redwall Abbey, 'tis the 'appiest place I've ever seen in all me seasons!"

Riffle could not resist rubbing his paws together gleefully. "Good egg! An' we're going to be there in a few days, wot!"

Faint but urgent a faraway cry echoed through the woodlands.

"Eulaliaaa! Rally the troops! Death on the wind! Eulaliaaaaa!"

Food and talk were instantly forgotten; weapons appeared as the Patrol leapt to the alert.

"Rally the troops! Eulaliaaaaaa!"

Captain Twayblade's long rapier thrust toward the cries. "Over that way, I reckon! Eulaliaaaaaa! Chaaaaaaarge!"

They took off like a sheet of lightning, blades and slings whirling, roaring aloud the war cry to let Perigord know help was on its way.

"Eulaliaaa! 'S death on the wind! Eulaliaaaaa!"

Despite his bandaged paw, Tammo was up with the front-runners, Twayblade, Riffle, and Midge. Straight on they raced, through bush and shrub, loam flying, leaves swirling, twigs cracking, and startled birds whirring off through the trees. Pawsounds thrummed fast against the earth like frenzied, muted drumbeats. Sunlight and shadow wove together as they hurtled onward, bellowing and baying like wolves to the hunt.

25

Bursting over the brow of a humpbacked ridge, the wild charging hares crashed through a grove of rowans down into a narrow rocky defile and flung themselves like madbeasts into the fray. Major Perigord was backed into a small cave; beset by yelling vermin, he held the entrance gallantly. A broken javelin tip protruded from his right shoulder, and he was slashed in several places, but still he wielded his saber like a drum major's staff, fighting gamely against overwhelming odds, which threatened to bring him down and get at whoever was behind him inside the cave. Smashing into the rear of the vermin and scattering them like ninepins, the Long Patrol hares arrived to their officer's rescue.

"Eulaliaaaa! Give 'em blood'n'vinegar! Eulaliaaaa!"

Tammo's dirk, Twayblade's rapier, and Riffle's dagger claimed the first three foebeasts. Rockjaw Grang slew two with ferocious kicks from his mighty hindpaws. Lieutenant Morio had his face laid open by a cutlass slash as he brought down another with his lance. Perigord flung his saber after the remainder, who were scrabbling off up the far side of the small ravine. He fell on all fours, shouting hoarsely, "Run 'em to earth, keep after the scum!"

More than a score of the remaining vermin ran off through the woodlands, with the hares hard on their heels. Sergeant Torgoch ran alongside Twayblade, trying to keep his eye on the escapers as they fled into the deep tree cover. "They're splittin' up, Cap'n. What now, marm?" he shouted.

Twayblade kept running, watching the vermin starting to fan out, issuing orders as she went. "Lieutenant Morio stayed behind with the Major, so with Russa that makes us eleven. Torgoch, you take Rubbadub and Midge . . ."

Tammo interrupted, his face full of concern. "But where *is* Russa?" he said. "Has anyone seen her?"

"Probably off somewheres finishing off a few dozen vermin with that stick of hers," said Twayblade, sounding more confident than she felt. "Torgoch, Rubbadub, Midge, keep after those to the left. Riffle, go after those who've gone right—Tare'n'Turry, go with him. Tammo, Pasque, Rockjaw, stay with me, there's about ten of 'em bunched together keepin' straight ahead. We'll stick with them, and everyone keep your eyes skinned for Russa."

Knowing they were running for their lives, the fleeing vermin dashed helter-skelter, south into Mossflower. Tammo was beginning to feel weariness weighting his paws, owing to the headlong dash to the defile and the subsequent fighting. However, he was running with the famed Long Patrol, so he tried hard not to show signs of fatigue. Keeping his mouth closed, he breathed hard through his nostrils and whacked both footpaws down resolutely.

As Twayblade shot ahead, a rat tripped over some protruding tree roots in front of her. Before the creature could recover, she was upon him, dispatching him as he tried to rise. Tammo noted a weasel breaking off from the main body and slipping behind a hornbeam. Shooting off to one side, he watched the tree as his companions raced past it. Slowing his pace, Tammo came around the hornbeam. The weasel was smiling, thinking he had shaken off his pursuers. Turning to head east, he ran straight into Tammo. A look of surprise crossed the vermin's ugly face and he grabbed for the hatchet shoved through his belt, but too late. Tammo slew him with a single thrust. The chilling feeling took control of Tammo as he dashed to join the others, teeth chattering and limbs trembling uncontrollably. He sighted them up ahead; they were halted, retreating slowly. Rockjaw Grang saw him and called, "Stay where thee are, Tamm, 'tis bad swampland 'ereabouts!"

Tammo walked forward another few paces until the ground became squishy, where he joined his companions. Farther out in the swamp the remaining vermin had rushed heedlessly into a dangerous quagmire.

Twayblade nodded in their direction. "Nothin' we can do about 'em now, chaps. Put up y'weapons."

Horrified, Tammo stood watching. Nearly all eight of the vermin were in over their waists. They shrieked and struggled, making the position worse for themselves, grabbing at one another as the bottomless ooze sucked them remorselessly down. One, a nimble ferret, pulled himself up onto a rotting log and managed to scramble along its length as his weight pushed it down. Behind him, his comrades, who had only their heads showing above the treacherous surface, yelled piteously to him.

"Rinkul, 'elp us, mate, do somethin', 'elp us!"

But the ferret was intent on saving only his own skin. Hauling himself upright, he streaked the length of the sinking trunk, flinging his body forward in an amazing leap. He landed in some bushes where the ground became firmer and ran off, hop-skipping wildly until he was clear of the main swamp. Turning, he watched, as did the hares, the remaining vermin gurgle horribly as the muddy depths claimed them for its own. Seconds later there was nought but a smooth gray-brown patch amid the green rotting vegetation to indicate where they had gone down. The ferret, Rinkul, turned and shrugged.

As he squelched his way off over the swamp's far side, Tammo noticed that he was twirling something.

A sick feeling swept over the already trembling young hare, and he fell down on all fours. Pasque was right beside him, wiping his face with some damp grass.

"Tamm, what is it? Are you wounded?"

Tammo's face seemed to have aged several seasons as he fought to stop shaking, muttering words at the ground in front of him.

Captain Twayblade assisted Pasque to pull the shivering hare upright. She cocked an eyebrow at the younger creature. "I say, can y'make out what he's chunnerin' on about, wot?"

Tears began brimming in Pasque Valerian's soft brown eyes. "Oh, Cap'n, he said that the ferret was carryin' Russa's stick!"

Twayblade sheathed her rapier, grim-faced. "Come on, Rock, we'd best get back to the Major, post haste. Stay with Tammo, young gel, take y'time bringin' him back, we'll go ahead. If y'see the others, tell 'em where we are."

The kindly Rockjaw Grang took off his tunic and draped it about Tammo's quivering shoulders. It was so large that it lapped his footpaws, but it was thick and warm. "There thou goes, sunshine, thee tek it easy now!" he said, patting Tammo's face.

It was full noontide when Pasque and Tammo made it back to the defile, accompanied by Sergeant Torgoch, Rubbadub, and Midge, whom they had met up with on the way. Perigord was seated in front of a fire, his right paw in a sling that held a large herbal pad to the shoulder. On seeing the Major, Tammo was able to say only one word.

"Russa?"

Perigord's normally languid face was pale and drawn as he nodded toward the cave. Breaking free of Torgoch and Pasque, the young hare staggered into the little chamber. A strange scene confronted him. Lieutenant Morio, with a bandage 'round his face that ran beneath his chin and ended in a bow between his ears, was nursing a tiny badger. Looking for all the world like an old harewife, he placed a paw to his lips.

"Sshh! I've just got him t'sleep!"

In a corner there was a still form, covered by a ragged homespun blanket. Close to it, Russa, also wrapped in a cloak, was sitting with her back against the sandstone wall. Tammo gave a deep sigh as he sat down next to his squirrel friend.

"Whew! Thank the seasons you're alive, mate!"

Russa blinked slowly through clouded eyes. "Not for long, young 'un. They hit me good this time—two arrows an' a spear. But I gave good as I got, sent a few of 'em along in front t'pave the way for me."

Tammo put a paw around the squirrel's narrow shoulders. "Russa, don't talk like that. You'll be all right, honest, you will!"

Russa Nodrey smiled, coughed a little, then swallowed as if clearing her throat. She took Tammo's free paw, saying, "None o' your nonsense now, sit still an' lissen t'me, Tamm. Tell yore mama I did the best I could, an' if y'see Osmunda again, tell 'er I sent my regards. Make yore family proud of you, Tamello De Fformelo Tussock, never do anythin' you'd be ashamed to tell 'em. One other thing: you don't 'ave to be a Long Patroller if'n y'don't want to. Mebbe there's other things y'do better."

Russa stayed Tammo's reply by squeezing his paw feebly. "Oh, I've seen you fight, Tamm, yore one o' the best, but you've 'ad a different upbringin'. You ain't no slayer like those hares out there—at Salamandastron they're brought up to it."

Tammo tried to choke back the tears that fell on Russa's paw. "You'll be fine, matey. I'll tell Pasque to get all her medicines an' herbs an' we'll . . ."

Russa managed to wink at him. "Medicines an' herbs won't do me no good now, Tamm. I wish you'd stop soakin' me paws an' carryin' on like that. I've got other places t'go, I've always been a wanderer, so I wants t'see what 'tis like on the sunny hillsides by the still meadows. . . ."

Outside the hares sat listening as Major Perigord related what had happened.

"Russa an' meself were scoutin' ahead when we heard roarin' an' screamin'. Of course it wasn't the vermin doin' the noisemakin'. We reckoned 'twould be innocent creatures captured by those villains, so we'd no choice except to try an' rescue 'em. On m'word, we ran straight into it! Thirty-odd assorted blackguards, tormentin' an' torturin' an old badgerwife an' a babe. Scoundrels! We gave 'em a taste or two o' their own medicine, I can tell you! Trouble was that we were outnumbered by about eighteen t'one—they'd slain the old badger. Well, we fought 'em off best as we could an' I pulled the poor dead ol' badger into the cave with the little 'un still clinging to her. Russa was protectin' my back, that's when she took two arrows. Then we turned and tried to hold 'em off, shoutin' Eulalias like nobeast's business, hopin' you chaps'd hear us. Sadly Russa took a spear through her middle, so I bundled her in the cave with the badgers. That's when I got the lance in me shoulder, took another few slashes too. Just look at me best green velvet tunic. Good job you arrived when y'did. I was about ready to go under. By the by, did y'get 'em all?''

Twayblade took the tunic from her brother's shoulders and inspected it. ''Ripped t'bits, be a long time before you get another like it. Ah, the vermin. Yes, they split up, but so did we, got 'em all barring one, a ferret, he escaped through a swamp. I shouldn't think a lone villain would bother the Redwallers a good deal, wot?''

Sergeant Torgoch poured himself hot mint tea from the canteen by the fire. ''Don't think 'e would, marm. Some o' those big otters that 'angs about the Abbey'd be only too glad to accommodate 'im, if'n 'e showed 'is nose 'round there.''

Tammo came walking from the cave, dry-eyed and stone-faced.

''Russa Nodrey has just died, sah.'' His voice trembled as he tried to be a soldier worthy of the Long Patrol, but tears streamed down his face.

Perigord closed his eyes tightly and stood, head bowed.

That night they sealed up the cave with earth and rock. On the front of the pile, Rockjaw Grang placed a huge flat slab, which Tammo and Pasque had worked on, scraping deep into the sandstone with knifepoints a simple message:

> Russa Nodrey and an unknown badger lie within.
> They died fighting for freedom against cruelty.
> Seasons may pass, but we will remember them.

The baby badger slept on, between Pasque and Tammo, wriggling in his slumbers to get closer to them. Tammo had never seen a badger before; he stroked the infant, glad to have a creature near who knew nothing of killing and war before that day.

26

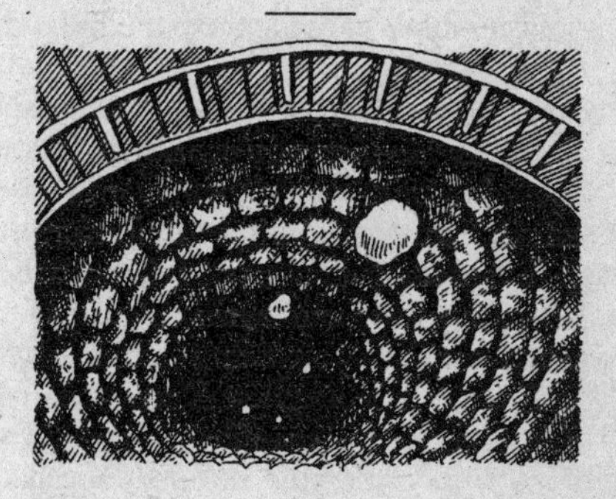

Beneath the Abbey's south wall, Foremole Diggum and his team held the lanterns out over the underground cavern. Holding on to the moles' digging claws, Tansy and Arven leaned out at the edge of the shored-up timber platform that the moles had built at the end of the small tunnel down which they had come. They peered down into the shadowy depths of what appeared to be a huge abyss, wide, dark, and mysterious.

Far below them water could be heard. Foremole tossed a turnip-sized boulder into the yawning chasm. They listened, but only silence followed.

Tansy turned to the solemn-faced mole leader. "Where has that rock gone to?" she asked.

Her question was followed by an echoing distant splash. Foremole shook his head gravely. "Daown thurr summwhurrs, marm, hurr, that'n be's a gurt deep 'ole."

They stood awhile, then Tansy backed off the platform gingerly. "Dear me, that's enough of that! It's like looking down from a high building and not seeing the ground. I was beginning to feel quite woozy!"

Foremole Diggum and his crew assisted her back to the

surface, offering his irrefutable mole logic as he lit their way. "Urr, 'tis better feelin' woozed up on furm ground for gennel beasts such as ee, marm. Oi thinks us'n's be 'appier talkin' abowt et all in ee Abbey, thurr be things oi've gotter say regardin' yon gurt 'ole!"

Intrigued by Foremole's words, they all followed him indoors.

On entering the Abbey, Tansy walked straight into a dispute that had broken out in the kitchens. Amid much paw-wagging and whisker-twitching, the Abbess placed herself between the dormouse Pellit and a sturdy squirrel called Butty, whom Mother Buscol was training in the ways of the kitchen. Both creatures argued fiercely, glaring truculently at each other.

"I won't be able to get on with me work, she'll be in the way!"

"Work? Huh, when did *you* ever work? You spend half y'time sleepin' on empty veggible sacks by the back oven!"

"You young skipwaggle, keep a civil tongue in yer head when yore talkin' to elders'n'betters!"

"Listen, you might be older'n me, but we'll soon find out who's better if you call me a skipwaggle again!"

Tansy grabbed a copper ladle and struck it on a cooking pot with a resounding clang. "Silence, please, this instant! Now, one at a time. What's this all about? Pellit, you first."

The dormouse adopted an air of injured innocence. "Mother Abbess, all I said was that the bird shouldn't be allowed to live in our kitchens, 'taint right. For one thing, we need the space in that cupboard for storage, there's little enough room fer that down 'ere as it is . . ."

Tansy's hard stare and upraised paw halted Pellit. "You're speaking in riddles, sir. Butty, begin at the beginning!"

The young squirrel explained as best he could: "Well, marm, 'tis the owl Orocca. She's been lookin' 'round the Abbey for somewheres t'put her nest an' eggs. She searched high'n'low but nowheres suited her until she discovered our kitchens an' that big corner cupboard where we store apples. Anyhow, me an' Shad shifted her in there, owl, eggs'n'nest. Then before y'know it, old whinin' whiskers Pellit is moanin' an' complainin' an' reportin' the matter to Sister Viola."

Redwallers gave way as Tansy swept regally across to the

ıpboard. She opened the door and was confronted by the eat golden eyes of Orocca. The owl snuggled down right- ɔusly atop her nest on the middle shelf, and said, "Hmph! ou've already wrecked one homesite where I lived, now I ıppose you're going to eject me from this one?"

With a wry smile hovering on her lips, Tansy turned to ellit. "D'you know where an auger or a drill can be found?"

The dormouse answered her hesitantly, "Er, yes, marm, urrbowl an' Foremole Diggum keeps 'em in the wine cellars ɔr borin' bungholes in barrels, marm."

Tansy tapped the cupboard door. "Good! Then go and get ɔme form of drilling tool from them and bore lots of holes this door, so that our guest has plenty of fresh air to breathe her new home. Well, don't stand staring, Pellit, hurry along ɔw!"

Turning back to the owl, Tansy bobbed a small curtsy. "I ɔpe you'll be comfortable here. If you need anything at all, ıst ask. I'll detail Mother Buscol to take care of you; should ɔu want to leave your nest, I'm sure you'll be able to trust ɛr to keep an eye on the eggs until you return."

Orocca blinked rapidly, her head bobbing up and down. My thanks to you, Abbess. This will be a good warm home ɔr my eggchicks when they break shell. If any of your crea- ıres sees my husband, Taunoc, perhaps they would tell him here I am."

Craklyn, who had witnessed the quarrel, patted Tansy's paw dmiringly as they made their way down to Cavern Hole. Well, you took care of that wonderfully, but poor old Pellit's ɔt a face on him like a fractured tail. Did you see him?"

Tansy folded both paws into her wide habit sleeves. "Ac- ıally I'm glad Orocca caused that disturbance. For some time ɔw I've been thinking of making certain changes in the kitch- ıs. Mother Buscol is a bit old to be in charge of all the ɔoking, and young Butty is a good hardworking creature and fine cook. I think he'll make an excellent Friar given the ıance."

Craklyn agreed with Tansy, though she had reservations. What about Pellit? He's older and has worked in the kitchens ɔnger than Butty. Won't it cause bad feelings if you promote ıe young squirrel over the dormouse's head?"

But like a wise Mother Abbess, Tansy had a reason for everything she did concerning her beloved Redwall. "I don't think so, Craklyn. The trouble with Pellit is that he's fat, getting on in seasons, and of course he's a dormouse. That's why he's always nodding off in the warmth from the ovens. If I left him in the kitchen he'd injure himself someday. So I've decided that he shall be Viola Bankvole's new assistant—he's always chatting to her and hanging about the Infirmary, and the job's an easy one, so he'll have plenty of time to rest. Mother Buscol can look after Orocca and the eggchicks when they arrive. That way she'll be in the kitchens a lot to keep an eye on our new Friar, Butty."

Tansy spoke to Mother Buscol and Viola, and then to Butty and Pellit, before taking her seat in Cavern Hole. Everyone seemed happy with the new arrangements. Craklyn sat with the other creatures, very impressed with the know-how and wisdom the seasons had bestowed upon her old friend.

Word had passed around regarding the chasm beneath the outer south wall, and now everybeast was familiar with the news. Arven opened the discussion.

"So now we know what was causing the wall to collapse. I suppose the continuous action of the water wore the ground away and formed the big hole. What d'you think, Diggum?"

"Well, zurr, oi thought the same as ee at furst. But me'n'moi moles, we h'explored ee sides o' the gurt 'ole, an' guess wot? Us'n's found that part o' ee sides o' yon pit wurr square stones. Aye, they'm been builded thataway boi summbeasts long gone, hurr!"

This announcement caused a buzz of speculation. Tansy hid her surprise and silenced the gossip.

"One moment, please! Thank you. I was about to say that this casts a whole new light on things, but it only seems to deepen the puzzle. Let us not get carried away with wild speculation, friends. Has anybeast a sensible suggestion to offer?"

Skipper of Otters ventured an idea. "Supposin' me'n'my crew put some long ropes together an' went down there tomorrer, marm. We might find where all that water's flowin' to, an' who knows wot else?"

The mole Bunto scratched his nosetip with a hefty digging

claw. "Gudd idea, zurr, an' may'ap ee'll take a lukk at ee carvens on yon stones."

Foremole Diggum donned a tiny pair of glasses and peered over the top of them at Bunto. "Yurr, ee never told oi abowt no carven on walls!"

Bunto smiled disarmingly, saying, "Probberly 'cos you'm never arsked oi, zurr!"

Foremole took Bunto's answer quite logically. "Hurr, silly o' me. No matter, next toim oi'll arsk ee!"

That seemed to settle the matter. Tansy looked around the assembly. "Right then, Skipper and his crew will look into it tomorrow. Any more questions, suggestions, or business? Good, then I'm off to my bed. It's been a long day."

An amazingly cultured voice rang out from the doorway: "Excuse me, I do beg your pardon for interrupting, but does anybeast know the whereabouts of an owl named Orocca, last seen perched on a nest containing three eggs?"

A trim and very dignified-looking male Little Owl opened the door wide and bowed courteously to the Redwallers. Tansy had long ago given up being surprised by anything; she simply returned his bow with a polite nod of her head.

"Ah, I take it your name is Taunoc, sir. Welcome to Redwall Abbey. This is our Foremole, Diggum, he will take you to your wife. Main kitchen, far corner, right in the apple cupboard. You'll probably find a dormouse there drilling holes. If he disturbs you, then please send him away."

The Little Owl bowed once more. "My thanks to you, marm. I bid you a pleasant good night!"

When he had departed with Foremole, there was a moment's silence. Then both Tansy and Craklyn burst into helpless laughter. "Whoohoohoo! Oh, hahahaha! Great seasons, did you see the face on him, and such beautiful manners. Heeheehee! Oh, dear, what next?"

Craklyn widened her eyes and did a perfect imitation of Taunoc. " 'Last seen perched on a nest containing three eggs?' Hahahaha!"

Tansy rose, supporting herself weakly on the chair arm. "Heeheehee! No more business! No more questions! No more anything, please! I need my bed! Oh, whoohoohoohaha! Sorry!"

Leaning against each other, Recorder and Abbess left Cavern Hole, tears streaming down their faces as they giggled and whooped.

Bunto looked blankly at Drubb. "Hurr, oi'm glad they'm 'appy, b'aint you?"

"Burr aye, but wot they'm a larfin' anna chucklen at oi doant know. 'Twas on'y summ owlybird a looken furr 'is missus."

Gradually the spring night cast its spell over Redwall. Lanterns flickered, fires guttered, and a stray draft moved the tapestry in Great Hall before passing on. All was peaceful, calm, from dormitory to cellars.

Beneath the south wall, far down in the stygian gloom of the chasm, something moved. Something cold, slippery, and long . . . Something moved.

27

awn's half-light was barely peeping over windowsills when
ıe young squirrel Butty pounded on Tansy's bedroom door.
ulling the coverlet over her head, Tansy complained in a
leep-muffled moan, "Go 'way, 'taint light yet, I've only just
losed my eyes!"

But the new Friar persisted, thumping the door and shout-
ng, "Mother Abbess, marm, new owlbabes have arrived in
ur kitchens! Oh, please come quick, I dunno what t'do!"

Tansy's footpaws found her old slippers as she threw on a
ressing gown and dashed to the door.

"Rouse Sister Viola, Mother Buscol, and Craklyn, and
ring 'em straight down to the kitchens. Go quickly and try
ot to waken the others!"

Completely in a dither, Butty raced off, yelling aloud, "Owl
abies! Just arrived in the kitchens! New little 'uns!"

Abbess Tansy peered around the half-open cupboard door.
rom beneath Orocca's fearsome talons, three sets of massive
olden eyes stared unblinkingly back at her. All of Redwall,
lad in a variety of nightshirts, tasseled caps, dressing gowns,
ld sandals, and slippers, packed into the kitchens, hopping

up and down eagerly to catch a glimpse of the new arrivals.

Mother Buscol complimented the owl on her eggchicks: "My my, wot beautiful liddle birds. They've got yore eyes, too!"

A brief smile flitted across Orocca's solemn features. "Thank you, Buscol. These are my first brood, and I'm glad they're all fit and well. My husband, Taunoc, will be pleased, when he eventually gets to see them."

Craklyn raised her eyebrows in surprise. "Taunoc hasn't seen his babes yet? Where is he?"

Orocca lifted her talons, allowing the chicks to stumble forward. "Poor Taunoc was in a worse tizz than that young squirrel of yours. The moment he heard eggshells cracking he took off in a fluster, muttering about hunting to feed five beaks now. He'll be back."

The little owls were mere fuzzballs, with eyes practically larger than their bodies. When they were not dumbling and stumbling to stay upright, they were huddling together to keep their balance. Orocca knocked the door open wide with a sweep of her wing.

Now all the Redwallers could see the three chicks clearly, there were exclamations of delight, particularly from the Dibbuns, whom Skipper and his otters had lifted onto their shoulders so they could get a clear view.

"Burr, can they'm owlyburds coom out t'play with us'n's?"

"Why don't they say noffink yet?"

" 'Ello, likkle owlyburds, d'you want some brekkfist?"

Viola Bankvole, keeping a safe distance from Orocca, took charge. "A sensible idea, why don't we all go in to breakfast and leave Orocca to clean up her nest?"

Viola and Tansy ushered the crowd out, while Mother Buscol and Gurrbowl Cellarmole stayed behind to help the owls.

Skipper of Otters whacked his tail down hard upon the tabletop. "Stow the gab now, mateys, yore Abbess wants a word!"

Nodding thanks to Skipper, the Abbess tucked paws into her dressing-gown sleeves and stood to address the Redwallers. "Listen carefully now—this won't take long. Summer's nearly here, 'tis a beautiful day outside, so here's my plan. I say we cancel all work and worries until tomorrow, and let today be one of feasting and celebration for the three little lives that have arrived into our Abbey. A triple birthday party out in the orchard!"

Cheers of joy rang to the rafters of Great Hall.

Brother Ginko was Redwall's Bellringer. Today he didn't stand below and pull on the ropes; instead, he climbed the stairs to the steepletop chamber, stood on the beams between the two bells, and operated them by pushing with both paws. The warm brazen sounds rang out over Mossflower.

Larks took to the meadow air, and woodland birds fluttered out over the green tree canopy, adding their morning songs to the bell tones rising into a bright sunlit sky.

Below in the line of trees skirting the east ramparts, a furtive figure slunk close to the wall's edge. Rinkul the ferret, last of the vermin band being pursued by the hares, fled south along the woodland edge. Dried swamp mud clung to his matted fur as he hurried on, chewing roots and berries and casting fearful glances backward. Rinkul hoped the bells were not ringing to denote that he had been spotted—he could see the figure of Brother Ginko framed against the open arches of the steeple chamber. He held still awhile, then, satisfied he had not been detected, Rinkul left the shelter of the Abbey wall to cut off over the south common lands, where he could see a stream that would provide him with drinking water.

With the sun warm upon his back and the bells booming in his ears, the ferret lay flat on his stomach, drinking greedily of the fresh stream water. After a while he rose into a crouch, checking that he was still alone. He stared hard and long at what he saw. It seemed incredible, but he trusted the evidence of his own keen sight. Redwall's battlemented south ramparts were collapsing. The line of high, thick masonry had been breached by the fall of a massive tree, and farther along, the wall dipped and leaned inward, as if messed about by some colossal paw.

Rinkul backed into the shallows, still staring at the fractured outer wall. Following the stream course southeast to hide his tracks, he tucked Russa Nodrey's hardwood stick into his belt.

"Got to find the Rapscallion armies," he muttered delightedly to himself. "This information'll make me an officer, a Rapmark!"

Brother Ginko had his back to the fleeing ferret. He shielded his eyes and stared hard at the two figures loping steadily down the path from the north toward the Abbey. Hares—it was two hares!

Halting the toll of one bell, he continued ringing the other singly, warning of creatures approaching. Skipper and Shad came racing out of the Abbey, hard on the heels of Arven, who was belting on the great sword of Martin the Warrior.

The squirrel Champion cupped both paws around his mouth and yelled upward, "Strangebeasts on the path, Ginko?"

The Bellringer leaned outward, pointing. "Aye, two hares come out o' the north!"

The look of concern melted from Skipper's tough face, to be replaced by one of comic dismay. "Did you say 'ares, messmate? Lock up the vittles an' stan' by fer a famine, prepare to be eaten outta 'ouse'n'ome!"

Breaking cover from the woodlands, Tammo stared excitedly at the soaring towers and gables of the red sandstone building farther down the path. Pasque's voice at his side echoed both their thoughts.

"Golly, is that Redwall Abbey? 'Tis even bigger'n I thought it'd jolly well be. What a beautiful sight!"

Sergeant Torgoch kept his eyes ahead as he said, "None more luvverly, miss! Right, fall inter twos an' let's see us marchin' up there like Long Patrol an' not a bunch o' waddlin' ducks on daisy day! Chins up, chests out, shoulders back, tails twitchin' smartly! Keep up at the back there, Grang!"

The giant hare Rockjaw Grang was carrying the baby badger in a sling across his chest. He frowned at the Sergeant. "Beggin' thy pardon, Sarge, but could y'keep thy voice down? Sithee, ah've just gotten yon tyke asleep for his mornin' nap!"

Major Perigord, who was marching at the head of the column, smiled whimsically at the thought of Rockjaw as a nursemaid. "Don't fret, Rock. If Galloper Riffle an' Turry are already there, they'll have no shortage of blinkin' badgerminders t'take the little 'un off y'paws, then you can sit down to good ol' tuck-in with the rest o' the chaps, wot?''

A dreamy look crossed Rockjaw's face as he wiped a paw cross his lips. ''Redwall Abbey vittles, by 'eck, lead me to em!''

28

Abbess Tansy and Arven, with a deputation of otters and elders, stood in the open gateway to greet the Long Patrol. Captain Twayblade broke ranks to embrace the Abbess warmly.

"Mother Abbess, so good t'see you, old friend. You look wonderful!"

"Twayblade, what a lovely surprise. Welcome to our Abbey again!"

Old friends met old friends, and new ones were made as introductions flew thick and fast. The dashing hares of the Long Patrol were much admired by the Redwallers as they stood there chatting in the Abbey gateway, leaning on their weapons, smartly clad in their tunics, with medals and ribbons on display. Secretly, even the most humble Abbeydwellers wished they too could present such a picture—jolly, courteous, and kind, but feared by their enemies and totally perilous.

Major Perigord winked at Skipper. "What d'ye say, old lad, d'ye think everybeast here would like to march in with us, make a jolly good entrance, wot!"

Skipper stood smartly to attention at the Major's side. "Good idea, matey. Ahoy, form up in a line o' fours, let's ring our guests 'ome in style. Arven, Shad, up front 'ere with e'n'the Major. Great seasons, I wish we 'ad a band!"

Perigord drew his saber with a flourish and a rattle. "Your ord is my command, sah. Rubbadub, beat us in with your est drums, if y'would!"

Dibbuns whooped in delight and amazement as Corporal ubbadub milled about, waving his paws and setting up a dust nd a din.

"Baboom! Baboom! Baboombiddy boombiddy boom! rrrrrapadapdap! Drrrubbadubdub! Bababoom! Bababoom! ababoom!"

Cheering aloud and stamping their paws in time to the beat, e cavalcade marched across the lawns to the Abbey in fine ilitary style. Tammo and Pasque strode alongside Friar Butty nd the molebabe Gubbio, chatting animatedly. The young quirrel Friar had excellent news for them.

"You've arrived at a good time, friends. Today we're avin' a great feast to celebrate the birth of three liddle owl-hicks."

Pasque's normally soft voice was shrill with excitement. "I ay! Y'mean we're actually goin' t'be guests at a famous Red-vall feast?"

Gubbio grabbed her paw as he hop-skipped to Rubbadub's rums. "Ho aye, marm, ee'll 'ave such vittles'n'fun as ne'er fore!"

As soon as they were inside the Abbey, those hares who ad never visited Redwall were led off on a grand tour by a ang of eager Dibbuns. Other Redwallers went about their asks to prepare for the festivities, while Abbess Tansy and er elders retired to Cavern Hole with Perigord, Twayblade, ockjaw, and Torgoch.

The hares were offered light refreshments of candied fruits nd red-currant cordial as they exchanged news and informa-ion with their hosts. Tansy listened carefully to the account f the skirmish in the defile, shaking her head in sorrowful ewilderment at the death of Russa Nodrey, who had visited edwall many times in bygone seasons. When the tale was old, Rockjaw opened the sling, which he had held easily con-ealed beneath his tunic, and presented the Abbess with his recious burden.

"Sithee, marm, this is the babby. A grand likkle male an good as gold for company on a march, 'e is!"

Tansy could not wait to hold the tiny bundle. She placed a cushion in her lap and laid him on it. He was no more than a season old, hardly any age at all. Lying flat on his back, the babe yawned and opened his soft dark eyes as the Abbess inspected him. The badger's back was silver gray, and his chest and paws were velvety black. He had a moist brown nose and a snow-white head, sectioned by two thick black stripes running either side of the muzzle from whiskers to ears, covering both eyes.

Craklyn touched the upturned footpads. "Seasons of winter! Just look at the size of these paws! He's goin' to be big as an oak when he grows to full size!"

Tansy chuckled fondly as she tickled the babe's tiny white-tipped ears. "Welcome to Redwall Abbey, little sir, and pray what name do you go by?"

The baby badger held out his paws to her, growling, "Nunnee! Nunnee!"

"The little chap's said that several times," Major Perigord explained, "only word he seems t'know. We've surmised that it means Nanny, the old badger he was with. She was prob'ly his grandmother or nurse—'fraid we haven't a clue as to who his parents are. There was certainly no sign of them where we found him. Had there been two grown badgers with him, those vermin would've given the place a wide berth, wot!"

Foremole Diggum placed a honeyed hazelnut in the babe's paws, and immediately he began chewing the nut hungrily.

"Burr," said Diggum, " 'ee may be a h'orphan, but thurr b'aint nuthin' amiss wi'ee appetoit, no zurr!"

A bowl of creamy mushroom soup was sent for, and Tansy fed the babe while other matters were discussed. The Redwallers knew nothing of Rapscallions, nor had any other vermin been sighted in the region of late. Arven related the dangerous position of the Abbey's outer south wall and their plans to rebuild it.

By the time the discussions were near their close, the little badger had licked the soup bowl clean and gone back to sleep in the Abbess's lap. Major Perigord had listened pensively to e problems faced by Redwall and its creatures. He stood ruptly, having reached a decision.

"Well, chaps, my duty as Commanding Officer, Long Pa-ol, is pretty clear. Until your wall is rebuilt and the Abbey fe'n'secure once more, me an' my hares will guard Redwall ' patrol the area night and day. Couldn't do any less, wot! dy Cregga'd have me ears'n'tail if I didn't. So, marm, if u are willin' to accept us, me an' my troop are at service!"

Bowing low, Perigord presented his saber hilt-first to the bbess. Abbess Tansy touched the handle, signifying her ap-oval.

"My humble thanks to you, Major. I am sure that I speak r all Redwallers when I say that we are assured of safety by ur presence, and your gallant offer is warmly accepted!"

Foremole Diggum threw in a gem of mole logic: "Gudd! nen if you'n's be afinished usin' gurt long apportant words, ay'ap us'n's best go an' get ee feast ready, ho urr aye!"

idge Manycoats sucked his paw ruefully. "Huh, I've just en pecked by perishin' owlbabes!"

Chuckling, Friar Butty replaced the lid on a steaming pan. You must taste good to 'em, Midge. Come over 'ere an' lend paw. I'm showin' Tammo an' Missie Pasque how t'make ossflower Wedge."

Both hares were intrigued by the goings-on in Redwall's tchens; it made such a pleasant change from marching and ghting. Pasque had lined a rectangular earthenware dish with astry, which Butty was viewing approvingly.

"Well done, missie, we'll make cooks of you hares yet. ammo, are you ready with the first layer?"

Tammo wielded a ladle, enjoying himself immensely. Wot? I'll say I am. Now don't tell me, Butty, just watch is!" He spread the chopped button mushroom and grated arrot mixture on its pastry base, making sure it was level.

"There! Righto, Pasque, you an' Midge chuck in the next yer!"

Watched by the Friar, the two hares spread sliced white rnip and chopped leeks as a second layer. Then Butty placed third layer of diced potato and slivered white cabbage.

He winked at Tammo and stood back, wiping his paws on a cloth. "Go on then, Tamm, I'm not tellin' you what's next. 'tis up t'you."

Tammo took the lid off a panful of dark rich gravy. "Mmm. smells absolutely super duper! Stand clear, please!" He poured the gravy over the layered vegetables evenly, watching it soak through, pulling his paw back swiftly to avoid a slap with Butty's damp cloth.

"No takin' secret licks at the pan, or I'll tell yore Sergeant an' he'll have yore tail for supper, or wotever it is he does. C'mon now, take an end o' this cover each."

Gingerly they lifted a big pastry top between them and flopped it gently over the dish. Butty took a knife and trimmed it while Tammo and Midge crimped the edges. Pasque borrowed Butty's knife to cut a series of arrowhead slits in the center, then she brushed the top with a mixture of light vegetable oil and finely chopped spring onions.

The squirrel Friar shook their paws. "Well done, good effort for y'first Mossflower Wedge. Now, how long does it stand in the oven?"

Pasque and Tammo spoke out together, "Until it tells you it's done!"

"Right! And when's that?"

"When the crust is golden brown an' shiny, an' there's no more steam coming out of the slits in the middle!"

"Correct! See, I told you I'd make Redwall cooks out of you. Now, let's see how good y'are at makin' Abbey Trifle. . . ."

A single lantern had been left burning at the platform dug by the moles beneath the south outer wall. The pale light flickered, sending its radiance down into the depths of the darkened chasm, where it shone feebly on the spray-drenched stones by the rushing water. In the dim light, bunched wet scales glistened, savage rows of ivory-hued teeth showed briefly, and two slitted eyes filmed over. The creature had heard the furry creatures above, it had seen them, so it waited hungrily, knowing that sooner or later they would be descending into the gloomy rift. Coiling its sinister length around a rock to prevent it being swept away . . . it waited.

29

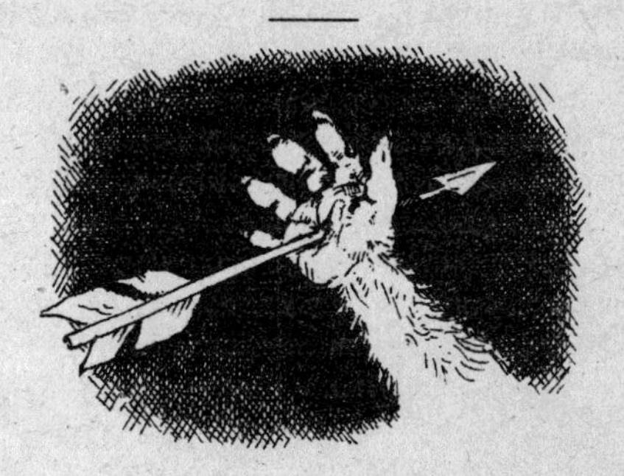

Sneezewort sat on the hillslope enjoying the mid-morning sunshine. In an old upturned helmet he was boiling up a broth of frogspawn and some stream vegetation on his fire. The rat watched his companion approaching, then turned his gaze upon the helmet, pretending to be engrossed with the task of cooking.

Lousewort came damp-furred and shivering. An enormous lump showed between his ears as he squatted by the fire to dry his shivering body.

Sneezewort spoke to his former companion without looking up. ''Thought yew was supposed ter be an officer gettin' punished.''

Lousewort peered hungrily at the mess bubbling in the helmet. ''Er, er, well, I ain't a ossifer no more, mate. Er, er, that looks good. I'm starvin'.''

Sneezewort stirred the broth with his dagger. ''Don't you 'mate' me, I ain't yore mate no more. Why aren't yer still stannin' up t'yer neck in chains inna river?''

The other rat shrugged noncommittally. ''Er, er, they all

escaped durin' the night, with Borumm an' Vendace, but I got left be'ind.''

''Left be'ind? Didn't yer wanna go wid 'em? Better'n freezin' yore tail off inna stream, I woulda thought.''

''Er, well, I got knocked over me 'ead an' left senseless.''

''Harr, harr! Wouldn't take much t'leave *you* senseless. Wot 'appened then?''

''Er, er, well, I woke up an' shouted the alarm. Lord Damug sent Skaup the ferret out wirra 'undred or more, to 'unt 'em down. Er, Lord Damug said t'me that at least I was loyal, stoopid but loyal 'e called me, an' 'e said that I wasn't fit ter be an ossifer an' told me I'd got me ole job back, servin' in the ranks. So 'ere I am, mate, we're back together, jus' me'n'you.''

Sneezewort snorted as he picked the helmet off the flames between two sticks and set it down by the fireside. ''Hah! So y'think yer can come crawlin' back t'me, eh? Where's all yer brother officers now, tell me that? An' anudder thing, don't think yore sharin' my vittles, slobberchops! Go an' get yore own, y'big useless gully-wumper!''

Lousewort sulked by the fire, looking hurt and touching the lump between his ears tenderly. Then, as if remembering something, he reached into his sodden garments and drew out a big dead gudgeon, its scales glistening damply in the morning sunlight.

''Er, er, I stood on this an' killed it when I jumped off the rock in the stream. D'yer think it'll be all right to eat?''

Sneezewort nearly knocked the helmet over as he grabbed the fish. ''Course it will, me ole mate. Tell yer wot I'll do, I'll shove it in wid this soup an' cook it up a bit on the fire, while you scout for more firewood, mate. You kin 'ave the 'ead'n'tail, those are the best bits, I'll 'ave the middle 'cos yew prob'ly damaged that part by jumpin' on it, mate!''

Lousewort rose, smiling happily. ''Er, er, then we're still mates?''

Sneezewort's snaggle-toothed grin smiled back at him. ''I was only kiddin' yer a moment back. We wuz always mates, me'n'you, true'n'blue! If yer can't find a spot by yer fire an' a bit t'spare for yer ole mate, then wot sorta mate are yer, that's wot I always says. You nip along now an' get the wood!"

Damug squatted at the water's edge, honing his swordblade against a flat piece of stone as he conveyed his orders to the Rapmark Captains.

"There's plenty of food and water here. We'll camp by this stream until they bring back Borumm and Vendace and the others. When they do I'll make such an example of them that no Rapscallion will ever even think of disobeying me again. Gaduss, we've got no scouts at present, so you take fifty with you and go north. I want you to do a two-day search in that direction, but if you find anything of interest before that, report back immediately."

The weasel Gaduss saluted with his spear. "It shall be done, Firstblade!"

Nearly a full day's journey up the same stream bank, the water broadened, running through two hills whose tops were fringed with pine and spruce trees. Log-a-Log, Chieftain of the Guosim shrews, was busily cleaning moss from the bottom of a beached and upturned logboat, assisted by another shrew called Frackle.

They paused to watch the other shrews fishing. Frackle wiped moss from her rapier blade, nodding toward them. "Lots o' freshwater shrimp in that landlocked stretch o' water," she said.

Log-a-Log ran his paw along a section of hull he had cleaned off. "Aye, freshwater mussels, too. Minnow an' stickleback were there in plenty last time I fished that part. Take a stroll over there, Frackle, easy like—an' don't look up at yonder hill on the other bank, we're bein' watched by some o' those thick-'eaded Rapscallion vermin who tried attackin' us yesterday."

Frackle sauntered away, murmuring casually, "Aye, I see the glint o' the sun on blades up in those trees at the 'illtop, Chief. What d'ye want me to do?"

The shrew Chieftain went back to cleaning his boat. "Just take things easy, mate. Tell the crews not t'look suspicious, pass the word to the archers t'drift back to their boats an' git their bows'n'arrers ready. We'll give those vermin a warm welcome if they comes down offa that 'ill an' tries crossin' the stream."

Panting and breathing heavily after their long run, Vendace, Borumm, and forty-odd Rapscallion fugitives lay flat among the trees on the hilltop, watching the shrews below.

Borumm stared at the packs that had been unloaded from the boats. "There ain't time fer us t'stop an' forage in this country. We needs those packs o' vittles if'n we're gonna circle an' make fer the sunny south."

One of the fugitives crawled up alongside the weasel. "Cap'n Borumm, those are the beasts that set on us. They kin fight like wolves wid those liddle swords o' theirs. Huh, you shoulda seen the way that ole Chief one finished off Hogspit!"

Vendace curled his lip at the vermin in a scornful sneer. "Stow that kinda talk, lunk'ead, yore with real officers now. Huh, 'Ogspit? I coulda put paid to 'im wid both paws tied be'ind me back. Bunch o' river shrews don't bother me'n'Borumm none, do they, mate? Phwaw! They're bakin' sumthin' down there, I kin smell it from 'ere. Mmmm! Biscuits, or is it cake?"

Borumm smiled wickedly at the fox. "Wotever it is we'll soon be samplin' it. Right, let's make a move. Keep 'idden climbin' down the 'illside, play it slow. I'll give the word ter charge if they spots us."

The shrewboats were all cleaned and anchored in the shallows. Log-a-Log and his shrews stood around the cooking fire, all acting relaxed, but keyed up for action.

"Scubbi, Shalla, take the archers an' use our boats fer cover. Spykel, Preese, get be'ind those big rocks wid yore sling team. Lead paddlers, stay back 'ere with me an' Frackle, ready to jump in the boats an' launch 'em. Those vermin are startin' downhill, too far out o' range yet. If we 'ave to make a run fer it, stay out o' midstream and use the current close t'this bank."

A rat named Henbit came running to the hilltop. His eyes took in the situation at one quick glance. Turning, he dashed back pell-mell to where the ferret Skaup was leading the main party at a run, hot on the tracks of the fugitives.

Henbit dashed up and threw a hasty salute. "Borumm an' Vendace straight ahead, Cap'n! They've jus' left that 'illtop to cross the stream an' attack those shrews!"

Skaup acted quickly. "You there, Dropear, take fifty an' run on ahead. Don't go up the 'ill, go 'round it—come at 'em along the shore. I'll take the rest an' make for the shore from 'ere, that way we'll get 'em between us. Never mind the shrews, we're 'ere to bring those traitors back, not to fight wid a gang o' boatmice. Get goin'!"

Vendace and Borumm were almost down the hill when the fox whispered to his partner, "D'yer think they've seen us? I coulda swore I saw the ole one lookin' over this way once or twice."

Borumm waved his paw to the vermin scrabbling downhill, urging them to move a bit faster. "Nah, if'n they'd seen us we'd 'ave known by now, mate. Best stop our lot when we reach the stream bank, that way we can all charge together. That water looks pretty shallow t'me."

It took more time than Vendace liked for the last vermin to get down off the hill onto the shore. He fidgeted impatiently, conveying his anxiety to Borumm. "All of a sudden I don't like this, mate. Those shrews gotta be blind if they ain't seen us by now. Lookit our lot too, barrin' for me an' you an' a couple o' others, there's scarce a decent blade between us—they're mostly armed wid chunks o' wood or stones."

The weasel glared bad-temperedly at the fox. "Fine time ter be tellin' me you've got the jitters. Wot's the matter, mate, don't you think we kin take a pack o' scruffy shrews? Straighten yerself up! Come on, you lot. *Chaaaaaarge!*"

Bellowing and roaring, they made it into the shallows—then they were besieged on three sides. Log-a-Log and his Guosim loosed arrows and slingstones across the water. The charging line faltered a second under the salvo, then they were hit by the forces of Dropear and Skaup coming at them from both sides. It was a complete defeat for Vendace and Borumm's vermin.

"Stay yore weapons, Guosim," Log-a-Log called to his

shrews, "this isn't our fight no more. But stand ready to bring down any vermin tryin' to cross the stream!"

The fugitives could run neither forward nor sideways. Some tried running back uphill, where they made easy targets for arrow and lance. The remainder, knowing what fate would await them at the paws of Damug Warfang, fought desperately, trying to break free and run anyplace.

Across the stream the shrews sat in their logboats, paddles poised as they watched the awful carnage.

Frackle averted her eyes, as if she could not bear to watch. "They're from the same band. Some of those creatures must've fought together side by side. How can they do that to one another?"

Log-a-Log watched the slaughter through narrowed eyes. "They're vermin, they'd kill their own families for a crust!"

There were only ten of the original fugitive band left alive—the rest lay floating in the stream or draped on the hillside. Skaup grinned evilly at Borumm as he noosed his neck to the others, forming them into a line. "Firstblade Damug'll be well pleased to see you an' the fox safe back under 'is paw, weasel."

Bound paw and neck, the prisoners tottered painfully along the shore, driven by spearbutts and whipped with bowstrings. Skaup turned to stare across the stream at the Guosim sitting in their logboats. "You got off light t'day, but you've slain Rapscallions. We'll settle with you another day!"

Log-a-Log's face was impassive as he picked up a bow and sent an arrow thudding into Skaup's outstretched paw. "Aye, we've slain Rapscallions, an' we'll slay a lot more unless you get gone from this place. I warn ye, scum, next time I draw this bowstring the arrow won't be aimed at yore paw. Archers ready!"

Guosim bowbeasts stood up in the logboats, setting shafts to bowstrings, awaiting their Chieftain's next command.

Skaup's face was rigid with agony. He looked at the shrew shaft transfixing his paw and the Guosim with bows stretched, and slunk off, his voice strained with pain and anger as he yelled, "We'll meet again someday, I swear it!"

A ribald comment echoed across the stream waters at his

back: "Be sure t'bring that arrow with ye, 'twas a good shaft!"

Skaup was close to collapse when he made it back to his party. Dropear threw a paw of support around his shoulders. "Siddown, Cap'n, an' I'll dig that thing outta yore paw."

The ferret pushed him roughly aside and staggered onward. "Not here, fool. Let's get out o' sight farther down the bank!"

Log-a-Log and his shrews stood watching them until they were behind a curve in the stream course. The shrew leader stroked his short gray beard. "Hmm, what we saw 'ere t'day tells me somethin', mates. If they could afford to slay more'n thirty o' their own kind, then there must be more of 'em than I thought—a whole lot more! Right, let's get these craft under way midstream, where the current runs swift. Watch out for a weepin' willow grove on yore port sides. We'll take the back waterways an' sidecut off to Redwall Abbey. I think I'd best warn 'em there's trouble comin'."

30

Algador Swiftback cast a fleeting glance backward as he marched on into the gathering evening. "Whew! I say, we've covered a fair old stretch today. Salamandastron's completely out o' sight!"

Drill Sergeant Clubrush's voice growled close to his ear. "The mountain might be out o' sight, laddie buck, but I'm not! No talkin' in the ranks there, keep pickin' those paws up an' puttin' 'em down. Left right, left right, left right . . ."

More than five hundred hares of the Long Patrol, some veterans but mainly new recruits, tramped eastward into the dusk, with Lady Cregga Rose Eyes, axpike on shoulder, always far ahead.

The lolloping young hare named Trowbaggs still had difficulty in learning to march properly. He put his left paw down when everybeast was on their right, and vice versa, and for the umpteenth time that day he stumbled, treading on the footpaws of the hare marching in front.

"Oops! Sorry, old chap, the blinkin' footpaws y'know, gettin' themselves mixed up again, right left, right left . . ."

Deodar shook her head in despair as she watched him.

"Trowbaggs, y'great puddenhead, it's left right, not right left!"

Clubrush's stentorian voice rang out over the marchers: "Long Patrol—halt! Stand still everybeast—that means you too, Trowbaggs, you 'orrible liddle beast!"

Thankfully, the marching lines halted, standing to attention until the order was given.

"First Regiment, stand at ease! Water an' wood foragers fall out! Duty cooks, take up chores! Lance Corporal Ellbrig, pick out yore sentries for first watch! The remainder of you, lay out y'packs an' groundsheets, check all weapons an' arms! Four neat rows now, clear away any nettles an' prickles over there—that's yore campsite for tonight, you lucky lot!"

Hares dashed hither and thither on their various duties as Sergeant and Lance Corporal roared out orders. In a short time, military precision resulted in camp being set up.

Algador sat with his companions by the shallows of a small pond, everybeast cooling off their footpaws and resting on their packs.

Furgale lay flat on his back, complaining to the stars: "Oh, my auntie's bonnet! I thought ol' Clubrush was goin' to march us all bally night. Look, there's steam risin' out of the water where I'm dippin' me pore old paws!"

The Sergeant's tone was almost an outraged squeal. "Get those dirty great sweaty dustridden paws out o' that water! It's for drinkin', not sloshin' about in. Trowbaggs, what'n the name o' seasons are you up to, bucko?"

"Wrappin' m'self up in me groundsheet, Sarge. Good night!"

Veins stood out on the Sergeant's brow as he roared at the hapless blunderer, "Sleepin'? Who said you could sleep, sah? Get that equipment cleaned, lay out yore mess kit, line up for supper! Forget sleep, Trowbaggs, stay awake! Yore on second watch!"

Trowbaggs groaned aloud as he searched in the dark for his mess kit. "Somebeast's pinched me flippin' spoon. Oh, mother, I want to go home. Save me from all this, I wasn't cut out for it, wot!"

"Never mind, scout," a kindly older hare named Shangle Widepad whispered to him, "it gets worse before it gets jolly well better. Here, I'll swap with you. I'm on first watch. You do it and I'll take second sentry for you, that way you'll be able t'get a full night's sleep.''

When the camp had quieted down and was running smoothly, Clubrush went to sit beside Lady Cregga at the pond's far side. She looked up from polishing her axhead and asked, ''How are they doing, Sergeant?''

''Oh, they'll shape up, marm, never fear. First day's always the longest for the green ones. P'raps if we don't march 'em as 'ard an' far tomorrer . . .''

The rose eyes glinted dangerously. ''They'll learn to march twice as hard and fast, aye, and fight like they never imagined before I'm done with them. I never brought them along on any picnic, and the sooner they realize that the better. Dismissed, Sergeant Clubrush!''

The Sergeant stood to attention and saluted. ''Aye, marm, thank ye, marm!''

Clubrush went to where his equipment was neatly laid out. Somebeast had carefully folded his groundsheet so that he could retire immediately without making it up into a sleeping bag. Being an old campaigner, the Sergeant upset the sheet with his pace stick. A pile of nettles and some soggy bank sand flopped out on the ground.

He lay down on the clean dry part of the sheet and shouted, ''Oowow! Who put this lot in me bed? You 'orrible rotten lot, I'll march yore blatherin' paws to a frazzle in the mornin'!''

Smothered giggles sounded from the recruits' area. Sergeant Clubrush smiled as he settled down. They were good young 'uns; he'd do all he could to help them make the grade.

Obeying Damug's orders, Gaduss the weasel had scouted north with his patrol all day, reaching the southern edge of Mossflower Wood by nightfall. He allowed no fires to be lit in the small camp set up at the outer tree fringe. The night passed uneventfully.

In the hour before dawn, the scouts broke camp and pressed on. They had not been traveling long when the weasel gave a signal. Dropping flat in a patch of ferns, the vermin patrol watched Gaduss wriggle forward. Through the mist-wreathed tree trunks a silent figure moved, seeking shadows between shafts of dawn light.

Gaduss unlooped from his belt a greased strangling noose fashioned from animal sinew. Winding it around both paws, he inched forward until he was shielded by an ash tree, directly in the traveler's path. Timing it just right, he leapt out behind the unwary creature and whipped the noose over his head and 'round his neck.

Rinkul was fortunate in that it also looped over the stick he was carrying. In panic, he pushed outward with the piece of polished hardwood, preventing the sinew from biting into his windpipe.

Both beasts went down, rolling over and over in the loam, kicking, snapping, and scratching at each other. The vermin broke cover and dashed to assist their officer, tearing the fighting duo apart. Seconds later the two were face-to-face, Gaduss wide-eyed with surprise.

"Rinkul, wot'n the name o' blood'n'claws are you doin' 'ere?"

The ferret massaged his neck where the noose had bruised it. "Findin' me way back ter Gormad Tunn an' the army. Nice reception yer gave me, mate, 'arf choked me ter death!"

Gaduss stuffed the noose back into his belt. "You 'aven't 'eard, then. Gormad's dead, so is Byral, 'tis Damug Warfang who's Firstblade of Rapscallions now. Where've y'been?"

Rinkul sat down on a rotting stump. "Been? That's a long story, mate. Our ship was driven off course an' wrecked up near the northeast coast. I've been through a lot o' things an' I'm the onlybeast left alive out o' a shipload. But that's by the by. Get me ter Damug Warfang, I've got news fer 'is ears alone—urgent news!"

31

In the orchard of Redwall Abbey the tables for the owlchicks' feast had been laid. Friar Butty supervised his helpers 'round a firepit, over which the hot dishes were being kept at a good temperature. Apple, pear, and plum blossoms were shedding their petals thickly on the heads of the feasters. It was a joyous sight.

The three owlchicks sat on cushions inside an empty barrel alongside their mother's place at the table; the badgerbabe lay in an old vegetable basket lined with sweet-smelling dried mosses. Tammo and Pasque sat together, with Arven and Diggum Foremole on either side of them. Mother Abbess Tansy occupied her big chair, which had been specially carried out. She looked very happy, clad in a new cream-colored habit, belted with a pale green girdle cord. The Dibbuns had made her a tiara of daisies and kingcups, which she wore proudly, if a little lopsidedly, on her headspikes.

Good Redwall food had the tables almost bent with its weight. Rockjaw Grang grabbed spoon and fork in a businesslike way. Gurrbowl Cellarmole nodded to him as she and Drubb rolled a barrel of October Ale up to its trestle. "Hurr, ee lukk ready t'do a speck o' dammidge to yon vittles, zurr!''

Sergeant Torgoch eyed a large spring salad longingly. ''You'll 'scuse me sayin', marm, but 'e ain't the only one 'ereabouts who's lived on camp rations fer a season, eh, Rubbadub?''

The fat hare's smile matched the sun in the sky. ''Rubbity dubdub boomboom!''

Abbess Tansy nodded politely to the Major. ''As our guest, sir, perhaps you'd like to say the grace?''

Perigord's mouth was watering furiously, but he wiped his lips on a kerchief and drooped an elegant ear in Tansy's direction. ''Quite, er, thank ye, marm!''

''Thanks to seasons an' jolly good luck,
We've all got a sword an' a head,
An' the way we'll tuck into these vittles
Will show that we're living, not dead.''

''Haharrharr!'' Shad the Gatekeeper chortled. ''Short'n'sweet, that's 'ow I likes it, mate. Dig in!''

Everybeast did so with a will. Redwallers had no strict rules about dining: sweet was as good as salad to start, stew as acceptable as cake, and all shared the feast with one another.

''Here, mate, try some o' this plum slice with black-currant sauce!''

''Whoi thankee, zurr mate, may'ap you'm aven summ o' moi deeper'n ever turnip'n'tater'n'beetroot pie. Hurr—that be th'stuff!''

''Mmmm! Well, what d'you think of our Mossflower Wedge, eh, Pasque?''

''Excellent. I never knew I was such a jolly good cook, wot!''

''I say, this Abbey Trifle is absoballylutely top hole!''

''Just give me good ol' fresh crusty bread an' ripe yellow cheese, oh, with some o' these tangy pickles, an' a plate o' salad, an' maybe some stuffed mushrooms. Put that fruitcake on the side, I'll deal with it later. More October Ale, please!''

''Damson an' gooseberry pudden with meadowcream, that's f'me!''

"Ahoy, Dibbun, drink any more o' that strawberry fizz an' you'll go bang!"

"Awright den, me go bang. Ooh, likkle berryfruit tarts, me like 'em!"

Taunoc dropped in and peered at the owlchicks in their barrel, saying, "Goodness, what handsome chicks. I think they resemble me strongly."

"Wot a pity," a raucous voice called out. "Shame they don't look more like yore missus, hahaha!"

The Little Owl sniffed pityingly. "There speaks a beast with all his taste in his mouth."

"Have you decided on names for the little ones yet, marm?" the Abbess called across to Orocca.

Orocca took her beak out of a hazelnut turnover long enough to reply, "Owls never name their eggchicks. They'll tell us their own names once they are ready to speak."

Tansy gave her a charming nod and a smile, then, pulling a wry face, she turned to Craklyn. "Oops, excuse me for asking, but what about our badgerbabe? We're going to need a name for him soon. Anybeast come up with a good idea yet?"

Craklyn paused from her rhubarb and maple crumble. "D'you see the giant hare over there, the one they call Rockjaw? Well, I think he's thought up a name for the little fellow."

At their request, Rockjaw emerged from behind a pair of platters piled high with salad, bread, cheese, cake, and pasties and wiped his mouth daintily on the tablecloth hem. "By 'ecky thump, marms, there's only one thing better'n food—*more* food! Sithee, I've dubbed yon likkle tyke well. 'E's to be named Russano."

Captain Twayblade nodded her agreement. "Aye, 'tis a good strong name. Russa Nodrey saved his life, so her name'll live on in the badger. 'Twas clever of ol' Rock, really, he took Russa's first name an' the first two letters of her second. Russano, I like it. Here's to Russano!"

Everybeast raised their drinks to toast the babe's new name.

"Russano! Good health, long seasons!"

"May he always remember his pretty ol' nurse, Rockjaw Grang!" Lieutenant Morio added, then ducked quickly beneath the table as Rockjaw picked up a pie.

"Ah've never struck a h'officer wi' an apple an' red-currant pie afore, but there's allus a first time, 'tenant Morio!"

Amid the general laughter, Craklyn got up and sang an old Abbey birthing song.

"O here's to the little ones,
Sunshine on all,
As we grow old'n'small,
May they grow tall,
Not knowing hunger or winter's cold bite,
Fearing no living thing, by day or night,
Strong in the heart, and sturdy of limb,
Making us proud to know of her or him.
Here's to the life we love, honest and new,
Grant all these hopes and dreams come true,
With each fresh dawn may joy never cease,
Long seasons of happiness and peace!"

Perigord thumped the tabletop with his tankard. "Splendid, well sung, marm! Long Patrol, let us honor little Russano in Salamandastron style. Draw steel!"

Tammo was not sure what to do, though he felt privileged to be part of the hares' brief ceremony. Pulling forth his blade, he held it flat over the vegetable basket like the rest. Gazing solemnly up through a crisscross of deadly steel, the badgerbabe watched Major Perigord as he intoned:

"We are the Long Patrol, these are our perilous blades,
Pledged to your protection across all the seasons,
Our lives are yours, your life is ours.
Eulaliaaaaaaaaa!"

"Blister me barnacles, mate," Skipper of Otters whispered to Arven. "I felt the fur rise all along me back when those warriors shouted their battle cry!"

The Champion of Redwall smiled. "Aye, me too, but did y'see the little Russano? He never batted an eyelid. He'll grow to be a cool 'un, I wager."

"I've heard that hares can't sing," Ginko the Bellringer called out. "Is that right?"

Pasque Valerian threw a paw across Rubbadub's shoulders. "An' where pray did y'hear that, sir? Everybeast up on y'paws an' form two rings, one inside the other. One ring goes left, the other circles right. Midge, Riffle, you show 'em. Rubbadub, you beat time an' I'll do the singin'. 'Hares on the Mountain.' "

Whooping and leaping, the hares gripped their Redwall partners' paws.

" 'Hares on the Mountain,' beat it out good'n'fast!"

Rubbadub grinned massively, striking up his drum noises. "Rubbity dubbity dumbaradum, rubbity dubbity dumbaradum . . ."

Both circles began moving counter to each other with the beat, at every third step banging both paws down hard and doing a double clap. Soon the Redwallers had the hang of it. When the circles were moving to Pasque's satisfaction, she sang out loud and speedy:

" 'O mother, dear mother, O mother come quick,
Calamity lackaday bring a stout stick,
There's hares on the mountain, they're all rough'n'big,
A cuttin' up capers an' dancin' a jig!

They wear rusty medals an' raggy old clothes,
There's one with an apple stuck fast to his nose,
Another's got seashells all tied to his back,
There's hares on the mountain alas an' alack!'

'O daughter, my daughter, now listen to me,
Such rowdy wild pawsteps I never did see,
Run into the house quick an' cover your eyes,
An' I'll give those ruffians such a surprise!'

A hare in a frock coat so fine an' so long
Scraped on a small fiddle an' banged a big gong,
He seized the poor mother an' gave a loud cry,
'Let's warm up our paws with a reel, you an' I!'

'O mother, sweet mother, oh may I look now?'
'Come stir y'stumps, daughter, an' look anyhow,'

As she whirled around the good mother did call,
'There's a handsome one here with no partner at all!

'So batter that drum well an' kick up your paws,
I'm reelin with mine an yore jiggin' with yours,
A leapin' an' twirlin' as cares fly away,
Those hares on the mountain can call any day!' "

All through the grounds of the Abbey, the warm sunny afternoon resounded with the joyous sounds of feasting and laughter. Sloey the mousebabe filled her apron pockets with candied nuts and dashed off with the other Dibbuns to play hide-and-seek.

Gubbio and the rest drew straws to see who would be denkeeper. A tiny hedgehog named Twingle drew the short straw. Covering his eyes with a dock leaf, he began counting aloud in baby fashion.

"One, three, two an' a bit, four, sixty, eight, three again, an' a five-seventy-nine . . ."

Squealing and giggling with excitement, the little creatures dashed off to hide before Twingle finished counting.

"Four, two an' a twelve, don't knows any more numbers, I'm a cummin' t'find youse all now!"

Back at the table the moles were broaching a great new cask of October Ale, singing uproariously along with the Redwallers, showing the Long Patrol hares what good voice they were in.

"October Ale, 'tis brewed when summer's done,
From hops'n'yeast an' barley fine,
With just a pinch of dandelion,
A smidgeon of good honey, a taste of elderflower,
An' don't forget the old wild oat
Culled at the dawn's first hour.

We puts it up in casks of oak,
All seasoned well with maple smoke,
Then lays it in cool cellars deep,
Ten seasons long to sleep.

October Ale, no drink so good'n'cheery
In winter by the fireside bright
To warm your paws the whole long night,
Or after autumn harvesting, to rest an' take your ease.
Just sip a tankard nice'n'slow,
With crusty bread an' cheese.

'Tis wholesome full an' hearty
For any feast or party.
We'd tramp o'er forest hill an' dale
For good October Ale!"

Gurrbowl wielded her mallet, knocking the spigot through the bung with a satisfying thud. Skipper and his otters lined up with tankards and beakers as the foaming dark brew splashed forth. Sergeant Torgoch brushed his bristling mustache with the back of a paw, smacking his lips and clunking beakers with Galloper Riffle as they sampled the new barrel's contents.

Torgoch placed a coaxing paw around the Cellarmole's shoulders, saying, "Wot d'ye say, marm, 'ow about comin' to be Head Cellar Keeper at Salamandastron? Just think of all those poor hares who ain't never tasted yore October Ale. Take pity on 'em, I beg yer!"

The molewife was so flustered by the compliment she threw her pinafore up over her face. "Hurr, go 'way, zurr, you'm a turrible charmer, but oi wuddent leave this yurr h'Abbey for nought, so thurr!"

With a twinkle in her eye, Abbess Tansy chided Torgoch: "Shame on you, Sergeant, trying to rob us of our Cellar Keeper! But seeing as you like Redwall's October Ale so much, here's what I propose. You may take as many barrels back to Salamandastron as you can carry."

Rockjaw Grang placed his paws around a barrel. Grunting and straining, he was barely able to move it. The Sergeant pulled a mock mournful face. "Thankee, marm, yore too kind, I'm sure!"

Suddenly, Twingle the hedgehog Dibbun came stumbling up to the table, waving his paws wildly and shouting, "Come a quick, 'urry 'urry!"

Arven picked him up and sat him on the tabletop. "Now then, you liddle rogue, what's all this noise about?"

Twingle struggled down from the table, yelling urgently, "We was playin' 'ide-seek an' Sloey falled down d'big 'ole!"

Shad the Gatekeeper lifted the Dibbun with one big paw. "What, y'mean the pit under the south wall, Sloey fell down there?"

Breathless and tearful the Dibbun nodded. "All a way down inta the dark she gone!"

Like a flash the otters and hares were away, running headlong with Arven leading them.

Sloey's fall was broken by the rushing waters far below. The swift current was about to whip her off into the bowels of the earth when suddenly she was plucked from the roaring torrent by her apron strings and flung up on the bank. Half conscious, the mousebabe struggled upright and screamed with fright as a coil, heavy and scale-covered, knocked her back down. Something licked her paw, and she caught the dreadful waft of stale breath, hot against her quivering nostrils. A long, satisfied sigh sounded close to her face.

"Aaaaaahhhhhhh!"

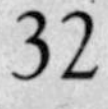

Tammo was with Arven, Perigord, and Skipper as they hurried onto the platform over the chasm. Shad could be heard calling behind them, "Stay back, too many'll collapse the platform! Stay back, mates!"

Grabbing a rope, Major Perigord knotted it through the carrying ring of the lantern left there by the moles. He swung the light out into the gorge, paying the rope out. Everyone leaned over the edge, peering down as the lantern illuminated the abyss.

Arven bellowed down, "Sloey, can you hear me? Sloey?"

A wail of terror drifted upward as the lantern traveled lower.

Perigord grabbed Skipper's paw. "Great thunderin' seasons! Look!"

A big yellow river eel was menacing the mousebabe on the bank, its brown back and muddy umber sides rearing up snakily, the gashlike downturned mouth open, revealing glittering teeth. It swayed slowly, as if savoring the anticipation of a meal, while its eyes, amber circles with jet-black center orbs, focused on the helpless mite.

Skipper wiped a nervous paw across his dry lips, calling

oarsely, "Keep quiet, liddle 'un! Stay still, don't move!"

Arven stared anxiously down at the horrendous scene. "Oh, nercy! What'll we do?"

Skipper of Otters acted swiftly. Grabbing the dirk from Tammo, he climbed up onto the rail of the platform. "I'll orrow yore blade, matey, speed's the thing now. One of you ollow me down by usin' the rope. Rescue the Dibbun an' get er back up 'ere. Can't stop t'chat, mates, 'ere goes!"

With the long knife between his teeth, Skipper dove head-irst into the gorge.

Something flashed by Sloey and landed in the water with a ooming splash. Instantaneously the big male otter surfaced nd bounded clear of the rushing stream. The eel was about o strike down on its prey when Skipper hurled himself on the oiling monster.

"Redwaaaaaaallllll!"

The eel struck, burying its teeth in the otter's shoulder and vhipping its coils around his body. Skipper had sunk his teeth nto the eel's back and was stabbing furiously with the dirk. Eel and otter went lashing and thrashing into the churning vaters, locked together in a life-and-death struggle. In a flash hey both were gone, swept away underground.

Arven and Perigord took hold of the rope together, but Tammo ducked between them and slid over the platform, linging to the rope.

"I'm lighter than you chaps. Stand by t'pull me up when I get the Dibbun!"

Paw over paw the young hare descended, looking down to vhere the babe lay and shivered in the light of the bobbing antern. Tammo dropped lightly beside Sloey and, taking off is tunic, he wrapped her in it, talking in a soft, friendly tone.

"There now, that nasty thing's gone, thank goodness. I now, we'll make you a nice seat so they can pull you up, vot!"

Sloey turned her tearful face to her rescuer. "I falled downa ole an' nearly got eated up!"

Tammo detached the lantern, knotted a fixed loop into the ope's end, and sat the mousebabe in it. "Yes, I know, but ou're safe now, Sloey. You go on up an' have some more ood at the feast, that'll make y'feel lots better."

He signaled and the Dibbun was lifted up in the makeshift sling, clinging tightly to the rope and calling back down, "Tharra naughty fishysnake, me 'ope Skipper smack its bottom good'n'ard!"

Lying flat on the rocks, Tammo allowed the waters to drench him as he held up the lantern and squinted away to where the boiling torrent raced off downhill into the darkness. Nowhere could he see sight or sound of Skipper or the yellow eel.

A pall had been cast over the golden afternoon. The feast lay abandoned as Perigord explained what had happened. In stunned silence the Redwallers heard the news.

Abbess Tansy stood by her chair, wide-eyed with disbelief. "Oh, poor Skipper, is there nothing we can do?"

Tammo wiped his wet paws on the grass. "I stayed down there an' took a good look, marm. The water goes straight down underground—'fraid Skipper's gone. What a brave beast he was, though. Never considered his own safety at all!"

Arven leaned against a table, his eyes downcast. "I saw his face before he jumped. I could tell that there wasn't anything he wouldn't do to stop little Sloey from being hurt. Skipper of Otters was a true Redwaller!"

Major Perigord gripped his saber handle tightly.

Some distance southeast of Redwall Abbey, the streams, brooks, and back channels became less rapid, flowing placidly through Mossflower Wood. It was here that they converged on the margins of a sprawling water meadow. Log-a-Log, the Guosim Chieftain, gave orders to ship oars and let the little fleet of logboats drift. He sat in the prow of the lead vessel, conversing with his friend Frackle, their voices a low murmur, as if to preserve the sunlit peacefulness that hung over the flooded meadows like an emerald cape.

A half-grown dragonfly landed on the boat, close to Log-a-Log's paw. It rested, unconcerned by the shrews, its iridescent wings fanning gently.

"Hmmm, nothin' like a bit o' peace," the shrew leader sighed. "I never yet rowed through this place, always let the boat drift. See, Frackle, 'tis summer, the water lilies are startin'

open, an' look over there 'twixt the fen sedge an' bul-
shes—yellow poppies sproutin' with the cudweeds. I tell
ou, matey, this is the place to take a picnic on a quiet noon-
de!''

Frackle let her paw trail in the dark water, swirling a path
mid the minute green plants that carpeted the surface.

Then a white-fletched arrow hummed, almost lazily, through
e still air, burying itself in the prow of the logboat, and a
ruff roar rang out from somewhere behind the banks of fern
nd spikerush: ''Thee'd ha' been dead now hadst thou been a
ebeast!''

Log-a-Log stood up in the bows of his logboat, reassuring
e other Guosim with a quick wave of his paw. Then, sitting
ack down, he pretended to stifle a yawn as he replied idly,
Yore brains are all in yore boots, Gurgan Spearback. If I'd
een a foebeast I'd have spotted the smoke up yonder creek,
om the chimneys o' those clumsy floatin' islands you call
fts!''

Hardly had he finished speaking, when one of the rafts came
irting the reeds and headed for the logboats. Propelled by
x hedgehogs either side with long punting poles, the craft
immed lightly and fast, belying the awkward nature of its
onstruction.

There was a hut, a proper log cabin with shuttered windows
nd a door, built at the vessel's center, with a smokestack
himney sprouting from its roof. Lines of washing ran from
r'ard to aft, strung between mast timbers. Between the rails
the raft's edges, small hedgehogs, with safety lines tied
bout them, could be seen playing. It was obvious that several
rge families were living aboard.

The leader of the Waterhogs was a fearsome sight. Gurgan
pearback wore great floppy seaboots and an immense brass-
uckled belt, through which was thrust a hatchet and a scythe-
laded sword. He had long sea gull feathers impaled on his
eadspikes, making him look a head bigger than he actually
as. His face was painted white, with scarlet polka dots
aubed on.

Gurgan leaned on a long-handled oversized mallet, its head
section of rowan trunk. As the raft closed with the leading
gboat, the Guosim Chieftain sprang over the rail and hurled

himself upon the Waterhog leader. They wrestled around th raft's deck, pummeling each other playfully while they mad their greetings.

"Thou'rt nowt but an ancient blood pudden, Log-a-Lo Guosim!"

"Gurgan Spearback! Still lookin' like a spiky featherbe wid boots on, you great floatin' pincushion!"

More rafts joined them, sailing out from a creek on the fa side. Soon they were joined into a square flotilla, with th logboats tied up to their outer rails. Food was served on th open decks, hogcooks bustling in and out of their huts, carry ing pans of thick porridge flavored with cut fruit and honey the staple diet of Waterhogs. This was accompanied by ho cheese flans and mugs of rosehip'n'apple cider.

The little hogs wandered between groups, eating as if the were facing a seven-season famine. Big, wide-girthed father and huge, hefty-limbed mothers encouraged them.

"Tuck in there, Tuggy, th'art nowt but a shadow, get som paddin' 'round thy bones, young 'og!"

Log-a-Log refused a second bowl, patting his stomach t indicate that he had eaten sufficiently. "Phew! I wouldn' chance a swim after that liddle lot, mate!"

Gurgan snatched the bowl and dug in with a scallop-shel spoon. "So, what brings thee'n'thy tribe around these 'er parts?"

Log-a-Log patted a passing young one's headspikes an winced. "I could ask you the same question, messmate, bu we're chartin' a course close to Redwall Abbey to warn th goodbeasts there. Did y'know there's Rapscallions on th move?"

Gurgan licked the empty bowl and hiccupped. "Aye, that did. We've been four days ahead o' yon vermin since the burned their fleet on the southeast coast. Damug Warfang ha o'er a thousandbeast at his back, too many for us. I wa lookin' to avoid 'em someway."

Log-a-Log nodded gravely. "Perhaps the answer is to joi forces and go after the vermin. We'd have a chance together."

Gurgan began licking his spoon thoughtfully. "Aye, tha we would. But hast thou seen the number o' liddle 'uns we'r earin' now? 'Twould not be right to put their lives in danger.''

The shrew sipped pensively at his beaker. ''Aye, but think on this a moment, Gurgan. Warfang an' his army are like to weep the whole land an' enslave all, 'less they're stopped. If Mossflower were conquered an' ruled by Rapscallions, wot inda country would that be to bring young 'ogs up proper?''

Gurgan's paw tested the sickle-edged blade at his belt. 'Thou art right, Log-a-Log. What's to be done?''

''We'll take yore young 'uns up to the Abbey an' lodge em there. That'll leave you free to fight!''

Paw met paw; Log-a-Log winced again as Gurgan's big mitt rushed his with right good will.

''Thee've an 'ead on thy shoulders, comrade. Thun-er'n'snowfire! Ah'll give yon Warfang an' his ilk some death ongs t'sing!''

33

Half the Guosim were left on the water meadows with th
fighting crews, while the old and very young were conveye
toward Redwall in the logboats. Twilight was upon the lan
as they paddled upstream. Not too far off, Redwall could b
seen, framed by Mossflower Wood on its north and east side
The logboats lay in a small cove, where the stream took
bend on the heathlands before turning back to the woodland
Gurgan waddled ashore, leaning on a long puntpole he ha
brought along. "This looks as close as we'll hove to yon Ab
bey. Best leave the boats here an' walk the rest o' the wa
Come hither, young Blodge, an' quit messin' about there!"
The young Waterhog Blodge had jumped ashore ahead c
the rest and was poking about with a stick at the foot of
hillock by the stream bank. Waving the stick, she came scu
rying along. "Look ye, I finded water comin' out o' yond
hill, sir!"
Log-a-Log and Gurgan went to investigate. Blodge ha
found a trickle of cold fresh water seeping out of the moun
and flowing into the stream. She probed it with her stick unt
it became a tiny fountain, spurting from the hillside.

Log-a-Log took a drink. "Good water, sweet'n'fresh, cold too. It must be comin' from some underground stream, runnin' fairly fast, by the look o' it."

Gurgan Spearback placed his long pole against the water. It sprayed out either side of the butt. "Ah've ne'er seen ought like this," he said, shaking his great spiky head. "Stand aside there, I'll give it a good prod."

They stepped out of his way and he pounded the pole home into the hole with several powerful thrusts. Water squirted everywhere from the enlarged aperture, soaking them. A warning rumble from somewhere underground caused Log-a-Log to grab Blodge and leap back aboard the logboat, yelling, "Come away, Gurgan, mate! Quick!"

The rest of his warning was lost as the hill burst asunder with the awesome pressure of water building up inside it. Mingled with rocks, soil, pebbles, and sand, a mighty geyser of roaring water smashed sideways, demolishing the hillock and immediately swelling the stream to twice its size as it ate up the banks and the land close around.

Skillfully the Guosim oarbeasts rode the flood, turning their boats in midstream and beaching them on the farther side. Shouting and screaming, the young Waterhogs scrambled ashore, away from the danger. Gurgan Spearback was picking himself up and trying to wade upstream, when he was clouted flat by a mud-covered mass, shot from underground like a cannonball. Blowing mud and water from nostrils and mouth, the sturdy Waterhog fought to get the weight off him; it was pinning him down in the shallows, threatening to drown him.

Log-a-Log and several shrews came rushing to his rescue and grappled with the great muddy object, managing to free Gurgan.

Waist deep in icy water, Log-a-Log wiped his eyes and gasped, "Are you all right, mate? Yore not bad injured, are ye?"

"Ho don't fuss now, I'll be all right when I cough up this mud, matey!"

Gurgan looked at Log-a-Log. "Who said that?"

Skipper of Otters staggered to the bank, grunting under the weight of a dead yellow eel whose coils were still wrapped tightly around his sodden frame. He collapsed on dry land.

"I said that! Well, don't stand there gettin' wet an' gogglin', lend a paw t'get this slimy h'animal off me, mates!"

Log-a-Log was never one to panic. He took the situation in his stride. Relieving Skipper of Tammo's dirk, he began prising the stiff coils apart, talking to the otter in a matter-of-fact way.

"Ahoy, Skip, it's been a season or two since I clapped eyes on ye. So this is what yore wearin' these days, a serpent fish. What's the matter, ain't a tunic good enough for ye anymore?"

It was not often that the Abbey bells rang aloud once night had fallen, but Skipper's return proved the exception. Ginko the Bellringer swung on his bell ropes, sending out a joyous clangor across the land until his paws were numbed and reverberations hummed through both his ears.

The new arrivals were welcomed into Great Hall, while the heroic Skipper was carried shoulder high by the hares and his otter crew, down to Cavern Hole. He sat stoically as Sister Viola and Pellit cleaned, stitched, and salved his wounds, answering the volley of questions, of which Tammo's was the first.

"Did you bring my dirk back, Skip? How was it?"

With some reluctance, the otter returned Tammo's weapon. "I tell you, matey, that piece o' steel saved my life. 'Tis a blade t'be proud of an' I'd give ten seasons o' me life to be the owner of such a fine thing!"

The young hare polished his dirk hilt proudly before restoring it to his shoulder belt.

Shad poured hot mint tea for his friend. "I'll wager that old snakefish kept you busy, matey?"

Skipper held his head to one side as the Sister ministered to a muddied slash the eel's teeth had inflicted. "Aye, he did an' all. A real fighter that beast was, a shame I had t'slay it. The snakefish was lost an' 'ungry; 'twas only his nature t'seek prey. Yowch! Go easy, marm!"

Sister Viola placed an herbal compress on the wound. "I'm sorry. There, that's done! It was extremely brave of you to act as you did, sir. Little Sloey owes you her life. I don't often ay this to fighting beasts, but it has been an honor to treat our injuries."

Captain Twayblade pounded the table enthusiastically. 'Well said, marm, we can't afford to lose a beast as perilous s the Skipper. I propose y'make him an Honorary Member f the Long Patrol, eh, what d'ye say, Major?"

Amid the roars of approval, Abbess Tansy entered. Smiling rough her tears, she clasped the otter's paw affectionately. 'So, you old rogue, you came back to us!"

Skipper stood slowly, flexing his brawny limbs experimenally. "Of course I did, Abbess, marm, an' I'll thank ye next me I'm gone that y'don't cancel the feast in me absence. eggin' yore pardon, but y'didn't finish all the 'otroot soup, id ye?"

Shaking with laughter, Rockjaw Grang strode off to the itchens, saying over his shoulder, "Sithee, riverdog, sit ee ere, I'll fetch ye the whole bloomin' pot if y've a mind to up it!"

iurgan Spearback peeped around the door of the spare doritory where the young Waterhogs had been billeted. "Hoho! 'here they be, fed'n'washed an' snorin' respectfully. My anks to thee, goodbeasts."

Mother Buscol shuffled out, carrying a lantern, followed by 'raklyn, who was holding a paw to her lips. "Hush now, sir, e've just got the little 'uns to sleep."

Gurgan carried the lantern for them as they went downstairs. 'They Abbey be full o' babes—Dibbuns, my Waterhogs, ree liddle owls, even a badgerbabe. How came you by im?"

Craklyn kept firm hold of old Mother Buscol's paw as she egotiated the spiraling steps. "That's our little Russano, he's ery special to us."

Log-a-Log interrupted them as they entered Great Hall. 'Council o' War's to be held in Cavern Hole straight away!"

34

Sneezewort and Lousewort, like the rest of the Rapscallio horde, were stunned by what they had witnessed. Both rats sa by their cooking fire in the late evening, discussing in hushe tones the terrible retribution Damug Warfang had inflicted o the ten runaway rebels whom Skaup and his hunters ha brought back.

Sneezewort shuddered as he added twigs to the flame: "Good job you never went with 'em, mate. Nobeast'll eve think o' crossin' the Firstblade after the way 'e dealt wit Borumm an' Vendace an' the eight who was left!"

Lousewort gazed into the fire, nodding numbly. "Er, e that's true. Though if I 'ad gone wid 'em I'd 'ave sooner bee slain fightin' to escape than . . . Wot was that word Damu used?"

"Executed, mate, that was wot 'e said an' that was wot ' did. Ugh! Imagine bein' slung inter the water like that, wid great rock tied around yer neck, screamin' an' pleadin'!"

Lousewort ran a paw around his own neck and cringed a the thought. "It was cruel, 'ard an' merciless an', an' . . cruel!"

Sneezewort moved closer to the fire and shrugged. "Aye, ut that's 'ow a beast becomes Firstblade, by bein' a cold-looded killer. I was watchin' Damug's face—that'n was en-oyin' wot 'e did."

Damug Warfang was indeed enjoying himself. Everything eemed to be going his way. Not only had he brought the scapers to his own harsh justice, but his scouting expedition nder the command of the weasel Gaduss had yielded a double esult.

Rinkul the ferret, whom he had supposed long dead, was ack with news of Redwall Abbey. Damug had never seen edwall, though he had heard all about the place. What a prize would be. From there he could truly rule. If all he had heard om Rinkul was true, then it would not be too difficult to onquer Redwall, seeing as the entire outer south wall looked ke collapsing.

There was also the prisoner that Gaduss had brought in with im, an ancient male squirrel, but big and strong—one of ose hermit types living alone in Mossflower.

Damug circled the cage that held the creature, idly clacking is swordblade against the seasoned wood bars. The squirrel y on his side, all four paws bound, ignoring the Warlord, his yes shut stubbornly.

Damug leaned close to the bars, his voice low and persua-ive. "Food and freedom, two wonderful things, my friend, ink about them. All you have to do is tell me what is the bbey's strength, how many fighters, what sort of creatures. 'ell me and you can walk free from here with a full stomach nd a supply of food."

The reply was noncommittal: "Don't know, 'tis no use as-in' me. I've never been inside the place. I live alone in the oodlands an' keep meself to meself!"

The swordblade slid through the bars, prodding the captive. You saw what I did to those creatures earlier on. Keep lying me and it could happen to you."

The old squirrel's eyes opened and glared scornfully at the reatrat. "If you think that'd do ye any good yore a bigger ol than I took ye t'be. I've told you, I know nothin' about edwall!"

The swordblade thrust harder at the squirrel's back. "There

are ways of making you talk, far slower and more painful tha
drowning. Has that notion penetrated your thick skull?''

''Huh! Then try 'em an' see how far it gets ye, vermin!''

Damug knew his captive spoke the truth. The old squirr
would die out of pure spite and stubbornness rather than tall
Controlling his rising temper, the Firstblade withdrew hi
sword. ''A tough nut, eh? Well, we'll see. After you've bee
lying there a day or two watching the cool fresh stream wate
flowing by and sniffing the food on our campfires, I'll com
and have another word with you. Hunger and thirst are th
greatest persuaders of all.''

In a circle around a fire on the stream bank, the Rapmar
Captains squatted, subdued by the memory of Damug's ho
rible executions, but eager to know more of the big Abbe
whose wall was weakened to the point where it looked lik
falling. Rinkul sat with them, though he would not say any
thing until Damug allowed him to.

Damug Warfang strode into the firelight, flame and shado
adding to his barbarous appearance: red-painted features an
glittering armor surmounted by a brass helmet that had a grin
ning skull fixed to its spike. Gathering his long swirling blac
cloak about him, he sat down, eyes flicking from side to sid

''Three days! Just three more days, then we march to tak
the greatest prize any Rapscallion ever dreamed of. The Abbe
of Redwall!''

Beating their spearbutts against the ground, the Rapmark
growled their approval, until a glance from the Firstblade si
lenced them.

''In three days' time every Rapscallion will be rested, we
fed, fully armed, painted for war, and ready to do battle. Yo
are my Rapmarks; this is your responsibility. If there is an
more desertion or mutiny in this army, one soldier unfit c
unwilling to fight and die for his Firstblade, then I will loo
to you. You saw what happened to Borumm and Vendac
today; they were once officers too. Let me tell you, they go
off lightly! Should I have to make any more examples yo
will all see what I mean! Remember, three days!''

Damug swept off to his tent, leaving behind a circle c
Captains staring in silence at the ground.

• • •

Mid-morning of the following day found the columns from Salamandastron marching under a high summer sun. Lance Corporal Ellbrig watched young Trowbaggs suspiciously. The youngster was actually skipping along, but still keeping in step with the rest, waggling his ears foolishly and twirling his sword. Ellbrig narrowed one eye as if singling out his quarry.

"That hare there, Trowbaggs, you lollopin' specimen, what d'you think you're up to?"

The Long Patrol recruit chortled in a carefree manner, "G'mornin', Corp, good t'be jolly well alive, wot?"

Ellbrig scratched his chin in bewilderment. "I was always a bit doubtful about young Trowbaggs, but now I'm sure. He's gone doodle ally, completely mad!"

Deodar, who was marching alongside Trowbaggs, reassured the Corporal: "He's all right, Corp, it's just that he's learned to march properly and his footpaws aren't so sore anymore. Sort of got his second wind, haven't you, old lad?"

Trowbaggs gave his sword an extra twirl and sheathed it with a flourish. "Exactly! Y'make the old footpaws go left right, 'stead of right left. A good night's sleep, couple of lullabies from the Sergeant, pinch some other chap's spoon an' fork, scoff a bally good breakfast, an' heigh ho, I'm fit for anything at all, wot!"

Drill Sergeant Clubrush had caught up with Lance Corporal Ellbrig and had heard all that went on. "Very good, young sir, fit fer anythin' are we?" he said.

Trowbaggs leapt in the air, performed a pirouette, and carried on skipping. "Right you are, Sarge, brisk as a bee, bright as a button, an' carefree as crabs on a rock, that's me!"

The Sergeant smiled and exchanged a wink with the Corporal. "Right then, we're lookin' for bushtailed buckoes like you. Fall out an' relieve some o' those ration pack an' cookin' gear carriers in the rear ranks. Look sharp now, young sah!"

The irrepressible Furgale stifled a giggle. "Poor old potty Trowbaggs. Serves him jolly well right for openin' his silly great mouth, I s'pose."

Sergeant Clubrush's voice grated close to Furgale's ear. "Wot's that, mister Furgale? Did I 'ear you sayin' you'd like t'join Trowbaggs? We're always lookin' for volunteers, y'know."

"Who me, Sarge? No, Sarge, I never said a blinkin' word Sarge!"

The Drill Sergeant smiled sweetly, an unusual sight. "That's the spirit, young sir, less o' the loosejaw an' more o' the footpaw, left right, left right, keep those shoulders squared!"

The columns did not break step until well into the afternoon. Halting to rest and take light refreshment, they sprawled gratefully on a high hilltop amid wide patches of scented heather. Lady Cregga Rose Eyes climbed onto a rock and surveyed the terrain ahead. Sighting two running figures, she summoned Clubrush.

"Runners coming back, Sergeant. We'll stop here until they report and rest. One of them's young Algador Swiftback, but I don't recognize the other, do you?"

Clubrush shielded his eyes and watched the Runners. "Aye, marm, 'tis one o' the Starbuck family. Reeve, I think."

Algador and Reeve put on an extra burst of speed for the last lap, running neck and neck uphill. The Sergeant dropped his ears flat in admiration.

"Look at 'em go, marm. Only Salamandastron hares can run like that. Ho fer the days o' youth an' t'be a Galloper again, eh!"

Dashing up with scarce a hairbreadth between them, the pair skidded to a halt in a cloud of dust, throwing up a joint salute.

"Found 'em, Lady Cregga, marm!"

"Rapscallion tracks, great masses of 'em!"

Leaping down from the rock, the huge badger confronted them, her eyes turning from pink to red as the blood rose behind them. "Where did you see these vermin tracks?"

Trembling under the Warrior's glare and still breathless, Algador and Reeve continued with their report.

"Comin' up from the south an' east, marm!"

"When we cut their trail 'twas about four days old, but it was Rapscallions right enough, travelin' north, marm!"

Cregga's mighty paw gripped the axpike haft like a steel vise. "Where would be the best place to cut their trail short?"

Algador stuck a paw straight out, turned slowly a few de-

rees to his right, and, narrowing both eyes, sighted on a lo-
ation. "Right there, marm! If they're marchin' due north, the
losest place we can cut trail would be between those two hills
onder."

Without waiting for anybeast, Cregga strode off downhill,
eaded for the distant spot. Sergeant Clubrush ruffled both the
Runners' ears.

"Well done, you two. Rest here an' tell cooks to leave you
ood an' drink. Follow us when y'feels ready to go agin.
ance Corporal, get 'em up on their paws an' formed in mar-
hin' order. Come on, you slack-pawed, famine-faced web-
vallopers! Are you goin' t'sit around all day while yore good
ady Commander is off alone an' unprotected? Hup two three,
ast one in line's on a fizzer!"

Clubrush tugged Trowbaggs's ears as he passed by. "Leave
he carryin' to the carriers, Trowbaggs. Back up with the rest
n' be'ave yoreself now."

Trowbaggs hurried along, saluting furiously many times.
'Behave m'self, Sarge, yes, Sarge, very good, Sarge, thank
ou, Sarge!"

Clubrush and Ellbrig marched at the rear, helping and en-
ouraging any stragglers. The Sergeant peered ahead through
he column's dust. "I knows I shouldn't be sayin' this, Corp,
ut did you see 'er? She wasn't bothered whether or not she
ad one or five 'undred at 'er back. Not Lady Rose Eyes,
traight off she went, grippin' that axpike like she was stran-
lin' it, eyes blazin' red, jus' longin' t'be destroyin' any ver-
nin she catches up with!"

Ellbrig stooped on the march, retrieving a beaker some re-
ruit had dropped, and continued without breaking step.
'Well, you said it, Sarge, though you spoke for me 'cos I was
hinkin' the same thing. We're led by a beast who's liable to
un out o' control at any moment. But what can we do?"

The Drill Sergeant blinked against the dust, keeping his eyes
traight ahead on the winding downhill path. "Our duty, Cor-
oral, that's wot we can do. Obey Lady Rose Eyes's com-
nands an' look after those who 'ave to obey us. Best thing
ve can do is the thing we do best. Turn these recruits into
eal Long Patrol hares who can take care o' themselves in
attle. Teach 'em discipline an' comradeship an' 'ope most of

'em come out o' this mess alive, experienced enough to teach those who'll come after them.''

Clubrush raised his voice, bellowing out in true Drill Sergeant fashion so all could hear him: ''Come on, me lucky buckoes, move those dodderin' footpaws, yore like a load o ole molewives out pickin' daisies! Pick up that step now Shangle Widepad, you an' the older veterans, give 'em the 'Moanin' Green Recruit' song, see if'n these whippersnapper can keep up with the pace!''

The tough-looking hare who had helped Trowbaggs on his first night by standing second guard for him struck up the tune Clubrush had requested. Shangle had a fine deep bass; his comrades joined in. Soon the entire column was moving faster every young hare in the ranks not wanting to be identified with the object of the mocking air, the Moaning Green Recruit

''O 'tis up at dawn every morn,
The flag is flyin' high,
Why did I join this Long Patrol,
O why O why O why?

I march all day the whole long way,
Me footpaws red an' sore,
If I get home I'll never roam
No more no more no more!

O watch that line, step in time,
Through sun'n'rain an' snow,
Would I sign up again to go,
O no no no no no!

The Corporal shouts, the Sergeant roars,
As like a snail I creep,
Just get me to that camp tonight
An' let me sleep sleep sleep!''

As a result of the quick-marching dogtrot, the column moved ahead speedily like a well-oiled machine, throwing up a dust cloud in its wake. Darkness was falling fast, and the twin hills were near. Lady Cregga would either be waiting fo them in the valley between the hills, or she might have continued pursuing the trail of the Rapscallions. In any event, Clubrush had decided that was where night camp would be pitched.

Trowbaggs was marching directly behind Shangle Widepad when the veteran stumbled. The younger hare saved him as he fell backward. "I say, old bean, are you all right?"

Shangle grimaced, breaking into a hop to keep up with the pace. "Oofh, me flippin' footpaw, I just ricked it on a sharp stone!"

Trowbaggs supported him, nodding to Furgale. "What ho, Furg, lend a paw here, this chap's hobblin', wot!"

The two recruits took Shangle's weapons and pack, sharing them and bolstering up the veteran between them.

"C'mon, bucko, we'll get y'to camp, not far now."

"Rather, you just lean on me'n'ole Trowbaggs, that'll give us five footpaws between us."

Shangle threw his paws gratefully around their shoulders. "Thanks, mates, I'll do the same fer you sometime!"

Good-natured as ever, Furgale winked at the older hare. " 'Course y'will, old lad, when this is finished y'can piggyback both of us all the way home, wot!"

Lady Cregga was not at the rendezvous. It was a fine dry night, and the ground was still warm from the sun's heat. Lance Corporal Ellbrig was left in charge while Clubrush headed off alone after their leader.

Ellbrig watched Trowbaggs and Furgale staggering in with Shangle between them. "Well done, you two! Shangle, sit down there an' I'll take a look at that footpaw. The rest of you, cold supper, no fires, sleep on the ground with yore groundsheets as pillows, don't unroll 'em. We'll be movin' out sharpish at first light."

Deodar and a hare named Fallow were on first watch. They jumped up, weapons at the ready, as two figures loomed up through the gloom.

"Who goes there? Step forward an' be recognized!" Fallow ordered.

Algador and Reeve jogged out of the darkness.

"What ho the camp, 'tis only us Gallopers. Well, did y'catch up with Lady Rose Eyes?"

Fallow snorted. "You're jokin', of course. Sar'nt Clubrush has gone ahead to see if he can find her. You two best get some shut-eye; whole caboodle's movin' out at dawnlight."

Algador unshouldered his pack and let it drop. "Seasons o' slaughter, what drives Lady Cregga on like that?"

Deodar yawned, stretching languidly. "Search me, but whatever it is, we're bound to follow!"

35

Cavern Hole was packed tight for the Council of War. As Champion of Redwall, Arven sat at the Abbess's right paw, his weapon, the great sword of Martin the Warrior, laid flat on the table in front of him. As guests and experienced fighters, Major Perigord and his hares held the right side of the table, Log-a-Log and his shrews with Gurgan Spearback and the otter crew facing them.

The Guosim Chieftain had something to say before the main meeting got under way. "About that water runnin' beneath yore south wall, I think I've found the answer t'the problem. Today we found where the water comes out—good job we did, too, or Skipper woulda never been seen agin. So, I figgers that I knows the waterways of Mossflower better'n most. Any-'ow, I put on me thinkin' cap about that stream. If'n it's got a place t'come out, stands to sense there must be a spot where it flows in. Heed me now, I think I knows where that very place is, 'tis on the river north an' west o' Redwall. I've sailed it a few times an' seen where it splits off. With yore permission, Abbess, marm, I'd like to take some o' yore otters an' molefolk with me to dam it off an' stop the water flowin' under yore wall. We'll go first light tomorrer, sooner the better!"

Mother Abbess Tansy signaled for her helpers to begin serving supper all 'round. "You have my permission and may fortune go with you and yours, Log-a-Log. The Guosim have always been special friends of Redwall. Skipper, Foremole Diggum, will you assist the shrews?"

"Aye, marm, my crew's willin' an' ready!"

"Bo urr, ee can count on us'n's, h'Abbess!"

Tammo was sitting between Perigord and Pasque. He sipped hot red-berry cordial and nibbled a wedge of heavy fruitcake, not feeling really hungry. Cavern Hole seemed overfull, rather muggy, warm, and distant. Tammo's eyes drooped, then he swayed slightly and settled back as the talk became a soothing murmur, as if it were echoes from far away. Then a butterfly flew gently by in his sleep-laden imagination; soft, delicate, and silent. It settled on the pink flowers of an almond tree, closing its fragile, pale gold wings. The flowers fell, drifting slowly through still noon air, lighting with scarcely a ripple on the tranquil waters of a shady stream. Catching a small eddy, butterfly and flowers together went 'round and 'round in lazy circles.

Both Log-a-Log and Gurgan Spearback had told the meeting of Gormad Tunn's death and everything they had seen of Damug Warfang and his Rapscallions. All eyes turned to Major Perigord and Arven, who were already deep in conversation. The squirrel Warrior, as Champion of Redwall, would naturally be consulted on the Abbey's defense. Finally Perigord leaned forward, nodding his head shrewdly. "Hmm, we've defeated those vermin at Salamandastron not s'long ago, but you'll forgive me sayin', we had the full force o' the Long Patrol an' Lady Cregga Rose Eyes full o' Bloodwrath when we did it. How many Rapscallions d'you estimate Damug has on call?"

Log-a-Log scratched his head reflectively. "Best ask Gurgan, he's seen 'em firsthand."

"Aye," said the Waterhog, "we've watched 'em on the move and when they camped. Oft times they looked to number like leaves in an autumn gale. Hark now, 'tis not my wish to afright these gentle Redwallers, but my mate Rufftip, she counted 'em as they moved out from the coast. Damug Warfang has a few score o'er ten 'undred to do his biddin'."

A stunned silence settled upon Cavern Hole. Nobeast had envisaged a vermin army of more than a thousand on the march. Arven shot Major Perigord a quick glance. Something had to be done before panic set in. Perigord understood and rose to the occasion.

"Well now, chaps, that sounds like a tidy old bunch, wot! However, there was half that number again when they came at Salamandastron, ships too, but we still managed to send the rotters packin'. Main thing is not t'be scared by numbers, after all, 'tis quality that counts, not quantity!"

Pellit the dormouse challenged him. "You could stand 'ere all night talkin' like that, but it still won't stop all those Rapscallions attackin' Redwall. Point is, wot are you goin' to do about it besides talk, eh?"

Abbess Tansy glared frostily at Pellit. "Perhaps, sir, you would tell us what *you* propose to do?"

All the dormouse could do was bluster in his own defense. "I ain't no fightin' beast, marm, most of us Abbeydwellers don't know the first thing about battlin'. Wot d'you expect us t'do?"

Arven stood up slowly, frowning at Pellit, who cringed under the Redwall Champion's stern reproof.

"Major Perigord has pledged himself and his patrol to help us. I would expect that you have the good manners to give him a hearing, unless you have a better or more helpful suggestion to assist your Abbey in this crisis."

Pellit lowered his eyes and shrugged. The Abbess smiled apologetically at Perigord. "Forgive the interruption, Major. You were saying?"

But the hare had slightly lost track of his speech. To gain time he stroked his whiskers thoughtfully and pursed his lips.

Suddenly all eyes turned on Tammo. He rose and walked 'round to stand beside Arven, gazing at the great sword that lay upon the table. In a calm, measured voice, he began speaking:

"Aye, Sire, it shall be as you say."

Arven could tell by the look in Tammo's eyes that he was still sleeping. The young hare moved toward the steps leading up to Great Hall. Placing a paw to his lips, Arven warned everybeast to hold their silence. Then he gestured with his other paw to clear a way. Redwallers fell back to either side as Tammo went by them, unaware of all about him. Craklyn uttered a single word as she followed in his wake:

"Martin!"

Lanterns burned dimly in Great Hall, casting shadows around the sandstone columns and recesses, and moonlight shone through the high windows onto a floor worn smooth by countless generations of paws. In complete silence the Redwallers grouped behind Tammo, who stood staring up at the tapestry on the wall. It was a marvelous piece of work, fashioned by Abbey creatures in the distant past. Martin the Warrior, Redwall's founder hero, was depicted there, standing armor-clad and leaning upon his sword.

"I brought you quill and parchment," Viola Bankvole whispered to Craklyn, passing her writing materials. "You may need them!"

The Recorder nodded her thanks as Tammo started speaking.

"Spring is done now, summer calls,
This season fraught with wartime's fear,
Fate says Damug will ne'er see our walls,
Battle must take place, though not here.

Manycoats will know the way,
So go with him, De Fformelo.
A soothsayer knows what to say,
Secrets Warfang longs to know.
One day Redwall a badger will see,
But the badger may never see Redwall,
Darkness will set the Warrior free,
The young must answer a mountain's call."

A vagrant night breeze waved the tapestry once, then all was still and quiet. Tammo sat down upon the floor. He rubbed his eyes and stared at his surroundings in bewilderment.

"What the . . . Who brought me here?"

Arven sat beside him, pointing to the figure on the tapestry.

"Martin the Warrior did, he had a message for us."

"Oh, y'don't say, an' what was the message?"

"You should know, friend, 'twas you who delivered it!"

"Me? I say, that's a bit blinkin' much. I don't remember a single thing. What did I, I mean he, say?"

Craklyn spread her parchment in front of the young hare. "Don't worry, Tammo, I recorded every word. Martin the Warrior is the guiding spirit of our Abbey. In times of trouble he will often choose somebeast to deliver his message to us. You must be a very special creature for Martin to single you out."

Tammo nodded absently as he scanned the parchment. "Hmm, never thought of m'self as jolly well special, marm. Hey, Midge, it mentions you here. It says, 'Manycoats will know the way.' "

Midge was far shorter than the other hares, but none the less brave. He laughed excitedly. "Hahaha! Wonderful! It's just come to me in a flash, yes, I certainly do know what t'do!"

"Well bully for you, laddie buck!" Perigord checked him hastily. "But there's no reason t'be worryin' our friends with a lot o' balderdash. C'mon, chaps, all pop along an' get some shut-eye now, it's rather late y'know. Leave this to us, we'll sort out the details, wot!"

Abbess Tansy nodded in agreement. Some of the Redwallers looked rather reluctant, but one glance from their Abbess told them she was in no mood for argument.

Skipper, Foremole, Log-a-Log, Gurgan, and the hares followed Arven, Craklyn, and Tansy back down to Cavern Hole. Once there they made themselves comfortable by the fire embers.

Perigord stirred the logs with his saber tip, saying, "Speak y'piece, Midge. Tell us what came t'you in a flash."

The small hare did so readily. "Listen, Martin said that the battle mustn't take place at Redwall, it's got to be fought elsewhere, see!"

Arven placed the great sword on the fireplace lintel. "That makes sense. We wouldn't stand much chance with over a thousand Rapscallions charging a collapsin' south wall. What do you intend t'do about it, Midge?"

"Here's the wheeze, old chap. Damug Warfang, like all Warlords, is prob'ly very superstitious. Well, what if an old ragged soothsayer puts a word in the ear of somebeast close to him?"

Perigord frowned. "What sort o' word?"

"Well, sah, the sort o' word tellin' where a battle might take place an' sayin' how unlucky 'twill be to look upon Redwall Abbey until the battle is won, an' how the chosen battle place'll be lucky for a certain Rapscallion leader . . ."

The Major shook his head at Midge's quick-wittedness. "Enough, enough, I've got the drift now. Well done, Midge Manycoats! Spot of action for you, young Tammo; the rhyme says you've got to go with Midge. Don't worry, he'll disguise you pretty well."

Eyes shining, Tammo clasped his dirk hilt. "Y'can rely on me, sah!"

Perigord ruffled Tammo's ears fondly. "Splendid! I knew I could. Y'know, you look the image o' your mother sometimes, not half as pretty, but somethin' about the eyes. However, can't let you two go alone. Rockjaw, you are our best tracker. Go with 'em, find the camp, and keep y'self close. We'll use you as a go-between. Very good! Sar'nt Torgoch, you an' Lieutenant Morio go right away at dawn an' scout out a good location for the battle. We'll get news of the chosen spot to you, Rockjaw. Taunoc, with his sharp eyes and knowledge of the woods, will be messenger. Meanwhile, Midge, you can be workin' y'self into the vermin's confidence. Shouldn't be too hard for a hare with a head on his shoulders like you have, wot. We'll get word t'you as soon as a good location's been staked out. That's all, chaps. Get some rest now, busy day ahead of us tomorrow. Dismissed!"

BOOK THREE

The Ridge

36

Two hours after dawn the next day, four logboats plied the waters of the broad stream north by west from Redwall. Foremole Diggum and his team crouched uneasily in the boats, some of them with cloaks thrown over their heads. Moles are not noted for being great sailors, preferring dry land to water.

"Boo urr, 'taint natcheral t'be afloaten abowt loik this!"

"Hurr nay, oi'm afeared us'n's moight be a sinkin' unnerwater!"

Log-a-Log dug his paddle deep, scowling at them. "Belay that kind o' talk, I ain't never lost a beast off'n a boat o' mine yet. Quit the wailin' an' moanin', willyer!"

Skipper stuffed bread and cheese in his mouth, winking at his otter crew as they gobbled a hasty breakfast. "Ooh, 'e's an 'eartless shrew, that'n is! Ahoy there, moles, come an' join us in a bite o' brekkfist, mates."

Gurgan Spearback, swigging from a flask of October Ale, noted the moles' distress.

"Hearken, Skip, yon moles were a funny enough color afore ye offered 'em vittles—don't go makin' 'em any worse!"

Log-a-Log's companion Frackle pointed with her oarblade. "There 'tis, see, two points off'n the starboard bow!"

Part of the stream forked off down a narrow tributary. Steering the logboats into it, they followed the winding downhill course of the rivulet, wooden keels scraping on the bottom as they went. After a short distance, Log-a-Log waved his oar overhead in a circular motion.

"Bring all crafts amidships, sharp now, bow'n'stern broadsides!"

Four logboats were soon wedged lengthways against the flow, their stems and sterns resting on opposite shores of the narrow waterway. Gratefully, the moles scrambled ashore, kissing the ground in thanks for their safe landing. Skipper and his otters went ahead to the point where the stream disappeared into a hillside.

"This is it, mates," announced Skipper. "Spread out an' search for a big boulder!"

By the time the rest arrived, the streamflow had dwindled a bit, owing to the course being blocked by the logboats.

Gurgan waded through it and climbed the hill to admonish Skipper. "Thou'rt still hurted, thee shouldn't ha' come!"

The tough otter scratched at one of his wounds, which was beginning to itch. "Coupla scratches never stopped me doin' what I like, mate. Ahoy there, mates, that's a good ole boulder ye found!"

The stone was partially sunk into the earth, but Foremole Diggum and his crew soon dug it out. Using a smaller rock as a chock, the otters levered the roundish mass of stone uphill, using shrew oars to move it. Gurgan threw his added weight into the task, while Foremole marked out a spot on the hilltop, calling, "Bring ee bowlder up to yurr!"

Once or twice the heavy stone rolled back on them, but they were determined creatures. Otters, shrews, moles, and the Waterhog Chieftain gritted their teeth and fought the boulder, fraction by fraction, until it rested on Foremole's mark. Sighting with a straight twig, Foremole ordered the boulder moved a bit this way and a bit that way. Finally satisfied, he took an oar and gave the boulder one hard shove with the paddle end. The great rock toppled down into the stream, sending up a shower of water; then it rolled back downhill and lodged itself quarely across the spot where the flow vanished underground. Ioles and otters dashed down to pack the edges with a mix-ıre of mud, pebbles, and whatever bits of timber came to aw.

The flow of the stream halted and backed up on itself until became a becalmed creek. A short celebratory meal at the reekside would have been appropriate, but the otter crew had aten all the food, so they drank the last of the October Ale nd plum cordial, then got the boats headed out. Log-a-Log alled out to the moles, who had remained onshore, "Come n, mateys, back to the Abbey. 'Twill be a fine fast sail down-ver, we'll be back afore ye knows it!"

Foremole wrinkled his nose, trundling off along the bank-de. "You'm go, zurr Log, an' gudd lukk to ee. Us'n's be 'alkin' back even if'n it takes ten season t'do et. No more ıilin' fur molers!"

ammo watched, fascinated, as Midge Manycoats applied his isguise before a burnished copper mirror in Sister Viola's ormitory. The small hare explained as he went along.

"Alter the face first, that's half the trick. See, I roll my own ırs down and put on this ole greasy cap with false ears ickin' out the side of it, one's only half an ear an' the other ıs a slice out of it, just like some smelly ole vermin. Now, rub m'face with this oily brown stuff—pass me that candle, amm. Singe the whiskers down an' rub 'em 'til they're rubby. Good! Put a patch over one eye, and paste a thin bit bark over the other, givin' it a nasty slant. Aye, that's more ke it. Look, a little black limpet shell, stick it on the end of y handsome nose with a blob o' gum, an' presto! Snidgey ointed vermin hooter, wot! Few bits o' darkened wax over e teeth, two long thorns stuck in the wax just under the top ɔ. Haharr, fangs! Pass me that greasy charcoal stick, hmm, o wicked downcurved lines, one either side of the mouth, at's it! Righto, I throw this filthy tattered sack over me, belt with a loose cob o' rope, crouch down a bit, hunch shoul-rs, shuffle footpaws. What d'you see, Tammo?"

The young hare gasped in amazement. Standing before him as an aged vermin creature, neither wholly rat, ferret, or oat, but definitely vermin of some type.

"Great seasons o' soup! No wonder they call you Midg Manycoats!"

Midge adopted the whining vermin slang. "Harr, wait'll ye sees yerself when I'm done wid ye, cully!"

Rockjaw Grang was having what he figured would be his la good hot meal for a while, working his way through an im mense potato, mushroom, and carrot pastie oozing rich dar herb gravy. Dibbuns surrounded the big hare, watching hi throat bob up and down as he polished off a tankard of dar delion and burdock cordial. Gubbio the molebabe pushed steaming cherry and damson pudding in front of Rockjaw, an Sloey, none the worse for her adventure, poured yellow me dowcream plentifully over it.

"Whoo! A you goin' to eat alla dat up, mista G'ang?"

Rockjaw sat the mousebabe up on the table. "Sithee, ju you watch me, liddle lass, but keep out of t'way, else I'll sco thee an' all. Aye, y'd be right tasty wi' a plum in yore mou an' some cream o'er yore 'ead!"

Clapping their paws and jumping up and down, the Dibbu chortled, "Goo on, mista G'ang, eat Sloey alla up!"

The giant hare set Sloey back down on the floor. "Only she's very naughty. 'Ey up, wot's this?"

Two thoroughly evil-looking vermin shuffled into the kitc ens and began dirtying their blades by coating them with ve etable oil and soot from the stovepipes. The Dibbuns shrieke and leapt upon Rockjaw, clinging tearfully to his neck. H patted the tiny heads soothingly.

"Shush now, liddle 'uns, 'tis only Midge an' Tammo acti at bein' varmints. You go an' play with the babby owls a Russano now. I'll eat those two up if'n they frightens a more Dibbuns."

Shad the Gatekeeper took Abbess Tansy and Craklyn down the platform beneath the south wall. They lowered two la terns on a rope and saw that the water had dwindled away a mere trickle.

Shad grunted with satisfaction. "Y'see, marms, they fou the stream an' likely blocked it off. Soon it'll be dry dow there. May'aps then we'll go down an' take a look around.

don't mind tellin' you, I'm real curious t'see wot 'tis like. I know you are too, miz Craklyn.''

The old Recorder peered down at the drying stream bed. ''It's my duty to see what's down there. Everything has to be recorded and written up for future generations of our Abbey. Which leads me to think I've been looking in the wrong place to find out more about this—the answer might lie in your gatehouse, Shad. I suspect that if we look through Redwall's first records, the truth about all this may emerge.''

Tansy kissed her old friend's cheek. ''But of course! What a clever old Recorder you are, Craklyn.''

The Recorder of Redwall turned away from the pit, signaling Shad to escort them aboveground. ''You're no spring daisy yourself, Mother Abbess. Come on, we've a long dusty job ahead of us.''

Shad hastily excused himself from the task. ''Beggin' yore pardons, but I got other chores t'do. You ladies 'elp yoreselves to anythin' y'need in my gate'ouse. I can't abide the dust an' disorder when you starts unpackin' those ole record books'n'scrolls off the shelves, miz Craklyn.''

Tansy watched the otter hurrying off across the Abbey lawns. ''Other chores to do, indeed, great wallopin' waterdog!''

Craklyn chuckled as she took her friend's paw. ''Don't be too hard on poor Shad. Otters never made good scholars. He's probably off to play with little Russano and the baby owls.''

37

The south wallgate had been jammed shut by the subsidence so Tammo, Midge, and Rockjaw were leaving by the little eas wallgate. Major Perigord and Pasque Valerian saw them off Perigord was none too happy about Tammo going.

"Now remember, you chaps, keep y'heads down an' don' attract too much attention to yourselves. Normally I woulc have sent Tare or Turry with Midge, but as the rhyme name: you, Tamm, well it seems you're the one to go. So take i easy, young bucko, an' report back to Rockjaw whenever yo can. We'll get news of the battleground to you as soon as w hear back from Torgoch and Morio. Look after 'em, Rock I've no need to tell you of the danger they'll be in."

Rockjaw Grang saluted the Major. "Never fear, sah, y'ca rely on me!"

The soft brown eyes of Pasque looked full of concern Tammo winked roguishly at her from beneath his vermin dis guise. "Don't fret, chum, we'll be back before you know it!'

Perigord watched them threading their way south throug the woodland until the three figures were lost among the trees He locked the east wallgate carefully, then, turning to the de ected Pasque, he chucked her gently beneath the chin. "C'mon now, missie, you'll bring on the rain with a face like that, wot! Your Tammo'll be back in a day or two, full o' tales of how he outwitted the Rapscallions. Cheer up, that's an order!"

Midge Manycoats had done an excellent job of disguising Tammo, making him look old and thoroughly evil by giving him shaggy beetling brows to hide his eyes and a matted straggling beard. To this he added a greasy flop hat, lots of jangling brass ornaments, and an old dormitory blanket that was literally in frayed tatters, after he had finished trouncing it about in the orchard compost heap. Tammo not only looked villainous, but smelled highly disreputable.

Both hares found themselves gasping for breath under their camouflage. Leaning against an oak tree, they pleaded with the long-striding Rockjaw.

"I say, Rock, ease off a bit, will you, you've got the pair of us whacked with that pace o' yours!"

"Aye, slow down, mate, or we'll perish long before we find the vermin camp. Whew! I'm roasted under this lot!"

The big fellow turned and retraced his path, halting several paces from them and wafting a paw across his nostrils. "By heck, you lads don't mind if'n I stands well upwind of ye?"

Tammo leered nastily and tried out his vermin accent. "Ho harr, me ole matey, you don't expect us t'go sailin' inter a Rapscallion camp smellin' like dewy roses now, do yer?"

Beneath his disguise, Midge winced at the pitiful attempt. "I think you'd best keep your lip buttoned an' pretend to be my dumb assistant, Tamm. That vermin accent o' yours is awful!"

Rockjaw agreed with Midge's assessment. "Aye, yore too nice-spoken, Tammo, prob'ly 'cos you was well brung up!"

Young Friar Butty brought a tray to the gatehouse that afternoon because neither Tansy nor Craklyn had been back to the Abbey building for anything to eat. Both windows and the door were wide open to counteract the dust. Butty blinked as he entered, and looked about for somewhere to set the tray down.

"I was beginnin' t'get worried about you, marm, an' yo
too, miz Craklyn. So I brought you a snack. There's turni
an' carrot bake, cold mint tea, some blackberry tarts, an'
small rhubarb an' strawberry crumble I made special for you
They're fresh strawberries from the orchard, nice an' early thi
season."

Tansy looked up over the top of her tiny glasses. "Than
you, Friar Butty, how thoughtful. Just put the tray on tha
chair, please. Let's take a break, Craklyn."

While they ate their food, Butty looked around at the pile
of books, ledgers, scrolls, and charts piled everywhere, lots c
them browny-yellow with age.

Craklyn watched him as she sipped gratefully at a beake
of cool mint tea. "Those are our Abbey records going righ
back to when Redwall was first built. Unfortunately they'r
mixed in with lots of old recipes, poems, songs, herbalists
notes and remedies. Help yourself to any recipes that yo
like—they may come in useful when you get stuck for cookin
ideas."

Butty, however, was looking at the latest piece of writing
the parchment on which Craklyn had recorded the words se
via Tammo from Martin the Warrior. He read aloud the secon
part of the verse.

"One day Redwall a badger will see,
But the badger may never see Redwall,
Darkness will set the Warrior free,
The young must answer a mountain's call."

Abbess Tansy glanced up from her seat in a deep armchai
"Why did you pick that part of the poem to read, Friar?"

The young squirrel tapped the parchment thoughtfull
"Well, it seemed to me at the time that the first part of th
thing was all that you were interested in, that bit about th
battle taking place elsewhere and Tammo goin' along wi
Midge Manycoats. Nobeast took an interest in the second pa
What d'you suppose it means?"

Craklyn pointed out the first two words of the ninth lin
"See here, this line begins with the words 'One day.' So w
take that to mean at some distant time in the future. All w

vere looking for in the poem was Martin's immediate message ɔ save Redwall from danger. But you're right, Butty, it is a 'ery mysterious and interesting part you read out. Alas, we annot see the future, so we will just have to wait for time :self to unroll the message it contains."

Friar Butty put the parchment down and riffled through the ıass of papers piled on a nearby shelf. He withdrew a thick nd aged-looking volume, blowing the dust from it. "Aye, I uppose you're right, marm, time reveals all sooner or later, robably even the secrets that this old volume contains."

Tansy liked young Butty; he was a fast learner. "My word, ıat is an ancient-looking thing. Does it say who wrote it? The ame will be inside the front cover."

Butty opened the book and read the faded script therein. ' 'The journal of Abbess Germaine, formerly of Loam-edge.' "

Mint tea spilled down Craklyn's gown as she jumped up-ight. "The architect of the Abbey! That's the very volume /e're looking for! Well done, young sir!"

Hurrying out into the sunlight, the trio seated themselves on ıe broad stone steps leading to the gatehouse threshold. Crak-'n turned carefully to the first page. "I'll wager an acorn to bushel of apples that the answer to what lies beneath our ɔuth wall is in these pages somewhere!"

•

'he crews of the logboats strode into the kitchens, refreshed y their fast trip downstream and hungry as hunters. Skipper 'hacked his rudderlike tail against a big pan. "Ahoy, Friar ›utty, any vittles fer pore starvin' creatures?"

Mother Buscol waddled from the corner cupboard, waving threatening ladle at the otter. "Look, you great noisy riv-:rdog, Butty ain't 'ere, see. So don't you come with yore ɔugh gang a shoutin' an' hollerin' 'round these kitchens when 'e just got the owlbabes takin' their noontide nap!"

Gurgan Spearback touched his headspikes respectfully. 'Thee'll 'scuse us, marm, we'll be well satisfied t'sit out in our dinin' room an' wait t'be served by one as pretty as oreself."

Taken by surprise at the Waterhog's courtly manner, Mother uscol smiled and dipped a deep curtsy. "Indeed to goodness,

sir, I'll just warm up the pasties and heat some soup. Woul
you be takin' gooseberry cordial with it?''

Gurgan bowed, sticking one of his immense boots forwar
as he made what he considered to be an elegant leg.

" 'Twould be more'n sufficient, m'lady, 'specially if it wer
served by yore own fair paws!''

Chuckling, the old squirrelmother set about her task.

Log-a-Log nudged Gurgan. ''You fat ole flatterer, all sh
was about t'give us was a swipe with 'er ladle. 'Ow d'you d
it, matey?''

Gurgan led them out to the tables, winking slyly. ''A smid
geon o' sugar's worth ten barrels o' rocks, friend. Lackaday
who did that to yore nose, Shad?''

The burly otter Gatekeeper was seated at the table, feedin
candied chestnuts to the little badger Russano. He touched th
dock leaf wrapped tenderly 'round his snout. ''Never lean to
close to owlchicks, matey, they got beaks on 'em like liddl
scissors. I just found that out when I was playin' with 'en
Savage beasts they are, they'll eat anythin' at all!''

Skipper laughed and tickled the badgerbabe's footpaw
''An' 'ow's my liddle mate 'ere behavin' 'imself, eh?''

Shad patted Russano proudly. ''I just taught 'im a ne
word. Watch!''

He held a candied chestnut up, just out of Russano's reac
The tiny fellow reached out his paws, uttering the wor
gruffly. ''Nut! Nut!''

The otters and shrews thought Russano's new word was
source of great hilarity. They gathered 'round him, chantin
''Nut! Nut! Nut! Nut!''

The two little owls, Orocca and her husband, Taunoc, cam
flying out of the kitchens. They landed on the tabletop, con
tracting and dilating their massive golden eyes and flexin
their talons.

''Whichbeast is making all the noise out here?''

''Waking our eggchicks with that silly nut-nut call!''

Straightfaced and serious, all the otters and shrews pointe
at the badgerbabe Russano, who lay innocent and smilin
" 'Twasn't us, it was him!''

38

Skaup the ferret and a dozen or more Rapscallions were out foraging, roaming farther than they usually did. Skaup was pleased: they had slain several birds and in addition had two clutches of waterfowl eggs and a fat old perch they had found floating dead in a stream. They were seated in a patch of shrub that had a blackberry sprig growing through it. Although the berries were only partially ripe, the vermin crew readily picked and ate them, the reddish-purple juice staining their paws and mouths.

Suddenly a stoat pointed to the left. "Over there, three beasts. Look!"

Rockjaw Grang dropped swiftly out of sight at the sound of the stoat's shout. He scurried off backward, bent double. "I ain't sure they got a proper glimpse o' me. You'll have to bluff 'em, Midge. Good luck, you two!"

Swords drawn, the Rapscallions advanced on the pair. Midge muttered urgently to Tammo, "Remember, you're dumb. Leave this t'me!"

A moment later the tip of Skaup's blade was touching Midge's throat. "Who are yer an' where'd you come from?"

Midge stood his ground fearlessly, curling his lip at the ferret. "I could ask you th' same question, bucko!"

"You ain't in no position to ask questions, rag'ead," Skaup sneered back at him. "There was *three* o' yer. Where'd the other one go to?"

Ignoring the swordtip, Midge shook his head pityingly. "If you seen three of us then you've either bin swiggin' grog or yer eyes are playin' tricks on yer. I'm Miggo an' this is me matey Burfal. There ain't nobeast with us."

The stoat who first sighted Rockjaw scratched his head. "I'd swear I saw another, a big 'un 'e was, I'm sure of it!"

Midge pushed Skaup's blade aside and grabbed the stoat, pulling him close. "Ho, so yore the one seen three of us? Well wotta useless lump you are! I wager yer don't even know there's a chestnut in yore ear, do yer?"

Reaching out quickly, Midge gave the stoat's ear a sharp tug. The vermin yelped in pain, but his companions stood goggle-eyed, staring at the candied chestnut which the stranger had apparently pulled from the stoat's ear.

Tammo caught on right away to Midge's trick. Sliding a candied chestnut from the pouch under his blanket, he hobbled past Skaup, who had lowered his sword. Midge noted what Tammo had done, and gave the ferret a snaggle-toothed grin. "Look at yer swordpoint, mate!"

Skaup lifted the sword level with his eyes and found himself gazing at a candied chestnut impaled upon it. "But . . . 'ow did that get there?"

Midge cackled as he performed a shuffling little jig. "Hee-heehee! An' how did two of us turn up 'ere when we're sup-posed ter be three? I dunno, do you, mate?"

Midge looked so comical that some of the vermin started laughing. Tammo joined in with his friend's dance, the pair of them whirling and stamping, rags and tatters jouncing and twirling. Soon all the vermin were laughing at their antics, even Skaup.

From his hiding place behind a stately elm, Rockjaw smiled. Midge and Tammo were safe for the moment. Keeping a safe distance, the big hare shadowed the party as they made their way back to the Rapscallion camp.

Skaup trudged alongside Midge, eyeing him curiously.

"Yore a clever ole beast, Miggo. Let's see yer pull a chestnut out o' my ear, go on!"

Midge's unpatched eye twinkled slyly. "No need to, bucko. Look, there's one stuck to yer cloak!"

Skaup shook his head in wonderment as he pulled the sticky nut from the cloak across his shoulders and munched happily on it. "Yore pal there, Burfal, why don't 'e never say anythin'?"

Midge passed a paw across his throat, grinning wickedly. "We 'ad an argument when we was both young 'uns. Burfal called me some bad names, so I cut 'is throat. Haharr, 'e lived through it, but 'e ain't never spoke a single word since that day. Heeheehee! Ole Burfal won't call anybeast bad names no more!"

It was getting toward evening when they reached the Rapscallion camp on the hillside above the stream. A shudder passed through Tammo as he followed Skaup's party. There were countless vermin crouched around fires, cooking, resting, squabbling, and arguing with their neighbors. Drums throbbed ceaselessly, and hideously painted faces glared curiously at the two disguised hares. Everybeast was armed with an ugly array of weaponry, from cutlasses and spears down to what looked like sharpened hooks set on long poles.

Smoke from the fires swirled around them as they reached the stream bank. Skaup halted his party in front of a tent with four rats guarding the entrance, and laid the supplies they had foraged for on the ground.

Tammo and Midge were pushed forward. Suddenly the tent flap was thrown back and they found themselves face-to-face with Damug Warfang, Firstblade of all Rapscallions. Though the fur on his back stood rigid with fright, Tammo could not help being impressed by Damug's barbarically splendid appearance. The Greatrat was wearing the helmet with a skull on its spike, and his slitted feral eyes glared at them out of a scarlet and blue painted face. He wore a close-meshed tunic of silver mail, belted about with a broad snakeskin band. Sandals and gauntlets of green lizard skin covered his paws.

Damug Warfang leaned forward, his powerful frame like a coiled steel spring as he pointed at the hares with his symbol of office, the sword with two edges, one straight, the other like the waves of the sea.

"What do you want here? You are not Rapscallions!"

Midge nodded his head knowingly as he spoke out boldly, "I was a Rapscallion long afore you was born. I served under yore father, Gormad Tunn. Wait now, don't tell me, you'll be Damug the youngest son, or was it the eldest? I forget. Didn't you 'ave a brother? Haharr, I remember now, 'twas Byral. Where's 'e got to these days?"

Damug's eyes glinted dangerously. "You ask a lot of questions for a ragged old creature. Silence is the best policy for one such as you when I am holding a sword!"

Midge sat down on the ground. He pulled an assortment of colored pebbles and some carved twigs from beneath his sacking gown, and tossed them in the air. Totally ignoring the Warlord, he studied the jumble of wood and stone on the grass in front of him. Then in a sing-song voice he said, "I got no need to ask questions, my signs tell me all. The moon an' stars, the wind in the trees, an' water that runs through the land, all these things whisper their secrets to me."

Midge could tell by the look in Damug's eyes that he had captured the Warlord's interest. The Greatrat sheathed his sword. "You are a Seer, one who can look into the future?"

"Somebeasts have called me Seer. Maybe they're right, who can tell?"

"Who is that beast with you, is he a Seer also?"

"Not Burfal. He is called the Silent One an' must be allowed to roam free an' unhindered. Burfal, go!"

Tammo sensed that Midge was giving him an excuse to find Rockjaw and report to him. Smiling foolishly he wandered off.

Damug turned to Skaup. "Let nobeast harm Burfal; he may go where he pleases. Seer, what do they call you?"

"My name is Miggo. 'Twas given to me on the night of the dark moon by a black fox."

Damug stared at Midge for a long time, then beckoned to him, "Come into my tent, Miggo. You there, bring food and drink for this creature. The rest of you, get about your business."

Tammo's footpaws shook as he made his way through the camp. He could feel Skaup watching him, so instead of traveling in a straight line he wandered willy nilly. The aim of his walk was to take him over the hilltop, away from the camp, where he would seek out Rockjaw Grang.

Night had fallen now, and all over the hillside the vermin campfires burnt small islands of light into the darkness. Tammo was threading his way 'round one fire when he stumbled awkwardly. A hardwood stick had been thrust between his footpaws by one of the vermin seated at the edge of the fire. It was the ferret Rinkul. As Tammo tried to pull himself upright, Rinkul kicked him flat.

"Wot are you doin' skulkin' 'round our camp, yer dirty ole bundle of smells? Well, speak up!"

Tammo shook his head wildly, pointing dumbly to his mouth.

One of Rinkul's friends, a wily-looking vixen, snatched the dirk from Tammo's rope belt and held it to the firelight. "An ole slobberpaws like you shouldn't be carryin' a blade like this'n 'round. Bit o' cleanin' up an' this'll make a fine weapon fer me."

Suddenly Skaup was on the pair of them, whacking both Rinkul and the vixen heftily with his spear haft. "Don't y'dare put a paw near Burfal again, either o' ye!"

Tammo retrieved his dirk from where the vixen had dropped it, then he staggered off into the night as Skaup continued beating Rinkul and the vixen.

"Owch! Yaagh! We was only 'avin' a bit o' fun. Yowch! Aargh!"

"Fun, was it? I'll give ye fun! Firstblade's orders is that nobeast is to bother ole Burfal. Either o' ye lay paw on 'im agin an' Warfang'll slay yer good'n'slow. See!"

Skaup thwacked away with the spearhaft until he decided they had been punished thoroughly.

Tammo was relieved to be away from the Rapscallion camp. It was calm and peaceful on the other side of the hill; only the distant throb of drums on the night air reminded him of the vermin encampment. Suddenly a big dark figure detached itself from a clump of boulders and waved to him.

"Sithee, Tamm, over here, mate!"

Good old Rockjaw Grang. They crouched together in the outcrop, and Rockjaw dug oat scones, cheese, and cider from his sizeable pack. He shared the food with Tammo as the young hare made his report.

"Midge has got his jolly old paws well under the table there. Damug thinks he's some kind o' Seer. Any news of the battleground yet, Rock?"

The giant hare demolished a scone in one bite. "Nay, 'tis too early yet. May'aps the Major'll get word to me on the morrow."

Tammo squinted uncomfortably from beneath his odious rags. "Sooner the better, wot. I don't want t'stay in that foul place a moment longer'n I have to, chum."

"Aye, well, that's wot y'get for runnin' with Long Patrol, young Tamm. You'd best finish up vittlin' an' get back afore yore missed. I'll be here tomorrow night, same place."

39

Midge knew he was playing a risky game. Damug was no fool. He sat staring at the disguised hare across a small fire, which was laid in a pit at the center of his tent.

"Speak to me, Miggo, tell me something."

Midge stared into the flames awhile, then he spoke: "I see a mountain and a badger Warrior with eyes like blood. I see Gormad Tunn and a fleet defeated there."

Damug Warfang rose and, reaching across the fire, seized Midge around the neck. Lifting him high, Damug shook him like a rag. "Anybeast could have told you that, you sniveling wreck. Tell me of my future and tell me quickly, before *your* future ebbs away as I strangle you!"

Fighting for breath and with colored lights dancing before his eyes, Midge Manycoats dangled above Damug's head. Grabbing what he needed from beneath his ragged garb, he planted the object, at the same time kicking out with a footpaw and catching the Warlord in one eye.

Midge managed to shout hoarsely, "I see! I see your future!"

Damug dropped him, squinting hard, and pawed at his eye

make sure no damage had been done. Midge sat up, massaging his throat. Damug was sitting in his former position, the eye watering and smarting slightly. He stared unruffled at Midge, unwilling to let him see that he had been hurt.

"Well then, what do you see? Tell me."

Midge went back to his former seat at the other side of the fire. Again he took out his pebbles and twigs, tossing them in the air and watching how they fell. He spoke like one in a trance.

"Here are ten twigs, each of them represents one hundred Rapscallions; this means you command a thousand. These stones are red, the color of blood, the color of a red sandstone Abbey. Only one stone can rule that place, that is your stone, the brown one. Brown, the color of the earth and the symbol of the Firstblade who will conquer all the earth."

Midge closed his eyes and lapsed into silence. After a while, Damug became impatient, wanting to know more.

"Where is this brown stone? I see only twigs and red stones on the floor. Tell me quickly, Seer, where is the brown stone?"

Reaching into his rags, Midge cast a pawful of powder into the fire. The flames gave forth smoke as they burned blue.

"Aaaahh! 'Tis up to ye to find it, Firstblade. The stone cannot be found in yore heart. Allbeasts know that a Warlord's heart is made o' stone, so how can a stone be found within a stone? But 'tis also known that you are wise—mayhaps the stone is in yore brain. Can you look inside yore skull, Damug Warfang?"

Mystified, the Greatrat took off his helmet and placed it on the ground. He touched his own head, back, front, and beside both ears, all the time glaring through the firesmoke at Midge.

"Find a brown stone inside my own skull? Do you take me for an idiot? Let me warn you, Miggo, if you think you're going to pull something from my ear, I've seen that done before—try it and you're a deadbeast!"

Midge folded his paws, staring back at Damug. "I'll sit over here, Sire. If I tried anythin' you'd say it was a trick. My voices tell me the brown stone is inside yore skull; more'n that I cannot say."

Damug touched his head again, this time more carefully—

running both paws along his jawline, around his eyes and the base of his skull. Suddenly he jumped up angrily, shaking his head. "This is stupid! You talk in riddles. How could there be a brown stone inside my skull? Rubbish!"

He kicked the war helmet to one side. From the mouth of the rabbit skull impaled on its spike, a brown stone rolled forth.

Trying not to show his immense relief, Midge pointed. "See, the skull belongs t'you. Did I not say the brown stone could be found inside yore skull?"

Midge Manycoats had guessed correctly. Damug Warfang was like any other conqueror, superstitious and ready to believe in omens and signs.

Damug picked up the simple brown pebble and gazed in wonder at it. "You spoke truly, Miggo. You have the gift of a Seer. What is my future? Tell me—I must know!"

Midge knew now that he had his fish well hooked. Closing his eyes, he sat back, remote and aloof. "I need food and drink now, rest too. Have quarters prepared for me and my friend, Burfal the Silent One. Tomorrow we will talk."

Rinkul the ferret was smarting from the beating he had received, but that did not stop him. He limped about the Rapscallion camp, looking for the one called Burfal. There was something about the dumb creature that disturbed him. Using the hardwood stick to aid his walking, he crisscrossed the hillside, checking the creatures around their campfires. Maybe it was something in Burfal's eyes, in the way he had looked at him.

"If yer after vittles, we ain't got none 'ere, mate!"

Rinkul ignored Sneezewort and questioned Lousewort. "May'aps you've seen a raggy ole beast about, one o' the two who came inter camp earlier on? Did 'e pass this way?"

Lousewort sucked on a fishbone and thought for a moment. "Er, er, y'mean the Silent One? Stay away from 'im, matey, Firstblade's orders. Did you 'ear, Cap'n Skaup knocked the livin' daylights out o' a few smarty-chops that tried interferin' wid that dumb beast. Stupid fools, serves 'em right, I say!"

Rinkul's hardwood stick rapped Lousewort's nose viciously. "When I wants yore opinion I'll ask for it, mud-bottom. Now, which way did the dumb beast go?"

Sneezewort pointed toward the stream. "Went by us a moment back, 'eaded thataways."

Supported by his stick, Rinkul hobbled off to the stream. Lousewort hugged his nose tenderly as he watched the ferret go. "There wath no need for him to do that, wath there!"

Tammo had seen the caged squirrel on the stream bank. Pulling faces, and pushing the two stoats guarding the cage, he made it clear that he did not want them around. The guards retreated a distance to the nearest fire, where they sat warming themselves. Word had got around regarding the Silent One, and they were careful not to offend him.

Drawing his dirk, Tammo pushed it through the bars and began prodding the old squirrel, pretending to have some cruel fun with him. Moving to the cage's far side to avoid the blade, the old creature cast a withering glance at his tormentor.

"Do yore worst, vermin. I ain't afeared of ye!"

Tammo's whisper barely reached his ears. "Sorry, old chap. Can't speak up, they think I'm dumb, y'see. I'm no vermin, this is a disguise. Really I'm a hare of the Long Patrol. I'll help you if I can."

Lying flat, the squirrel rolled over, closer to Tammo so that he could whisper back. "Get me some food an' a blade!"

"I'll try, but don't attempt anything on your own. Leave this to me an' my friend—he's disguised like me."

Before he spoke further, Tammo took a swift look about and saw Rinkul leaning on his stick, watching him. Throwing caution to the winds, Tammo dashed at the ferret and dove on him. They went down together. Tammo grabbed Rinkul, pulling him on top of himself and uttering little mute squeaks of distress.

A Rapmark stoat named Bluggach, who was seated by the fire with the two guards, grabbed his cutlass. "Lookit that, the addle-brained oaf, don't 'e know no better? Damug gave orders not t'touch the dumb 'un! Cummon, mates!"

Rinkul found himself roughly hauled off Tammo, his protests lost among the angry roars of Bluggach and the two guards as they thrashed him with the flats of their blades.

"Git off that beast. Wot d'yer think yore doin'?"

"We've all been ordered to stay clear of 'im!"

"You wanna dig the soil out'n yore ears, ferret!"

"I ain't gonna report this or Lord Damug'd kill yer, but you gotta learn to obey orders. Teach 'im a lesson, mates!"

Gathering his rags about him, Tammo fled the scene.

Midge stuck his head out of a canvas shelter that had been erected between a bush and a rock. He peered into the night at the lumpy figure ambling aimlessly about.

"Tamm, over here, pal! We've got our own special quarters!"

Tammo scrambled gratefully into the shelter and crouched by the fire. Midge passed him some rough-looking barley-cakes, a piece of cooked fish, and a canteen of strong grog, but Tammo put it aside, saying, "Thanks, Midge, but I've already eaten. I contacted Rockjaw and he gave me supper. But tell me your news first—how did y'get on with old thingummy Warface?"

The friends exchanged information, telling each other all they had experienced since arriving at the Rapscallion camp. Tammo tightened his paw 'round the dirk handle, gritting his teeth. "Those vermin we were tracking—remember the one that got away? I've seen him, the ferret they call Rinkul. He was the last of the murderers who slew the old badgerlady and my friend Russa; the scum still carries her stick. First chance I get I'll make him pay for them!"

Midge shook his head. "That's not what we were sent here for, Tamm. You'll get your chance at Rinkul, but not here—it could cost our lives an' the safety of Redwall. Let's rest up a bit, then when all's quiet we'll take food to the squirrel. I've got a small blade with me, we'll deliver that to him as well. Rest awhile now."

Long after the midnight hour had passed and the sprawling Rapscallion camp lay silent, two figures made their way carefully down to the prisoner in his cage by the stream.

40

Redwall's twin bells had tolled out the midnight hour, but their muted tones were heard only by the three creatures who were still awake. Abbess Tansy, Friar Butty, and Craklyn the Recorder sat around a table in the kitchens, studying the journal of Abbess Germaine. It had been written countless seasons ago when the Abbey was actually under construction. The little owl Orocca had watched them awhile, waiting for Taunoc, who had gone off under the command of Major Perigord. When it became apparent he would not be returning that night, Orocca retired to care for her three owlchicks in the kitchen cupboard.

Butty selected some hot muffins, which his helpers had baked for next morning's breakfast, took a bowl of curds, flavored it with honey, and stirred in roasted almonds. He brewed a jug of rose-petal and plum-flower tea and set the lot on the table, inviting his friends to help themselves.

"It's sort of half breakfast an' half supper, suppfast, I calls it, when I'm up very late cookin' down here. Tell us more about this place called Kotir, marm."

Craklyn opened the journal at an illustrated page. "This is

what it must have looked like, an old crumbling castle, damp, dark, and ruled over by fearsome wildcats, backed by a vermin horde. Martin the Warrior and his friends destroyed it and defeated the enemy, long before Redwall was built. They diverted a river and flooded the valley in which Castle Kotir stood. It sank beneath the waters and was never seen again. Redwall was built from the north side first, I think the south wall was to have been bordered by the lake that had covered Kotir. But our Abbey was not built in one season, nor ten, nor even twenty. You can see by these sketches farther on that by the time the north wall was erected, the lake had begun to dry up. Abbess Germaine states that all the soil and rock dug up for the Abbey foundations was dumped into the lake. Well, over a number of seasons the lake became little more than a swamp, the only trace of it being a spring that bubbled up in a hollow some distance from the original lake site. This kept throwing up clear water until it became incorporated in the Redwall plans as an Abbey pond."

Tansy blew upon her tea and sipped noisily. "The very same pond we have in our grounds today, how clever! But carry on, Craklyn. What happened next?"

"Hmm, it says here that by the time the main Abbey building was in progress, a drought arrived after the winter. Spring, summer, and autumn were intensely hot and dry, not a drop of rain throughout all three seasons. Even the Abbey pond shrunk by half its length and breadth. What had once been swamp became firm and hard ground, with tree seedlings taking root on its east side. So they ignored the fact that Castle Kotir, or a lake, or even a swamp had once been there, and carried on to build Redwall Abbey."

Craklyn closed the journal and dipped a hot muffin in the sweetened curd mixture. Friar Butty flipped through the pages; yellowed and dusty, they seemed to breathe ancient history. He paused at one page with a small illustration at its chapter heading.

"Here 'tis, see! A sketch of the completed Abbey with a dotted line representin' Kotir an' where it once stood. There's the answer!"

Abbess Tansy brushed muffin crumbs from the parchment. "Well, I never. They built the south wall right over the part where Castle Kotir's northwest walltower stood. So after all these seasons the ground has decided to give way, and that hole we were looking down must be the inside of Kotir's walltower. It would be fascinating to climb down there if it was dry and safe enough."

Orocca's head appeared around the partially open cupboard door. "You'll beg my pardon saying, Abbess, but I wish you'd stop all your noisy yammering and go now. These eggchicks need their sleep!"

Tansy began gathering up the remains of the meal carefully. "I'm sorry, Orocca. Right, let's away to our beds. We'll take a look down there first thing in the morning. Shad and Foremole will go with us, I'm sure."

As dawn shed its light over the flatlands west of Redwall, Major Perigord sat up in the dry ditch bed where he had passed the night. Captain Twayblade was balancing on a thick protruding root, scanning the dewy fields in front of her.

Perigord reached up and tugged her footpaw. "My watch I think, old gel. Any sign of 'em yet?"

Twayblade climbed down from her perch. "Not a bally eartip. Where d'you s'pose they've got to, sah?"

The Major drew the rags of his once-splendid green velvet tunic about him and yawned. "Who knows? Torgoch an' Morio are a blinkin' law unto themselves when they're on the loose together. I say there, come on, Taunoc, you jolly old bundle of feathers, up in the air with you an' scout the terrain, wot!"

Taunoc peered from under his wing, then struggled from beneath the ferns where he had been sleeping, and blinked owlishly.

"Strictly speaking, I am a nocturnal bird, not widely given to flapping about in dawnlight like a skylark. What is it you want?"

With a flourish, Perigord drew his saber and poked at the sky. "I require your fine-feathered frame cleaving the upper atmosphere, lookin' out for any sign of our friends. That too much trouble?"

With a short hopping run the little owl launched into flight. "After a night in a ditch, nothing is too much trouble."

He soared high, wheeling several times before dropping like a stone. "Your Sergeant and Lieutenant are coming now, west and slightly south of here. I suggest you wave to denote your presence, Major."

Perigord climbed out of the ditch and waved his saber. It glittered in the early sunlight as he hallooed the two hares. "What ho, you chaps, what time d'you call this to come rollin' back home? Come on, Torgoch, on the double now!"

Sergeant and Lieutenant came panting up to the ditch. Throwing themselves flat in the damp grass, they lay recovering breath.

Morio raised himself up on one paw, his normally saturnine face glowing with pride. "We found the place, sah, day an' a half's march sou'west o' here. There's a rock stickin' up like an otter's tail top of a rollin' hill range, and beyond that a valley with a gorge runnin' through. Looks somethin' like this." In the bare earth of the ditch top he scraped out a rough outline with his knifepoint.

Twayblade nodded approvingly. "Well done, chaps, looks a great spot for a picnic, eh, wot?"

Perigord studied it, obviously pleased by what he saw. "Aye, we could shell a few acorns there! Stretch our forces along the ridge and send out a decoy party t'lead 'em into the valley from the south side. If we can get 'em with the gorge at their backs and the hill in front, 'twill be an ideal battleground. Taunoc, time for you t'do your bit, old lad. Fly out an' scout this place. When you're satisfied as to its location, seek out Rockjaw Grang and tell him exactly where the battlefield is to be. Got that?"

Once again the little owl heaved himself into the air. "I think I am reasonably intelligent enough to understand you, Major. After all, I am an owl, not a hare!"

When the owl was well away, Sergeant Torgoch grinned at Twayblade. "Well curl me ears, marm, there goes an 'uffy bird if ever I saw one. Bet 'e counts 'is feathers regular!"

"You, sir, would find yourself counting your ears after an encounter with me, I can assure you!"

Torgoch almost leapt with fright as the owl landed beside him. The bird stared accusingly at Perigord. "You gave me the location and told me to whom I should deliver the information, but you did not mention when the battle is to take place.''

The Major bowed courteously to Taunoc. ''Beg pardon, I stand corrected. Shall we say three days, or however long after that the Rapscallions can be delayed? We need to play for all the time we can get. My thanks to ye, sir!''

Long after the owl had flown, Sergeant Torgoch looked mortified. ''I really opened me big mouth an' put me footpaw in it there!''

41

Abbess Tansy and her party were ready for the descent into the pit beneath the south wall. Friar Butty was armed with a stout copper ladle, his chosen weapon. Foremole Diggum and Shad the Gatekeeper had lengths of rope, lanterns, and a fine rope ladder that Ginko the Bellringer had loaned them. Tansy and Craklyn had donned their oldest smocks, and between them they carried a hamper of food.

It was a good hot summer morning. Tare and Turry of the Long Patrol were pushing a wheelbarrow about on the lawn. Three little owlchicks and the badgerbabe Russano sat on a heap of dry straw in the barrow, taking their daily perambulation.

Tansy waved to them as they passed. "See you later. Bye bye!"

Waving back, the babies repeated the word they used most often. "Nut! Nut!"

Craklyn fell about laughing. Shad opened the food hamper and tossed a pawful of candied chestnuts into the barrow for them. "Bye bye, hah! These liddle tykes know wot's good for 'em!"

Having lit the lanterns, Friar Butty strung them at regula intervals upon a long rope and lowered it into the depths providing illumination all the way down. Shad secured th rope ladder and let it unroll into the void. "I'll go first," h said. "Butty next, then Abbess an' Craklyn. Foremole, yo follow last. Remember now, take y'time an' step easy!"

One by one they descended into the silent pit, lantern ligh and shadows dancing eerily around the rough rock walls tha surrounded them. Scarcely a quarter of the way down, Fore mole pointed a digging claw at the wall in front of him.

"Yurr, thurr be's ee writin' that Bunto see'd!"

Foremole Diggum had remembered that Bunto, one of hi mole crew, had seen writing carved upon the wall.

Craklyn studied it. "See these broken rock ends and bits c shattered timber? There must have been a spiral stairway run ning from top to bottom of the walltower once. There's a spac that may have been a window, all blocked with earth now This carving is beside it—probably some vermin soldier di it while he was idling away the hours on guard duty at tha very window."

Tansy tweaked at her friend's footpaw, which was directl above her head on the ladder. "Never mind the architectur what does the writing say?"

The Recorder's voice echoed boomingly as she read o aloud.

"Turn at the lowest stair,
Right is the left down there,
Every pace you must count,
At ten times paws amount,
See where a deathbird flies,
Under the hunter's eyes,
Radiant in splendor fair,
Ever mine, hidden where?

Verdauga, Lord of Kotir."

Clinging to the ladder, Tansy looked up at her friend as th echoes faded to silence in the strange atmosphere. "Sounc like some sort of riddle to me. Craklyn, what are you doing up there—writing?''

''Scrap o' parchment and a stick of charcoal always come in useful,'' the old Recorder muttered busily as she scraped away. ''I never go anywhere without them. This won't take long. Hmm, Verdauga, he was mentioned in Abbess Germaine's journal, some sort of wildcat who ruled Mossflower before Martin the Warrior arrived. There, I've got it!''

Foremole Diggum, who was last on the ladder, grunted impatiently. ''Ho, gudd for ee, marm. Can us'n's git down thurr naow? Oi'm not gurtly pleased 'angin' 'round up yurr!''

It was a long and arduous descent. When they touched ground at the pit bottom, Friar Butty peered upward to the platform. It looked very small and far off.

''Phew!'' he said, nodding in admiration. ''Just think, Skipper dove from up there, what a brave an' darin' beast! I think if I tried it I'd prob'ly die of fright halfway down.''

Shad tapped his tail against the mud-coated rocks. ''Since the waters dried up, mate, you'd die fer sure if you landed 'ere. Right, let's git the lay o' the land.''

He lit another lantern and they moved gingerly on the slippery stones of the dried streambed, staring at their surroundings. It was little more than a stone chamber, with a gaping hole at eye level where the water had flowed in from the right, and another hole beneath their paws to the left, where the stream had exited downward.

Tansy found a dry rock and sat down. ''It's very smelly and cold. We'd best watch we don't slip and fall down that hole—goodness knows where we'd end up. Well, anyone got some bright ideas? This place looks like a dead end.''

Craklyn studied the verse she had copied, then took a careful look around. She pointed to a spot not far above their heads. ''Look there, up to the left. There's a hole in the wall, but it's blocked by rubble and old timbers. I think that was where the stairs finished originally. We must be standing below the old ground level now, where the water carved the floor away.''

Shad climbed back up the ladder, swinging it inward until he could reach the hole in the side of the wall. He secured the rope ladder to a splintered wood beam that stuck out. ''Aye, yore right, marm, this is where the last stair was. I think we might've found a passage 'ere. Stand clear while I try an' unblock it.''

Huddling beneath an overhang at the cave's far side, they watched rock, timber, and masonry pouring from the hole as the husky otter cleared away the debris. It was not long before he called down to them, ''Haharr, 'tis a passage sure enough—dry, too. C'mon up, mateys!''

One by one Shad helped them from the rope ladder into the passage. Foremole discovered a shattered pine beam and, using a dash of lantern oil, soon had a fire burning cheerily.

''Thurr ee go. Oi thinks us'n's be 'avin' a warm an' summ vittles afore us do ought else, bo urr!''

Abbess Tansy warmed her paws gratefully. ''What would we do without a good and sensible Foremole?''

Friar Butty unpacked a latticed fruit tart, some nutbread, and a flask of elderberry wine, which he set by the fire to warm. As the friends ate they discussed the verse that Craklyn had copied.

''So,'' said Tansy, ''it wasn't an idle sentry who carved those words, it was the Lord of the castle himself. But why put it there in plain view?''

Craklyn explained what she had seen. ''It wasn't exactly in plain view, though. I noticed some spike holes in the stone; there must have been a wall hanging or a curtain hiding the verse. Maybe Verdauga was getting old and he carved it there to remind himself.''

Foremole sliced the tart evenly, shaking his head. ''Hurr, 'tis a gurt puzzlement tho', marm. 'Roight is ee left daown thurr,' wot do that mean?''

''I know it sounds odd, but it's not really. Creatures who hide something and write about it usually try to trick others by arranging the words so they sound strange. 'Right is the left down there' means that the left passage is the right one to take. I could say that two ways; either the left is the right one to take, or as Verdauga put it, right is the left to take. See?''

Butty poured out small amounts of the warm wine for them. ''I'm with you, miz Craklyn, 'tis right to take the left passage, an' that's the one we're in now, lucky enough. I think I've got the next two lines as well. 'Every pace you must count,

At ten times paws amount.' Everybeast has four paws, so add ten to that an' it makes fourteen paces we must count."

A smile hovered on the Recorder's lips as she challenged the Friar. "Is that right? Go on then, young Butty, take the lantern and walk fourteen paces down this passage. Tell us what you find."

The young squirrel marched off, counting precisely. He was lost to sight at the count of eight, where the passage took a bend. Shortly he returned to sit by the fire, scratching his chin. "Hmph! Wasn't a thing there, nothin' except stone walls!"

Craklyn shook a paw at him in mock severity. "That's because your arithmetic was wrong, Friar. Work it out properly now. You have four paws, and the line says 'Ten times paws amount.' *Times!*"

The answer dawned upon Butty suddenly. "Of course, ten times four is forty—it means take forty paces!"

Tansy passed him a slice of tart. "Well done, sir, but let's have our meal, then we'll all go and count it out together."

Beyond the turn a long passage stretched before them, dark and gloomy, layered with the dust of untold ages. So intense was the silence that they paced on tip-paws, whispering out the count. Tansy looked left and right at the forbidding bare stone walls and the worn paved floor. What sort of creatures had walked them in the distant past? How long had it been since a living beast set paw down here?

"Thirty-eight, thirty-nine, forty!"

"Well wallop me rudder, look at this, messmates!"

A great shuttered window stood before them, broad and high, its lintel, sill, and corbels intricately carved with sinister designs. Shad unlatched the shutters, announcing jokingly, "Wonderful view o' Mossflower countryside from 'ere. Take a look!"

Cobwebs parted as Shad drew back the creaking shutters, revealing the entire frame, packed solid with stone and dark earth. He shut them again and pushed the rusty latch into place.

"Too far down even for roots or worms to travel. Question is, wot are we supposed t'look for now?"

Craklyn repeated the fifth and sixth lines of the verse:

"See where a deathbird flies,
Under the hunter's eyes."

Tansy shuddered as she held up the lantern to inspect th sill. "These carvings are skillfully done, but they're horrible See here, there's a snake swallowing a little mouse, and here two rats are cutting up a skylark with curved knives. Every where you look there's cruelty and murder being done. N wonder Martin and his friends fought so hard against the ver min who lived here. But where's the deathbird and th hunter?"

Piece by piece they went over the grisly scenes until Shad being the tallest, stood on the sill and held up the lantern t view the lintel overhead.

"Is this wot yore lookin' for, marm?"

He was pointing to a picture of a raven. The big black bir was trying to fly away, but it was trapped by a leaping wildca that had bitten deep into the raven's back.

Craklyn clenched her paws tightly, fascinated yet repulse by the dreadful image. "Yes, that's it, Shad! The wildcat i the hunter, and the raven has long been known as the deathbir for the way that it feasts upon carcasses of dead creatures. I'n sure that is it!"

They sat upon the windowsill, looking at one another in th flickering lamplight. Tansy read out the final two lines:

"Radiant in splendor fair,
Ever mine, hidden where?"

Young Friar Butty hunched his shoulders, shivering slightly "I couldn't imagine anythin' radiant or splendidly fair dow here, but if there is I'll bet 'tis behind the carvin'!"

Shad took out his knife and stood up on the sill. "Well let's see, shall we!"

He tapped with the knife handle, rapping the corbels an the surrounding wall, finally hitting the lintel several smar raps. "Aye, yore right, Friar. Sounds as if there's a cavity wal above this lintel. Pass me the lantern."

The light was passed up to Shad. He dug and scraped awa

with his blade until they were forced to vacate the sill beneath him.

"You'm sendin' daown a turrible dust, zurr. Wot be you'm a doin'?"

"Oh! Sorry 'bout that, mates, but there's a big stone that's stickin' out a bit up 'ere. I'm just diggin' out the mortar wot's holdin' it in. I reckon wot we're after lies be'ind it."

"Yurr, oi'll coom up an' 'elp ee. Lend oi yore young shoulders thur, Butty, let oi git moi diggen claws worken on et."

Butty stood on the sill, grunting as Foremole Diggum clambered up onto his shoulders.

Shad and Foremole blinked mortar dust from their eyes as they dug, tugged, and probed. The otter grasped the lantern ring in his mouth to leave both paws free.

Craklyn watched them anxiously. "Do be careful now, mind your paws don't get jammed in the cracks."

"Stan' asoide, lukkee owt naow, yurr ee comes!"

With a few mighty heaves the two creatures pulled the big oblong wallstone free and dropped it.

Boom!

It shattered a section of the paved floor as it fell, sending up a choking dust cloud, through which Shad could be seen, one paw rummaging deep in the hole as he held out several glittering objects with the other.

"Ahoy there, hearties, lookit wot I found! Owowooh! Me paw!"

There was a rumbling, crumbling sound as the stones above collapsed down, trapping the paw Shad had buried in the wall space. He hung there awkwardly, gritting his teeth against the pain. Then everything happened without an instant's notice.

Foremole slipped from Butty's shoulders and fell backward as, with a dull roar, the entire wall and ceiling disintegrated in an avalanche of stone, mortar, and thick choking dust!

42

Vermin snored and muttered in their sleep, fighting imaginary battles, some of them even singing snatches of songs as they lay around their campfire embers in the warm summer night. The guards of the cage were still at the fire of the stoat Bluggach, within easy distance of the prisoner they were supposed to be watching. Like Bluggach, they too were flat on their backs, mouths open wide to the sounds of their painful rasping snores.

The old squirrel watched the two ragged figures' silent approach to his cage. He grabbed at the food they pushed through the bars to him, and his throat moved up and down as he gulped water from a canteen, drinking until the vessel was empty. With his head bent low he gave a long sigh of satisfaction, then began chewing the food slowly, while Midge whispered questions at him.

"What do they call you, and how did y'come to be here?"

"My name is Fourdun. I live alone in Mossflower. They took me by surprise—I must be gettin' old."

Midge passed the small knife through to him. "We're both Long Patrol hares. I'm Midge, he's Tammo. Listen to me, old feller—don't do anythin' silly. We'll get you free. Maybe tomorrow night or the night after, but we'll do it. So watch out for us an' don't try escapin' by yourself."

Nudging Midge, Tammo hissed urgently, "Look out, that big stoat Cap'n's awake!"

Bluggach woke with a throat that was both sore and dry from snoring. Coughing hoarsely several times, he staggered down to the stream. Crouching in the shallows, the stoat pawed water into his mouth until he had drunk enough, then he straightened up and belched.

There was no place for Tammo or Midge to hide—one movement from either of them and they would be discovered. Midge shoved Tammo toward the stream, muttering to him, "Sit by the water an' look as if you're meditatin'—hurry!"

Tammo walked straight for the stoat, bumping into him as he slumped by the shallows, and stared intently into the water. Bluggach was about to say something when Midge strolled up.

"Pleasant night to ye, Cap'n. Take no notice of ole Burfal, 'e goes off doin' odd things any hour o' the day or dark."

The stoat drew his cutlass, eyeing Midge suspiciously. "Wot are yew doin' 'round 'ere?"

Midge produced the flask of grog he had been about to give Fourdun. "Oh, jus' keepin' an' eye on Burfal, seein' 'e don't disturb nobeast. 'Ere, take a pull o' this, sir, Warfang's own private grog. 'Twill put a throat on ye like a cob o' velvet."

Bluggach was still not quite convinced by Midge, but he took a good swig of the fiery grog as he weighed the ragged beast up. "You'll be the Seer, then? Some sez yore a magic creature."

Smiling craftily, Midge moved close to the stoat and reached out. "I ain't magic, Cap'n. You are, though. Wot's this candied chestnut doin' in yore earlug?"

Grinning widely, the big stoat tossed the nut into his mouth and gave Midge a friendly shove that almost knocked him flat. "I knew you was magic the moment I clapped eyes on ya, haharrharr!"

Midge laughed along with him, urging Bluggach to drink some more. "Bein' magic ain't as good as bein' a Rapmark Cap'n like you, sir."

The stoat warmed to the tattered Seer. Throwing a paw about him, he said, "Ho, ain't it though? I tell yer, matey, sometimes I wish I c'd magic some discipline inter this lot. Lookit those two, snorin' like weasels at a weddin', an' they're supposed t'be on guard! But tell me more about yore magic. Y'know wot I like, haharr, I likes beasts like yerself who know clever riddles. Go on, do a riddle fer me. 'Tis ages since I 'eard a good 'un."

Midge tapped a dirty paw against his stained teeth. "Hmm, a riddle, now lemme see . . . Ah, 'ere's a riddle fer ye. Wot goes gurgle gurgle snuffle trickle blubber ripple scrawf scrawf? D'yer know the answer to that one, Cap'n?"

Bluggach took another good pull at the grog and sat down, narrowing one eye and scratching his head. Midge beckoned Tammo silently, and together they began moving away. The stoat Captain drank some more, halting them with an unsteady wave.

"Er, burgle sniffle truckle sprawl, wot goes like that? Hah! That's a good 'un, mate. I dunno, tell me the answer."

Midge pointed at the two sentries sleeping by the fire at the water's edge. "There's yore answer, Cap'n. Two fat lazy guards sleepin' their 'eads off by a stream all night. C'mon, Burfal, time we was goin'."

They departed as the joke's punch line dawned on Bluggach, and made their way back to the shelter and their own fire with the stoat Captain's laughter ringing out behind them.

"Oh harrharrharr, that's a good 'un, hohohoho! Wake up, you two, an' lissen t'this. Harrharrhohoho! Wot goes grungle snirtle, worf worf an' sleeps like youse two by the stream all night? Yarrharrhahaha! Betcha don't know the answer, do yer?"

Sitting beside their own fire, the two hares discussed their plans.

"If Rockjaw gets a message from the Major tomorrow, we'll be able to quit this place once I've worked more of my magic on Warfang."

Gathering his rags about him, Tammo lay back to rest. "Aye, but we'd best wait until late night to make our escape. That'll be a good time to break Fourdun out, too—we can't leave him there for the vermin to starve an' torment, he must go with us."

Midge smiled at the determination on his young friend's face. "Of course Fourdun's goin' with us, wouldn't have it any other way, Tamm. But it ain't goin' to be easy, by the left it ain't!"

By mid-morning of the following day, Rockjaw Grang had shifted his hiding place. Moving farther downhill, he settled himself in a dip, surrounded by rock and bushes. Not knowing how long it would be before he could once more sample the good food of Redwall, the giant hare ate sparingly. Munching on a russet apple, he checked his weapons. He laid out his heavy arrows and counted them, then rubbed beeswax on the stout string of his great yew bow. Rockjaw tested his sling, refilled the pebble bag, and set himself to honing a long dagger on a smooth stone.

Taunoc appeared beside him suddenly. Without raising an eye, the big fellow continued whetting his blade, commenting drily, "Sithee, bird, where'st thou been? Much longer sittin' 'ere alone an' I'd be talkin' to mahself!"

The little owl folded his wings rather moodily. "Continue with that attitude and you *will* be talking to yourself, sir! My late arrival was due entirely to the tardiness of your own compatriots. However, I am not here to bandy words with you. I bring important news, so listen carefully."

Lady Cregga Rose Eyes was lost in strange country. She had plunged forward in the darkness, driven by the Bloodwrath, running all night until she could go no farther. Now, with her massive axpike clutched in both paws, the Badger Warrior lay amid the ferned fringe of an ash grove. She slept a fevered sleep, shivering, with her tongue lolling out and eyes half open, but unseeing.

From the grove, a colony of rooks watched, hoping the badger was so ill that she would soon be weak and dying. A young rook made as if to hop forward, but the leader, a hefty older male, buffeted him flat with a single wingsweep.

"Chakkarakk! We wait, take no chances with a stripedog.

When the sun sets we will fall on that one. Never have we tasted stripedog; there will be plenty there for all!"

The Long Patrol had risen at dawn. Picking up Sergeant Clubrush's trail, they pressed forward on the double. The Drill Sergeant was sitting cooling his paws in a brook. He watched them approach, gnawing his lip in disappointment. Ellbrig halted the column in front of Clubrush, who shook his head.

"Must be gettin' old lettin' 'er give me the blinkin' slip. I lost Lady Cregga's trail sometime in the night. But even if I 'adn't, what beast can keep up with a badger travelin' at 'er speed?"

"Sah, beg t'report," Trowbaggs called out from the back ranks. "Lady Cregga's tracks are here to the left, travelin' due west by the look of it!"

The veteran Shangle Widepad inspected the torn-up grass and scratched rocks. "Well spotted, young 'un. She's well off course, though."

Clubrush limped slowly over to the spot. After a quick glance he gave his verdict to Ellbrig in an undertone.

"Bad news for us, Lance Corporal. Looks like the Bloodwrath's full on 'er. Take four with you an' find 'er. We'll wait 'ere."

Trowbaggs, Deodar, Furgale, and Fallow jogged in a line abreast with Ellbrig. In broad daylight the trail of Rose Eyes was clear: ripped-up moss, flattened bushes, and trampled heather all told the story of the badger's flight.

The irrepressible Trowbaggs chatted constantly as they forged on. "I say, looks like a flippin' herd o' badgers passed this way, wot? This Bloodwrath thing, Corp—what's it all about?"

Ellbrig eyed the grinning recruit, about to tell him to mind his words, then he thought better of it. "You've as much right as the next beast t'know, I suppose. Bloodwrath is more a sickness than anythin', 'tis a terrible sight t'behold. I think 'tis mainly Badger Warriors suffer from it, though I 'ave 'eard o' otherbeasts taken by the Bloodwrath. Imagine hatin' an enemy so much that even if he had ten thousand at his back, y'd charge at 'im, aye, an' destroy many to get at 'im. They say a beast taken in Bloodwrath can fight on, even though wounded almost to death. Aye, they battle on still, as if they was fresh as a daisy, slayin' anybeast that stands afore 'em. Red-eyed, full of the lust for death, an' scornin' fear, that's Bloodwrath. Worst thing that c'n happen to a creature, I think!''

Trowbaggs was subdued by the Corporal's statement, but only for a moment. He nudged Furgale, saying, ''Hard luck on the foebeast, I'd say, but blinkin' useful to have a hefty dash o' the Bloodwrath on our side. Wot, wot!''

In the late afternoon, Ellbrig stopped to scan the weaving, meandering trail. ''Hmm, the fires appear t'be dyin' down. These tracks are all over the place, willy nilly. She can't be far ahead.''

Fallow pointed to the distant ash grove, set in a vale between three low-lying hills. ''I'll wager we find her there, 'tis where I'd make for if I was tired'n'weary. What d'you think, Corp?''

''Aye, I'd say you made a good bet. Let's get a move on. I think there's big birds flyin' low over that way.''

They increased the pace. Drawing closer to the grove, Ellbrig put on extra speed, roaring out an order. ''Out slings, it's rooks, they're attackin' somethin'!''

Yelling Eulalias and loosing off stones, the five hares leaped to the fray. Shrieking harshly, the rooks fled from their prey in a dark flapping mass, beating at one another with wing and talon in an effort to regain the safety of their grove.

A few bold ones remained, sticking out their necks and menacing the hares with their pointed beaks. Charging into the ferns, Ellbrig and his companions battered at the birds with loaded slings. Several rooks were slain before the birds finally fled.

Cregga Rose Eyes was surrounded by dead and dying birds. The big badger was ripped and pecked in a dozen places. Using her axpike for support, she staggered from the ferns with the hares assisting her. Ellbrig watched her carefully as she drank from a small canteen he had brought along, and he noted that her face was calm and her eyes had returned to their normal rose pink.

''Sar'nt Clubrush sent us, said you'd lost y'way, marm.''

Cregga looked slightly bewildered. Wiping a heavy paw across her eyes, she blinked at the Lance Corporal. "Lost? Yes, I suppose I was, in a way. Where are all the others?"

Ellbrig pointed in the direction they had come from. "Nearly a full day's march back that way, marm. Can y'make it?"

The badger set out slowly, her head bowed wearily. "Yes yes, you carry on, Corporal. I'll be fine."

Drill Sergeant Clubrush sat finishing a fine supper of forager's stew, washed down with some good mountain cider. He wiped his platter with a chunk of rye bread.

"By the fur'n'feather, that was a better meal than I ever knocked together in my recruit days. Top marks to you'n' yore crew, young Algador, there's hope for ye yet!"

As Algador saluted he cast a quick glance to the huge form of Lady Cregga, fast asleep on a pile of groundsheets by the fire. "Thanks, Sarge. Will we be movin' out at dawn?"

Clubrush continued wiping his already clean platter. "Y'move when I say, laddie buck, an' I move when she says. Though the seasons only knows when Lady Cregga'll waken. She looked fair done in. Thank the fates that she's normal agin."

43

Rinkul was festering with hatred for the ragged pair of mystics who had entered the Rapscallion camp. He gathered a dozen of his cronies about him and issued secret orders. "Let me know every move that pair make, see. An' the dumb one, keep a keen eye on 'im, 'specially once it gits dark!"

Tammo managed to give Rinkul's cronies the slip. He slid off at twilight, while the hillside camp was still teeming with Rapscallions going about the business of cooking, fishing, and foraging for supper.

Rockjaw Grang was awaiting his arrival. He fed the young hare from the last of his supplies and passed on the information Taunoc had vouchsafed to him. Getting back was more difficult. Tammo could see Rinkul and his band searching for him as he peered over the hilltop. There was only one thing for it. Keeping bent double, Tammo shuffled into the camp, trying hard to look inconspicuous. He was doing fine until a heavy paw descended upon his shoulder. It belonged to the big, slow-witted rat Lousewort.

"Er, er, tell me a funny riddle like you tol' Cap'n Bluggach."

His companion Sneezewort shook his head in disgust. "Oh belt up, seedbrain, that 'un can't talk—that's the dumb 'un!'

Lousewort was not convinced. "But he's magic like th otherbeast. Maybe he kin put a spell on hisself so that 'is voic comes back!"

Lousewort's voice was so loud that he attracted the attentio of Rinkul and his gang. Immediately they spotted Tammo an began making their way toward him. The young hare acte quickly. Moaning and uttering dreadful croaking sounds, h waved his paws wildly at Lousewort and Sneezewort. Unsur of what the ragged creature was about, the two rats backe off nervously. Rinkul and his vermin tried to shove past them and seize Tammo, but he pushed Sneezewort and Lousewor into them and ran off. Extricating themselves from the tangle Rinkul and two others gave chase.

Tammo threw himself into the shelter, where Midge wa waiting. He barely had time to gasp out the information whe Rinkul appeared. Ducking his head under the canvas awning the ferret drew an ugly-looking blade.

" 'Tis time ter settle up wid you two ragbags!"

Midge gave an evil cackle and raised his paws dramaticall "Beware o' my magical powers, fool. Raise that blade at m an' I'll turn yer into a toad, right where y'stand!"

Sneeringly, Rinkul began raising the blade. Midge als raised his paws higher, threatening his adversary. "Don't sa I didn't warn ye. Snakeblood an' lightnin' come strike thi abode, an' turn yonder ferret into a fat toa—"

"What's going on here?"

At the sound of Damug Warfang's voice, Rinkul swiftl sheathed his blade. Lowering his eyes humbly, he shrugge and said, "Just a bit o' fun, Sire. The ragged one was gonn show me'n'my mates a few spells an' tricks."

Damug strode between them, eyeing Rinkul suspiciousl "Get out of here and leave these creatures alone!"

Rinkul and the other two vermin bowed and hurried off relieved that the Firstblade had not sensed their intentions Damug bade the two hares to be seated. He stared at Midg for some time, then asked, "Could you have turned Rinku into a toad?"

Cocking his head to one side, Midge returned the star

boldly. "That's my business, Warlord. Now I'm really goin' to show yer some magic. D'you want to know where t'meet the Redwallers?"

Damug leaned forward eagerly. "Aha! Your voices have spoken to you, Seer! Tell me!"

Midge shook his head knowingly. "Not so fast, Damug Warfang. Answer my questions an' you'll find that you already know, the information'll come out by itself."

For the first time, Damug looked puzzled. "You speak in riddles, Miggo. What do you mean?"

"Be silent, an' speak only when I ask you a question!"

Tammo was as mystified as Damug. He feared that Midge had gone too far with their dangerous game. But as he listened, Tammo was surprised by his friend's skills.

Midge tapped the patch that covered his eye. "Tell me, Firstblade, 'ow many good eyes 'ave you'n'I got between us?"

The Greatrat answered without hesitation "Three."

Midge cackled knowingly. "Haharrharr! You said it. Three! That's the time you'll meet those Redwallers, three days from now!"

Damug's voice quivered with excitement. "What are their numbers—how many will they be, Seer?"

Midge Manycoats eyed him scornfully. "What if they 'ad twice yore number? Redwallers are peaceful creatures, they toil at growin' things in earth. Yore a Warlord wid a thousand at yer back, all warriors. But 'earken t'me, Damug, if we're talkin' in hundreds, then three is still yer lucky number."

Damug thought about this a moment, then grinned wickedly. "Three hundred peace-loving beasts!"

Midge nodded. "You said it, Warfang, an' 'tis little use lyin' to yerself. Wot's three 'undred farmers agin a thousand soldiers?"

Damug drew his sword, pointing it at Midge. "If there's only three hundred, then why can't I just march on Redwall Abbey and take it, tell me that?"

Midge brushed aside the swordpoint contemptuously. "Go if ye will, fight 'em there! Wreck the place, smash it, burn Redwall t'the ground. What'll ye have then, mighty one? Go on, you tell me that!"

Sullenly the Warlord sheathed his weapon. "Mayhaps you are right, it is difficult to control a thousand when they sense plunder in battle. So, where is the place to be?"

Squatting by the fire, Midge tossed in a pawful of salt. Blue flames rose from it. "Beneath a blue sky west o' here lies a valley. I see a hill with a rock like an otter's tail atop of it, and three 'undred standin' by, waitin' for yore blades to bring 'em death. Now I see yore father, Gormad Tunn, tellin' you t'make the Rapscallions great again. Keep the rift at yore back, my son, that's wot 'e says, keep the rift at yore back!"

The blue flames from the salt died down, and Midge shrugged. "That's all, I see no more."

Damug continued staring into the fire. "So why should the whole of Redwall be waiting for us in this field?"

Midge smiled. "Think, great one. The Redwallers have friends throughout Mossflower. They have been informed that a great army is gathering to attack. They will not risk allowing you to reach their sacred gates. Tomorrow they will hold a Council of War, this I have seen. The quickest route to Redwall is through that field. The next day they will decide upon an ambush there. The third day they will set forth. All this I have seen."

Damug sneered. "Well, what's to stop us taking Redwall when the fools are all away playing soldiers in this field?"

Midge toyed with his cap while he rapidly thought of an answer. "Think again," he said finally. "You are destined for complete victory, to be the unchallenged ruler of all Mossflower. Do you really want to deal with bands of insurgents, resistance fighters who know these woods better than their own right paws? No! Better to slay and take prisoners for slaves to serve you and your great army. True victory only comes through conquest, great Lord!"

Convinced at last, the Greatrat recounted the information. "Three days from now I will face the Redwallers west of here. They will be on a hilltop; I must keep the rift at my back. What does my father mean—keep the rift at my back?"

Midge closed his eyes, as if exhausted. "I can't tell yer, that's all I know."

"Hmm," Damug grunted. "Well, I will field a thousand,

but the Redwall creatures number only three hundred. Are you sure you can tell me no more, Seer?''

Midge shook his head several times. ''Nothin' except a certain victory for you an' yore army.''

Damug strode to the entrance of the dwelling and summoned two guards; then he turned to Tammo and Midge. ''So be it. Pray to the fates that you have seen truly. These two guards will watch you and never leave your side until Redwall is mine. If you have tried to play me false, I will have you both skinned, roasted, and fed to my army.''

He fixed the two guards with a cold stare. ''If either of you let these two out of your sight for a moment, I will make you curse the day you were born. Is that clear?''

Sneezewort and Lousewort (whose turn it had been to stand guard duty) bobbed their heads vigorously as they croaked, '' 'Er, er, yes Sire!''

Immediately after Damug had left, the two rats leveled the heavy guard spears they had been issued with at Tammo and Midge. ''Sit still an' don't bat an eyelid, you two, or yer deadbeasts!''

The two hares sat with spearpoints almost touching their throats, knowing that the nervous rats were capable of anything in their highly strung state. Tammo stared beyond them. Outside he could see Rinkul and his gang lurking. In a barely audible whisper, he said to Midge, ''Touch an' go, old chap, wot?''

Midge blinked his eyes in agreement. The situation was extremely dangerous. If they escaped the guards it would be like jumping out of the frying pan into the fire. Yet they had to escape and take Fourdun with them before dawn, when the Rapscallion army would break camp and march west.

''Time t'put the old thinkin' caps on, bucko!'' he murmured back to his friend.

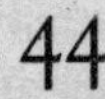

44

Spitting pebbles and dust, Foremole Diggum worked furiousl in the darkness. When the tunnel collapsed, he had bee thrown partially clear, but he was trapped below the waist b the mountain of debris that stretched from floor to ceiling. Th mole's powerful digging claws tore at the rubble, showerin stone and mortar either side until he pulled himself free. Hi head struck the lantern; it had gone out. Grabbing the cove off, Foremole blew gently on the smouldering wick, and spark showed. Slowly he coaxed the flame back to life.

"Ahoy there, mate, move aside, I'm comin' down!" Sha the otter emerged from the top of the pile and slithered care fully over the slope of the cave-in, favoring his injured paw "C'mon, let's git diggin' fer the others!"

Glittering pieces of booty sparkled in the lantern light. Sha seized a heavy gold platter and, using it as a scoop, he attacke the pile.

Foremole dug alongside him, calling out, "Whurr are ee you'm gennelbeasts? Call out naow!"

A muffled but urgent cry came back at them from insid

the pile: "Go easy, there's only a beam protectin' us. Dig careful, friends!"

Shad grunted as he tunneled into the jumble of earth and stone. "Take care o' miz Craklyn an' the Abbess, young Butty—we'll soon have ye out o' there!"

They hauled aside a block of masonry between them, and pulled and tugged at timbers and rock slivers. Foremole flinched suddenly. "Yowch! Oi be stabbed in ee tail!"

Shad held up the lantern to see what it was. An ornate silver spearhead, studded with peridots and tasseled with silk, was poking out of the debris, its point waving and shaking.

"In here, we're in here! Hurry, the air's runnin' out!"

Shad held on to the spearhead while Foremole dug swiftly around it. The good mole was an expert digger, and he soon had a small tunnel through to the three trapped creatures. Shad began enlarging it, scooping aside earth with his gold platter.

There was an ominous creaking of timber, then the sound of Abbess Tansy's voice calling to them, "You'd best be quick—Craklyn's been knocked senseless and I think this beam is about to break under the weight of rubble!"

Shad thrust the lantern through and squeezed in after it. Bent double, he sized up the situation.

The cave-in had fallen around a huge baulk of timber, leaving a small space. Butty and Tansy were crouched in it, supporting the limp form of Craklyn. Suddenly, unable to bear the weight of collapsed material, the beam gave a splintering crack, showering them with soil and mortar dust.

Foremole scrambled in alongside Shad. Moving Tansy aside, he took her place so that he and Butty were supporting Craklyn. "Hurr, et be gurtly bad in yurr, marm. Do ee get owt quick loik!"

Shad assisted Tansy into the escape tunnel, and the timber beam began to groan like a living thing as it shifted. The hefty otter threw caution to the wind. Wedging his back beneath the beam, he strained upward and took the weight upon himself.

"Get 'em out, Diggum, mate. Don't argue. Go!"

They scrambled out, dragging Craklyn between them, through choking dust and a rain of pebbles.

Foremole and Butty grabbed the silver-headed spear, thrusting the pole back toward Shad, who had been forced almos flat. Butty shouted instructions: "Grip tight to the spearpole mister Shad. You push, we'll pull. Ready, one, two, push!"

Shad held the spearpole like a vise as, forcing himself fre of the beam, he gave a mighty shove. Foremole and Butt heaved on the other end, knowing their friend's life depende on it.

Covered in earth and battered by stones, Shad flew out o the tunnel as the beam broke and everything collapsed inwar behind him. He was practically shot out of the hole like a arrow from a bow, landing in a heap atop his rescuers.

Butty found the remains of a flask of elderberry wine, whic had been thrown clear. While Tansy bathed Craklyn's brov with it, Shad took stock of their situation.

"Well, messmates, that's wot we get fer goin' treasur 'untin'. We're blocked in this passage better'n if we'd bee walled in by builders. Still, we're alive, an' the air is fit t breathe."

Licking her lips, Craklyn came back to consciousness "Mmm, I taste like elderberry wine, that's strange. What hap pened? Is everybeast all right?"

Tansy breathed a sigh of relief and hugged her old squirre friend fondly. "Everyone is fine, though you were knocke out when the tunnel collapsed. How do you feel?"

Craklyn stood up and dusted off her gown. "Fine, neve felt better! Dearie me, looks as if we're trapped down here though. What in the name of seasons are you up to, youn Butty?"

The squirrel Friar pointed proudly to the small heap of glit tering objects he had gathered from the rubble. "Collectin treasure, marm. 'Tis rare pretty stuff!"

Foremole wrinkled his snout at the precious trove. "Phwurr Pretty is all et be. Us'n's caint eat et, hurr no, so 'tis of n use at all down yurr!"

Craklyn ignored the mole. She dug out of her pocket th rhyme she had copied, shaking her head knowingly. " thought so. Treasure, that's what we missed. Look at the firs letter of each line, reading downward.

''Turn at the lowest stair,
Right is the left down there,
Every pace you must count
At ten times paws amount,
See where a deathbird flies
Under the hunter's eyes,
Radiant in splendor fair,
Ever mine, hidden where?''

She folded the scrap of parchment triumphantly. ''So that's the riddle solved. Treasure! And we've found it!''

Shad picked up the empty wine canteen. ''Well good fer us, marm, but Foremole's right, treasure ain't goin' to feed us or get us out o' this mess. So, wot next?''

Craklyn and Butty gathered up the treasure and wrapped it in a cloak—having found it they were not about to leave it behind. The young Friar gazed at the heap of debris blocking the passage. ''We'll take this with us. Hmm, bet there's lots more of it buried in there, pity we can't dig it out.''

Abbess Tansy tweaked Butty's ear playfully. ''You greedy young wretch! Come on, let's explore farther down this passage and see where it leads. Bring the lantern, Shad.''

There was neither dawn nor dusk far beneath the earth; time had no meaning. It was only by hunger and thirst that the five companions could judge how long they had been down there. Long, dark and dreary, dry, dusty, and silent, the passage wound on a downward slope. Occasionally they arrived at a cave-in that had not quite blocked the way, and then they found themselves scrambling up hills of broken stone, forcing their way through narrow apertures close to the tunnel ceiling.

Foremole tapped the walls regularly and probed the tight-packed earth at window and door spaces, but without any great success. Being the strongest of the party, he and Shad forged ahead in front of the others, to make sure the way was safe.

The big otter was wearied from his exertions fighting the crushing beam. ''I don't like it, Diggum,'' he murmured in a low voice to Foremole. ''Looks like we're goin' nowheres down 'ere. We ain't got food nor drink, only the air we breathe, an' that lantern light ain't goin' to last forever.''

Dust rose from his back as the mole patted it. "Hurr, oi knows that, ole riverdog, but us'n's be bound t'put ee brave face on, lest ee froighten an' scare ee uthers. Coom now, let's set an' rest awhoile."

They waited for the others to join them, then all five sat with their backs against the wall, tired and dispirited, each with his or her own thoughts, which were rather similar. Green grass, sunlight, fresh air, clear water, and the happy world of Redwall Abbey, so far above them that it all seemed like a dream.

45

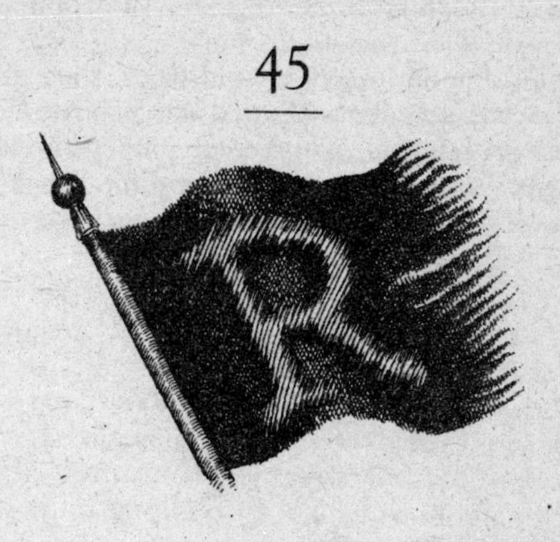

Major Perigord stood in the gap of the south wall with Captain Twayblade. Together they watched the shrews and Waterhogs from the water meadows being led up the slope by Log-a-Log and Gurgan Spearback to join the Redwall army. Perigord attempted a rough head count as they turned west to the main gate.

"About a hundred an' ten, maybe twenty, not many really. Let's go an' see what Morio has mustered up."

Lieutenant Morio was seated in the orchard with quill and parchment on an old tree stump. Pasque was assisting him in compiling the figures on what number of fighting beasts were available.

Perigord looked questioningly at the two hares. "Make y'report, be it good or ill. Speak up, chaps."

Morio wiped an inky paw against his tunic. "Well, it ain't good, Major, but they all seem fit'n'able. There's fifty Redwallers, and thirty squirrels come in from 'round Mossflower, all pretty fair archers an' good slingers, well equipped too. Skipper's rounded up a few more otters, bringin' his strength up to twoscore. Wish we had more otters—they look like they know their way 'round a fight."

Perigord straightened his green velvet tunic, now practically in tatters after all it had been through. "Wishes don't win wars, Lieutenant, we make the best of what we've jolly well got. Have y'counted all the shrews'n'hogs?"

"I have, sah. One hundred an' sixty-three all told, and if you add our twelve, well, that's the total strength. Always providin' that Tammo, Midge, an' Rockjaw make it back from the Rapscallion camp in one piece."

Perigord did a quick mental calculation. "Well, that makes nearly three hundred we can put in the field. Pasque, me pretty one, how's the jolly old armory?"

Pasque Valerian had slightly better news. "Top o' the mark, sah. Everybeast carries their own weapon, an' there's a chamber in the bell tower crammed full of arms, all manner o' blade, spear, and bow. Ginko the Bellringer says you're welcome to 'em all, sah!"

Twayblade drew her rapier, and flicking an apple from a nearby branch, caught it deftly and polished it on her sleeve. "Three hundred, eh. Wish I'd told Midge to let the Rapscallions know there was only two hundred of us, but I said three, hopin' we might have had four. Always nice to keep a hundred as a surprise reserve. Ah well, no use worryin' over spilt cider, wot."

Perigord took the apple from his sister and bit into it. "Indeed, we'll just have t'give ten times as good as we get off the vermin. Hello there, what's amiss here?"

The Galloper Riffle was trying to restrain Viola Bankvole from reaching Perigord.

"Sorry, marm, y'can't see the Major right now, he's busy."

Viola thrust her jaw out belligerently. "Stand aside, young sir, or I'll take a stick to you. I must see your officer right now!"

Perigord gestured Riffle to one side. "At y'service, marm. You wanted to see me?"

Viola shot Riffle a haughty glance before addressing the Major. "It's our Abbess. She's missing, and so are Shad the Gatekeeper, Foremole Diggum, Craklyn the Recor . . ."

Perigord cut her off with a wave of his paw. "Enough

marm, enough! Just tell me how many altogether.''

''Well, there's five of them. They're nowhere to be seen, I've searched the Abbey grounds high and low. Now, what do you intend doing about it, sir?''

Perigord answered her gently, seeing that Viola was upset. ''Beggin' y'pardon, lady, but there ain't a lot I *can* do. We're about to march off an' fight a war. So as y'see, I can't spare anybeast to go off searchin' for your friends.''

Viola Bankvole's paw waved under the Major's nose as she ticked him off. ''Well, that's a fine how d'ye do. But mark my words, sir, I will gather more reliable searchers and look for them myself. Good day!''

She flounced off through the orchard, calling to the older ones. ''Gurrbowl, come here! I need you to search with me, and you, Mother Buscol, you too, Brother Ginko. Follow me!''

Captain Twayblade chuckled as she rescued the apple back from her brother. ''I say, chaps, I think we'd best stay here an' search. Send *her* off to face the vermin. She'd soon send 'em packin', wot!''

Perigord nodded admiringly as he watched Viola bullying half the Abbey elders into service. ''Aye, she's a bold perilous creature right enough. But to business now. Pasque m'dear, would y'be good enough to assemble the leaders? We'll have to get geared up an' movin' shortly.''

The last full meal had been produced in Redwall's kitchens by Guosim shrew cooks. They had filled six huge cauldrons with a thick stew of leeks, mushrooms, carrots, turnips, water shrimp, onions, potatoes, and lots of herbs, enough to feed an army. October Ale casks were broached and served in beakers with rough batch loaves and wedges of autumn nut cheese.

As the Redwall force ate, Perigord consulted with their Chieftains: Skipper of Otters, Log-a-Log of the Guosim, Gurgan Spearback of the Waterhogs, and Arven, Champion of Redwall, bearing with him the great sword of Martin the Warrior. There was not a lot to say that had not already been said; they all knew what they had to do, and even in the face of overwhelming odds they were prepared to do it, or go down fighting.

Mother Buscol had evaded Viola. She stood on the sidelines, with Russano the badgerbabe and Orocca's three young owls in the straw-lined wheelbarrow, enjoying the sun. The rest of the Abbey Dibbuns crowded 'round, hanging on her apron strings, in the absence of anyone else to mind them. Together they listened to the Major address his troops.

"Right ho, chaps, for those who don't know me, let me introduce m'self. I'm Major Perigord Habile Sinistra of the Salamandastron Long Patrol, commandin' this entire operation, though your orders will prob'ly reach you through your own leaders an' chieftains. Now I'll make this as short as possible, wot! There's a thousand Rapscallions sweepin' upcountry, an' Redwall Abbey's in their path. So to save the place I've . . . ahem . . . arranged for the jolly old fracas to take place elsewhere. According to Taunoc the blighters are on the move, and we've found the ideal place to meet 'em head on. So that's what we'll jolly well do, if y'follow me. As you know, we'll be outnumbered by more'n three to one, but by jingo we won't be outclassed! We won't be outfought! An' as long as I can stand with a saber in me paw, we won't be driven backward a single pace!"

Every creature listening leapt up cheering and brandishing their weapons.

"No surrender! No retreat!"

"Eulalia! 'S death on the wind!"

"Boi 'okey they'm furr et!"

Perigord gestured for silence. "Thank you, friends. But as you know, not all of us will come marching home. War is war, and that is a fact. So if there are any of you with families or young 'uns to look after, well, nobeast will think less of ye if you go home to them now."

A rough-looking otter stood up. "Beggin' yore pardon, Major, but I got a wife an liddle 'uns, an' if I didn't go with ye then I'd think less of meself. 'Cos we ain't fightin' the vermin just to protect Redwall, we're facin' 'em to make the land safe an' rid of their kind."

Mother Buscol trundled her barrow of babes through the army ranks, followed by a flock of Dibbuns. She halted in front of the Major and presented him with a cloth bundle.

"Indeed to goodness, sir, you can't 'ave an army without a flag to march under, oh dear no you cannot!"
Skipper and Arven unrolled the bundle. It was a dark green tablecloth with a big red letter R embroidered upon it. Inside the bundle was another smaller package, which Buscol gave to Perigord. "It ain't velvet, sir," the old squirrelmother said, shrugging awkwardly, "but may'ap 'twill be of service."
Arven grabbed a long pike and began fastening the flag to it. "Here, Skip, lend a paw, you can tie better knots than me." The banner was lashed to the pikestaff, and Arven waved it high over the crowd. Back and forth it fluttered in the sunlight as the massed shouts rose to a concerted roar:
"Redwaaaaaalll! Redwaaaaaalll! Redwaaaaaalll!"
Major Perigord slipped out of his tattered tunic and donned the one that Mother Buscol had made for him. It was blue linen, homespun, but beautifully fashioned from an ancient bed quilt. Fastening on the medals from his old tunic, he bowed gracefully and kissed the squirrel-mother's paw. "My thanks to ye, lady, I'll wear it with honor an' pride. Mayhap I'll even return here with it unharmed."
The Dibbuns dove upon the Major's old tunic.
"Me wannit, 'smine, gitcha paws offen it, Sloey!"
Perigord eyed them sternly. "Silence in the ranks there, you fiends! Y'can wear it a day each at a time. Sloey first." Even the search party led by Viola left off their task to see the Redwall army on its way. Elders and Dibbuns alike lined the path to the main gate as the warriors marched past four abreast, every creature well armed and carrying provisions. Arven and Perigord stood to one side, each drawing his blade to salute the flag, which was being borne by Skipper. The stout otter dipped the colors, awaiting orders as the columns formed up on the path outside.
It was a high summer day, and the sun shone out of a sky that appeared bluer than it had ever been. They stood waiting in silence, listening to grasshoppers chirruping and skylarks singing on the western flatlands. Many Redwallers straightened their backs, breathed deeply, and blinked to prevent a tear appearing, wondering if they would ever see the old Abbey on such a beautiful day again.
All the good-byes had been said, though Major Perigord

bowed to Sister Viola and spoke a last few words. " 'Tis always hard to leave a place, marm, particularly when certain friends are not there to wish you farewell. I wish you every good fortune in your search for the Mother Abbess and her companions. In happier, more peaceful times, myself and the patrol would have been at your disposal to help find them, but alas it was not to be. I hope you bear me no ill will, marm. I must bid ye good-bye."

Sister Viola smiled at the gallant hare. "How could any true Redwaller bear ill will to a brave soldier marching to defend our home and our very lives? Never fear, sir, I will find our lost friends. I bid you success and good fortune along with my good-bye. You are a perilous creature, Major."

Sergeant Torgoch's stentorian roar rang out through gateway and path: "Flagbearer three paces forward! All offisahs to the vanguard! In the ranks . . . Atten . . . shun! Corporal Rubbadub—beat the advance! By the right . . . quick . . . maaaaaarch!"

Shouldering blades, Perigord, Arven, Gurgan, and Log-a-Log formed the first rank of four behind Skipper's banner, with Rubbadub behind them setting up a fine, paw-swinging drumroll.

"Barraboom! Barraboom! Drrrappadabdab! Buboom!"

Galloper Riffle called out through the rising dust cloud. "Permission for the Company to sing 'O'er the Hills,' sah!"

"Permission granted, Galloper," Perigord's voice rang back at him. "Sing out with a will!"

"O'er the Hills" was a famous marching song, and close to three hundred voices roared it out lustily:

"O'er the hills an' far away,
'Twas there I left my dearie,
An' as I left I heard her say,
'Come back to me d'ye hear me,
Y'may eat cake an' drink pale wine,
But come back home at autumn time,
An' on fresh bread'n'cheese you'll dine,
For no one brews good ale like mine.'

O fields are green an' skies are blue,
Ole woods are high an' full o' loam,
But hearken friend I'll tell you true,
Ain't no place in the world like home.

O'er the hills an' far away,
'Tis there my home's awaitin',
The season's shorter by a day,
Whilst I'm anticipatin'
A logfire made from cracklin' pine,
An' washin' dancin' on the line,
As blossoms 'round the door entwine,
Hurrah, for there's that dearie mine!"

Redwallers old and young stood out on the path waving kerchiefs, aprons, and headscarves until the marchers diminished to a faraway dust cloud, with their song a faint echo on the hot air.

Viola could not help sniffling into a lace kerchief, "Oh, they made such a brave sight going off like that!"

Ever the practical creature, Gurrbowl Cellarmole shooed the Dibbuns back inside, remarking, "Hurr aye, they'm did, an' let us'n's 'ope they'm lukk ee same on ee day 'em cumms back!"

46

The two rats Sneezewort and Lousewort kept their weapon firmly centered on Midge and Tammo, suspicious of thei every move. It was a stalemate that was lasting far into th night, with little hope of the two hares escaping.

Eventually the fire inside the canvas-and-brush shelter be gan to burn low. From beneath his heavy disguise, Midg Manycoats winked significantly at his friend. It was time t make their move. Tammo edged slowly around until he judge that Rinkul the ferret and his cronies, who were hovering out side, could not see him.

Midge stood upright. Sneezewort's spearpoint menace him, a fraction from his throat. "Siddown, ragbag, where d'ye think yore goin'?"

Midge stood his ground, nodding at the guttering flames "Need more wood fer the fire, matey."

The rat considered Midge's request, then jabbed with hi spear so that his prisoner fell back in a sitting position. "I'n not yore matey, an' you ain't goin' nowhere. Lousewort, kee an' eye on 'em. I'll get the wood."

Once Sneezewort had gone outside, Midge turned to hi

slow-witted partner. "You ain't afeared of us, are yer, bucko?"

A slow smile spread across the rat's dull features. "Er, er, scared? Huh, why should I be scared o' two rag-bottomed beasts like youse? Yore no bother at all t'me."

Midge moved closer to him, chuckling in a friendly manner. "Of course we ain't, a dumb ole vermin like me mate there, an' a pore one-eyed wreck like me. Fat chance we'd 'ave agin a fine big strappin' beast like yerself, armed wid a great spear like that 'un. But lookit, yore spear shaft's cracked right there!"

Lousewort lowered his head, following Midge's pointing paw. "Where? I don't see no crack."

Midge's other paw came swinging over, clutching a stone he had picked up from where he had been sitting.

Whump!

He hit Lousewort a hefty blow between the ears. The rat's body wobbled, and he staggered dazedly. Using the handle of his dirk, which he had kept well hidden beneath his cloak, Tammo sprang forward and dealt Lousewort a smart rap between the eyes.

Midge caught the spear, lowering the senseless rat quietly down. "Quick, Tamm, put that fire out and get this spear!"

Tammo kicked earth over the embers, then, grabbing the spear, he stood to one side of the entrance. Midge positioned himself on the other side, holding the fallen rat's cloak at the ready. Almost as they did, Sneezewort ducked inside, carrying a few twigs. "Hoi! 'Taint arf dark in 'ere, wot's go—*Mmmmffff!*"

Midge had flung the cloak over the rat's head. Tammo gave him two good hard knocks with the spearhaft to make sure he went out.

Then they lay still, peering outside at Rinkul and his band, who had made a fire some distance away—careful after Damug's warning to stay away from the prisoners. Tammo watched them until he was sure they had noticed nothing amiss. Midge passed him Sneezewort's cloak and spear, and donned Lousewort's cloak himself.

"Get rid o' those rags now, Tamm. We'll have to shift pretty fast!"

Discarding their disguises, they slid under the rear of the canvas shelter and wriggled off into the night, hugging tight to the ground until they were well away. Midge threw the hood of his cloak up. "Now t'get old Fourdun free. Right, Tamm, straighten up there! Make it look as if we're two sentry-type vermin takin' a duty patrol 'round the camp, wot."

Picking their way boldly 'round Rapscallions sleeping by campfires, the pair made their way down to the stream. Blug-gach the Rapmark Captain was snoring next to his companions by the water's edge, their fire untended and burned to white ashes.

Tammo crept up to the cage and identified himself to the old squirrel. "It's Tammo an' Midge. C'mon, old chap, time to go!"

A few swift slices of Tammo's dirk severed the ropes on the cage door, and Fourdun crawled out, having already freed himself of his bonds with the small knife they had given him earlier.

Positioning themselves either side of Fourdun, the hares gripped his paws and marched him off quietly, Midge whispering to him, "If anybeast stops us, leave the talkin' to me. We're two Rapscallion guards takin' you to Damug 'cos he wants to question you. I'll bluff us through, don't worry."

Lousewort had two things going in his favor: an extra-thick skull and remarkable powers of recovery. Staggering from the dark smoky shelter, he sat on the ground, nursing his head and grunting with pain.

Rinkul, who had been watching the darkened shelter suspiciously, came bounding over. "Where's the two prisoners? 'Ave yer still got 'em?"

Shaking his head gingerly, Lousewort peered up at him. "Er, er, I dunno, it went dark all of a sudden!"

Rinkul ran back to his fire and snatched a blazing brand. Kicking Lousewort aside, he rushed into the shelter, and seizing Sneezewort cruelly by one ear, he struck him several times with the burning stick until the rat came 'round with a yelp.

"Bunglin' idiot," Rinkul snarled into Sneezewort's frightened face. "Y've let 'em escape, 'aven't yer! Best thing you can do is take off fast afore the Firstblade learns they're gone, or Damug'll slay you'n'yore mate fer sure. Go on, beat it, an' don't raise no alarms. Leave those two t'me, I'll settle wid 'em!'' He signaled to his waiting band. ''Arm up an' let's go, they've escaped. Don't go shoutin' an' roarin' all over the camp. I wants those two ragbags fer meself. We'll catch 'em an' take 'em somewheres nice'n'quiet where I'll do that pair 'ard an' slow afore dawnbreak. Now go silent!''

Lousewort staggered upright, and Sneezewort leaned on him for support. ''That's us finished wid the Rapscallions, mate. Let's be on our way afore Warfang wakes an' decides to 'ave us fer brekkfist!''

Without another word, they stumbled off, south, as far as they could get from Damug Warfang's vengeance.

The three escapers made their way uphill through the still-sleeping camp. Tammo felt that all was going well, too well, and that worried him. Fourdun peered around into the darkness and suddenly saw Rinkul and his band striding through the camp, coming in their direction.

Thinking swiftly, the old squirrel pulled his two friends down beside half a dozen vermin lying 'round a fire, and scrambled beneath Midge's cloak. ''Lie still, some o' the scum are comin' this way!''

Hardly daring to breathe, they stretched on the ground amid the slumbering Rapscallions. Rinkul actually trod on the hem of Tammo's cloak as they went by, and Tammo heard the ferret murmur to one of his companions as they passed, ''I've got a feelin' they'll be down by the stream where that ole squirrel's caged up!''

Raising his head carefully, Midge watched them from the back as they headed toward the water. The trio rose slowly, avoiding the outstretched paws of a stoat who was acting out a dream. The stoat snuffled and turned away from them, kicking out with a footpaw that came into contact with a glowing log.

''Yowch!''

At the sound of the creature's yelp, Rinkul and his party turned.

Midge saw they were discovered. He took off at a run, hissing to his friends, ''Fat's in the fire, chaps, make a dash for it!''

Silently and grimly the chase of death began as they shot off uphill.

The stoat was clutching his scorched footpaw, hopping about. One of Rinkul's band whacked him with a cudgel as he passed, and snarled, "Go back ter sleep, mate!"

Though Fourdun was a strong old beast, he was not half as fast as the two hares, so they were forced to run at his pace. With the enemy hard on their heels, they got clear of the encampment and made the brow of the hill. Midge turned and threw his spear, and it pierced a vixen who was running alongside Rinkul. This slowed their pursuers momentarily and bought them a second's time.

Breasting the hill, Tammo called out as they ran, "Rock! Rockjaw Grang!"

Lower downhill, the giant hare heard Tammo. Leaping from cover, he bounded uphill to meet them. Rinkul was first over the hilltop. He had pulled the spear from the dead vixen; taking aim at Midge, he threw the weapon skillfully.

"Sithee, Midge, look out!"

Rockjaw flung himself in a flying tackle, bulling into Midge and knocking him sideways. The spear took Rockjaw through his side.

Hatred welled up in Tammo. He heaved his own spear straight at Rinkul. It struck the ferret through his middle, snapping off as he fell and rolled downhill toward them.

Rockjaw brushed Midge and Fourdun aside as they tried to lift him. Close to a dozen vermin were dashing down upon them now. The big hare unslung his bow, crying, "Get goin', I'll hold 'em off!"

The lifeless carcass of Rinkul the ferret halted its downhill roll in front of Rockjaw. He forced the hardwood stick from its death grip and tossed it to Tammo. "Good throw, young 'un. Russa woulda been proud o' ye. Now leave me an' run fer it, I'm bad hit!"

Fourdun ducked an arrow as he inspected Rockjaw's side. He looked up, shaking his head at Tammo. " 'Twould kill him to pull the spear out!"

The big hare sat up and sent two arrows in quick succession at the vermin. Notching another shaft to his bow, he glared angrily at the two friends standing either side of him. "Sithee, 'tis not yore night to die. Now get out o' here an' don't stand there wastin' my time. Leave me t'my work!'' Ignoring them completely, he fired the arrow and selected another.

Fourdun tugged at their paws, whispering urgently, ''Can't y'see he's dyin'? If we stay here we'll all be slain. That beast doesn't want or need yore 'elp. Come on!''

Attracted by the shouts of their comrades, the vermin from the camp edges near the hilltop appeared. Rockjaw laughed wildly. ''Hohoho! Come t'the party, buckoes, the more the merrier! Tammo, Midge, tell the Major I took a few wid me. Good fortune, pals—run straight'n'true an' remember me!''

Tammo, Midge, and Fourdun had to run for it before the Rapscallions encircled them. They ran like the wind into the night, shouting, ''Give 'em blood'n'vinegar, Rock!'' Soon they were lost among the groves and knolls, charging headlong across darkened country until there was no sound save the thrumming of their paws against the earth.

Rockjaw Grang sat on with his back against a jutting boulder, the arrow quivers of two dead vermin beside him, his sling and stones ready for when he ran out of shafts. Completely surrounded, and wounded in four places, he fought on.

''Come on, thee cowardly scum. Ah'll wager nobeast warned ye about Goodwife Grang's eldest son. Eulaliaaaaaa!''

As the foebeasts closed in on him, Rockjaw drew the spear from his side and hurled himself upon them like a creature taken by the Bloodwrath.

'' 'S death on the wind! Eulalia! Eulalia! Eulaliaaaaaaa!''

He bought the time for his friends to escape safely, for even within sight of Dark Forest gates, Rockjaw Grang was a perilous hare.

47

Lady Cregga Rose Eyes sat bolt upright from the bed of gras
and soft mosses she had been laid upon for a day and a night
It was but a few hours to dawn as the great badger roared out
"Eulaliaaaa!"

Corporal Ellbrig and Sergeant Clubrush, wakened from thei
sleep, rushed to her side.

"Lady Cregga, what is it?"

Her strange eyes looked all 'round before settling on Clu
brush. "A bad dream, Sergeant, a very bad dream!"

She rose and stared over his shoulder in a northwesterl
direction. The Drill Sergeant was very concerned. He watche
Cregga's eyes carefully, though it was still too dark to se
them clearly.

"Are you all right, marm?"

She moved to the nearest fire, nodding to reassure him
"I'm fine, Sergeant, but very hungry. How long to breakfast?"

Corporal Ellbrig busied himself at the fire. "Right now i
y'like, marm, you h'aint eaten in two days."

Deodar and Algador had just finished their sentry watch, s
they joined the trio at the fire. Young hares are always willin

to eat an early breakfast when they smell it being cooked. Lady Cregga seemed in a rather mild, thoughtful mood, which was unusual for her. She passed scones and honey to Deodar, followed by a beaker of hot mint and dandelion tea.

"Breakfast tastes good after being on sentry, eh?"

Through a mouthful of scone, the young hare sipped her tea. "Rather, marm, 'specially when you can have an hour's sleep before reveille an' join the jolly old queue for more."

Lady Cregga smiled at Deodar's honesty. "Tell me, young 'un, do you ever have dreams?"

"Dreams, marm? Well, yes, I s'pose I do."

The badger stared down at her huge paws. "I had a dream just now, and I believe it to be true."

Algador paused from ladling honey onto a hot scone. "Really, marm? May I ask what it was about?"

The Sergeant was about to upbraid Algador, when Cregga spoke. "I'm afraid I couldn't tell you the parts that aren't clear, but I know a brave creature died. I shouted Eulalia with him as he went down. Somewhere over there to the northwest. And the more I think of it, the more certain I am. That is where the army of Rapscallions is at this very moment. I can feel it!"

The two young hares exchanged puzzled glances with the Corporal and Sergeant until Lady Cregga caught their attention once more. "When the sun is up and my hares are fed, we will go there."

Trowbaggs spooned hot oatmeal in at a furious rate, eyeing a last scone that lay between him and Furgale. "Well lucky old us, it's heigh-ho for the northwest on the strength of a bally dream, wot! I think I'll dream tonight that I've been sent back to Salamandastron to take up the blinkin' job of head food-taster. D'you think it'll work?"

Drill Sergeant Clubrush tweaked the cheeky recruit's ear. "Strange y'should say that, young sir. H'I've just 'ad a dream that you was on pot-washin' duty an' you volunteered to carry my pack all day. Wot d'you say to that, young Trowbaggs?"

"Er, haha, silly beastly things dreams are, Sarge, er, that is unless Lady Cregga dreams 'em up, wot!"

The Sergeant's pace stick tapped Trowbaggs's shoulder

lightly. "Right y'are, bucko, an' don't you forget it!"

The Long Patrol hares assembled after breakfast for their final orders before marching. Lady Cregga and Corporal Ellbrig looked on from the sidelines as Drill Sergeant Clubrush lectured them.

"Listen carefully now. From this moment we march silent an' quick. An' when I say silent—Trowbaggs an' some o' you other young rips—I means it! Foolish an' thoughtless noise or playactin' could get us all ambushed or slain. Shangle Widepad, you an' the other seasoned veterans keep an eye on our recruits, 'tis yore duty to show 'em the ropes. Everybeast make sure yore weapons are in good order—slings, javelins, swords, bows'n'quivers. Soon we'll be in enemy territory an you may need 'em. Right, that's all. Unless you got anythin' t'say to 'em, Lady Cregga, marm?"

For the first time, the Badger Warrior addressed the five hundred hares who formed her traveling army. "So far you have all proved worthy and well, my thanks to you. Soon we will be facing Rapscallions in battle. Make no mistake about them—vermin they may be, but they are trained killers. To bring peace to these lands we must slay them, or be slain. From this moment you are hunters and warriors, and there will be no marching songs, Eulalias, or campfires. That is all."

They marched then. No commands were called; a nod, the wave of a pace stick, or a signal from the Sergeant's paw was all that they required. They kept to grassland, ferns, and rocky terrain wherever possible, so that a tell-tale dust cloud would not betray their position. Trowbaggs strode silently alongside Shangle Widepad. After a while the irrepressible young hare found himself humming a little ditty called the "Fat Frog's Dinner," and he winked at Shangle and grinned. The glare he received from the grizzled veteran silenced him immediately. Grim-faced and determined, the five hundred pressed on.

Rapscallion drums pounded savagely, throwing out their wild challenge to the summer skies. Pennants and war banners fluttered in the breeze, bedecked with tails, skulls, and hanks of animal hair. The little rat informant Gribble slunk about outside the Firstblade's shelter, waiting for him to emerge.

Damug Warfang strode out, his face streaked purple and re

for battle. Unsheathing his sword, he cast an approving eye over the ranks of snarling vermin before turning to the rat groveling on the ground in front of him.

"Speak your piece quickly, Gribble, then get out of my way!"

The rat was already shuffling backward to avoid a sudden kick. "Great Lord, the Seer and the dumb one are gone, so are the two guards you left to watch them. Also the ferret Rinkul and several others are missing from camp."

Damug faced west across the valley slope and nodded curtly. "Well, let's hope they catch those two, for their own sakes. If they've deserted I'll find them when this is all over. But now I march west, to find out what these Redwallers are made of. Stand aside—death waits on anybeast barring my way!"

The Greatrat hurried to the forefront of his vast eager army, with their roars drowning out the pounding drums: "Warfaaaaang! Warfaaaaang! Warfaaaang!"

Away to the west, a green valley basked in the warm sun. Light breezes rippled the vale ferns and stirred the blossoms of gorse and pimpernel on the broad hillslope. A single rock with moss and lichen clinging to its sides stood out on the long high ridge like a raised ottertail. Far below, wispy tendrils of mist arose from where the sun's warmth penetrated a deep rift that ran like a jagged scar along the valley's far edge. Small birds, redstart, stonechat, and wheatear, chirruped and chattered, perching on gorse thorns with sure-clawed skill, bright beady eyes constantly searching for minute insects. Butterflies and bumblebees visited the flowers of the vale, and sunlight glinted off the iridescent wings of hoverflies seeking aphids.

The life of the valley hummed peacefully on, lulled by summer's warmth, unaware that three armies were marching toward it.

48

Trapped in the tunnels of old Castle Kotir, far beneath Redwall Abbey's south ramparts, five creatures sat dozing fitfully in the gloom. Giving off an occasional flicker, their lantern warned that its light would soon be out.

Abbess Tansy gazed ruefully at the small golden tongue of flame as it gently swayed. "I should never have encouraged you to come on this silly venture, friends. I'm sorry."

Craklyn snorted, wagging a paw at her old companion. "*You* encouraged us, *you?* Hah! Let me tell you, Tansy Pansy, we're all down here because we wanted to come. We encouraged ourselves!"

Tansy clasped the old squirrel Recorder's paw affectionately. "Dearie me, 'tis some long seasons since anybeast called me Tansy Pansy. D'you remember when Arven was a Dibbun, he was always saying that name? Now what was it he used to chant at me?"

Craklyn thought for a moment, then chuckled. " 'Tansy Pansy toogle doo.' Hahaha, he was a proper little wretch."

Foremole wrinkled his nose severely at the pair. "Beggin' ee pardun, but do you'm be soilent, oi can yurr summat."

There was a moment's silence. Young Friar Butty looked around. "Aye, I c'n hear somethin' too. Sounds like water drippin'."

Shad pressed his ear to the tunnel wall. "That's water, all right, on the other side o' this 'ere wall. I can 'ear it drip-drippin' away. Sounds like 'tis fallin' a far way down. Wot d'ye think, Abbess, marm, shall I 'ave a go at breakin' through the wall?"

Foremole Diggum waved a digging paw hastily. "Ho no, zurr, you'm'll be a bringen ee tunnel topplin' on us 'eads agin fur sure!"

Shad scrambled upright and retrieved the lantern. "P'raps yore right, mate. You all stay 'ere an' I'll scout about further down this tunnel t'see wot I can see."

While Shad was gone, the remaining four creatures sat in complete darkness without the lantern. To keep their spirits up, Tansy sang a simple little ditty.

"If I were a leaf upon a tree,
Then I would live right happily,
I'd grow up flat and green and big,
Unless of course I was a twig,
A twig with a leaf upon its end,
And then the leaf would be my friend,
I'd grow to such a wondrous length,
And from my branch I'd take my strength.
If I were a branch upon a tree,
With leaf and twig for company,
I'd grow so round and fair and trim,
Sprouting from a great stout limb,
But if I were a limb all thick and wide,
Branch, twig, and leaf I'd hold with pride,
And they would all depend on me,
And the mighty trunk of my big tree.
Then if I were a tree with bark for husk,
I'd stand up firm from dawn 'til dusk,
And limb, branch, twig, and leaf would be,
All through the season part of me!"

She had barely finished singing when Shad's voice boomed up the passage and they saw the welcome glow of the lantern.

"Ahoy there, mates! Come an' see this—I've found a way down!"

Stumbling through the half-light behind the fading lantern, they followed Shad down the corridor. He halted in front of a heavy wooden door, swinging it open with a jarring creak to reveal its other side, covered in fungus.

"Welcome to the ole castle cellars, me hearties, though I don't see wot good they'll do us. We should be goin' up, not down'ards!"

Dropping his bag of treasure, Friar Butty pushed past the otter. "Look, torches!"

From rusted iron rings in the wall he pulled four hefty wooden bundles, their ends coated thick with pine resin. Tansy took one and lit it from the last dying lantern flame. "Of course, it makes sense to leave torches at the entrance to cellars. By the seasons, they do burn brightly!"

Brilliant yellow light radiated around, revealing their position. Far larger than Great Hall, the cellars stretched above and below them. Water dripped from long stalactites hanging from a high-hewn rock ceiling, falling down from a great height to splash far below where they stood. The five questors were on a narrow step jutting from the wall. Other steps wound their way downward, hugging the wallsides until they ended in the depths below.

Shad lit another torch from the one Tansy carried. "Only one way t'go, mates: down. C'mon, foller me."

Placing their backs to the wall, they descended carefully, step by step, each holding the other's paws. The stone stairs seemed never-ending, and by the time they had covered three-quarters of the distance, wet moss and slime made the going treacherous.

Shad stopped and rested by crouching against the damp walls. "Phwaw! This place is enough t'give a crab the creeps. You got any rope left, Diggum?"

The Foremole unwound a coil from 'round his waist. "Yurr, oi gotter liddle len'th."

Shad took it and knotted it 'round his middle, then passed it back. "Best rope ourselves together fer safety—*Yaaaaar!* Gerraway, yer filthy scum!"

A large, gross toad with sightless eyes was trying to gnaw the end of the otter's tail. With a swift flick of his rudderlike appendage, Shad tossed the amphibian in the air and batted it off the step. The toad whirled in an arc, then hit the liquid below. It vanished with a squelching plop, leaving a small dimple on the surface.

Tansy held her torch out over the stair edge. "That isn't water down there, 'tis more of a swamp!"

Other toads were crawling upstairs toward them, the dreadful creatures apparently attracted by Shad's cry and Tansy's voice.

Craklyn hid behind Foremole, shuddering. "Ugh! Horrible monsters, keep 'em away from me!"

Butty had been carrying his treasure slung on the end of the silver-headed spear he had found in the rubble. Untying the bundle, he passed the spear along to Shad.

The otter Gatekeeper began clearing the toads off into the ooze below. Some spread their webs to prevent themselves from sinking instantly, and these were set upon and torn to shreds by creatures not half their size, who appeared in packs. At the same time they were being devoured, the toads began eating their tormentors.

The five friends watched, revolted but fascinated by the sight.

"Yurr, they'm all a h'eatin' each uther!"

"Aye, those small 'uns look like some kind o' mudfish, they're blind as the toads!"

"So they all live down here in this slimy darkness, feeding off one another. What an awful existence!"

"Yukk! What are we doin' in this terrible place? Let's get out!"

Foremole Diggum tugged against the rope as they began moving. "Hurr no, us'n's mus' gotter stay. Lookee!"

They followed the direction his paw was pointing, across the underground morass to a dark hole in the wall at the cellar's far side.

Tansy held the torch high. "What is it, Diggum?"

The mole's reply was prompt and confident. "That thurr's a tunnel dugged boi moles, oi'd stake moi snowt on et, oi surrtinly would, 'tis a mole tunnel, 'twill lead oopward!"

Shad shook his head doubtfully. "Are you shore 'tis a mole tunnel, mate? 'S a long way off."

Diggum Foremole would not be shaken from his belief. "Oi said 'twurr, din't oi, oi'm ee Foremoler, 'o'd know better!"

Friar Butty stared unhappily across the expanse of cannibal-infested bog.

"If that's the way out, then how do we get to it?"

A small meeting was being convened in the kitchen at Redwall Abbey. It was for elders, though the Dibbuns had invited themselves along too, because there were always plenty of tasty bits to nibble at in the kitchens.

Viola Bankvole presided. "Mother Abbess always appoints me in her place when she isn't here, so if you don't mind I'll take charge. Gubbio, get your head out of that oven, please!"

Mother Buscol shooed the little mole from the oven, nipping back to the table just in time to stop Russano the badgerbabe grabbing a bowl of soup. "Indeed to goodness, Viola," she said, passing a paw across her flustered brow, "what is it you're wantin' now? Can't you see we've got our paws full as it is?"

Viola shook her head primly at the old squirrel. "Abbess, Craklyn, Foremole, Shad, and young Butty are still missing. Sloey! Put that ladle down this instant! Now, have you all searched properly?"

Pellit the dormouse tried to wrest the ladle from Sloey's grasp. "Well, I searched the entire orchard and down as far as the gatehouse, Sister. I don't think Ginko was looking very hard, though."

Ginko the Bellringer glared across the table at Pellit. "I done my share o' searchin'. Found *you* asleep 'neath the stairs in my bell tower, didn't I!"

Gurrbowl Cellarmole, who was sitting with Taunoc and Orocca, tending the owlchicks, ventured a suggestion: "May'ap they'm losed theyselves unner ee gurt 'ole at south wall."

An owlchick fumbled itself loose from her and lumbered into the bowl of soup that lay nearby. Viola leaned over and fished the little bundle of downy feathers out. "Good job that soup was cold. Under the south wall, you say? Ridiculous! What would our Mother Abbess be doing grubbing about down there? Personally I think she may have gone up into the Abbey attics to look for something, and taken the others with her. Barfle, stop pulling Sloey's ears. She'll end up looking like a hare. What do you think, mister Taunoc?"

"About what, madam, the Abbess in the attics, or Sloey looking like a hare?"

"Silly! I'm talking about the Abbess in the attics!"

The Little Owl ruffled his feathers and blinked at her. "Silly yourself, madam! All this meeting has achieved is to get one of my chicks soaked with soup. Wherever the Abbess is at this moment, it will be exactly where she wants to be. Your Abbess is a hedgehog, old and wise. She will return in good time."

Russano looked at Taunoc and spoke the only word he knew. "Nut!"

Sloey the mousebabe managed to hit Pellit a good whack on his nose with the ladle he was trying to take from her. Reaching over to assist Pellit, Viola Bankvole upset the bowl of cold soup, and it spilled all over Mother Buscol's apron. An owlchick fastened its small sharp beak on Ginko's paw, who yelped with pain and woke the remaining owlchick, who had been sleeping. The owlchick set up a din. The meeting dissolved in disarray, with Viola Bankvole struggling to maintain her dignity in the position of deputy Abbess.

"Er, continue the search. I will inform you later of when the next meeting is to be held. Be about your business now!"

Viola was about to make a stately exit, when she slipped on a patch of cold soup that had dripped from the table, and sat down hard on the stone floor.

The molebabe Gubbio tried pulling her upright by the apron strings, lecturing the bankvole severely: "Doant ee play abowt onna floor, marm, you'm get dreffful dusty!"

The meeting ended with everybeast of the opinion that without a Mother Abbess to run things, Redwall Abbey would grind to a halt.

Underground, young Friar Butty made his way back up to a dry step, where he sat nursing his rumbling stomach. "Ooh, am I 'ungry, I've never been so 'ungry in all me life!"

Abbess Tansy sympathized with Butty, but she could not

show it. "We're all hungry, but sitting complaining about it isn't going to do us any good. Look at Shad. He's bigger and hungrier than the rest of us, but he isn't moaning, are you, Shad?"

The otter, who was perched on the bottom stair amid the mud, called back up to Tansy, "No I ain't, marm. I think I've got a plan t'get us across to yonder mole tunnel!"

Picking their way carefully down the muddy steps, Tansy and the others joined Shad. He shifted a big venturesome toad off into the swamp with his spearbutt before explaining. "See, about halfways along the wall there, 'tis a chain, hangin' from a ring set high in the stone. If'n we could get hold o' that chain, I reckon we could swing across to the ledge over yonder an' make our way along it to the mole tunnel."

Craklyn studied the scheme, looking doubtful. "It'd be a mighty big swing needed to get onto that ledge, and look, the ledge itself is piled high with those loathsome creatures. But the main difficulty would be getting hold of the chain. It's much too far away for us to reach."

The thin, rusty chain hung down into the mud, well out of reach by about eight spearlengths. Shad scratched his chin thoughtfully. "Hmm, yore right, marm. I could soon clear those ole toads off'n the ledge when I got there, but 'ow t'get the chain over 'ere, that's the problem. Any ideas, mates?"

"Burr aye, farsten summat to ee rope an' try to snare ee chain!"

Shad's hearty laugh echoed boomingly 'round the vast cellar space. "Haharr, leave it to our ole molemate. Good idea, Diggum!"

Knotting their own belts and habit ropes together, they fastened them to the rope Foremole had brought with him. Shad coiled it up. "That should be long enough fer the job. Now, wot we needs is an 'ook to tie on to our line. Let's 'ave a look at yore treasure trove, young Butty."

The squirrel Friar tipped a glittering heap of precious objects from their cloak wrapping and began sorting through them. "Nothin' here that looks like a hook, mister Shad."

Craklyn selected a long thin dagger. It was a beautiful thing, more ornament than weapon, with a hilt crusted with seed pearls and blue john stones. Its slim, elegant blade was made of solid gold. "Here, this should do. Gold is soft metal, it'll bend."

Shad took the dagger and, setting it in a crack between the stair stones, he bent it double with a few powerful shoves. The rope was tied tightly to the dagger handle, and Shad twirled it like a sling.

"Right, mates, let's go fishin'!"

The first few throws went short. Hauling the line back through the watery mud, the otter winked broadly. "I've got the range now, this time does it. Redwaaaaaallllll!"

Mud splattered all 'round as he swung rope and hook in a circle above his head. Shad let go, paying out the coil as his hook streaked out. It landed with a splodge, slightly beyond where the chain hung. Crouching down, he began drawing the rope slowly in.

"Easy does it, messmates. Come t'me, you liddle beauty . . ."

The chain moved toward them. Butty waved his paws wildly, crying, "Good throw, Shad, you've got it!"

It was indeed a good, or a lucky, throw. As the chain appeared from beneath the surface of the swamp, they saw that the point of the hooked dagger had actually passed through the center hole of a chainlink, snaring the chain securely. But Shad took no chances; he continued drawing the line in carefully until he could reach out and seize hold of the rusted and muddied object.

"Gotcha!"

Craklyn backed off, surveying the risky venture with a jaundiced eye. "Er, who's going to go first?"

The otter Gatekeeper tugged boldly on the chain to test it. "Bless yer 'eart, marm, who else but me, seein' as I'm the biggest an' 'eaviest? If the chain 'olds fer me, 'twill be safe fer all."

Without further ado Shad climbed up five stairs and stretched his paws high, holding the chain as far up as he could. Abbess Tansy had a sudden thought. "Here, Shad, you'll need the spear to clear those toads from the ledge. Stay there, I'll bring it to you!"

Shad bit down on the spearhaft and nodded, and the Abbess stood aside. He took a short run and launched himself from the stairs. Tansy watched the gallant otter swing out in a huge semicircle over the vast lake of liquid mud, with a spear clenched in his teeth and his tail standing out straight behind him, and knew she would never forget the sight. She held her breath. It looked as though the wide, arcing swing was about to dip downward and plunge Shad into the swamp. But on the final stretch he kicked out and up with both footpaws, jerking himself onto the ledge. The four friends on the steps cheered heartily. Shad held the chain in one paw and thwacked at the fat revolting toads that had already crawled up onto the ledge with his spear handle, sending them flying high and wide with dreadful hisses and croaks of protest.

"Shove off, ye great blobs of blubber, g'wan, jump fer it!"

The oozing surface boiled with writhing mudfish tearing at the toads who, in their turn, gobbled down as many mudfish as they could.

"Stand ready wid the 'ook an' line," Shad yelled across to Diggum Foremole. " 'Ere comes yore chain!" He swung the chain out in a wide arc. Foremole threw the line, hooking it as it came within range.

"Oi got 'er. Coom on, miz Crakkul, doant ee be faint'earted!"

Craklyn went next, aided by a mighty shove from her friends. She wailed and yelled the whole way across the ledge as she swung over the toads, mudfish, and deep morass.

"Whoooooeeeeeeeaaaaaa . . . Heeeeeeelp!"

"Well done, marm. Never fear, I've got ye, yore safe now!"

The old squirrel Recorder ceased her din, smiling sweetly at Shad. "There, it didn't hurt a bit. Send the chain back to Tansy now, mister Shad. I've never heard an Abbess scream, have you?"

Tansy was next to go, but when Foremole and Friar Butty pushed her from the step, she did not scream at all. Instead she clung on like grim death and closed her eyes tight. Shad and Craklyn caught her. She wagged a mischievous paw across at the Foremole. "Guess who's next, Diggum?"

When he had hold of the chain, Foremole looked pleadingly at Butty. "Oi 'opes they toadyburds an' muddyfishes doan't get oi!" As it was, Foremole probably had the best crossing of all, coming in to land so fast that he almost hit the wall.

Young Friar Butty was last to go. His was the most difficult trip, because he had nobeast to give him a good starting push. The fat little squirrel launched himself off, only to swing in a faint halfhearted circle and land back on the steps.

Abbess Tansy roared across at him, "Oh, come on, Friar, you can do better than that. Imagine twenty hungry hares are chasing you to cook dinner for them, and run."

Butty went at his task with a will; grabbing the chain high, he dashed from the step and leapt out, yelling, "Go an' get yore own dinneeeeeer!"

He flew across the swamp, but halfway across his paws began slipping down the muddy chain. Butty was still traveling inward towards the ledge when he plowed into the swamp and vanished.

49

Immediately the surface of the swamp began wriggling and roiling with toads and mudfish.

Shad seized the spear close to its blade. "Quick, you three grab the other end tight an' don't let go!"

Hanging on to the spear with one paw, Shad dipped daringly outward and grabbed the chain with his free paw. "Pull me in, pull me in quick!"

They hauled him from his almost horizontal position back onto the ledge. Wordlessly they all took the chain and pulled it in paw over paw, heaving madly at the rusted, mud-coated links. Butty was dragged forcibly to safety, practically unrecognizable. He was coated from head to tail in reeking sludge, roaring and spitting mud as toads and mudfish clung to him gnawing.

"*Blooaargh!* Gerrem off me, the filthy dirty swampscum!"

They brushed and wiped at him, cleaning him up as best they could.

"There y'are, matey, you'll live. The worst bit's over now!"

Butty winkled mud from both his eyes and glared at Shad. "How do you know?"

Toads proved the only problem on the narrow rock ledge. They congregated there in droves, perching on one another's backs, standing on the heads of those beneath them, blocking the way, sometimes five and six high. Sightless, filmed eyes, bulbous heads, damp spreading webs, and fat slimy bodies barred the path of the five Redwallers. The cavernous space echoed to the sound of venomous hisses and croaks.

However, Shad was made of stern stuff. He headed the party, battling a path for them along the slippery rock strip. Buffeting left and right with the spearhandle, he thrashed the creatures unmercifully until they were forced to flee into the swamp. Toads plopped and flopped in scores to the waiting mire below.

The four creatures walking behind Shad kept their backs firmly against the wall. Gripping one another's paws, they edged slowly along to the mole tunnel, encouraging their champion.

"Get that big scoundrel, Shad—that 'un there!"

"Watch out for that fat 'un, he's tryin' to slip past you!"

"Burr, you'm give 'em billy oh, zurr, 'ard'n'eavy!"

The hole was not too high up. Shad could see into it by pulling himself up tip-pawed, but it was dark inside.

Foremole Diggum produced one of the torches from the cellar. "Oi brung this'n o'er with me. Can ee set flame to et?"

With a few threads of Tansy's habit, a piece of flint which Friar Butty always carried, and the steel blade of Craklyn's quill knife, they improvised spark and tinder. Tansy set the smouldering threads on the resin head of the torch, and blew gently until it ignited.

Shad boosted them all into the mole tunnel, where they sat and took a breather. They all were tired, thirsty, and with grumbling, rumbling stomachs.

Friar Butty picked drying mud from his paws and spat out grit from between his teeth. "Ah well, we might yet see daylight if this tunnel goes anywhere."

Foremole wrinkled his nose and sat back confidently. 'Lissen yurr, Butty, if'n summ mole digged this tunnel, then you'm can lay to et thurr be a way out. Ho aye!''

It was a steep uphill climb, slippery at first, but growing easier once they encountered deep-sunk tree roots, which they could hold on to.

Craklyn explained the tunnel's origin to Tansy as they went. ''From the journals of Abbess Germaine, I gather that this is one of the original passages that the moles dug to flood Castle Kotir. They diverted a river down several tunnels and flooded the place out.''

The Abbess, who was traveling behind Craklyn, smiled wryly. ''Very interesting, I'm sure, marm, but will you try to stop kicking soil down the back of my neck!''

Friar Butty, who was traveling up front with Foremole, shouted, ''Fresh air! I can taste the breeze!''

Foremole, who was carrying the torch, suddenly backed up on to Craklyn's head, pulling Butty with him. ''Coom quick, zurr Shad, thurr be a surrpint up yurr!''

Scrabbling soil and bumping past the others, Shad, who had been bringing up the rear, fought his way to the front. ''A snake, ye say, matey? Where?''

The torchlight showed a sizeable reptile, coiled around a mass of roots, hissing dangerously. Butty was petrified by it. ''Sh . . . Sh . . . Shad, look, 'tis an adder!''

The otter seized the torch and thrust it at the bared fangs and beaded eyes. The snake's coils bunched as it backed off.

'' 'Taint no adder, that's a smooth snake. It don't carry poison in its fangs, but it can bite an' crush ye!''

''Hurr, you'm roight, zurr. Oi see'd ee smoothysnake once. Moi ole granma, she'm tole oi wot et wurr. Gurr, boitysnake!''

The fearless Shad stripped off his tunic. ''A bitin' snake, eh? Then we'll just 'ave to give it summat to bite on, mates. There y'go. 'Ow's that, me ole scaley foebeast!''

He hung the tunic on his spear and jabbed it in the snake's face. Instinctively the smooth snake struck, biting deep into the homespun material. Shad was on it like lightning. He bundled the snake's head in the tunic, wrapped the garment tightly, and thrust it forcibly into the crossed forks of some thick-twisted roots. The snake thrashed about madly, but only for a brief time. It settled down into a steady twitch as it tried to pull itself free of the encumbering tunic.

Shad pointed upward. "Come on—I can see a twinkle o' starlight up ahead there!"

They followed him, hugging the far side of the tunnel cautiously as they passed the slow-writhing reptile.

Even though they were sore and weary, the five companions leapt about gladly once they were aboveground in the moonlit woodlands.

Friar Butty was ecstatic. "O sweet life! O fresh fresh air! O green pretty grass!"

Foremole was used to being underground. He sat back and grinned at the young squirrel's antics. "Hurr hurr hurr! Wot price ee treasure naow, young zurr? Oi'll wager ee wuddent loik t'go back an lukk fer it."

Butty shook his voluminous Friar's habit and the cloakful of treasure fell out upon the grass. "I wasn't leavin' that behind! Why'd you think I slipped down the chain—it was the weight of this liddle lot!"

Shad tweaked the young squirrel's nose. "Yer cheeky liddle twister, we shoulda left you fer the toads an' mudfishes!"

Butty pulled loose and jumped out of the patch of moonlight they were standing in. His four companions looked shocked for a moment, then they started laughing uproariously.

He pouted at them indignantly. "What're you all laughin' at? I don't see anythin' funny."

Craklyn wiped tears of merriment from her eyes. "Oh, don't you? Well, take a look at yourself, you magic green frog!" Swamp mud, dried and crusted, and the dust on Butty's paws, was shining bright green in the darkness. He gazed at his small fat stomach in anguish. "I'm green, shinin' bright green!"

Craklyn patted his back sympathetically, and a cloud of green dust arose. "It must be some mineral in the mud that does it, phosphorus or sulphur, I suppose. Heeheehee! Lead on, Butty, we won't need a torch to show us the way, my small green-glowing friend!"

Butty waved a bright green paw at the Recorder. "One more word outer you, miz Craklyn, an' I'll give yore share o' the treasure to Sister Viola, so there!"

•

Two old moles, Bunto and Drubb, were sleeping in the gatehouse at Redwall Abbey when they were wakened by banging on the main gate. Bunto blinked from the deep armchair he was settled in. "Oo c'n that be a bangin' on ee gate inna noight?"

Drubb rose stiffly from the smaller of the two armchairs by the fire. He yawned, stretched, and said, "Us'll never know 'til us'n's open ee gate. Cummon, Bunto."

Stumbling out into the darkness, they unbarred the big gate and opened it a crack to see who required entrance to the Abbey. The other four had hidden themselves; Butty stood there alone. The two moles took one look and scooted off toward the Abbey building, roaring in their deep bass voices, "Whuuuooooh! Thurr be ee likkle green ghost at ee gate, an' ee'm lookin' loik pore young Butty. Murrsy on us'n's!"

A half of a dandelion wine barrel cut lengthways formed the badgerbabe Russano's cradle. Mother Buscol rocked it gently with a footpaw as she dozed on a pile of sacks in the dark, warm kitchens of Redwall. Only a faint, reddish glow showed from the oven fires, where the scones were slowly baking for next morning's breakfast. From his cradle, the little Russano sat up and pointed at the strange apparition that had appeared. He smiled at it and uttered the only word he knew.

"Nut!"

Mother Buscol half opened her eyes, inquiring sleepily, "Nut? What nut, m'dear?"

Then her eyes came fully open and she saw Butty standing there. "Waaaoooow! 'Tis young Butty, come back to 'aunt me! Ho, spare me, green spirit, don't 'arm me or the liddle one!"

The glowing phantom answered in a hollow, moaning voice, "Bring scones from the ovens, enough for five, honey too, an' woodland trifle if'n there be any about. Some strawberry fizz an' October Ale. I'll be outside. Remember now, enough for five!"

The specter faded slowly away to the small canteen outside the kitchens. Mother Buscol busied herself, complaining to a cockleshell charm she always wore around her neck, "Indeed to goodness, fat lot o' good you were. Lucky charm, indeed I was nearly eaten alive in me bed by an 'ungry ghost. Fifteen scones, that'll be three apiece, now where's that woodland trifle got to? Oh, dearie me, don't you fret, my liddle babby, I won't let 'im 'ave you!''

Russano stood up in his tiny nightshirt, chuckling. ''Yee-heehee. Nut!''

Accompanied by Taunoc and Orocca, the old squirrel-mother brought out a heaped tray. Shad had to take it and put it on the table, as she almost dropped it. In the lantern-lit area, Butty appeared normal.

Tansy waved at her. ''Hello, Mother Buscol, Orocca, and Taunoc, my friends. How are your eggchicks? Well, I hope?''

Taunoc bowed courteously and alighted on the table. ''We are all healthy, thank you, Abbess. Welcome back to Redwall!''

50

Major Perigord Habile Sinistra looked around the high ridge in the dawn light, sizing up the hillside and valley below.

"You an' Morio did well, Sergeant Torgoch. This ridge could be held against many by a few. Top marks, wot!"

Morio threw a languid salute. "Best place we could find, sah. Looks like we're first here."

Brisk as ever, Torgoch was issuing orders. "Scout around now, see if y'can find stones, any kind, from pebbles to blinkin' boulders. Put 'em in piles along the ridge—always useful t'chuck down on the vermin."

Perigord nodded approvingly. "Good show, Sar'nt, make use of the terrain, eh, wot. Chief Log-a-Log, what can I do for you, old lad?"

The Guosim leader nodded, shrews not being in the habit of saluting. "Thinkin' about food fer the troops, Major. Shall we risk lightin' cookin' fires?"

"Why not, old chap, why not, we want the blinkin' enemy to see where we are. Light some whackin' great bonfires, if y'please."

Log-a-Log took Perigord at his word, and soon three huge

fires were alight and blazing out like beacons in the gray of dawn.

Gurgan Spearback had a stroke of luck. His Waterhogs reported they had found a great, fallen pine trunk on the ridge's other side.

"Thee did well, 'ogs. Fetch rope an' wedges. Methinks I'd like yon timber atop o' the ridge—'twill come in useful."

Everybeast joined in to roll the big dead trunk uphill. Gurgan, painted for war, wearing his club and ax, supervised the job. "Put thy backs into it, thou slab-chopped ne'er-do-well rabble! A liddle twig like yon should give thee an appetite for when we breakfast. Worry not about gettin' lily-white paws dusty, by me spikes, come on, move it, afore I move *ye* to bitter tears!"

Captain Twayblade levered hard at the pine with a pike, smiling in high good humor at the fat hedgehog's insults. One of Skipper's crew working alongside her gritted his teeth as he threw his weight against the massive log, and muttered, "Wot's so funny, Cap'n?"

Twayblade leaned on the pikehaft, taking a short breather. "That Waterhog, old chap, Gurgan thingummy. I'd like to put him in a contest against our Sergeant Torgoch. I wager they could insult a regiment for a full day without jolly well repeatin' themselves. That Waterhog's a born Color Sergeant!"

Pasque Valerian sat alone near the tall standing rock at the ridge center, her breakfast untouched, watching the daybreak. Rising from behind a bank of dusky cream cloud, the sun appeared reddish-hued like a new copper coin, burning the morning dew into tiny wraithlike tendrils. It was the start of a high summer's day, but the young hare was downcast.

Arven, the Champion of Redwall, had already eaten. He wandered across to where Pasque sat, and, leaning against the rock, he watched her. "Gracious me, there's a long face! D'you want it to rain?"

The young hare looked up into the squirrel's kind features. "No sir, I hope the day stays fine."

"Lost your appetite too, I see?"

"Oh, I'll get 'round to eatin' it, sir."

"What is it, then? Are you afraid of the battle to come?"

"Not really, sir. I've seen quite a bit of action with Long Patrol."

Arven drew the Sword of Martin from its sheath across his back. He touched Pasque's paw lightly with the tip, smiling secretly. "D'you see this sword? Did you know that it has the power to make pretty hare maidens happy?"

Pasque cast her eyes over the legendary blade. "I've never known a sword do that, sir, but if you say it does, then I'll have to take your word."

Arven snorted impatiently and flourished the blade. "Hah! I see y'don't believe me. Right, I'll show you, missie. C'mon, up off your hunkers and see where my blade is pointing!"

Pasque arose with a small sigh. She did not feel like being forced to laugh at sword tricks.

Arven pointed the blade out and downward to the back of the ridge. "Place your eye level with my sword and look carefully."

The young hare did as she was bid, and in an instant she was wreathed in smiles, jumping about excitedly. "It's Tammo, he's coming! He's coming here!"

Arven watched the small figure below on the plain, running in front of two others like a true Long Patrol Galloper. "Y'see, I told you this is a powerful sword!"

Major Perigord had to lower his brows and glower a bit to prevent himself from smiling. "I say, Pasque, old thing, d'you mind lettin' go of young Tammo's paw, just while he makes his blinkin' report t'me, wot!"

Tammo flushed to his eartips and gave a smart salute. "Midge'll be here soon, sah, our mission was successful. Damug Warfang is headed this way with the Rapscallion army. Sorry to report that we lost Rockjaw Grang . . ." Tammo's voice broke for a moment. "He . . . he gave his life so we could escape. Brought a squirrel with us, name o' Fourdun; he was a prisoner, y'see. I cut your trail 'twixt here, south o' Redwall, and we've been runnin' like madbeasts all night t'get here. Sah!"

The Major turned aside and, taking out a spotted kerchief, he wiped his eyes. After a moment he faced Tammo again, his face pale. "Big Rockjaw Grang, eh? A good an' perilous hare. By my blood an' blade, we'll make the vermin pay heavily for him! Go an' get y'vittles, Tamm, you look quite done in. I'll get the fine details from Midge. Thank ye, y'may dismiss."

Bluggach, the big stoat Rapmark, made his way to the head of the marching Rapscallions, pointing as he came level with Damug Warfang.

"See, Firstblade, fires burnin' on that ridge in the distance!"

The Greatrat kept his gaze locked on the trio of smoke columns rising against the distant sky. "I saw them a while back. Send Henbit to me."

Henbit was a wily-looking Rapmark officer. He appeared at Damug's side with scarcely a sound. "Mightiness, you wanted to see me?"

"Aye, listen now. Take a score of trackers, good ones who are able to hide and run silent. Get over to that ridge, look for a rock like an otter's tail, and see how many are waiting for us there. Then check the valley, it should have a rift running along the far side of it. Take care that you are not seen. Go!"

Damug was confident that he could win. Who else could put an army of a thousand in the field? Where in all the country east of Salamandastron was any serious force of fighters to be found? As he strode at the head of his powerful force, Damug planned ahead.

He had learned the lesson of overconfidence from his father, Gormad Tunn, when they attacked Salamandastron with disastrous results. Though this battle would be different and his opponents fewer, that was no reason not to take precautions. He would split the army into two groups, sending them into the valley from both ends in a pincer movement. This would catch any of his enemy who were lying in wait on the valley floor and prevent the Rapscallions being outflanked.

Those Redwallers had a harsh lesson in death coming to them. Redwall—when the Abbey was his he would change its name. Fort Damug! That had a good sound to it. His name would live forever when the place was mentioned in far seasons to come. Fort Damug. Tales would be told of how he defeated the foe on open ground and took the Abbey without disturbing a stone.

A keen-eyed squirrel, one of the friends from Mossflower Wood, stood erect on top of the standing rock. Shading both eyes with a paw, he scanned all 'round. The way in which he halted, tail erect and head thrust forward, told Lieutenant Morio that he had spotted something.

Morio hailed him. "What ho there, Lookout, any sign o' movement?"

Holding his position, the squirrel called back, "Dust cloud comin' out o' the southeast, too faint yet t'see much!"

Morio's long face lit up momentarily. "Keep your eye on it, bucko, looks like our visitors are on their flippin' way. Report if you note any change!"

The big pine trunk had become a kind of social gathering place; hares, mice, hedgehogs, shrews, moles, and squirrels grouped about it when they were off duty. Perigord sat scratching his initials into the wood as he listened to Morio's report.

"That sounds like the blighters right enough. When d'you think we can expect them to arrive?"

"Can't say, sah, have t'wait on the Lookout's report."

The Major winked at his waiting warriors. "Well, whenever it is, we'll give the blackguards a warm welcome, eh?"

Ribald comments greeted this statement.

"Aye, we'll feed 'em a nice 'ot supper o' cold steel!"

"Haharr, we'll rap their scallions for 'em!"

"Give the villains rock cakes served with spearpoints!"

Perigord looked down to the thick end of the trunk. Several creatures were throwing weapons at a shriveled leaf, which they had pinned to the trunk. A selection of axes, knives, and javelins quivered from the wood all 'round the leaf.

A shrew called Spykel held up a ribbon of crimson silk. "First to pin the leaf dead center wins this!"

Log-a-Log balanced his rapier and threw it like a javelin.

"A hit! The Guosim Chief's hit it!"

Gurgan Spearback inspected the leaf. "Nay, 'tis not dead center, a touch left, I'd say. Stand away now, yon ribbon'd look fetchin' in my wife, Rufftip's, spikes!"

Gurgan stood on the ten-pace mark. Closing one eye, he

licked the blade of his ax, sighted, and flung it spinning. It struck the leaf, slicing it neatly in half through its middle. Gurgan pulled his ax loose and wound the ribbon on to his paw. "See, that's how a Water'og learns to cast his blade!"

Midge Manycoats stopped Gurgan strolling off with the prize. "If a chap could send his blade spot into the cut your ax made, would you give him that nice fancy ribbon, old feller?"

Gurgan chuckled so that his oversized boots quaked. "Hohoho! Hearken to this 'un! 'Taint possible, master 'are! Nobeast can cast a blade good as that in one throw!"

Midge winked at Tammo, who was standing nearby with Pasque. "Show the Waterhog how our patrol chuck a blade, Tamm, go on!"

The young hare blinked modestly. "Oh, really, Midge, I don't go in for showin' off."

From his perch on the trunk, Perigord interrupted. "Go to it, Tamm, win the ribbon for young Pasque!"

Three paces farther out than the mark, Tammo drew his dirk. "Oh, well, if you say so, sah . . ."

The weapon shot from Tammo's paw like chain lightning. It hissed through the air and thudded deep into the center of the split made by Gurgan's ax. A roar went up from the onlookers.

Bewildered, the Waterhog Chieftain inspected the throw. "Lackaday, I never seen a beast sling steel like that, young sir! What manner o' creature taught thee such a skill?"

Tammo grunted as he used both paws to tug the dirk free. "One called Russa Nodrey, a far finer warrior than I'll ever hope t'be. Keep your ribbon, Gurgan, 'twas you split the leaf."

But the Waterhog would not hear of it. He draped the crimson silken ribbon on Tammo's paw and bowed formally. "Nay, I'd like t'see thee give it to thy pretty friend!"

Tammo felt his ears turn bright pink as he draped the silk about Pasque Valerian's neck. Everybeast cheered him, and Perigord shook him warmly by the paw.

"Your mother'd be rather proud if she could see you now, Tamm!"

51

Furgale and Algador Swiftback had been out scouting the land ahead of the Salamandastron contingent. They returned at midnoon and made their report to Lady Cregga and Sergeant Clubrush.

"I'm afraid we haven't sighted the ridge you described, marm. It must be further than you estimated."

The badger leaned on her fearsome axpike. "No matter, 'tis there somewhere, I know it is. Did you sight vermin or anything else of interest?"

"Well, m'lady, about two hours ahead there's a dip in the land, sort of forming itself into a windin' ravine. It goes north and slightly west . . ."

Cregga exchanged a knowing glance with the Sergeant. "Good work! We'll camp there tonight and follow the course of this ravine you speak of. That way we won't betray our presence; 'twill keep us well hidden as we march."

Drill Sergeant Clubrush winked at the two recruits. "Top marks, you two, that's wot I calls usin' the old h'initiative. Go an' join yore pals in the ranks now."

Twilight was falling as they entered the ravine's shallow

end. Within moments nobeast within a league's distance could tell there were five hundred hares on the march. The columns were reduced to three wide in the narrow gorge; they pressed forward with the rough earthen walls rearing high either side of them.

Trowbaggs accosted Corporal Ellbrig in quaint rustic speech. "Hurr, 'ow furr be et afore us'n's makes camp, zurr?"

Ellbrig looked at him strangely. "Wot're you talkin' like that for, y'pudden-'eaded young rogue?"

Trowbaggs continued with his mimicry. "Hurr hurr hurr! 'Cos oi feels just loik ee mole bein' unnerground loik this, zurr, bo urr!"

The Corporal nodded sympathetically. "Do you now? Well you keep bein' a mole, Trowbaggs, an' when we makes camp you kin dig out a nice liddle sleepin' cave in the ravine wall fer yore officers."

Trowbaggs did a speedy change back to being a hare. "Oh, I say, Corp, why not let old Shangle do the diggin'? He looks a jolly sight more like a mole than I do."

Shangle Widepad fixed the young recruit with a beady eye. "One more squeak out o' you, laddie buck, an' y'won't be either mole or hare, y'll be a dead duck!"

It was chilly sleeping in the ravine. After a cold meal of thick barley biscuit and apple slices, the hares settled down for the night, wrapped in their groundsheets. However, Lady Cregga Rose Eyes felt her blood run hot as she lay there, dreaming of meeting Rapscallion vermin in a valley beneath a far-off ridge.

Standing as high as he could on the pine trunk at the ridgetop, Arven watched the Rapscallion campfires. They dotted the far plains like tiny fallen stars. Skipper of Otters climbed up beside him and passed the Redwall Champion a beaker of vegetable soup, steaming hot.

"All quiet down there, mate?"

Arven blew on the soup and sipped gratefully. "Aye, Skip. If they break camp just before dawn, I figure they'll arrive in the valley below at midday tomorrow. By the fur'n'fang, though, there's going to be a lot of 'em facin' us!"

The big otter set his jaw grimly. "Mebbe, but there'll be a

lot less of 'em by the time we're done! Wot makes 'em act like that, Arven? Why can't they just be like ordinary peace-lovin' creatures an' leave us alone?"

Paw on swordhilt, the squirrel Champion shrugged. "Hard to say, really, Skip. There'll always be vermin of that kind, with no respect for any creature, takin' what they please an' never carin' who they have to slay, as long as they get what they want. Peaceful creatures to them are weak fools. But every once in a while they come up against beasts like us, peace-lovin' an' easy-goin' until we're threatened. Win or lose then, we won't be killed, enslaved, or walked on just for their cruel satisfaction. No, we'll band together an' fight for what is ours!"

Far away from the ridge, in the safety and warmth of Redwall Abbey kitchens, the badgerbabe Russano lay in his barrel cradle, his soft dark eyes watching a chill blue mist forming across the ceiling. From somewhere, slow muffled drumbeats sounded, sweet voices humming in time with them.

A scene appeared out of the mists. The army from Redwall lay in slumber amid shattered spears, broken swords, and a tattered banner. Other creatures came then, warriors he had never met, yet a voice in the babe's mind told him he knew them. Martin, Matthias, Mattimeo, Mariel, Gonff, all heroic-looking mice. There were badgers, too, great fierce-eyed creatures with names like Old Lord Brocktree, Boar the Fighter, Sunflash the Mace, Urthclaw, Urthwyte, Rawnblade, and many more. They wandered the ridge, and each time they touched a creature he or she stood and went with them.

Finally they stood in a group together, pale and spectral, and another joined them. It was Rockjaw Grang, the big hare who had carried and nursed Russano on the long trek to Redwall Abbey. Though he did not speak, the little badger heard his voice.

"Remember us when you are grown, Russano the Wise!"

Mother Buscol was awakened by the babe's unhappy cries. Not knowing what he had witnessed, she laid him on her lap and stroked his head, whispering soothingly, "There, there, my liddle one, sleep now, 'twas only a dream."

Back and forth she rocked the little badger until he drifted back to sleep, far too young to tell her what he had seen. Russano had witnessed the Redwall army upon the ridge in the aftermath of battle; he had beheld all those who lived, and the ones who did not.

52

Dawn brought a mad bustle of activity to the army on the ridge, with fires being relit, Corporal Rubbadub beating all creatures to stations, and Chieftains roaring commands.

Damug Warfang had stolen a march on them. Perigord listened as the squirrel Lookout reported what he had seen at daybreak.

"Major, those fires last night were nought but a bluff. Damug must've lit 'em an' carried on marchin' forward. They split into two forces, and right now they're lyin' in the rift at both ends o' the valley, waitin' on some kind o' signal to move!"

On the right flank, half of the Rapscallion army crouched, led by the Firstblade himself. He sat motionless as the rat Henbit, who had headed the scouting expedition, told what he had discovered.

"Mightiness, there can't be more'n three 'undred creatures atop of that ridge—a few hares'n'otters an' some Water'ogs. The rest ain't much: squirrels, mice, an' moles, wid a scatterin' o' those liddle raggy beasts that sail the streams, shrews I think they call 'em. They got plenty of weapons, but no chance o' winnin' agin a thousand of us. Back side of the ridge is too steep an' rocky—you'd be best advised to attack from this side, Sire.''

Damug Warfang peered upward, noting the piles of rock heaped along the heights and the big tree trunk positioned at its center. ''A thousand won't be needed to conquer three hundred. Bluggach, you take half of this five hundred. Gribble, take word to Rapmark Skaup that he will send half of his force with Captain Bluggach's fighters. Between them they should take the ridge. That is my command. Go now.''

The little rat scurried along the defile to where the ferret Skaup lay waiting on the left flank.

Tammo stood with Pasque on one side of him and Galloper Riffle on the other. He leaned slightly forward and looked down the line. Tight-jawed and silent, the front rank waited, while behind them the second rank, mainly archers, checked shafts and bowstrings.

The young hare felt his limbs begin to tremble. He looked down and noticed that the footpaws of Pasque and Riffle were shaking also. Behind him, Skipper drummed his tail nervously on the ground.

''Me ole tail's just bumpin' about for the want o' somethin' t'do,'' the otter leader chuckled encouragingly. '' 'Tis all this waitin', I s'pose, mates. Can y'see 'em, miss Pasque?''

Gripping the cord of her sling like a vise, Pasque nodded. ''Indeed I can, Skip, they're lyin' in the rift down there, waitin' the same as we are. D'you suppose they're nervous too?''

Sergeant Torgoch was pacing the ridge, keeping an eye on the front rank. He winked as he halted in front of her. ''Nervous, missie? I can see 'em quakin' in their fur from 'ere!'' He waved his pace stick to where Perigord was perched on the pine trunk, leaning nonchalantly upon his saber. ''Wot d'ye think, sir, shall we tell 'em wot we thinks o' vermin?''

Waving back with his blade, the Major smiled. ''Capital idea, Sar'nt, carry on!''

Swelling out his chest with a deep breath, the Sergeant roared in his best drill parade manner at the Rapscallion army, ''Nah then, you scab-tailed, waggle-pawed, flea-ridden excuses fer soldiers! Are ye sittin' down there 'cos yore too stoopid t'move, or are yer afraid?'' Then he turned his back on the foebeast and waggled his bobtail impudently. Laughter broke out from the Redwallers' ranks.

Gurgan Spearback clumped up in his oversized boots, wielding the massive mallet that was his favorite weapon. ''Hearken t'me, all ye vermin wid half a brain to lissen. Remember what thy mothers told thee about climbin'. If you come climbin' our hill, we'll spank thee right 'ard an' send you away in tears!''

Hoots of derision from the ridge accompanied this announcement. Then Lieutenant Morio's deep booming voice called out a warning: ''Stand to arms, here they come!''

Five hundred Rapscallions clambered out of the rift from both flanks, and charged. They made a blood-chilling sight: painted faces, bristling weapons, and blazing war banners. Drums pounded as they screamed and howled, racing like a tidal wave across the valley floor toward the slope of the ridge.

Nobeast could stop it now. The battle was begun.

Captain Twayblade held her long rapier point down. ''Steady in the ranks there, let 'em come! Stand by the first three rockpiles! Slingers, wait my command! Steady, steady now, chaps!''

The vermin pounded up the slope, increasing their pace until they were running at breakneck speed, spearpoints, pikes, and blades pointing upward at their adversaries.

Tammo stood his ground, deafening noises thrumming in his ears, watching the hideous pack draw closer until he could see their bloodthirsty faces plainly.

Sergeant Torgoch's voice rumbled across the first rank. ''Wait for it, buckoes, wait on the Cap'n's command!''

A barbed shaft whistled past Twayblade's jaw. ''Front rank, let 'em have it,'' she shouted. ''Now!''

Slings whirled and a battering rain of stone struck the leading Rapscallions. Tammo saw the look of shock on the face of a lean scarred weasel as his round weighty river pebble struck it hard on the forehead. The creature toppled backward with a screech, rolling downhill, still clutching a broken bow. Loading the sling swiftly, Tammo swung out and hit a rat who was almost upon him.

Now Major Perigord was standing with the front rank, whirling his saber and calling to the moles who were behind the hills of stone. "First three rockpiles away!"

Boulders, rocks, soil, dust, and stones showered down on the advancing Rapscallions. The vermin were seasoned fighters, giving as good as they received. Ducking and dodging, they battled upward, thrusting with pike and spear, slinging, firing arrows, and hurling anything that came to paw.

Tammo was on his third sling when he heard Sergeant Torgoch bellowing, "Down flat an' reload slings, first rank. Second rank, shoot!"

Tammo and Pasque threw themselves down side by side, fumbling to load up their slings. Skipper and the second rank stood forward, shafts drawn back upon tautened bowstrings, and sent a hail of arrows zipping down into the massed vermin. From where they lay, the first rank twirled their slings and added to the salvo.

Then everybeast in the Redwall army grabbed for the spears lying on the ground between the ranks. Tammo, Pasque, and Riffle, like many others, did not have a proper spear, but the long ash poles with fire-hardened points served just as well. Staves, spears, pikes, and javelins bristled to the fore all along the line.

The Rapscallions were completely taken by surprise. They had expected their opponents to stand and defend the ridge, not to mount a counter charge with spears. Many a vermin heart quailed then as the war cry of Salamandastron's Long Patrol cut the air.

"Eulaliaaaaa! 'S death on the wind! Eulaliaaaaaa!"

The Redwallers' charge broke the Rapscallion advance. Drums from below in the rift pounded out the retreat, calling the vermin back.

Damug Warfang estimated that he had lost threescore in the first assault; the Redwallers had lost about half that number. Slightly more than he had expected, but the Greatrat was satisfied. Now that he had tested his enemies, he knew their strength and also their weakness. However, the Firstblade was surprised at his adversary; for peaceful Abbeydwellers they showed great ferocity in fighting and much cunning in their maneuvers. Despite this he was confident they would be unable to resist the might of his full army.

Arven sat still as a mole plastered boiled herbs to a deep graze in his side, lifting one paw up to allow the healer better access to his wound. The mole stopped bandaging, blinking at the sight in the valley below.

Damug Warfang was standing on the grassy sward with his entire army formed up behind him.

"Bo urr an' lackaday, zurr, lukkee, 'tis a turrible soight!"

It was indeed terrible, and impressive. Almost a thousand well-armed vermin, lined in columns, flags streaming, drums beating, with the Greatrat in full armor, sword drawn, out in front.

Log-a-Log stopped sharpening his rapiertip on a whetstone and glanced quizzically at Major Perigord. "Wot d'you suppose Warfang's up to now?"

The hare viewed the scene below dispassionately. "Tryin' to frighten us with a show of force, what else? That was only half their blinkin' number he threw at us in the first charge."

Sergeant Torgoch saluted with his pace stick. "Shall I stand the troops ready for action again, sah?"

Perigord sheathed his blade and started downhill. "I think not, Sar'nt, the blighter obviously wants to parley. Huh! We're all supposed t'be tremblin' in our fur at the size of his force. I expect he wants us to jolly well surrender."

Arven's voice echoed the Major's final word incredulously. "Surrender?"

Tare and Turry, the Long Patrol twins, helped Arven upright. "Hah, fat chance of that, old lad!"

About a third of the way downhill, Perigord halted, calling out, "I take it y've got somethin' to say, rat. Well spit it out an' be quick about it, a chap can't dally here all day, wot!"

Damug Warfang waved his sword eloquently at the massed Rapscallions backing him. "What need of words, hare, when we could destroy you in a single sweep!"

Perigord shook his head and smiled mockingly. "Oh, is that all you've got t'say? Wasted your breath, really, didn't you? Still, what else can one expect from vermin?"

The Greatrat smiled back as if he were equally at ease. "Just think for a moment what we will do to the ones you left behind at Redwall Abbey. I imagine they're the creatures not fit to fight, babes and oldbeasts. Have you considered them?''

Perigord seethed inwardly, but he did not show it. ''Oh, if it comes t'that, old thing, I wouldn't worry if I were you. Y'see I fully intend slayin' you, so y'won't be 'round to see it.''

Damug was still smiling as he played his trump card. ''I'm a bit ahead of you there, because I intend killing you. Now!'' He let his sword blade drop and nodded.

The rat Henbit had lain near the ridgetop, concealed among the dead vermin that littered the slope. He sprang up, poising himself to hurl the javelin he held, not three paces from the Major. Suddenly he sighed, as if tired of it all, and let the javelin slide carelessly backward as he fell, an oak shaft in his back.

Perigord stepped distastefully over the fallen rat. ''Don't like that sort o' thing. Sneaky. Well shot, Corporal!''

Rubbadub twanged a chord on the empty longbow string, grinning from ear to ear at his officer's compliment.

''Drrrrrrubadubdub!''

Then the Rapscallion army charged. As it swept across the valley, Tammo left off helping Pasque Valerian to bind wounded heads and paws and took up his position in the first rank, feeling slightly detached from it all.

Gurgan Spearback nudged him with a rough paw. ''Art thou all right, friend?''

The young hare shrugged in bewilderment. ''Strange, isn't it, but here we are facin' almost a thousand an' all I can think about is the time o' day. Look, 'tis almost evening, yet it only seems a moment ago it was mornin'. Can't get it off my mind, really. What's happened t'the rest o' today? Where'd it go?''

Gurgan stumped the ground with his mallethead like a batsman at his crease. ''Aye, I know what thou means. All I can think of is my wife, Rufftip, an' our seven liddle 'ogs, 'avin' a pickernick on our boat in the water meadows. Silly wot a body can think of at times like these—*Oofh!*''

An arrow protruded from Gurgan's shoulder. Tammo stared, aghast. ''You're hit!''

The Waterhog pulled the shaft out, snapped it, and flung it from himself bad-temperedly. ''Tchah! When a beast's as full o' spikes as I am, one more don't make much difference, though 'tis a great displeasure t'be shot!"

Before Tammo could reply, Sergeant Torgoch was bawling out orders. "First rank, sling! Second rank, stand ready! Keep 'em off the slope!"

At the point where valley met hillslope, the Rapscallions took the full force of the first stone volley. Owing to their numbers, Major Perigord had taken the decision to strike early and save his Redwallers being speedily overrun. He turned to the moles, saying, "How's the fire comin' along under that log, chaps?"

"Ee'm a burnen broight an' reddy t'go, zurr!"

"Capital! Splash all that vegetable oil over the trunk now, quick as y'like!"

Dry timber and resin gave a great whoosh as the oil buckets were hurled upon it. The evening sprang to light, sparks and flaming splinters crackling as they leapt from the blazing tree. Skipper and his otters rolled it forward using spearpoints and ash staves. It teetered a moment on the brow of the ridge, then took off with a crash, rumbling, rolling, bouncing, and spinning.

Lady Cregga Rose Eyes and the Long Patrol army had been plodding all day. The going was awkward and rough in the narrow rift; it seemed to stretch on forever. They had waded through mud and water, squeezed through narrow gorges, and climbed over collapsed debris.

Deodar was first to see it. "Look, Sergeant, up ahead, that light!"

A sudden bright glow lit the evening sky from a ridgetop in the distance. It flared brightly then disappeared, leaving the hares blinking against the gathering darkness. Sergeant Clubrush placed himself in front of Lady Cregga, blocking her way.

"Deodar, Algador, drop y'packs but 'old on to yore weapons. Scout up ahead, close to that ridge as y'can get. We need h'information quick as to wot's goin' on up yonder. So make all speed there an' back. Run lively now, young 'uns!"

As he spoke, the Sergeant had pulled Corporal Ellbrig and

several others past him to barricade the rift. Both Runners hared off.

Lady Cregga glared fiercely at Clubrush. "Stand out of my way, Sergeant!"

It would be said in later seasons that this was the first time a hare openly disobeyed a Badger Ruler. Sergeant Clubrush drew his sword.

"Sorry, Lady, but we got to wait 'ere 'til the Runners gets back. If you goes chargin' off now, not knowin' wot lies ahead, you could get y'self an' all these slain, recruits an' veterans. We must know wot's goin' on at that ridge first afore we goes at it. Now I know y'could snuff me out like a candle, marm, but I'll try to stop ye if'n I can, for the good of all 'ere!"

Lady Cregga Rose Eyes raised the terrible axpike high over her head with one paw. She brought it smashing down into the rift wall, knocking out a great quantity of soil-bound rock.

"So be it, we wait! But those hares of yours had better be quick, Sergeant, because I won't wait long!"

53

Vermin screamed and wailed as the blazing pine trunk cut a swathe through the Rapscallion ranks. It thundered off the hillside, over the valley, and disappeared with a crash of loose earth into the rift, where one side of the defile fell in on top of it.

This was followed by a frightening silence.

Galloper Riffle rubbed both his eyes, peering into the fallen night. "What's happenin'? Why's everythin' so bally quiet—I can't see a flippin' thing!"

A shrew standing by Riffle blinked hard several times. "Neither c'n I, matey, all's I see is colored lights, poppin' all round. 'Twas that burnin' tree wot did it."

Most of the Redwallers were grouped at the center of the ridge, in the place the otters had launched the trunk from. A shout from the far side of the ridgetop alerted them.

"Help! They're attackin' this end!"

With their sight growing clearer, the Redwallers rushed to defend that end of the summit, only to be hailed by another distress cry. "Yurr, on ee t'uther end, they'm up 'ere too!"

Damug had not been slow. Even as the burning trunk was

launched from the crest of the ridge, he had issued orders for his army to split up again and attack the summit from both ends. Now the Redwall army was in deep trouble. Damug's plan had worked; he had gained the precious moments he needed to put his Rapscallions on the ridge summit.

Tammo fought back-to-back with Pasque, sling in one paw, dirk in the other. Vermin came at them in mobs. Lieutenant Morio was surrounded and alone; gallantly he battled away, hacking at the encroaching Rapscallions with a cracked pike. Tammo and Pasque began forcing their way through to Morio's aid, but too late. The brave Lieutenant went down, fighting to the last.

"Eulaliaaaa! 'S death on the wind! Eulaliaaaaa!"

Captain Twayblade, too, was ringed by the enemy. Her long rapier darted and flickered as she wove it around cutlass and spear, slaying every vermin she touched. "Saha! Come an' meet me, sir vermin, I'll have ye crowdin' at Dark Forest gates this night!"

Tammo glimpsed a fox working his way behind Twayblade, and as the fox raised his sword, Tammo let fly with the dirk.

"A hit!" Twayblade laughed. "Over here, Tamm, come on, Pasque!"

They were joined by Skipper, and between them they smashed free of the crowding foebeasts. The otter pushed them toward the standing rock. "Over there, mates—get our backs agin somethin'!"

Perigord and Gurgan had been outnumbered and driven back along the ridge. Striving valiantly with what was left of their group, they too managed to reach the standing rock. The Major's saber decimated the ranks of vermin swarming to get at them. Blood ran from a cut above his eye as he stood shoulder-to-shoulder with Gurgan.

"Whew! I keep choppin' 'em down, but they're still comin'!"

The Waterhog's huge mallet hit the Rapmark Skaup, wiping him out. "Aye, there's nought left but to take as many as we can with us. Hearken though, I'd like t'get yon Damug atwixt my paws!"

Log-a-Log gritted his teeth, bringing down a weasel with his heavy loaded sling. "Y'won't get close to that scum, mate.

Damug's the kind who leads his army from be'ind, like the true coward he is! Tamm, did they get ye, bucko?"

Tammo almost collapsed as Pasque drew the pike from his leg. "Aaaagh! He got me, but I made sure I got him, the blackguard!"

They ringed the pair, fighting off the attackers as Pasque stuffed herbs into the awful gash and bound it with the red silken ribbon. "There, that'll hold you, sir. Lean on me. I knew that ribbon'd come in useful. Good job you won it for me, wot!"

Deodar and Algador slumped on the rift floor, gasping for breath after making their report.

Lady Cregga acted instantly. "Sergeant, take the right flank; Corporal, you take the left. I'll hold the center. Let's get out of this ditch and form up in a skirmish line, ten deep, fifty long. Double-quick speed, weapons out and ready. We'll come at that ridge from the back. Rapscallions haven't got the brains to think we'd attack that way!"

Still fighting for air, Algador and Deodar drew their blades. "We're comin' too, Sergeant!"

Trowbaggs nodded to Shangle Widepad. "Grab old Algy there, chum, we'll help him along. Fallow, Reeve, lend a paw to Deodar, there's good chaps!"

The night air thrummed to the paws of five hundred Salamandastron hares. Silent and determined, they sped off into the darkness.

Damug Warfang was delighted beyond measure. He stood back from the fighting, leaning on his sword by a fire. The Rapscallions had suffered heavy losses, but nothing to what the creatures of Redwall had sustained. From his position he viewed what he considered to be the last stages of the battle. His enemy would soon be soundly defeated and the famous Abbey of Redwall his for the taking.

Rapscallions crowded in on every side around the standing rock, but there was a space at the center between them and their opponents. The Redwallers had fought more fiercely than anybeasts they had ever encountered, and now, at this final part of the battle, many vermin were growing cautious, no wanting to be on the lists of the slain while their comrades enjoyed the spoils of victory.

The stoat Captain, Bluggach, was a bigger and more reckless beast than his confederates. Pike in one paw and a wicked steel hook in the other, he swaggered into the open space between the armies and began taunting his beleaguered enemy.

"Haharr, so yore the bold crew who were gonna spank us an' send us off in tears, eh? I wager the one who shouted that is 'idin' somewheres at the back now, prob'ly in tears hisself!"

Mass laughter and cheering from the Rapscallion horde prompted Bluggach to become bolder. He leered at the Redwallers, licking the tip of the hook he carried. "C'mon out an' face me, 'tis my turn t'do the spankin'!"

Gurgan Spearback was already out as he spoke, wielding his tree-trunk-headed war mallet. "Stoats be windy braggarts. Come an' spank me if thee thinks thou art warrior enough to do it!"

Bluggach gave a wild yell and charged the big Waterhog. Gurgan sidestepped and swung the mallet once. Just once.

Bluggach slumped to the ground, never to rise again.

But Gurgan's sidestep had carried him close to the Rapscallion mob. A crowd leapt upon him, overwhelming the Waterhog Chieftain.

The Redwallers could not leave their friend in enemy paws. They charged forward into the vermin pack, roaring, "Redwaaaaallll! Redwaaaaaallll!"

They were hopelessly outnumbered, but prepared to sell their lives dearly. Strangely, though, it was Damug Warfang who saved them.

The unpredictable Warlord strode among his vermin, lashing out with the flat of his swordblade. "Halt! Enough, I say! We will take these creatures as prisoners. Nobeast must touch them. I will keep them as captives to serve me!" The Greatrat halted in front of Perigord. "All except you, hare. Nobeast talks to me as you did and lives!"

Held fast by four Rapscallions, the Major still struggled to break free and get at his enemy, even though he was twice wounded. "So be it, foulface. Give me back my saber an' I'll fight you, blade-to-blade. Come on, vermin, let's have at it, wot!''

Damug looked Perigord up and down. Dried blood was caked over the Major's brow, covering his right eye, while the Redwall tunic hung from him in shreds, revealing a ragged scar on one shoulder. The Greatrat sneered contemptuously. ''Your fighting days are over, fool. I'm going to make an example of you in front of your friends. Conquered beasts always learn to behave better when they see their leader executed. Get him down in front of me and bend his head!''

A massive roar shook the night air, chilling the blood of every Rapscallion on the ridge.

''Eulaliaaaaaaa!''

Thundering forward, fifty paces ahead of her command, Lady Cregga Rose Eyes hit the vermin ranks like a lightning storm.

Tammo saw vermin actually fly through the air as the huge badger, her eyes blazing red with Bloodwrath, swung her ax-pike into them. Then she was upon Damug Warfang. Casting her weapon away, she seized the Firstblade with both paws and teeth.

''Spawn of Gormad Tunn! Evil murderer's kin! Come to me!''

Hacking furiously at the Badger Warrior's head with his sword, Damug gave an unearthly screech. Locked together, the pair hurtled into space from the ridgetop.

''Eulaliaaaa! 'S death on the wind! Eulaliaaaaaa!''

Booting aside a rat, Major Perigord grabbed his saber. ''Hares on the ridge, hundreds of 'em! Eulaliaaaaaa!''

54

The army from Salamandastron charged into the Rapscallions' midst to join the Redwallers. Galloper Riffle was down; a snarling weasel who was about to dispatch him with a dagger thrust fell forward, slain by a saber swing. Riffle felt himself pulled upright; he stopped a moment in the thick of battle, recognizing his rescuer. "Algador! My brother!"

The young Runner blinked, smiling and crying at the same time. "Riffle, thank the seasons you're alive!"

"Logalogalogalogalooooog!"

The shrew Chieftain, at the head of his remaining Guosim, tore into a pack of vermin and chased them the length of the ridge.

"Redwaaaaaalll! No surrender, no quarter, me buckoes!"

Skipper of Otters and his ragged band threw themselves headlong at another group of foebeasts, javelins forward.

Tammo had formed foursquare with Pasque, Midge, Twayblade, and Fourdun, battling madly against the desperate Rapscallions. They pushed their way with blade, sling, and tooth to where Corporal Rubbadub lay stretched on the ground, limp and trampled. While the others fought, Pasque stooped to inspect the big lump and the awesome cut across the back of Rubbadub's head. She looked up sadly at her friends. "I think poor old Rubbadub's gone!"

"Nonsense!" Twayblade kicked Rubbadub's paw roughly.

Turning over, the drummer rubbed his head, grinning widely. "Dubadubadubb! B'boom!"

Sergeant Torgoch found himself fighting alongside Drill Sergeant Clubrush. The pair fought like madbeasts but chatted like old pals.

"By the left, Sar'nt, yore young'uns are shapin' up well!"

"They certainly are, Sar'nt—they pulled yore chestnuts out o' the fire!"

Tare and Turry had formed up with Trowbaggs and Furgale. They pressed forward in a straight line, driving Rapscallions off the edge of the ridge. Determined to distinguish himself in this his first action, Trowbaggs pulled away from the others and began taking on four vermin single-pawedly. "Have at ye, y'scurvy rascals, Trowbaggs the Terrible's here!"

He managed to slay one before another got behind him and put him down with a dagger in his side. Corporal Ellbrig and Shangle Widepad rushed in to his aid, slaying two and sending the other one running.

Holding on to his side, Trowbaggs managed a weak smile. "Chap got behind me. Wasn't very sportin' of him, was it, Corp?"

Shangle provided cover while Ellbrig ministered to the recruit. "Trowbaggs, wot am I goin' t'do with you, eh? War isn't no game—there ain't no such thing as a vermin bein' sporty. Good job that dagger only took a bit o' fur'n'flesh. You'd be a goner now if'n that was an inward stab instead o' a sideways one. Come on, up on yore hunkers, me beauty, stick wid me'n'ole Shang."

Furgale and Reeve Starbuck were in difficulties. Heavily outnumbered, they fought gallantly. Tammo's party saw they were in a fix and dashed over to help, but too late. Both the recruits went under from vermin spear thrusts before they could be reached. Others came running to avenge their comrades, exacting a terrible retribution on the vermin spear-carriers with swords and javelins.

Clubrush saw Furgale twitch, and he knelt by him, supporting his head. "Y'did bravely, young sir. Be still now, we'll git you some 'elp."

Furgale tried to focus on Clubrush, his eyes fluttering weakly. "Get my old job back, servin' you an' Colonel Eyebright in the mess . . . won't shout too loud though, Colonel doesn't like that . . ."

The young recruit's head lolled to one side, his eyes closed. Drill Sergeant Clubrush hugged him tightly, tears flowing openly down his grizzled face. "I 'ope you've gone to an 'appier place than this blood-strewn ridge."

The tide of battle was turned. What was left of the mighty Rapscallion army fled from the hill, pursued by the hares and the Redwallers. Major Perigord and Captain Twayblade limped their way down the hill and across the valley, with Tammo and Pasque following them. They found Lady Cregga in the rift, clutching the mangled remains and broken sword of Damug Warfang.

Pasque Valerian was the only one of the four who was still fit and active. She climbed down to the bottom of the rift. Perigord peered over the edge, watching her inspect the badger.

"I say, Pasque, get a chunk o' that smoulderin' wood t'make a torch."

The young hare snapped off a billet of pine from the charred trunk and blew gently upon it until the flame rekindled itself. She looked closely at the still form of Lady Cregga, checking her carefully.

"Good news, sah! Though you wouldn't think it to look at her. Lady Cregga's alive, but Warfang must have slashed an' battered at her with his sword somethin' dreadful. Her face, head, an' eyes suffered terrible injuries, but as I say, she lives!"

The Major winced as he straightened up. "Well, there's a thing! Our Badger Lady must be jolly well made of iron. Tammo, see if y'can hunt up stuff t'make a stretcher and find some able-bodied beasts to carry it. Tamm, are you all right, old lad?"

Tammo sat at the edge of the rift, his head in both paws, shaking and weeping uncontrollably. "No, I'm not all right, sah. I've seen death! I've been in a battle, I've slain other creatures, seen friends cut down before my eyes, and all I can think of is, thank the fates *I'm* not dead. Though the way I feel right now I don't know if I want to go on living!''

The Major sat down beside him. ''I know what y'mean, young 'un, but think for a moment. Think of the babes at Redwall and the oldsters, think of all the families, like your own, who will never be frightened or harmed by the bad ones we fought against. You've done nothin' t'be ashamed of. The Colonel an' your mother would be proud to know they had a son like you. What d'you say, Pasque? Tell this perilous feller.''

Pasque Valerian paused from her salves and dressings, capturing Tammo with her soft voice and gentle smile. She pointed skyward. ''I don't have to tell you anything, Tamm. Just look up.''

Tammo felt the other three staring upward with him.

Fading from dark blue to light, dawn was breaking, with threads of crimson and gold radiating wide. Pale, cream-washed clouds lay in rolls to the east, their undersides glowing pink with the rising of the sun. Somewhere a lark was singing its ascension aria, backed by waking curlews on the moor, and wood pigeons in the copses.

The spell was broken abruptly as the little owl Taunoc swooped out of nowhere to land at the rift edge. ''I see by your returning warriors and the vermin carcasses lying everywhere that you won the battle.''

Perigord wiped his saber blade with a pawful of dewy grass. ''Aye, we won!''

Taunoc nodded sagely, preening his wings, ready for flight. ''I will carry the good news back to Redwall Abbey. Is there anything else you wish me to add?''

Tamello De Fformelo Tussock dried his eyes and smiled. ''Tell them . . . tell them we're coming home!''

55

Extract from the writings of Craklyn the squirrel, Recorder of Redwall Abbey in Mossflower Country.

Healing the wounds of war takes a very long time. It is four seasons since the victorious warriors returned to us, but still the memory of that terrible time is fresh in all our minds. When Lady Cregga was brought to our Abbey, we feared greatly for her. She spoke little and ate even less, lying in the Infirmary with her whole head swathed in bandages. Pasque Valerian and Sister Viola both knew Cregga would be blind, even before the bandages were removed.

Alas, when we did unbandage her, the rose-colored eyes were no more. They had been replaced by tightly shut eyelids. She no longer had the desire to slay, the Bloodwrath, they call it; all that was gone. Throughout the winter she remained in an armchair by the fire in Cavern Hole.

It was pure accident that a miraculous change was wrought in her. One day the baby Russano got loose and crawled off, and we found him perched in Lady Cregga's lap, both badgers entirely happy. Since then she lives only to rear and educate Russano. He is her eyes, and now that he can walk in a baby fashion, they are seen everywhere together. Tammo reminded me of the second half of the rhyme Martin imparted to him:

One day Redwall a badger will see,
But the badger may never see Redwall,
Darkness will set the Warrior free,
The young must answer a mountain's call.

After the battle, the Warriors buried the Rapscallions in the rift and our own on the ridgetop. When spring arrived, they returned to the Ridge of a Thousand (for that is what it is known as now). Major Perigord took Lady Cregga's big axpike. Moles chiseled a hole into the top of the standing rock on the summit, and they cemented the axpike in it, upright, with the old green homemade flag that bears the red letter R fluttering proudly from the piketop. There it will stand until the winds of ages shred the banner and carry it away with them.

The moles are good stonemasons; they carved Pasque Valerian's poem to the fallen on the rock.

Slumber through twilight, sleep through the dawn,
Bright in our memory from first light each morn,
Rest through the winter beneath the soft snow,
And in the springing, when bright blossoms show.

Warriors brave, who gave all you could give,
Offered your lives so that others would live.
No one can tell what my heart longed to say
When I had to leave here, and you had to stay.

Aye, there are memories that die hard and others that we want to keep forever. What courageous creatures they were; as the Long Patrol would say, perilous!

I wish that little Russano would never grow up, but that is an idle and foolish thought. One day he will have to take his place on that mountain far away on the west shores; he will be Lord of Salamandastron. Lady Cregga is certain of this. He is a quiet youngster, but he seems to radiate confidence, understanding, and sympathy to all about him. Already the hares call him Russano the Wise.

The owlchicks of Orocca and Taunoc are big birds now. My goodness, how quickly they grew and learned to fly! They chose the names Nutwing, Nutbeak, and Nutclaw, because "nut" was the only word they spoke for a full season. All three are fine birds, though not as well-spoken as their parents and inclined to be a bit impudent at times, but they are still young.

I am the official keeper of the medals, did you know that? I'll tell you about it. The treasure we brought up from sunken Castle Kotir was melted down by order of my good friend Abbess Tansy. She decreed that a solid gold medal, each set with a separate gem, would be made for everybeast who fought at the Ridge of a Thousand. Redwallers get a ruby, Waterhogs and otters a pearl, shrews a peridot, and hares a blue john, every one set in a small gold shield attached to a white silken ribbon. But I am left in charge of them all because they will not wear them to work!

What work, did I hear you say? Why, the rebuilding of our south wall, of course. Major Perigord, Skipper, Log-a-Log, Gurgan Spearback, and our own Arven all agreed that they cannot abide idle paws. So we have a veritable army working on the south wall, filling holes, tamping down earth, and relaying the massive red sandstone blocks. It will soon be completed, and then there will be double reason, nay treble, for festivities. One for the new wall, and two to celebrate the lives of those lost in the battle last summer. The third reason is so exciting that I can scarce bring myself to write about it.

Tammo and Pasque are to be wedded!

It's true! Taunoc flew off some time back to bring Tammo's family from Camp Tussock to attend the celebrations. Mem Divinia was very proud of her son, and even old Colonel Cornspurrey had to admit that his son was a true Long Patrol warrior. Abbess Tansy saved enough gold and three beautiful emeralds to make a paw bracelet for Pasque. She is the prettiest hare I have ever seen, and I personally think that she knows more of healing wounds than anybeast. But don't tell Sister Viola I said that. Alas, even Pasque can do nothing for Tammo's limp, which the spear wound in his leg caused. But Tammo just laughs when asked about his injury. He says that he never intended being a Runner and gets about better than most. I agree with him, the limp is hardly noticeable.

When the sad day arrives that Russano has to leave us, our Abbey will not be without a badger. Lady Cregga has decided to live at Redwall as Badger Mother. The Dibbuns adore her, and though she has massive strength, her gentleness toward them is touching to see. And talking about seeing, Mother Cregga is learning to see more without the use of her sight than most of us can see with two eyes!

The Guerilla Union of Shrews in Mossflower, or the Guosim, as they are known, have faithfully stayed at our Abbey to help rebuild the wall, as have the Waterhogs. Redwall is full of fast-growing Dibbuns with even faster-growing appetites. Log-a-Log has been hearing the call of the streams and rivers of late, though he says he will wait until Russano is ready to go, then the shrews can accompany him.

Gurgan Spearback keeps his houseboat on the water meadows, merely for the pleasure of his large family. What a quaint beast Gurgan is. He has relinquished Chieftainship of the Waterhogs to his eldest son, Tragglo. Gurgan's great interest now is being Abbey Cellarhog; he was so enthusiastic about brewing October Ale that old Gurrbowl has retired and passed the job on to him.

You will forgive me, but I am about to put aside my quill pen and scrub the ink from my paws. I have an appointment with Friar Butty. Together with the Friar and Captain Twayblade, I will help to plan the triple feast. There will be ten kinds of bread, from hazelnut and almond to sage and buttercup loaves.

Cheeses, well, last autumn's cheesemaking was the best ever. We have some huge yellow ones, with celery and carrot pieces in them, and all the different cheeses in between, ending with tiny soft white ones.

Friar Butty has drawn up a recipe for a South Wall Cake, it will be the centerpiece of the tables. Though if you could see the recipe and the amount of fruit, honey, and meadow-cream the cake will take, you would wonder how any other food could find room on our festive board. The seasons have been kind; there will be more than enough for every-beast, but then they deserve it.

What more is left to say, my friend? Redwall Abbey is as it has always been, basking in the shelter of Mossflower Wood, the gates ready to open any old sunny day to weary travelers, friends, and visitors, all good honest creatures like yourselves. Please come and feel free to stop for a season, any time. You are always welcome.

Craklyn Squirrel, Recorder of Redwall Abbey

Epilogue

Many a long season passed since Major Perigord Habile Sinistra had set eyes upon the mountain of Salamandastron. Straightening his scarlet tunic and brushing his slightly graying whiskers, he touched the long-healed scar line upon his brow and gazed up at the fortress on the far west shore.

"The old place hasn't changed a bit, wot!"

Captain Tamello De Fformelo Tussock and his wife, Lady Pasque Valerian, detached themselves from the throng of travelers. Standing to one side, they too viewed the mountain.

"So this is Salamandastron, m'dear. 'Tis all you said it would be."

"Wait until you see inside, Tamm—it's even more impressive. Oh, look, there's a welcoming party coming out to greet us!"

Old Colonel Eyebright headed the reception group, leaning heavily upon the paw of Garrison Captain Cheeva. Tammo was reminded of his own father as the old hare popped in his monocle and peered closely at the lines of shrews, Waterhogs, and Redwallers, led by Arven, who carried the Sword of Martin.

Then Colonel Eyebright's gaze shifted to the hares, and the monocle dropped from his eye to dangle on its string. "Well, 'pon my life. Perigord!"

The Major clasped paws warmly with his old friend. "Colonel Eyebright, sah, you're lookin' remarkably chipper. Brisk as a blinkin' barnacle on a big boulder, wot!"

Eyebright chuckled, shoving Perigord playfully. "Away with you, base flatterer! I'm as old as I feel and twice as jolly well old as I look. The owl Taunoc told us you were comin', but I didn't expect you until the start of winter. 'Tis still autumn!"

Drill Sergeant Clubrush and his companion Sergeant Torgoch saluted the Colonel smartly. "Beg to report, sah, we made good time, mostly by water with our pals the Guosim shrews an' the Waterhogs. Sah!"

"Aye, we remembered what you taught us, sah, save the old footpaws wherever possible. No doubt the owl gave you our message, sah, 'fraid we didn't bring 'em all back, two score an' a half lost in action . . ."

Colonel Eyebright nodded sadly. "So I heard, Sergeant. Perilous beasts, they'll live in our memories forever, wot. Your friends from Redwall will have to stay with us until spring—no good makin' that long trek back in wintertide. We'll make them welcome to share all Salamandastron can offer. You there, young chap, c'mere. What name d'you go by, eh?"

"Tamello De Fformelo Tussock, sah!"

"Hmph! No need t'shout, sir, I'm not deaf, well not completely. So, you'll be the laddo who stole the prettiest hare on the mountain. Wed to our Pasque, if I'm not mistaken. Hmm, Tussock, knew your father well, your mother too, she was as pretty as your wife."

Tammo and Pasque bowed respectfully to the Colonel as he gestured Cheeva to assist him walking through the ranks. The Colonel halted near the rear markers and, slowly bending his knee, bent his head down until he touched a massive footpaw with his forehead.

"My life and honor are yours to command, Sire!"

Immediately he was raised up by a gentle paw.

The old hare found himself gazing into a pair of dark hazel

eyes. He knew instinctively that they held more wisdom than he could have gathered in two lifetimes. The badger was tall, young, and slender, but his paw and shoulder structures dictated that in maturity he would be a beast of mighty girth and boundless strength. Shifting aside his homespun green traveling cloak, he walked toward the mountain entrance, with Eyebright leaning upon his paw for support.

Holding her Colonel's other paw, Captain Cheeva glanced across at the tall young badger, curiosity overcoming her. "Sire, it is said that Badger Lords always carry a great blade, spear, or mace, yet you carry no weapon. Why is that?"

Such was the calm and dignity radiated by the badger that everybeast was attracted to his presence. They all craned forward to hear him speak for the first time. His voice was deep and mellow.

"I have no need of a blade, nor any kind of great weapon. This is all I carry. You would be surprised what a creature can do with this. I have been brought up by good friends and instructed in its use." Smiling quietly, the badger drew forth from his cloak a short hardwood stick, well used and polished to a dull sheen. "It once belonged to a warrior, formidable and perilous."

Old Colonel Eyebright tightened his grip on the badger's wide paw. "It was written in the stones of Salamandastron that you would come here one day to rule. Truly you are named Russano the Wise, Lord of Salamandastron!"